RED RAIN

VOL.2

RED RAIN

VOL.2

RACHEL NEWHOUSE

rachelnewhouse.com

CONTENTS

FOX HUNT

RED RAIN #4

JUNE 2076

1

Of all the ways I had imagined spending my Sunday afternoon, getting a tattoo with Nic in the ghetto of a Martian city was nowhere on the list.

Well, "tattoo" was a bit of a misnomer; in reality, it was a minor cosmetic surgery. "Just like getting a nose job," the technician explained as he swiftly slid my fingers into the metal device that would keep them still for the delicate procedure. "Relax, babe."

I was doing no such thing. Lying in a cracked dentist's chair in the shuttered back room of a tattoo parlor with both hands strapped down was giving my anxiety a lot of material to work with. The only thing keeping my heart from forcing its way up my throat was the fact that Nic stood behind me, watching.

I was a bit surprised that he'd come with me, especially when the procedure was supposed to take several hours. But I wasn't about to complain. He stood with arms crossed and feet apart, eyes roaming the room in constant patrol. The bulge of the pistol in his pocket sent a clear message.

The technician finished strapping me in and rolled the surgery machine up to the chair. It was sleek and metallic—a single robotic arm with a microscopic needle on the end. The technician keyed a passcode into the control panel, and the device whirred to life. The robotic arm stretched and rotated, needle sliding in and out.

"Did you sanitize that?" Nic grunted.

The technician mumbled something as he fetched an alcohol pad and swiped it on the needle. I swallowed.

"Now this won't hurt much," the technician said for the tenth time. I noted that his qualifiers kept changing; five minutes ago, the procedure wasn't supposed to hurt "one bit."

"This laser-guided needle is going to alter your fingerprints—like a miniature skin graft. But first, we have to design your new set. And that's why you pay me the big bucks." He rolled his chair up to the control panel and typed eagerly.

"*How* much is this going to be?" I asked.

"It's fine," Nic interrupted, and I silenced.

"First, I scan your existing prints. Then I run them through a program that compares them to a global database so the algorithm can generate a new pattern. Of course, I always manually edit my designs to make sure they look as organic as possible. Purely autogenerated prints look fake—if you ask me."

He threw a pierced-lip grin at me that I didn't return. I had no idea if any of that was true, but I didn't have much of a choice. I had to get new prints taken before I could use my new file, and there weren't that many microsurgeons on Mars.

At least not many who were willing to do procedures off the record.

The technician guided the machine's arm until it hovered above my left hand. A patchwork of blue laser light fell on my thumb. A soft whir and a click, and then he moved on to the next finger.

I tried to control my rising panic as he scanned the rest of my digits. My fingerprints had been with me since birth. God had designed them Himself, and within three hours they would all be irreversibly altered.

After today, Philadelphia Smyrna would no longer exist, and Andromeda Nolan would take her place.

The design process took over an hour, during which I closed my eyes and prayed to keep myself from hyperventilating. There wasn't much else I could do with my hands bolted to the arms of the chair.

Finally, the technician called Nic over to approve the prints. He squinted at them, then angled the screen so I could see.

I stared at the eerie electronic rendering, as if I had any idea what I was looking for. *Dear God, I hope this is the right choice.* I looked up at the technician and nodded.

"One new ID coming up! Let me know if it starts hurting a lot."

The machine shifted gears. The laser changed from a grid to a dot, so focused I could barely see it. Then without any kind of warning, the needle sank into my skin.

I flinched as the thin metal started weaving in and out of my fingertip. My heart broke free and blocked my next breath, everything in me begging him to stop. I couldn't do this—I couldn't take who I had been my entire life and callously throw that person away like I was erasing a whiteboard.

I was Philadelphia Smyrna. I was.

But I couldn't be, not anymore. I knew that. I knew it wasn't safe. My "real" name and image had been plastered all over the internet, associated with several acts of terrorism against the United—some of which I was more or less responsible for. Even worse, I was their link to Red Rain.

If I didn't want to end up in an interrogation room giving the government the formula to melt entire cities with acid rain, I needed to become a new person. So I closed my eyes, bit down on my tongue, and said nothing.

It seemed like an eternity before the microscopic stabbing stopped. It hadn't hurt much—although I'm sure the pain medication Nic doped me up on before we left had an effect. The technician freed my hands from the machine, and I struggled to feel them. My palms tingled and shook, my fingertips flushed red and raw.

"And there you have it, Miss—what did you say your name was?"

I was about to answer when Nic stepped between us. "I'm paying." He held out his phone. The technician took it and keyed in numbers.

"How much extra to wipe the originals?" Nic waved his hand at the machine.

The technician licked his lip piercing. Then he grinned, hit another key, and handed the phone back to Nic.

Nic nodded and pocketed the device. "Let's go."

I tested my balance before standing up, then followed him out the door into the main storefront. The place was deserted except for another tattoo artist, who lay on her table scrolling through a phone.

"Want anything else done while you're here?" The technician came out behind us and waved his hand at the sketches plastered on the wall.

"No thank you," I said, even as my eyes scanned the gallery. Although most of it was downright bizarre, I had to admit that a few of the pieces—like a stunning blue-and-purple nebula wrapped around someone's wrist—were strangely alluring.

He shrugged. "Come back anytime if you change your mind."

Nic was already out the door, so I hurried to follow. "You know, he's not wrong," Nic commented as soon as we had blended into the anonymity of the alley. "A tattoo is a fairly inexpensive way to change your appearance."

"You want to sign the parental waiver on that?"

He grunted at me as he unlocked the transfer. Even though Nic had agreed to be Andromeda's legal guardian on paper, he did not like being reminded.

I grabbed the passenger door handle and winced, my tender fingertips protesting. I swallowed a grimace as I opened the door and hoisted myself over the treads into our bulky ride. Nic slid into the driver's seat.

"Besides," I said as buckled in, "I was hoping for less permanent options."

"If you want to spend an hour in the bathroom putting on your mask each morning, be my guest. Just be glad you don't pay the water bill."

He started the transfer and pulled out of the parking lot. I took one last look at the Martian city as we drove down the backroad towards the border. We were on the outskirts, where the buildings were smaller and cheaper, but it was still a sight to behold.

The architecture was a mishmash of designs, as if no one could decide what aesthetic Mars should adopt. Most of the buildings were paneled with large windows to let in as much of the distant sunlight as possible. Slabs of concrete traced out an informal network of roads, and numerous planter boxes and greenhouses attempted to lend some humanity to the inorganic maze. Here and there, the natural red earth seeped through the cracks in the road and the gaps between buildings, reminding us that we were ultimately foreigners superimposing our will on an unforgiving wilderness.

Above it all stretched a dome of glass. The honeycomb panels kept the thin atmosphere out and the heat in—or at least some of it. Despite the fact that we were near the equator and had been soaking in the sun all day, Nic had still advised me to wear my heaviest jacket. He cranked the heat up in the car as we neared the edge of the glass.

The border officer cleared Nic's credentials, then flagged us into an exit tunnel. We drove into a bay, and the doors behind us shut, plunging us into near-darkness. Nic double- and triple-checked that all the vehicle's windows were sealed and the doors locked. After a moment's hesitation, the lights on the wall flashed green. The doors ahead of us opened, and we drove out into the Martian countryside.

The town was one of three biodomes clustered in the valley. I watched the other cities glitter in the distance as we drove up the crude road that had been hewn into the side of the plateau. We crested the top and continued into the unsettled wilderness. Around us stretched miles of untouched dirt. There were no roads, no signs, no other indication that humans lived on this planet. The transfer's computer navigated off of some unseen satellite as it led us through the gathering darkness.

I risked conversation. "Thanks for your help back there."

"Oh, you're paying me back."

I turned to him. "That's not what I meant."

He didn't respond or look at me, so I kept silent and returned my attention to the shadowy outcrops rolling past.

It was dark by the time we got back to Base #9.6.11. It was the only research base for miles in this part of the country, and the light from the glass-domed central wing shone like a lighthouse in the wilderness. I swore the base looked bigger every time I saw it from the outside. New wings and biodomes were always being added, connected by snaking hallways, as if the base were a living organism sending out roots and multiplying.

The docking bay doors opened to receive us. We waited until they had closed again and the atmosphere had been restored before piling out of the car.

Nic opened the door to the base, took two steps into the lobby, and stopped.

"You know I'm not doing this just for you, right?" he said without turning around.

"Huh?"

"I'm not giving you all this tender loving care because I like you."

"Good, because I thought we were past the stage of having to like each other."

He glanced back at me. "If you screw this up, I go down with you."

That wasn't exactly what he said, but it was the child-friendly translation.

"If the United ever figures out who 'Andromeda' really is, they're going to investigate her relatives—and at the moment, that is, unfortunately, me."

"Is that why you didn't want me to pay?"

He nodded. "I don't want you logging any electronic activity off this base until your new file is online." He started walking. "Find Jean-Luc and have him scan your prints into the database. Have him text me when he's done. The sooner we get your new file online, the better."

2

It took me awhile to find Jean-Luc, if only because I had no idea who he was. Thankfully, my neighbor Mr. Sardis was, as always, happy to help me, and within an hour my new prints were imaged and uploaded.

I went back to the cafeteria to claim the tail end of dinner, then retired to my quarters. I braced myself as I waved my hand over the panel and opened the door. I hated seeing the empty room and being reminded that I lived alone.

I went to the bathroom and started stripping my "mask," as Nic called it. A whole process had gone into getting me ready to go to town. Temporary dye turned my long, dark hair an unnatural shade of maroon, and contacts had shifted my brown eyes green. A heavy layer of makeup contoured my face, and I'd cobbled together an ill-fitting outfit from pieces Mrs. Sardis had lent me. The whole process had taken over an hour, and taking it apart took at least half that—all so that nobody on the street would recognize me as Blue Fire, the girl from the videos.

Nic was right—I was glad I didn't pay the water bill.

Three shampoos later, my hair had been restored to its natural color, conditioned, and braided to dry. I wandered back to the living room to hear my tablet dinging.

I picked it up. I still wasn't sure that I liked the new device. It was as thin as a clipboard, with sharp edges and a too-bright screen. I missed the comforting warmth of my clunky old ereader, with its bulky case and clacking buttons. This tablet didn't even have a home button; it turned on as soon as it saw my face.

I sank down on the couch and swiped through the notifications. There weren't many, mostly because so few people knew how to contact me. Unfortunately, I had to keep it that way.

I did have a couple of new texts on my encrypted messaging app. The most recent was from Nic.

IT'S UP

I swallowed, feeling the significance of that settle in my stomach. As far as the government was concerned, I was now Andromeda Nolan.

I whispered the name to myself, still trying to get used to the sound. I didn't love the name, mainly because I didn't love the man who had given it to me. Director Thames Nolan had picked it when he'd forged the file. He had been intending to adopt me—after he used me to blackmail my father into completing the formula for Red Rain. It would have worked if I hadn't exposed Thames's secrets on livestream and turned him over to the United.

He'd taken the easy way out, and I had no choice but to assume the identity he'd designed for me. I hated using his last name; every time I said it, I thought of him and his sickeningly sweet wife. But Philadelphia's file was a mess, and I had to start over if I had any hope of surviving.

Nic sent another message.

WILL FIX YOUR TABLET TOMORROW AT BREAKFAST

I texted back a "k, thanks" and shoved the thoughts out of my head. I switched over to the other unread conversation: from Jayde—or "Aurelius," as he went by online.

HEY, YOU OKAY? HAVEN'T SEEN YOU ONLINE ALL DAY

I pondered the message before replying. I wanted to spill my whole day to him; telling a sympathetic ear how I had just wiped my fingerprints and become a new person would probably make me feel better about the ordeal. But Nic had been very, extremely, and somewhat violently strict about making sure I didn't mention Andromeda online. As long as the United still thought I was going by Philadelphia, they would be watching the wrong file.

So even though I trusted Jayde—the kindly guard had helped me out of more than one scrape—I'd obeyed Nic and not told Jayde I had new credentials.

After writing and rewriting my reply several times in my head, I settled for:

ALL GOOD, JUST TAKING CARE OF A FEW THINGS. ANY WORD?

I knew what the answer would be—if there had been any word, he would have blown my texts up—but the irrational amount of hope that gripped my life demanded I ask.

NONE. I'M SORRY, PHIL

I sighed. The breath grated against my buried emotion, and a half-formed sob ripped out of me. I closed my eyes and curled into the couch, trying to shut out the sight of the empty room, the heavy silence, and the crushing reminder that I had no idea where my family was.

It had been two weeks since Thames died, and there was still no activity on either my father's or brother's files. Nic's sister Cea had also gone dark. Last I knew they were on Earth; they'd escaped from Thames and gone off the grid. I thought, now that Thames was gone, they would realize I was safe and try to make contact—if not with me, then at least with our mutual friends in the underground.

But so far there had been radio silence.

Jayde tried to console me.

8 MILLION PEOPLE SAW YOUR LAST VIDEO THOUGH. EVERYONE'S TALKING ABOUT BLUE FIRE

I tried to muster the energy to be impressed by that. It didn't matter if a *billion* people saw my video if that number didn't include the three people I was searching for.

AND NO ONE'S SAID *ANYTHING*? NOTHING IN THE COMMENTS?

NOTHING YET. MY NETWORK IS ON HIGH ALERT—IF THEY MAKE CONTACT WITH ANYONE, WE'LL BE THE FIRST TO KNOW

I drummed my nails on the screen. It didn't make sense. Why *hadn't* they made contact with the underground? I knew Dad and Ephesus had to be careful; their files were as corrupted as Philadelphia's. But Cea had never been incriminated in the investigation into Red Rain. Her file was clean. She knew how to find Jayde. She could easily make contact—or even turn herself in at our old religious containment camp. So why hadn't she?

I banged my frustration out on the keyboard.

ANY OTHER IDEAS?

The typing dots appeared at the bottom of the screen, vanished, then reappeared several moments later.

YOU COULD TRY TELLING THEM TO ORDER PIZZA

I stiffened. "Order pizza" was their euphemism for calling for an emergency pickup. Cea and I had done it once, but that was before Stanyard, the former friend who used to "deliver" that pizza, had abandoned me in an alley to die.

Was he back in the game? I resisted the urge to ask; I knew Jayde couldn't tell me in so many words. Did it even matter? Stanyard had been quick to betray me before, and now the stakes were much higher. He was the last person I trusted with my family's safety.

I DON'T TRUST HIM

Jayde's response was quick.

SOMEONE ELSE RUNS THE SHOP NOW

CAN I TRUST THEM?

OF COURSE

I searched for a sense of peace about the whole thing and only found residual pain and bitterness.

I DON'T KNOW. I'D RATHER THEY CALL YOU

YEAH, BUT YOU CAN'T GIVE OUT MY PHONE NUMBER ON AIR

I sighed. *Nor mine.*

JUST TELL THEM TO ORDER PIZZA. THEY KNOW WHERE THE SHOP IS

He was right, and it was better than nothing. There was only so much I could do from Mars.

OKAY

I PROMISE WE'LL FIGURE THIS OUT, PHIL. WE'LL FIND THEM. YOU CAN TRUST ME

I tried to absorb his confidence. *Please, God. I need you.*

I thanked Jayde, said goodbye, pulled up Sydney's number. Sydney was a tech on base that I wouldn't know from Adam, except that he could run the soundboard in the recording studio. I preferred him over the other techs— mainly because he didn't talk much and had a tendency to be up late.

UP FOR A RUN?

After a few minutes, he responded.

SURE. LET ME FINISH THIS GAME

I thanked him and left my dorm to start the long trek back to Wing 74.

It had taken several tries—most of which ended with me calling Mr. Sardis to come rescue me—before I could walk there without getting lost. My route was definitely not the most efficient, but it was the one I could remember, so I stuck with it.

Nic had already started remodeling Wing 74. A good chunk of it had been demolished; the rest was being retrofitted and reconfigured. Hallways were rerouted, rooms were stripped and repurposed, and windows were added to wings that had formerly been denied the light of day. All with the intent of covering up what had really happened in these halls.

Nic said it was so that should Carnegie, his former assistant, ever rat us out and send officials to investigate the base, they wouldn't find anything linking the base to Red Rain or Thames. Me, I was just glad I was no longer locked on the wrong side of the door.

All of the doors in Wing 74 opened for me now. Nic had given me all access.

At my request, there was one room in Wing 74 that would survive the demo—the recording studio. Although I had no fond memories of that room either, it was currently my best hope for finding my family.

I pushed aside the drop cloth that shielded the door from construction dust and let myself in. While I waited, I straightened the greenscreen, centered the chair, and polished the lens of the gigantic robotic camera that hung from the ceiling.

Sydney arrived about the time I was satisfied with my work. He appeared in the plexiglass window of the sound booth and started flicking on monitors. "Tell me when you're ready to start," he said, which was probably the only thing he'd say to me all evening.

I nodded and arranged myself in the chair. The viewscreen of the camera flickered on, and I checked myself in the monitor. I hadn't bothered to put on makeup, so I looked ashen and tired in the stark glare of the studio lighting. I didn't care. Ironically, on camera was the one place I could be myself without a filter.

There was no reason to hide online; the world already knew who Philadelphia Smyrna was. Thames and Carnegie had forced me to record videos for their various and sundry evil schemes, and my name—and the hashtag #bluefire, which they'd evidently invented to channel the energy—had been trending for a few weeks now.

I was trying to use my forced popularity to my own advantage. Thames had been using my videos to try and find my father; surely I could do the same. Jayde and his friends were sharing my content religiously, and the internet loved my tragic life story. As long as I included some clickbait content about the ugly truth of the United—and what they did to unassimilated people like me—my videos blew up. Eventually my family had to see one of them.

Of course, I couldn't exactly leave a forwarding address or tell them to meet me at the corner of 18th and Vine, not when United officials would love to arrest and/or execute all of us. Maintaining a stable online presence had also proved impossible; the government banned all my accounts as soon as they found them.

But I wasn't about to give up. My family was out there somewhere; until the Holy Spirit told me otherwise, I would keep praying and sending up smoke signals.

I gave Sydney the go-ahead, took a deep breath, and stared straight into the camera. The *On Air* sign on the wall glowed to life.

"My name is Philadelphia Smyrna, and I'm looking for my father."

3

Nic met me for breakfast the next morning. He approached my table with a coffee cup in one hand and the other outstretched. I dutifully pulled my tablet out of my pouch and handed it to him.

He sat across from me, drained the last of his mug, and started toggling menus.

"Do you need more coffee?" I asked in lieu of the good morning he had noticeably omitted.

"This shouldn't be *that* hard," he said without looking up. "But if you're offering."

I got up and took his mug to the buffet to get him a refill. I had seen him drink enough of the stuff that I knew how he liked it—as black as it came.

I returned to the table and set the mug down in front of him, using the opportunity to watch over his shoulder as long as I could before he got annoyed.

"What are you doing to it?" I asked, trying to sound innocently curious. I'd gotten used to him messing with my stuff—it was his tablet, after all—but I still liked to know what he was changing.

"I'm officially registering this device on the United's database."

I was so appalled by that statement that I froze.

"Don't hover over my shoulder. We talked about this, Andi."

"You can call me Phil," I reminded him for at least the seventh time that week, "and why?"

"Because I can't work when you're reading over my shoulder. Now sit down."

"Not that," I groused, but did it anyway. "Why are you registering my tablet with the United?"

"For the same reason I call you Andromeda—so you can be legally compliant."

I tried to rationalize that on my own and failed. "Since when have you cared about making sure stuff is legal?"

He spared me a sharp glance over the edge of the tablet. "Ninety percent of my job is making sure this place stays legal. Believe me, if I didn't have to make sure we check all the boxes, I'd get a *lot* more done."

"So what box did you check when Ephesus 'died'?"

"'Deceased.'"

"Hilarious."

He shrugged. "That's what the United needed to hear. As governor, I'm responsible for everything that happens on base. That means I need to be able to reconcile everything—and everyone—that comes or goes. In the case of your brother, I needed to explain why I didn't have a living person *or* a body. Transit explosion was the most reasonable explanation at the time."

The tablet chirped at him. "Although in hindsight, I probably could have found a less dramatic solution."

It was my turn to shrug. "So you're saying there's a paper trail for everything that happens on base, even if the details are a bit embellished?"

"Mmhmm," he mumbled around a sip of coffee.

"How does registering my tablet help? Wouldn't it be easier to leave it in incognito mode or whatever and not tell them the device exists?"

"While you're on base, sure, because I'm the only one watching the internet traffic. But as soon as you connect to someone else's wifi, having an unregistered device will raise huge red flags. It's like walking into a bank with a mask on—they're going to assume you're up to no good."

He looked up and met my eyes. "What I'm about to tell you is very important. I need you to listen carefully, because I am *not* going back to jail because you did something stupid on TikTok."

I leaned back and returned his gaze. "I still don't know what that is, but okay."

"This device is now officially registered as belonging to Androméda Nolan." He held the tablet up for emphasis. "Which means, don't do *anything* on it that Andromeda wouldn't do."

"Got it."

"That means you're not Philadelphia, and Dr. Smyrna isn't your dad."

I flinched.

Nic was unmerciful. "I mean it, Andromeda. If you mention any names online—make any association with yourself and the Smyrnas—someone could make the connection, and then your whole online presence is ruined. Andromeda is only safe as long as you protect her."

"I know," I whispered, still shivering.

"Which means…" He laid my tablet on the table and resumed typing. "That boyfriend of yours needs to stop calling you 'Phil.'"

"Jayde?" I questioned, then blushed. "He's not my boyfriend. Stop making it weird."

"*He's* the one making it weird. He's been acting awful chummy for someone who is, at best, a lead." He flicked his finger across the screen, and I knew without asking that he was skimming my chat history. "He should know his chats could be watched."

My skin crawled, partially from fear and partially because I wasn't sure how I felt about Nic reading my conversations with Jayde. We hadn't talked about anything but finding my family, but I still didn't want Nic as a third wheel. "I thought you said that app was secure. Well, semi-secure."

"It's semi-secure because it disguises itself. It cloaks the data to make it look like you're playing a multiplayer game online instead of texting. That's how it hides the data exchange between two users. Most algorithms will glaze right over it—but if a censor does decide to investigate, the code isn't hard to crack."

He typed with both hands. "I'm going to wipe your chat history and create a new account for you. Don't worry—I'll let him know you'll be in touch when you need him."

I could tell by the amount of characters he was producing that he was also telling Jayde much more than that—no doubt reading him the riot act about revealing my identity online. I cringed and reached for the tablet. "Let me do it."

"Already done." He punched a button.

I hissed at him.

He arched an eyebrow.

I too was a little mortified by the sound that had come out of my mouth, but I was no less upset. "You could have let me talk to him."

"Sorry, but this was important."

That made it ten times worse. "Oh, so you don't trust me with important stuff?"

His eyebrow seemed stuck up there. "Don't be a child."

"Don't be a jerk," I shot back, and slumped in the chair. The deed was done, so it was pointless to argue, but the anger still sizzled in my nerves. Jayde was my friend, the one relationship I had outside of this base, and I didn't like Nic speaking on my behalf. If Jayde needed to be put in his place, I wanted to be the one to tell him; it was my relationship to manage.

Apparently Nic thought we were even on exchanging insults, because he let it drop. He clicked another button and handed the tablet back to me.

I looked at the screen. The messaging app was loaded under a brand-new account with no chat history. I couldn't even read what he'd told Jayde.

Nic returned to his coffee. "Now that you're online, you can pay me back for the procedure."

"Want to show me how?"

"I would love to."

I rolled my eyes. He was being tactless, as usual, but he had a point: I had money now, and I didn't even know how much.

He walked me through the process of downloading a banking app and claiming my credentials. I logged in, and multiple accounts appeared—a checking, a savings, and some random investments. All of them had balances with several zeroes at the end, not that I had any appreciation for how much buying power that was. It had been a long time since I'd dealt with real money.

Nic showed me how to wire money to him. The amount he asked for barely put a dent in my checking.

"Stupid question," I asked as I scrolled through the transaction history. "But am I… rich?"

"Richer than I am," Nic muttered.

That didn't give me a whole lot to go on, but I still recognized that it wasn't a good thing. "Really?"

"The funny thing about being in the experimental sciences is that you're rarely working with your own money—you're usually investing someone else's. And thanks to Carnegie's fallout, I'm severely lacking in investors right now."

I swallowed. There was a lot I was worried about right now, but the stability of the base had never been one of them. Should I add it to the list?

"It will be fine," Nic said, not one to be pitied. "Now that I'm back in charge, I'll solicit new projects. But in the meantime, I might charge you rent."

I looked back down at the screen and tried to appreciate just how much I had. Apparently Thames had left me a great deal of money, and I tried to fathom, again, what had inspired a corrupt politician to want to adopt me and leave me an inheritance. According to the transaction history, he'd been paying into the account for over two years, which meant he'd been planning this since Ephesus went to Mars.

That's probably when he started watching you. I shuddered.

Nic got up from the table. "I'll slide the bill under your door on the first of each month."

I glanced up at him as he walked away. "So is it safe for me to go to town and buy stuff now?"

"You can buy whatever you want," he said without looking back. "Just make sure it's something Andromeda would own."

He left the cafeteria. I scarfed my cold, abandoned eggs and got up to find Mrs. Sardis.

There was one thing Andromeda needed.

4

The Martian city glittered under the light of a thousand artificial suns.

We'd gone to one of the newer settlements. It had been designed for tourists, and no expense had been spared to replicate the Martian dream. The streets were lined with neon, and every window flashed with electronic displays. The terrariums housed a freak circus of genetically modified plants that looked like they could be native to Mars. The walkways were covered with solid arches of glass wherever possible, so seamless and clear that you almost forgot you were inside. Adding to the illusion was the glow of daylight-replicating streetlamps. They augmented the distant sunlight and bathed the entire city in brightness, making everything look even more plastic and fake.

I'd asked Mrs. Sardis to take me clothes shopping, and she'd been delighted to oblige. I owned all of three outfits, none of which I could wear in public. Two I had worn while streaming, and the other—one of the skirts I had inherited from Mama—was so far out of fashion that it "screamed unassimilated," or so Mrs. Sardis claimed.

Fortunately, now that I had money, my wardrobe was an easy thing to rectify.

We'd gone to the shopping center first, but the pickings had been slim. There were only a few stores, each of which had but a dozen styles in limited sizes. Mrs. Sardis explained it was because it was so expensive to ship goods to Mars; even with the improvements in transit travel, flights were costly and depended wildly on Mars's rotation. During the wrong time of year, a flight from Earth could take twice as long and cost three times as much. That meant shipments of nonessential goods—like fashion—were infrequent and cost a premium.

Like everything else in the city, the clothing was designed to fulfill tourist fantasies, which meant most of it was more art than covering. I enjoyed browsing the shimmering array of vinyl and nylon but left without buying anything. Maybe I was being picky, but I didn't fancy looking like an alien from a bad movie, at least not for the prices they were charging.

Our next stop was proving much more fruitful—the thrift store. They called it an upscale rehoming boutique or some such nonsense, and the prices had an extra zero compared to the last thrift store I remembered from Earth, but it was still a vast improvement over the shopping center.

I found several pairs of jeans, including one with intentionally ripped-out knees. I wasn't too keen on pre-destructed clothing, but Mrs. Sardis said they were vintage enough to be cool again. I picked up a black leather jacket to replace my old pullover, plus new boots that weren't falling apart in the soles.

Meanwhile, Mrs. Sardis went to work finding shirts. It took a few "discussions" for us to settle on a new aesthetic for me. At first she wanted me to embrace the other end of the rainbow—pinks and neons and gaudy contrasting patterns. I would have preferred to stay in the safe realm of neutrals, but she reminded me that the whole purpose of our trip was to give myself a new look.

So we settled on a compromise—lots of black I could layer with colorful vests and scarves. She also picked out several t-shirts with benign graphics on them—abstract planets and stars, innocent pop bands, forgotten brand names.

But her most important find was a kitschy little black backpack to replace my well-worn pouch.

I took it from her and instantly hated it. It was stiff and bulky and plasticky—fake, just like Mars. It was nothing like the comforting leather satchel I was used to.

But then again, that was the point.

I added it to the pile with a sigh and went to check out.

Our next stop was a drug store to buy more makeup. Mrs. Sardis had done her best with foundation we'd borrowed from another lady on base, but I needed stuff that was my "shade," whatever that meant. Thankfully Mrs. Sardis knew what she was looking at, so I let her do the work and fill my basket with an assortment of creams and powders.

"Let's see, what's left?" she chatted as we loaded our haul into the car. "Oh, we should get you some jewelry. Have you thought about getting your ears pierced?"

I gaped at her. I was *exhausted*. I hadn't done this much shopping in six years, since before they sent us to the containment camps. Going to one more store sounded like torture, especially if it involved needles.

I'd had enough of those for one week.

She saw my face and laughed. "How about lunch, then?"

We retired to a café around the corner. Like everything else in the city, it was ridiculously themed, but at least the food was normal. I ordered soup and a fruity lemonade drink that was their special for the season, and Mrs. Sardis had an elaborate salad. We chatted about the weather and her son's antics and the newest arrivals on base—basically anything but what had gone on over the past month.

"Thanks for all your help today," I said as we were wrapping up. "I'd have been absolutely lost in that makeup department."

She chuckled. "When we get home, I'll show you how to use it. I promise it's not hard."

"If you say so." I smiled. Our waitress approached, and I flagged her down. "Here, let me pay. It's the least I can do."

"That's really not necessary, sweetheart. I'm happy to help." Mrs. Sardis reached into her purse, but I put my hand up.

"No, really. Apparently I can afford it, and besides, I'm still learning how to use this thing." I turned on my tablet and pulled up the universal payment app all United establishments were required to accept. The government had long since abandoned cash and card in favor of an app so that they could easily monitor and tax all transactions. Or at least that's how Nic explained it. My device sensed my location and automatically pulled up the café.

"How was everything?" Our waitress stopped at our table and claimed our dirty dishes. She was a spunky blonde thing that reminded me of a diminutive version of Cea, but with more tattoos.

"It was great. What's the total?" I looked her in the eyes and gave her a smile, which she returned.

"Oh, if you put your table number in here, it will pull it up for you." She leaned over my shoulder and pointed while I followed the motions. I tried not to be too fascinated by the technology—I'd nearly given myself away twice today by being amazed at things that Mrs. Sardis claimed were commonplace.

Spending five years in a containment camp will put you really far behind on technology.

"How do I add a tip? Do people still tip?" I realized how that must sound and faked a laugh. "I mean, I don't know how people do it on Mars."

I looked up at our waitress with what I hoped was a disarming smile and found her staring at me.

I was so unnerved that I returned the favor for a moment. Then I managed to clear my throat and ask, "Is that okay?"

She blinked and shifted back so she was no longer in my bubble. "I'm sorry, I mean... No, that total's not right. The system must not be syncing. I'll be right back." She snatched the rest of our dishes and hustled to the kitchen.

I watched her retreat, a brick settling in my stomach where lunch should have been. I glanced at the receipt displayed on the screen. "It looks right to me."

Mrs. Sardis shrugged and sipped the last of her iced tea. "Maybe something was on special."

If that was the case, our waitress was awfully upset about us being overcharged.

A stirring in my gut prodded me. *Leave. Now.*

But we haven't paid! I argued with Him, long enough that our waitress emerged from the back.

"Sorry about that. System's being dumb, so I had to print you a paper receipt." She laid a slip of white paper on the table. "Come again if you ever need anything."

I returned her gaze intentionally this time. She searched me for an almost indiscernible flicker, then turned to leave before I could thank her.

"I'm surprised they still have paper receipts," Mrs. Sardis commented.

I looked down at the slip, and my heart stopped.

Our meal had been comped—all the numbers replaced by zeros. At the bottom, on the line where a tip would have been, she'd scratched a single word:

#BLUEFIRE

I jerked my head up and searched for her, but she'd vanished.

I snatched the receipt and stuffed it in my pocket. "We need to get out of here."

Mrs. Sardis looked up from her phone. "What's wrong?"

I stood, trying to make the motion look casual, but my fingers shook as I gripped the table for balance. I strode towards the door as confidently as I could, hoping Mrs. Sardis would follow without making a scene. I cast a glance around at the other diners, looking for any prying eyes, but they all seemed absorbed in their own food and conversation.

I shoved the door open and hurried to the transfer. I keyed the code into the keypad and unlocked it from my side, jumping in and slamming the door before Mrs. Sardis even made it to the car.

"Phil, what's wrong?" she said as she opened the driver's door.

"It's Andi," I reminded her, "and just drive."

She obeyed. I didn't risk conversation until we'd cleared the border and were a good ten miles into the countryside, even though I realized that was paranoid. The transfer was built to contain its own atmosphere—no one was going to hear a hushed conversation through the thick glass.

But then again, no one was supposed to recognize me with my contacts and hair dye.

"Are you going to talk to me now?" Mrs. Sardis asked after she'd checked the rearview mirror to make sure we were alone in the wilderness.

I opened my mouth to answer—and suddenly realized I was having a full-blown panic attack. The pressure clogged my throat and shoved all cognitive thought out of my head except for blinding fear. I pulled the receipt out of my pocket and shoved it at her, then clenched my jaw to stop my teeth from chattering.

She drove with one hand while she smoothed the paper out and read it. She muttered something inaudible under her breath.

"Either she's seen my videos," I stuttered, words clipped, "or she heard about it from the tattoo artist."

Given the amount of ink she had on her arms, both scenarios were equally possible, and neither of them was good.

Mrs. Sardis stepped on the gas. "Nic will know what to do."

Will he? Nic couldn't fix this. At least two people now knew who I was—and, more importantly, that I was in this quadrant on Mars, which limited the search field significantly. How many other people they had told? If any of them recorded a video or made a social media post…

"Guess I should have gotten that piercing," I said, and sobbed.

Mrs. Sardis laid a consoling hand on my knee as she gunned the vehicle towards the base.

I'd never been so happy to see the glittering metal-and-glass structure rise on the horizon, even as I fought back the dread lining my stomach. How long would I be safe on base? One slip-up would turn my haven into a prison again—and bring Nic and everyone else down with me.

I was out of the car almost before the atmosphere was restored. The door to the lobby opened, revealing a tall figure posed there as if he had been waiting for us.

Nic. I was relieved to see him at the same time guilt nipped my cheeks. Had he already heard what happened?

I darted into the lobby and was about to spill my confession, but he spoke first.

"There's something you need to hear."

5

The recording was crackly and clogged with static, as if it had been ripped and modulated several times. His voice sounded close and yet muffled at the same time, and there was heavy background noise—maybe a train, or a car. But it was him.

"Radio check. This is Catalyst. Tell Blue Fire 10-4. Tell Klez 10-106. All listening 10-5. Over."

Daddy.

He repeated the message two more times, then the recording went silent. I stared at the blank media player on Nic's screen, letting the sound of my father's voice echo in my heart. I braced myself for a rush of emotion—the elation, the worry, the desire—but it never came. All I had was a tense longing, as if I were posed on the edge of a cliff, expecting—hoping—for more.

I looked down at Nic, who sat at the desk, watching me. "What did he mean?"

"10-4 means you've received and understood a message. So, assuming 'Blue Fire' means you..." Nic had the grace to soften his voice. "He's telling you he saw your videos."

There was the tidal wave of emotion as a dozen lonely, one-sided conversations suddenly came to fruition.

He knew. Daddy knew. He knew, and he understood.

Thank you, Jesus.

I swallowed back tears. "Any idea who Klez is?"

"It's an infamous computer virus from the 2000s, so best guess is it's your brother." Nic gestured at the screen. "10-106 means your status is secure. He's probably telling him it's safe to make contact."

My heart started beating faster as the implications took hold. "How did you get this recording?"

He hesitated for a suspicious beat. "From a… friend." He choked on the word, as if he wasn't sure he liked the taste. "He still monitors the CB down on Earth."

"The what now?"

"Citizens band—it's an old form of local radio."

"Radio," I repeated, and marveled.

Nic misinterpreted my silence. "Yes, it's a dated form of communicating sound over the electromagnetic spectrum—"

I put a hand up to stop him. "I know what a radio is. I just didn't think anyone used them anymore."

"They don't—not officially. Which is probably exactly why your father is." He leaned back in the chair. "The United banned most forms of radio because it's difficult to track. There are ways to find a transmitter, but only while it's actively broadcasting. More importantly, it's almost impossible to pinpoint the *receiver*. Not ideal for a government that wants a comprehensive log of its citizens' communication."

I pondered that. "So why aren't more people using it? People like us, I mean."

"Because it's horribly imprecise and utterly unsecured. If my friend picked up this transmission, that means anyone with a receiver in a five-mile radius heard it too—including the government."

I shuddered, but Nic generously assuaged my fears. "Unless your father left this broadcast running continually, they can't track him from it. All it tells them is what general vicinity he is—or was—in, and that's if they even realize who 'Catalyst' is."

"Did your friend know?"

Nic shrugged. "He was just doing what the message asked."

When I gave him a sideways look, he added, "10-5 means to relay the message."

"How do you know all this?"

"I looked it up."

I stared at the computer screen, a million hopes, plans, and prayers competing for priority in my mind. "Can we send him a message back?"

"You want to radio your father… *from Mars*."

The pedantic tone of his voice told me everything I needed to know, but I didn't like being talked down to. "What? Radio waves travel that far. Right?"

"Oh distance isn't the problem," he grunted. "The problem is you have no way of telling him what channel you'll be on. That and the time delay with radio from up here is a bit tedious. But more important is the fact that you want to broadcast—from Mars—your identity, on a radio transmission that could be picked up by *literally* anyone."

"I get it, I get it." I sighed, and with that motion, the obvious solution settled into place. "Then I have to go back."

He didn't react, cold gray eyes searching mine. I repeated myself, mostly to anchor my own courage. "I have to go back to Earth."

"You actually don't," he returned.

I frowned at him. "Yes, I do. Dad's file is a mess—there's no way he could buy a transit ticket, even if I could make contact."

"Certainly not."

"And I know he doesn't have the money to forge a file."

"A reasonable assumption, but none of this necessitates that *you* have to go back to Earth." It was Nic's turn to sigh, like this whole thing was a necessary evil. "But I can see that you're going to."

I crossed my arms. "Do you have a better idea?"

"Several, including doing absolutely nothing." He turned back to the computer and started typing. "But what's your great idea?"

Well, it certainly doesn't involve sitting around doing nothing like you're doing. "I've got money, right?"

He grunted an affirmative.

"And you said it's easy to forge a file—maybe not one that looks legitimate, but at least enough of a shell to buy a transit ticket."

He glanced at the ceiling as if praying to some unknown god. "I did, unfortunately, say that."

"So if I can get back to Earth and make contact, I can buy him and Ephesus temp files and bring them back here."

I paused as the elephant in the room made its ungraceful appearance. "*Can* I bring them back here?"

"Well, let me think about that." His tone suggested he was actually giving it some thought, and I bit my lip. "If you bring your father and brother back here, I'll have all the loose cannons who could blow my cover under one roof where I can keep an eye on them. Yeah no—that sounds like a pretty good deal." He shot me a sideways glance. "Of course they can live here. Don't be petty. I'll even be nice and not force them to work against their will, since we're such good friends and all."

"Thanks," I said, trying to be genuine even though I wanted to slap him. "Where did your friend pick this up?" I gestured at the screen.

"Somewhere outside Boston."

"See? Dad hasn't even left the city—which means Ephesus probably hasn't either." Relief flushed through me as I ran the numbers. Thames's office was in Boston, which meant he had probably detained Dad and Ephesus somewhere nearby. Dad had stayed in the area to look for Ephesus, so Ephesus no doubt did the same. If they hadn't already made contact with each other, they soon would. All I had to do was go back to Earth and get them out.

I took a deep breath and straightened, the resolution solidifying in my stomach. "I'm going back."

Nic didn't look up, so I kept going. "I'm going back to find them and bring them home."

I mentally ran through the dozens of hitches to my plan. Radio wasn't private—I couldn't announce my identity and location on there any more than I could online. But I was currently on another *planet*, and Dad had still managed to make contact. If I could get down there and get within range, we could work together. I could save him and Ephesus. I had the money—and I even had the contacts.

"I'll call Jayde," I formulated my thoughts out loud. "He's got an altered file—he can hook me up with someone who can forge credentials for Dad and Ephesus. He can probably also get me a place to stay."

Nic stopped typing in the middle of a sentence and looked up. "You're going to do what?"

His tone made me second-guess everything that had left my mouth for the past five minutes. "I'm going back to Earth?"

"No, the next part."

"To find Dad and Ephesus and get them new files?"

"Keep going."

"And I'm staying with Jayde?"

He propped his arm over the back of the chair and regarded me. "I just need you to stop and appreciate the glorious stupidity of that statement."

"What?" I complained, although even as the word left my mouth, I realized how I must sound. It would sound less weird if everyone didn't have the annoying habit of calling Jayde my online boyfriend. "I won't stay with him *alone*, if that's what you're implying."

"Whether or not you have a chaperone is the least of my concerns," Nic scoffed. "What makes you think this is a good idea? No really," he said in response to my glare, "help me through your thought process. I'm learning how to communicate with a sheltered homeschooler."

I rolled my eyes at the same time I flushed red. "He's someone I trust—"

"Ahh! I'm going to stop you right there. That's your problem." Nic sat up and sketched in the air like he was writing on a whiteboard. "You see that word? Trust?" He spelled it out. "You're using it wrong. I don't think it means what you think it means."

I crossed my arms. "Oh? And what do *you* think it means?"

"Giving respect and access to someone who has proven themselves reliable," he said, which was a surprisingly biblical answer.

"Which Jayde has," I emphasized.

His eyebrows did their stupid little dance. "How so?"

"Did you miss the part where he saved us from Thames?"

"The way I see it, *you* saved us from Thames. But we can argue about how many star stickers you both get on your achievement charts later. The point is, you can't trust Jayde."

I trust him more than I trust you, I thought, and unfortunately the sentiment came out in words. "And what would you know about trust?"

He was unaffected. "I trust you."

I stopped.

"Look, I know he's cute and heroic and all, but you shouldn't trust him. Thank him if you must, but don't give him any slack. Whatever you think you're feeling, it ain't trust."

Then what is it? I challenged, and searched my spirit. I had no reason not to trust Jayde. He had been kind to me; he'd helped me break out of jail; he'd given me valuable information; and he'd helped me stop Thames. He'd never done anything to betray my trust. What more was I looking for?

Nic tried to help. "You don't *know* him, Andi. You realize that, right?" His tone suggested that he doubted my mental capacity to complete this self-assessment.

I met his gaze. "What do you mean? I met him when Thames arrested me."

"Yeah, but you have no idea if this is the same guy. Have you talked on the phone? Video chatted? No, you haven't. He could literally be anybody."

The realization that he was right dawned on me with a shiver that crawled up my spine. "But he knew my nicknames, and about Cea…"

"So did Carnegie."

I flinched.

Immediately, I started second-guessing every interaction I'd had with "Aurelius." What if it *wasn't* Jayde? Who else could it be? He acted like my friend, sure—but even Thames had pretended like he cared about me. What if I *couldn't* trust him?

But then, how did "Aurelius" know so much about Jayde? He'd known about the incident with Cea, and Jayde's job, and his security access. If it wasn't Jayde talking, the only other explanation was that "Aurelius" had done something *to* Jayde.

That was an extreme scenario, of course, but Nic was right. I didn't know. I didn't know anything. *Oh God, what have I done?*

Nic seemed uninterested in my self-flagellation. "If he's being helpful or offering useful information, take advantage of that. But if you want my advice?"

He paused. I waited. I did want it, but I wasn't going to beg for it.

Nic turned back to his computer. "Use him, but don't trust him."

He resumed typing while I marinated that admonition in silence. He was right—traveling *to another planet* to stay with a stranger wasn't my smartest idea, especially when I had a secret identity to protect.

"But I still need to get back to Earth," I continued the thought aloud.

"That's one solution," he said without looking up.

"Which means I need a place to stay."

"You've got money—book a hotel."

I did have the money, but staying in a hotel didn't sound much safer than meeting up with Jayde. Everyone saw you come and go at a hotel; if I was trying to slide under the radar, checking into public accommodations that were heavily surveilled was probably not my best option.

"You got any better ideas?" I shot back.

He stopped typing and stared at the wall for a minute.

"Well." He punched a key to end whatever he was doing on the computer. "You could stay with my parents."

6

Nic waited patiently for me to adjust my reality around that statement.

I cleared my throat. "So, this is going to sound dumb…"

"I'm used to it."

"…because I realize, factually speaking, everyone has parents…"

"That is how biology works."

"…but I didn't realize you, you know, *had* parents."

"You thought they were dead," he said patronizingly, like he was bargaining with a five-year-old.

"Yeah. And don't say I never asked." I cut him off with a finger wag. "Because when would we have had time to talk about that?"

"Exactly. My familial status has been completely irrelevant up until this present moment. Now that this information potentially has some value to you, I'm offering it."

"Thanks." Had it only been Nic involved, I would have accepted that explanation and moved on. However, Nic was not an only child. "Cea acts like your parents are dead."

"To her, they are."

The most likely conclusion washed over my nerves like liquid nitrogen. "Does she… know they're alive?"

For the first time since we'd met, Nic made the effort to look properly offended. "Of course she knows. What, you think I'd lie about that?"

"Wouldn't be the first time you faked somebody's death," I mumbled.

He paused to consider that. "Fair point, although I think your limited experience skews the data. But no." He leveled his voice, the one reliable marker of his intentionality. "She knows. She just decided it was easier to pretend they were dead than to contend with the uncomfortable reality of their existence."

"Why?"

"Coping mechanism. Yours is obsessive-compulsive reading. Hers is avoiding confrontation."

"No, I mean like, what happened?"

Nic sighed and rapped his finger on the desk, and I suddenly realized that Cea wasn't the only one avoiding things.

"They had neurosurgery," he declared finally.

I swallowed. "Why?"

He frowned. "You've met my sister—why do you think?"

I thought about the illegal Bibles Nic had on his database and smiled. "They're Christian."

"*Were*," Nic corrected, not returning my smile.

I searched his expression. "When did they undergo the procedure?"

"About eight years ago."

I did the math. Cea would have still been a teenager. More importantly, that was before neurosurgery had been deemed "safe."

I wasn't sure the procedure had ever gotten full federal approval as a legal corrective device. They talked about it periodically; usually it came up around election time to give the career politicians something polarizing but irrelevant to debate on TV. It had been a long time since I'd heard of anyone undergoing the procedure; the containment camps were a much more palatable option for reconditioning unassimilated people like me.

Nic wasn't volunteering any more information, so I knew I'd have to lead. "But they survived?"

"With flying colors—if you consider only their physical health. It could have been the celebrity case that inspired the legalization of the procedure, if it weren't for the annoying complication that they both forgot literally everything they know."

He glared at the unforgiving wall of his office. I gave him space and waited.

"Dad was an engineer. Brilliant—way more than me. The experiments I've done look like science fair projects compared to what he's accomplished."

That seemed like a stretch—considering the numerous diabolical heists Nic had pulled off—but maybe he was better at scheming than engineering. Still, it was the most endearing thing I'd ever heard him say about another human being.

"He helped designed stations like this." Nic waved his hand at the glass-and-metal dome that shielded us from the sparse Martian atmosphere. "He was one of the main scientists responsible for putting humans on Mars."

I gave that achievement the moment of silence it deserved. "Why would they risk putting someone like that through neurosurgery? That seems self-defeating."

"That's what I said. But you know how legalistic they are. Having your top-awarded scientist be unassimilated doesn't look good on press releases. I guess they were hoping they could cut the saint out of his brain but keep the doctor."

I knew exactly how the United was—but neurosurgery still seemed like a ridiculously ineffective solution to the problem. "Couldn't they have just locked him up in a containment camp and forced him to work for free?"

"Those weren't public knowledge yet—but believe me, they tried. Dad wouldn't have it and raised all hell." Nic regarded me with something that could almost be construed as affection. "You two would have gotten along."

I smiled, but that was as far as the sentiment went for Nic. His face returned to its natural state of condescension as he continued, "Dad never took no for an answer either—put him in a containment camp and he'd blow the place up. Which he did. Twice."

"I think I heard about that." I had vague recollections of seeing it on the news and overhearing Mom and Dad talk about it when they thought I wasn't listening. Of course, the news had vaguely referred to the camp as a "correctional facility"; I had no idea I'd be living in one a few years later.

"You probably did—he was too high-profile to keep out of the news. Eventually he told them that they'd have to put a bullet in his head if they wanted him to deny his religion, and Mom was right there with him. No amount of pleading from me *or* Cea could convince them otherwise."

I stiffened. "So they put them under?"

"Without consent or warning. I didn't get the call until the state realized they needed 24/7 care. Thought they could rope me into doing it for free because we're 'family.' I told them I was current on my taxes."

I imagined that was *not* what Nic had said to them, but I was grateful to him for not repeating the actual language he used. "They're braindead?" I reached the obvious conclusion.

"Oh no, their brains are functioning perfectly. They've just been wiped of any useful information."

I searched his face for any residue of emotion. "They don't remember you."

"Or any of their combined five doctorate degrees, or how to function in polite society, or how to survive as independent adults. They're doing better now, but it took almost three years of therapy and round-the-clock care to get them to the point where they could largely take care of themselves. Ever try to potty-train a forty-year-old?"

I cringed. If the bad PR wasn't enough to kill the legalization of neurosurgery, the fact that it ladened the state with costly dependents no doubt doomed it. It was cheaper to put people in a work camp—or kill them, if you were willing to deal with the paperwork.

"I'm sorry," was all I could think of to say, and it seemed the most inadequate.

Nic shrugged and sank in his chair, as if the emotional transparency had exhausted him.

I gave him a minute to recover. It certainly explained why Nic hated the United—although I'm sure there had been more than one grudge motivating his mastermind plan to cut Mars off from government control. And Cea—I was still surprised she hadn't said anything to me, especially after I'd been so frank about my own mother's death. But I could see why it was easier for her to pretend they were gone.

Sometimes it's easier to pretend people aren't there than to wish for a relationship you can't have.

I prayed for Cea, wherever she was, and then my present conundrum regained control of my thoughts. How did any of this help me in my search for a place to stay?

"Is it safe for me to stay with them?"

Nic barked a dry laugh. "Their house is probably the safest place on Earth. They're completely harmless and intolerably dull, and they'll forget you as soon as you leave the room." His eyes finally met mine. "Which for you is a big plus."

It would definitely be in my favor to stay with someone who couldn't tell the United—or Carnegie—where I'd been.

"Besides," Nic continued, "since I'm your legal guardian, no one will question why I sent you to visit my parents. So if anyone does happen to check your papers, it will make sense."

I nodded, convinced. "Okay."

Nic returned the gesture. "I'll make some calls." He resumed typing. "Mom might give you a hard time, but don't let her bully you."

I decided to avoid the obvious sarcastic response. "How do I buy a ticket back to Earth?"

"Ask Sardis."

"You don't know how?"

"No, I just don't want to help you with something so pedestrian. That's why I have people. Tell Sardis what you're doing, and he'll take care of everything. Just let me know when you leave the planet."

"Okay. And thank you." He didn't acknowledge that, so I turned to go.

"Andromeda."

I glanced back at him, expecting a heartless goodbye.

He didn't look up from his screen. "Tell my folks I said hi."

7

Three hours later, I had my transit ticket.

We could have accomplished it much sooner had the Sardises not spent the first hour trying to talk me out of going, and then the next hour and a half scouring the internet trying to find the best deal on a flight. I told them I had enough money—I could just buy direct from the transit line—but Mr. Sardis insisted on finding a discount. After we found one that satisfied his budget—and my itinerary—Mrs. Sardis walked me back to my dorm and helped me pack.

I couldn't take any of my old outfits, that was a given. I thought about throwing everything away, but Mrs. Sardis suggested I hang them in the back of the closet so I could have them "if" I came back.

She did not say "when."

She watched me as I folded my suite of unworn jeans and t-shirts into a carryon she'd loaned me. It was too risky to take Mama's purple suitcase—Carnegie was the only person alive who knew what it looked like, but he was one of the main people I didn't want to find me.

"Are you sure about this?" she said after several minutes of silence.

It was no use answering the question for the tenth time that night, so instead I returned with, "Do you think I shouldn't?"

Her sigh said everything. "What about Carnegie? We have no idea where he is. What if he's watching the base and follows you out there?"

That seemed unlikely. Nic had more than one layer of security around the base, and according to the proximity sensors, Carnegie had left when Thames died and not returned. It was far more likely that the cunning old man had fled to Earth to regroup and find new investors, but his file hadn't been updated one way or the other in the past two weeks. It wasn't out of the realm of possibility that he was still around.

But no matter where he was, I knew Carnegie was also after my father—and I couldn't let him get there first. "I have to find my dad before Carnegie does. Besides, if Ephesus and Cea are alive, they're probably still in the area. They may have heard Dad's message too."

I was fully aware of how many "if's" I'd crammed into that breath, but it didn't matter. Nothing she could say would have convinced me to stay. I had an opportunity to find my family, and I was taking it.

"But what if someone recognizes you?" She must have realized I wasn't responding to "what if's," because she abruptly changed tactics. "Someone *will* recognize you. Someone recognized you today—on Mars, where there *isn't* a security camera on every corner."

I looked up and caught my reflection in the mirrored closet doors. She had a point. The waitress today may have been tipped off, but millions of people on Earth had seen my videos. And that didn't count the dozens of United officials who were actively searching for me and my father.

Mars wasn't looking for me. Earth was.

I straightened and ran a hand over my hair, which was sticky and shiny from the cheap dye. I was still wearing my contacts and makeup from before, and even I could see that the façade only ran skin deep. Between my greasy hair and cakey foundation, I *looked* fake.

And if I was going to find my father before our enemies did, spending two hours in the bathroom every day putting on my face was probably not to my advantage.

But what else could I do? I'd tried everything to hide my appearance— everything that wasn't permanent.

My courage choked in my throat. Nic's angry words echoed back to me.

That girl is dead to you.

I pinched a chunk of hair between my fingers.

Let her die.

Mrs. Sardis mistook my silence. "Please, Philadelphia, reconsider."

I strode over to the desk before I could do exactly that. I threw the drawers open with a bang, rooting through the standard-issue tape and glue until I found what I was looking for: a pair of scissors.

I turned back to the mirror and held the scissors close to my ear. A flash of panic almost stopped me—that was ten years of growth I held in my fist.

Mrs. Sardis cautiously stood up. "Philadelphia…?"

I tightened my grip. "My name is Andromeda Nolan."

I slid the scissors down until they were just past my shoulder, closed my eyes, and cut.

Mrs. Sardis gasped.

I dropped the dead hair on the floor. I gave my heart a minute to calm down before I opened my eyes and turned to face her.

"How do you think I would look blonde?"

*

By morning, I was unrecognizable.

After Mrs. Sardis had cried over my cut locks and fussed about how I didn't have to do that—even though we both knew I definitely did—she ran to find someone to "fix" it. With the help of the lab techs and their chemicals, we bleached my hair to an ashy shade of blonde, and Mrs. Sardis tidied my hack job. My hair now fell just to my shoulders.

I'd also taken Mrs. Sardis's suggestion and gotten my ears pierced. Again, the techs had more than enough implements that could put a hole in my ear, so I got one stud on my left ear and two on my right. Mrs. Sardis said asymmetrical piercings were all the rage on Earth right now.

I had to admit, it matched the rest of my new aesthetic: ripped jeans, black jacket, generic band t-shirt. I switched my green contacts for a haunting blue and painted my nails an arrogant shade of purple. I'd gone lighter on the makeup, aiming for a look that was more natural, with a brush of bronzer to make it look like I'd seen Earth's sun in the last decade.

I spun before the mirror and tried to tell myself that I liked my appearance. I looked good—cohesive, convincing, like I was a real person. But something was missing.

I walked to my suitcase that lay open on the coffee table and rooted through my makeup bag. My fingers closed around a thin object. I pulled it out and held it up to the light: the mascara Narissa had given me. Her note was still taped to the end.

I twirled it in my fingers and tried to picture how she had done my makeup. There had been a lot more steps involved—more than I would ever be able to master on my own—but surely I could copy some of it.

I grabbed a black eyeliner and turned back to the mirror. Taking a deep breath to steady my hand, I drew a thin line under each eye. Then I found the eyeshadow palette Mrs. Sardis had picked out and painted my lids a murky purple with a hint of glitter.

I stood back and looked myself over again. The illusion was perfect. I looked moody, confident, calm.

Everything I wasn't feeling right now.

Swallowing a prayer, I sat down on the couch and picked up my tablet. The screen flickered on to a barrage of notifications. "Aurelius," as he often did, had sent me a tsunami of texts.

I'd messaged him briefly yesterday to give him my new username and apologize for Nic; mercifully, he'd taken the whole thing in stride. But in all the chaos of last night, I'd forgotten to check my messages until just now, and he had assumed the worst of my absence.

I skimmed the message history. It was clear he had also heard about Dad's transmission, which confirmed a couple of things. One, that the underground was still monitoring "the CB," and two, that people had obeyed the message and passed it along. That meant it was very likely Cea and Ephesus had heard it, if they were still in the area—but it also meant that Carnegie and the United officials had heard it.

This is why I have to get down there now.

I kept reading. I could tell when Aurelius's messages changed from friendly prods to concerned questions, concern that had gotten increasingly more frantic when I'd failed to respond.

It did look like he had taken Nic's warning to heart, though, because his messages were noticeably absent of names. Instead, he tried every way to tell me, without telling me, that he'd heard my father's transmission and was wondering what I was going to do.

HEARD THE NEWS. WHAT DO YOU THINK?

ARE YOU COMING TO THE PARTY?

SRSLY CHECK YOUR TEXTS

HEY. NEED TO KNOW IF YOU'RE COMING

EVERYTHING GOOD? ANYTHING I SHOULD KNOW?

I clicked in the text box and stared at the blinking cursor, writing and rewriting my reply in my head. How could I tell him discretely that I was on my way to Earth?

You don't know him.

I took my hand away from the keyboard. I didn't know Jayde—but then again, I didn't know anybody. I had no one. Everyone I used to know was either locked in a containment camp or on the run. I was going to walk into one of the United's biggest metropolitan areas, armed with a fake identity and some eyeliner, to stay with strangers who had been brain-wiped.

It would be nice to have an ally who had all his faculties.

He could literally be anybody.

But then again, I still had no idea why Jayde—if it was him—had even befriended me. All I knew was that he hated the United, at least enough to help me fight Thames. But how deep did that loyalty run? What skin did he have in this game? He had gone to an awful lot of effort and put himself at great risk for someone he'd only known for a few weeks. Why?

And in the meantime, he was also the dead man's switch on the bomb that was my new identity. He was the only person outside the base who knew my real name and had a way to contact me. He could reveal my location to anyone—and if he saw me in person, with my new hair and style, he could tell the United everything they needed to know.

Use him, but don't trust him.

Nic was right; Aurelius couldn't know I was on Earth.

I pondered sending a goodbye message but thought better of it. I closed the app before I could change my mind, turned my tablet off, and zipped it in my backpack.

Mr. Sardis met me in the docking bay. He hadn't seen me since yesterday, so he took in my new appearance with a wide-eyed stare. "You look great," he said finally, but I couldn't tell if he meant it. "Ready to go?"

There was a fake pause and even faker smile that punctuated that statement, and I knew that was a final plea for me to change my mind. I didn't trust my voice to be confident, so I just nodded firmly and handed him my suitcase.

He sighed and loaded it in the trunk.

A voice emerged from behind us. "When will you be back?"

I turned to see Nic standing in the doorway to the lobby. "Me?" I asked, and panicked. I had no idea when I would be back; I hadn't even stopped to consider it.

Nic shook his head and gestured at Mr. Sardis. "I expect about four hours, sir," he answered. "I'd like to see her off if you can spare me."

Nic nodded. Mr. Sardis tipped an imaginary hat and climbed into the driver's seat.

Nic reached into the pocket of his lab coat and withdrew a white business card. He wordlessly held it out to me. I took it and squinted at the small print. There was nothing on it except for a graphic of a mountain range and a phone number with a country code I didn't recognize. I looked up at him and raised an eyebrow.

"Don't call him until you're ready to buy new files," he said. "But when you do, tell him I sent you."

I nodded and slid the card into the inner pocket of my backpack. Then I walked to the transfer and opened the passenger door.

"Philadelphia," he called.

I glanced back at him, startled that he'd used my real name.

His eyes found mine. His voice held no ambiguity as he said, "Keep your head down."

Then before I could respond, he stepped back into the lobby and shut the door.

8

I stopped in the middle of the sidewalk and put on a great show of looking like I knew what I was doing.

The flight down had been uneventful. Mr. Sardis had carried my luggage to security, bought me a bag of candy for the ride, and given me a long, fatherly hug that I savored. Then he mercifully let me go without another word.

I'd given myself a little scare when I scanned my fingerprints and *Nolan, Andromeda* popped up on my ticket. That's what it was supposed to say, of course, but it was still weird seeing it in print.

I'd gathered my wits and passed through security without an issue. There were no glitches, no warnings on my file, and no wary glances from strangers. One of the attendants even complimented my asymmetrical piercing. Then I was ushered to my seat and left to my own devices.

I managed the three-day flight just fine—it wasn't the first time I'd made the trip—and even succeeded in navigating the labyrinthian transit hub in Boston to pick up my luggage. I found my way outside to the bus stop, and that was where my confidence ground to a halt.

I stood on the curb and was assaulted with the blare of car horns, the roar of launching airplanes, the throbbing of a crowd of people, and the crippling realization that this was the first time I'd been "outside" in nearly six years.

Unless you counted my brief stint in Stanyard's basement, I'd spent my entire teenage years either locked in a containment camp, fighting for my life in jail, or secluded on the base on Mars. None of which had done anything to prepare me for the challenge of navigating Boston's public transportation system.

In retrospect, I probably should have done some research on basic life skills—how to ride the bus, how to buy groceries, what music was trending—because right now, my greatest enemy was my ignorance. My official file now claimed I had nearly eighteen years of well-adjusted life experience, and the world was going to expect me to act like it.

I took a deep breath and let it out with a prayer. The Holy Spirit had gotten me out of a burning factory, among other inconceivable scrapes—surely He could help me figure out the bus.

I took my tablet out of my backpack. I typed the address Nic had given me into maps and routed walking directions. The internet rose to the occasion and populated a step-by-step path.

I laughed to myself. One benefit of living in a hyper-connected and heavily-surveilled economy was that you could give very precise directions.

I checked the digital signboard and found the bus I needed. The next one was due in mere minutes, so I shouldered my carryon and ran the rest of the way. I made it just as the bus jerked up to the curb, its electric engine buzzing at an annoying pitch. I joined the short line of people waiting to board and watched their motions.

The first two simply walked onto the bus without even glancing at the driver. A bar above the door chirped and flashed green as they passed.

The next man attempted to board, but the door flashed red and screeched at him. I reflexively cringed, the nightmare of a hundred rejections rushing back at me. The driver glanced up and gave the man a bored stare. The man grumbled, took off his overstuffed backpack, and rooted through it until he found a laptop. He made a dramatic scene of holding it up to the scanner, which accepted the sacrifice and turned green. The man continued to mutter as he dragged his backpack to a seat in the rear.

Then it was my turn. I panicked, even as my feet continued to move me forward. What if I needed a special app?

Too late to ask. I put my foot on the step and braced myself for the denial and shame—but the bus welcomed me warmly. The driver acknowledged me with a jerk of his thumb towards the back, and I stumbled to an empty seat, trying not to shake with relief. I sat down just as the bus lurched forward.

There, I told myself and the Holy Spirit. *One step done.*

I would be riding this bus for a while—the first stop was a transfer hub twenty minutes away—so I settled back in the seat and watched out the window. Boston had been my city all my life, but I rarely got to see it like this.

It was approaching six o'clock, and the world was caught in the twilight. The sun was just beginning to set, but the streetlights had not yet turned on, so the city was bathed in soft glow and shadow. Rush hour had given way to the post-dinner stroll. People—beautiful, disparate, unique people—milled on sidewalks and crowded taverns. A few children still played in parks and chased electric scooters down the sidewalk. The scenery was both welcoming and foreign at the same time.

With my anxiety pacified, my consciousness had room for curiosity. If there wasn't a special app, how did the bus know I was cleared to ride? I knew there was no ticket fee—they'd taught us that much in school—but the door had scanned *something*.

I pulled out my tablet and flipped through my recent notifications. There was a location ping stating that I'd boarded bus #763 at stop 1112 for the westbound 64 route. I clicked on the notification, and it pulled up my personal file.

There I was, Andromeda Nolan, with all my recent travel activity dutifully logged. Since I owned this file, I could see every piece of information that was associated with my name—at least, every piece of information the United wanted me to see.

It made you wonder how much information the United was recording that they didn't disclose.

But how did the bus know it was me? The only explanation was that it had scanned my tablet—which was now officially registered as belonging to Andromeda Nolan.

I thought back to the warnings Nic had given me before I left. Between him and Mr. Sardis—who had given me a safety lecture on the ride to the transit hub—I'd compiled a lengthy list of rules for my trip.

Rule 1: Remember that any time you make an electronic transaction or pass under a censor bar, you're making a permanent log under Andromeda. Don't do anything or go anywhere that she wouldn't.

Well, if anyone was watching Andromeda's file, they now knew she was back on Earth. It was that sinisterly simple—all I had to do was board a bus, and the United knew exactly where I was and where I was going, if they cared to look.

I shuddered, but there was no avoiding it, so I packed the feeling down and tried to ignore it. No one was looking at my file. The trick was to keep it that way.

It was nearly dark by the time I'd transferred buses and gotten off in a ritzy subdivision in Allston. The houses weren't large—most of them were hardly bigger than the concrete boxes we'd had in the containment camp—but they were single-family, which for downtown was a luxury. The homes were tall and narrow, with barely a hair's breadth of yard between them. Most of them had been built in the 1900s, and even though they had been plastered over with metal siding and solar panels, their age showed. Far nicer (and larger) condos could have been obtained at a fraction of the cost, but apparently the privilege of genetically modified grass was worth paying for.

Nic's parents lived in a house at the end of the street. Their porchlight wasn't on, but I wasn't expecting it to be. Nic said he'd called to let them know I was coming, but he also said they would likely forget as soon as they hung up the phone.

In other words, I was calling on this poor couple unannounced, expecting to be given a place to stay.

And I absolutely did not have a backup plan if they refused.

I took a deep breath. *Holy Spirit, pave the way.*

I walked up to the door and waved my hand over the touchless doorbell. The words "please wait" danced across the screen. The admonition was moot, because the door opened not ten seconds later.

A quaint elderly couple appeared in the doorway, backlit by the warm glow of their living room lamps. They looked so perfect and kind and stereotyped that it was easier to imagine them as characters in a TV show than as real people. Even their motions seemed scripted as the wife pulled open the door, her husband calling *"Who is it, honey?"* as he approached from behind.

I answered before either of them could ask. "Hi, Mrs. Von Nieuwenhuyse. I'm Andromeda Nolan. Nic sent me—he said he called."

Roseanne—Nic had mercifully given me a rundown of their names— opened the storm door but didn't step out onto the porch. She was a more elegant, refined version of Cea, her graying curls styled primly around her contoured face. Her eyes were piercing, and she gave me a once-over so sharp that I'm surprised the motion didn't give her whiplash. "Who are you? And who's Nic?"

I swallowed as I remembered Nic's second rule.

Rule 2: Don't try to explain to my parents that they have a son. You'll get stuck in that conversation forever. Just tell them I'm a colleague of his and we used to work together.

"He worked with you after college." I turned my attention to Paul, who was crowding his wife's shoulder in the doorway. "You were partners in a big space station project."

"Really?" Paul mused, but he sounded more like he was fascinated by the idea than recognizing that it belonged to him. He looked like a police sketch of Nic aged thirty years. He had a nearly identical fluffy mustache with an afterthought of a goatee. Both were washed a comforting salt-and-pepper gray, but his wayward hair still had a bit of blond left in it.

Roseanne glanced back at him. "Space stations? Since when have you worked on space stations?"

"I've been working on space stations since..." Paul started, then realized he had no idea.

I tried to grab the conversation and reel it back in. "I just came from a Martian base you helped design," I boasted—which, according to Nic, was essentially the truth. "It's an honor to meet you."

"Mars!" he crowed. "I've always wanted to see Mars."

"That's news to me," Roseanne muttered.

Paul either didn't hear her or chose to ignore her. He gave me a second look, as if I had suddenly gotten far more interesting. "You live up there? Maybe I should come visit you on my next vacation."

I imagined the Von Nieuwenhuyses visiting their son on Mars and couldn't decide if that would be endearing or disastrous. "Nic would love to have you. He spoke very highly of you."

"Oh, did he now?" Paul's eyes twinkled, and I knew I'd won him over.

I returned his grin. "He has the utmost respect for you and your work, and he wanted me to tell you he says hello."

Paul looked positively tickled, but Roseanne hadn't caught up yet. "He sent you all the way from Mars just to tell us that? Does he know emails exist?"

Her tone could have cut sheetrock, and I suddenly realized which parent Nic took after.

Also just like Nic, her sharpness made me falter and question everything about myself. "No, I... he suggested you would be a safe place to stay while I... applied to Harvard." That was the story Nic had told me to repeat, but it suddenly sounded lame to my ears.

"Good luck getting in there," she huffed. "And this man, Nic, he's your... father?"

"Ew no," I said, too quickly. "I'm his..." *What am I?* I stalled, then settled for a partial truth. "My parents used to work for him. He took me in when they died."

The light in Paul's eyes flickered like a threatened candle. "I'm very sorry to hear that, dear, but it sounds like you're in good hands. He must be a very kind man."

When he wants to be.

My tragic backstory did seem to soften Roseanne a bit. "Yes, a very kind thing of him to do. I'm sure his parents are proud. But I'm just not sure we're set up to accommodate guests right now." She glanced up at her husband, silently prodding him to verify her statement.

I jumped in before he could answer. "I can cook and clean. I won't be any trouble."

Even as the word left my mouth, I imagined Nic laughing doubtfully.

The mention of food distracted Paul from the silent signals his wife was sending him. "Well now, that sounds like a pretty good deal!"

Roseanne dropped her pretense of subtlety. "Paul! We can't just invite strangers into our home!"

"I'm not—" I started, but Paul was quicker on the draw.

"She's not a stranger! She's a friend of Nic's. Besides, we can't turn her away now—it's late."

"It's 6pm," she deadpanned.

Paul was already walking back into the house, waving at me to follow. "Come on, it's cold out."

Roseanne made a last-ditch effort, even as she stepped out of the way to let me pass. "It's sixty-five degrees!"

"Well, I'm cold!"

She sighed, then frowned down at me. I picked up my carryon and found my most charming smile. "Thank you, Mrs. Von."

Rule 3: Don't waste your breath calling them Mr. and Mrs. Von Nieuwenhuyse. Mr. and Mrs. Von is just fine.

"Should I start calling you Dr. Von Nieuwenhuyse?"

"Not unless you want to be put up for adoption."

Mrs. Von offered me a smile that was about as genuine as most of Nic's, but she did let me in.

Mr. Von must have taken me literally on my offer to cook, because before I could even shed my jacket, he was showing me around the kitchen and asking me what we should make with the ground beef they had thawed. I could tell by the various implements and spices that were out on the counter that Mrs. Von had already started something—although whether or not she remembered what she was cooking was another story. I didn't want to step on her toes more than I already had, so I deferred and instead offered to wash the dishes.

Dinner was a production. It involved me reintroducing myself twice (to each of them on separate occasions), and I'm pretty sure the dish we ended up with was not the one Mrs. Von had intended to make when she started. But it was edible, and the comforting camaraderie of sitting around a dining room table with a family was worth the hassle.

Mrs. Von was more than happy to let me do all the cleanup as penance for my imposition, and by the time I was done, they'd both retired to the living room in front of the TV and completely forgotten about me. I bid them goodnight to a chorus of vague "Yes dear's" and went to show myself around the house.

There were two unused bedrooms on the second floor. Both of them had been shut up for years and, as such, had been spared the misery of forgetfulness. Unlike the rest of the house, which had been edited and rearranged by a woman who didn't know who she was, these bedrooms had been sealed like a time capsule, with Nic and Cea's childhood embalmed within.

Nic had the bedroom on the left. It was almost as austere and undecorated as the man himself, but the air of studiousness was as thick as the layer of dust that had settled on the furniture. The carpet near the wall was indented with the ghosts of overladen bookcases. There was a large desk, an even larger drafting board, and an advanced telescope that had, in its day, been top-of-the-line. All of it was arranged with exacting precision like hands on a clock.

Cea's bedroom was on the right. It gave the impression that she had attempted to be a girly girl in high school and then never bothered to change her wallpaper, even as her aesthetic drifted in another direction. A guitar with a snapped neck—signed by some emo heartbreaker—had been mounted on the wall right over pink psychedelic decals with curling edges. Memorabilia for bands from the previous decade competed with dolls and decaying makeup compacts on the dresser. And scattered here and there were trophies from her stint as a cheerleader—a signed jersey, dusty pompoms, and a frilled uniform hiding in the back of the closet.

I tried to imagine Cea in a short skirt performing somersaults on a football field, but I couldn't reconcile that image with the sharpshooter I knew now. I supposed that cheerleader didn't exist anymore, just like her parents, who were downstairs wandering lost in their own living room.

I decided it was more appropriate that I stay in Cea's room, even though Nic's felt strangely more familiar. I debated leaving my clothes in my suitcase—how long would I be staying?—but realized it would look better if I put on a pretense of settling in. I shoved Cea's old outfits to the side and hung mine up in the closet, arranged my makeup on the dresser, and set up the charging dock for my tablet on the nightstand, right next to a highschool-era picture of Nic and Cea that I was sure I'd seen hanging somewhere on base.

After I dismantled my hair and makeup, I settled on the bed and turned on my tablet.

Aurelius had sent numerous messages, all of which were variously-worded pleas begging me to respond—as he had been doing for the past five days. I cleared the notifications and ignored them, even though my heart twinged a little when I did it. Then I switched over and read the text from Nic.

DID THEY LET YOU IN THE DOOR?

NOT FOR LACK OF TRYING ON YOUR MOM'S PART

I WARNED YOU

YOU UNDERSOLD IT. EVEN YOU'RE MORE FRIENDLY THAN SHE IS

He didn't respond, which either meant I'd gone too far, or he didn't want to admit that he did, in fact, know how to be nice to me. I attempted to salvage the conversation.

THANKS AGAIN FOR THE HELP

JUST REMEMBER IT TAKES LIKE 5 MINUTES FOR THE WATER
TO RUN HOT IN THE UPSTAIRS SHOWER

I acknowledged that with a thumbs up, and he went offline. I closed the app and was suddenly reminded that I was very much alone on Earth.

The basket cases downstairs hardly counted.

And now what? I had gotten in the door and secured a safe place to stay—at least until they forgot about me and called the cops on their home intruder—but now I had to come up with a plan to find my dad, the most wanted man in the district. All without blowing my cover and ruining Andromeda's spotless reputation.

I picked Nic and Cea's picture off the nightstand. I tapped the glass over their stoic faces and wondered, not for the first time, how much easier this would be if either of them was here.

I set the picture down on the nightstand, flopped back on the pillow, and picked up my tablet. I reflexively went to open my Bible reader—then hesitated.

Rule 4: Remember that the Bible is illegal media, so take your reader offline if you're going to read it. But also remember that offline devices are illegal, so use them sparingly.

I glanced at the clock; it was late enough that nobody would expect me to be online. The algorithm better get used to the fact that Andromeda went to "bed" early every night.

I took my device offline, opened my reader, and started a conversation with the one person I knew wouldn't leave me.

9

The smell of bacon burning drew me out of sleep before my alarm did. I lay there, staring at the faded unicorn sticker preteen Cea had stuck to her ceiling fan, and waited until I heard Mrs. Von cussing herself out in the kitchen before I got up.

I sat on the edge of the bed and brought my tablet back online. My messaging app nearly choked on itself as it chimed multiple notifications at once. I knew without looking who it was; Aurelius had sent his usual barrage of angsty good mornings.

I sighed, managing to feel annoyed and guilty in equal proportions. Would it hurt just to let him know I was okay? I could at least tell him that I was safe; he didn't need to know anything else.

I opened the chat. Nic had showed me how to turn off the feature that let the sender know I'd read the message, so I could skim the notifications in private.

> I TAKE IT YOU'RE NOT COMING TO THE PARTY. ANY REASON WHY?

> EVERYONE'S ASKING ABOUT YOU. THEY WANT TO KNOW IF YOU'RE COMING. DO YOU NEED A RIDE?

> IS THIS ABOUT WHAT I SAID EARLIER? IF SO, I'M SORRY

I gripped my tablet with both hands, my heart dropping to the pit of my stomach.

> I WON'T DO IT AGAIN

> JUST PLEASE TALK TO ME

> I'M WORRIED ABOUT YOU

My next breath snagged on an unwelcome sound.

Just tell him you're all right. Tell him it's not his fault. If it's really Jayde, he'll understand.

I clicked in the text box, but before I could type a character, a new message came through.

HEY, DID YOU GET THE NEW INVITE?

I mentally scrolled back through our conversation and easily deduced what that meant: Dad had been on the CB again. And I needed to know what he said.

I hesitated with my finger over the screen. What would Nic say about texting back?

If he's offering useful information, take advantage of that.

NO I DIDN'T. WHAT DID IT SAY?

The app did a somersault as it coughed up multiple messages in short succession. Aurelius sent a swear word, followed by a run-on "you're okay I was so worried." Then, as if realizing neither of those messages was a good look, he attempted to save face with:

SO YOU *HAVE* BEEN GETTING MY MESSAGES

I fought back a wave of frustration. I knew he wasn't aware of everything going on—he didn't know I'd adopted a new file I needed to keep hidden—but he should understand how much was at stake. He knew how much danger I was in, never mind my father.

THIS ISN'T ABOUT YOU. WHAT DID THE INVITE SAY?

He ignored my reproof but mercifully answered the question.

THE PARTY'S BEEN MOVED

IS IT STILL IN TOWN?

FOR NOW

I drummed my fingers on the back of the tablet to channel my nervous energy. Dad was still in town—but he was on the move, which meant that if I didn't make contact soon, I might lose him again.

HAS ANYONE I KNOW RSVP'D?

BESIDES ME? I DON'T THINK SO

So Ephesus and Cea still hadn't made contact—which meant it was up to me to catch Dad before he left town.

Aurelius had the same thought.

YOU NEED TO RSVP. NOW

He was right, but I wasn't going to do it by proxy. I needed to find a radio.

I closed the chat without responding and leapt out of bed. I threw myself into some semblance of order and tumbled down the stairs, halting just outside the kitchen door. Mr. and Mrs. Von were sitting at the island, chatting in tune to the morning news that was broadcasting from the TV on the counter. I swallowed a prayer and braced myself for the anxiety of being reintroduced.

Be consistent, Nic had instructed. *They do have some short-term memory, but space is limited. The more consistent you are, the more likely they are to develop a pattern.*

I put on a smile and walked in like I belonged there. "Good morning, Mr. and Mrs. Von."

They both stopped midsentence and turned to stare at me.

"It's me, Andromeda, Nic's friend?" I offered.

Mrs. Von's eye twitched. "Oh, you're still here," she said finally. I passed it off with a fake laugh.

Mr. Von considered me for only a fraction of a second before he decided he still liked me. "Well, good morning! You're just in time for breakfast. Roseanne made my favorite." He finished his cup of coffee and stood to refill it.

"All food is your favorite." Mrs. Von indulged in an eyeroll that was clearly directed for me to see, and I wondered if she hated me slightly less than she did the night before. I pulled another stool up to the counter and sat down.

"Do you want some coffee…?" Mr. Von glanced back at me and squinted.

"Andromeda," I repeated.

The light returned to his eyes. "Ahh, right. How do you take it?" He grabbed another mug from the rack and started filling it before I even answered.

I hesitated. *What options are there?* "Uhh, black," I blurted, only because that's how Nic took his, and it was all I could think of.

He filled the mug nearly to the brim and slid it across the counter towards me. I accepted it and took a cautious sip. The strong, bitter flavor hit me in the teeth almost as hard as the scalding heat did. But I didn't want to look like an idiot, so I swallowed the mouthful with a smile and took another drink.

"Well, I've got to get to work. See you lovely ladies for dinner." Mr. Von grabbed a jacket from the rack and marched out of the room.

"You're retired," Mrs. Von called after him without turning around.

Mr. Von barely missed a beat. "Then I shall work on finishing this show!" He continued his stride into the living room as if that was where he had intended to go all along.

Mrs. Von turned the stove off. "Bacon or sausage, Miss…?"

"Andromeda, and bacon, please."

She nodded and, after opening and closing three separate cabinets, found a plate. She filled it with two eggs and a link of sausage and set it in front of me.

I ate the greasy meat without complaint, gears turning. If Mrs. Von couldn't remember what I'd said sixty seconds ago, she probably wouldn't remember if I asked her about an illegal radio.

"Do you know where I could get a radio?" I asked.

She gave me another whip-like stare, and I wondered if my question hadn't come off as casually as I'd intended it. "You kids still listen to the radio?" she scoffed.

I relaxed a bit. "No, no, I need it for a… school project." I took another brave sip of coffee.

She accepted the excuse with a snort. "Well, good luck with that—the last time I saw a radio was in a 2000s truck. Maybe try the junkyard."

It wasn't a terrible idea—but a young girl walking up to a junkyard asking to buy an illegal part off an old truck would probably push the bounds of suspicion. "I kind of need one that works. Any other ideas—"

I looked up and realized she wasn't listening to me at all. She stood there, deep in thought, grease dripping off her spatula.

I reached for a napkin. "Mrs. Von—?"

"Now where would he have put it?"

"Put what?"

She slapped her spatula on the counter. "Paul!" she shouted into the other room. "Didn't you used to have a radio?"

My heart restarted, and I strained to hear his answer.

"A what now?" he hollered back.

"A radio! You know, one of those walkie-talkie things. Right?" She glanced at me, looking for confirmation. I nodded encouragingly.

"I haven't seen a radio in years! Whatcha need one of those for?"

Neither of us bothered to answer him. Mrs. Von turned back to me with a shrug. "Maybe look it up online?"

That was also out of the question, but the gears were turning. Of course Mr. Von wouldn't have seen a radio in years—it had been eight since his neurosurgery. But before then he'd been a rebel, according to Nic. It wasn't out of the realm of possibility that he'd used a radio back then.

But would he still have it? He'd been a high-profile criminal; no doubt his home had been searched by government agents multiple times over the years. If there was still a radio in this house, it would have to be hidden very well.

Somewhere that had not been touched in over a decade.

I shoveled my eggs into my mouth and chased them down with a gulp of coffee. "I'll come back for the dishes," I told Mrs. Von as I stood up. "There's something I need to do for school."

She mumbled an affirmative. As soon as I left the kitchen, I heard her opening the dishwasher.

I muttered another prayer for her mental health and darted up the stairs to Nic's room.

The door creaked as I opened it, a signal I was about to step back in time. The room clearly hadn't been touched since Nic left for college, which would have been prior to his parents' surgery. It was possible the room had been overlooked by the censors.

I started at the door and searched all the way around the room, but unfortunately there wasn't much to look at. The closet was empty except for a band uniform that had been discarded like a prison jumpsuit. There were a few dried-out pens rolling around in the desk drawer, and school awards lined one shelf. The rest of the surfaces were bare.

I got down on the ground to look under the bed. *Nothing*, I groaned. *Except...*

From this angle, I could see that there was a bump in the carpet where the bookcases had been.

I knelt down and traced the rectangular indents in the carpet. There were three of them; three identical narrow bookcases must have once stood side-by-side. The carpet underneath was slightly less dusty than the rest of the room, as if the bookcases had been removed several years after Nic had moved out.

And the indent in the middle was clearly not level with the others.

I dug my fingernail into the crease and hit hard wood. I scraped and picked at it, ignoring the splinters, until the carpet loosened. I got one finger underneath the edge and pried it up. With a crack and a groan like an old man being wakened from sleep, a square panel came loose from the floor.

Underneath the floorboards was a storage compartment, filled to the brim with vintage electronics.

I reached in to grab the first object—and nearly screamed when I realized it was a gun. I carefully set it to the side and removed the rest of the objects one by one.

There was a laptop, two more guns, several ancient smartphones, and, at the very bottom, a radio.

At least, I *assumed* it was a radio. I'd never seen anything like it. It was an unmarked black box, about the size of Grandpa's vintage DVD player, with a couple of dials on the front. A corded handset was clipped to the side.

I turned one of the dials, but nothing happened. Did it need to be plugged in?

I flipped it over and looked at the back. There were several cut wires sticking out of the case; maybe the thing *had* been ripped from an old truck. But someone had turned an old laptop battery into a redneck power source with wires and electrical tape. I flipped the crudely marked "on" switch and tried the dial again.

This time I was greeted with a shower of static, and the front display lit up with the number "40."

I set the device on the edge of the bed so I was eye-level with it and started playing with the buttons. The one marked "Vol" was self-explanatory, but the rest were Greek to me: "SQ," "RF Gain." "PA." I could get the number on the display to change, but all I got through the speaker were various tones of static.

I rapped the display with my finger. It couldn't be that complicated—there were only so many options—but I couldn't just look it up on the internet. Andromeda wasn't supposed to have a radio; she certainly wouldn't look up the instructions for how to run one.

I was so engrossed in my frustration that I didn't hear the approaching footsteps over the static. The door creaked, and I nearly fell backwards into the hole in the floor.

Mr. Von stood in the doorway. He tipped his head to the side and squinted at me.

I hastily stood up and brushed off my knees. "Andromeda," I offered before he could ask.

"I know that," he said, although it was hard to tell if he meant it. "But what are you doing up here?"

"I uh… said I was going to help clean so… I thought I'd dust in here." I clapped my dirty hands together for emphasis.

He chuckled disarmingly. "You are an ambitious woman. I like it." He took two steps into the room and stopped, taking a cursory glance around. The insecurity returned to his eyes. "I don't remember what we even used this room for."

I swallowed. "I don't think it's been used in a few years," I offered.

He snorted an affirmative and glanced down at the bed. "Whatcha got there?"

I hesitated. A half-hour ago he couldn't even remember that he *had* a radio; would he remember how to work it?

I picked up the device and held it out. "Do you know what this is?"

He walked over and took it from me. He turned it over in his hands—once, twice—and my hope faltered.

Then a shot of light flashed across his face. "Ahh, my old CB! I didn't know I still had this."

Apparently the United didn't either. "Do you know how to work it?"

"*Does* it still work is the question we should be asking. This thing's older than you." He winked at me.

I smiled back. "Well, so are you, but you still work."

His large laugh filled the room. "Then there's still hope for it. Let's try it."

He sat down on the edge of the bed, and I joined him. I watched as he flipped switches and adjusted dials, trying to memorize his movements. He pressed the button on the side of the handset and coughed a "check, check" into the speaker.

Then he grabbed the largest dial and started turning it slowly. The number on the display started counting up from 1, but still all I heard was static.

"Does the static mean it's broken?" I asked after he'd gotten past 10.

"No, it just means no one's talking. Be patient."

He continued to cycle channels—and just when I'd given up hope for the fifth time in so many minutes, he hit channel 19 and I heard voices.

There were a few muttered words, like we'd jumped in at the end of a conversation. Then, loud and clear, a new voice cut through the static.

"Radio check. This is Catalyst. Are you receiving?"

"Dad," I breathed, then caught myself. I looked up at Mr. Von to see if he'd heard, but he wasn't paying attention to me. He was squinting at the device, face contorted in a frown.

There was some interference, then a voice I didn't recognize answered. "Catalyst, this is Data. 10-2, standing by."

"Thanks, Data. Requesting 10-13, Brighton and Malvern. Over."

I had no idea what 10-13 meant, but Brighton was a major road less than a mile from here.

Dad's here—he's right here!

I grabbed Mr. Von's knee. "Can we talk back?"

He didn't respond. He held the device up and pressed his ear to it, even though the volume was on max.

The stranger on the other end of the line spoke again. "Does anyone have a visual on Brighton and Malvern?"

There was silence—a long silence—and I thought we'd lost them. I grabbed the handset and held it to my lips—then realized I had no idea what to say. I couldn't just announce my location and tell Dad to meet me on the street corner. But he was *right there*—I had to do something.

A third voice joined the conversation before I could decide. "Catalyst, be advised we've got bears. Over."

"What's a bear?" I wondered aloud. It had to be some kind of code—there was no way there were actual bears in downtown Allston.

"It's a cop," Mr. Von mumbled.

I stared at him. Was he remembering?

"What's 10-13 mean then?" I pressed, hoping to milk more out of his window of sanity. But he said nothing more—I don't think he realized he'd spoken at all—and continued to gaze in wonder at the device in his lap, as if he'd just given birth to it.

There was broken chatter, and then Dad clipped in again. "10-4, thanks for that."

I tried to piece the information together. Dad must have been asking if that intersection was clear to pass through—which, apparently, it wasn't.

How could I tell him I was nearby and safe?

"Catalyst, this is Data again. 10-25 Blue Fire?"

I froze. He was asking about me.

The pause before Dad responded was palpable. "Negative, Data."

My heart broke. *I'm right here, Dad!*

Data sighed into the line. "Roger that. Data over and out."

Even I knew what that meant—they were about to hang up. Who knew how long it would be before Dad would sign on again—and if he moved out of range, I'd never be able to reach him on the radio.

I can't lose him again!

I pressed down on the handheld. "Catalyst, this is Blue Fire. I'm here."

10

The silence was deafening, so much so that I thought they'd already signed off. I was about to repeat myself when multiple voices started competing at once.

"Oh my—"

"Blue Fire, this is Data, 10-20?"

"Green Dragon, are you reading this?"

"10-45, we need a fox hunt."

"Blue Fire, this is Data, do you copy?"

And through it all my father's voice cut like a knife. "Blue Fire, 10-41-32, *now.*"

I hadn't heard that tone of voice in almost ten years—not since that one time Ephesus had goaded me into sneaking into Grandpa's attic and we'd broken an irreplaceable antique. That was the tone of voice you did not disobey—except I had no idea what he was asking me to do.

I'd forgotten Mr. Von was there until he lurched, bouncing the radio on his knees. "Switch to channel 32!" he declared gleefully, and then thankfully did just that—since I was still figuring out how to change the channel.

He flipped a dial, and my father's voice came in mid-sentence. "—you copy? Blue Fire!"

"Da—I mean Catalyst, it's me, I copy," I cried into the receiver.

"What are you doing?" There was that tone of voice again. "You need to get off the radio—now."

"It's fine, I'm safe." I glanced at Mr. Von, as if to confirm my statement. He was watching me with a wild grin, as if this was the most fun he'd had in years.

"No, you're not!" Dad seemed to realize he was shouting. He lowered his voice and sped up his words. "Listen, we only have a minute before they figure out we're on this channel. Stay off the radio. Tell no one where you are. Don't trust anyone."

Use him, but don't trust him.

I swallowed back fear. "I know, but it's okay, I found a safe place. I need you to meet me here. I can get us out of this."

"It's *not* safe. I need you to lay low; they know you're in this neighborhood now. Don't log any electronic activity. They're looking for you."

I wanted to blurt the truth—that I had a clean file, and money, and I could get us back to Mars, if only we could make contact.

Dad didn't give me a chance and kept talking. "Don't use the radio—they can track you as long as you're transmitting. I'll call you on Tuesday, at 20:30, channel 2."

Tuesday? That was a whole three days from now. I opened my mouth to object—but the Holy Spirit washed over me with all the truths I couldn't deny.

You can trust him.

You can trust Me.

"10-4, Catalyst," I said with a peace I did not feel.

He sighed, and for a second there was a crack in his armor. "I love you, Blue Fire. I'm so sorry—"

Other voices cut into the line and talked over him.

"Blue Fire, do you read?"

"Catalyst, hold your position."

"10-45, anyone tracking?"

I barely caught Dad's "over and out" through the clamor. I hung there, listening to their frantic chatter, fighting competing waves of loneliness and joy. Then I reached down to turn the device off, silencing the noise.

Mr. Von sat there for another minute, still grinning wildly, as if he expected there to be more. When nothing happened, he seemed to come back down to Earth, and whatever buoyancy had been sustaining his sanity faded. The dull and distracted look returned to his eyes, and he offered me a weak smile.

"Well, that was fun. Thanks for letting me play." He stood up and handed the radio to me.

I took it. "Sure. Thanks for the help." I set the device, which suddenly felt light and cheap, in my lap. The handset slid off and dangled by its coiled cord.

He gave my shoulder a squeeze and left.

I watched the handset bounce until the motion stilled. *Tuesday?* I wouldn't hear from Dad again until Tuesday night, and what was I supposed to do until then? I had to stay off the radio, and Andromeda couldn't do anything suspicious online. I probably shouldn't even go outside.

Apparently the best thing I could do was absolutely nothing, and that felt utterly wrong.

I picked up the handset and clipped it on the radio. Dad said he would call me Tuesday—which meant he would still be in the area. He wouldn't do anything without me, not this time.

I knelt down and put the rest of the gadgets back under the floor. I picked up one of the old smartphones and turned it over in my hand. Cea had used a phone just like it when she called for help. After some thought, I set the phone aside, then put everything else away and replaced the panel.

I took the cellphone and radio and hid them under the far corner of Cea's bed, in a box of off-season clothes. I didn't figure the Vons got many visitors, but the last thing I needed was someone walking in and seeing the radio on the counter.

As soon as that task was finished, anxiety and restlessness tried to shove their way back into my vacated brain. I knew I had to keep myself busy, so I decided to do what I'd promised: Clean.

After asking Mrs. Von where her cleaning supplies were (and then spending ten minutes finding them myself because the closet she indicated wasn't the correct one), I started in Nic's room. I'd disturbed enough of the dust crawling around on the floor that my footprints in the carpet led like a treasure map right to the hidden panel. I dusted the room top-down, shook out the comforter, and vacuumed three times in an attempt to restore the carpet to its original shade. The bookcase-size dents in the floor still seemed obvious to me, so with some effort I managed to drag the drafting board across the room and cover up the panel.

By then it was lunchtime, during which Mr. Von subjected me to another cup of coffee because apparently he was ready for his third (or fourth). This time I had no excuse not to stay at the table and eat slowly like a well-adjusted person, so I forced myself to finish the whole cup.

I took over dish-duty and then decided to continue the trend and clean the whole kitchen. Mrs. Von had done her best to keep up with it, but the inside of the fridge was a nightmare. It was clear grocery shopping was a struggle for her. She had six or more packages of all the common ingredients. Most of them were dated only days apart, as if she bought a new one every time she went shopping. There were numerous expired items, some of which had grown into a biohazard. It took me several hours to get it back in order and wipe down all the shelves.

After that I needed a bath. Nic had, as usual, undersold the faultiness of the upstairs shower; I was practically done before the water was anything more than tepid. But then again, it took me half as long to wash my hair now that it was so short.

I came back to my room just in time to hear my tablet vomit up several notifications. I skimmed the lockscreen and was unsurprised to find a tirade from Aurelius. He had evidently heard about my brief radio appearance and was less than pleased that I'd come back to Earth without telling him.

I skimmed the messages, several of which were punctuated with foul words, until I got to the bottom.

LOOK, I KNOW YOU'RE HOME FROM COLLEGE. YOU CAN COME TO THE PARTY. WHY WON'T YOU LET ME PICK YOU UP?

THERE'S A MALL NEAR YOUR PLACE. WHY DON'T WE MEET THERE TOMORROW? I'LL BUY YOU LUNCH

I cringed. There was, in fact, a mall near here—which he would know because I'd given away my general area by being on the CB.

It was unavoidable that he knew I was in town, but I didn't like the fact that he was watching my every move, trying to deduce my whereabouts like I was a math problem to be solved. Couldn't he take no for an answer?

Maybe Nic had been right about him all along.

I muted Aurelius for twenty-four hours and closed the app.

By the time I got back downstairs, Mrs. Von was cooking again. Just like Nic had predicted, she seemed less startled to see me each subsequent time I walked in the room, as if the repetition were softening her nerves. She actually let me help with dinner, and I was able to keep us on track and follow the recipe through to completion. Mr. Von was delighted with the results.

Mrs. Von wouldn't let me clean up; she'd said I'd "done enough," which made me wonder if she'd noticed the inside of her fridge and managed to put two and two together. I tried to excuse myself, but Mr. Von haggled me into the living room to watch a sitcom. It was censored media, which meant it was lifeless and boring and agonizingly politically correct, but I enjoyed watching him guffaw after every punchline.

Sunday and Monday went much the same, with Mr. Von giving me way too much coffee (he didn't even ask this time) and Mrs. Von making a concentrated effort not to hate me. I cleaned the living room, dining room, Cea's room, and the upstairs bathroom. Mrs. Von wouldn't let me anywhere near their master, but I hoped she would change her mind after she saw how beautiful the rest of the house looked. I was running out of places to clean.

Monday night, I voluntarily followed Mr. Von into the living room after dinner. Mrs. Von joined us and read on her tablet. We spent the evening in companionable silence, with me wondering if this was what Nic's childhood had been like.

Surely there was a point in time when Mr. Von wouldn't have been content to sit in front of a TV all day. You didn't put humans on Mars by being idle. How much of this man's personality had been artificially manufactured by the neurosurgery? What had he been like before then? Could that man be ever brought back?

I turned on my tablet and started researching neurosurgery. I figured no one would question my internet history when my file clearly stated I was staying with people who had undergone the procedure.

The theory behind the pseudoscience was simple: If a person was noncompliant, perhaps they could be rewired to fit the mold. After all, according to the government, all the troublesome things that made us individuals—religion, nationality, race—were figments of our imagination, fictitious constructs we created around flawed thinking. To them, the human brain was little more than a stubborn computer, and computers could be reprogrammed.

Unlike the failed brainwashing attempts of the 2060s, neurosurgery didn't "erase" memories. Instead, it rewired the neural pathways to avoid problematic triggers. The theory was that if you could block out a person's emotional reaction to words like "God" and "Bible," they'd cease to be Christian, or at least stop behaving like one.

The problem was that test subjects also stopped doing a lot of other things—including, in some cases, breathing. Everyone who had undergone the procedure ended up like the Vons or worse. Apparently you couldn't just cut people's identity out of their brains like ripping a page from a book.

But if the surgery didn't touch long-term memory, that meant the memories were still in there, weren't they? Could those neural pathways be reconnected? If a brain could be reprogrammed once, surely it could be reprogrammed again.

A quick internet search revealed that other people had been asking the same questions. As of yet, experimental therapy had been unsuccessful—but at least they were trying.

Unlike Nic.

I was deeply engrossed in some stupidly-hard-to-interpret medical journal when someone jangled a key in the back door.

I froze and told my irritable pulse that I'd heard wrong. But then I heard the door open and the screen door slam shut, and I jumped up.

Mr. and Mrs. Von either hadn't heard or weren't concerned, because they both just gazed at me curiously.

"Someone's here," I hissed.

Mr. Von shrugged. "Probably grocery delivery."

"It's nine o'clock at night!" I returned, and realized I sounded exactly like Mrs. Von.

I briefly considered running. I didn't know who could be visiting the Vons—after dark, and coming through the back door—but whoever it was, they didn't need to know I was here. But the only place to go was the kitchen, and light footsteps were already coming down the hall.

Both Mr. and Mrs. Von stood up as a woman strode into the living room. She threw the hood of her dark jacket back, revealing a halo of tangled blonde curls.

"Mom and Dad, I'm home."

11

"Cea!"

She looked as surprised as I was to see a visitor in her parents' living room. She flipped her jacket back and put her hand on the gun she was not-so-subtly carrying in her pocket.

"Who are you?" she demanded. She took in my bleached hair and angsty outfit and, apparently, didn't recognize me at first glance. I would have been flattered if I didn't think I was about to get shot.

"It's me." I put my hands up and spoke slowly so she could hear my voice.

She took me in again, and her eyes lit up. "Philadelphia!" she cried, a burst of raw emotion garbling the word. She ran at me and engulfed me in a hug.

"Who are you?" Mrs. Von demanded, at the same time her husband said, "Who's Philadelphia? I thought your name was…"

"Andromeda," I said, giving Cea's shoulder a warning squeeze.

She separated herself from me. "Right, Andromeda, sorry." She took a sharp breath to compose herself and turned to her parents with a plastic smile. "Hi, Mom and Dad, it's me—Cea—remember?"

When it was clear they didn't, I stepped in. "Remember that doctor I told you about? Nic? He's her brother."

All three of them repeated Nic's name with various inflections. Mr. Von acted like this was the first he'd heard of the man—Mrs. Von looked like she might remember, but that only made her more suspicious—and Cea went unhinged.

"Nic! He's okay? Have you seen him?"

I silenced her with a warning glance.

"This man sure gets around," Mrs. Von muttered, then shifted her scrutiny back to Cea. "How'd you get in?"

"You gave me a key, remember?" Cea held up the tiny silver object.

Mrs. Von frowned at it but couldn't deny its existence, so she shifted gears. "And what are you doing here?"

Cea sighed and pocketed the key. "I came back for a visit."

"I'm sensing a trend here." Mrs. Von glanced at her husband, but to no avail. He'd already settled back in his armchair.

"If she's a friend of Nic's, she's welcome here! Andi, show her upstairs, why don't you."

"Of course." I grabbed my tablet and led the way up the stairs before Mrs. Von could attempt any more negotiations.

As soon as the bedroom door shut behind us, Cea started gushing again. "Phil! I can't believe you're all right. How did you get here?"

"Nic sent me." I gestured at the bed, hoping she'd sit down and remember to breathe.

"Nic *sent* you? Where is he? Is he all right? Does he—"

I put my hand up to stop her. "Why don't you let me explain from the beginning?"

She let out the breath she apparently forgot she was holding. "Sorry. You're right. It's just... been a week." She shed her coat and sat down on the bed, then looked around the room. "What are you doing in my room? Couldn't you have picked Nic's?"

"I liked your style of decorating better," I laughed, even though that wasn't exactly the truth.

She smiled as I sat down next to her. She wrapped me in another hug—softer and longer this time. After a minute, she sat back and studied me.

"You look different. I like your earrings."

"Different was the intent." I studied her in return. She looked like she was in one piece, but the blood and dirt under her broken fingernails told a different story. "What happened to you?"

She gave a morbid chuckle. "Going to make me go first, eh? What have you heard?"

I paused to take my tablet offline, just in case. "Only what Thames told me. He said you escaped, but I never knew how much of that was the truth."

She nodded. "It happened pretty much like you think it did. The virus—that was you, wasn't it?"

"More Nic than me, but yeah."

She smiled, the implications not lost on her. "They had me in solitary. The virus made a mess of the security systems and had all the guards running around like chickens with their heads cut off—it wasn't that hard to slip out."

I sent up a prayer of thanks. "So where have you been?"

"I went off the grid. I wanted to see how things would blow over—and then I heard about your videos. I was sure Nic and I were going to get flagged in the investigation—but we never did. Then suddenly Thames was dead, and I realized no one was looking for me. So I decided to come here."

"Why didn't you call Nic?" I asked.

She shot me a look. "First of all, I didn't know he was back on Mars. Second of all, my file still says I live in a containment camp. If I logged any electronic activity, they would have arrested me and thrown me back in prison."

I flinched. "So that's why you've been offline."

She groaned and popped her neck. "You have no idea how freaking long it takes to walk across this city."

"I'm so glad you're safe." I indulged in a laugh, but the sound died halfway through when I remembered someone else. I sat up and grabbed her arm. "Have you heard from Ephesus?"

"No," she said quietly, as if she were afraid to let me down. She looked at her hands and traced the scratches on her knuckles. "Your dad was being held somewhere else, and Ephesus was still in the hospital—or so they said."

My heart fluttered weakly. "Was he—"

"He's alive," she corrected. "They said he had a few broken bones and a smashed nose, but nothing internal. I'm sure he's fine now." She reached up and squeezed my hand.

I tried to console us both with a smile. "He must have escaped, or we'd have heard about it. His file says he's still missing."

She nodded but did not return the smile. "And your dad?"

I straightened. "I just heard from him. He got on the CB a few days ago—that's why I'm here."

"The CB?" she said, in exactly the same tone I'd used when I first heard it. "That means he's still in Boston?" Without waiting for an answer to that question, she spilled several more. "And how did *you* get here? Where was he keeping you? Your file is a mess, girl. You can't even sneeze in public without getting the cops called on you. How did you—"

"Whoa, maybe it's my turn to explain." She conceded with a nod, so I continued. "I have a new file."

"So that's Andromeda?"

"Yeah, Andromeda Nolan." I let the name hang in the air.

She jerked. "Nolan? You're kidding, right?"

"I wish."

"Well, this will be a good story." She yanked her muddy boots off, fluffed the pillows up against the headboard, and settled back. "I'm listening."

I folded my legs under me and told her everything that had happened since we'd been separated—including how I'd come to acquire my enemy's last name.

"That explains why Mrs. Nolan was so nice to you, and why Thames let her get away with so much," Cea mused.

"Unfortunately," I muttered, trying to keep the bitterness out of my voice.

"Guess we owe her a thank you." Cea tipped her head. "Do you know what happened to her?"

"Hopefully she ran when the government busted Thames's office," I said, avoiding her eyes. I really did hope the woman had escaped—I had no desire for her to be hanged for her husband's crimes—but I also didn't want to see her again. I hoped wherever she went had taken her far away from me.

"She visited me a couple times before I broke out." Cea detangled her curls with her fingers. "Gave me updates on Ephesus."

I nodded and hoped that was the end of the conversation.

"So Nic…" Cea sat up straight. "…is governor again? He's still on Mars? Can you get ahold of him?"

"Yes, yes, and yes." I grabbed my tablet and brought it back online. "Carnegie kept the base clean—the United has no idea anything happened on Mars. Nic was able to basically pick up where he left off—minus the plot to start World War IV with acid rain."

A dry smile tugged at her lips. "Let's hope so."

I opened the messaging app. There was a fresh batch of notifications from Aurelius, but I ignored them and started an audio call with Nic.

It rang through the first time. I glanced at the dark sky outside the window and wondered what time it was over there. Not that it mattered; I'm sure even if it was 3am he would be glad he took this call.

I dialed him again. This time he answered after one ring. "This better be important, Andromeda." He sounded fully awake, and I heard other people talking in the background. "Because there's a lot of money hinging on this meeting."

"Of course it's important." I enabled video and angled the camera to face Cea.

"Nic," she called.

He swore. There was clattering and hurried apologies to the others in the room, then footsteps. A door slammed, and his camera blinked on.

"Laodicea." His voice was soft, but his face was hard as he searched her, as if making sure it was really her.

"Nic," she repeated. She took the tablet from me and held it up to her face. "You're okay."

"Never better. Where are you?"

"Mom's house. I realized the United wasn't after me or you, so I made my way here."

"Watch what you say," he reminded her coldly. "But I'm glad you're safe. Now come home."

The abrupt suggestion killed Cea's smile. "I'm sorry, what?"

"Come home," he repeated in exactly the same tone as before.

"You want me to jump on a transit and come back to base?"

"Unless they've invented another way to get to Mars, that's what I'd recommend."

She rubbed her forehead with one hand. "Nic, I can't just 'come home.'"

"Why not?" he responded, which was exactly what I was wondering.

"My file still says I live—"

"A clerical error. You've signed the file, have you not?"

"I mean yeah, but the transit ticket—"

"I'll buy it," I offered.

Nic cleared his throat. "I'm not *that* poor, Andi." I couldn't see the screen from where I was, but I could perfectly imagine what expression went with that attitude.

"No, you don't get it. I can't come back yet, Nic. I've got to find Eph—"

"He's a grown man, last I checked. Let him find himself."

I flinched. He wasn't wrong—he rarely was, it seemed—but I would have said it with a lot more grace. I tried to translate. "Nic's right. Let him come to you. He'd want to know you're safe."

Cea looked up at me. "Yeah? And what are *you* doing here?"

I opened my mouth, then realized I had no good answer to that. *Exactly what I just told you not to do...*

"Andromeda has her own affairs to attend to," Nic said. "Yours are up here. Come home."

Cea wagged her head. "No. I'm not leaving until everyone is safe."

"Then you'll be waiting a very long time, which is exactly why we're not going to have this conversation."

She glared at the screen. "You're right, because I've made my decision."

"Cea."

"Nic, I'm serious."

"Cea," he repeated, harder and slower.

"I'm not coming home, Nic."

He sighed. "Don't make me do it."

I could have sworn Cea turned white, but she held her ground. "Do what, Nic? What are you going to do?"

He prefaced with some expletives. "You're *really* going to make me do this, aren't you?"

"Do, uh, I need to leave?" I offered.

They both ignored me. "I'm not *making* you do anything, Nic. You're the one being a jerk."

"Fine! Fine, fine, fine, fine…" His voice faded and returned, as if he'd gotten up to take a lap around the desk. "You want me to be the bad guy? I'll be the bad guy."

I swallowed. Being the villain hadn't gone well for him last time—and I could tell it was about to go very poorly now.

"Laodicea," he said, using the name like a threat.

She gave him one last warning. "Don't."

"I'm *ordering* you to come home."

Now it was Cea's turn to growl, drop the tablet, and storm around the room. "You can't tell me what to do!" she screeched.

"Actually, as the commanding governor of the base you're supposed to be stationed on, I can."

I cringed as Cea's face flushed redder than the surface of Mars itself. "You know I *hate* it when you do that."

"I honestly don't care what you think right now," he returned, although I had long since figured that out for myself.

Cea spun back around and gestured emphatically at the tablet, even though she was nowhere in view of the camera. "And what about Phil, huh?"

"Andi," both Nic and I said at the same time.

"You want me to just leave her here alone?"

"Please don't bring me into this…" I said, entirely to myself.

Nic shrugged. "She got there just fine on her own."

"She's a child, Nic!"

"Excuse me?" I grunted.

"In more ways than one," Nic agreed. "But unlike you, I can't tell her what to do."

The delicious irony of that statement was too great to resist. "Uh, actually, you can," I said, fully realizing I wasn't helping.

"Andromeda, don't you dare—"

Cea shot me a look.

"Technically, he's my legal guardian right now."

Nic muttered something foul under his breath.

Cea stood frozen in the middle of the room for a beat. She looked at me, then back at the tablet. "Well, nice to see you two have kissed and made up."

"Yes," Nic regained his composure, "and our newfound friendship is going to be the death of me. I would be happy to tell you all about it if you would *just come home!*"

At that moment, our bedroom door creaked open. "Girls? What's all this shouting? Are you all right?" Mrs. Von stepped into the room, backlit by the much brighter light in the hallway.

Cea waved her off. "It's nothing, we're just talking…"

"Hi Mom," Nic chirped from the tablet.

Mrs. Von cocked her head. "Who's that?" She walked over to the bed.

My heart lurched. "Remember that doctor I was telling you about? The one who took me in after my parents died?" I snatched the tablet and held it up for her to see. "This is him. This is Nic."

She leaned over and squinted at his image.

Nic stared back calmly, letting her study him. "How is Paul?"

She seemed tickled that he asked. "Oh, he's good. You knew him, right?"

I jumped. Did she remember our earlier conversation? I cast an eager glance at Cea, but she was just watching her mom blankly, eyes dry and glazed.

"Very well," Nic responded. "He's a brilliant man."

Mrs. Von straightened. "That was a nice thing you did for Andromeda, taking her in. She's a good girl."

"Despite her best efforts," Nic agreed. I blushed.

Mrs. Von smiled. "I bet your parents are very proud of you for taking care of her like that."

Cea sucked in a crippled breath. I searched Mrs. Von's face, looking for any emotion, any recognition of what she was saying.

Nic was slow to respond, but when he did, his voice was filled with more confidence than I expected. "I know they are."

"Well." Mrs. Von walked away. "You girls try to keep it down. Paul's asleep in his armchair like he always is. And don't stay up too late—it's a school night."

"Yes ma'am," I called as she closed the door behind herself.

I turned back to Cea. Her face was unreadable, but the interaction seemed to have taken the fight out of her—which for the moment was probably a good thing. She sat back down on the bed.

"Come home, Cea," Nic said again, this time at least making an attempt to be polite.

She sighed. "I just don't feel good about leaving Ph—Andromeda here alone. She's a teenager, Nic, and she's looking for the most wanted man on the eastern seaboard. You want me to just leave her out here to find her dad by herself? She could get killed, Nic."

I couldn't tell by her expression whether she was actually afraid for my life or just using me as bait. She was obviously scared—but of what?

Nic remained calm. "I am fully aware of the immense risk she's putting herself in. Unfortunately, the last time I tried to keep her here against her will, she blew up a lab, depressurized an entire wing, and I spent six months in jail. Hence, I am reserving that as a last resort."

I chuckled dryly, but Nic cut me off mid-laugh. "That said, if you pull another stunt like you did Saturday, Andi, I *swear* I will send Sardis down to get you."

Cea arched an eyebrow at me. I felt my neck grow hot as two revelations—both of which should have been obvious from the start—suddenly dawned on me.

Nic hadn't wanted me to go.

And he was keeping an eye on me from afar.

"Yessir," I mumbled, somewhat culled.

"Well, what do you think happens if you keep *me* up there against my will?" Cea inserted herself back into the conversation.

"Same thing that always happens," Nic said without hesitation. "You don't talk to me for three weeks."

Cea huffed, and suddenly their relationship made a whole lot more sense.

"But I think I can live with that if I know you're safe."

She was silent.

Nic sighed. "Look, I'm aware Andromeda has put herself—and, quite frankly, the rest of us—in a dangerous position. But that was her choice."

I tensed. His statement lingered in my soul and stirred an emotion I couldn't quite identify.

"But I can—" Cea started.

"I can't begrudge her for taking care of her family," Nic interrupted. "But I need to take care of mine."

She finally looked into the camera again.

"Come home, Cea. Please."

She didn't say anything for a long moment. Then, finally, she nodded.

He released the emotional tension with a sigh. "Thank you. Text me once you have your itinerary."

She nodded again, then stood up and walked across the room. I picked the tablet up.

"Andromeda."

I looked down at the screen to find him staring at me, hard.

"Remember what I said."

"Yessir," I said again, and he hung up.

I set the tablet down and waited for Cea to speak first.

She spent a long minute staring at one of the many rock band posters plastered on her wall. "I need a shower," she declared finally. She grabbed some of her old clothes from the closet and stormed out of the room.

My tablet dinged with a message from Nic. He said Cea's file had been corrected and asked if I could please book her transit ticket right away. He added that he would pay me back.

I acknowledged the message and pulled up the travel site Mr. Sardis had shown me. The earliest flight was for Thursday afternoon. The price was significantly higher than what I had paid a mere week before—she could save several thousand if she waited a few more days—but I went ahead and bought the ticket. I took a grand off the amount I told Nic and hoped he wouldn't question it.

Cea returned shortly after, her hair hanging in wet waves around her face. She flopped backwards on the bed with a grunt.

"I hate him," she announced.

"Don't we all. You're leaving Wednesday." I put my tablet on the charger.

"I'm kicking you out of my room tonight." She rolled over on her side and looked at me. "So what's your plan, exactly? You said your dad's on the CB? How'd you find this out?"

For an answer, I got down on my knees and pulled the box of sweaters out from under the bed. I tossed the radio and the old smartphone on the comforter.

She sat up. "Where did you get these?"

"They were hiding in the floor in your brother's room."

"So that's where Dad hid his gear." She flipped the phone over in her hand. "Were there more phones?"

"Yeah, a couple."

"Good, I'm going to show you how to set up a burner phone." She powered the device on. "Old smartphones make the best burners because of one key feature—emergency calling."

The lock screen brightened. She held the home button until the "Emergency Call" text appeared. "It's the law that every phone has to be able to dial 911, even if the user is out of cell service or data or whatever."

"So? Even my tablet can do that." I picked up my device and pressed the "emergency" icon on the home screen. The screen flashed white and asked me if I wanted to contact emergency services.

Text in the corner caught my eye: *Emergency Contact.* I clicked on it.

Nic's profile appeared. I smiled.

Cea didn't notice. "Yeah, but United cell service is free, so it's kind of a moot point. Newer devices just treat it like any other call. The old phones basically bypass all verifications and connect to whatever signal they can find when you activate emergency mode. That means, with a bit of messing around in the settings, you can get it to make calls *without* registering the device on the database."

I made a noise of admiration.

"Trouble is, when an unregistered device like a cellphone connects to the network, it raises massive red flags in the algorithm. They're almost always going to investigate it—which means they'll see what phone number you're using, who you called, what you said, and, if you keep using the same device, probably track the signal."

"So use it to order pizza and then ditch it," I concluded.

"Exactly." She opened the menu and showed me how to change the settings. I made her repeat the steps twice so I could memorize them. Then she powered off the device and pocketed it. "Now I need a real phone. If I'm going to fly to Mars, they're going to expect me to be online."

"I can buy you one tomorrow. Do you want some better clothes, too?" I eyed the garishly juvenile outfit she'd chosen.

"Sure, let's have a girl's day out, why not. Here, you should take this." She got up to root around in the dirty clothes she'd tossed on the floor. She found her parents' house key and pressed it into my palm.

"Why do I need this?"

"So you can get in when they're not home—and without leaving an electronic log." She sat back down on the bed. "Nic took the keypad on the back door offline years ago so we could keep using the manual lock. If you go through the front or garage door, there will be an electronic log associated with your fingerprints. Of course, if you want to stay completely offline, you also don't want to connect to the home internet with any registered devices."

I nodded. I grabbed my backpack and hid the key in an inner pocket where it wouldn't get lost.

Cea picked up the radio. "This thing still works?"

"Surprisingly. Do you remember your dad using it?"

"A little." A tangle of vague emotions clouded her voice. "I wasn't around for most of my parents' rebellious phase. As soon as things started getting serious—and Dad started getting in real trouble with the law—Nic petitioned child services to put me in boarding school. He took custody of me as soon as he became governor. The government, of course, was happy to hand me over."

I couldn't decide whether that was endearing or horrifying—or a sinister combination of both—so I stayed silent.

She ran her hand over the device. "I guess that's one thing we have in common now—Nic's decided it's his job to take care of us."

I snorted doubtfully. "I'm sure as soon as my dad's back online Nic will be more than happy to give me up."

"About that." Cea set the radio aside. "Your file must have cost millions to forge—there's no way you can concoct the same thing for your father *and* Ephesus, at least not on short notice. What's your plan, girl?"

"I just have to get them back to Mars," I said with resounding confidence, hoping the strength in my voice would convince both me and her. "Nic says it's not hard to forge a temp file. It might not look legitimate under scrutiny, but if it'll buy a transit ticket, it'll do. Nic already agreed they can come live on base."

A genuine smile briefly brightened Cea's features before vanishing back into obscurity. "Do you have someone who can forge a temp file?"

I rooted around in my backpack until I found the business card Nic had given me. I held it out to her. "I'm supposed to tell him Nic sent me."

She took the paper and squinted at it. Her eyes lit up, and she turned back to me with a grin. "Want to get a tattoo?"

13

If I thought the tattoo parlors on Mars were sketchy, the ones in the inner city of Boston were even worse.

It was the next day, and Cea and I had ventured downtown. Our first stop had been a gas station across the street from her parents' house, where Cea traded a scan of her fingerprints for a bus pass. I was impressed those still existed, but Cea explained that they were exactly for situations like this. If a citizen lost their electronic devices—or couldn't afford any—the United still wanted to track their movements. Most people were happy to trade security for a free ride.

We took the bus to a shopping center, where I bought Cea a new cellphone. The bored sales rep made her register it on the database before he removed the security tag.

After that, we took the bus to a different shopping center across town to buy clothes. We bounced from mall to mall until we had everything Cea needed, avoiding staying in one place for long. I was a wanted woman, after all.

I'd spent the first hour of our trip guiltily scanning the crowd, foolishly hoping I'd see Dad or Ephesus and desperately hoping I wouldn't see Jayde. But of course I didn't see anyone I knew—and no one else seemed to recognize me either. No one gave me a second glance, not even the store clerks who looked me right in the eye. Apparently my dark eyeliner, ripped jeans, and ashy hair had me blending in with the mall crowd perfectly.

I was just beginning to relax when Cea took us to a part of town I definitely knew we shouldn't be in.

The street reeked of decay. The buildings seemed to draw in on themselves, leering over the broken sidewalk as if they were trying to block out the sun. Trash clogged the gutter, and the sewer smelled rancid. And the men at the bus stop definitely stared—although not, I'm sure, because I reminded them of Philadelphia Smyrna.

"You sure about that tattoo?" Cea grinned at me as she continued walking, as if the decrepit atmosphere had no effect on her.

"No—I mean yes." I yanked my eyes away from the street and tried to pull myself together. "No tattoos. Final answer."

I followed her into an alley. The row was lined with several shops—none of which looked like places I should be patronizing.

"Suit yourself. I have a fun one on my shoulder blade."

"You do?"

She winked at me. "Don't tell Nic."

She led me to the shop at the end of the alley. The tinted windows were marked with same mountain range that was on the business card. Cea shoved the door open, and I followed, muttering a prayer for protection under my breath.

The interior was somehow both dank and neon-lit at the same time. It was definitely a tattoo and piercing parlor—not unlike the one I visited on Mars—although judging by the various advertisements on the wall, they also did other augmentations as well. One sign even suggested they offered experimental brain implants. Mercifully, the shop was vacant.

A stocky man in a kilt emerged from the back. I couldn't help but stare—it had been at least a decade since I'd seen anyone wear a kilt in public. Regional costume wasn't technically illegal, but it was a good way to get yourself reported for a hate crime—even if you were a native.

"Like it, lass?" he said, laying the accent on thick for my benefit. He was muscular, with a fierce short beard and a proud manbun. Most of his visible skin was decorated with a kaleidoscope of Celtic knots, dragons, and ancient symbols of horses, men, and eagles.

"Progressive," I said, and he winked.

"Andes." Cea's voice dripped with enough butter to bake a potato. She sidled up to the counter and leaned on it. "Remember me?"

He squinted at her, eyes nearly disappearing behind his chiseled cheekbones. "Got any of my work on ya?"

She rolled up her sleeve until she revealed a tiny symbol on the inside of her upper arm—somewhere almost no one would have seen. It looked like a bird with a lightning bolt, but she pushed her sleeve back down before I could get a better look.

Andes broke into a grin. "Well, if it isn't my favorite wayward girl, Laodicea. Your brother ain't anywhere around, is he? You know how he feels about you getting work done."

"Actually, he sent us."

The atmosphere in the room changed immediately. Andes's smile faded. "The great Dr. Von referred me? I don't believe that for a minute," he said, although the clipped tone of his voice implied the opposite.

Cea nodded at me. I reached into my backpack, withdrew the business card, and threw it on the counter.

Andes glared at it but didn't pick it up. His jaw tensed, causing the tattoos on his neck to ripple. "And what if I say I'm not in business anymore?"

Cea sighed. "Andes, please, this is import—"

I put my hand up to stop her. I found the man's gaze and held it. "I'll pay in advance."

He barked a laugh. "You?"

I pulled out my tablet, opened the payment app, and handed the device to him. "Name your price."

His wolfish smile returned, and some air came back into the room. "You sure do know the way to a man's heart, lass."

He reached below the counter and pulled out a thick rubber mat. He unrolled it and laid my tablet on it. "Phone, please," he grunted at Cea.

She nodded and tossed her device on the mat. At my quizzical stare, Andes explained, "Dampening field. I don't take chances." He pulled his phone from his pocket and added it to the pile.

"And neither do we," Cea resumed control of the conversation. "We need two temp files and fingerprint alterations to go with them."

"Two? Are these credentials for you lovely ladies?"

Cea snorted derisively. "Our affairs are in order, thank you."

"I'm sure they are. How long do these files need to last?"

"Long enough to buy a transit ticket," I answered, and hoped that wasn't revealing too much.

"To where?"

"Nowhere you're going."

He ran a tongue over his teeth. "And when do you need this done by?"

I looked to Cea. "We'll let you know when we're ready," she replied with a toss of her curls.

"Say no more," Andes chuckled, which was good, because I wasn't comfortable giving him any more information. He reached under the counter again and pulled out a vintage paper logbook. It was filled with names and data from some business that had probably died before computers were born.

Andes flipped to a page in the middle and stabbed his finger at a random entry. He glanced up at me. "Guy name, gal name, or don't care?"

"Male names, please." It didn't matter a whole lot, but Ephesus would have a very hard time convincing anyone that his real name was even remotely feminine.

"How about… Michael Eddington for lucky guy number one, and…" Andes slid a pencil out of the spiral of the logbook and added a number next to the entry he'd picked. Then he flipped to a new page and selected another random name. "Reginald Barclay for wingman number two."

"Sure," I said dismissively, as if I had any idea what a convincing fake name sounded like. I hadn't exactly had a hand in inventing my own.

Andes picked up the business card and copied the numbers from the logbook onto the back. "When you're ready, tell the boys to call Andes and say they have an appointment with these confirmation codes. I'll take care of the rest."

He slid the card across the counter. I pinned it with my finger. The process sounded simple enough—except for the fact that I would probably have to give my father and brother this information over the radio. "And what if someone were to overhear me telling them to 'call Andes'?"

He was prepared for the question. "Andes isn't my real name, and this number isn't traceable—at least not to anywhere on this continent."

"And what if another one of your clients happens to be eavesdropping? I can't be the only girl so lucky as to secure your services."

"My clients know better than to interrupt a deal. Not when I know who they used to be." His eyes glittered wickedly, as if he would relish the chance to make someone pay.

"Duly noted." I picked up the card and returned it to the inner pocket of my backpack. "Thank you."

"No, thank *you*." He picked up his phone and started typing. "Let me draw up the contract for your surgery so you can sign off on it, and we'll get you paid up."

"My *what*?" I said, casting a nervous glance at the lewd advertisements on the walls.

"Don't worry, a lot of girls your age get it. No one will question it on your file." He winked. "It is quite expensive, though."

I caught up. "Worth every penny."

Cea and I reclaimed our devices. Andes handed me his phone, and I signed off on a lengthy contract I was too nervous to read. Then I wired him the money without questioning the amount. My checking had definitely taken a hit over the past few days, but I wasn't hurting by any stretch of the imagination.

I rearranged my face into the cold, confident expression he was no doubt expecting from someone with money and power. "And what guarantee do I have that you'll fulfill your end of the bargain?"

He spread his hands. "What guarantee do you need?"

"Nic and I are very close," I said, which in some twisted irony was the truth. "Don't make me call him."

Andes stiffened, which I took as a good sign. "I wouldn't dream of it, lass."

I nodded curtly, then turned to go without another word.

Cea thanked him and hurried after me. I stepped out of the shop and heard voices—the alley that had been blissfully abandoned moments before now had a few people milling around in it. I resisted the urge to glance their way and strode towards the main road like I belonged in this part of town.

Cea caught up to me. "Good job."

I took in a deep breath—not that the air in the alley was much cleaner than the air in the shop—and hoped it would clear the anxiety out of my chest. "You sure about this guy?"

"He's your best bet for fifty miles. He's been in the business for a while—I doubt he's eager to blow it now, especially when you're willing to pay a premium. He's probably more interested in earning your loyalty so you'll bring him repeat business."

"I hope I never need his services again," I muttered, and stopped on the curb.

I glanced both ways, looking for the bus. I was eager to get out of this part of town and back to the Vons. I needed a shower and—

"Cea." I grabbed her arm.

She jerked. "What?"

I gestured with the barest nod of my head down the road.

At the end of the block stood a cop, watching us.

14

He stood in the middle of the road like he'd risen from the sewer. His stance was almost comical; his hands hung limply at his side, and a garish balloon of red-orange hair covered his head, like he was a clown posed to deliver the jump scare in a bad horror movie.

I was certainly terrified. Only one thought formulated over the roar of fear and what-if's:

We should have checked for bears.

I registered the screech of brakes and rush of air as the bus jerked to a stop. Cea yanked me back from the curb. "Come on."

I turned around and followed her down the street in the opposite direction. She walked crisply, like she had a meeting to catch. I struggled to match her stride, even though my legs wobbled like a newborn calf. *Oh Jesus, help.*

"Where are we going?"

"We're losing him."

She turned a corner, and we came upon an entrance to the subway. She scanned the square, then started down the steps.

Feeling like Lot's wife, I stole a sinful glance behind me. The cop was walking our way.

I scurried down the damp steps after Cea. "He saw us enter!"

"It won't matter in a minute." She pushed through the turnstile and merged with the crowd.

I fought to keep up with her as the smell of must and grease assaulted me with foggy memories. It had been years since I'd ridden the subway, and my anxiety was making the tunnel feel claustrophobic.

The station was a blindingly lit cave of concrete crammed with five o'clock commuters. We cut into the middle of a line, and the crowd funneled us through checkpoints that flashed green approvingly. I struggled to follow as

Cea snaked her way through the throng. She shoved her way to the front just as the next train screamed to a stop at the platform. She was on before the carload of passengers had even disembarked.

It took me another minute to fight through the crowd and get on the train. Thankfully Cea had taken a seat right inside the door and saved a spot for me—despite the disgruntled looks of other passengers.

"Try to keep up next time," she whispered.

The doors whooshed shut, and the train took off with a lurch. I scanned the receding platform, but if the cop followed us into the station, I couldn't see him through the crowd.

We rode the line several stops down, then got off, waited for the next train, and immediately got back on. Then we exited the station, looped around to the northbound line, and went back the way we came. We repeated this process a few more times until I could have sworn we'd visited every station within a two-mile radius. Finally we got back on the southbound line and let it carry us to Allston.

I didn't speak until we'd emerged from the underground onto the darkening sidewalk. Cea thankfully knew exactly where we were, and we walked the rest of the way to her parents' house.

I found myself scanning the shadowy yards as we passed. "Do you think we lost him?"

She actually laughed. "We lost him thirty minutes ago. And besides—he wasn't looking for us."

I did not share her humor. "How do you figure?"

"If he was chasing us, we would have known as soon as we walked away. You have to remember—as far as he knows, we're legal citizens. We have no reason to be afraid of the cops. But you can never be too careful—which is why you should always take the subway instead of the bus if you think you're being followed."

I made a concentrated effort to stop looking behind me and stared at her instead. "How's it any safer?"

"First, it's easier to hide in a crowd. Second, even the United has trouble tracking the subway. They scan you when you enter and exit the station—but none of the platforms in between are regulated. Even if they saw us enter, they'll have to sort through the hundreds of other passengers that walked through that checkpoint during the same ten-minute window. That's why the subway is the best place to arrange a drop-off, at least around here."

We came in sight of the Vons' house, and I was surprised to find the porchlight on. I fished the key out of my backpack and let us in.

"There you are!" Mrs. Von exclaimed as we entered the kitchen. She gave Cea an annoyed look, as if she were surprised she came back, but she offered me an expression that resembled a smile. "I thought you were going to help with dinner."

"I mean… of course," I stuttered. I had told her as much before Cea and I left this morning—did she remember?

I glanced at Cea, but the nuance was lost on her. She returned her mother's glare, then stormed out of the room with a sniff that threatened to turn teary. I heard her stomp up the stairs and sent a prayer up after her.

Cea didn't come back down for dinner, so the Vons and I went through our routine. I excused myself before Mr. Von could pull me in front of the TV. I went upstairs to find Cea lying on her bed, jacket and shoes still on, as if she'd thrown herself down on the pillows and refused to get up.

"Do you want anything to eat?"

"Go sleep in Nic's room," she snapped.

"I need the radio. Dad's calling me soon." I knelt down and grabbed the box without waiting for permission.

She sighed and sat up. "I'm sorry, Phil, I just—"

"I get it." I clutched the radio to my chest and kicked the box back under the bed.

"Now you know why I never mentioned them."

I chewed my lip and gave the Holy Spirit time to speak. "Maybe it's time to start talking about it."

She glanced sideways at me. I sat down next to her on the bed. "I know it's hard, but they'll never remember you if you're never here."

"Just as well," she muttered.

"Is it?" I wondered aloud, even though I hadn't meant to.

Her expression clouded. "You saw how she looked at me, like I'm breaking and entering. I'm not their daughter anymore."

"But you are."

"You don't get it, Phil!" Tears sprang to Cea's eyes, and she tried to cover them up with violence. She yanked her shoes off and flung them into her bookcase, upending several figurines. "They're gone. I don't know who that is down there in the living room, but they're *not* my parents. My parents are dead. You have no idea what that feels like."

I waited for her to realize her error.

She washed white. "I'm sorry. I didn't—"

I folded her in a hug. I waited until her breathing had slowed before I spoke again. "I do understand. But your parents aren't dead—they're right there."

I pulled away and studied her. She stared at her hands in her lap.

I pinched her shoulder. "They *do* remember things—if you repeat them enough. She remembered I was coming back to help with dinner. I think she left the porchlight on for me."

Cea didn't appreciate the sentiment. "That's not remembering, Phil—that's habit. Of course you can program them to have habits. What do you think they were in therapy for three years for? Their entire existence is just a bunch of patterns. Right now you're part of the routine—but as soon as you leave, they'll get on without you. But that's not the same as accepting me as their daughter." She wiped her eyes. "Nic's right—Mars is where I belong. I'm going home."

I looked down at the radio in my lap and idly twisted the dials. Maybe she was right—maybe I was reading too much into Mrs. Von's actions. But I couldn't imagine leaving my parents to die, letting them rot away in their quaint suburban prison, when I knew I still had a chance.

It had been almost a decade since their surgery; neuroscience had advanced leaps and bounds since then. Surely there was some kind of therapy they could try—if only Cea or Nic would take the time to look.

"When was your dad going to call?" Cea asked, as if she knew where my train of thought was going.

I glanced at the clock. "8:30—any minute now."

I reached down to turn the radio on, but Cea laid her hand across mine.

"Let your dad know you're with me, but don't say my name on air."

I searched her face and waited.

She spoke slowly, as if trying to work it out for herself. "A lot of these people know I'm Nic's sister. If they find out you're with me... it won't take a master's degree to work out that Nic's involved somehow."

"Andes knows about Nic." I tapped my finger on the device. *And so does Aurelius.*

"Yes, but Andes has reasons to stay quiet. We don't need anyone else digging into Nic's file and finding he suddenly has a new dependent."

I nodded, once again glad I'd followed Nic's advice and kept Aurelius at a distance. *It's almost over. As soon as I can get Dad and Ephesus on their new files, I won't need Aurelius anymore.*

I turned the radio on and tuned to channel 2.

At first there was only static. I listened for one minute, two. Cea shifted beside me. I checked the time: 8:33. Did I have the wrong channel? Did he tell me the wrong time? What if something happened to him?

Take it easy... I swallowed a breath and put the handset to my lips. "Radio check."

The response was instant. "This is Catalyst, receiving."

I pinched my eyes shut in relief as the familiarity of his voice rushed through me. "This is Blue Fire."

"Good. We only have a few minutes, so listen closely." His voice was firm but comforting, so I followed his lead. "Are you in a safe place?"

"Yes." I glanced at Cea. "I have a friend with me."

"I see." A beat. "Do I know this friend?"

"Yes." I searched my memory banks, struggling to think of a mnemonic only he would know. "Remember how you said I make 'convenient' friends?"

He answered me with silence, so I tried again. "And you were glad I'd found someone who had taken a liking to me?"

"Ahh." The recognition dawned in his voice. "Is your friend safe?"

"Yes."

"Does she have her affairs in order?"

I remembered what Cea had said to Andes this afternoon and inferred what he meant. "Yes, she does."

"Does she have a safe place to go?"

"Yes."

"Good. I want you to go with her."

The receiver suddenly felt cold to the touch, as if my hand had frozen around it. "What?"

"I want you to go with her and lay low until I find you."

His voice held no uncertainty, but I could think of a million excuses. "I can't leave you."

"You have to. I need you to be safe."

Cea gave me a pointed look that I ignored. "I'm safe here, I promise."

"Not for long. Look, Blue Fire, there's more going on than you realize, things I can't discuss on here. And this time, I mean it when I say I'm not withholding this information to hurt you."

But you don't have all the information this time. "No, you don't get it. Things have changed. I have mo—"

Cea squeezed my knee sharply, so I backpedaled. "I have *resources*. I have the means to get you and Eph—Klez to a safe place if you'll just meet up with me."

I gave him a chance to argue. When he didn't, I seized my window of opportunity. "My friend helped me arrange everything. It's all in order. I just need you to make contact with me."

He prefaced his reply with a heavy breath. "Is this true?"

"Absolutely," I said, hoping the confidence was viable in my voice.

"And you're sure the place you're staying is safe?"

"Yes. I'm fine, I promise. Please don't make me leave without you."

I tried to maintain the same professionalism he had and failed as the poisonous memories came rushing back.

I won't leave you!

We don't have a choice.

"I won't go. Not this time," I whispered, tears punctuating my words. Cea slid her arm around my shoulder.

Help me, Daddy, please!

Just go. Please. Before you get hurt.

"Okay." Dad collected his nerves with a sigh. "I won't make you leave without me. But I need you to promise me that you'll stay right where you are."

"Of course." I wiped my eyes with the heel of my hand.

"Don't move. Don't hang out in public spaces. Stay off the radio. Don't go online."

"Yessir."

"I will contact you when it's safe to meet. I don't know how long that will be." The doubt crept back into his voice, and I silently begged him not to change his mind. "I need to find Klez first. I have a lead, but these things take time. It could be weeks before we can see each other."

He stressed the end of the sentence hard, and I knew he was now silently begging *me* to change my mind. But I couldn't. Not when I'd come so far—not when I had the means to save him. How was he going to get to Mars without me? He didn't have the money or the contacts to forge a file. He needed me.

"I understand, sir," I said by way of deferral.

He didn't sound pleased, but he didn't argue. "And one more thing."

I waited, receiver clenched in my hand.

"If you sense *any* trouble—feel like someone's following you, or anything compromises your position—I need you to leave. I need you to promise me that you'll buy the next available ticket and go home to your friend."

Cea rubbed my shoulder. I swallowed.

"I will find you." Dad's voice reached out to me, but the bad memories got there first.

If I come back, I will find you.

"I promise," he repeated. "You can trust me."

Philadelphia, I will not leave you.

Dad wouldn't take silence for an answer. "Promise me, Blue Fire."

Not if I have a choice.

"I promise," I whispered. *Please, God, don't make me do it.*

"Thank you." The relief in my dad's voice was palpable, and it gave me a little courage. "I need to get off now. Stay where you are and wait for me to contact you."

"How will you contact me?" I asked, scrambling for a thread of security, something to hang on to while I sat around and did nothing.

"If there's any update, I'll try to reach you on this channel, same time. You can tune your radio to listen once a night—but other than that I want you to stay off. Don't say anything unless you hear from me first."

"What if it's important?" I realized how childish that sounded, so I quantified. "Like Klez makes contact with me."

"You can try this channel. But be very careful what you say—someone is always listening. And you can't trust—" There was a blip of static, and I thought I lost him.

"Trust who? Catalyst?"

He came back in with a sigh. "I can't be more specific on here. Just remember that not everyone who calls you Blue Fire is your friend."

You don't know him. "I understand."

"Good. I'm trusting you to be smart about this. If anything happens—you feel like you're in any kind of danger—just leave. Don't try to send a message. Just go and I'll catch up with you."

Just go.

I fought to keep the emotion out of my voice. "Yessir."

"Thank you. I love you." He crammed a year's worth of affection into the phrase. "Catalyst over and out."

"Over and out," I mumbled to the room, even though I didn't bother to press down the handset. I dropped it in my lap and listened to the static, wishing the thrum would drown out my other thoughts.

Cea finally reached down and turned the radio off, bringing back the unwelcome silence. "It's not too late to change your mind. You can come with me."

"You know why I can't," I snapped, more harshly than I intended.

She graciously absorbed the bitterness. She leaned over and gave me another hug that I weakly returned. "You'll be safe as long as you stay with Mom and Dad," she said, more to convince herself than anyone else. "Just lay low. Your dad knows what he's doing."

And so do I. I have money. I can fix this. "I'll be all right. The basement really needs to be cleaned anyway." I pulled away from her and offered her a smile.

She took it. "We'll all be on Mars together again soon."

I glanced at the starry sky peeking through the blinds.

And maybe, just maybe, we would never come back.

15

"You don't have to drop me off," Cea said, probably to relieve herself of any guilt. I could tell she was glad I'd come along.

I smiled at her as we climbed onto the bus. "You'd do the same for me."

We sat near the front. It would take several transfers to get all the way to the transit station, but it was worth it to get out of the house and spend one last afternoon with Cea. The rest of my week was probably going to be spent watching TV with a man who couldn't remember what he had for breakfast— I'd take the companionship while I had it.

"Got everything?"

She patted the suitcase at her feet. "Yes—and thank you. I'll pay you back."

"Don't," I said, a bit too aggressively. "I mean, you don't have to. Nic makes a big deal out of it because he'd rather die than admit that he needed me, but you and I can be adults about it."

Cea laughed. "Fine. I'll just take you shopping when you get home."

I joined her. "Deal."

We transferred at the next stop and took an aisle in the middle. A fully armed cop got on behind us and took the row next over.

I tensed. I started to turn towards Cea, but she grabbed my knee warningly. She pulled her phone out of her pocket and typed rapidly, then held the screen out for me to see.

DON'T STARE. REMEMBER, YOU'RE LEGAL

I made a quiet noise of acknowledgment. She gave me an encouraging wink, leaned back in her seat, and started scrolling on her phone like there wasn't a man with two guns and a taser sitting less than five feet away from her.

I tried to follow suit. I unzipped my backpack and made a pretense of rooting around for the lip balm I definitely didn't need in June. I told myself over and over there was nothing to be afraid of—we weren't doing anything suspicious, and no one had recognized me yet. The cop wasn't even looking at us; he had his cap pulled down low over his eyes as he stared out the window.

Thankfully, Cea distracted me by chatting about everything and nothing. We were so engrossed in our laughter that we almost missed our last transfer and had to shout at the driver to stop. We got off, giggling—and the cop followed.

Cea ran to our transfer without looking back, so I don't think she saw him. But I keenly felt his presence as we joined the line of passengers waiting to board. Cea took the first open aisle. The cop let two or three other people board ahead of him, and then he walked to the back of the bus. I kept my eyes on my tablet as he passed.

Should I say something to Cea? I decided against it. If he was following us, pointing in his direction and whispering probably wasn't a good look. And if it was nothing, I didn't want to get her riled up. He was probably just headed to the transit station—that's the only place this bus went.

The twenty-minute drive seemed to take twice that. Finally, we arrived at the transit station, and Cea and I disembarked with the majority of the other passengers. The cop did not follow; he remained on the bus until it pulled away from the curb.

I let out my breath. *You're jumping at shadows.*

I walked Cea to her gate and made sure she had everything she needed. I bought her a snack and an ebook and then wired her some extra spending money when she wasn't looking. I was sure I'd hear about it from her (or Nic) later, but it was the least I could do.

We stopped outside of security to exchange one last hug. After a minute, I'd had my fill and started to pull away—but she wouldn't let go.

"Phil," she whispered in my ear. She hesitated, then tightened her hug. "Are you sure about this?"

I wiggled out of her grasp. "It's Andi, and I'll be fine."

She kept her hand on my shoulder. "I know, I… you ever just have a feeling that something's not right?"

I did, although I usually attributed it to the Holy Spirit. But I didn't have that feeling now.

"It'll be okay. You helped me take care of everything. I just have to sit back, watch sitcoms, and wait for Dad to call. Honestly, I'll probably be bored." I really would be, and that was honestly the most concerning thing about the whole venture. Last time I was bored, I wandered into Wing 74 and started a war.

She was still struggling. "Look, I know I sound paranoid, but... I really wish you'd come with me. I bet we can still get a ticket. I'll buy you a toothbrush."

I tried to brush it off with a laugh. "Don't be like Nic—at least not in that way."

"Nic would want you to come."

I took a step back. "Nic understands why I have to do this."

She let go of my arm. I tried to patch the bridge. "But I know who to call if I need help."

She smiled. "We're here for you—both of us."

I put on my most confident grin. "I'll see you soon."

She lifted her suitcase. "Can you relay a message for me?"

"Of course."

"If you see Ephesus, tell him I love him."

I squinted at her. "What inflection do you want me to put on that...?"

She grinned coyly. "Whatever inflection you what." She turned to go.

I stood there and waved until she had disappeared behind security. My bravado wavered as soon as she was out of sight—but probably because I didn't relish the idea of being alone again. At least this time I knew where she was, and I could call her whenever I wanted.

I sent her a goodbye text just to make myself feel better, then routed my way back to her parents' house. I squeezed into a seat on the full bus and let the dissonant chatter of a dozen strangers distract my thoughts. I tried to pray, but I couldn't figure out what to talk about. My mind felt full and empty at the same time.

My attempts at divine conversation ended when I got off the bus at the first transfer hub and saw the same cop sitting on the bench.

Don't be ridiculous, it can't be the same one. They all look the same anyway.

As if he knew my thoughts, he reached up and pulled his cap off, releasing an explosion of red-orange curls.

The cop from yesterday. And he was staring straight at me.

I ran across the lot and picked the closest bus. I had no idea what line it was, but it didn't matter. I climbed on and sat as close to the driver as I could.

The cop did not get up and follow. He did, however, lean over and talk into the handset on his shoulder.

The bus jerked away from the curb, and I grabbed the pole to keep from falling over. Surely I was overreacting. It was just a coincidence that it was the same cop, wasn't it? He couldn't be trailing me—if he was, he would have gotten off at the transit station with us. He'd have no way of knowing I'd come back to this transfer hub—

Except he did. The route to the transit station was a continual loop; it only went back and forth from this transfer hub. The cop would have known I'd come back.

And apparently he wasn't interested in Cea.

What did I do? I mentally replayed my day, trying to figure out where I had gone wrong. What had I done to arouse suspicion? Did he recognize me? Surely if he thought I was Philadelphia Smyrna he would have arrested me on the spot.

If he was chasing us, we would have known as soon as we walked away.

No, I was definitely jumping to conclusions. If I were in real trouble, he would have caught up to me already.

Besides, even if he saw which bus I got on, he'd have no way of knowing where I got off.

I mapped the route I was on and saw that it passed through downtown— perfect. There were tons of subway entrances downtown. I could get off the bus, take the subway, and lose them just like Cea had shown me.

I waited until the bus had carried me into the heart of the city and got off on a busy intersection in front of a crowded mall. *It's always easier to hide in a crowd.* I stepped into the bus shelter and pulled up my map. The closest subway station was two blocks down. *Thank you, Jesus.*

I walked to the curb and looked both ways—and there was another cop.

He sat across the road on a bench where he had a perfect view of the bus stop. He crossed his arms and stared at me, unblinking.

The crossing light turned green. I felt a rush of people push past me, but I didn't move. The light turned red again, and I was left standing alone on the sidewalk. The cop continued to stare, waiting.

I turned and ran into the mall.

I took a lap around the lower level, searching for another entrance. I finally found one on the opposite end of the building. I pushed open the first set of double doors—and froze.

Two more cops stood outside on the sidewalk, talking into their handsets.

"Hey, watch it!" An angry teen grunted at me as she tried to push past me in the doorway.

I mumbled an apology and turned around.

I joined a crowd of shoppers coming through the door and let them carry me back to the main concourse. I paused by the nearest gondola and pretended to browse the wares, running my fingers over the gaudy necklaces to hide how badly my hand was shaking.

They had the building surrounded. They were definitely looking for me.

I had to get to the subway without them seeing me. That was my only hope. Surely there was another way out of this building.

I walked to the nearest map and scanned the diagram, searching for any possible exit. No doubt they had all the street entrances blocked, but—there. The parking garage. The ramp out of the parking garage dumped onto the next street over, right around the corner from the subway station.

Would they have thought to watch the parking garage? I didn't want to walk over there and find another cop; the last place I wanted to get caught alone with a police officer was in a parking garage with no people around.

I needed someone to look for bears.

Of course, I was nowhere near a radio, so that didn't help me. *Unless...*

Aurelius had access to a radio. He could ask for me.

I glanced around the concourse, then ducked into the nearest shop and hid among the cluttered clearance racks. Pulling out my tablet, I opened the messaging app and skimmed my chat history with Aurelius. He'd slowed his roll over the past twenty-four hours, which I took as a good sign; there was nothing in his recent texts that indicated he'd heard my last conversation with Dad. Mainly he was just pleading with me not to do anything stupid—as if Nic and Cea hadn't done enough of that already—and reminding me that he was here to help.

I need your help now. But if I asked him about that intersection, he'd know where I was. I wasn't keen on giving him a pinpoint, but I wouldn't be in that intersection for long. As soon as I got on the subway, I'd be hard to find. Plus, he didn't know what I looked like anymore.

I clicked in the textbox.

I NEED YOUR HELP

I hoped he would take the bait and bypass his usual guilt-tripping.
It worked. He responded within minutes.

WHAT'S WRONG? ARE YOU OKAY?

I'M FINE. I'M JUST WONDERING IF THIS PART OF TOWN IS SAFE

I hoped he would infer the meaning. I was still trying to phrase things like socially-compliant Andromeda would.

He seemed to understand and asked for the location. I took a deep breath, hoped I wasn't making a grave mistake, and sent him the cross streets.

ARE YOU THERE RIGHT NOW?

I cringed. *Don't be like this...*

NO, IT'S FOR A FRIEND

HANG ON

A minute later, he added:

THEY'RE CHECKING. HANG TIGHT

THANKS

He tried to capitalize on the opportunity.

ARE YOU SURE EVERYTHING'S GOOD?

YEAH WE'RE COOL

WANNA MEET UP LATER?

What do you think?

THIS WEEK ISN'T GOOD FOR ME

He opted not to acknowledge that.

YEAH, THAT PART OF TOWN IS LEGIT. YOU SHOULD BE FINE

THANKS

I closed the chat before he could say anything else and walked to the parking garage.

I hovered near the door until someone entered. I stole a glance around the corner while the door was open; no cops that I could see. Taking a deep breath, I grabbed the door handle and stepped out.

I shivered in the concrete-cooled air. Pulling my jacket around me, I strode towards the opposite end as fast as I dared, trying to walk with purpose. My boots echoed disturbingly loud on the pavement. A car honked on another level, and I jumped.

You're almost there.

I slowed as I neared the exit. A van entered the garage, and I stepped up on the curb to let them pass. I pressed myself against the wall and scanned what I could see of the street.

No one, except a gaggle of women walking past with their shopping bags. I swallowed my next breath and stepped out behind them.

I followed them for a block until they crossed the street. I kept walking, tossing one more glance around me. I was alone, so I picked up my pace. The subway entrance was just a block ahead around the corner.

Almost there.

I passed the last alleyway and heard a shout.

"Blue Fire!"

I instinctively turned my head—and by then it was too late.

Two men emerged from the shadows behind a dumpster. One pointed a gun at me.

"Don't scream, or we'll shoot," he said, advancing.

Oh Lord, help.

"What do you want?" I eyed them. They definitely weren't cops; they were my age, with barely enough facial hair between them to constitute a mustache, and their weapons were at least a decade old.

The second man put his hands up. "We just want to talk. We don't want to hurt you."

I don't believe that for a second.

They took another step towards me. "We've been looking for you."

"Who's we?"

But even as the word left my mouth, I knew.

They're looking for you.

I remembered the scrambling on the radio, the strangers demanding to know where I was, and Dad's cryptic warnings. He wasn't talking about the United when he told me to be careful. He was talking about the underground.

Not everyone who calls you Blue Fire is your friend.

The underground had been looking for me this whole time.

And Aurelius had led them right to me.

Why they wanted me, I couldn't fathom, but I wasn't going to play that game. Anything that involved holding me at gunpoint couldn't be good.

"What do you want, really?" I demanded.

"We need you," the first admitted with a smile, and I didn't like the sound of that at all.

The Holy Spirit rushed at me with a burst of wisdom. I drew myself up straight. "Is that so?" I said with a coldness I did not feel. "Put the gun down and maybe I'll talk."

They exchanged a glance—too long. "I don't have all day," I hissed. "You may need me, but I definitely don't need *you*."

The second one nodded. The first looked annoyed but obeyed. He bent over to put his weapon on the ground, but apparently someone else wasn't interested in peaceful negotiations, because they shot first.

I screamed as a gun fired from farther down the alley. The bullet shattered the concrete a few feet away, grazing my arm with shrapnel.

The two guys whipped around and shouted. I didn't wait to see who the other gunman was.

I turned and ran.

I darted around the corner and pounded down the steps into the subway without looking back. The station was not nearly as crowded as I'd hoped. I stood out like a fish swimming against the current as I shoved my way through the turnstile and tried to blend in with the passengers scattered on the platform. I listened for an approaching train, but the tunnels were eerily silent. Had I just missed it?

Please hurry! I bounced unsteadily on my heels, trying to conceal the adrenaline. I kept my eye on the entrance. *Please don't follow, please don't—*

A group of people descended the stairs—just as the screech of brakes echoed down the corridor. I pushed past the person in front of me and ran to the edge of the platform. I crammed my way onto the train as soon as the doors opened, ignoring the complaints of disembarking passengers.

I fled to the far corner of the cab and collapsed on the bench. It seemed like we were stalled in the station for an eternity as a million people got off and on. Finally, the train lurched away from the platform, and I stole a glance out the window. The group on the stairs turned out to be a bunch of schoolkids. There were no cops anywhere. No one ran after the departing train, shouting.

I took a scan of the other passengers, but they were all absorbed in their own business.

The adrenaline broke. I sagged against the wall, my arms shaking in time to the rattling car. The fog of blinding terror cleared just enough for me to put my fear into words.

They were shooting at me.

My nerves seized up again. *Breathe. Breathe!* I swallowed the fear and tried to smother it with the only emotion that was stronger: Anger.

I yanked my backpack off and grabbed my tablet. My sweaty fingers slipped across the screen as I struggled to unlock it.

In some cruel irony, there were no new messages from Aurelius. This time, I initiated.

I THOUGHT YOU SAID IT WAS CLEAR

He responded immediately.

WHAT? DID SOMETHING HAPPEN?

DON'T PLAY STUPID! YOU LED THEM RIGHT TO ME!

WHAT? WHO?

Before I could even fight through my rage to come up with a reply, he sent several more messages.

ARE YOU OKAY?

WHERE ARE YOU?

TALK TO ME

I never should have talked to you.

DON'T PLAY ME! I JUST GOT SHOT AT!

The typing dots appeared and vanished again. *Why are you still talking to him?* The Holy Spirit begged me to leave it alone—just walk away before someone got hurt. But I had to see his reply. I wanted—needed—there to be a good explanation, some miraculous happenstance that could make this all go away and prove that he was still my friend.

He, of course, didn't have one.

WHAT? ARE YOU SERIOUS?

ARE YOU OKAY?

CALL ME

Then without waiting for a response, he started an audio call, which I promptly ignored. He tried again—twice—then resorted to typing.

PLEASE TALK TO ME

I SWEAR I DON'T KNOW WHAT HAPPENED

JAYDE SAID THE INTERSECTION WAS CLEAR

The world lurched to a stop at the same time the train did. I lunged forward and nearly fell off the bench. I braced my boot against the floor and waited for everything to restart. The train did. My heart didn't.

You don't know him.

He didn't seem to realize what he'd said and was waiting for my reply. I finally found the coordination to type the words.

I THOUGHT YOU WERE JAYDE

He could be anybody.

He swore.

I'M SORRY I LIED TO YOU

Use him, but don't trust him.

The typing dots appeared, but I didn't wait. I hit the drop-down and blocked him.

The chat grayed out, and his avatar went dark. I hastily closed the app and shoved my tablet into my backpack.

I felt the hot tears slide down my cheeks. I covered my face, struggling not to be a spectacle. Nic was right—he had been right all along. I didn't know Aurelius. I'd given him my location and almost gotten killed. I couldn't trust him. I couldn't trust anyone.

The underground wasn't my friend; it was the enemy. They'd come for me—and they'd surely be going after Dad next. They'd shot me on sight; they wouldn't hesitate to kill my father.

We had to get off this planet.

16

I let myself in the back door and ran up the stairs before the Vons could talk to me. I dragged the radio out from under the bed and tuned it to channel 2.

"Catalyst, come in, this is Blue Fire. Please respond."

Static. I sat down on the bed and repeated myself. "Catalyst, it's me, Blue Fire. Please come in."

It was a stab in the dark—Dad had said to use this channel if I needed to reach him, but I had no way of knowing if he was monitoring it now. But it was my only hope.

I tried again. "Emergency, emergency! Catalyst, do you copy?"

A stranger answered me. "Blue Fire, this is Data, where are you? What's your status?"

I growled under my breath. *Not now!* "Stop clogging the channel."

He wasn't deterred. "Blue Fire, we need to make contact. There's been an incident—"

I should say so! I spoke over him. "Emergency, emergency! Catalyst, come in!"

Data must have brought friends, because suddenly multiple voices started competing for bandwidth. "Someone get Green Dragon on the line!"

"All units, 10-25 Catalyst?"

"Green Dragon, I'm prepped for tracking."

"Belay that, Watts. Blue Fire, do you copy?"

I ignored them all. "Catalyst, please acknowledge!"

The voices continued to bicker—one minute, two—and I started to lose hope. I gripped the receiver with both hands. *Please, God! This is my only chance!*

"Blue Fire! What are you doing? Get off the radio, now!"

Daddy. "Catalyst, something's happened. We need to talk."

New voices jumped on the line, but Daddy spoke over them. "Then you know what to do. Leave and I'll catch up with you."

"No, you don't understand—change to channel 10."

I did it without waiting for him to acknowledge. He followed and spoke first. "Blue Fire, I told you not to send a message. I need you to get on a plane and—"

"No, listen. You can't trust these people."

He was still talking, a sure sign he hadn't heard me. "—leave tonight if you can. I'll catch up, I promise."

He paused to take a breath, and I jumped in. "Dad! Just listen! The underground—"

The other voices invaded our privacy. "Channel 15!" I shouted, and switched.

This time I spoke first. "Dad, don't speak, just listen. Something's happened. You can't trust the underground. They've been stalking me." I decided to omit the fact that I was almost murdered.

"I know they are," he responded, voice thick with worry. "That's why I need you to leave."

"You don't get it! I'm trying to tell you that *you're* not safe here!"

"It's not your job to protect me."

"Dad, things aren't how you think they are. I can help you. My..." I struggled to recall the phrase, "affairs are in order."

"Blue Fire," he snapped.

I couldn't detangle the emotion attached to the name, but I didn't care. "I've arranged for your affairs. Everything's in order and we can be out of here tomorrow. But I can't tell you on this line—I need you to call me privately."

Andes claimed his other clients wouldn't interfere—but I didn't trust anyone who would shoot me in an alley in cold blood.

There was a breath of silence—long enough for me to panic. "Dad, please, you have to trust me."

He rattled off a number.

"What?"

He repeated it more slowly—a phone number. I grabbed my tablet and wrote it down while he dictated. "Text—don't call. I'll turn my device on in exactly fifteen minutes and leave it on for five minutes. Text me what I need to know. Then turn your device off and wait. I will text you back at 21:00 to arrange a meeting. If you don't hear from me at 21:00—run."

This time, I didn't patronize him. "I won't. I'm not leaving without you."

I'll never know if he would have argued—another voice jumped onto the channel and said something I couldn't make out. I didn't wait for Dad's acknowledgment and turned the radio off.

I went to Nic's room and fished one of the smartphones out from under the floorboards. Leaving the panel ajar, I took the phone back to Cea's room. I sat down on the bed, powered on the device, and altered the settings just like Cea had shown me. Then I opened the default texting app and drafted my message.

If what Cea said was true, the United would almost certainly read my text after my activity triggered their censorship programs. Andes had said his name was fake and his number untraceable, but I still had to word the message carefully.

CALL ANDES. YOU HAVE AN APPOINTMENT, CONFIRMATION NUMBER 0422

I added the phone number from the business card, then saved the message as a draft and checked the time. I still had five minutes to wait.

My heart was racing and my fingers shaking from adrenaline, so I ran through the next steps in my mind to give my nerves something to focus on. I would bring the phone online—send the text—wait for Dad's confirmation— and then turn the phone off so they couldn't track it.

Track it! If the United looked into my activity, they'd see that the text was sent from the Vons' internet connection. I couldn't bring them into this—I had to connect to another hotspot.

I remembered what Cea said about old smartphones connecting to any signal they could find. If I got out of range of the Vons' internet, the phone should connect to the nearest cell tower instead.

I had three minutes before Dad was expecting my text. I stuffed my devices in my backpack and raced down the steps.

Mrs. Von intercepted me at the bottom of the stairs. "There you are! It's almost time to start dinner!"

I wiggled past her. "I'll be right back—I need to grab something at the gas station."

She didn't buy it. She gave me a once-over, and her eyes fell on the scratches on my arm from the shrapnel.

I pulled the sleeve of my jacket down. "I tripped on the sidewalk, it's fine."

She tipped her head to one side, as if my behavior didn't fit in a pattern she could process. "Try to be more careful..."

I threw her an apologetic smile and raced out the back door.

I jogged down the street towards the bus stop. I had no intention of getting on, but at least I wouldn't look like an idiot for running towards it. I reached the bench just when fifteen minutes had passed. I brought the phone online, sent the text, and said a prayer.

The response was instant.

GOT IT

I wanted to say more but knew we couldn't risk it. I sent another text to Andes's number and told him to expect a call for appointment 0422. I didn't get a response, but I wasn't worried. I powered the device off and hid it in my backpack. Then I decided I'd better go to the gas station and buy something, just in case Mrs. Von was having a good day and remembered.

She didn't—but she was nonetheless pleased with the chocolate I brought her. She commandeered me as kitchen help as soon as I walked in the door, and I was grateful. It would be over four hours before I'd hear from Dad, and I wouldn't know how to contain my nervous energy otherwise.

I kept telling myself it was going to be all right. I had everything set up and in order. Dad's temporary identity was paid for, and neither the underground nor the United had any idea what was going on. As soon as Dad's new file was online, I could buy us transit tickets and we'd be on the next flight to Mars.

We still had to find Ephesus, but Nic was right—Ephesus was a grown man. He'd been smart and not gotten tangled up with the underground; he wasn't in immediate danger, not like Dad. Once we got back to base, I could go back to looking like Philadelphia and record videos again. Ephesus would see them.

I excused myself from the living room at 8:30 and went upstairs to pack. I put my clothes and makeup in the suitcase and left it on the bed, then took my tablet off the charger. I glanced at the messaging app and realized I'd missed a notification from Nic—he was asking if Cea had left.

I responded with an affirmative, then debated letting him know we were coming. After a minute, I decided against it. He would *not* be pleased when he heard about the risk I was taking, and I didn't want him asking questions until our itinerary was set in stone. No use ruffling his feathers when it wouldn't change anything.

I slung my backpack over my shoulder and left out the back door, trying to be quiet and not disturb the Vons.

I walked to a different bus stop this time, one a few blocks over, so they wouldn't pinpoint my burner phone to the same location. It was long past dark, and the street was comfortably deserted except for some kids hanging out in front of a gas station down the way. I sat down on the bench under the streetlight and powered on the smartphone.

8:58—still early. Andes had responded to my text with a thumbs up a few hours ago, which I took as a good sign. 8:59. I checked to make sure my connection was good and refreshed the app.

9:00. Nothing yet—but clocks could be off. I waited three more minutes. Still nothing.

I decided to initiate.

YOU GOOD?

I waited several more minutes. No response.

I checked my connection again. I had full bars.

If you don't hear from me at 21:00—run.

No—I wasn't going to leave him behind just because he was five minutes late texting me. I already told him I wouldn't go.

9:08. I got up and started walking. If the United was tracking my signal, I needed to be a moving target.

I walked another three blocks down the road. 9:15.

Maybe his appointment with Andes was running long. It had taken a couple of hours to get my prints altered—if Andes hadn't gotten him in until later in the day, Dad might still be tied down in the machine and couldn't text back.

I dialed Andes's number. He picked up immediately and barked a gruff greeting that was probably Scottish.

"Andes, we spoke earlier. I set up the appointment for 0422."

"Lass!" His bellow filled the line. "All good on your end? I'm still waiting."

"What?" The sound came out more breath than word.

"Your man hasn't showed. Did you give him the right number? If he calls I can give directions."

I hung up.

17

I dialed Dad's number. It rang through—but that meant the phone was on, wasn't it?

I tried again. It rang only three times before sending me to voicemail. I switched back to text.

ANDES SAID YOU DIDN'T SHOW. WHERE ARE YOU?

No response.

I dialed again. This time it cut me off on the first ring—and a text immediately came through.

It was an address.

I mapped it on my tablet and was relieved to see that it was only ten minutes away by bus.

Another text came through.

THIRD FLOOR. HURRY

I powered off the smartphone and started running.

I darted across the street to catch the bus heading in the other direction. Thankfully the lines were still running, and the next bus was due within minutes. I practically fell into the road waving the driver down as he came around the corner.

I took the first seat, not caring that it was marked for the elderly. The bus zoomed towards the outskirts of town, and I prayed there would be no one waiting at the other stops so that we'd get there faster.

Oh God, please let him be alive! Please let me get there in time!

The address took me to a shell of an office building on the edge of town. It was vacant, the dusty for sale sign in the window sending up a weak S.O.S. All of the windows were dark, and several had been bashed in.

I would have thought I'd come to the wrong place if the front door weren't propped open.

I ran inside and scanned the lobby. No one was in sight. There was no power to the elevator, so I found the emergency stairs and raced to the third floor. The only lights in the stairwell were the emergency exit signs, and I tripped three times in the dark.

I shoved open the door to the third floor. It dragged on its hinges with a hideous squeak like I'd raised it from a dead sleep.

A quick scan of the floor made it appear empty except for the frames of abandoned cubicles and a couple of bereaved desks. The halls in every direction were dark; the only light came from the glare of the streetlamp outside the bay windows that lined the wall on the left.

"Dad?" I called, and my voice echoed back to me hollowly. I crept down the left side of the room, staying close to the light. I tensed as I passed each cubicle, expecting the worst—but it never came. There was no sound, no movement, no evidence that anyone had been here in months.

I reached the opposite end of the room and peered into the dark hallway beyond. "Dad?" I tried again.

At first, silence—then the most sickening sound I could have imagined: muffled shouting, and the smacking of a hand on glass.

"Dad!" I ran. I looked in every office I passed, searching for any sign of life. Finally, I saw a faint blue glow flickering from around the corner up ahead. The shouts came again, closer this time, and I thought I heard my name.

"I'm coming!" I stumbled around the corner into an empty lab. Most of the equipment had been swept away into the corners to die, but one machine was alive and throbbing. It was a hefty glass-and-metal tube, propped up at an angle. And my dad was trapped inside.

I screamed. He saw me and banged on the glass, shouting something that was still too muffled to hear. I ran to him, tripping once on the way there, and collapsed against the side of the machine.

"Are you okay? What happened? Who did this to you?" I pressed myself against the cold glass and searched his face for answers. He seemed alert, his eyes wild and dilated. There was a smear of blood on the inside of the glass that matched the small wound on his forehead. But otherwise he seemed unhurt.

He put his palms against the glass to match mine. "Philadelphia, listen to me." His words chattered along with his teeth, and his breath clouded the air inside the tube, briefly making him invisible.

"What is this thing?" I stepped back and scanned the machine. The tube itself was little more than a glass coffin with a single keypad on the side, but it was hooked to several other machines and a flashing control panel by a tangle of wires. A thick hose ran out the back and connected the tube to a large metal canister. I didn't recognize the chemical symbols on the side, but I didn't like the look of it—or the fact that the whole apparatus was absolutely *freezing.* My fingers grew numb against the frosty glass, but I refused to move.

"We have to get you out of here."

"The control panel," he said. I touched the keypad on the side of the tube, and he gestured wildly. "No, the computer. Abort the process." He coughed, as if those words had taken all the breath left in his lungs.

What process? I didn't have the stomach to ask. I turned to the control panel and swiped through the open menus, looking for anything with a "stop" button or red X. Everything was timers and readouts and nothing I could control.

Oh, God, help. "I can't find—"

"Philadelphia!" My father's voice changed pitch into a shriek.

I turned my head—right into the barrel of a gun.

Before I could even process what I was seeing, someone grabbed me from behind. The gun was rammed under my chin, scaring away any cry that attempted to leave my lips.

"Hello, Philadelphia," my captor said by way of greeting.

My heart was beating too loudly in my skull for me to identify the voice. Thankfully he put his lips close to my ear and repeated himself. "Not so clever now, are we?"

Carnegie. I daren't turn to look, but in my peripheral I could see the wrinkled hand holding the gun and knew it was him.

"Carnegie, please don't hurt her." My father fought to keep his voice level even as it shook from exhaustion. He struggled to stay upright. I could see now that he was turning white and blue in all the wrong places.

Carnegie savored the spectacle. "You had your chance for peaceful negotiations—twice now. Although I suppose I can't really blame you for the fiasco on Rott." His strangely warm hand fingered my neck.

I resisted the urge to swallow. "What do you want?"

He barked a laugh. "I have what I want. What I would *love* is to kill you right now and let you bleed out while he watches."

He jammed the gun into my throat, causing me to gag. My dad made an unutterable cry of agony. I pinched my eyes shut.

Jesus Jesus Jesus.

"But." Carnegie loosened his hold, and I sucked in a gasp of air. "Revival is expensive, so I suppose we could still make a deal."

Revival? Somehow I knew he wasn't talking about church.

He turned back to my dad. "Give me Red Rain, and I'll let her live."

Dad didn't even flinch, but I felt my soul freeze over. *No. Not again.*

"I'll put her under for a week—just so there's no incidents—and if you give me the formula, you can both go free. I'll even buy you a transit ticket to Mars as a gesture of goodwill." I felt the chuckle vibrate in his chest. "You can tell Nic I sent you."

Dad's eyes flickered back and forth between me and Carnegie.

"Well, doctor? What will it be?" Carnegie taunted, twisting the gun against my throat.

Dad opened his mouth—but I spoke first.

"No."

Carnegie dug his fingernails into my neck, but I ignored him. I swallowed and straightened as best I could. "We won't do it."

"I wasn't asking you." His spit landed on my ear.

I flinched. "And I wasn't talking to you." I met my dad's gaze and held it with all the conviction and sincerity I could muster. "Don't let him win."

Help me, Dad. Fight with me.

His face was pinched in an expression I couldn't interpret. I kept going. "My life isn't worth millions of others."

"It is to me," he said, voice clogged with a lifetime of heartbreak. He coughed again. Carnegie laughed cruelly.

I jerked against him to shut him up. "I know, but this is what's right."

Don't let them use you. Don't let them blackmail you.

Dad didn't argue. He put both palms flat against the glass, even as they trembled.

"This is my choice," I said. The adrenaline sapped the courage from my voice, but I kept speaking from the conviction I knew was hiding under the blinding roar of death.

Whatever they tell you, whatever they say they're going to do to me, don't listen.

"Don't do it. Don't give him Red Rain."

Don't let him win.

"I will drop her right here and now," Carnegie said, as if there was any doubt. "And I'll be happy to make it slow and painful. So make your choice, doctor."

Dad closed his eyes and leaned his bloody forehead against the glass. I saw his lips moving and followed suit.

With great effort, Dad pushed himself upright. When he opened his eyes again, he focused them straight at Carnegie.

"I won't do it." His voice still quavered from the cold, but it had the strength of a thousand men. "I won't give you Red Rain."

I smiled at him through my tears.

Thank you, Jesus.

Carnegie made a noise of annoyance. He hesitated, and for a brief moment hope shot through me. Had we called his bluff?

Then he adjusted his grip on the gun and regained control of the situation. "Well, at least that answers one question."

Neither I nor my father replied. The terror returned to my father's face as he realized what he'd done.

I heard the smile in Carnegie's voice. "Thank you for letting me know your daughter is expendable."

Dad uttered an oath. I closed my eyes and braced myself for the inevitable that never came.

"But luckily for you, I hate her," Carnegie clenched his hand around my throat, "more than I hate you, so I'm going to let her watch you die—instead of the other way around."

Before I could comprehend what he meant, he lowered the gun just long enough to punch a button on the screen. The machine kicked into high gear. He pressed the gun to my neck again and dragged me back a few steps so I had an agonizingly clear view of the horror that was unfolding.

The machine throbbed. The pipe on the back went stiff as the canister drained its chemical contents into the line.

Dad yelled. I turned my attention back to him and saw that the glass tube was filling with liquid. It was thick and slimy and the horrid blue-green shade of evil. It crawled up the side of the tube—too fast to stop, but slow enough to send Dad to hell in his own mind. I almost vomited as all the emotions of a man facing death contorted his face. He rammed his fists, then his shoulder, over and over into the glass, but it did nothing.

I sobbed and fought against Carnegie, but he held me back.

The liquid reached Dad's neck. In panic he threw one last plea towards Carnegie. "Please—"

Whatever he was going to say was drowned out as he swallowed a mouthful of liquid. He thrashed as he went under. There was a flash of light and a hideous crack—and then silence.

Carnegie released me. I stumbled forward and crashed into the machine, swiping furiously at the frost that clouded the glass. But no matter how hard I wiped, all I could see was a solid block of greenish ice inside the tube.

"You killed him!" I screeched, but the sound came out garbled like a strangled animal.

"Not exactly." Carnegie approached from behind and tapped the control panel. "He's frozen for safekeeping. When I'm ready to use him, I'll bring him back."

I snarled. I whipped around to punch him, but he was ready. My punch bounced weakly off his arm, and then he reached out to trip me.

I landed hard and struggled to get up, but he kicked me sharply under the ribs. I wailed.

"Oh, Philadelphia, you know this is all your fault, right?"

I squinted at him through the tears.

He kicked me again. "You led me right to him."

I scrambled backwards until I was in the middle of the floor. He just watched me and smiled. "I knew you wouldn't listen to Nic. I knew you couldn't sit still. And when I gave you that scare in the alley—I knew you'd pull the trigger and flush my fox out in the open."

The world was spinning in time to the pain that was radiating through my body. I pushed myself up on one knee and fell down again. "I don't—that was you?"

He spread his hands, face consumed in a proud grin. "Those cops work for me. I've been following you this whole time, Philadelphia—or should I say, *Andromeda.*"

I managed to stand even though I was shaking uncontrollably.

He answered my unspoken question. "Of course I knew. It was part of my deal with Thames—he gave me my weapons, and I gave him the daughter he always wanted. Shame he never got to claim his prize."

Carnegie's laugh filled the room along with the thunderous roar of my guilt.

He's right. This is all your fault.

He checked to make sure his gun was still loaded and ready. Then he aimed it at me. There was nowhere to run—he stood between me and the hallway.

"You should have stayed on Mars, sweetheart."

You should have listened to Nic.

Carnegie put his finger on the trigger—and someone else fired.

The deafening explosion ripped the scream from my throat. Carnegie lurched forward one drunken step, planting his foot as if he could save himself by keeping his balance. His eyes flashed, then glazed. He coughed blood.

Then he collapsed face first on the concrete, a bullet lodged in his back.

Stanyard stood behind him, panting.

A pistol smoked in his hands. He kept it aimed, hands steady despite the shaking of his chest, as if he expected Carnegie to come back for more. The room was silent except for the ringing in my ears. We both stared at Carnegie until the amount of blood seeping through his lab coat made his state of life clear.

Stanyard finally looked at me, eyes burning. "What do you think you're doing?" he yelled, more colorfully than necessary. "Why didn't you call for help?"

He was shouting—and he sounded very, very angry.

"Call for help?" I squeaked. I wasn't sure whether to be afraid, offended, or confused—and then I realized I was all three with a vengeance. "How could I have called for help? I didn't even know you were *alive*." My volume rose to match his.

He put his hands up. "I'm sorry. I'm sorry. I'm sorry." With each repetition, he lowered his voice until it was an acceptable level. He swiped at the sweat on his forehead. "I just… I thought I lost you again."

His words ricocheted around the lab, louder and more terrifying than the gunshot. My ears started ringing again, and I remembered.

I thought I lost you.

I'm sorry, Phil, I really am.

I'm sorry I lied to you.

I took a step back, feeling sick and unsafe all over again. "It was you. Aurelius—that was you the whole time."

He looked down, but only for a beat before he lifted his eyes to meet mine. He nodded.

I tried to attach an emotion to that revelation and failed. I would have taken any emotion—fear, anger, betrayal. Any concrete feeling would have been better than the swirling pressure in my chest, like a vacuum had been created that was sucking out my ability to process and breathe and be my own person.

"You lied to me," I finally managed, but it did nothing to direct the storm.

He nodded again.

"Why? Why not just tell me?"

It was a genuine question—the correct answer to which could have reset the universe. Unfortunately, he didn't have a good answer.

"You said yourself you didn't trust me," he mumbled.

You're right, I don't.

Suddenly, a recognizable emotion formed in my throat, and I grabbed it. "You almost got me killed!" I screeched.

"I swear I don't know what happened. Jayde said—"

"I thought you were Jayde!" Suddenly, icy fear clashed with the anger burning in my veins like lava meeting water. "Does he know? Where is he? What did you do to him?"

"Whoa." Stanyard slid back. "Jayde's fine. What, you think I'd hurt him?"

Well, you hurt me. "I don't know what to think," I said, which was the truth.

Stanyard searched my face. He didn't look offended, as if he'd seen this coming all along. "Jayde's safe. He's back with the others. And yes, he knows. He was with me the whole time."

"Oh, so you all agreed to lie to me." I wanted to be angry about that too, but suddenly I just felt *tired*. Stanyard had lied to me *again*, and Jayde had lied to me, but then they'd both come back and tried to save me, and then Stanyard had just now *actually* saved me, and apparently we were all going to be together again.

All of these things seemed important, and yet not important, and meanwhile Carnegie was still lying on the floor between us, dead and getting deader.

Stanyard didn't wait up for my mental composure. "Look, can we talk about this later? We need to get out of here. Whoever he's working for—" He shook his pistol at Carnegie, "—knows you're here. As soon as they realize he's gone dark, they'll have this place surrounded."

He took a step towards me, and suddenly I remembered who else was in the room. "Dad!"

I ran to the machine. Stanyard turned to follow and muttered an oath. "Did he—?"

"He's frozen," I stated the obvious. I swiped more frost from the glass, then instantly regretted it. Dad's face was faintly visible through the block of solid cryoprotectant. He floated eerily, like he was suspended a few inches under a frozen lake. The rapid process had turned his fear into a stone monument—his eyes screaming in terror, mouth agape, body twisted in pain.

A sound I couldn't remember summoning wrenched out of me.

Oh God.

Stanyard approached the tube slowly and looked in. "Oh Phil," he breathed. "I'm sorry."

I muttered in tongues under my breath, then swallowed the rush of courage. "We have to get him out. Help me." I reached for the control panel.

"Don't touch that!" Stanyard lunged forward, hand reaching to block mine—then realized he was still holding a gun. He quickly set the safety and stuffed it in the belt of his jeans. "You can't just thaw him out—that's not how that works."

I stared at him, my heart racing again—this time in tune to an entirely new breed of panic.

"There's a whole process to thawing someone out. It's not like defrosting a turkey—you can't just let them come to room temperature. He'll need neurotherapy and blood transfusions and a bunch of stuff."

"But he's only been frozen for a minute!"

"Doesn't matter! We're going to have to take him to a reviving facility."

"But I can't just leave him here." I couldn't leave him—not after I'd just found him—and if Carnegie had people, they would surely be coming. I wouldn't let them have Dad, frozen or otherwise.

Stanyard knelt and rooted around on the floor. "You won't have to." There was a grunt, and he stood up. "This is a mobile transport tube. It can be unplugged for several hours." He held up a thick, multi-pronged cord for emphasis.

The display on Dad's tube chirped and changed color. It glowed yellow, and a timer started counting down from three hours. I watched the seconds tick, then glanced back up at Stanyard.

"Carnegie wasn't planning on keeping your dad here," he said.

I swallowed. "I know." Where would he have taken him? Had he found more allies? Who was he working with?

Stanyard started disconnecting the other hoses and wires that anchored the tube to the machine. "The other guys are on their way—I sent them my location. They can move him."

"I'll wait with him."

"No, you won't." A pipe hissed at him as he released the seal. "Phil, if they find out you're still alive, they'll either finish the job, or they'll take you who-knows-where. We need to get you out of here, now."

"But Dad—"

"The guys will take care of him. Please, just come with me." He pulled out the last plug and turned to extend a hand to me.

I stared at it, his palm streaked with sweat and gunpowder, and suddenly I was back in that dreaded alley as he reached to help me out of the car.

Phil, if you don't come now, I'll leave you behind!

I could tell by the look in his eyes that he was there too. He dropped his hand and wiped it on his jeans. "This way. The car's out back."

He started walking. With one last glance back at Dad, I followed.

18

Stanyard mercifully stayed silent as he drove us back to base. I spent the ride gripping the passenger door handle, trying not to choke on residual adrenaline. It didn't help that my muscles had memorized what happened the last time I'd ridden in a car with Stanyard.

"Base" ended up being a nondescript brick-and-steel office building, not unlike Thames's headquarters. What surprised me was that it was located smack-dab in the middle of a busy thoroughfare on the fringes of downtown.

Stanyard answered my quizzical stare with a shrug. "It's easier to hide in plain sight."

He drove underneath the building into the parking garage. Jayde stood in the middle of the lot, waiting for us.

He opened my door as soon as Stanyard parked. "Blue Fire! You made it! We all thought you were going to go dark."

I almost did. I got out and studied him, trying to decide if I was happy to see him or not.

He didn't wait for an emotional reaction. "I owe you an apology."

That was a cold open I couldn't ignore. I shifted my eyes to his face.

He returned my stare. "Those men that stopped you in the alley this afternoon? They were my guys."

"What?" I yelled—or tried to yell. The word caught on my throat, raw from processing death and terror, and came out weak and raspy.

He nodded. "We've been trying to find you since you came back to Earth. Stanyard was our only contact, and when you kept ghosting him, I realized I'd have to do it the old-fashioned way. Stanyard radioed to ask if that intersection was clear, and I figured this was my only chance. I sent guys to pick you up. You almost fooled them with your new look—but thankfully you answered to your name."

My fists and jaw tightened again. I had a dozen questions—and I suspected none of them had good answers. "So you were going to kidnap me?" I put several steps between us and wondered—yet again—if I'd made a mistake going with Stanyard.

Jayde put his hands up. "No, but you weren't safe out there."

"I was doing just fine until your guys nearly got me killed!" *Dad was right about you. You're not my friend.*

"We didn't know Carnegie was trailing you too!" He raised his voice, as if shouting over my panic would fix it. "If I had known—"

"What? You would have sent your goons to stalk me another day?" I couldn't decide whether I wanted to throw up or start running. I glared at Stanyard, who stood several feet away. "How could you? You said—"

"He didn't know!" Jayde lunged between us. He stopped, took a deep breath, and forced his voice back down to a normal level. "I told him that intersection was safe. He didn't know I had guys out looking for you. Be mad at me if you want, but he wasn't involved, I swear."

The disgusted look on Stanyard's face suggested that was the truth, so I accepted it.

"I know you think I'm a creep," Jayde drew my attention back to himself, "but I think you'll forgive me when you see who's inside waiting for you."

My heart rammed against my chest. "Ephesus," I whispered, and desperately hoped it was true.

Jayde grinned. I shoved past him and raced for the elevator. Both boys ran to catch up and barely made it before the doors closed. Jayde called level six, and I braced myself against the wall as we shot upwards. I was already shaking and crying and didn't care what either of them thought.

The doors beeped and opened. I shoved my way through and ran down the hall, screaming. "Ephesus! Ephesus!"

My name echoed back to me from the far end of the hall. "Philadelphia!" He stepped out of a room. His right arm was in a cast, his hair had been buzzed short, and he had a lumpy bandage over his nose. But it was him.

I screeched and collapsed into him. He sat down on the floor and pulled me into his lap like he had when I'd found him on Mars. He rocked me with his good arm as I released all the terror of the past few weeks in an unending stream.

"Philadelphia," he whispered when I'd slowed down enough to hear him. His voice was nasally but gentle. "It's okay. You're okay."

"No it's not!" My tears returned with a vengeance when I realized I had to tell him what I'd done. "Dad—he's—I can't—" I gasped for breath.

Ephesus jerked his head up and looked at Stanyard. "He's frozen," Stanyard admitted. "Carnegie vitrified him. The guys are bringing him back now."

I felt Ephesus stiffen and cried harder. "Ephesus—I'm sorry—it's all my—"

"It's not your fault, Phil," Stanyard interrupted. "I should have told you who I was."

He should have, but would that have prevented anything? Carnegie was already watching. It was only a matter of time before he caught up to me.

Ephesus kept his arm around me protectively. "And Carnegie is…?"

Stanyard just nodded. I swallowed another sob.

Ephesus set me upright. "We'll fix this. Dad's not dead—we can bring him back. We just need a revival tech."

I nodded rapidly and rubbed both eyes with the heels of my hands. *Please, God, please. Help me fix this!*

Ephesus brushed my sweaty hair out of my face. "Did he hurt you?"

The bruise under my ribs was throbbing, but it seemed inconsequential. I shrugged and turned the questions on him. "Are you all right? Cea said—"

He gripped my arm. "Cea? You've seen her? Where is she?"

"She's safe—she's on a transit back to Mars right now." *Where you should be.*

Relief brought some color back to his cheeks. He let go of my arm. "Mars? So it's true about Nic. He's back on base."

I nodded, then remembered that no one else was supposed to know about Nic. "How did you find out?"

"They told me." He gestured with his bandaged elbow at Stanyard and Jayde.

I glanced at them and realized I was missing a big piece of the story. "Why didn't you tell me you'd found Ephesus?"

Stanyard raised his hands. "I just picked him up this afternoon."

I frowned at my brother.

He nodded to corroborate the story. "I've been in the area for the past several weeks, trying to make contact with Dad. I knew my file was flagged, and something was going on in the underground—so I was trying to avoid letting anyone know I was here. But when I overheard your last conversation, I knew something bad had happened—so I took a risk and ordered pizza."

Stanyard's lips twitched.

Something wasn't adding up. "If you knew I was in trouble, why didn't you come? Why'd you send—"

"Stanyard was closer," Jayde answered. "He was at my apartment across town—a good five miles closer to where you were. There was no way any of us would have made it in time."

"Besides," Ephesus tapped his cast, "this is my shooting arm. I couldn't have fought Carnegie in this condition."

I shuddered, finally remembering to be grateful. *You saved me, Jesus.* I looked up at Stanyard and focused on his face for the first time in several minutes. "Thank you."

He shook his head. "I wasn't fast enough. Had I figured out where that bus line was going—"

"Wait. How'd you know I was on the bus?" I sat up straight and turned to face them. "How did you know where to find me?"

He met my gaze and spoke slowly. "I was tracking Andromeda's file."

My blood ran cold as the last fragment of my privacy was ripped from my grasp. "How long have you known?"

"When you told your dad your 'affairs were in order,' I realized you must be using new credentials."

I remembered the harsh tone of voice Dad had used when I'd said it and writhed. *What have I done? How many other people know?*

But wait—just because they knew I had a new file didn't mean they knew what name it was under. "How did you figure out I was Andromeda?"

He opened his mouth, and someone else spoke.

"I told him."

I froze. I knew that voice—and she was the last person I wanted to see right now.

Stanyard glanced over his shoulder and stepped aside.

Mrs. Nolan stood at the end of the hall.

"Hello, daughter."

CATALYST

RED RAIN #4.5

MAY 2043

1

I laughed when she said she was Catholic.

It was outlandish. In a world where being even a casual Christian was social suicide, going the extra mile and being Catholic felt flamboyant.

But even funnier was the way she said it, like she was crying *"Leprosy! Unclean!"* in the marketplace. She hadn't even offered her name; as soon as she saw me approach, she turned around and threw up that verbal stop sign, palms forward. It was like she was giving me every possible reason to reject her before I even asked her to prom.

I guess the way I sidled up her table at lunch made my intent clear.

I grinned and sat down across from her, slinging one leg over the bench. "Yeah? Well, I'm Pentecostal, which if you ask the Baptists is just as bad."

She returned my smile and lowered her hands. "Sorry, I just... don't like to lead people on."

I doubted she had ever done anything of the sort, but I knew what she meant. I was three rejections into my search for a prom date, and of the three, I thought two of them *were* Christian.

Apparently they weren't Christian enough to want to be seen with me. Word had gotten out about the marks I'd gotten on my file for praying for people in the hallway, and it was making it royally hard to find a prom date.

Perhaps an ardent Catholic would be daring enough to give me a chance.

I offered her my hand. "Well, now that we got that out of the way... I'm Thomas."

It was her turn to laugh as she accepted the shake. "Abigail."

I held her hand for an extra half-beat to preface my offer. "Can I take you to prom, Abigail?"

She didn't hesitate. "No."

I was surprised at the amount of rejection that steamrolled through my body. After all, she hadn't been my first choice for a date. But as my palms began to sweat and all the other uncomfortable symptoms of puberty radiated through me, I realized how much I was hoping she'd say yes.

I tried to play it cool. "Why not? Did you get a better offer?"

She snorted. "No."

"Aha! Then that means I'm the best offer."

She whipped her head around, as surprised as I was by my forwardness.

There was a beat, long enough that I wondered if I'd shot myself in the foot—and then she relaxed and put her chin in her hand. "Maybe you are."

My pride might have imagined it, but I could have sworn she gave me a once-over with her eyes. I wasn't chiseled; I cared too much about my grades for that. But I was lean, and just tall enough, and I'd bothered to put gel in my dark hair this morning. Apparently that, combined with my crisp button-up, was doing it for her.

The flattery gave me my courage back. I propped my elbow on the table and leaned towards her. "Well, since I'm currently the highest bidder, is there anything I can do to tempt you to change your mind? Flowers?"

She arched one eyebrow.

"Chocolate?"

Both eyebrows went up.

"Convert to Catholicism?"

She stopped, leaned back, and opened her mouth. I could tell I was about to seal the deal—before a whiny voice interrupted us.

"Hey, who's this guy?"

Abigail audibly rolled her eyes as a wiry nerd of a middle schooler joined us at the table. I could barely see his face under his mess of unkempt dark hair, but I vaguely recognized him as someone from a few grades below us.

Abigail patronized him with a sigh. "He's fine, Bart. I said he could sit here." She hadn't actually said that—because I hadn't asked—but I took the compliment.

"Bart, eh?" I said, trying to be a gentleman. "Is that short for something?" I offered my hand.

He stared at it like it was a dead fish. "For *you*, it's short for Tower."

It was a lame comeback, made even lamer by the squeak hormones put in his voice, but I wasn't about to let a twelve-year-old friendzone me. "Tower? What's that, your streamer name?"

"Obviously."

Abigail flicked her hand like he was a fly she could shoo away. "He plays this dumb game with a goat. It doesn't even have a storyline."

He *tched* and tossed his hair, which flopped around like a wet mop. "That's because it's a *physics simulator*, and I have twenty thousand subscribers now. Unlike 'Blue Fire,' who has, like, ten." He jerked his thumb at Abigail.

I arched an eyebrow at her. "'Blue Fire'?"

"Never mind, I don't even play." She coughed to clear the flush from her cheeks, then turned her frown on Bart. "Don't you have a remedial language class after lunch?"

It was his turn to blush, which made his eyes look even more sunken. "Mom wasn't supposed to tell you…"

"She told me so that I could make sure you did it. Now go."

He threw another sour glance at me, as if I was the cause of his misery, and sulked off.

"Sorry, little brothers." Abigail turned back to me with a shrug.

"Occupational hazard." I grinned, not that I had any idea what it was like to have siblings. My only brother had died in the war in Asia before I was old enough to appreciate him, but I wasn't going to burden her with my sob story. "You were telling me when mass was."

Her eyebrows returned to their locked and upright position. "You were serious about that?"

"Depends on how serious you are about not going to prom with me."

She weighed me with a sharp gaze, then reached into her backpack and fished out her phone. "What's your number?"

I was so stunned that I forgot what my digits were. After leaving her hanging for an awkward moment, I pulled myself together and took my phone out of my pocket. I held it out to her so she could tap the back and get a download of my file.

She fidgeted with a strand of her long hair. "Ahh, that feature doesn't work on mine. It's… old."

I could clearly tell that her device wasn't old, which meant the only other explanation was that it was unregistered.

"Well, aren't you full of surprises," I said with a grin. Some cities still allowed adults to have unregistered devices, but the government had long since made it mandatory for students.

She shrugged. "I keep it offline."

"But why?" Not that I wasn't in favor of sticking it to the government, but the punishment for possessing an unregistered device on school grounds was suspension. That was a hefty price tag to pay for an offline device.

She scrolled nervously. "I just don't like them knowing what I'm reading all the time."

Reading?

I slapped my hand on the table. "It's you."

She flinched and cast a glance around the cafeteria, but as usual the cool kids had given us a wide berth.

I dropped my voice and leaned in. "You're the one who keeps uploading Bibles to the school's cloud." The Bible had been banned from the school library because it wasn't inclusive, but someone kept uploading copies to the database. It was driving the principal insane.

"Me and a couple friends, yeah." Abigail searched my eyes for a reaction.

"Rebel," I smirked. Maybe I wasn't the only one in school with a marked file.

I gave her my number verbally. She smiled shyly as she typed it in. "And what's the last name, Thomas…?"

"Smyrna," I answered. "Thomas Smyrna."

JULY 2045

2

"Blue Fire, eh?"

It was a 2005 Ford Thunderbird convertible in perfect condition. Her chrome shone like a mirror, and her stormy blue paint was immaculate. I longed to run my hand along her dash and grip her leather-padded wheel, but if I wanted to stay on Mr. Berg's good side, I knew I shouldn't touch his belongings.

That included his daughter Abigail, who leaned on the hood. Her long, chocolate-colored hair pooled on the windshield as she tipped her head back and gazed at me with saucy honey-brown eyes.

I stuffed my hands deep in my pockets. "So your dad nicknamed you after the car?"

She chuckled and ran her hand along the hood. "Yeah, he said I was almost born in the backseat of this thing."

"Born? Is that what your mother told you?"

I turned to see the broad silhouette of Mr. Berg standing in the doorway to the shed, backlit by the hazy summer sun.

Abigail klutzily stood up. "Yeah, she said you were late to the hospital."

He bellowed a laugh. "Really."

Abigail bleached white, as if she were afraid her whole world was about to bottom out. "That's why I'm your little thunderbird..."

"Oh, you're our little thunderbird all right." He stepped into the shed, a smirk wrinkling his face. "But maybe you should go ask your mother if that's what really happened."

All of the color came back to Abigail's cheeks in a rush. Mr. Berg winked at me, and I laughed, which only added insult to Abigail's injury.

Mr. Berg spared her further misery by jerking his head towards the house. "Go find out when dinner will be ready."

She fled the room, too embarrassed to even look at me. I watched her retreat.

Mr. Berg grabbed a rag and wiped off the fingerprints she had left on the hood. "Do you love her?"

I jumped. I'd been expecting the question, but his abruptness still sent my heartrate into orbit. I gulped down a breath and forced my voice to be strong and convicted. "Yessir, I do."

He crossed his arms across his chest. "How do you know?"

I straightened and took my hands out of my pockets. "Well, she's smart, and kind, and caring..."

I could tell by the arch of his eyebrows that he wasn't buying my greeting card answer. I closed my eyes and tried to condense the woman I knew into words.

"I love her because... she's pure. When I'm with her, I feel like I'm getting the whole person... that *I'm* a whole person. She's honest and transparent and she always thinks of others first. I've never met anyone like her."

It was true. Ever since that first prom date—where we'd given up a half-hour in and gone to a nearby coffee shop to talk—I felt like I'd been handed an unlocked diary. In a world constantly connected online, everyone was always trying to filter and hide pieces of themselves, if not from the government then from each other. Abigail was never like that. She always felt present and complete, like she existed entirely in the moment and nowhere else. She was trusting, and as soon as she started piecing out that trust to me, I knew I was in love.

"Okay," Mr. Berg jerked me back to the present. He sounded bored, as if I'd just answered a math problem correctly. "So what are you going to do about it?"

I frowned. "What?"

"You love my daughter—so now what?"

That was not on the list of questions I expected to get from my future father-in-law. "Well... for starters, I'd like to marry her."

"Please do."

"After I ask your permission."

"I appreciate the gesture."

I searched his face for any emotion but found none. "And then I'm going to buy a house—"

"If you can find one," he cut me off.

I frowned. What was he expecting of me? "I'll be able to afford it. I already have a great job offer lined up as soon as I get my degree, and they're even paying me to intern this summer."

He was not impressed. "That's if they don't suddenly decide the position is only open to people who have signed the file."

He had a point there.

Mr. Berg sighed. His stern expression broke, revealing a father whose back had been bent by years of worry. "That's all well and good, son, and I'm proud of you. I really am. But there's coming a day when love won't mean holding down a job and paying the mortgage. It's going to require so much more of who you are."

I tried to track what he was saying. "You mean like going to war?"

He shook his head. "If only it were that simple. But we're long past that stage. We gave up war when we surrendered in Asia."

"It's not a surrender—it's a treaty." They had beaten that into our heads at school. The United States hadn't lost World War III; instead, the world powers had amicably agreed to merge into a global conglomerate to avoid nuclear apocalypse. The newly-christened "United" promised to end all wars by eliminating discrimination and disparities. The theory was that we wouldn't fight each other if we were all the same.

But as the surveillance—and religious discrimination—of communist China had increasingly become the world standard, I began to wonder if we'd lost more than just our national identity.

"Countries that go to war are countries that have something to fight for. America isn't willing to fight anymore—and that's what scares me for my daughter."

Mr. Berg grabbed a can of polish off the workbench and dumped some on his cloth. He knelt and began rubbing the headlights. "I can't tell you where the world will be in ten years, son. I don't know if people like you and me are going to be able to hold jobs and buy houses. I don't even know how much longer we're going to be able to go to church without being fined—or worse."

I nodded, feeling a worm of dread crawl into my stomach. The Bergs' Catholic church had closed not two weeks ago. Thankfully I'd already convinced Abigail to attend my church—a conversion that had alienated her brother but surprisingly not her father—but I didn't know how much longer we'd be able to afford our building. The United claimed it had no intention of making the private practice of religion illegal, but the crushing taxes and slippery anti-discrimination laws were sending the opposite message.

Mr. Berg stared at his curved reflection in the chrome bumper. "Soon being 'unassimilated' is going to mean more than paying higher taxes and being unable to run for office—and there's nothing we can do to stop it."

His words hit me like a punch to the gut. I'd known it—ever since I was old enough to drive and have a job and experience the world for myself, I'd seen the signs. I knew our culture was on a slippery slope we couldn't pull back from, but I sure wasn't going to go down with it. I always believed I would stand up for what was right and be the last man standing. But what if that wasn't enough? Was it really too late for people like us?

"But I need my daughter to be with someone who's going to try anyway."

I looked up to find Mr. Berg's deep brown eyes searching mine.

"That's why I asked what you were going to *do*. Saying you're a Christian isn't enough. Not in this world. If you're going to hold on to God, you have to *do* something—and be willing to fight for those who can't."

He stood up and walked over to me. I held still. Tossing the greasy cloth over his shoulder, he gripped my arms with his weathered hands and tipped me back until our faces met.

His voice dropped to a hoarse whisper. "Are you willing to fight, son? Will you fight for my Blue Fire?"

SEPTEMBER 2049

"Where have you been? I thought you were dead!"

That was an exaggeration—I'd only been offline for twenty-four hours, not nearly long enough to send out a search party. But the utter anguish in my wife's voice told me that she had, in fact, assumed the worst. Her shriek made the connection crackle as she continued to scream into the phone.

"I don't get a call, text, nothing. I tried to call you twenty times!"

That was *not* an exaggeration. As soon as they'd given me my devices back, I'd turned on my phone and knew I was in trouble. Abigail had tried to call me at least once an hour, and judging by the timestamps on her barrage of texts, she hadn't slept all night.

I ducked into an alcove behind a potted plant, the only place in the hallway not in full view of a security camera. "Baby, I'm so sorry, but I promise it's fine—"

"It is *not* fine! You go offline while you're in Beijing with all those communists—"

"Abigail," I said, raising my voice to make myself heard. "Remember this is a work line. It's recorded."

She let out a breath that turned into a sob. "I know, I know, I'm sorry, I just... what was I supposed to think?"

I didn't blame her. Being an unassimilated in Beijing, the seat of United politics in the East, was about as safe as walking the streets of Roxbury alone at night. By all accounts, I shouldn't be here. But the government's desire to see an important chemistry research project finished had outweighed their need to be legalistic, and I'd gotten special clearance.

"I know, baby, I'm sorry. Some government officials came to oversee the project, and there was a communications blackout."

"And you couldn't warn me?"

I weighed the tone of my voice before speaking. "They didn't give us any heads up before going in."

Abigail muttered something under her breath, but thankfully she seemed to accept that explanation.

I hated lying to my wife, but she was so scared already. I couldn't imagine what she'd do if she found out the truth.

"Smyrna!" Liu, one of my lab partners, rounded the corner. "How was solitary?"

I slapped my hand over the phone and glared at him. Thankfully he'd barked it at me in Mandarin, but it'd be just my luck that Abigail would remember enough from high school and be able to translate.

"What's going on?" Her muffled voice came from the speaker.

"Just a second, honey, I need to give something to a coworker." I muted the call.

"Sorry," Liu muttered. "I just wanted to know if you still had the notes for the project."

I searched his face. "Which ones?"

He cast a glance around the deserted hall. Turning his back to the security camera, he opened his tablet and pulled up a screenshot. It was a crude drawing of a bird with a lightning bolt in its claws: a thunderbird.

I nodded and swiped through menus on my phone. I knew the officials had deleted my download when they searched my devices, but they clearly hadn't found the backup copies I'd stashed in various places all over the company server.

If they had, I would have been in solitary for much longer than a day.

I found one and initiated the file transfer. I held up my phone, and Liu tapped his tablet on the back of it.

"Thank you," he whispered.

I closed out the window and erased the download. "If anyone else needs it, tell them Chen has backups."

Chen was the lead scientist on the project and a top United official. He'd be mortified to learn that I'd hidden a download link for a Bible on his company profile page, but he was also the person least likely to get implicated if anyone ever found it.

As near as I could tell, they didn't suspect me for transmitting—not yet. They'd caught me reading the Bible on my personal device, which, while a violation of my probationary employment, was hardly something they could imprison me for. I had too many letters after my name to be swept away with the other dissidents. Instead, they added another felony to my file, charged me a huge fine, and stuck me in "special custody" for a day—the United equivalent of a slap on the wrist.

I knew they wouldn't be so merciful if they caught me doing it again, but I couldn't pass up the opportunity to spread Operation Blue Fire in China.

Liu thanked me with a wave and hurried off. I unmuted the call and brought the phone back to my ear. "Sorry about that. I'm here now."

She had apparently used the moment of silence to calm her nerves, because when she spoke her voice was steadier. "You're sure there's nothing I need to know about?"

"I promise," I said with the confidence I knew she was craving. "Everything is fine."

I listened to the silence on the other end of the line and tried to gauge her reaction. Abigail knew what I was doing—sort of. She knew I was transmitting through work, and she knew I'd codenamed the operation after her, in honor of the Bibles she'd shared in high school.

But she had no idea how big the operation had become. She had no idea we'd built a massive network of people willing to transfer restricted media. And she had no idea I was transmitting in China, where the officials were a lot more trigger happy when it came to punishing infractions.

For the sake of her sanity, I didn't want her to find out.

She finally relinquished with a sigh. "I'll just feel better when you get home."

"Which will be very soon." I pumped some reassuring cheer into my voice. "The project is almost done." I probably would have completed it already had I not wasted a perfectly good workday in solitary.

"Good." Her voice caught on the word. "Baby, there's something I need to tell you..."

I stiffened. "What is it? What's wrong?"

"Nothing's wrong," she said, too quickly. "It's just..."

I rattled off a prayer to dampen the panic spiking my nerves. "Do you not want to tell me on a recorded line?"

"No, no, nothing like that. It's..." She sucked in a sharp breath and found her courage. "I'm pregnant."

NOVEMBER 2058

4

It was an unpleasant surprise when Bart showed up for Thanksgiving.

It wasn't officially called Thanksgiving, of course. The United had disbanded most traditional holidays in the name of being culturally neutral. But no one could stop us from cooking a turkey around November 28, and doing so was a delicious act of rebellion.

I hadn't seen Bart in years. He came home periodically when he was on leave from the military, but he somehow managed to time his visits for when I was away on long assignments.

Unfortunately for both of us, our vacations happened to fall on the same week this year.

Abigail put herself between us at the dinner table, trying to form a bridge with her presence. Mr. Berg sat across with a watchful eye, daring either of us to start something. I for one had no intention of talking to Bart if it could be avoided.

The only one not affected by the tension was Ephesus. He'd only met his uncle once or twice, and the mystery had turned the man into legend. Ephesus was enraptured with Bart's uniform and standard-issue guns and demanded to know all about life in the military. Much to my chagrin, Bart was obliging with stories and unnecessary detail.

"Ephesus, you need to eat," Abigail inserted, with a side glance at her brother that he willingly ignored.

Ephesus shoveled his forgotten mashed potatoes into his mouth and spoke around them. "I want to join the military when I grow up!"

Abigail turned her pleading eyes to me.

I reached over and brushed the back of my son's head. "No, you don't. Because you'd have to sign the file." I shifted my glare to Bart, who returned it in kind.

Mr. Berg cleared his throat.

Bart jerked his head towards the front porch. "Do you want to take this outside?"

I stood. "Let's."

Abigail reached for me. "Thomas, please..."

"It's fine, Abi," Bart said, rising. "He and I need to talk about something."

Mr. Berg watched us leave.

I led the way to the front porch and shut the door behind us. Bart glanced around the yard, as if to verify that it was indeed deserted, before turning back to me. "Look, I know this isn't fun for anyone, but I came to warn you."

I dropped all my defenses and straightened. "What's wrong?"

"Von's down."

"Dear God, no," I muttered, not realizing I had said it aloud.

Bart searched my face. "They found his server and busted him a couple of days ago."

I pinched my temples, as if I could stop the blood from pounding in my ears. "Is he okay?"

Bart shrugged. "Last I heard they put him in solitary. The whole case is classified—no one knows anything. I can't figure out what they did with the missus."

Oh Lord, have mercy.

"But that's not why I came." Bart shifted. "They've already used his data to track down three of his associates—you could be next."

My heart restarted. "And you're just now telling me?"

"I couldn't exactly text you that on a company line, now could I? I'm not risking my career for you. Do you know what they do to soldiers who betray their command? Way worse than what you'll get for copying and pasting some Bibles."

He was right, but that didn't stop the heat from sizzling in my nerves. They'd already had several days to scour Von's data—it might already be too late.

"Look," Bart made a heroic effort to soften his voice, "just take the server offline and wipe it. If they track you, they'll find nothing. Where did you set it up?"

I involuntarily glanced towards the Bergs' shed.

Bart followed my gaze and muttered something foul. "You didn't."

"He agreed," I shot back. "He registered an electric car—explains the power drain."

Bart roared and dug his fingers into his greasy hair. "I can't believe you dragged Dad into this!"

"I didn't get dragged into anything." The screen door squeaked as Mr. Berg joined us on the porch. "What's going on?"

Bart skipped the preamble. "You need to bring that server offline and wipe it, now. The feds could be tracking it as we speak."

Mr. Berg looked past him, and his face folded into a frown. "No time for that."

I turned and saw what he was looking at—the dust trails of two cars approaching on the country road. Even from this distance I could tell they were police cars.

Bart swore again. "Dad, you need to run. Take Abigail and hide in the attic—I'll talk to them."

"No, I don't want you tangled up in this. You've done enough already." He opened the door and waved us inside. "I want you—both of you—to go back to the kitchen and stay put. No matter what you hear, I don't want anyone to come out on this porch, you understand?"

Bart lost what little color his skin had. "Dad, please, don't—"

"He's right," I said, even though my throat was closing in panic. "It's my server; I should take the blame."

"It's on my property," Mr. Berg returned. "They'll believe me if I say it's mine."

I could think of a million more objections, but he didn't give me a chance to voice them. He grabbed my shoulders and shoved me into the house.

I tripped over the threshold. I struggled back to my feet and turned around. "Andrew, please, I'm sorry..."

He shook his head. "Abigail needs you."

Then he grabbed the door, slammed it shut, and locked it from the outside. I heard the muffled bleep of a siren as the police turned onto the driveway.

"Andrew!" I yelled, and yanked on the door handle. *Oh God, what have I done?*

Bart dragged me back. "You heard him!"

Abigail appeared in the kitchen doorway, Ephesus clutching her skirts. "What's going on?"

"Get back in the kitchen!" Bart shouted. He ran through the living room and yanked the blinds shut, but not before I saw three armed cops emerge from their vehicles and walk towards the porch.

Ephesus craned his neck to get a look. "Who's that?"

I herded him back from the doorway. "Come on, son, you need to finish your dinner." I cringed when I realized how much my voice was shaking.

"But I'm not hungry!"

I ignored his pleas, scooped him up, and deposited him back in his chair.

Abigail searched my face. "What happened?"

I grabbed her hand and sat her in the chair next to me. "It's going to be okay—" I started, but a shout from outside cut me off.

"Police, stand down!"

Abigail instinctively grabbed Ephesus's hand. "Thomas...?"

Bart was quick to throw me under the bus. "Your beloved 'Catalyst,'" he spat out my callsign like it was a curse, "set up a server of illegal media in Dad's shed."

"You did what?" Her shriek sent stabs of accusation into my heart.

"It's just Bibles," I assured her. "Transmitting is a light sentence—he'll be fine."

"Don't lie to her!" Bart shouted. "He's got too many other marks on his file."

Abigail washed white and began to tremble.

Ephesus glanced between us. "Is Grandpa going to be okay?"

"Yes," I said.

"No," Bart snapped at the same time. He turned his dark eyes on me. "You and I both know they won't let him off easy."

Ephesus gasped. Abigail broke down sobbing, and I knew what I had to do.

I stood up. "I'm going to tell them the truth. They'll let me off easier."

"No!" Abigail shrieked at a pitch loud enough to shatter glass. She grabbed my arm and pulled me back down. "You can't go!"

I laid my hand over hers. "Baby, it'll be a week tops in solitary, I can handle it—"

"No, you don't get it, I need you here." She sucked in air and tried to find her words. "Dad knew. That's why he went..."

"Knew what? What did he know?" I glanced at Bart, but he looked as lost as I felt.

She gripped my arms with both hands like she expected a hole to open up in the floor and swallow us all. She wouldn't look either of us in the eye as she announced, "I'm having another baby."

Silence washed over the room.

How? How did this happen?

Abigail took one look at my face and started crying again. Bart made the sign of the cross.

Ephesus, oblivious to his mom's distress, jumped up and grabbed her arm. "I'm going to be a big brother?"

I straightened. "Ephesus, take your uncle to the basement and show him your video games—*now*."

Somewhat to my surprise, they both obeyed me. I waited until the door had slammed behind them before I pried Abigail off my shoulder and sat her upright. "Baby, are you sure?"

She rubbed at her tears with the heels of her hands. "I'm sure. I've even had an ultrasound."

I did the math. "Wait, how long have you known?"

She looked down at her stomach. "Since August."

We were so careful…

She didn't wait for me to formulate a sentence. "I'm so sorry, I wanted to tell you, but you've been gone so long, and I didn't want you to worry…"

Shame flooded me like I'd plunged through the ice on a frozen lake. My own wife, scared to tell me about our *baby?* What had I become?

I vaguely registered the sound of a police siren starting and fading away down the road.

It wasn't supposed to be this way.

"It's all my fault," Abigail continued to stutter, words blurred with tears. "I must have miscounted, or…"

I pulled her into my arms before she could accuse herself anymore. She wept into my shoulder, muttering *"sorry, sorry, sorry"* in between each gasp for breath.

I pressed her to my chest. "Sweetheart, please stop saying that. Everything's going to be okay."

She gave up talking and just continued to cry.

I ran my fingers through her hair, feeling her whole body shake. Every shiver sent guilt ramming into my soul, and I wanted nothing more than to steal her grief and swallow it myself. "Baby, please," I breathed in her ear. "It's not your fault."

I glanced across the table at her father's abandoned place.

It's mine.

MAY 2070

5

"Don't you dare touch my daughter!"

That's the only thing I remember saying the day they took us into camp. I must have said—and done—a lot more, since I got a misdemeanor for resisting arrest and a concussion from the hilt of an officer's gun.

But those words were the only thing I could remember when I came to in the hospital hours later. My mind restarted with a jump, my heart racing and my whole body sweating as if I were still caught in that moment. I saw the tears on Philadelphia's ashen face and heard the fear in her voice as she cried in pain. I saw the officer cruelly dragging her by her arm and felt the burning rage, the primal instinct to protect her, and the crushing realization that I had failed as a husband and father.

There's nothing we can do to stop it.

They kept me in the hospital for a day and solitary confinement for three more, probably to intimidate me. It wasn't working, but I knew it was putting my wife and daughter through hell, which was why I nearly jumped the officer who came to bring me my meal on day three.

"Whoa, dude, it's me."

I recognized the sullen voice, even though I hadn't talked to him since Philadelphia was born. I gave him the courtesy of looking him in the eye. "Bart?"

"I know we're not friends, but shanking me is a bit much," he grunted from somewhere under his mop of tangled hair.

I relaxed and sat back down on the bed. "How did you get here?"

"As soon as I heard they were taking you into camp, I asked to be transferred back home." He set my dinner tray on the floor.

"I can't believe they approved that."

He shrugged. "They have no reason to question my loyalty."

I swallowed a nip of rage; now was not the time. "What do you want?"

He glanced behind him, then stepped into the cell and kicked the door shut. "Hold out your arm."

"What?"

He extended his hand and wiggled his fingers impatiently.

I hesitantly rolled up my sleeve and lifted my arm.

He grabbed my elbow with his clammy fingers. "Don't tell Abi I did this."

"What are you—"

Before I could react, he grabbed his baton from his belt and thwacked my upper arm—hard.

I yelled something I am not proud of. "That's going to bruise!"

"Exactly. If anyone asks what we're doing in here, tell them I beat you for being unruly."

I rubbed the tender skin. "That was the best plan you could come up with?"

He didn't grace me with a response. "Listen, we don't have much time. We need to talk."

I eyed him. "What is it?"

He closed his eyes, took a deep breath, and pinched his fingers together, as if it took every ounce of courage he possessed to say the next three words. "I need you."

I wasn't flattered. "Well, you're a little late. In case you haven't heard, my new forwarding address is a prison. No thanks to our inglorious military."

"Would it make you feel better if you got a swing in at me?" He held his baton out. "Look, I know you don't approve of my lifestyle choices, but I promise I haven't been idle."

He paused, as if listening for footsteps in the hall. "It's time for Operation Blue Fire to come back."

I threw up my hands. "Absolutely not. I told Abigail I would stop transmitting after what happened with your father."

"But these won't be just any Bibles."

I frowned at him. "I don't follow."

He licked his chapped lips. "The United went too far with the containment camps. People are angry—people who normally don't care. They'll act, but they need a lightning rod."

I sat up slowly. "What are you proposing?"

"It's going to take time," he deferred. "But meanwhile, we need an information network. And we think Bibles are the safest way."

"Define 'safe.'"

He grinned. "Think about it—what does the United do when they find Bibles? They delete them. And they sure aren't reading every single page before they do."

I caught on. "And transmitting is a lighter sentence than espionage."

"Significantly."

I searched his face. "Why do you need me?"

"You have experience—and your employer is high enough up the food chain that their company server is an ideal launching point."

A pressure filled my chest, but I couldn't decide if it was the Holy Spirit or my own fears.

Bart mistook my silence. "Look, I know we haven't gotten along in the past, but you have to trust me on this one. This could work—this could get you out of that camp. Think about Philadelphia—do you want her to grow up in there?"

"Why do you suddenly care?" I snapped, louder than intended. "You haven't even met her."

He took the accusation in stride. "Abi's still my sister. I let Dad down once—I'm not going to let my family down again."

And I can't let them down either.

Bart found my eyes. "This is all or nothing, brother. Are you with me?"

*

"Daddy!"

Philadelphia threw herself into my arms before I was even all the way in the door. She grabbed me around the neck and bawled, her whole body racked with sobs.

"Oh Philli." I sank to the floor and pulled her into my lap, wishing I could crush out her fear with my embrace. "It's okay, Daddy's here."

I heard dishes clattering and a shout of "Praise God!" from the kitchen. I looked up to see Abigail stumbling towards us. She collapsed next to me, and I pulled her in with my other arm and gave her a long kiss.

She finally leaned back to look at me. "You're all right," she breathed in a tone that begged me to assuage all her fears.

I met her gaze. "Perfectly fine."

She traced my unshaven chin with her finger. "They wouldn't tell us anything."

My heart broke. Philadelphia sprung up and thrust herself in my face. "What happened, Daddy? Are you in trouble?"

I reached up to brush the tears from her cheeks. "No, no, Daddy's fine. I just got a good bonk on the head, and they kept me in the hospital for a few days."

She leaned back on her haunches and studied me. I couldn't tell if she believed me; she was maturing, and my playful sarcasm wasn't working as well as it used to.

I turned the conversation back on her. "What about you, sweetheart? Are you okay? Did they hurt you?"

She shook her head, making her long hair flop about. "No. I just have a little bruise. See?" She took off her sweater and showed me the fading mark on her arm where the guard had grabbed her.

My nerves flared with anger, but I played it off. "Well, that's okay, because now we match. Daddy has a bruise just like it." I rolled up my sleeve and showed her the blue-purple lump Bart had so graciously given me.

Abigail started to say something, then caught herself.

"I got it just for you, so we could be twins." I winked at my daughter.

This time, the humor landed. She arched one eyebrow, and I saw a twinkle of a smile creep back into her eyes.

I turned to my wife. "Have you heard from Ephesus?"

"He's fine. They moved him to a new dorm, but he says not much has changed. I guess they have so many regulations at school that it was basically a concentration camp anyway."

I snorted; that was exactly the kind of thing my witty, headstrong son would say.

I struggled to rise. Abigail quickly stood and pulled me to my feet. "We need to call him. He needs to know you're okay."

I nodded, then stifled a groan. As I straightened, all the aches and pains of being stuck in a tight cell for three days came back to remind me that I was not a young man anymore.

"Are you okay, Daddy?" Philadelphia asked.

I closed my eyes, waiting for the flashing colors to dissipate. "Daddy's fine, I promise. I'm just tired."

"I'll go get you some water." Abigail squeezed my arm and ran into the kitchen.

Philadelphia found my hand. "I'm worried, Daddy."

I glanced down at her face and almost lost my balance. She looked so much like her mother that it startled me. She gazed up at me like I held the power of life and death itself, her eyes searching for the secret answer to an unutterable question.

I gripped her hand and struggled not to drown under a wave of guilt. My daughter was the best thing that had ever happened to me, and now I was failing her miserably. How could I let my precious baby girl grow up in a prison?

"I'm worried," she repeated, tracing the scratches on my knuckles with her fingers. "I'm worried about us, and I'm worried about Ephesus, and I'm... I'm worried about you."

I wanted to lie to her. I wanted to swear on my life that everything would be okay, that Daddy had it under control, and that there was nothing to fear.

But we were past that point. There was no lie I could utter, no reassurance I could give, that could explain away what had happened. She was only eleven, but she'd seen too much already. I couldn't bring back her innocence.

But maybe I could prevent her from losing more.

She clenched my hand in both of hers and looked up into my face. "What are we going to do, Daddy?"

Movement fluttered in my peripheral. I turned to see Abigail standing in the doorway to the kitchen. She was calm, a radiating pillar of peace—because she had to be, for our children.

But I could tell she needed to hear my answer as much as Philadelphia did.

Dear God, give me strength.

I met my wife's eyes as I slid my arms around our daughter's shoulders. "I will fight for you."

OCTOBER 2072

6

<hr>

"Radio check. This is Catalyst. Come in, Tower."

"Tower here."

His voice was crackly, like he was on the edge of receiving range. I sat down on the bed and fiddled with the controls, trying to reduce the static. It didn't help that my radio was jerry-rigged from laptop parts, duct tape, and the receiver from an old truck.

When you're smuggling supplies into a containment camp, you make do with what you can find.

Bart said something that was garbled beyond translation, followed by an unhelpful: "Roger so far?"

I gave the machine a thwack. "Tower, say again."

He did, and his voice was mercifully clearer than before. "We need to postpone the drop."

A wave of fear washed over me, inspired more by the tone of his voice than the content of his sentence. "Why?"

"I can't make it today." He offered no more explanation, which was less than comforting. "We'll do it tomorrow—same instructions."

The flash drive in my pocket suddenly felt like it weighed more than a brick. The drive contained a dozen Bibles, all carefully edited to include the instructions for the next—and hopefully last—phase of Operation Blue Fire.

Unsurprisingly, I didn't relish the idea of keeping it in my possession any longer than I had to—especially since I lived in a containment camp where unannounced bunk checks were the guards' idea of a fun night out.

"Can you send someone else?" I suggested.

"I don't trust anyone else—no offense," he added for the benefit of any associates who might be tuning in.

I didn't blame him. We'd been planning this last phase for months, and every cog needed to move with precision. If we were successful, it could mean an end to the containment camps.

If we failed, we would all be executed.

"10-4," I said, making sure my displeasure was crammed into each syllable.

He heard, and the annoying little brother came out. "You've had it for a week now," he groused. "If anyone shows up, you know what to do."

As if manifesting my worst fear, the front door slammed.

A prayer warped with panic ripped out of my throat. I grabbed the flash drive from my pocket and prepared to destroy it—and then I heard my wife's voice.

"Honey? Are you still home?"

I let out my breath. Pressing down on the handset, I whispered into the radio, "Catalyst over and out. Blue Fire's home early."

"Tell her I said hi."

I flipped the device off. I had no intention of telling her anything. Abigail didn't know I'd been working with her brother for the past two years—much less that we were planning a coup.

I would tell her when all the pieces were in place and it was time to run.

I hastily shoved the radio under the furthest corner of the bed. I didn't have time to put it back in its hiding spot in the ceiling in the closet; Abigail was already halfway up the stairs. I slid the drive in my pocket, brushed my pants off, and donned a relaxed smile as she walked in the door.

"Baby!" She waltzed over and planted a kiss on my cheek. "I thought you would have left for work already."

I returned the affection. "We had a late start today," I said, which was the truth—all part of the plan so Bart could take me to work and collect the drive. "I'll leave soon. What are you doing home?"

"They're overstaffed today—so of course I take the pay cut." She shed her jacket and reached up to undo her meticulous bun. Her thick locks tumbled over her shoulder, and abruptly I remembered how beautiful my wife was.

I reached for her waist, but a knock on the front door interrupted me.

Abigail slipped out of my grasp. "That's probably your ride."

I fumed. *Of course they'd be early.*

She saw my expression and giggled. "I'll go tell them you'll be down in a minute."

She floated out of the room. I shoved my disappointment aside and bent down to retrieve the radio. I needed to hide it properly; knowing my wife, she'd use her day off to clean the entire house and would find it under the bed.

The front door banged open. I grabbed the device and walked to the closet—and then Abigail screamed.

I dropped the radio and ran.

I stumbled down the stairs and nearly collided with Commander Ambrose. His large frame blocked the way as he leered up at me. "Well, Smyrna, you've done it now, haven't you?"

There was scuffling and a whimper. I looked past him. Two armed guards filled my entryway—and one of them had my wife pinned against the wall at gunpoint.

Two years of pent-up primal rage came back in a rush. "Don't touch her!" I shoved all my weight into Ambrose, but he grabbed me by the arm and threw me to the floor. I slammed my chin into the tile and tasted blood.

"Thomas!" Abigail squeaked.

Ambrose wasted no time in asserting his dominance. "I know about the Bibles, Smyrna."

My nerves clenched. *Oh Lord. No no no...*

"Thomas? What does he mean?" Abigail's voice wavered, like she was trying to hold onto the edge of a crumbling cliff.

I took a deep breath. I couldn't panic; there was no reason to panic. We rehearsed this. This was exactly why we used Bibles to share information; transmitting was a light sentence.

"It's okay, baby, it's nothing—just a few Bibles." Out of the corner of my eye, I saw the heartbreak and betrayal on her face and knew the damage had been done—but I could still fix this. I lifted one hand in surrender and used the other to push myself to my feet. I turned to Ambrose and painted my voice to be soft and contrite. "I'll show you where they all are—just leave her out of this."

He laughed—a deep, full-throated laugh, like he had been saving up for this moment. "Oh doctor, you and I both know these aren't just any Bibles."

I lost all sense of feeling as the world swayed in and out of time.

His face warped in a smile. "Don't you think I know what you and your friends have been up to? Don't you think I've been listening to your little game of telephone?"

"Thomas?" Abigail made no attempt to hide the terror in her voice. "What's he talking about?"

Ambrose glanced between us. "She doesn't know?" He spat out another laugh. "She doesn't know! You surprise me, doctor. I thought you Christians were supposed to be the honest ones."

I found the courage to look at my wife's face. She was already crying.

Oh baby, I'm so sorry.

"Where is it?" Ambrose demanded.

The world restarted, and with it came a rush of adrenaline. They couldn't find the drive—if they saw what was on there, we were all dead.

One of the guards grabbed my arm, but I jerked my elbow free and jabbed him where it hurt. He lost control—just long enough for me to yank the drive from my pocket, throw it on the floor, and smash it with my foot.

Ambrose bellowed. He whipped his gun from its holster and barreled into me, slamming me backwards into the wall. Before I could even find my balance, he had the gun shoved under my chin. Abigail wailed.

Ambrose's stale breath was hot on my face as he snarled, "I've been waiting two years to shoot you, Smyrna. Is today the day?"

Not if I can help it.

I found my footing and shoved, knocking him off balance. I grabbed his wrist and tried to wrench the gun from his hand—and he fired it.

The shot ripped the air, and Abigail screamed.

Everyone stopped. The guards instinctively drew back. She stood there, tottering, her last breath stopped in her throat. She stared straight ahead, as if she were afraid to look down and see the blood seeping through her blouse.

This time, I was the one who screamed.

She collapsed, crumpled in on herself like a house of cards falling. Her head hit the tile with a crack, and I roared. I lunged for her, but I never made it. One of the guards held me back while the other knelt beside her. I heard Ambrose shouting, and the harried calls for an ambulance, and my own oaths uttered over and over.

Jesus, what have I done, Jesus, don't let her die, Jesus, don't do this...

The guard lifted her limp body from the floor, and my rage turned into pleas for mercy.

Please, just let me go with her, please, she's dying, please, I need to be with her...

All I heard over and over was "no... no... no..." although whether it was Ambrose or my own anguished cries, I'll never know. I fought against them like an animal. She had moments, if even, and I needed to be the last one to touch her, to hold her hand, to kiss her.

Ambrose finally put me out of my misery and tranquilized me.

The last thing I heard before the world went dark was a voice I didn't recognize whispering, "She's gone."

7

When I came to, I was cuffed to a chair in an interrogation room.

An underpaid clerk sat across from me at the table. He looked bored stiff, as if he'd almost fallen asleep while waiting for me to come around. He rubbed his face and blandly informed me that Abigail had died on the way to the hospital.

He asked if I had any questions, but there was nothing to say. When I didn't speak, he left and locked the door.

I buckled and put my head between my knees, struggling to breathe as reality ran me over. Abigail was dead. My beautiful, innocent wife was dead, and I killed her.

Guilt clawed at my mind as my subconscious scrambled to find a place to affix the blame. I tried to figure out where I'd gone wrong, but the more I replayed the events, the more sins I tallied.

I shouldn't have joined Operation Blue Fire.

I shouldn't have offered to alter the Bibles.

I shouldn't have postponed the drop.

I shouldn't have lied to my wife.

I lied. I did exactly what I said I wouldn't do, and then I covered it up because I thought that, if I had a little more time, I could save us all. Her last moments were filled with terror and betrayal—apologies I would never get to make—all because I kept her in the dark.

I failed her. I failed everyone. Operation Blue Fire was over. The plans were destroyed, and my family's hope of freedom was gone. We were never getting out, not after this. My daughter would grow up in a prison without her mother and, unless the Lord had mercy, her father.

All because you lied.

The government seemed to know that the worst punishment was leaving me alone with my thoughts, which they did, for hours. I do not know how long

I sat in that chair in the unnatural silence of the soundproofed room. The knowledge that there were probably people watching on the other side of the glass kept me from expressing my grief. Instead I twitched and fidgeted, unable to even wipe my agitated eyes. Each of my labored breaths scraped against the thick silence in the room, grating on my ears and reminding me that I was one lungful away from shattering.

Exhaustion almost made me lose my battle with my tears. Several escaped down my face just as the door opened. Commander Ambrose entered, grinning hungrily at my damp eyes, as if he had waited for this exact moment to arrive.

He settled into the chair across from me. I drew a fruitless sniff and said nothing.

He flung the obliterated drive on the table. It skidded towards me and spun to a stop.

"I know there's more than Bibles on this drive," he threatened.

I looked up at him.

"But unfortunately I can't prove it." He grunted and slouched in the chair. "I've already searched all your devices and confirmed that you were smart enough to wipe the originals. So, credit where credit is due, Smyrna."

I wasn't careful enough. If I had been more careful, Abigail would still be alive.

"However," he shook a flushed finger at me, "I have recordings of all your radio conversations, and that gives me more than enough material to work with."

I waited. I wanted to beg him to get to the point and issue my sentence, but I wasn't about to give him the gratification of watching me grovel.

"I could have you executed. I should shoot you right here and now." He flipped his gun from its holster for emphasis.

I tried to conjure up a normal, human reaction to that and failed.

He fingered his weapon. "But that would be a mercy, wouldn't it?"

He was right. A quick death would be a mercy—to everyone except my children, but I'm sure they were far from his mind.

He laid the gun on the table. "Besides, I was hoping to leave early today. So if it's all the same to you, I'd just as soon save the unnecessary paperwork."

I caught up. By crushing the drive and keeping my tracks clean, I'd taken one victory from him: He had no proof of my plans, and he had no way to track my associates. Our radio conversations had been vague and coded; as long as the others were smart, I was the only one that would get caught. Ambrose could certainly put me away for using an illegal radio, but he'd be in more trouble with his superiors for allowing a rebellion to ferment in his containment camp for two whole years.

Unless, of course, he conveniently didn't report it.

"So I think, since you seem to have brought enough punishment on yourself, I'll write this off as a simple transmitting violation. Are we agreed?"

I held his gaze. What did he want me to say? I didn't exactly have a choice in the matter.

He picked the drive up off the table. "I trust you won't be needing this anymore."

"No," I said, the meaning not lost on me. "I won't."

"Then we understand each other." He pocketed the drive and stood up. He came and leered over me, his broad shoulders blocking the light. I forced myself to look up at him.

"Let me be clear, doctor: I'm doing this for me, not you. If you give me *any* trouble, know that I can put you away forever. So unless you want that lovely daughter of yours to go into the system, I suggest you keep your head down. Understood?"

*

The entryway was covered in blood.

I nearly slipped in it when I came in the door. They'd made no effort to clean it up. They'd simply left it to coagulate and rust, their boot prints tracing a macabre dance on the tile.

I dropped to my knees, overwhelmed by the smell and screaming memories.

Abigail, my Abigail, how could I...

I dragged myself back up. I couldn't grieve, not yet. Philadelphia would be home from school within the hour, and I couldn't let her walk into this. I couldn't let her see how violently her mother had died.

I fumbled about, gathering every towel and rag I could find and using them to sop up the blood. I fought vacillating urges to vomit and rage as I sprayed the walls and mopped the floor. I prayed Philadelphia would be too distracted to notice the smell of bleach when she walked in the door.

It was almost 3pm by the time I was done, and I looked horrible. There was blood under my fingernails and dried stains on my shirt.

I hurried up the stairs and threw my shirt in the laundry basket, burying it under the other dirty clothes. I found a clean sweater and pulled it over my head—and that's when I saw the radio.

It was posed in the precise center of the bed, its cord neatly coiled, which was not where I had dropped it a few hours before. The guards must have found it and left it behind, but why?

It took me only seconds to read the unspoken threat.

Have I not been punished enough, Ambrose?

I sat down on the bed and turned on the device. A flurry of noise erupted. Multiple voices, some I recognized, fought for bandwidth as they called *emergency, emergency* and cast frantic 10-codes at each other.

I took a deep breath and pressed down the handset. "Break, break," I yelled, conjuring up the last of my strength to raise my voice. I waited until the line hushed, then said, "Tower, come in."

There was static and scraping on the other end of the line, as if he was fumbling with his receiver. "Catalyst! What happened? I saw the call go out for an ambulance to your area, but no one could tell me anything. I was so—"

He abruptly stopped, as if remembering that I couldn't answer him while he was talking.

I swallowed and weighed my words, only to realize that there was no way to soften the blow. No amount of lying or reframing would make the news any easier to swallow.

I spit out the truth before I could choke on it. "Blue Fire is down."

There was a long silence—too long. When he realized I had no more to add, he resumed sputtering with a vengeance. "Down? What do you mean? What happened? Is she okay? What hospital did they take her to? I'll see if I can—"

"Tower!" I yelled, and waited to make sure he heard me. "She's dead."

Someone else on the line uttered an oath.

The tears returned to my voice, and I made no attempt to hide them. "They knew we were planning something. They came for the drive."

"What did you do with it?" a young male voice I didn't recognize demanded to know.

My knuckles went white as I clenched the receiver. "I crushed it, just like I was supposed to. And in the process my wife got *shot.*" I gagged on the word.

He didn't appreciate the sacrifice. "Yeah, and the rest of us would have too if you—"

"Green Dragon, get off the line!" another stranger scolded him.

Bart ignored them all. "Catalyst, we need to get you out of there. I can arrange a pickup, tonight, 19:00."

I remembered Ambrose was probably listening and cringed. "Belay that, Tower, I'm fine. They can't prove anything. Don't come for me. Stay out of this."

"No, I'm serious, I'm coming to get you. I'm tired of playing this game from the other side of the wall. I'm taking you both to safety, and then you're done."

A brief shot of hope rippled through me, but it was immediately drowned out by a torrent of cold fear. If Ambrose suspected we were up to anything, he'd have Philadelphia in custody before I could blink. She'd never even make it off the bus.

I slammed down on the receiver. "Tower, no! Don't come for us, and don't try anything. That's an order."

"Don't boss me around, old man. I—"

"Don't you get it?" I shrieked. "They know what we're doing. They're probably listening right now. If I try anything, my daughter goes into the system."

There was silence. When Bart spoke again, his voice was softer, and I could tell he was also fighting tears. "She's already in the system."

"Yeah, well at least she's alive," I hissed, and then slapped a hand over my mouth when a worse sound threatened to come out.

His sigh made the line fuzz. "Catalyst, please. I promise I can do this safely. Let me come get you."

"No," I repeated with gravity I hoped was understood by everyone on the line. "Operation Blue Fire is over. We're not going anywhere."

Is that what you want to hear, Ambrose?

"Catalyst—"

I wasn't about to repeat myself. "I'm done—and I don't want you to contact this family ever again."

There was a beat, barely. "It's my family too."

The front door slammed. "Mom, I'm home!"

Philadelphia.

Bart muttered some Catholic prayer under his breath.

I tightened my grip around the receiver. "Catalyst over and out."

I turned off the radio before he could respond.

Philadelphia continued to search for her mother, her voice making a lap around the lower level. I stood and threw the radio on the ground, then slammed my heel into it with all the strength I could find. I put a sizable dent in the middle of the casing, hopefully crushing enough of the internal contents to make it unusable.

"Over and out," I muttered again to the empty room.

Footsteps pounded up the stairs. I kicked the radio under the bed out of sight.

Philadelphia appeared in the doorway. "Dad! You're home early."

The pleasant surprise in her voice broke my heart. I forced myself to look at her.

She smiled. "Where's Mom?"

I sighed—too hard. I saw the worry flicker in her eyes and knew there would be no delaying the conversation.

I sat down on the bed and patted the blanket next to me. She took the invitation and leaned her head on my shoulder. Her weight settled against me, and with it the crushing realization that I was all she had left.

This was it. I couldn't afford any more felonies, any more time in solitary. If there was a war to be fought, someone else would have to fight it. I had to be there for my daughter.

I couldn't let her get hurt anymore.

She noticed my silence. "Dad? What's wrong?"

I wrapped my arms around her and held her to my chest. What was I going to tell her? What was I going to tell my son? I would have to call Ephesus at school and repeat the whole story again. What story was I going to give them?

What story did they need to hear?

They couldn't know about Blue Fire. They couldn't know about their uncle, or the rebellion, or Ambrose's threats. They couldn't know that their mother had died a senseless death, a morbid accident wasted on my carelessness and lies. Ephesus might be able to handle the truth, but Philadelphia? It would crush her.

I had to protect her.

I tried to whisper a prayer and choked on it. I swallowed the shame and found my voice.

"Philadelphia, we need to talk."

JUNE 2076

8

For the first time in my life, I praised God for the United's merciless laws.

They'd shut down a little coffee shop on Warren. Who knows what for—it was so easy to get yourself fined out of business these days. The eviction must have happened recently, because the building hadn't been gutted and the power hadn't been turned off.

That meant the public wifi was still on, and the manager's computer might still be functional.

Muttering a prayer for forgiveness, I smashed the glass on the back door and twisted the lock. I shoved the door open and waited for the wail of a security system—but there was none.

After checking the alley behind me, I crept down the hallway and peered around the shop, careful to stay out of sight of the front windows. It looked like everyone in the place had been raptured. Half-full cups and soiled napkins were scattered on the tables. Dirty dishes floated in the sink. Stale coffee languished on warmers—one of which was still on.

No wonder they forgot to set the alarm.

I flicked the warmer off, sending up a prayer for the owners, and went to find the office.

It was unlocked, door drifting in an unfelt breeze. I stepped into the cramped space and was relieved to find that the computer was up and running, along with the security cameras. A monitor offered a comprehensive view of the building, including both entrances.

I shut and locked the office door behind me. I was still cornered at the end of a hall, but at least if anyone found me, I'd see them coming.

I tapped the computer monitor. A login screen appeared with the manager's credentials mercifully autofilled. I desperately prayed the poor soul hadn't been blacklisted. Depending on how badly he or she had offended the United, their file could be flagged, just as mine was. If so, any activity on a computer registered to their name could send the police running.

But it was a risk I had to take. I had to find my daughter, which meant I had to get online.

After surveying the security monitor one last time, I settled in the desk chair and brought up a web browser. I typed her name into the search bar and hesitated.

I knew she was alive—at least she had been a week ago. Thames had sent her to Rott, a prison island deep in the Atlantic. It was not the kind of place I wanted my daughter to be, but it was the ideal place for her to die.

The United didn't expect anyone to come back from Rott, so they wouldn't question it when my daughter met an untimely accident there. "Philadelphia" would be quietly swept under the rug, and my baby girl would come home as "Andromeda."

Except she wouldn't be my baby girl anymore. She would have a new name and a new guardian powerful enough to protect her: Thames.

But I'd have visiting rights, which was far more than I could expect to get if Thames turned me over to the United to be tried for my crimes involving Red Rain. So we'd struck a bargain: I gave him his weapon, and he gave my daughter a new life.

What a fool I'd been.

That had been over a week ago, and I hadn't heard any word since. I'd been told to wait, which I did for several agonizingly lonely days.

And then, suddenly, the entire complex had gone offline.

Every electronic in the whole building gasped and gave up the ghost at once, like the angel of death had come to claim the firstborn. Computers blacked out, digital appliances started malfunctioning, and the security system caved in on itself.

I'd seen something like it before and knew my son's programming was likely involved. Someone had dealt new cards into the game, and that meant the deal with Thames was off.

I'd run—well, more like walked—out the door. The building was in chaos, and it wasn't hard to escape to the streets. I'd stayed in the area for a day or two, vainly hoping Ephesus or Cea had been detained nearby, but I'd heard no word of them.

I'd taken the hint and gone offline. I knew my file was marked with blood, and if I so much as tried to board the bus, the United would arrest me. So I'd hung off the grid, begging favors and sleeping in alleys, searching for a way to get online without being seen.

Now I had it—but this might be my only chance for a while.

I hit enter, calling on every mercy of the Lord while I waited for the page to load.

I was both elated and terrified when the first result was a video with her face on it.

It had been uploaded today, which most likely meant she was alive—but she shouldn't be online. If she was with Thames, she should have altered her appearance and adopted the name Andromeda. If the tides had shifted and she'd escaped, as I dared to hope that she had, she should be off the grid like I was.

I swallowed a lump of panic and clicked on the link. *Dear God, let her be safe.*

It was clearly a staged video, a high-quality one at that, which made me suspect that Thames or someone else with money and power was still involved. She was posed in front of a greenscreen, the fancy camera and bright stage lighting projecting her fear in high definition. It didn't look like she'd been hurt; her eyes were clear, her hair had been curled, and someone—not her—had done her makeup. But no amount of blush and powder could hide the waver in her voice and the crease in her lips.

They were using her, and she was terrified.

My heart hurtled to my throat. *Oh Philli—I did this to you.*

I shook the guilt from my head and tried to focus on what she was saying. It sounded like she was reciting her life story, going all the way back to the day we were contained in the camp. She spoke stiffly, as if reading off a script, and her voice tripped every time she noticeably avoided a proper name.

But why? Who would want a video like this, and why was the United letting it be aired?

I kept the video running and tabbed back to the search results. A quick skim proved me wrong: The United *didn't* want this video shown. All of the available videos were reposts, many from dummy accounts. I clicked on several and found over half of them had already been flagged or removed.

I refreshed the results and read through them again, looking for anything official, anything original, anything that wasn't a repost of a ripped video.

Halfway down, a link title caught my eye:

#BLUEFIRE

My heart stopped as all the air was sucked from my lungs.
Dear God, no.
I clicked on the video. It was another repost, but the comments section was on fire. With a hasty scroll, I saw dozens of names, callsigns, and hashtags I would have preferred to forget.
Please no.
I whipped back to the search results. I saw it everywhere now. All the newer videos were using the hashtag. The image results were drowning in

crude sketches of thunderbirds. And judging by the views and interactions, the movement was gaining steam.

People are angry—people who don't normally care.

This couldn't be by accident. Someone was orchestrating this, and I began to wonder if that person wasn't Thames.

They'll act, but they need a lightning rod.

Someone was trying to bring back Operation Blue Fire, and they were forcing my little girl to be their thunderbird.

I shoved the chair back, as if getting farther away from the screen would dampen the horror. This couldn't be happening. Philadelphia was never supposed to know about any of this. She was never supposed to find out about her mother, or the rebellion, or my crimes. She had no idea what she was getting into—because I never told her.

And now she had no idea how much danger she was in.

BLUE FIRE

RED RAIN #5

JUNE 2076

1

The last person I wanted to see was my mother.

She wasn't my biological mother, of course; that woman had been dead for years. No, Mrs. Nolan was my mother in name only, and not by choice. I hadn't wanted to be adopted. I hadn't wanted to change my name and use the file Thames—Mr. Nolan—had forged for me.

But I'd had no choice. I'd had no choice, because Thames had forced me to record videos taking responsibility for the destruction of the factory on Rott. He'd sacrificed me as a scapegoat so that the United wouldn't know he'd been manufacturing a world-ending superweapon. He'd let me take the blame and turned my whole family into public enemies.

That's why I recorded a video and revealed his identity to the government. That's why he killed himself. That's why I altered my fingerprints, assumed the identity he'd created for me, and ran.

I never wanted to see Mrs. Nolan again, but now she stood at the end of the hall, between me and the only exit. Why was she here? She had no reason to be here. We were in an office building on the fringes of downtown Boston that had been converted into a base for the underground. It was supposed to be a safe place, or at least that's what my old classmate Stanyard had said when he'd brought me here.

Now I was beginning to wonder if I'd walked right into another prison.

I scrambled up from the floor and braced myself, feet apart. Mrs. Nolan didn't move. She studied me, not saying anything for a cold minute. She looked exactly the same as she had the last time we'd met. Her hair had been flat-ironed into submission, and her lips were a perfect shade of pink.

Only this time, she wasn't smiling.

"Andromeda," she said, using my adopted name. There was no emotion attached to it.

I clenched my fists. "What do you want?"

She took me in once, twice; I swore I saw her grimace in displeasure. "We need to talk."

"No, no—you need to leave me alone." I'd spent the last several weeks fighting to get away from the Nolans; I wasn't going back.

"Philadelphia," my older brother Ephesus called to me from where he sat on the floor.

I glanced back at him. He met my eyes and spoke slowly. "It's okay. She's with me."

The hallway flashed out of focus as the universe shattered around him.

No. Don't do this to me.

"She's *with* you?"

He nodded.

My heart throbbed in my ears. I glanced at the others in the room, willing them to discredit the story.

Jayde, the soldier who was supposed to be in charge of this place, just shrugged.

I turned to Stanyard. His dark eyes were guarded as he said, "She helped us find you."

I sucked in a breath but didn't get any air. "You led her right to me."

You betrayed me. Again.

"Phil, it's okay," Ephesus repeated. "I promise you can trust her."

His words pierced my chest like a needle. "Trust her? You have no idea what she's done!"

"What did I do, Andromeda?"

I spun around. Mrs. Nolan crossed her arms, expression calm and pale. "What did I do to you?"

I gaped at her as the rejection filled my lungs like water. "What did you do to me? Do you have *any* idea how much hell your husband put me through?"

"Phil!" Ephesus exclaimed.

"Wow, someone's upset," Jayde remarked.

"They kidnapped me! They drugged me and took me to another *planet*," I screamed, as if I had to justify it. Why did I have to justify my feelings? Why didn't anyone understand?

Why doesn't anyone care?

Mrs. Nolan was unmoved. "Sweetheart, you know it was for your own good."

The butter—the sugary compromise that I knew all too well—slipped back into her voice, and my stomach hurled. "My own good? You used me as blackmail, and now the government wants to kill me. It's your fault I had to change my name. It's your fault Philadelphia's gone."

You planned this. You planned it this way all along, and you know it.

She shook her head. "And you *would* be dead if it weren't for that file my husband forged for you. We only did it to protect you."

"Protect me?" I screeched, but my voice broke at the end. My throat burned, and every breath made my bruised rib hurt. It didn't matter anyway—no one was listening to me.

Ephesus grabbed my hand and tried to drag me back down to the ground beside him. "Phil, please, I promise I can explain everything."

I wrenched my hand from his grasp. "No, you can't." *There's nothing you can say that will fix this.*

The realization hit me like a fresh kick to the ribs. There was a time when my big brother could have fixed anything. Now he sounded just like one of them.

I started to cry.

Stanyard put his hands up. "Hey, it's okay. You need to sit down, breathe."

He took a step towards me. I backed away—right into the wall. My pulse shot to my throat.

I don't trust you. I don't trust any of you.

"He's right." Ephesus pushed himself to his feet with his good arm, and suddenly the hallway seemed a lot narrower. "Let's all step back and regroup."

He touched my shoulder, and I threw him off. "Don't touch me!"

Jayde reacted. "All right, that's enough." He reached forward to grab me, one muscular hand sliding reflexively towards his holstered gun.

I ran.

I turned and sprinted down the hall. Someone shouted my name, but I wasn't sure who. I heard heavy footsteps behind me and willed myself to be faster.

At least Mrs. Nolan had the decency to get out of the way.

I'd never make it on the elevator. I turned the corner and followed the exit signs to the nearest stairwell. I threw the door open and slid down the stairs, taking them three at a time. I had to get out of sight before they figured out which floor I was on. The building was huge; surely there was some place to hide.

I descended until I reached the basement. I slid around the door and shoved it shut behind me, pausing to listen. Shouts echoed from further up the stairwell, but they were several floors away.

The corridor was dark except for a lone security light. I stumbled around until I found an alcove out of sight of the stairwell and collapsed on the ground.

The adrenaline broke, and in its place rolled waves of pain. My injured side was screaming. It wasn't the first time I'd been kicked in the ribs, but the pain was infinitely worse than I remembered. Ambrose's kicks had been fat and clumsy. Carnegie wasn't strong, but he was cruel. He had known exactly where to kick to make me bruise.

I braced myself against the wall and struggled not to vomit. I was shaking and sweating and saw flashing colors, even though the hall was dark.

Oh God, help.

What was I going to do? I was stranded on Earth with a dozen enemies. The government was hunting for me; the underground had compromised my position and almost gotten me killed; and my own brother was partnering with the one woman who could reveal my identity and condemn me to death.

Meanwhile, my dad, the person I had come back to Earth to save, was cryogenically frozen, and the one man who could probably fix everything was on another planet.

You should have stayed on Mars, sweetheart.

"Philadelphia."

I screamed. Ephesus stood over me. He looked terrifying backlit by the weak security lighting, with his shaved head and bandaged nose and everything that was strange and unfamiliar.

I hid my face. "Leave me alone!"

He knelt beside me. "What's wrong? You're white. Are you hurt?"

He reached towards me. I jerked back and winced. "Please don't touch me," I whimpered. It was a plea this time, not a command. *Everything hurts so bad.*

"Phil, please, you need to see a doctor. Let Mrs. Nolan look at you."

"No!" She was the last person I wanted to touch me.

He sighed. He sounded annoyed, which just made me want to cry. "Phil, I promise she won't hurt you."

You don't know that. I tucked myself further into the corner. "You don't understand."

"You're right—I don't."

I stopped and looked up at him.

He searched my face. "I have no idea what you've been through—because I wasn't there."

The statement held no accusation, only heartbreak. He sat cross-legged on the floor next to me. "I have no idea what happened between you and Thames. Cynthia—Mrs. Nolan—told me what she knows, and I saw your videos, but I know that's only half the story. I know you've been through a nightmare, and I wasn't there to help you."

His voice cracked. "We've barely seen each other these past two years, and that kills me. Honestly, Phil, when you came around the corner back there," he gestured at the floors above us, "I didn't even recognize you."

I grimaced, but I wasn't surprised. In the process of becoming Andromeda, I'd chopped my long, dark hair and bleached it nearly white. I wore blue contacts and had three piercings in my ears; not to mention, my new aesthetic of ripped jeans and angsty t-shirts was a far cry from the industrial skirt and jacket I used to wear. I didn't look anything like the girl he'd left behind.

You aren't the girl he left behind. That girl is dead.

Ephesus's eyes glistened in the dark. "I don't even know you anymore, and it's my fault. I feel like I failed you. You had to fight for your life, and you had to do it alone."

But you weren't alone, the Holy Spirit reminded me. Nic had been there for me—or at least he had been until I'd run away to Earth because I thought I could fix everything.

A fresh sob ripped out of me.

"Oh Philli." Ephesus gently took my hand. "I know I wasn't there for you, but I'm here now. You don't have to do this by yourself. We'll get through this together. Just please, let me—let us—help you."

I flinched. That was the exact same thing Thames had said to me.

Let me help you.

I took a deep breath and tried to steady my thoughts. I didn't trust Mrs. Nolan. I had no idea what she expected to gain by partnering with Ephesus, but it couldn't be good. I also didn't trust Jayde or the underground; they'd already lied to me more than once. And Stanyard—he'd saved my life today, but only after he put it in danger. I still didn't know where he stood.

But even if I couldn't count them as friends, I knew I could trust Ephesus. He'd made mistakes, but he was still my brother. And that was something even a name change couldn't take from me.

I opened my mouth to respond, but approaching footsteps interrupted me. Stanyard rounded the corner.

"I'm sorry," he panted with a nervous glance at me, "but they've brought your dad in."

2

He's not dead, he's not dead, he's not dead.

I chanted it over and over to make myself believe it. He certainly looked dead. His petrified face screamed out from beneath the glass, and the shadow of his twisted body was faintly visible through the solid block of green-blue cryoprotectant. To make matters worse, the flickering displays and throbbing controls made the whole apparatus look like it was glowing. Dad's terrified features appeared rotten and taut in the green light, like he'd fallen into a vat of acid and burned alive.

I stumbled and braced myself against the doorframe. *He's not dead, he's not dead. Dad's not dead.*

They'd dragged Dad's preservation tube up to a lab on the fifth floor of the base. The microscopes and racks of bottles had been swept aside to make room for the bulky machine. The coffin-sized tube was propped up at an angle and connected to a computer terminal by a net of wires. Mrs. Nolan stood at the screen, tampering with the monitor.

"Get away from him!" I screeched.

She glanced over her shoulder. "What this man needs is a doctor, and I'm the only one you have right now."

I opened my mouth, but Ephesus squeezed my arm. "Phil, please, let me handle this."

He walked over to Mrs. Nolan and whispered something. I didn't like the way he approached her. He stood close, too close, their shoulders nearly brushing, and he spoke to her like they'd been friends for years. He really did trust her.

Do you not have any idea who she is?

A lanky teenager I didn't recognize was wiring the machine into the wall. He finished and straightened with a grunt. "You'd better come up with a good excuse for this power drain, or you can expect an audit in the morning," he declared to no one in particular, his words thickened by a Russian accent. He couldn't have been more than thirteen or fourteen, and puberty had not yet altered his voice. The preteen squeak undermined the gruffness of his accent, and the effect was like salt on a wound.

He wiped his greasy hands on his jeans and turned to face me. He sized me up with eyes the color of faded denim. "Blue Fire," he acknowledged with a nod.

I stiffened. "Blue Fire" was the callsign the underground had invented for me on the radio, and I had no love for it. I eyed the young man. "Who are you?"

"Lev," he replied. "But you know me as Watts." He ran a hand through his buzzed blond hair and waited for a reaction.

My whole face tightened in disgust. Watts had been one of the many voices on the radio, one of the members of the underground who had stalked me and led me right into the path of a bullet.

Yet another person I can't trust.

Jayde inadvertently diffused the room. "I'll take care of the power drain. Good work, man," he said, and gave Lev a hefty pat on the back. Lev nodded and saw himself out, giving me one last look as he passed.

I found the courage to step into the room. Stanyard, who had been hovering behind me in the hall, followed at a safe distance.

Mrs. Nolan went back to maneuvering the controls. Ephesus leaned over the tube and looked in.

I approached his side. He stood there, staring, for minutes that felt like hours, not making a sound. I willed him—or me—to say something. Scream, accuse, demand, apologize, anything. But I couldn't come up with the words.

Ephesus, I'm so sorry.

Finally, his lips moved, but no sound came out. It took me a minute to realize he was praying.

He took a deep breath and turned to Jayde. "We need a revival tech. Do you know anyone?"

Jayde stalled by chewing on his lip. "There's someone I can call. But his track record is not... great."

I grabbed Dad's tube with a protective hand, then regretted it when the frost bit my fingertips. "No! Dad only has one chance. We can't risk it."

Ephesus nodded. He wiped a hand across his pallid forehead. "She's right. He's better off frozen than poorly revived."

Mrs. Nolan stabbed at the screen. "No, he's not."

I turned to her. She glared at me with eyes colder than the machine beneath my hand. "The longer he's frozen, the more therapy he'll need. More of his skin will have to be regenerated, and he'll lose most of his organs. He'll need additional transplants—and the longer he's under, the more his likelihood of surviving those procedures drops."

Her words sent despair rippling through my nerves, but I forced a straight face. "We're doing it right—with a technician I trust."

If she heard the insult, she didn't react. Ephesus glanced between us before turning to Jayde.

"I'll make some calls," he grunted, then left.

Stanyard moved aside to let him pass, then looked at me. "Can I get you some water, Phil?"

"I'm fine," I said without pausing to ascertain if that was true.

He tried again. "Have you eaten? You're still pale. You need to rest."

"He's right." Ephesus laid his hand gently on my shoulder. "You should lie down."

"I'm not leaving Dad," I declared with all the authority I could muster, but my voice came out paper-thin.

Ephesus shook his head. "There's nothing you can do for him right now."

"But I—"

"He's right," Mrs. Nolan inserted. "None of us can do anything until the machine stabilizes. It has to recalibrate after it's been unplugged for transport. I can't even get into the diagnostics until it finishes its cycle." She swiped fruitlessly at the screen.

Ephesus tried to steer me out of the room. "Come on, let's find you someplace to sleep."

"No!" I screamed, then paused to figure out why that thought filled me with such dread. I grabbed Ephesus's arm. "Don't leave me alone—please."

He searched my face, his own expression pinched. "Okay."

Stanyard excused himself. Ephesus took my hand and led me out of the lab. I followed him down a floor to a lounge stuffed with couches and recliners. Ephesus turned off the lights and propped the door open so that the room was lit only by the gentle glow from the security lamps in the hallway. He rooted around in a cabinet until he found a blanket, then gestured at the biggest couch. I sat down, and he settled in next to me.

He draped the blanket over my knees and put his good arm around my shoulder. I collapsed against him, just like I'd always done with Dad.

It wasn't the same.

He didn't say anything for a long moment. "You need to rest."

"I don't want to sleep."

"Okay." He didn't ask for an explanation. "You don't have to." He shifted so he was settled back in the cushions. I tried to copy him, but I felt stiff and rigid, no matter how much I willed my nerves to relax.

Ephesus noticed. "Try talking to me. Tell me everything that happened."

I didn't want to recap the nightmare again, but Ephesus needed to know. I wanted him to know.

He rubbed my shoulder. "Start from the beginning."

*

I was drowning.

I was submerged in a sea of green-blue. I fought and twisted, but I couldn't see any source of light, any sand on the floor, any indication of which way was up. I gasped but didn't swallow anything—no air, no water. No sound left my lips, and I panicked.

Somebody help me!

The water was thick and slimy. Each stroke was exhausting, and the more I pushed, the more the water pushed back. *Is the water getting harder?*

"Philadelphia?"

I heard my name and a distant knocking, but I couldn't tell which direction it came from. I screamed fruitlessly.

You have to help me!

I stretched my hand forward—and rammed my knuckles into something solid. The sea of green had become cold, hard, and slick.

Ice.

I swung my other arm and slammed my elbow into more ice. I tried to kick my legs, but I couldn't move them at all. The water seized around me in a solid block of ice. I couldn't move my arms, or my head, or my lungs. I couldn't breathe, and it was getting colder.

You're freezing. You're going to die—

"Phil!"

A warm hand touched my shoulder, and the nightmare shattered.

I jerked upright, reality washing over me like a bucket of water. There was someone close—too close—and I didn't recognize the room, and my heart was still pounding, and I—

"Whoa, hey, it's okay, you're okay."

I focused on the face. It was Stanyard. He stood over me, which did nothing to ease the panic. I scooted away from him. "What are you doing here?"

He put his hands up. "I'm sorry, I tried to wake you by knocking on the door, but you were out."

I took another stock of the room and finally remembered where I was. I was alone on the couch, the blanket tucked around me. Daylight illuminated the hallway outside. "Where's Ephesus?"

"I can't find him—that's why I came to get you."

I heard the tremor in his voice and looked up. "What's wrong?"

His eyes took a full lap of the room before they met mine. "There's a problem."

3

I threw the blanket aside and stood up, ignoring the flash of pain in my ribs. Stanyard took the cue and led the way.

I followed him back to the lab. They'd hooked Dad's tube to half a dozen additional monitors; the tiny room was now crammed with machines. Their motors hummed at an unnatural pitch and their displays flickered with unstable readouts—an irritable pulsing that perfectly matched the adrenaline that was still draining from my system.

"What is it?" I asked, fighting to keep my voice calm, even though my mind leapt to a dozen apocalyptic conclusions.

Stanyard pointed at the main control panel. "The machine is password-protected. We can't thaw it without the code." He dropped his arm. "And I'm guessing that code was Carnegie's."

Who is very, extremely, dead.

My heart thudded against my ribcage, all the panic and distress and grief battering to get out. I took a quick breath—too quick, the sound coming out like a sharp gasp. Stanyard flinched.

I took another breath, slower this time. "Can you hack the password?"

"I can try running a decryption program. I just wanted to ask you first."

I answered him almost before he finished the sentence. "Yes, please."

He nodded. "It will take a while for the program to run, depending on how long and complicated his password is. I'll come get you when I have something to report. You should go back to bed—"

"I'll wait."

He studied me for a beat. "Okay. I'll go get my computer."

He returned ten minutes later with a backpack overflowing with wires and gadgetry. I watched from a safe distance as he pried a panel off the control monitor, exposing an access port. He fished through his bag until he found the right adaptor and plugged it in. Then, with a swift and confident hand, he started weaving a Medusa's head of wires. He plugged different cords and adaptors together—feeding some through flashing devices he procured from his bag—before finally connecting a cable to his laptop.

"I'm surprised all of this isn't wireless," I commented in fascination.

"You don't want a machine like this to be wireless." He turned his laptop on. "If it was, anyone on the internet could hack into it."

I swallowed. I definitely didn't want a stranger halfway across the planet to have access to Dad's tube.

Stanyard wheeled a desk chair up to the control panel, propped his laptop on his knees, and started typing. I figured he didn't want me staring over his shoulder the entire time, so I dragged another chair to the other side of the machine and sat down next to Dad.

I didn't look at him; I didn't need his terrified face etched in my nightmares any more than it already was. Instead, I traced my fingernail through the frost on the glass and prayed silently. The only sound in the lab was the irregular clack of Stanyard's keyboard.

I glanced over the machine at him. He was angled away from me, his uncombed dark hair fringed in a blue glow from his laptop screen. I thanked God that Stanyard was willing to help, even as I wondered if he would be able to do it. Stanyard had been hacking for as long as I'd known him—he'd gone to detention for messing with the school's computers more times than I could count—but there was a big difference between altering someone's algebra grades and breaking into a secured cryogenics tube.

But then again, he'd accomplished some intense hacking for me while I was on Mars. Altering the door lock database couldn't have been easy—unless that was Jayde's handiwork.

With a flush of frustration, I realized I still had no idea how much of "Aurelius"—the mysterious online user who had helped me escape from Thames—was Jayde and how much was Stanyard. For all I knew, Jayde had done the heavy lifting.

Either way, I deserved to know.

"Hey."

"Yeah?" he responded without looking up.

"While I was on Mars…"

He stopped typing.

"How much of that was you talking?"

"Jayde dictated a little." There was an audible beat. "The rest was me."

I drew circles in the fog on the glass, replaying all of the messages I had received from Aurelius over in my mind.

I'D RATHER NOT WATCH THAMES KILL YOU ON LIVESTREAM
IF IT CAN BE AVOIDED

"Did you do all that hacking yourself?"

He scrolled on his laptop, but I could tell he wasn't really working. "It was a team effort. Jayde had access to the programs, but I did a lot of the legwork."

DID YOU SLEEP AT ALL?

DID YOU?

YEAH ACTUALLY

GOOD

Suddenly his late-night efforts and quick responses took on a new meaning, and I wondered why I hadn't seen it before.

I NEVER GOT A CHANCE TO SAY THANK YOU

DON'T

But then again, why would I think it was him? He was the last person I expected to help. All he'd ever done was prove that he didn't care about me, and he'd abandoned me time and again when I needed him most.

I never once imagined he'd come back to get me.

IT'S THE LEAST I CAN DO

An unease gripped my chest. "Did you mean what you said?"

"Which part?" he responded, too quickly.

"Everything," I said firmly.

I'M SORRY PHIL. I REALLY AM

He was silent. I stared at the back of his head—waiting, as always, for him to turn around.

Finally, he did. "Everything I said was the truth."

"Except the part about you being Jayde."

His eyes drifted again. "I never actually said I was…"

I sighed. "Why didn't you just tell me?"

"I didn't…" He stopped and recalculated, as if he wisely deduced that I wouldn't buy any more excuses.

He slammed his laptop shut. "I was scared. Okay? I was afraid that if I told you it was me, you'd block me—or give me the look you're giving me now."

I tried to figure out what expression was reading on my face, but I had no idea how I felt. I had no idea how I felt about any of this.

"All I wanted was the truth," I squeaked, and suddenly started to cry, hard.

"Phil…" I heard the desk chair roll across the floor and felt him in front of me. His fingers brushed my shoulder.

"Don't touch me!" I screeched, and slapped him away. The sharp sound of flesh on flesh broke through the throbbing in my ears, and I realized what I'd done. Stanyard had saved me from Carnegie, and now he was trying to save my dad, and all I'd done was scream at him.

What is wrong with you?

"I'm sorry, I'm sorry, I'm sorry," I gushed, trying to stuff the emotions back where they came from. But the more I tried to silence the anger and the fear, the more it roared. I felt scared and unsafe and exposed, and all I could do was sob and wish the tears would break something down inside of me.

They didn't.

It was several minutes before Stanyard spoke again. "Philadelphia."

He waited until I stopped crying. I swallowed the last sob and wiped my eyes, then stared at my hands in my lap.

He knelt to get in my line of sight. "Philadelphia, I'm sorry. I'm sorry I lied to you. I'm sorry I left you behind. I almost got you killed, and I've never regretted anything more in my life."

I believed him, but it didn't make me feel any better—or make me feel anything at all.

He didn't wait for a response. "I'm sorry for everything." And then, without missing a beat, he added: "Will you forgive me?"

Time stopped, and I gaped at him. No one had ever asked me to forgive them. Ephesus hadn't. Dad hadn't. Nic certainly hadn't, but I wasn't going to wait up for that one. Sure, I knew all of them were sorry by their actions—just like I knew Stanyard was sorry by his—but none of them had never *asked*.

Of course, it was a rhetorical question, wasn't it? Obviously, I had to forgive him. The Bible left no room for interpretation on that matter.

I opened my mouth to give the reflexive response, but he put his hand up. "No," he said, very firmly. "I don't want you to say it just because we're Christians and that's what we're supposed to say."

I frowned at him. "How do you want me to say it, then?"

He didn't hesitate. "I want you to say it like you said it to your dad."

I instinctively glanced at the block of ice beside me. I pictured the recording studio, with the camera whirring and my eyes blurring and the rage burning inside of me—and through it all a strong, confident feeling that I was doing the right thing, even if it broke me down to the core of my soul.

I forgive you.

I swallowed. "I don't… I don't know if I trust you like that." *Yet*, I should have added, but didn't.

He wasn't offended by the omission. "You weren't sure if you trusted your dad, either."

I still didn't—at least not in the same way I used to. There was still a lot I didn't understand, a lot we needed to work through. But as I stared at his body, mercilessly enshrined in glass, I knew without a doubt that my hurt and my pain wouldn't come between us, no matter how long it took to heal.

Because I'd forgiven him.

"I know I need to earn your trust back." Stanyard's whisper caused me to look back at him. "That could take months, years—I don't care."

"Then what do you want from me?" *What are you expecting?*

His dark eyes were raw and unfiltered as he declared, "I want you to give me a chance."

I searched his face.

"I know it will take time. But if you're going to say you forgive me, I need you to mean it. I need to know that you're wiping that from my account and letting it go. I need to know that when I try, you're not going to remind me of all my past sins—that every time I hold out my hand, you're not thinking of the time I left you behind."

He glanced down at his own hands then, and the images flashed before my eyes unbidden.

"I… don't know if I can do that," I stuttered. "Because right now, that's all I see."

"I know," he whispered, voice beyond broken.

I struggled to piece my feelings together. "I know you tried to make it up to me on Mars, but our whole relationship was based on a lie. And now every time I look at you, I have to ask myself if you're still lying."

He didn't defend himself, but he lifted his face to meet mine.

I quickly looked away. "And what am I supposed to do? Tell you I never want to see you again? I need you to hack Dad's tube. I need you, and I hate that I need you, but I don't have a choice. I *have* to forgive you."

There, at least I said it.

His tone was firm and unflinching as he responded. "I'll do everything I can to save your dad whether you forgive me or not. This isn't conditional. But if you're going to forgive me, I need you to mean it. I need you to give me the opportunity to earn your trust."

The silence was pregnant, so I knew I had to look at him. "And what if I don't?"

Rejection flooded his eyes. My conscience writhed, but I didn't back down. I had to know. I had to know if I really had a choice.

"Then I guess I'll have to live with that," he whispered. "But at least I asked."

The pain in his voice stabbed me, but at the same time, I felt powerful, like he'd handed me a gun with the safety off. For the first time in years, I had a choice. It was my decision, and the only person I had to answer to was God.

And there was always a choice with God.

Stanyard pinched his eyes shut. When he looked at me again, his expression was deep and clear. "I'm giving you my weapons, Phil. If you're going to shoot me, do it. But don't say 'I forgive you' if you don't mean it. I can't live that way." He took in a sharp breath and let it out. "Not with you."

Something caught in the back of my throat, but for once, I didn't fear the feeling.

"Philadelphia," Stanyard said again, his tone resetting the room. "Will you forgive me?"

I inhaled and sat up straight. "Yes, I will."

He didn't smile, but I saw the life creep back into his eyes. "Thank you."

He stood up before I could think of anything else to say. "It's going to take me a little while to get my decryption program set up. I need to reconfigure it to work with this OS."

I took the hint this time. "I should go find Ephesus. Text me when you make progress." I stood up and walked to the door.

He returned to his chair and started clacking on his laptop again. I stopped in the doorway and watched him work for a fraction of a second.

"Hey."

He paused and glanced up.

"Will you let me say 'thank you' now?"

Something close to a smile stretched his lips. "You're welcome, Phil."

I smiled back, then left, shutting the door behind me.

4

Ephesus found me as soon as I walked out of the lab. He came jogging down the hall, calling my name.

"There you are! What's wrong? I had a dozen missed calls from Stanyard, and then you were gone…"

I swallowed and forced the truth out before I could choke on it. "Dad's tube is password-protected."

He stopped in front of me and ran through the requisite cycle of emotions, finally settling on bitterness. "Carnegie."

I nodded, and the motion shook more tears loose. "Ephesus, I'm so sorry—"

"Phil, stop, please." He touched my shoulder and glanced through the window into the lab. "Is Stanyard trying to hack it?"

I nodded again and rubbed my eyes. "He's configuring his password programs to work with the system."

"Then we should let him work." Ephesus steered me down the hall. "Come get breakfast."

I glanced up at him as we walked into the elevator. I thought about asking him where he'd been, but I answered my own question when I saw his buzzed hair was glistening wet.

For the first time, I took a moment to acknowledge the changes in his appearance. I missed his fluffy hair already, and I wondered how mutilated his nose was under the bandage.

He caught me staring and reached up to touch it. "I promise it's not bad. They just splinted it to keep it from getting bent out of shape while it healed."

I stepped onto the elevator after him. "And your arm? Can't they just regenerate the bone?"

"Sure, but you have to go to a special facility for that." He adjusted the strap of his gaudy orange sling as we descended a few floors. "Thames was trying to keep this whole thing off the radar, so he couldn't risk checking me into a 'real' hospital. So it's the old-fashioned cast and sling for me."

The elevator door dinged and opened, and we stepped out into the hall. I heard chattering voices and clattering dishes from up ahead.

"I promise I'm fine. Cynthia—Mrs. Nolan says she'll probably take the splint off my nose this week." He looked down at me with that generous, trustworthy smile that used to solve all my problems—but now I could barely feel the warmth.

I weakly returned the gesture, just so he wouldn't worry.

We rounded the corner into a small cafeteria. A few people I didn't recognize littered the tables. Mrs. Nolan and Jayde stood around the prep counter, talking. They both stopped and looked up at me.

"Blue Fire!" Jayde boomed, tipping his coffee mug towards me.

I flinched. "Don't call me that."

Jayde opened his mouth, but Ephesus came to my defense. "Her name is Philadelphia."

"It's actually Andromeda," Mrs. Nolan returned.

The dissonant names ricocheted around in my head, making the world spin as a dozen conflicting realities collided like black holes. I wanted to slap my hands over my ears and shut them all out.

You have no idea who I am.

Jayde must have read my expression, because his face softened. "You're right, I'm sorry—you haven't even had coffee yet." He took the carafe off the warmer. "How do you take it?"

I took in a full breath and let it out, expelling all the fluttering thoughts with it. "Black, please."

Jayde blinked. "Whoa, hardcore."

Ephesus blanched. "Black? My little sister takes her coffee *black*?"

I glanced up at him, unsure what warranted the enthusiasm. "That's how I like it?"

"No way. You just don't know how to make it right. Here, I can fix this." He grabbed a clean mug and dumped equal amounts of coffee and creamer into it. He gave the mug a quick swirl and slid it towards me.

I picked it up and sniffed it skeptically; the drink was almost as white as I was. I took a small sip and almost barfed it back into the cup. It was sticky and sweet and didn't even taste like coffee.

"No thanks," I gagged, and shoved the mug back at him.

He took it with a grumble. "Who taught you how to drink coffee?"

I pondered that as I gratefully accepted the fresh mug Jayde handed to me. *Nic did.* I stared at the steaming brown liquid and managed a smile that felt genuine.

"How's your rib?" Mrs. Nolan's voice jerked me out of the pleasant memory.

I glared at her. "How did you know about that?"

"Ephesus told me," she said with a gesture in his direction.

I gripped the hot mug with both hands. "It's fine," I said, forcing the lie to sound placid and not bitter.

"I need to look at it." She took her plate to the sink and dropped it in the soapy water. "I want to make sure you don't have any fractures or internal bleeding, and I have some breathing exercises I want you to do. I can tell you're breathing shallowly, and if you do that too long, you'll get pneumonia."

I sucked in my breath involuntarily and was instantly reminded how much breathing *did* hurt.

She studied me. "Come to the infirmary after breakfast and I'll get you some pain medication."

That was definitely a bribe to get me to show up, and unfortunately, it would probably work. Thankfully Ephesus spared me the necessity of giving her a verbal reply by handing me a plate loaded with food. He gestured over to an empty table, and I followed, sliding onto the bench next to him.

He crammed a scoop of eggs into his mouth and then gestured at my plate with his fork. "Eat up. You need your strength."

"I promise I had three full meals yesterday." Eating didn't appeal to me—especially since swallowing *also* hurt—but I bravely stabbed the mound of nearly-white, gummy scrambled eggs and took a bite.

Jayde joined us at the table and set my tablet down in front of me. I frowned up at him; my tablet had been in my backpack, which I'd abandoned somewhere in the halls last night. Had he been digging in my stuff?

He put his hand up. "I just charged it." He took a sip of coffee. "And looked up who it was registered to."

I grabbed my device and self-consciously wiped his fingerprints off the screen with my sleeve. "You could have asked me."

He shrugged. "You were asleep."

"So you went digging in my purse?"

His jaw tensed, making his neck look even more muscular. "Look, keeping this place off the radar is a lot of work, so forgive me if I take digital security seriously."

Heat flashed across my cheeks, and I looked down at my plate.

He sat down across from me and leaned forward. "Hey, I'm just trying to keep everyone safe—including you."

"I know," I mumbled.

He leaned back and sighed. "I'm sorry to make you do this, but you can't keep that tablet here. All the internet traffic in the building is filtered, but it's not bulletproof. We can't have any activity from 'Andromeda' showing up on our log."

I looked up. "Can't I just take it offline?"

"That's even worse," Ephesus inserted. "If you go offline for large portions of the day, it will trip the algorithm."

Jayde nodded. "And I don't want the United to check your file and see that Andromeda takes the same bus route every day and then suspiciously drops offline when she reaches this address."

Ephesus tapped the screen. "I can set it up with a program that will run background activity all day—games, movies, that kind of thing. It will make it look like you're just hanging out at home for the summer."

"But…" The protest came to my lips and died. *But my Bible…*

"It will be safer if you leave it plugged in at the Vons'. Which, we need to talk about them." Ephesus put his fork down. "I think you should sleep at their house."

"What?" both Jayde and I protested at the same time.

Jayde was quicker to recover. "We need her here."

Who cares what you need? "I need to be here. Dad—

Ephesus put a hand on my shoulder to stop me. "Phil, there's nothing you can do about Dad."

But it's my fault. "I—"

"He's right."

I looked up. Mrs. Nolan stood a respectful distance away, leaning against the counter, but she had clearly been listening. "There's nothing you can do about your father. We can't even begin to work on him until we get that tube unlocked, and even after he's thawed, he'll be in revival therapy for several weeks. There is literally nothing you can do but wait."

She met my eyes, and for the first time since yesterday, her expression was neither cold nor bitter. "I promise."

I looked away. Ephesus squeezed my shoulder. "And you'll be safer waiting at the Vons."

"But what about you? I can't leave you."

"I promise I'm not going anywhere. Look, if my file wasn't a mess, I wouldn't be here either. But until I can safely get online, I have to stay off the grid."

I sat upright—a little too quickly. I concealed a wince. "I can fix your file. I bought you new prints."

Jayde's eyebrows formed a bright orange knot on his forehead. "From whom?"

"Andes," I said, and watched for a reaction.

His face relaxed. "How'd you get in? He told me he's not taking work anymore."

"I had a referral," I said, and for a brief moment felt powerful.

"Where'd you get money for prints?" Ephesus demanded.

I turned to him. "I have plenty of money. Thames—"

I caught sight of Mrs. Nolan in my peripheral and stopped.

Her expression darkened again. "No need to be ashamed of it. It's your money." She slammed her mug on the counter and walked out.

Ephesus watched her leave before turning back to me. "I take it you inherited more than their last name."

"Yeah, basically." I brushed off the uncomfortable emotions. "Point is, I bought new prints for you and Dad from Andes."

"So that's what you meant when you told Dad you arranged for his affairs. Was he supposed to meet Andes last night?"

"Yeah, but Andes said he never made it." My face numbed as the realization flooded me. "Carnegie must have intercepted him before he got there."

Memories of Carnegie's cruel laugh and final words rushed over me.

Oh, Philadelphia, you know this is all your fault, right?

"But how?" Jayde slapped a hand on the table. "Even I didn't know you'd been talking with Andes, or I'd have gotten there first."

That was hardly a comforting thought, but I knew the answer. "He was watching my file. He knew about Andromeda."

You led me right to him.

Carnegie was right: It was all my fault. He'd been following me the whole time; he'd seen me visit Andes. When he overheard me talking to Dad on the radio, he knew exactly what was going to happen. All he had to do was send men to watch Andes's shop. Dad walked right into their hands, because I led them there.

You should have stayed on Mars, sweetheart.

Ephesus slid his good arm around me, but I could barely feel it. *Oh Daddy, I'm so sorry.*

Ephesus rubbed my shoulder, as if that could coax some life back into me. "It's going to be okay. I'll just get my prints altered somewhere else."

"No, Andes is still your best bet," Jayde argued. "I can provide cover. There's a back way in. We'll go this afternoon."

I pulled away from Ephesus. "I'm going with you."

"Absolutely not. I'm taking you back to the Vons'."

"Ephesus, please—"

Jayde spoke over me. "I still think she should stay here."

"You don't get to decide," I snapped. "And I'm going to Andes's. I need to find out if that's what really happened—maybe he saw something." I looked into Ephesus's eyes and pleaded with him. "Please. I have to fix this."

He relented with a smile that was more sad than affectionate. "Okay."

My tablet flickered on, vibrating with a silent notification. I picked it up and saw a text from Stanyard.

GOT EVERYTHING CONFIGURED. GOING TO START RUNNING THE PROGRAM NOW

A prayer lifted some of the weight off my heart. *Thank you, Jesus. It's going to be okay.*

Ephesus leaned over to read the screen. "I'm going to go help him." He stood up and clasped my shoulder. "Please eat."

I grunted and forced myself to swallow another forkful of now-cold eggs. Ephesus grabbed his coffee cup and hurried out.

I sent Stanyard a thank you, then went back to methodically eating. I figured if I ate one bite at a time in a rhythm, I'd eventually get it all down.

Jayde watched me labor for a minute. "Do you want fresh coffee? It's probably cold by now."

"It's fine," I said, even though I took a sip and realized it wasn't.

He pushed his empty mug aside and leaned his arms on the table. "We need to talk."

I stabbed my toast with my fork, even though that was definitely not the recommended way to eat bread. *Do we have to do this now?*

"I know you're not a fan of the way I... followed you."

Just say it like it is. You stalked me. You stalked me, and you lied to me, and you almost got me killed.

"But the truth is, there's a lot going on. Stuff you don't know about—stuff your dad didn't tell you about."

I stopped when I remembered my dad's cold words on the radio.

Look, Blue Fire, there's more going on than you realize, things I can't discuss on here.

I looked up at Jayde.

His green eyes held mine. "Your dad isn't who he says he is. He's done this before."

"Done what?" I asked, but my tablet cut me off. I looked down to see another text from Stanyard.

YOU NEED TO GET UP HERE

5

I didn't bother to respond. I grabbed my tablet, swung my legs over the bench, and started running.

"What is it?" Jayde called.

"Dad!" I shouted as I darted out the door.

I ran to the elevator and back to the lab, ignoring the burning in my side. As I approached the window, I could see Stanyard and Ephesus standing over the tube. I felt a rush of hope soiled with fear. Had they cracked the password already? It couldn't have been that easy—could it?

I shoved the door open. Stanyard looked up and declared, "We have another problem."

"What now?" I gasped, out of breath from the sprint. I winced and braced myself against the doorframe, struggling not to drop my tablet.

Stanyard frowned at me but didn't comment. "It only lets us attempt the passcode three times before it locks us out for twenty-four hours."

He pointed at the control panel; it was glowing an angry red with an ominous counter ticking down. Ephesus stood with his back to me, glaring at the monitor.

Jayde jogged up behind me. "Didn't it warn you after the first two attempts?"

Stanyard flushed almost as red as the screen. "Yeah, but I missed it."

"How?" Jayde spat with absolutely no mercy.

Stanyard's eyes flittered around the room, looking anywhere but in my direction. "I had to patch my program to work with this OS, and I messed up the code for the warning relay."

Ephesus came to his defense. "We can adjust the program to space out the attempts so it doesn't trigger the lockout, but it won't do any good."

"Why not?" I burst, my last shred of hope imploding with the question.

Ephesus finally looked up at me. "Do you know how long it will take to try all of the possible potential passwords if we can only attempt one every five minutes?"

I wasn't good at math, but even I knew that it would take an eternity to crack the password at that pace. And time was one thing we didn't have.

All of Mrs. Nolan's warnings about Dad being under too long thundered in my skull.

Jayde took a minute to appreciate the gravity of that statement, then grunted. "Is there another way in?"

Ephesus grunted. "Yeah, but I don't like it. We could pry the casing off and try wiring into the machine directly. If we can find the right relays, we could bypass the computer and trigger the defrost procedure manually—but that's as good as killing him."

The gasp I made was involuntary. "Why?"

"Bringing him back to temperature is an incredibly delicate process. These machines are designed to run hundreds of diagnostics and adjust the procedure automatically based on how the body is responding." Ephesus rapped the monitor with his knuckles. "If we bypass the computer, we'd have to replicate all of that manually—and we won't have access to any of the sensor readouts."

"We'd not only need an incredibly skilled revival technician who can do everything by hand, but we'd also need a mechanic familiar with the tube design. And I don't know where we'd find either of those off the radar." Stanyard looked to Jayde.

Jayde shook his head, and I swallowed my heart.

"I can also try extracting the memory dump," Ephesus added, voice loud but devoid of any optimism. "There's no telling if that will work, but I can't even attempt it until tomorrow."

Stanyard dragged his hands through his already-matted hair. "Until then, I'd recommend collecting some educated guesses as to what Carnegie's code might have been. Randomized attempts aren't going to work."

It took me a minute to wade through the blinding fog of fear and realize that all three boys were staring at me.

"I hardly knew him... You worked with him longer." I turned pleading eyes to Ephesus.

He sighed. "Yeah, there's some things I can try—but it would be a lot easier if I were online."

Jayde took charge. "We need to get your prints fixed. I'll make the arrangements—we leave in an hour." He strode from the room without waiting for a response.

Stanyard waited until Jayde's footsteps faded down the hall before he turned to me. "I'm sorry, Phil."

I looked up and gave him a weak smile. "Thanks."

"No, I mean… *I'm* sorry. If I had known Carnegie had this password-protected…"

He heaved a sigh, his shoulders nearly caving in on themselves. I noted how pale his face was and how red his eyes were and realized he blamed himself.

"You had no way of knowing, man," Ephesus consoled him.

"I know!" Stanyard pinched his eyes shut. "But if I had, I would have—"

"Would have what?" I interrupted. "Let Carnegie shoot me instead?"

He opened his eyes and stared at me.

"You did what you had to do," I declared, as much for myself as for him.

His lips twitched.

"So what now?" Ephesus tapped the frosty glass. "I'll do some digging, but frankly, I'm not optimistic that I'll be able to find anything. Most of my time on Mars was spent on the wrong side of the door."

I knew exactly what that was like.

"Do we have any of the Wing 74 data left? Did any of Thames's servers survive the virus?" Stanyard suggested.

The obvious answer hit me with a wave of relief. "Nic!" I cried.

They both stopped and looked at me. I held up my tablet. "I can call Nic. He was Carnegie's boss—surely he has some of his old passcodes."

I unlocked my tablet and opened our encrypted messaging app. My pulse quickened as hope flowed through me. Nic would know what to do. He had a whole server's worth of data on Carnegie; surely he could find something. He could fix this…

After you tell him what you've done.

I hesitated with my finger over his profile picture. Nic had no idea what happened yesterday. Last he knew, I was lazing around his parents' house, waiting to hear from my dad. I was going to have to explain to Nic that I'd ignored every piece of advice he'd given me and nearly gotten us all killed.

I knew you wouldn't listen to Nic. I knew you couldn't sit still.

My palms left a sweaty smear on the back of the tablet. Nic had been right about everything, especially me.

Stanyard wheeled a desk chair over to me. "What's the matter, Phil?"

I gratefully sat down. "I'm going to have to tell Nic what happened."

"Why?" Ephesus sputtered. "He doesn't need to know the details. You don't owe him anything."

"I don't know, I just… feel like he deserves to know." I couldn't quantify the emotion; I couldn't quantify anything around the anxiety that suddenly swelled in my throat. I quickly clicked on Nic's profile and started an audio call before I could change my mind.

We all stayed silent while it rang once, twice, three times. I involuntarily let out my breath when he answered.

"Who died?" he asked as soon as he picked up.

I was so stunned that I almost forgot to acknowledge him. "Uh… what?"

"It's the middle of the night over here." He cleared the grogginess out of his throat. "So either you forgot to look up interplanetary time zones, or someone's dead."

The morbid accuracy of his assessment made me shudder. "Well, no one's dead yet—that's why I need your help."

There was a beat. "What happened?"

His tone shifted—firmer, quieter, as if he'd expected this all along. I flushed as my neck and ears started to burn.

Stanyard leaned towards the speaker. "I can explain if you want."

"Who's that?" Nic barked.

"Stanyard," I said, and wondered if he'd even remember who that was.

It took him a minute. "The kid?"

"Wow, specific," Stanyard muttered.

Nic was happy to clarify. "The one who abandoned you in the alley—"

"Yes, yes," I cut him off. "Ephesus is here too."

Nic swore.

"Love you too," Ephesus shouted from across the room.

"Well, this ought to be an excellent bedtime story." There was rustling on the other end of the line, as if Nic had gotten up and walked across the room. I heard a keyboard clacking. "Start from the beginning, Andromeda."

When I hesitated, he added, "And if you were thinking of holding anything back, let me remind you that this app encrypts calls."

"You said it wasn't bulletproof…" I mumbled.

"It's a risk I'm willing to take. Start talking."

I swallowed and obeyed, beginning when I dropped Cea off at the transit station yesterday. I omitted the gorier details, but there was no way to paint the story in any fashion that sounded heroic.

"Carnegie must have picked him up outside of Andes's," I admitted halfway through.

"Oh, I'm quite sure that's exactly what happened," Nic snapped with more anger in his voice than I'd heard in a long time. He hadn't been that angry with me since I'd broken into Wing 74.

I gripped my tablet, the apologies tumbling out before I could stop them. "I know, I'm sorry, I should have—"

"You should have waited to contact Andes until you had your father with you, like I *told* you to do!" Nic was shouting now.

Ephesus straightened. "Hey! Lay off of her."

Stanyard tried to help. "It's not her fault—"

"Would you just let me finish the story?" I cut them all off. I had to get through this before I started crying again.

I stumbled through the rest of the tale, ending with how Carnegie had frozen my father.

I paused, waiting to see if there would be any more scolding. Instead, there was silence.

"Where is Carnegie now?" Nic finally asked.

His voice had returned to normal, which relieved some of the tension in the room. My pulse slowed. "He's dead. Stanyard shot him."

"Well, at least that much is a happy ending. How'd the kid find you?"

"He knew about Andromeda—Mrs. Nolan told him."

There was a hacking cough, as if he'd tried to take a drink of water and regretted it. "Nolan? Well, that explains everything and nothing."

"I know." I let out my breath and didn't offer up any more explanation. Ephesus was right—I didn't owe him anything.

Nic didn't wait. "Well, let's see if we can't keep everyone else alive and thawed. Do you know what kind of cryoprotectant he used? Who's the tube manufacturer? Was it a controlled slow freeze, or did he vitrify him?"

I only knew what half of those words meant. I glanced at Ephesus.

"Hang on." He walked over to the terminal and started swiping through menus. "Looks like a Kaylon Core brand... model FM-2030."

I heard typing on Nic's side of the line. "It definitely wasn't a 'slow freeze,'" I offered. "It happened almost instantly." I rubbed my arm and hoped he wouldn't ask for a more detailed description of the process.

"I've got a schematic for the makeup of the cryoprotectant here," Ephesus said. "It looks like it's dimethyl sulfoxide based..."

Nic swore, and I knew we were in trouble.

"No need," he muttered. "That model number tells me all I need to know."

I swallowed until I had enough courage to ask, "What do *I* need to know?"

"Because I don't hate you, I'm going to give it to you straight." He gave me only a beat to prepare myself before he declared, "I don't think your father is coming back."

The boys were graciously silent while I came up with a million excuses as to why he was wrong. "Mrs. Nolan said he was going to need some skin grafts and a blood transfusion..."

"He's going to need a lot more than fresh blood if he's going to breathe again," Nic snapped, then sighed. "Listen, Andi, that tube wasn't designed to preserve people for revival. It was designed to preserve people for harvesting."

I reflexively looked at my father's petrified face.

"Preserving people for revival is a *process*. You need to prep the body, replace some of the fluids with inert gases—you can't just flash-freeze them. The amount of tissue and organ damage that causes is astronomical."

"But that doesn't make any sense," I cried. "Carnegie needed my father."

"He needed his *brain*."

Everything dropped to the pit of my stomach.

Nic continued, more slowly this time. "All he needed was the formula for Red Rain—which is in your father's memory banks somewhere, or at least the pieces needed to reconstruct it. He could have easily hooked your father's brain to a computer and transferred a lot of the data—that's at least real science. Or—never mind."

He cut off with a grunt. Every fiber of my being told me I shouldn't ask, but I did anyway. "Or what?"

He mumbled under his breath before answering. "Or he could have thawed your father and kept him in a vegetative state. That's the economical option. All he would have had to do was feed your father key images or words, and the brain would have supplied the needed memories. Any old synaptic device could read them. Your father wouldn't have to be 'viable' for that to work—it's all subconscious."

I turned to Ephesus, silently begging him to tell me it wasn't true, but he'd washed as white as a sheet. We both knew what method Carnegie would have chosen. Stanyard breathed a frantic prayer.

A cold tear slid down my cheek. "What do I do?" I whispered.

"Start making funeral arrangements?" Nic barked, then caught himself. "Look—I won't tell you not to try. Kaylon is a legit company, and their equipment is state of the art. If you have any hope, it's going to be in the quality of their materials. But you're going to need a wickedly good revival technician."

Where was I going to find one of those? Jayde said he was going to make some calls, but he himself admitted his contact wasn't skilled. Even if we could find someone willing to do a very expensive procedure off the record, would they be good enough? What if my father died simply because we botched the procedure?

I would never forgive myself.

"I'm going back to bed now," Nic said when he realized I didn't have anything else to contribute.

"Wait," Stanyard called. "There is one thing you can help us with."

"Yeah?"

"Carnegie password-locked the cryotube. We can't even begin to thaw it out until we crack it, and so far hacking has only triggered security lockouts. Do you have any idea what he might have used for a passcode? Any common codes he's used before?"

"At 3 am I don't know anything. But in the morning I'll start digging around in his files and see what I can find."

"Thank you," I offered with as much sincerity as I could around the gathering tears.

He hesitated. "Of course," he said, and hung up.

6

There was silence in the lab except for the humming of the machines. I sat there, barely breathing, feeling like I could cry but that the tears were just out of reach. My sinuses were clogged with emotion, like the apologies and guilt and shame were frozen in there.

Frozen and unviable. Just like Dad.

Stanyard was the first to speak. "Phil, I'm so sorry." He reached a hand towards my shoulder, then caught himself. He quickly stepped back.

Ephesus walked over to me. He knelt beside the chair and wrapped his good arm around me. I buried my face in his shoulder, willing myself to cry, apologize, *something.*

Only one thought solidified. "He's dead, isn't he?"

Ephesus didn't answer. I felt his shoulders tense.

I pulled away. "Daddy's dead."

And I killed him.

"No," Ephesus said, but not quickly enough.

Stanyard tried to cover for him, voice artificially loud. "There's still hope. Even Nic said there's a chance, and he is not known for his optimism."

"He just said that to make me feel better," I muttered, even though Nic had literally never made any effort to make me feel better about anything.

"I don't think so." Ephesus tapped the darkened screen of my tablet. "Nic has a lot of vices, but I don't think he's lying to you."

A tiny sliver of warmth crawled into my soul when I realized he was right. Nic would lie about a lot of things to a lot of people, but he wouldn't lie to me. Not anymore.

Ephesus stood up. "We need to find a revival technician—which means I need to get online and make some calls. I'm going to go find Jayde and see if he's ready."

I nodded. "I'll go find my backpack."

"What you need to find is a shower—and a change of clothes." Ephesus wrinkled his nose at me.

I should have been offended, but a glance down at myself proved he was right. I'd nearly died in this outfit, and you could tell.

"I'm sure Mrs. Nolan has something you can borrow," Stanyard offered.

I grimaced. I did not relish the idea of sharing clothes with Mrs. Nolan, but I didn't have much of a choice. I couldn't go to Andes's looking like this.

"Fine," I relinquished, "but don't leave without me."

Ephesus led me to the girls' locker room and left me to it. It was probably the most degrading shower I'd ever taken; the tile floor was freezing, and the generic soap they had in the dispenser on the wall smelled like a hospital. But I'd rather smell like a hospital than reek of death and terror.

I emerged to find a pile of toiletries on the bench. Someone had left a comb, deodorant, and a toothbrush, along with an oversized gray hoodie. It didn't look like anything Mrs. Nolan would wear, but at least it was clean. I sponged out my jeans, whipped my hair into a stubby braid, and brushed my teeth. I pulled the hoodie over my head and instantly felt more human; it was thick and soft, and I could hide my arms inside it like a hug.

Jayde was waiting for me outside. "Let's roll."

Lev, the young Russian I'd met yesterday, and a burly soldier twice his size accompanied us. We piled into a giant black SUV, the kind bad guys in movies drove. Jayde did, in fact, know a back way into Andes's; we parked at an abandoned warehouse two blocks away and entered through the alley. The precaution felt unnecessary, however; with three heavily-armed military guys accompanying us, we probably could have just gone through the front.

"Lass! You're all right!" Andes's booming voice filled the shop as soon as we entered. Thankfully he didn't have any other customers. He strode up to me, blithely ignoring the men, and grasped my hand in both of his. "Don't you know it's rude to hang up on a man like that?"

"I'm sorry, there was a mishap. But I've brought you some work." I gestured at Ephesus.

Andes released me and turned to size Ephesus up. "You must be the lucky lad!" He offered his tattooed hand, then pulled it back when he realized Ephesus's dominant hand was in a cast. "Have we met?"

"Not in the flesh." Ephesus stepped forward and whispered something in Andes's ear.

Andes's face split in a grin. "Klez! Well, isn't this my lucky day."

I glanced between them. "You two know each other?"

"Everyone's heard of Klez. Best coder in Boston." Andes slapped him on the back, a gesture which both looked and sounded painful.

Ephesus covered a wince. "That's hyperbole, but thank you."

Andes opened his mouth to say something else, then stopped. His eyes and face darkened like a storm had blown over the moor. "But if you're Klez, then that makes you…" His finger drifted to me.

Jayde stepped up. "This is Blue Fire."

Andes grunted something that wasn't English, but it definitely didn't sound polite. "I take it my no-call, no-show from last night was Catalyst." He spat out my dad's callsign like it was a piece of unchewable food.

"Yes," I admitted with a swallow.

Andes rubbed the bulging veins in his temples. "Why didn't you tell me?"

"It was none of your business." I glared at Jayde.

"Lass, I know you're new here, but let me teach you some etiquette about dealing outside the law." Andes crossed his arms over his thick chest and frowned at me. "When your client is on the United's ten most wanted, it's customary to let people know what they're getting into."

Desperation burst in my mind, but then I remembered that I was the one with the money. I held the power in this relationship.

I straightened and pulled my shoulders back. "If you're not confident enough to handle my case, then I'll take my business elsewhere."

The glitter returned to his eyes. "Oh no, I know where my loyalties lie."

He pulled the collar of his shirt down to reveal a tattoo below his right clavicle. It was a mystical-looking bird with a lightning bolt clutched in his talons—the same tattoo Cea had on the inside of her arm.

I searched his face. The image meant nothing to me, but if both Andes and Cea had one, it must be important. It probably meant both of them were part of the same sect in the underground. Cea was someone I still trusted, so hopefully that meant I could still trust Andes, too.

"Glad to hear it," I said.

He adjusted his shirt and glanced at Ephesus. "We need to get you fixed up—follow me."

He led us into one of the private booths off the lobby. Shoving the table aside, he reached up and pushed on a ceiling tile, revealing a metal ladder. With one yank, he pulled it down. He gestured at me. "Ladies first."

I glanced at Ephesus, who nodded. I grabbed the rungs and hurried up.

Above the ceiling was a glittering lab that looked like it belonged in the base on Mars. Overhead fluorescents drowned the room in sterile light. A dozen shiny machines competed for floorspace, and the air thrummed with electricity. In the middle of it all was an exam table that looked like a prop from the torture bay in a bad movie. The only thing not metal in the whole room were the brick walls, which lent a strange steampunk vibe to the space.

The rest of the group joined me. "I thought you said you were out of business," Jayde groused.

Andes pulled the ladder up behind us. "I never said I was out of business. I just said I wouldn't work for your prices." He pointed at a chair in the corner. "You, sit."

Ephesus obeyed, and Andes went about prepping a machine that looked exactly like the one the technician on Mars had used when I'd gotten my prints altered.

"Dare I ask what happened to Catalyst last night?" Andes glanced over his shoulder at me as he worked.

I took a deep breath. "Actually, I was hoping you could tell me."

I gave him a simplified version of the story, saying only that we believed an enemy had gotten to Dad first. Andes didn't need to know specifics.

He let out a growl from deep in his throat. "I'm afraid I can't help you. He called to make an appointment for 7 pm, but he never showed. I kept the shop open all night, but when you called and seemed as surprised as I was that he wasn't there—I assumed something had gone wrong."

He rolled the laser arm over to the chair. He eyed Ephesus's cast disdainfully. "This is gonna hurt, lad."

He took Ephesus's broken arm out of the sling and carefully bent it so that it was flat on the arm of the chair. Then he started sliding Ephesus's fingers into the clamps that would hold them still for the procedure. Ephesus did his best to swallow a wince.

Once he had Ephesus strapped down, Andes pulled a chair over to the computer terminal and started typing. "I'm sorry, lass. If there's any word on the street, I'll let you know. But if the United got ahold of him—I wouldn't be optimistic."

"I know." I wasn't optimistic anyway, but for once the government was not the cause of my misery.

He ignored me to focus on his work. I knew from experience that the procedure would take several hours, so I amused myself by wandering around the shop. Jayde, Lev, and their partner settled in chairs by the exit and engaged in a whispered conversation that apparently didn't involve me, which was just as well.

I found a binder of tattoo designs on a table and started flipping through it. They were all print-outs—pixelated ones at that, like they'd been run on an old copier—probably because the images were too sensitive to be stored on a computer. The first few pages were filled with flags and national symbols, emblems the United had long since branded as illegal. I lingered on a sketch of the American flag, a banner I had never seen fly in real life. Even my father was too young to remember when the United States was truly free.

I kept looking. The designs got progressively more seditious: crosses, the star of David, the Muslim crescent and star. There were words in foreign languages and symbols that looked like code. And there it was again—that bird with the thunderbolt.

I traced the image with my finger, wondering what it meant. I thought about asking, but Andes had his nose to the screen, editing one of Ephesus's prints.

I turned the page to find a picture of a brain. It was far too complex to be a tattoo; it looked more like a schematic, with annotations and arrows crisscrossing the neural pathways.

The next few pages were more of the same. There were markups of brains, lungs, even kidneys. And then I came to a sketch for an artificial heart.

That's definitely what it was, and an advanced one at that. I skimmed the list of features and remembered Mrs. Nolan's words.

He'll lose most of his organs. He'll need more transplants...

"Andes... do you do organ transplants?"

He didn't look up from his work. "I don't, but I know someone who does. Why, you need something done?"

Oh Jesus, please let it be.

I kept testing the waters. "And what about a skin grafter?"

He glanced back at me and arched an eyebrow.

I sighed and tossed the binder on the table. "I need a revivalist—and a good one."

The soldiers stopped talking and watched.

Andes punched a button on the machine to pause the procedure. He swiveled his chair around to face me and planted his hands on his knees. "I think you'd better tell me the whole story—from the beginning."

I looked to Ephesus, who gave me a subtle nod.

So I told Andes the truth—how "Catalyst" was back at base, frozen in a block of ice. When I was done, Andes reached up to massage the veins in his temples, which were even more swollen than before.

"You know how I said you should disclose all the relevant details about your clients? *That* was a relevant detail."

I shrugged. "Can you do it?"

He sighed. "Yes, we can."

Hope raged through me. *Thank you, Jesus!* I shared an eager look with Ephesus, who mouthed praises.

Andes cut off our celebration with a flick of his finger. "But I'm warning you, it will not be pretty. We've worked with that brand of cryogenics before—it's not the first time we've brought back someone the government iced. But it's a very harsh process, and we'll have no idea how badly he's been damaged until we get in there."

"I know," I said, even as my soul squeezed.

"And if you're wanting to do this all under the radar, you're going to have to take what you can get when it comes to replacement body parts. I can't guarantee that his skin will be all the same color when we're done."

The thought of my father being stitched together like a puppet made me want to throw up, but I fought the feeling down. "I understand—just get it done."

He studied me. "It's going to cost a fortune."

"I don't care."

"*How* much is this going to be?" Jayde asked.

"It's fine," I snapped, and realized I sounded exactly like Nic.

Andes was still watching me. "And one more thing—I guarantee you he'll suffer some memory loss."

I swallowed. "How much?"

He didn't sugarcoat it. "I've seen all ends of the spectrum."

I thought of the Vons and flinched. What if Dad ended up exactly like Nic's parents—barely able to take care of himself? What if he didn't remember Ephesus? What if he didn't remember me?

I pinched my eyes shut. It didn't matter. I couldn't give up on Dad. I had to fix what I'd done, and if that meant spending every penny and walking with him through therapy for three years, so be it.

I breathed through my nose until the anxiety subsided. I opened my eyes and met Andes's stare. "You're hired."

7

Ephesus insisted I get home to the Vons before dark. After we got back to base and checked on Dad, he gave me a tight one-armed hug and promised he would call me immediately if there was any change. I couldn't bring myself to tell him goodbye; I was choking on the irrational fear that as soon as I walked away, he would disappear from my life again. I knew it was ridiculous, and that we were all as safe as possible given the circumstances, but my emotions had long since abandoned reason.

Stanyard respected my need for silence as he drove me home. He parked in front of the Vons' house and turned to me. "I'll come pick you up at nine tomorrow."

"Thanks," I whispered, and got out. He idled on the road until I disappeared around the back of the house.

I let myself in the back door with my key and was instantly met by screeching.

"Where in the world have you been?"

I looked up into the flushed face of Mrs. Von. She blocked the hall, feet apart and hands on her hips. She made a grand attempt to leer over me, even though she was about an inch shorter.

"Where have you been?" she repeated, using language that would have made Nic proud.

While "a secret rebel base across town" would have been the truthful answer, I had a feeling that wasn't the answer I should give her.

Unsurprisingly, she didn't wait for an explanation. "You were gone all night, and when I went up to check your room, your suitcase was packed... What was I supposed to think?"

I gaped at her. I hadn't expected her to even notice I was missing. "I'm sorry, I—"

"Is that her?" Mr. Von called from the kitchen.

"Yes, finally," Mrs. Von muttered, and I realized that was the closest to an "I was worried about you" that I'd get from her.

Mr. Von was a little more obvious with his affection. He ran out into the hall and embraced me. "I'm so glad you're safe. When you didn't show up for breakfast..."

I connected the dots. I'd broken the pattern by disappearing, and it had sent their fragile minds into a tailspin. I returned Mr. Von's hug, ignoring the pain in my ribs. "I'm sorry, I was sleeping over at a friend's house. I thought I mentioned it..." I stepped back and gave Mrs. Von a sheepish shrug and smile. "It won't happen again."

She accepted the penance. "Well, I'm glad I didn't call the police."

I flinched. *Me too.* The last thing I needed was the police out looking for Andromeda.

"Well, you're just in time for dinner!" Mr. Von, evidently fully recovered, led the way back to the kitchen. "We're having... what are you making again, dear?"

Mrs. Von threw up her hands. "I don't even know anymore." The order in her universe had been restored, and now she just looked exhausted.

I took a bold risk and lightly touched her arm. "I'll finish cooking."

She eyed me for a minute, then smiled.

Even I couldn't figure out what Mrs. Von had been trying to make, but thankfully it wasn't that hard to retrofit the half-browned ground beef into another recipe. After dinner, I let Mr. Von talk me into watching two episodes of his current sitcom; I wasn't in the mood for TV, but I felt like I owed it to him.

After I finally excused myself, I went upstairs to take a longer, more satisfying shower. I threw every stitch of clothing in the wash and took my time scrubbing my fingernails and treating my scratches with antibiotic cream.

By the time I was done, my rib was in agony. I looked in the mirror and traced the giant welt on my side; it was already starting to turn a horrid shade of purple. I'd avoided going to see Mrs. Nolan earlier in the day—and had surprisingly gotten away with it—but now I was regretting not getting pain medication. I raided some ibuprofen I found in the bathroom cabinet and prayed it would take the edge off.

I went back to Cea's room and took my tablet off the charger. The notifications informed me that Ephesus had added me as a contact and reminded me to ask Nic about the password.

I sat down on the edge of the bed and sent Nic a message.

DID YOU FIND ANY PASSCODES?

The response was instantaneous.

CALL ME

I rolled my eyes and did as I was told, starting an audio call.

"Where are you?" he barked.

I sighed. Nic wasn't one to start conversations with hello, but the least he could do was not yell at me. "At your parents' house."

"Good." A popup appeared prompting me to enable video.

I stared at the screen in surprise. *Why...?* I hit accept. My video flickered on, and I realized I was nowhere in frame. I tried to lean back against the headboard and managed to pinch my bruised side. A cry of pain left my lips before I could filter the sound.

"Did he hurt you?"

"Huh?" I managed as I blinked away the flashing colors.

"Carnegie. Did he hurt you?"

I started to say "I'm fine," then realized I was tired of saying that. "He kicked me in the ribs."

Nic didn't answer. I looked down to find him glaring at the camera. "Andromeda," he said finally.

I couldn't read his tone of voice, but he didn't sound happy. I glanced away as my cheeks began to burn again. "Look, can we not do this? I know what you're going to say... I should have come back to Mars with Cea."

"The door's still open."

I looked back down at the screen.

He sighed and leaned back in his desk chair. "What's the plan?"

I carefully propped a pillow against my injured side and settled against the headboard. "Andes thinks his people can do it. They've worked with this kind of preservation before. He says Dad might suffer some memory loss, but almost everything else is replaceable."

I tried not to dwell on the fact that Dad might end up like Nic's parents—or with a body frankensteined from parts not his own.

"How much is that going to cost?"

My head was aching too much for me to remember numbers. "I don't know—a lot."

"Do you need money?"

My face flushed again, this time for a completely different reason. I brushed past the comment. "I don't owe him anything until we get the tube unlocked. Did you find anything?" I shoved the ball back in his court and hoped he would do the talking for a while.

"Yes, I'm going to send you a list of all the passwords I could retrieve from the database." His finger danced across the screen as he swiped through menus in the background. "He left some personal devices here—I'll try searching those tomorrow. But I have to warn you that Carnegie was not the type to reuse passwords."

I acknowledged that with a groan. "Any better ideas?"

"None worth mentioning. But I do know that if it's possible to hack around it, your brother will figure it out."

I realized that was the best compliment Nic had ever paid my brother and smiled.

"When are you coming home?"

The question startled me. "You mean to Mars?"

He rubbed his forehead. "Do you have another permanent residence I'm not aware of?"

Do I have anywhere else to call home? It was a meta question I was definitely not capable of processing right now. "I... I don't know. I can't transport Dad while he's frozen."

"Actually you can," he grunted. "But regrettably, I don't know any revivalists on Mars."

The thought of packing everything up and running back to Mars was tempting, but I needed Andes's help. "I guess as soon as Dad's revived we'll come." *That's if Dad survives the process.*

"I'd recommend leaving as soon as he's viable, even if he's still in physical therapy. As long as he's stable enough to make the trip, we can fix the rest when you get here. I'd recommend you book separate flights—all of you are wanted by the law, and their files are shoddier than yours. If one of you trips a censor, you don't want all three of you to get caught..."

His words blurred together. I dropped the tablet on the bed and pinched my temples. He was asking me to make adult decisions about a reality I couldn't even fathom yet. I was exhausted and in pain and had a growing headache; I couldn't wrap my mind around tomorrow, let alone a few weeks from now.

It took me a minute to realize he'd stopped talking. "I'm sorry, Andi."

"What?" I mumbled, not caring that I wasn't in frame.

"I'm sorry about your father."

I let his tone of voice sink into me. "I know you are."

"Make sure you get at least eight hours of sleep and keep your calorie intake up. You should probably start doing some stretches and breathing exercises so you don't get a deflated lung..."

I groaned. Now he sounded like Mrs. Nolan. "Fine, I get it, Dad," I sassed, and then instantly regretted it. It was a cruel joke to make when my own father was dying in a block of ice.

What's gotten into you?

Nic didn't respond for a long moment. "Call me tomorrow night with an update."

It wasn't a suggestion. "Yessir," I promised.

There was another beat, and then he hung up.

I shoved my tablet aside and turned the lamp off. Gingerly, I slid under the covers, but it took me only seconds to realize that lying down was too painful. I nested myself in the pillows until I was partially propped up and marginally comfortable. The ibuprofen was working, sort of, at least enough that I could breathe without wincing.

I looked up at the darkened ceiling and suddenly realized that it was quiet—too quiet. I was alone, again, and I knew exactly what nightmares would await me as soon as I fell asleep.

My eyes started burning, but they were dry. I needed to cry, or pray, or something. Anything but this precarious waffling between life and death.

"Jesus, please... I need you."

I waited for the rush of peace that usually followed prayer, but it never came. I couldn't feel Him there, or anything at all. All I could sense was the block of grief that seemed to have permanently replaced the air in my lungs.

I tried again. "God, I'm sorry."

I know it's my fault.

"I'm so sorry... Please help me. I have to fix this."

Nothing changed. The silence was terrifying.

I fumbled for my tablet and turned it on, desperate for some noise. I took my device offline, then searched Nic's music archive until I found an old worship album. I could only hope the lyrics would fill the void where I could not.

I hit play and tossed my tablet towards the end of the bed. Pulling the blanket up to my chin, I closed my eyes and waited for darkness to come.

8

Mrs. Von almost didn't let me out the door in the morning.

"What time will you be home?" She stood in the middle of the entryway, arms crossed.

"Before dinner, I promise." I tried to sidle past her; Stanyard was already waiting for me.

Mrs. Von sidestepped to make my exit impossible. "I said what *time*."

I sighed. "Five o'clock."

She nodded curtly. "All right. And watch your attitude, young lady."

I swallowed. "Yes ma'am, sorry ma'am. I promise—it's just a school project."

She wasn't buying it, although whether that was because it was a bad lie or because I was a poor liar, I couldn't tell. "Well, make sure you keep your device on you. If you're a minute late, I'm calling you."

"Yes ma'am, I will." It was another lie. I wouldn't have my device on me; Jayde said I couldn't have any registered electronics on base. My tablet was up in Cea's room, charging; Ephesus had installed a program that would simulate innocuous activity all day.

I wasn't thrilled about leaving it behind; I felt naked walking out without my device, my too-light backpack slipping off my shoulders. But I knew it was safer this way. Besides, Mrs. Von wouldn't even know how to call me if she wanted to; I hadn't given her my number, not that she'd remember it if I did.

She finally stepped back and let me reach the door. I darted out onto the porch before she could change her mind. "I'll see you tonight!" I called with artificial cheerfulness.

She loomed in the doorway. "Who's that?" She jabbed her finger at Stanyard's car.

"A classmate," I answered, which was surprisingly not a lie.

Stanyard rolled down the window and waved. "Hi, Mrs. Von Nieuwenhuyse."

She did not return the greeting.

I slid into the passenger seat and quickly put the window up. "I have to be home by five, or she's calling CPS."

He chuckled as he pulled away from the curb. "They must really care about you."

I processed that. "Yeah, I guess you're right." *Thank you, Jesus.*

"Did you sleep okay?"

"Yeah," I fudged, and hoped I wasn't about to be interrogated. I'd gotten plenty of sleep; the problem was what I dreamed about while I was under. "And I swear I ate all my breakfast."

That seemed to satisfy his minimum requirements. He braked at the end of the street and twisted around to grab something out of the backseat. "I brought you something."

I turned to him and tried to figure out why the idea of him giving me gifts made me nervous.

He set a book in my lap.

A Bible.

A real, paper Bible. A muttered exclamation left my lips as I picked it up.

It was beautiful. It was black leather-bound, with a gold cross and the initials *EMH* embossed on the cover. It was in excellent condition, with only a little creasing on the spine and a trickle of water damage on the corner.

I looked up at him. "Where in the world did you get this?"

He grinned. "There's a black market for everything." He turned his eyes back to the road. "I knew you had to leave your tablet behind, and, well... I know how you get when you don't have your reader."

I flushed. There was no denying it, but I was surprised Stanyard had noticed. I'd never talked books with him, not even when we were children. That's what I had my girlfriend Cami and Stanyard's sister Mira for.

Unless Stanyard had been listening the whole time.

I pressed the book to my chest. "Thank you," I said, which seemed wholly inadequate to express my gratitude. I had a Bible again—and not only that, but a *physical* copy. I hadn't seen a paper Bible in years.

I opened it. According to the inscription, it had been gifted to someone's "Favorite Auntie" in the 2050s. Whoever the owner was had methodically filled the margins with penciled notes and multicolored highlighting. I fanned through the pages, breathing in the smell of aged paper and skimming the annotations filled with faith and hope.

I stopped when I came to Ephesians. The highlighting was heavier here, as if she'd been over the book multiple times. I settled on chapter one and started reading.

For our struggle is not against flesh and blood, but against the rulers, against the authorities, against the powers of this dark world...

I had finished the book and started Philippians before I realized I'd been reading in silence for the past twenty minutes, completely ignoring Stanyard. I glanced at him out of the corner of my eye and wondered if I should apologize.

He was watching the road, smiling.

Ephesus and Jayde met us as soon as we got in the building. Ephesus welcomed me with a hug. "You look better."

I felt better, probably because I'd just spent the last half-hour reading a physical Bible. "Any luck dumping the memory?"

He scratched his buzzed head. "It's called extracting the memory dump, and I hope so. I whipped up a program that should help, but I can't try it until the lockout releases here in a half hour."

"We should get on it," Stanyard said, and led the way towards the elevator.

I started to follow him. "I'm coming with you."

Ephesus stuck his arm out to stop me. "Oh no you're not. You're going to see Mrs. Nolan."

I grimaced. "I'm fine."

"I don't care. I got an earful this morning because you apparently never got checked out yesterday, and I'm not in the mood for another scolding. I promise I'll come get you if there's any progress."

"But—"

He ignored me and looked over my head at Jayde. "Make sure she gets there."

I turned to Jayde with a scowl I hoped was threatening. "Don't you dare."

He rubbed his neck and waited until Ephesus and Stanyard had disappeared in the elevator. "If you want... I could conveniently come up with new 'orders' for you. Despite what he thinks, I am in charge around here."

I let out my breath. "Please."

He jerked his head and led the way. I followed him to an elevator at the opposite end of the hall. We stepped in, and he called B3. According to the keypad, there were at least four subfloors beneath the ground level, making me wonder just how deep the building went.

"Where'd you get this building?" I asked as we descended.

"We acquired it when the company that used to own it went out of business. A benefactor 'bought them out,' and now we use all their infrastructure as a shell." He tapped the floor of the elevator, where the company's faded logo was printed on the scuffed linoleum.

I put the pieces together. "So the government thinks the company is still in operation?"

He nodded. "I have a dozen full-time people whose sole job it is to keep this place clean on paper."

The elevator dinged, and I followed him out into the hall. "How many people work for you?"

"I've got a troop of about a hundred that report directly to me, but there's several other lieutenants that work out of this building." As if reinforcing his statement, his phone beeped. He pulled it out of the pocket of his cargo pants and swiped through notifications.

I glanced around the dank hallway and tried to reconcile that information with what Cea and Stanyard had told me. "Stanyard said the underground was just an informal network of sympathizers."

"For him, it is." Jayde didn't look up from his device as he continued to walk and talk. "People like Stanyard and Andes are civilians. They have day jobs and help on their own terms. But for people like me and Lev, this is our life."

I recalled the day we'd met in Thames's office. "So when you hired yourself out to Thames…"

"Wasn't the first time I played double-agent, and it won't be the last." He pocketed his device and looked up at me. "Resistance isn't a hobby for me. And it shouldn't be for you either."

My skin prickled. "What?"

He didn't clarify. "We're here." He paused at a thick steel door and swiped his thumb on the keypad. He held the door open for me, and I reluctantly stepped inside.

Beyond was a cavernous room the size of a gymnasium. It was long and narrow and made entirely of concrete. The front of the room was sectioned into booths by steel dividers. At the far end, the floor and ceiling met in a sharp V, like the whole room was a funnel. Tracks ran the entire length of the ceiling, and from them hung targets of various sizes, all laced with bullet holes.

Suddenly, I knew where we were, and my stomach tried to cram itself up my throat.

Oh no, I can't—

"Here, put these in." Jayde dropped a pair of earbuds into my hand. They were so tiny and smooth that I feared they'd fall into my ear.

"Jayde, I don't—"

"Unless you want to go deaf, put them in." He popped his own pair in. "You'll still be able to hear me."

I shrugged my backpack off. With shaking hands, I slid the plugs into my ears and discovered he was right. I could no longer hear the echoing of our footsteps, which was incredibly disorienting, but his voice came through clearly.

"You need to learn to shoot." He pulled his pistol from his belt and pressed it into my hands.

I stared at the cold, heavy weapon and wondered if I'd rather go see Mrs. Nolan.

"Jayde, I don't know if I can—"

"Blue Fire," he snapped, and I flinched. "Stanyard and I aren't always going to be around to protect you. I can't have you out there on the streets unable to defend yourself."

The gun shook in my hands, and that's when I realized my whole body was trembling. *But I can't shoot people. I can't... kill.*

He studied me, and his voice softened. "Think of how differently things might have gone if you'd had a gun when you met Carnegie."

My throat clenched shut. He was right—I might have been able to save my dad had I been armed, or stronger, or more aware of my surroundings, or *something*, anything.

You could have prevented this.

I took a breath that sounded more like a gasp and wrapped my sweaty fingers around the gun. I pointed it straight ahead and cupped the hilt in my palm, just like I'd seen Cea and Stanyard do.

"First rule of gun safety—don't point unless you're prepared to shoot." Jayde pushed the barrel of the pistol down with his finger. "Point down."

"Right, sorry," I mumbled. My voice sounded disembodied through the earbuds, like I was having an out-of-body experience.

He spun me around to face the range. "For now, just practice shooting in the right direction. Aim for the slit in the bullet trap." He pointed at the funnel at the end of the room.

I nodded and stationed myself in one of the booths.

"Feet apart and put your right foot slightly back."

I obeyed, my sneakers sliding on the floor.

"Bend your knees and lean forward slightly." He demonstrated.

I tried to mimic him, but I felt clumsy and unstable. My knees were still shaking, and I looked more like a newborn calf than a fighter.

"Both hands on the hilt. Keep your finger off the trigger until you're ready."

I'll never be ready. I gripped the hilt, but the metal felt cold and slippery in my hands.

I can't do this.

"Remember, shoot for the wall." He took a step back. "Ready, aim, fire."

I didn't move my finger. "Are these real bullets?"

He arched an eyebrow. "I said *fire*."

Oh God, help, I prayed, and squeezed the trigger.

I could barely hear the explosion, but the recoil sent shockwaves through my arm. I dropped the gun and stumbled back, yelling when my bruised side protested.

You shouldn't be doing this.

Jayde retrieved the gun and put it back in my hands. "Again."

"Jayde, I—"

"Again."

I winced and put myself in position. I tried to brace myself physically and emotionally, but it didn't soften the blow. I didn't drop the gun this time, but my rib absorbed the brunt of the force. I bit down on my tongue to keep from gasping. My eyes started to water as I forced myself to do it again and again. It was a good thing I wasn't trying to hit a particular target.

The muffled explosions echoed in my ears, and I tried not to think about the fact that each bullet fired could have ended a life.

It's fine, it's just a wall, no one's getting hurt...

I expended the bullets in the chamber and handed the gun back to Jayde. *There, you happy?*

He pulled a fresh clip from his belt, snapped it in the weapon, and held it out.

I groaned. My fingers were cramped, and I was sweating profusely. My ears rang in tune with my headache.

He wiggled the hilt. "You want to do this? You have to learn to be like us."

I took a step back. "But I don't want to do this. I'm not like you."

He grabbed my wrist and shoved the gun into my palm. "You will be."

I opened my mouth to argue, but a slamming door interrupted me. "What in the world are you doing?"

I turned. Mrs. Nolan stood in the doorway. "You should not be shooting."

For once, I completely agreed with her.

Jayde was undeterred. "She needs to learn."

"Not while she's got a bruised rib she doesn't." She dropped her medical bag on the floor.

I eagerly let go of the gun and backed away. Jayde's jaw tensed, but Mrs. Nolan cut him off before he could formulate words. "No. She needs to rest. Now you get out of my way and let me do my job, or I'm taking her home right now."

Jayde sized her up and wisely decided not to pick a fight. "Fine. You'll practice more tomorrow." He glared at me, as if I had any say in what was going on.

"She'll practice when I say she's well enough to practice."

Jayde didn't acknowledge the comment. He holstered his gun and strode out of the room.

Mrs. Nolan waited until his footsteps faded down the hall before she turned her frown on me. "You were supposed to come see me yesterday."

I put on a brave face as I took the earbuds out and put them in my pocket. "I felt fine."

"I can tell by the pace of your breathing that that's not true."

I made a concentrated effort to take a slow, deep breath. "I just pushed myself too hard, that's all."

That wasn't a lie, but she didn't buy it. "I need to make sure nothing's fractured." She bent and unzipped her medical bag.

I was pretty confident nothing was fractured; it didn't hurt *that* badly. "It's just a bruise, I checked. It'll heal on its own in a few days."

"Just let me scan you to be safe." She produced a small med scanner from her bag. It looked like an oversized digital thermometer with a bulky display. "The last thing you need is a punctured lung. Now come here."

She held out her hand. I took a step back.

"Andromeda," she said in the same tone of voice one might use with a toddler. "What is wrong with you? You were never like this before. You used to be such a polite girl."

My blood boiled. "Yeah, well, a lot has happened since we last met."

She let all her frustrations out in a sigh. "Andromeda, I'm only trying to help you."

"That's exactly what your husband said," I snapped.

She winced, and I almost took it back. *No—I'm tired of lying about how I feel.* If she wanted the truth, she was going to get it.

I straightened and found my courage. "You've never done anything to help me. You've been lying to me and using me, and you've never once cared about how I felt."

She didn't deny it. She tipped her chin back and waited.

"You kidnapped me to use as blackmail to make my father work for you. When that didn't work, you sent me to Rott." The horrid memories of the burning factory and scalding acid rain washed over me, and my voice wobbled. "How was that 'for my own good'? I almost *died.*"

"You were supposed to," she whispered.

I froze and looked at her.

She dropped the med scanner back in her bag. "Philadelphia was supposed to die on Rott. You were supposed to have an untimely 'accident' so you could come back as Andromeda."

It all made sense—horrid, ugly sense. I let the bitterness and pain bleed into my voice. "Right, so you could 'adopt' me and take me from my father."

There was a pause—too long. "He never told you, did he?"

Ice rippled up my arms. "He who? Told me what?"

She shook her head. "Thames. He never told you about your father."

"What about my father?"

Oh God, not again.

To her credit, her eyes looked wistful and sad as she relayed, "Your father knew about the whole thing. He agreed to work on Red Rain in exchange for us giving you a new life."

My pounding heartbeat echoed in the concrete room like a bullet ricocheting off the walls.

"We didn't 'take' you, Andromeda," Mrs. Nolan said. "Your father gave you up."

9

"You're lying!" I screeched, and desperately needed it to be true.

But I knew that it wasn't. I remembered my father's indifference, his dry eyes, his cold willingness to let me get shipped away to Rott, and I recognized what I should have seen all along.

My father knew exactly what was going on. He knew what he had done—what he had done to me.

Just go.

"I have the paperwork," Mrs. Nolan said.

Tears raged down my face. "Well, thank God my paperwork now says something else." I'd never been more grateful that Nic had agreed to be Andromeda's guardian; anything to keep this woman from having legal power over me. I swiped at my eyes and ran for the door.

She let me go, but she called after me. "You can't keep running from this, Andromeda."

I threw the door open. *Yes, I can.*

"You can't keep running from me."

I hesitated in the doorway and glared back at her. She stood there, arms wide. "We're family now."

I slammed the door shut again. "So that's it? You want me to just say 'I forgive you,' and we walk out of here as mother and daughter?"

Her eyes glittered with tears. "I would love that."

My gut hurled. *You will never be my mother.*

She spoke before I could formulate words. "But I know it can't be that way."

She took a deep breath and sponged her eyes with the back of her hand. "Things weren't supposed to be this way. You were never supposed to go to Mars. You were supposed to come home, become Andromeda, and start over. My husband was going to wait until things calmed down and then give your father and brother new jobs. You were even going to be able to visit them." She blinked away the last of her tears and looked at me. "We never intended to keep you from your father. You must believe me when I say that."

I did believe her, and that scared me.

I should have listened to Mrs. Nolan and insisted you stay on Earth. None of this would have happened if you hadn't gone to Mars.

"But after you released the virus, Carnegie wanted to use you as a scapegoat—and as bait to find your father."

Her choice of words startled me. "So you *did* know exactly what you were doing," I accused, and waited for her to defend herself.

She didn't. "Yes, we did."

For the first time since we'd met, I felt validated and understood—and a tiny bit less afraid.

My heart rate began to slow even as my mind sped up. "But that doesn't make it any better. You—Thames—could have prevented all of this. He could have told Carnegie no."

"I know," she admitted, "and he should have. That's why I know things can never be the same between us."

She released her breath, and her whole body seemed to sag. "I know you suffered terrible things up there. You were mistreated, and you've had to fight for yourself and make horrible decisions no young woman should ever have to make—all because of what my husband did to you. As soon as they released that first video, I knew your life was ruined, and I'd never get to bring my Andromeda home."

Her tears returned, and they seemed genuine. I let her weep silently and struggled to decide how to think, how to feel.

"What do you want from me?" I whispered.

She looked up through her veil of tears, not bothering to wipe them away this time. "I want you to let me help you."

I shook my head. "You can't—"

She put up her hand. "No, it's your turn to listen. You don't know me, Andromeda. You don't know how I feel or why I did what I did. And while I don't expect you to understand, I need you to know that I did it because I genuinely wanted to help you."

Every muscle in my body tensed, but the Holy Spirit brushed by my ear with a warning.

Wait.

Mrs. Nolan coughed. Her voice came through clear and unashamed as she explained. "I know you see me as a predator, but when I first met you, what I saw was a poor young girl who was growing up in prison. I saw a girl who had to live in poverty and go to school at *gunpoint* because someone with power hated her religion."

The obvious implication hit me. "And you *don't* hate my religion?"

She glared at me. "Since when have I ever implied that I hate your religion?"

I scrolled back through our conversations and realized that the Nolans had never once tried to get me to deny Christ. They'd never even asked me to sign the file, at least not directly.

Come with me, Philadelphia, and you can keep your Bible in peace.

"But why?"

She regarded me with a lifetime of sadness. "Do I need a reason not to hate you?"

Everyone else does.

She spread her hands. "You won't believe me when I say it's because I love you, but I do. I knew your father wasn't coming back from Mars, and I knew that if you stayed behind, Ambrose would place you with a family whose sole job it was to bully you out of your identity. And if that failed and you aged out of the system, you'd get thrown back in prison to be tried as an adult. Do you know how that makes me feel as a mother?"

Her eyes wandered the shooting range as she measured her next words. "To me, it was no different than adopting any other orphan. I had the money and privilege to give you what others could not: a clean file. I believed—knew— that you'd be better off with me than on your own."

I might have accepted that explanation, if it weren't for one fatal flaw in her logic. "But I wasn't an orphan."

She didn't sugarcoat it. "You soon would have been."

"But you had the power to change that." My eyes burned with the pain of a reality she still refused to see. "Thames was controlling the whole thing. He could have saved my dad. He could have kept us together. The only reason I needed to be adopted was because of the things *he* did. How can you expect me to believe that's love?"

"I'm not asking you to."

I threw my hands out. "Then what are you asking?"

She met my eyes. "I'm asking you not to hate me."

I stared back.

Get rid of all bitterness, rage and anger...

She shook her head. "Andromeda, you're the one that's trying to reconcile your beliefs with mine. I'm not asking you to justify me. I'm not asking you to agree with me. I did what I thought was right, and you did what you thought was right, and I don't expect us to ever see eye to eye on it."

...brawling and slander, along with every form of malice....

"I hope we can be friends," she continued, her voice strained under the weight of regret, "but if we can't, I understand. But don't refuse medical help because you hate me. Don't walk around with a fractured rib just because you're mad at me."

Be kind and compassionate to one another...

She retrieved the scanner from her bag. She turned it on and extended her hand one more time. "Let me help you."

...forgiving each other, just as in Christ God forgave you.

I took a step towards her.

She didn't smile, but something flickered across the back of her eyes. "Let me see."

I gingerly lifted my shirt to reveal the bruise that was spreading across my side.

She toggled the settings on the scanner, then knelt next to me so she was eye-level with my wound. "Take a deep breath and hold it for ten seconds."

I obeyed. She panned the device slowly over my ribs, brow furrowed as she focused on the readouts.

"All right, you can let it out." She fiddled with the device for a minute, then put it back in her bag. She retrieved a wireless stethoscope and put on the earpiece. "Take three slow breaths for me."

I put my shirt back down and focused on taking deep, long breaths. She stood in front of me and moved the stethoscope around my chest. Then she stepped back and pulled the earpiece out.

"Well, you're right—it's not fractured, and your lungs sound good. But I want you to do some breathing exercises so you don't get in the habit of breathing shallowly. That will lead to even worse problems."

"Yes ma'am."

She took out her phone and started typing. "I'll send the instructions to your tablet—you can do it when you get home. Feel free to ice frequently, and you might try sleeping partially upright for the next few nights."

"Okay. Do you have any pain medication?"

That time, she smiled. "Yes, I do. I'll send some over when I get back to the infirmary."

"Thank you." I hesitated—feeling, wondering if there was more to say. "I'll bring your hoodie back tomorrow."

"What hoodie?" she said without looking up from her phone.

"The gray one you loaned me yesterday. I'm washing it."

She shrugged. "Wasn't mine."

Then whose is it?

I waited for a second more. When I realized neither of us was going to say anything else, I picked up my backpack and let myself out.

"Andromeda," she called as I stepped out into the hall, "no more shooting until I say so."

I glanced back. "Doctor's orders?"

She winked. "Doctor's orders."

I smiled, thanked her again, and left.

10

The shred of peace I'd managed to scrape together evaporated when I walked into the lab and saw Ephesus with his head in his hand, muttering.

He sat next to Dad. I glanced around the room; Stanyard was nowhere to be seen. I rapped my knuckles on the doorframe. "Ephesus?"

He broke off and looked up at me with bloodshot eyes. "Hey, sis. Sorry, just talking to Dad."

I wanted to ask him what he'd said, but somehow I felt that his grief was not mine to share. He was an innocent victim; none of this was his fault.

"Any luck with the memory dump?"

He gestured at an empty chair; I dragged it over and sat down next to him.

"No," he admitted. "This OS is completely foreign to me. And since it's a proprietary—and potentially lethal—device, Kaylon hasn't exactly been generous with publishing its code on the web." He paused. "But I'll keep trying," he added, more to himself than to me.

The last sentence held absolutely no hope at all, so I didn't bother to acknowledge it. "Did you try the passcodes Nic sent?"

He nodded. "All of them. No luck. Stanyard's program is trying a randomized password every five minutes."

I didn't need him to tell me how futile an effort that was. *What do we do now, Jesus?*

"Did you go see Mrs. Nolan?" Ephesus's voice was starched with cheerfulness.

"She found me, yeah," I said, and didn't elaborate, even after he questioned me with a raised eyebrow. "She says nothing's fractured and my lungs sound fine."

"Good." He sighed and leaned back in the chair, his eyes on Dad's.

I watched him. "Why are you and Mrs. Nolan..." I backpedaled when I realized how accusatory that question sounded. "How did you find her?"

"She was treating me while I was sitting in jail, waiting for Thames to decide what to do with me." He tapped the bandage on his nose. "She brought me info on Dad and Cea."

That matched what Cea had told me, but it didn't explain how Mrs. Nolan had been promoted from prison nurse to friend. "Why is she here?"

He turned to me. "She helped me escape. When you released that virus on Rott, it sent Thames's headquarters into a panic, and Mrs. Nolan helped me slip out. She hid me at one of their rental properties while we tried to figure out what happened with Dad and Cea—but they both dropped off the grid."

"Cea was looking for you." With a laugh that wasn't quite happy, I remembered the message I was supposed to pass along. "She wanted me to tell you that she loves you."

A smile slowly warmed his features. "What inflection did she put on that?"

"What inflection do you *want* me to put on that?" I said, eying him.

He dodged the question. "When did she leave for Mars?"

I fumed playfully at him, but the only response I got was a wink. With a grunt to express my displeasure, I answered, "Wednesday."

"She should land tomorrow or Sunday then—I'll call her."

Seeing I wasn't going to get any more romantic gossip out of him, I circled the conversation back around. "So you've been at the Nolans' apartment this whole time?"

He shook his head. "No, when the government busted Thames's office, we both dropped off the grid. I saw your livestream and knew Thames was dead, and she'd be next. So I convinced her to come with me, and we..."

He kept talking, but his words were lost in the torrent of emotion that rushed through me. Mrs. Nolan was a widow. I knew that, of course—I was there when it happened.

Ephesus touched my shoulder. "You did the right thing, turning Thames in," he said, as if reading my thoughts.

"I know." There was no room in my cluttered subconscious for guilt or regret over Thames's death. But I had never stopped to acknowledge that Mrs. Nolan had lost a loved one, too—and unlike my father, there was no hope that Thames could come back.

"Any luck?"

I started and looked behind me. Jayde stood in the doorway.

Ephesus straightened. "No. Kaylon's code is completely proprietary, and none of my backdoors work."

"Did you try the passcodes from Q?"

Ephesus shook his head. "Nothing."

Jayde grunted.

"Nic will send me more tomorrow," I offered. "He said he was going to search Carnegie's personal devices…"

I tripped over the word. Both boys looked at me. I grabbed Ephesus's arm. "Carnegie's phone."

He wasn't impressed. "Huh?"

"Carnegie—surely he had a phone on him when he died. Did you search the room when you went back for Dad? Can we still get into that building?" I swiveled to face Jayde.

He shrugged. "I can send some guys, but I'm sure his allies have razed the place—if the cops didn't get there first. But we can try searching his phone again."

"Again?" I asked, and suddenly realized I probably didn't want the answer.

He raised an eyebrow, as if my incompetence amused him. "We've got his body in the morgue."

*

There he was, lying on a slab, looking only slightly paler in death than he had in life.

I'm not sure why I wanted to see him. My subconscious did not need any more morbid images to warp into nightmares. Perhaps I just wanted to reassure myself that he was one figment of my past who wouldn't be coming back to haunt me.

I nodded at Jayde, who pulled the sheet back over Carnegie's face. Ephesus muttered something under his breath.

Stanyard and Lev had joined us in the morgue—although "morgue" was a luxurious term for what was clearly a storeroom that had been retrofitted with tables and a walk-in freezer. I didn't ask if the freezer had been repurposed, or if it had been specially installed for storing bodies.

"Why do you have him in here?" I asked.

Jayde wheeled the gurney towards the freezer. "I figured if we cleaned up the evidence, it would give his allies a bit of a chase."

"Although I'm sure they've figured out he's gone dark by now." Lev dragged the freezer door open; I deftly avoided looking inside.

"Here's his personal effects." Stanyard dropped a box on an empty exam table.

I walked over, Ephesus a step behind me, and scanned the contents. There wasn't much: a keyfob, an expensive pen that looked like it was more for show than for writing, and two phones.

"We've got his car out back." Stanyard picked up the keyfob. "But it's empty except for a carjack and some cold coffee."

I took the phones out of the box. One was shiny, slim, and new. The other was old, chunky, and scratched—not unlike the early 2000s touchscreens we used as burners.

I glanced at Jayde. "Can I turn them on?"

He nodded. "Yeah, I took both of them offline and disabled the passcodes."

Ephesus picked up the newer device and frowned at it. "How'd you do that? Wasn't this thing locked?"

Jayde arched his eyebrow, a gesture I was quickly learning to loathe. "It's not like I don't have Carnegie's thumbprint."

Stanyard pulled a face that perfectly represented the disgust that shivered through my stomach.

Ephesus powered the phone on. I picked up the older device and did the same.

Jayde leaned his knuckles on the table. "We searched them once already and didn't find anything—but at the time I didn't know we were looking for a passcode."

Ephesus rapidly swiped through menus on the newer device. The old phone was still stuck on the loading screen.

After a minute, Ephesus shook his head and handed the new phone to me. "He had all his apps set to auto-purge data every twenty-four hours. Taking the device offline seems to have stopped the last purge, but there's almost nothing there."

Stanyard drummed his fingers on his arm. "It's like he was expecting to get caught."

"Smart man," Lev muttered.

I clicked on the texting app and saw that Ephesus was right. There were only a handful of active conversations, all dated from Wednesday. None of the numbers were associated with named contacts, but the meaning of the messages was obvious.

WE'VE GOT THE BUILDING SURROUNDED

SHE JUST RADIOED FOR BACKUP. EXITING VIA BOYLSTON. HER FRIENDS ARE WAITING

LET THEM GET THERE FIRST. IF YOU HAVE A CLEAR SHOT, TAKE IT

I clenched my hand around the device.

CONFIRMED, HE'S MAKING THE DROP TONIGHT, BEFORE 21:00

ARE YOU IN PLACE?

WE ARE

My forehead grew clammy at the same time my cheeks grew hot. *You led me right to him.*

MACHINE IS INSTALLED AND WARMING UP. WILL BE READY TO FREEZE IN THREE HOURS. WILL EMAIL THE INVOICE

WE'VE GOT HIM. HE'S OUT, BUT NOT FOR LONG

I SAID YOU DIDN'T HAVE TO BE GENTLE

I pinched my eyes shut to keep the tears from escaping. *Daddy, I'm so sorry.*

There was one more conversation. It was between Carnegie and a foreign area code.

WHEN SHOULD I EXPECT DELIVERY?

SHOULD BE READY BY 22:30

The recipient hadn't acknowledged the text. They didn't reply until after eleven o'clock—late enough that Carnegie was long dead.

Apparently, the recipient was aware of that fact.

YOU FOOL

I turned the screen off.

"I can hook it up to my computer, run some diagnostics," Stanyard offered.

"Please," I said, and handed the device to him. I picked up the older phone, which had finally decided to come to work.

"That's just a burner," Lev offered. "There's nothing on there."

I opened the most recent text and instantly knew whose phone it was.

THIRD FLOOR. HURRY

Dad.

A quick skim of the chat history showed that he had, in fact, confirmed an appointment with Andes. Then there was silence except for my frantic messages to him. Carnegie must have taken the phone from his unconscious body and sent me the address.

I sucked in my breath.

You should have stayed on Mars, sweetheart.

"What is it, Phil?" Ephesus said from over my shoulder.

I quickly closed the chat. "Nothing. It's just a burner, like he said."

Jayde's eyebrows went up again. Ephesus, thankfully, didn't notice. He turned to Stanyard and started rambling about the various programs they could run on Carnegie's phone.

I angled myself away from him and opened the app again.

I scrolled to the bottom. Unlike Carnegie, Dad hadn't wiped his message history—probably because most of his messages had gone unanswered. Most of the texts appeared to be cold calls, asking if the number still belonged to a friend or if he could claim a long-expired IOU.

THIS IS CATALYST. I'M WONDERING IF I CAN COLLECT THAT FAVOR

Most of the texts didn't receive a reply. Several numbers were undeliverable. Of the few who did answer, most of them quickly fizzled into dead ends.

IT'S GOOD TO HEAR FROM YOU, BUT I'M NOT IN BUSINESS ANYMORE

CAN YOU AT LEAST TELL ME IF THERE'S BEEN ANY UPDATES ON HER FILE?

SORRY MAN, I CAN'T HELP YOU

The text history did tell me one thing: Dad had a large network, even if most of it had gone cold. Where had he gotten all these numbers? He'd texted dozens of people, which meant he'd either had their numbers memorized or knew where to look them up. How did he know so many people? I couldn't recall him ever mentioning having allies, let alone friends. We'd always been alone in the world; Dad used to warn me that there was no one outside the containment camp walls we could rely on.

That was, apparently, another lie. He had known these people once—and some, it seemed, still knew him.

IS THIS STILL BART'S NUMBER?

I WAS WONDERING HOW LONG IT WOULD TAKE YOU TO CALL

I pondered the message, which Dad had never answered, as Jayde's words from yesterday came floating back to me.

Your dad isn't who he says he is.

I jumped to the most recent conversations—the ones that had gotten replies.

IT'S GOOD TO HAVE YOU BACK, CATALYST

I'M NOT BACK, I JUST NEED A FAVOR

BUT WE NEED YOU

I'M JUST TRYING TO FIND BLUE FIRE

WE NEED HER TOO

I gripped the phone. Dad hadn't acknowledged the message, but the stranger hadn't given up, sending several more texts in short succession.

IT'S TIME TO COME BACK

YOU NEVER SHOULD HAVE QUIT

WE CAN STILL DO THIS

He's done this before.

IT'S TIME FOR OPERATION BLUE FIRE TO RETURN

I dropped the phone. It clattered on the metal exam table, sound like gunfire in the silent room.
Ephesus and Stanyard stopped and turned around.
I looked up. Jayde was staring at me, waiting.
I grabbed the edge of the table. "What's Operation Blue Fire?"
He straightened and gestured at the door. "Come and see."

11

The command center was both dank and blinding at the same time.

The overhead lights were off, as if they were trying to hide in the dark, even though there were no windows in the cavernous place. The temperature was at least ten degrees colder than the hall as the air conditioning fought to keep the blinking wall of servers cool. The chill, combined with the incessant whir of electronics that thrummed like a plague of locusts, made the place seem claustrophobic, even though it took up the entire top floor of the building.

But despite the fact that the corners were enshrouded in shadow, the center of the room was drowning in irritating blue light from hundreds of backlit screens. Dozens of computer stations were scattered around the room, and a circular command module dominated the open floor. At hand-height was a ring of control panels and touchpads, its buttons and levers glittering like a diamond necklace. Above it hung a seamless jumbotron. Random inputs flickered across it constantly like an overactive heart monitor, adding to the anxious chaos.

"It's smaller on the outside," Stanyard muttered from behind me.

There were about twenty people, most in military fatigue, working around the room. Jayde stepped in ahead of us and clapped his hands. "Captain on the bridge!"

Everyone stopped and stood at attention, a fluid motion honed by discipline. The man standing nearest to us—an officer, judging by the number of pins and bars on his uniform—turned and spotted me.

"Blue Fire," he acknowledged, and saluted.

Around the room, everyone else followed suit.

I clenched my fists. "Don't call me that." I felt angry, but my voice just came out small and weak. Scared.

The officer turned to Jayde with a confused frown. Jayde jerked his thumb towards the door. "Clear the room."

They obeyed. Stanyard, Ephesus, and I stepped out of the way to let them pass. I felt all eyes on me as they walked by, even though I stubbornly avoided returning any of their stares.

As soon as the room was empty except for Lev, I turned to Jayde. "Can't you tell them not to call me that? We're not on the radio."

He shrugged. "It's who you are to them." He turned his back on me and walked over to the command module. He swiped on a touchpad, and a video I knew all too well started playing on the monitors: the security footage from Rott.

He gestured at the screen. "As soon as this video started trending, you became Blue Fire."

"I don't understand," I said, and frankly, I didn't want to.

"I was in the room with Thames when you and Q blew up the factory on Rott. I saw the livestream of the security footage at the same time he did—and managed to rip it before he classified it." He looked at me and waited to see if I understood the implications.

I did. "You're the one who leaked the video."

He nodded. "Stanyard and I uploaded it to our social media."

I glanced back at Stanyard. He did not avoid my gaze. "We—I—thought you were dead. I wanted the world to know why."

I studied him, trying to gauge his emotions, but Jayde wasn't interested in letting us have a moment. "We weren't the only ones. We spammed our contacts, and they repeated the process. You were an instant phenomenon."

I knew that; I'd seen the views on some of my videos. What I didn't know was that my fame had been manufactured by the underground.

Ephesus was tracking the same thoughts. "Surely Thames helped promote her," he argued.

Jayde shrugged. "Maybe, but we could have done it without him. Everyone loved you." He turned to me again. "I had contacts I hadn't heard from in years asking me how they could help. That's when I knew you were the new Blue Fire."

Stanyard made a noise that could best be described as a growl. "You told me you made up that callsign—"

I put up a hand to stop him. "'New' Blue Fire?" I repeated, my eyes on Jayde.

He didn't make me wait. "Your father was the first."

I wanted to deny it. I wanted to scream that he was lying and slam the door in his face, just like I'd done with Mrs. Nolan, and Thames, and Carnegie, and everyone else who had come before him. They had all lied to me. Everyone had—including Daddy.

But somehow I knew that Jayde wasn't. For the first time in my life, someone was telling me the honest truth, and it was terrifying.

"Dad?" Ephesus breathed.

Jayde toggled more menus, and Dad's file appeared on the screen. "Your father has been transmitting Bibles since high school. He and several others built a network of people willing to share censored media across the globe. They called it Operation Blue Fire."

That wasn't entirely news to me, although I'd never heard it spelled out in so many words. I knew Dad was a transmitter, and always had been, but I thought he only did it for friends and local contacts through his job. He had done more when he was younger, but that was before I was born—before Grandpa Andrew had gotten convicted for transmitting.

I had no idea he'd built an international network around it.

It's good to have you back, Catalyst.

"Anyone who knew the symbol could get a download." Jayde scrolled down, but I knew what I was going to see before the image even loaded: that haunting bird with a lightning bolt in its claws.

"A thunderbird," Lev answered my unspoken question.

There it was, on my father's file, the same image that Cea and Andes had. Were they both part of the same transmitting network? Had they worked with my father? Surely Cea would have mentioned it if she knew my father was involved.

I glanced at Ephesus to see if the image meant anything to him, but he was squinting at the screen, looking as pale and lost as I felt. Clearly, Dad had lied to both of us.

I shoved the queasy emotion aside. "But what does this have to do with me and my videos?" I'd transmitted a few Bibles in my lifetime, but it certainly wasn't what I was known for.

"Your father wasn't just transmitting any Bibles." Jayde clicked a button and entered a passcode, and my father's file, which was already long and peppered with warnings, doubled in length and lit up like a firework. "After you were taken into camp, they developed a plan to use censored media to spread coded information. The Bibles would be edited to include hidden messages and then distributed on the network. The theory was that if the government found illegal Bibles, they'd just delete them, never realizing they contained classified plans."

"Clever," Ephesus murmured, and he sounded sincere. I couldn't decide if that idea was sacrilegious or brilliant. It was at least a little more practical than scorching Earth with chemical warfare.

I took a deep breath and braced myself for the drop. "And what exactly were these plans for?"

Lev was the first to answer. "Revolution," he said, his Russian accent slurring the word into something thick and sinister.

Ephesus went completely still, as if he'd died standing up. Stanyard sucked his breath in sharply through his nose. All eyes turned to me and waited, as if expecting me to have a reaction.

I didn't know what to say.

Lev walked over to the other side of the control module and started typing. A map of the East Coast engulfed the screen, the topography muddied by dozens of crosses, lines, and coordinates written in bloodred. "The unassimilated camps made everyone angry—they were ready to act. So we came up with a plan to liberate the camps and end them for good."

Ephesus and I shared an involuntary look. *End the camps?* I'd never dreamed that was possible. I couldn't even imagine a world without religious persecution, a world where my identity wasn't illegal and shunned.

Could freedom like that be possible?

Stanyard jumped to the obvious conclusion. "What went wrong?"

"Catalyst dropped out," Jayde said, the bitterness unveiled in his voice. For a brief moment, the light went out of his eyes as he turned his glare on me.

You never should have quit.

I held his stare. "Why?"

Compassion rushed back into his expression as he whispered, "Your mother."

My face and hands grew numb as everything snapped into place. The lies, the blood splatter in the entryway, the police report on my father's file. All the deception to cover up the real reason my mother had died.

Ephesus moaned. "Oh, Mom…"

Jayde tapped the screen, and a crackly audio recording started playing. I walked up next to him to listen, even though I couldn't remember willing my feet to move.

There was a shower of static, and then the recording began in the middle of someone's sentence.

"—happened? I saw the call go out for an ambulance to your area, but no one could tell me anything. I was so—"

The person abruptly silenced. My mind strained at the voice; I'd heard it before, somewhere. "Do you recognize him?" I asked Ephesus.

His face was pinched in confused agony. "I—I'm not sure."

My dad was the next to speak, the heartbreak obscuring his words more than static ever could. *"Blue Fire is down."*

"Mom," Ephesus whispered.

I glanced at him.

"It was Mom's childhood nickname," he whispered, as if he were afraid to admit that it was true.

"Your father named the operation after her," Jayde echoed. "In honor of the Bibles she transmitted in high school."

The room swam as tears flooded my eyes. I pinched them shut and listened.

The other caller continued sputtering. *"Down? What do you mean? What happened? Is she okay? What hospital did they take her to? I'll see if I can—"*

"Tower! She's dead," my dad yelled, and my world stopped.

My eyes flew open. "Dad knew Tower?"

Jayde paused the recording. "They were in charge of the whole thing."

Stanyard stepped up beside me. "How do you know him?"

"He was a guard on Rott. He helped us destroy the factory." I replayed all our interactions in my mind and tried to sift out any signs of familiarity. He had been kind, of course, and willing to help, but he hadn't acted like he knew me. Did he not realize who I was, who my father was?

Lev and Jayde shared a glance, then Jayde hit play.

My father's voice came in again. *"They knew we were planning something. They came for the drive."*

I remembered the incident report on my father's file.

Police had been dispatched with a warrant to arrest Dr. Thomas Smyrna for the charges of transmitting illegal media...

Suddenly, Jayde's voice joined the recording. *"What did you do with it?"*

"I crushed it, just like I was supposed to," my father snapped, rage replacing the grief in his voice. *"And in the process my wife got shot."*

I slapped a hand over my mouth. Ephesus muttered an oath.

Dr. Smyrna resisted arrest. Officers drew weapons in an attempt to subdue him, and Abigail Smyrna was unintentionally shot...

Jayde had apparently wasted no time on grief that day. His recording was quick to demand, *"Yeah, and the rest of us would have too if you—"*

"Green Dragon, get off the line!" a stranger mercifully silenced him. I turned to Jayde. He was staring at the screen, face expressionless.

Tower continued. *"Catalyst, we need to get you out of there. I can arrange a pickup, tonight, 1900."*

"Belay that, Tower," Dad snapped. *"I'm fine. They can't prove anything. Don't come for me. Stay out of this."*

Tower was undeterred. *"No, I'm serious, I'm coming to get you. I'm tired of playing this game from the other side of the wall. I'm taking you both to safety, and then you're done."*

My heart skipped a beat. "You both" could have only meant Dad and me; Ephesus had been away at college at the time. Tower had been willing to come save us.

Dad's response was quick and panicked. *"Tower, no! Don't come for us, and don't try anything. That's an order."*

"Don't boss me around, old man. I—"

"Don't you get it?" Dad's shriek cracked the line. *"They know what we're doing. They're probably listening right now. If I try anything, my daughter goes into the system."*

I gasped. All eyes were on me again.

Ephesus touched my shoulder.

Tower's response was crushed with remorse. *"She's already in the system."*

"Yeah, well at least she's alive," Dad hissed.

I felt sick as the weight of the world dropped to my stomach.

Stay here. We're waiting for the officers to arrive.

"Catalyst, please," Tower begged. *"I promise I can do this safely. Let me come get you."*

"No," Dad snapped in a tone I knew all too well. *"Operation Blue Fire is over. We're not going anywhere."*

I'm not letting either of you get hurt anymore.

Jayde switched off the recording. I closed my eyes and willed the room—and everyone in it—to vanish.

Daddy, why did you lie to me?

Ephesus kneaded my shoulder, but his fingers felt cold and clammy. Stanyard was the first to speak. "Phil," he breathed. "I'm so sorry."

I drew an ugly sniff and tried to dam the tears back where they came from. I turned to Jayde. "What do you want with me?"

He spread his hands. "We need you to be the new Blue Fire."

I groaned. "What does that even mean? I still don't understand what any of this has to do with me," I said, even though it very clearly had *everything* to do with me. My father started all this—but that was in the past. That was before Mama died.

Now, I just wanted this conversation to be over.

"Why her?" Ephesus demanded, but not skeptically.

"Your videos made people angry," Jayde explained, all his focus still on me. "They're paying attention again. They'll act—if we give them a reason to. And you're that reason."

Only because you manufactured me into an idol.

"Operation Blue Fire is ready to launch," Lev echoed. "And you need to take your father's place."

I didn't appreciate his choice of words or the tone he used to say them. "Well, then you've got the wrong girl," I snapped. If they wanted a leader, they should have picked Ephesus. He'd done this before; he knew people in the underground.

I didn't know anything. I didn't belong here. I should be on Mars, keeping my head down, just like Nic told me to.

I brushed at the tears on my cheeks, even though more quickly fell to replace them. "I'm not my father. I don't know how to transmit, not like that. I don't have any contacts."

"You don't need them," Jayde said. "You're enough."

He put my video back on the screen and let it play. "People respect you, Blue Fire—they understand you. You're not some fancy hot shot with privilege and power who can buy your way out of trouble. At least Philadelphia isn't. She's a normal girl from the bottom of the food chain. An unassimilated. A nobody. A nobody who should be *dead.*"

He fast-forwarded to the part of the recording where the platform snapped, flinging me out of frame to my apparent demise.

"But you're not." He switched to another recording, the one I had strictly avoided rewatching.

"Their contact is a government agent named Thames. He has an office somewhere in the Boston metropolitan area..."

I pinched my eyes shut, knowing what was coming. Stanyard moved beside me. "Jayde..."

Jayde kept his hand on the button and left the video rolling. "You got up and kicked back. You had everything to lose, but you put yourself on the line to stop Thames and Carnegie—just like you fought Ambrose and Nic before them."

"He's right," Ephesus murmured, as if he'd never seen it before. His voice sounded far away, like he was also a video from my past.

Maybe he was. He didn't know me anymore. He didn't know who I'd become.

"It's not like that," I argued, but no one was listening to me. My own voice drowned me out as the video continued to play.

"You ruined yourself."

I slapped my hands over my ears.

"You don't understand. I could have helped you!"

"That's what people need to see," Jayde continued, raising his voice to be heard. "They need someone to show them that it can be done, to prove that there's something worth fighting for."

My scream ripped through the recording. There was a crack as I dropped the tablet, and the recording went dark. But the sound kept playing.

"We would have loved you!"

"Jayde, stop." Stanyard lurched forward and punched the control panel, shutting off the recording. But the damage was done. My memories supplied the gunshot, the screams, the blood.

Jayde took a step towards me. I jerked back. "Leave me alone!"

"I can't," he admitted. "I need you."

I stumbled into Ephesus, who braced me. "Phil, just listen to him. Maybe—maybe he's right."

I gaped up at him. *Are you on his side?*

Jayde came closer. "People won't follow me; they don't know me. But they know you."

"Then fine! Use my recordings. I don't care," I snarled, even though I definitely did. I just wanted to run. I just wanted to run and never see him or this place again. I slipped out of Ephesus's grasp.

"We need new recordings," Lev said. "We need you to get on air and rally everyone to the cause."

Horror rippled through me. "I can't go on air! Look at me!" I yanked on my short, ashen-blonde hair. "If the government finds out about Andromeda, I'm dead. Nic's dead."

Jayde grimaced. "Who cares about Nic?"

"I do!" I screeched, and realized it was true. "Don't you get it? I'm responsible for him—for everyone. It's my fault my dad's down there, frozen in a block of ice." I pointed and slammed the floor with my foot. "I did that. It's my fault he's almost dead, because I didn't listen to Nic and lay low."

"That's not your fault, Phil," Ephesus argued.

"Yes, it is," I declared, and for once, it wasn't guilt that ripped through me. It was rage.

Ephesus was wrong; they were all wrong. About Dad, about Blue Fire, about me. My dad wasn't a hero. He was a liar. He'd lied and put our entire family at risk, and now my mom was dead.

I wouldn't make the same mistake.

"But they'll follow you!" Jayde pleaded. "Look, I promise I know what I'm doing—"

He had the audacity to reach for my hand. I slapped him away. "No! I won't do it. As soon as Dad's thawed, we're going back to Mars. If you need a revolutionary, you're going to have to find someone else."

I turned and ran for the door, praying none of them would follow.

"Philadelphia," Jayde called, tone changing. He took a breath. "Please."

I gripped the door handle. "My name is Andromeda," I snapped without looking back. "And I am not your Blue Fire."

12

"Thanks for getting me home on time," I said as Stanyard pulled up to the curb in front of the Vons'. According to his dashboard clock, it was 4:52.

"Don't tell her I ran that last yellow light," he snarked as he put the car in park.

I acknowledged his weak attempt at humor with a half-smile, but the gesture felt like rolling a boulder uphill.

"Here." He fished something out of his pocket. "I think you should have this."

He laid it in my lap: Carnegie's phone.

"I pulled a memory dump and have the computer running some decryption programs on it, but..."

"But you don't think you'll find anything," I finished for him. I flipped the device over in my hand.

He didn't answer. He didn't need to. I unzipped my backpack and slid the phone into a pocket next to Dad's burner.

"Did you..." Stanyard drummed his fingers on the wheel and tried again. "Did you and Ephesus... talk?"

It was my turn to shrug. "Not really."

It was an exaggeration—Ephesus and I hadn't talked about anything. As soon as I'd run from the command room, I'd stumbled around until I found a bathroom. I'd locked the door, hid in the corner, and sobbed until I was too tired to feel panicked anymore. Then I'd washed my face and used the concealer I had in my backpack to cover up any signs of emotion.

I'd gone back to the lab, where Ephesus found me soon after.

"Did you know?" I demanded as soon as he walked in the door. I knew the answer, but I had to hear it from him. I had to know at least one family member hadn't lied to me about Mom's death.

"No," he said, his pain equal to mine. "Dad told me the same story as you."

"Do you think Mom knew?"

His answer was longer in coming. "No."

"He killed her," I said, even though the words scraped like knives on my throat. "It's his fault she's dead."

Someone had to say it.

Ephesus sighed. "Phil, I—"

"I'm not doing it," I cut him off. I could feel him staring at me, but I refused to look up.

"Is it because of Nic?"

"Yes," I said, even though that was only half the answer.

The real reason was I didn't want to be like my dad.

Ephesus took a breath like he was going to say something more, then wisely decided not to. He sat down at the computer and went back to his programming, typing one-handedly with agonizing slowness. We didn't speak again until it was time for me to leave. I spent the rest of the afternoon sitting with my knees to my chest, staring at Dad's body and silently begging him to explain to me why he hadn't told me the truth.

"Phil." Stanyard drew me back to the present with a sigh, the gesture more sound than name. "You know you don't have to, right?"

I turned to him. "What?"

He met my eyes. "Jayde. You can tell him no."

"I thought I just did."

"Do it again if you have to. You don't have to do this."

I searched his face. "Do you think I shouldn't?"

"I don't know." His answer was quick—prepared.

I waited. When he didn't elaborate, I decided to push the question I'd been harboring all afternoon. "Did you know? About Blue Fire. About… my dad."

He shook his head. "Jayde didn't tell me anything until today. I knew about the hashtag, but I thought he made it up. I didn't expect your videos to blow up like they did." His eyes wandered as he traced the dust on the dash with his finger. "And I don't think Jayde did either."

"You don't?"

"No. I don't think he expected it to work. I think he threw the hashtag on there to see if anyone would answer—and they did." He looked up at me again, eyes filled with admiration that bordered on fear. "He underestimated you, Phil. We all did."

A sharp rap on the window scared me out of my wits—and the need to reply. I turned to see Mrs. Von leering on the sidewalk, nose nearly smudging the glass.

I cringed and rolled down the window.

"You're late," she declared.

I glanced at the clock. *5:01.*

Stanyard leaned over. "I'm sorry, Mrs. Von Nieuwenhuyse, it's my fault."

"Uh huh." She straightened and started walking back towards the house. "Well, come on, you two. It's time to set the table."

"You… two?" I repeated.

She was already on the porch. "I'm not sending him home hungry. I'm no swine." The screen door slammed behind her.

Stanyard turned to me with a raised eyebrow.

I opened the door. "You'd better come in. If you don't, it'll throw off their groove, and they'll be unmanageable all evening."

He laughed and unbuckled his seat belt.

I'm not sure what Mrs. Von thought was going on, but whatever it was, she pulled out all the stops for it. The recipe she had been preparing was deemed unsatisfactory; she literally dumped the half-cooked food in the trash and switched to a fancy shrimp pasta instead. Mr. Von was delighted to have another man in the house and kidnapped Stanyard as soon as he walked in the door. He showed him the garage, and the basement, and the backyard, and then the garage again, because of course he forgot where he'd already been. Stanyard got three full tours of the house before dinner was done.

It was nice to have another body around the table, but I couldn't get a word in edgewise as the Vons spent the entire meal drilling Stanyard with questions. He fudged the answers to some of them—especially the inquiries about his own parents—but everything he said seemed to delight them. The leftovers had long since grown cold before they let us up from the table.

Stanyard tried to make a break for it, but they wouldn't have it. Mrs. Von shooed us both out of the kitchen, claiming it was "her turn to clean up." Before Stanyard could even make a move towards the front door, Mr. Von grabbed him by the shoulders and steered him towards the living room. No sooner had Mr. Von queued up a movie than his wife appeared with bowls of ice cream. She handed one to each of us, winked at me, and waltzed back out of the room.

Stanyard stared at his mound of whipped cream and chocolate syrup. "Are they like this every night?"

I stabbed mine with my spoon. "No, they never bring out the ice cream for me."

He chuckled. "You've been spending too much time with Nic."

My brain restarted when I remembered that I was supposed to call him. I picked up my tablet, which I'd set on the coffee table, and was unsurprised to find a new message from him.

I TOLD YOU TO CALL ME WITH AN UPDATE

I was too tired to be anything but truthful.

I FORGOT

He immediately came online and responded.

WELL, LET ME JOG YOUR MEMORY

I let the silence hang for a minute while I figured out how to respond. I didn't want to talk. The last thing I wanted to do was rehash the trauma all over again and suffer through Nic's biting commentary on my trainwreck of a family.

Nic waited patiently for me to fulfill my duty. I was somewhat surprised that he didn't initiate a call just to establish dominance.

I finally settled on a half-honest answer.

I'M EXHAUSTED. THERE'S NOTHING TO REPORT

Nothing except my dad is apparently a revolutionary who tried to overthrow the government, and that's why my mom is dead, and now they want me to finish the job.

Nic would want to know. He'd have to know eventually. But I didn't want to talk about it, not now. Not when I couldn't even talk about it with my own brother.

Nic, unfortunately, was feeling social.

I TAKE IT NONE OF THE CODES WORKED

NO

I'LL SEND MORE IN THE MORNING

THANKS

I tabbed away, but no sooner had I opened another window then more messages came through.

HOW'S YOUR RIB?

I begrudgingly switched back to the chat and responded.

I GOT IT TREATED

HOW ARE YOU FEELING?

That question could have meant several things depending on the inflection, but none of the plausible answers were information I wanted to divulge. I wasn't about to give him a detailed breakdown of my physical *or* emotional state.

I JUST NEED SLEEP

He didn't respond, but I could see he was still online, waiting.

I took the initiative and closed the chat.

Stanyard excused himself as soon as the credits rolled. I caught him in the entryway.

"Do you know whose hoodie this is?" I asked, holding it out. "Mrs. Nolan says it's not hers."

"Oh, it's mine."

I gripped the fabric and tried to decide how that made me feel.

He shrugged. "It was the only clean shirt I could find. You can keep it if you want."

I did want; it was the comfiest piece of clothing I'd ever worn. "But... why?"

He scrunched his nose. "Why not?"

There was no good answer to that, but I hung my mouth open like I had one.

He chuckled. "If you don't want it, I'll take it back. But if you like it, keep it. It's that simple."

Is it that simple?

The Holy Spirit laughed in my ear.

Yes, it is.

"Okay," I said, folding it over my arm. "Thank you."

He grinned.

My heart skipped a beat when I realized this was the second gift he'd given me in the last twenty-four hours. Since when had Stanyard been so generous? The only thing he'd given me when we were growing up was a hard time.

Stanyard seemed to have no such reservations about the whole ordeal. Without another word, he turned and went to open the door, then stopped.

"It's unlocked," I said after the silence had gotten awkward.

He spun back around. "Do you want to go to church with me tomorrow?"

He blurted it so fast that it took me a minute to translate, and then a minute longer to realize it had been years since I'd heard the word.

"Church...?" I repeated.

He nodded. "Yeah, I heard of one that's meeting across town tomorrow."

I ran the math and remembered what day it was. "Are we Seventh-day Adventists now?"

He shrugged. "You take what you can get in the apocalypse."

"I guess so." I struggled to wrap my mind around what he was proposing. "I just... didn't realize there were any churches left."

I tried to remember the last time I'd been in anything that resembled a church service. Public religious gatherings had been branded as seditious long before I was born. We'd tried to skirt the law, of course; I remembered meeting in basements, abandoned warehouses, old barns—even sketchy motel rooms in parts of town I probably shouldn't have been in—all to gather with the few friends we had left.

We'd gotten caught several times. Twice we managed to escape. The next time, only a few of us were left behind—not enough to prove that there had been a "gathering." They'd fined the adults and slapped felonies on everyone's files, including mine.

The final time—the last service I could remember attending—they surrounded the building and arrested everyone. Stanyard's family had been there too. My father and Mr. Dass spent over a week in prison, and for several days my mother feared they wouldn't be released.

They finally were, and my mother begged Daddy not to attend any more services. I don't remember what he said, but I clearly remembered what Stanyard said to me the next day at school.

"I'm never going to church ever again. It's not worth it."

Was it worth it now?

I searched his face. "Is it safe?"

"No less so than being on base."

He had a point there.

"I invited Ephesus. If it helps."

It did. "When do we need to leave?"

He smiled. "I'll come get you at 8 am."

13

It was unlike any church service I'd ever been in.

They were meeting underneath an abandoned parking garage, in a service tunnel that had once connected to the subway. It was accessible only by the stairwell, where they posted guards who looked suspiciously like subway maintenance crew. Stanyard showed them a text on his phone—proving that he'd talked to someone who knew someone—and they flagged us in.

The twang of an electric guitar floated up to us as we descended the last flight of greasy stairs. When we reached the landing, another guard used a handheld device to scan us for electronics and weapons. I wasn't surprised to find that Stanyard was carrying, but I was surprised when he surrendered his pistol without complaint.

Ephesus was less joyful about turning over his devices, of which he had a physically improbable number stuffed in his coat pockets. I only had Carnegie's phone and Dad's burner on me, but they still forced me to add them to the pile.

Satisfied we were clean, the guard ushered us through the door. We stepped into the tunnel, and I was instantly assaulted with the moan of collective prayer. A decent group of people—at least forty or fifty—had already gathered. The tunnel was wide enough for two trucks to pass, but the shape of the room still made the crowd look like a disorderly line. They clustered around the far end of the room, where the tunnel ended in a brick wall.

The floor sloped downward as the tunnel descended, allowing us to see all the way to the front. A crude stage had been erected from palettes and plywood, on top of which played an even cruder band. The drum kit was an eccentric combination of actual drums and vaguely acoustic buckets, and the electric guitar was hooked up to an old car battery. The band members, all two of them, warmed up with a wordless tune while a black man paced the stage, evidently leading the crowd in prayer.

"Lord, You said when two or three are gathered, You're going to show up. So I declare protection over this building, protection over the people who risked their lives and their freedom and their jobs to come here…"

More people shoved their way through the door. I watched the melting pot of skin color and affluence flow past and wondered where all these people had come from. Why weren't they in containment camps? Had they all signed the file?

Stanyard interrupted my thoughts. "Is that a fog machine?" He pointed to the corner of the stage.

It sure was, although it looked like it was made out of more duct tape than plastic. It intermittently hacked smog over the crowd, adding to the visual chaos.

"More like a smoke machine," Ephesus commented, and coughed.

"Don't insult Penelope! She's been through a war!"

I jumped when someone spoke from behind me—then breathed a prayer when I recognized the voice.

"Two wars, in fact," his partner said.

"Wait, what was the second one? Have you been to a war I don't know about?"

I turned around. "John? Dowe?"

They immediately went into battle mode, putting their hands up like a pair of clumsy superheroes. "Hey! How'd you know our code names?" one of them—God knows which one—said.

"Wait. Those are our code names?" The other lowered his arms and stared at his partner. "I thought those were our real names."

"I honestly can't remember," the first said without missing a beat.

"John," I said slowly, and watched to see which one reacted. "Dowe. It's me."

They sized me up with a squint, just like they had when we first met on Rott, and rightfully so. After some deliberation, I'd decided to go as Andromeda, piercings and all. If we were caught, it would be better for Andromeda to be fined for attending an illegal service than for Philadelphia to hang for her family's crimes.

It took a second—a long, painful second—but I was eventually rewarded with identical grins.

"Philadelphia!" they boomed together, and then rushed me in a hug. They both squished me at once, and while my soul appreciated the affection, my bruised rib did not.

"Ow, rib, ow," I complained, loud enough to be heard over their gushing.

"Sorry, sorry," Dowe said, and they freed me. "We're just so happy to see you. You know you've died, like, three times in the past month, right?"

"I think she's up to four," John argued. "There's Rott, and then that stunt on the TV, and then—"

"Don't mind if I ask, but..." Ephesus shoved himself physically and verbally into the conversation. "Do you know these guys?"

John sniffed at him, as if he could judge him by his smell. "The question is, do *you* know these guys? Because you should. We're awesome."

"You're something all right," Stanyard muttered.

Both John and Dowe turned on him in choreographed unison. "Well, what do you know," Dowe remarked. "She's brought another guy home."

"I swear she has a new one every time we meet her," John agreed.

Ephesus raised his eyebrow, Stanyard turned red and white at the same time, and I blanched. "I'm not 'bringing him home'!"

They weren't listening. "At least he's more her age than Q was."

"Yeah, but Q has a *base*."

"Fair, fair. She should really reconsider."

Stanyard shook his head to rattle his composure back into place. "Will someone please tell me what's going on?"

I took control of the conversation. "This is John and Dowe. I met them on Rott. They're friends." I looked to them, giving them a chance to prove me wrong.

John smiled. "The originals."

"But how did you get here?" I asked, reality catching up with me— although reality was always a slippery concept with John and Dowe. "What happened to Rott?"

John shrugged. "The cops told us we didn't have to go home, but we couldn't stay there."

"What he means to say is, we found out our sentence was up... *six years ago.* We could have gone home any time, but *someone* forgot to tell me." Dowe thwacked John in the back of the head.

"You're kidding, right?" Ephesus said.

I shook my head. "They never are."

Stanyard scratched the back of his neck. "I may have picked the wrong church..."

"Nonsense! This is the finest congregation this side of the Charles. Just wait until you meet our pastor." John turned and started screaming into the crowd.

"Never mind it's the only church this side of the Charles," Dowe muttered with a wink at me.

Ephesus turned to Stanyard. "Are you sure this place is safe? It's awfully... *loud* for something that's supposed to be off the radar."

"If you wanted quiet, you should have gone back to your concentration camp."

We turned to see a tall black man emerge from the crowd. I recognized him as the man who had been on the stage a moment before. He was built slim but powerful, his button-up tightly cuffed over his muscular arms. His head was shaved and his beard trimmed to perfection, and a gold chain glinted around his neck. He didn't look anything like what I had imagined the pastor of an underground church to be, but he did look like he meant business.

Ephesus sized him up. "What did you say?"

"If you wanted quiet, you should have gone back to your concentration camp," the man repeated, not unkindly. "We don't do quiet here."

Ephesus shifted but did not back down. "Aren't you afraid of getting busted?"

The man shrugged. "If Daniel was afraid of getting caught, he would have closed the window. Name's DeMarcus." He went to offer Ephesus a handshake, then settled for a pat on the shoulder instead.

Ephesus studied him for a beat more, then smiled. "Klez. Are you the pastor here?"

"Something like that," Pastor DeMarcus said with a twinkle. "I just bring the preaching. These saints organize the meeting." He gestured at John and Dowe.

"You... organized this?" I said, and wondered if I'd underestimated them all along.

They bowed with a flourish. "That's us—John and Dowe, your friendly neighborhood event coordinators! We have over thirty years of experience. Worship services, coups, weddings, distractions—you name it, we can plan it!"

I grinned. I knew from experience that they did, in fact, know how to plan a good distraction.

Pastor DeMarcus extended his hand to Stanyard. "And you must be Augustine. They told me you'd be bringing friends."

Stanyard accepted the handshake, and Pastor DeMarcus pulled him into a manly slap on the back. Then he turned to me. "And you are?"

"Andromeda." It felt weird to be the only one not using a callsign, but I wasn't about to admit that I was Blue Fire.

"Ooh, pretty," John or Dowe crowed.

Pastor DeMarcus held out both his hands. I stretched mine forward—and winced when the gesture pulled on my rib.

Pastor DeMarcus frowned.

"Just a bruise," I fudged.

"Could we pray for you?" Then, without waiting for an answer, he turned and gestured at someone across the room.

"I mean, sure," I fumbled. I couldn't remember the last time someone, let alone a complete stranger, had asked to pray for me.

A beautiful woman came to stand beside the pastor. Her skin was caught somewhere between black and white, and her raven-dark hair fell over her shoulders in heavy curls.

"This is my wife," Pastor DeMarcus said by way of introduction. He bent and whispered something in her ear.

She stepped towards me, hazel eyes searching me softly. "Is it okay if I put my hand on your rib?"

"I mean, sure," I said again, not sure what else to say.

She did, laying her warm fingers gently on my wound. She raised her other hand in the air as she started praying in tongues, her face set in concentration. Pastor DeMarcus followed suit, putting both arms up.

I just watched. I didn't know what to do except let it happen.

Abruptly, she switched to English. "Jesus, you are our healer. Come and heal this daughter of yours. Pain *goes*. Swelling *goes*. Strength returns."

Ephesus came up behind me and put his hand on my shoulder. Stanyard tentatively raised one hand halfway.

Across the room, the band kicked in. Someone jumped up on the stage and shouted a welcome that was answered with a rousing *Amen*. The guitarist began to sing a chorus, and the rest of the crowd joined him. Soon the entire room was clapping in beat, the sound echoing around the concrete structure and multiplying like rain turning into a storm.

Our God is an awesome God, He reigns from heaven above...

The woman took her hand away. "How do you feel?"

Dizzy, would have been the appropriate response. The music was thunderous in the narrow tunnel, and I felt warm all over. I took a deep breath, hoping for a miracle—but it still hurt to breathe. What was I supposed to expect?

"I don't know," I finally answered.

She smiled. "Give it time. It's good to have you all with us." She acknowledged everyone with a nod, then squeezed her husband's arm and blended back into the crowd.

Pastor DeMarcus turned to follow. "Let's worship."

We watched him walk away. The stragglers around the room were all flowing towards the stage, leaving our group alone on the outskirts.

"Let's go!" John and Dowe encouraged. "You can stand with us."

One of them took my arm. I allowed them to pull me towards the crowd. Ephesus and Stanyard mercifully stayed close behind.

We joined the edge of the throng. There was no cohesiveness to the crowd at all; everyone seemed to have their own idea of what worship meant. Some had their hands to the sky; others, their face to the floor. Some danced with as much passion as you would at a club; others were so still I might have thought them dead. Everyone sang at different volumes. Some weren't singing in English at all.

What am I supposed to do?

Dowe playfully jostled me. "Sing with me! This is my favorite song."

"But I don't know the words," I panicked.

I saw the Lord, seated on His throne... He was clothed in glory, and exalted high...

"Then make up your own!" John chirped, and started doing just that. He put his hands up and started babbling about how good God had been to him, in a key that didn't match the band at all. Dowe was doing the same, although he was closer to being in tune.

Ephesus watched them for a moment. Slowly, he lifted one hand. "God, thank you for saving me." He made no attempt to sing, but his voice grew louder as he recited his blessings—just like he would if he were praying at the kitchen table. "I should be dead, but you rescued me. Thank you for protecting me, and my sister..."

Something nipped at my cheeks and my ears and neck began to burn.

I opened my mouth, but I couldn't think of anything to say. I had a million things to be thankful for—didn't I?—but none of the words would form. I normally didn't have a problem talking to Jesus. Why couldn't I now? Was it the music? Was it the crowd? Was it too loud in here? No one else seemed to have any issues praying or singing. Was I doing something wrong?

His name is Jesus... His name is Wonderful, Counselor, Almighty God...

Pastor DeMarcus climbed on the stage. Abruptly, the singing tapered off, lowering the ambiance. He didn't have a microphone, but he didn't need one as his powerful voice boomed over the crowd.

"If anyone needs prayer, if anyone needs healing, the front is open. Don't let this moment pass you by! Don't leave here the same person you came in."

"Don't have to tell me twice!" John cheered. "Hey Klez, wanna come?" He grabbed Ephesus's good arm.

"I, uh—" Ephesus stammered.

He needn't have bothered; neither of them was listening. Dowe slapped his shoulder. "Don't worry, we'll go with you! Come on, Andromeda."

"I already got prayer," I blurted without even thinking.

John shrugged. "They don't charge for refills." Without waiting for my response, they dragged Ephesus into the crowd and disappeared. I was left with Stanyard on my side and a frantic throng pressed all around me, screaming the words to a song I didn't know.

How great is our God, sing with me, how great is our God...

This couldn't be right. There was so much noise, so much movement, so much shouting and crying and tears. What kind of church was this? Everyone around me seemed so excited. All I felt was a heavy weight in my chest, like I was breathing in lead.

Stanyard's voice broke through the chaos. "We should go up there."

"What?" I turned to him.

"We should get prayer." He was fidgeting, his face and hands twitching as if he'd been tased. I'd never seen him like that, like he'd lost the ability to stand still, and it only fed my anxiety.

Suddenly, he seemed to regain control of his body. He straightened and drew his shoulders back. "I'm going."

He took two steps—then stopped and turned around. "Come with me."

"What?" I gasped again.

"Come with me," he repeated.

I gripped the straps of my backpack. "Stanyard, I don't... I can't..."

"Come on, we won't get another chance. You need this as much as I do."

"What's that supposed to mean?" I squawked. I felt like I should feel offended, but I just felt terrified. There was no way I was going up there, in front of all these people.

"Come on, they've got a bunch of people up there, praying for everyone. Let's go." Stanyard looked over his shoulder towards the front. I saw the tension in his body and knew he was about to run and leave me behind.

And for once, I wished he would.

"You go, then," I said, drawing back.

"No, if we go, we go together."

I started and looked up at him. He turned back to face me and shifted his feet, posture firm.

"I want you to come with me," he said, and held out his hand.

I stared at it, memories of screams and sirens and tears ricocheting in my head.

Phil, if you don't come now, I'll leave you behind!

I looked up into his face.

His dark eyes met mine, open and unafraid. "I won't go without you."

Give me a chance.

I reached out and grabbed his hand.

He gripped my fingers and dragged me into the crowd. He swam through the throng like he knew what he was doing as people instinctively parted to let us through. I hung onto his hand like a rope, afraid that if I let go I would drown.

The sound grew deafening as we neared the stage, but it wasn't because of the music. If anything, the rickety drums and screeching guitar grew warped and distant as the thrumming inside my head drowned everything out. My heart was pounding, and my ears were ringing, and my lungs were burning with a pressure that was both familiar and foreign at the same time.

What's going on?

Everything shattered when we broke through to the front. There was a gap between the crowd and the stage, and the void seemed cavernous. I suddenly felt like I was alone, even though Stanyard still held my hand. A cold breeze swept across the concrete, and I felt weak, chilled, and exposed.

If God had been there a moment ago, I couldn't feel Him now.

Stanyard abruptly let go of my hand. I turned to him in a panic. Pastor DeMarcus had him by the shoulders, his face to his.

"You know you're forgiven, right?" Pastor DeMarcus declared, voice as authoritative as it was quiet.

Stanyard started to say something, then changed his mind and swallowed instead.

Pastor DeMarcus shook him gently. "Why are you still trying to earn it?"

"I don't... I'm not..." Stanyard stuttered, then finally settled on, "I'm sorry."

His voice cracked in a way I'd never heard before, and I started to panic.

Pastor DeMarcus smiled. "He doesn't want a slave. He wants a *son*."

Stanyard shattered. He collapsed, and the pastor let him fall. Stanyard dropped to his knees and started to *cry*, the sobs raw and unashamed.

I gaped at him, feeling like my world was crumbling out beneath me. The Stanyard I knew would never let anyone see him cry. He was cold and stoic and sarcastic, and that was safe.

This wasn't safe.

This can't be God, can it?

Pastor DeMarcus stepped towards me. I tried to back away, but there was nowhere to go. *No, please don't*, I wanted to beg, but I couldn't find the words.

He smiled at me—a soft, gentle gesture that was completely dissonant from the violent noise in the room. "No, He's not safe. But He's good."

I flinched. "How did you—"

"He's already given you everything you need," he continued as if he hadn't heard me. "But you have to let go."

"Let go of what?"

He didn't answer. He'd already moved on to the person next to me, leaving me feeling like I'd missed an opportunity I could never get back.

The thrum continued unabated, each song seeming to have no beginning and no end. The singing and the praying and the drumming swirled into a homogenous beat, until I couldn't distinguish one from the other.

Everyone seemed to be having an experience except me. There was moaning and crying and dancing and speaking in tongues. Even Stanyard was lost to the world as he beat the ground with his fists.

I felt nothing. The only thing I heard was my own anxiety chattering; the only thing I could sense was the ache in my head and the burn in my ribs. What was wrong with me? Everyone around me was passionately in love with a God I wasn't even sure I knew. Why wasn't He speaking to me? Was He mad at me?

Nic was. Dad would be, when he thawed out. Surely God was grieved with the mess I'd made of things.

This is all my fault.

I don't know how long I stood there in silence, wishing God would say something and yet fearing what He would say if He did.

Finally, I turned around and walked away.

14

I left the tunnel and collected my devices from the guard. Shoving past a cluster of latecomers, I climbed the stairs until I found a floor of the parking garage that was deserted. As soon as the door shut behind me, cutting off the distant music, my anxiety broke. My pulse slowed, and I took a full breath.

I couldn't decide whether to be grateful or guilty. Since when had I been relieved to get out of *church*?

I shoved the thoughts aside and strode for the railing. I needed fresh air.

The ledge was wide enough to sit on, so I carefully climbed up and swung my legs over. I was three stories up, and the height should have terrified me, but there were too many other emotions competing in my head to leave room for acrophobia.

I leaned my head against the cool pillar and closed my eyes. I counted down, willing the throbbing behind my temples to slow. I focused on the breeze and a distant car horn and the omnipresent sound of traffic—anything but the chaotic singing and frantic praying that still echoed in my ears.

You have to let go.

Let go of what? The whole reason we were in this mess was because I had been careless. If I'd been more aware, or prepared, or in control of the situation, Dad would still be alive.

But I hadn't, and he wasn't, and there was no one else I could trust to fix it. No one on this planet, anyway.

"Phil! Where are you?" It was Stanyard, his shout echoing up the stairwell.

I groaned and sat up. The door slammed, and his sneakers squeaked on the asphalt as he ran to me. "Phil! Get down!"

"I wasn't going to jump," I groused, but I swung my legs back around. He grabbed my arm and helped me down.

He let go as soon as my feet were on solid ground. "What's wrong? I got up and you were gone, and Ephesus hadn't seen you leave..."

"It's fine, I'm sorry," I said, even though I didn't mean either statement. "I just had a headache."

"Anything I can do?"

"Take me back to base."

He searched me. "Okay."

We collected Ephesus and walked back to the car. Both boys were silent during the drive. I watched Ephesus in the rearview mirror and wondered what he thought of the service, but he seemed fine, relaxed even. Whatever the problem was, it was apparently only with me.

Jayde met us at the door. "You're late."

I glared at him. I wasn't in the mood to talk to him, much less receive orders from him.

Stanyard came to my defense. "I didn't realize she ran on your schedule."

Jayde ignored the comment. He gestured at me and started leading the way down the hall. "There's someone here to see you."

I reluctantly followed him back to the lab, the boys a step behind me. We came around the corner to see a tall, dark-haired man standing over Dad's tube, and I recognized him instantly.

"Tower!"

He turned. He looked so different up close. When he was two stories high in his lookout, it was hard to tell how old he was; now, I could see that he was only a few years younger than my dad. His sunken eyes were framed with crow's feet, and his unruly mop of hair was graying underneath. His skin was hardened from years of working in the sun, his knuckles bashed and scarred.

"Phil," he acknowledged, his hands finding a home in the pockets of his army pants.

Ephesus stepped into the room. "So you're Tower."

Tower studied him up and down, eyes lingering. "To her, yes. To you, I should be Bart."

I looked to Ephesus in alarm. "You guys know each other?"

Ephesus shook his head. I could see the gears ticking behind his eyes, but his face remained blank.

"You don't remember me, do you?" If Tower was disappointed, he wasn't showing it.

Ephesus shrugged. "Should I?"

"Not if your father had any say in it. It has been..." He frowned at me. "How old are you again?"

"Seventeen."

"Seventeen years," Tower finished. "But I always was the cool uncle."

My whole world bottomed out and then sprung back again like a rock on a trampoline.

"Uncle Bart?" Ephesus croaked.

Tower acknowledged him with a nod. "Nephew."

I watched the emotions play out on Ephesus's face and wondered if that was what I had looked like when *he* came back from the dead.

As for me, I couldn't even conjure up the energy to be surprised, and apparently, neither could Stanyard. "Next we'll find out you've got an evil twin," he muttered.

I glanced back at them where they waited in the doorway. Jayde shrugged. "It was news to me too."

Ephesus sputtered like a broken sprinkler. "I thought you were dead!"

Tower wrinkled his nose. "Is that what your father told you?"

"I mean, not in so many words, but..."

"And what about you?" Tower arched an eyebrow at me.

I shrugged. "I mean, Mom talked about you sometimes, but..." I knew Mom had a brother, but she hadn't seen him since before I was born. My parents had always spoken about him in past tense, so I'd assumed he was either dead or didn't care about us.

My dad had strongly implied it was the latter.

"Jerk," Tower muttered.

"But why didn't you tell me?" I demanded. "I was there, on Rott, and you said nothing. You had access to my file. You knew who I was."

He shrugged. "I didn't want you to worry."

I crossed my arms. "Well, let me make up for lost time."

He eyed me with a look that wasn't quite affectionate. "Okay, Q," he snarked. "Forgive me for not wanting to see you cry at my funeral."

"What?"

He took his hand out of his pocket to scratch his neck. "Don't take this the wrong way, but I didn't expect your plan with the virus to work—not that well. I knew that if my superiors reviewed the logs, it wouldn't take a detective to realize I'd let a whole floor of prisoners out of their cells."

I replayed our interactions in my mind—the long, contemplative looks I had thought so little of at the time. "So when I asked you to help..."

I was asking you to die.

He studied me from somewhere under his mop of hair. "It was a sacrifice I was willing to make."

I shivered. "Thank you," I said, and it felt wholly inadequate.

Ephesus's internal processor seemed to have rebooted. "But what are you doing here now, after all this time?"

Tower straightened. "I heard Blue Fire needed my help."

I flinched.

"And it looks like Catalyst does too." He looked down at Dad and made the sign of the cross.

"You're Catholic?" I asked.

"One of the many reasons your father and I didn't get along." Tower reached inside his jacket and pulled out a rosary. He slid it over his head and laid it across the top of Dad's tube.

I tracked the obvious implications. "Does that mean Mom…"

"Yes, before your father and the Bible-thumping Baptists got ahold of her."

The distaste was palpable in his voice, and Ephesus laughed. It was a genuine sound that brought a little life back into the room.

Tower tapped the machine's control panel. "No luck cracking the passcode?"

"No," Ephesus sighed. "Our best bet right now is extracting the memory dump, but the OS is completely foreign to me."

"I put a request out yesterday asking for any code anyone had," Stanyard said from the hall. "I got a few responses, but I don't know if any of it is useful."

"Worth a shot," Ephesus muttered, in a voice that suggested he was prepared to fail. "Let's go look. I'll be right back."

The latter statement was directed at me, which I acknowledged with a nod. He turned to Tower. "Thanks for coming back."

Tower clapped his shoulder. "We'll talk more later."

Ephesus nodded and left, taking Stanyard and Jayde with him.

Tower waited until they were out of sight down the hall before turning to me. "You know why I'm here, right?"

"What?"

"As happy as I am to see you, I didn't come here for a family reunion."

The severity of his tone sucked all the warmth out of the air, and suddenly, I knew what this was about. "Jayde called you, didn't he?"

He nodded.

I folded my arms over my chest and pinched my eyes shut. "You think I should do it. You think I'm the next 'Blue Fire.'"

"And you don't?"

My eyes flew open, startled by the question.

His sunken eyes searched me. "Why not you?"

I gaped at him. He of all people should understand. "You know why. You were *there*. I heard the radio conversation. I know what happened."

He looked down at the frozen glass coffin beside him. "And what do you think happened?"

I swallowed and forced myself to speak the painful truth. "I think Operation Blue Fire was a failure. I think it's my dad's fault Mom is dead."

"And I think it's mine."

I looked up at him. There was no grief on his face as he stared into Dad's tube, but his words were stretched, each syllable labored.

"I was supposed to pick up the drive that day. But I postponed the drop because there were whispers—I thought someone might be on to me."

He pressed his clenched fist to the frosted glass. "I could tell your dad was nervous about it, but I ignored him. Like I always did."

I bit my lip.

"Next thing I know, there's a call for an ambulance, and Thomas doesn't check into work, and no one's answering the radio, and my sister is dead."

He slammed his fist down with a crack. He bent over, his matted hair hiding the tears I could clearly hear in his voice.

"I should never have let him be in charge of the files!" he shouted. "I should have known he'd get caught. I should have known he wouldn't tell Abi."

"Why didn't he?" I whispered, the accusation piercing the air between us.

"Same reason he didn't tell you why she died." Tower planted both hands on the tube and pushed himself up. "To protect you."

"A lot of good that did," I snapped, and regretted it. I gagged as the guilt and fear clogged my stomach.

"I didn't say it worked."

I pressed the heels of my hands to my eyes to stop the tears from falling.

Tower turned to face me. "Your dad made mistakes, Phil. But so did I. I should have come and got you that day. I could have picked you up at school and had you out of town before Ambrose even knew what was happening. None of this—Red Rain, Mars, Rott—would have happened if I'd gotten you out."

I tried to imagine a version of my life where I hadn't grown up in a concentration camp. A version where I'd been rescued and protected. A version where someone, anyone, had stood up to Ambrose. But I couldn't.

"I shouldn't have given up on you. I shouldn't have given up on my family." Tower's gaze wandered again, and the penance in his voice offered the apology it was too late to give. "And I never should have given up on Blue Fire."

His eyes returned to mine, and I saw the truth I wanted so badly to deny. "You don't think Dad should have quit."

"No," he said, unashamed. "I don't."

When I didn't answer, he rolled up the sleeve of his jacket. He licked his finger and rubbed it on the inside of his arm, right above the elbow. A layer of thick foundation peeled away, revealing a tattoo I knew all too well.

He held it out for me to see. "We could have done it then. We can do it now. All we need is a voice."

It was my turn to look away as all my excuses died on my lips. My arguments suddenly seemed fragile and frail, but I couldn't push past the fog of fear that surrounded my mind like the containment camp walls.

"I don't—I don't want to," I managed finally.

"Then don't."

I looked back up at him.

His eyes were reserved behind the shadow of his hair. "If you're going to do it, it has to be your choice. I'm not here to convince you."

"Then why are you here?" I challenged.

"To remind you that you're not alone."

If that was his goal, it wasn't working. I felt more alone and confused than ever before. Why couldn't anyone understand why I didn't want to do this?

He didn't seem to expect a response. He pushed his sleeve back down and strode towards the door. "I'll be in the command center if you need me."

I watched him leave, too afraid to give a definitive goodbye. "How long are you staying?"

"As long as you are." He paused in the doorway. "If you do it..." The emphasis was on the "if," but barely. "If you choose to become Blue Fire, promise me one thing."

I steeled myself. "What?"

"Don't make the same mistake your father did."

"Which one?" I said, and winced.

He glanced over his shoulder. "Call me more than once a decade."

I searched his face.

"Your father and I were enemies." His eyes took one last look at the tube before returning to me. "But you and I don't have to be."

Then without waiting for a response, he turned the corner and left.

15

Ephesus returned a few minutes later with Stanyard, and they rigged up their various computers and devices. It was a horribly complicated process that quickly fizzled into inglorious failure. They modified and patched and rewrote their program again and again, and each time it coughed up more errors.

After a few hours of misery, Stanyard slammed his laptop shut and stood up to pace. Ephesus raked his hand through what was left of his hair. "What about patching into the circuit board?"

Stanyard shook his head. "Same problem—all their circuitry is proprietary."

"But you've done some hardware hacking before, haven't you? Can't you at least try—"

"Yeah, but nothing like this. If I pry this thing open, I'll have no idea what I'm looking at." He jabbed his finger at the machine. "What if I cross the wrong wire? I can't play with your dad's life like that."

The frustration evaporated from his muscles, leaving him looking deflated. "I'm sorry," he said, voice bent towards me. "I'm not good enough."

I wanted to comfort him, but I didn't know what to say. There was nothing I could say that would make this any better.

Ephesus didn't say it, but I could read it on his flushed face: We were running out of options. The boys couldn't hack around it, and we couldn't keep trying random passwords. We would soon exhaust the codes Nic had given us, and then we'd be back to square one, picking away at mathematically infinite possibilities.

Meanwhile, the longer Dad stayed under, the more damage he would suffer—until, at some point, he may as well just stay frozen.

Ephesus kicked me out of the lab and told me to go eat a late lunch. I begrudgingly obliged. Then, wanting to avoid everyone, especially Jayde, I found an abandoned office and curled up in a desk chair with the Bible Stanyard had given me.

I fanned the pages, looking for answers. I didn't find any, but at least it distracted me until it was time to go back to the Vons.

I walked back to the lab. I came around the corner to find Stanyard lying face-first on the floor.

My heart shot to my throat, and I started to call out to him—but then he moved. I hung back around the edge of the doorway as he picked himself up and sat cross-legged next to Dad's tube. His face and eyes were red, but it didn't look like he'd been crying. He sat there for a long minute, gaze in another universe.

I was just about to say something when he spoke.

"God, please. I don't know what to do."

He broke off into mutters, much of which wasn't English. He ran his hand along Dad's tube—then made a fist and pounded it into the floor.

"God, save him, please, for Phil's sake. You know it will kill her if he dies. And she's been through so much already. You have to save him—save *her*."

I slid my hand over my mouth.

His bloodshot eyes went to the ceiling and lingered there. When he spoke again, his voice was an unfiltered whisper.

"I'm worried about her."

I gripped the doorframe, desperate to say something. I wanted to reassure him, tell him that he didn't have to worry about me, that there was nothing to be concerned about. He didn't have to take care of me.

But none of those statements were true, and I knew it.

Stanyard started muttering again. I watched him as he bent over, hands raking his unruly hair, and tried to assimilate the man on the lab floor with the moody, impenetrable boy I thought I knew.

The Stanyard I'd gone to school with would never pray for me, not like this. He would never have given me a paper Bible. He would never have invited me to church. And he would never, ever have wallowed on the prayer floor and let me see him cry. The Stanyard I used to know never opened up to anybody, not even God.

And certainly not me.

I'm giving you my weapons, Phil.

I eased away from the door until I was out of sight of the lab windows. Then I turned and fled down the hall, careful to be light on my feet.

Tower took me home. I made him drop me off a few blocks away; the last thing I needed was Mrs. Von asking questions about Tower's muddy military jeep.

Thankfully, I was home before five, so Mrs. Von didn't have any questions. I went through our dinner routine and then managed to concoct a reasonable excuse to get out of watching TV. I escaped to Cea's bedroom and took my tablet off the charger.

It exploded in a shower of notifications, all of which were from Nic.

He had sent me more batches of codes throughout the day, which made me wonder when he had slept. His first few messages were simply business, but when I'd failed to respond—even though my tablet clearly showed as being online—his tone had turned from informative to interrogative to downright antagonistic.

DID YOU RECEIVE MY LAST MESSAGE?

IT'S CUSTOMARY TO ACKNOWLEDGE PEOPLE WHEN THEY'RE ASSISTING YOU

IF THERE'S BEEN AN ISSUE, I NEED TO KNOW. PREFERABLY IMMEDIATELY

DO I NEED TO SEND SARDIS?

ANDROMEDA VERITY NOLAN, IF YOU DON'T ANSWER MY MESSAGES, I SWEAR I WILL GROUND YOU FOR A MONTH

Who on Mars is Verity? I thought, before realizing it was probably Andromeda's middle name. It was no doubt on my file; I'd just never bothered to look it up.

The fact that Nic had was both hilarious and terrifying.

I typed back.

SORRY, I DIDN'T HAVE MY TABLET WITH ME

I watched his avatar flicker green as he came online. I was not at all surprised by his next words.

CALL ME

I obeyed and decided to save myself some trouble by initiating video.

He appeared, posed perfectly in the center of the frame with his arms crossed, like he'd been waiting all day for me to call. When he didn't offer any greeting, I sighed and answered the implied question. "I left my tablet at home, sorry."

"But you were online all day. And watching the most *inane* movies. I expected better of you, although at this exact moment I'm not sure why."

"Yeah, Ephesus installed a program that makes it look like 'Andromeda' is relaxing at home. Sorry, I forgot to tell you."

"I'm sensing a trend here." He unfolded his arms. "And what were you doing all day where you didn't need your tablet?"

"I'm not supposed to have registered electronics on base."

I could tell by the slant of his eyebrows that he didn't like that anymore than I did. "Stanyard and Ephesus are there the whole time," I added, desperate to reassure him, or me, or someone.

"Neither of those names brings me any comfort," he grunted. "But at least now I know you're not dead."

His expression relaxed, and I let out my breath. Even though there were only about three muscles that distinguished Nic's disgruntled face from his default one, I could tell the difference, and it made me a lot less nervous when he wasn't tense.

He picked up his coffee mug. "You're still grounded. As soon as you get home, you're not leaving your room for a month."

I acknowledged that with a humorless chuckle. "At this point, that sounds like a vacation."

He studied me. "What's wrong?"

"Nothing," I muttered, entirely out of habit.

He slammed his mug on the desk with a crack so loud I nearly dropped my device. "Do you think I'm stupid?"

The anger had returned to his voice, so the only response I could squeak out was, "Huh?"

He leered at the camera. "Do you honestly believe I'm going to fall for that?"

I threw up one hand in surrender. "Fall for what?"

"A woman who is 'fine' is, statistically speaking, the exact opposite. And you haven't been 'fine' in…" he glanced at his watch, "at least two months. So start talking."

I cringed. "I don't… want to," I fudged, which wasn't the truth, but it was at least closer to it.

"I don't care. I've got a fresh pot and all day. I'll wait." To demonstrate, he grabbed a carafe from somewhere out of frame and refilled his mug.

I stared at the screen, feeling cornered even though he was over a million miles away.

"Andromeda," he said, and it was a threat.

"Nic, I…" I mentally ran through all the things he didn't know, and all the anxiety and terror and confusion and *Jesus* of the last forty-eight hours crushed me like a load of bricks. My tears returned, hot and shameful, and I hid my face in my arm.

Nic let me sob for several minutes. "Phil."

I made a gasp that sounded like I'd been stabbed, appalled that he'd used my real name. I squinted at the screen through a veil of salty water.

His deep gray eyes searched mine. "Talk to me."

I gulped back another sob.

"I can't help you if you don't tell me what's going on."

Let me help you.

I pinched my eyes shut and waited until the world stopped spinning, anchored by the one fact that hadn't changed over the past week:

Nic could help me. And he would.

I coughed to clear the ugly tears from my voice and tried to decide where to start detangling the mess. "Well," I said, finally settling on the most bizarre revelation I had to share, "I've got an uncle."

"Living?"

"Yes," I replied, and then realized how hilarious that was. Without warning, all the anxiety of the past two days shattered into hysterical laughter. I dropped the tablet as I buckled over and howled. It sounded absolutely terrifying, but it felt so good.

Nic waited until I came up for air. "I take it your rib doesn't hurt anymore," he commented over the rim of his coffee cup.

I abruptly stopped when I realized he was right—it didn't hurt anymore. I lifted the hem of my shirt and looked at my side.

The bruise was gone.

Pain goes.

"Andi?" Nic questioned, the speaker muffled by the blankets.

"He healed me," I murmured.

"What?"

"He healed me," I repeated, louder, as if that could make it all make sense.

"He who? Look at me when I'm speaking to you."

"Sorry." I grabbed the tablet. "I don't know how to tell you this…"

"You never do."

"But…" I licked my lip and braced myself for the rejection. "Jesus healed me."

To my surprise, he didn't laugh. "Meaning…?"

"Just that," I said, gesturing with one arm. "A lady prayed for me today, and my bruise is gone. It doesn't hurt at all."

He blinked twice. "That wasn't what I was expecting you to say, but at least it's not bad news."

I opened my mouth, then changed my mind. He could take it or leave it. I knew what God had done for me.

"So." Nic shifted in his chair. "Bob's your uncle?"

I dragged my mind back to the present. "Actually, his name is Bart."

"That's even worse."

I parsed out the next words, watching for his reaction. "But we know him as Tower."

Nic wretched, gagging most of his mouthful back into his cup. "Tower is your *uncle*?"

"Eyup."

"Mom or dad's side?"

"Mom's."

"Weird but okay." He wiped his mouth on his sleeve. "Why didn't he tell you?"

"He didn't think he was going to make it off of Rott alive."

"Oh ye of little faith," Nic muttered, "but fair point." He drew his eyebrows together as he reprocessed everything I had just said. "I take it you never met him growing up."

I shook my head. "I knew Mom had family, but Dad always told me they were all dead."

Nic propped his elbow on the arm of his chair and put his chin in his hand. "And I thought I was the only one keeping skeletons in the closet."

I huffed. "You should sue for plagiarism."

"I'll add it to the list of complaints I have for our next parent-teacher conference." He leaned forward and tented his fingers. "Listen, I realize this would normally be considered in poor taste, but given the amount of resurrected family members you have, I need to ask…" He cleared his throat, and for a brief moment, the sarcasm left his voice. "Is your mom actually dead?"

"Yes," I whispered, "she is." I sighed, expecting tears, but instead I just felt *dry*.

He watched me carefully, eyes tracking like a cursor. "Did it happen like it says in her file?"

I swallowed. "Not exactly."

Nic waited.

I tried to force the words up my throat, but they kept catching there, thickened by the fear and the confusion and the guilt. He was going to be so mad when he found out I'd kept all this from him.

You have to let go.

But he needed to know. I needed him to know.

I sat up. "That's actually what I need to talk to you about."

"Hang on." He bent over out of frame, and I heard a drawer sliding on a track. There was rustling, and a second later he reappeared, notebook in hand. He crossed one leg over the other, leaned back in the chair, and clicked a pen open. "Continue."

I smiled and did as I was told.

I told him everything—about Dad, about the rebellion, about Operation Blue Fire. I told him about gun training, about talking to Mrs. Nolan, about finding the truth on my dad's phone. I told him about Tower and the real reason my mother was dead. I even told him about going to church and meeting John and Dowe. I held nothing back, and by the time I was done, I felt like I could breathe again.

He didn't say much, only interrupting to ask a couple of clarifying questions. Surprisingly, he had the most questions about Stanyard and the church, even though that was the most innocuous part of my story. When I was done, I sat back and gave him space to speak—but he didn't.

I waited until he'd finished scribbling in his notebook before prompting him. "Well?"

He arched his eyebrows but didn't look up.

"Don't you have an opinion?"

"Several passionate ones." He clicked his pen shut and tossed the notebook on the desk. "None of which I intend to share."

A fireball of frustration imploded in my chest. "Oh, so *now* you're deciding to mind your own business? I just told you they want me to lead a war, and you decide now's a good time to take a vow of silence."

He finally looked up and met my gaze. "Do you want me to tell you what to do?"

My next comeback died on my tongue. *Is that what I want?*

He didn't wait for me to decide. "Because I won't."

I clicked my teeth shut and waited.

"I won't tell you what to do, because based on past experience, that increases the probability that you'll do the exact opposite."

I flushed poppy red when I realized he was right.

"But." He lingered on the word as he refilled his mug. "I think you know what I would do."

When are you coming home?

"Yeah," I said quietly, eyes on my lap. "I do."

"Any progress on unlocking the tube?" he prodded, as if predicting my next objection.

I shook my head. "Ephesus still hasn't been able to hack the memory dump or whatever."

"Don't tell him I said this, but that surprises me." Nic blew on his cup of coffee and waited for the ripples to subside. "I guess Carnegie really wanted to make sure no one else could get their hands on your father."

I grimaced. Nic was right, and in a cruel twist of fate, Carnegie had succeeded. Password-locking the tube ensured that if he couldn't have Red Rain, no one could.

"Do you have any idea who he was working with? Any idea what his plan was before you ingloriously ruined everything?"

I knew Nic was trying to make me feel less horrible, but it wasn't working. "None. He had his phone set to purge data every twenty-four hours…"

Time stopped when I remembered the one important conversation that was still on Carnegie's phone.

WHEN CAN I EXPECT DELIVERY?

Nic started to swear, then let the sound fizzle out into a hiss. "I can tell by the look on your face that I'm about to regret everything I just said."

"Yeah, probably." I gnawed on my lip and started calibrating all the ways my idea could go horribly wrong. There were dozens, but the more I thought about it, the more I realized it was my best chance.

I opened a note program to start writing things down—then stopped, closed my eyes, and did something I hadn't done in days.

Jesus, give me wisdom.

"Well?" Nic grunted.

I started. I'd almost forgotten he was there. "What?"

"If you're concocting another suicidal idea, I'd like to know what it is, so I can at least start prewriting your obituary."

The words were biting, but his expression was anything but. I searched his eyes and found the truth he could not say.

Talk to me.

I held his gaze. "I think I know how to get the code."

I told him my idea, walking through the details slowly until it was cemented in my own mind. He made a heroic effort to keep a rigid face during the whole conversation, but I saw the light behind his eyes flicker. He looked sad, which told me I was right: This was my only hope.

"Well?" I prompted when I'd finished.

He groaned and shifted in the chair, looking away from me for the first time since we'd started the call. "What did I just say about not telling you what to do?"

I grunted. We both knew I wasn't waiting for permission.

But we also knew that wasn't what I was really asking.

I chewed on my words until I could rearrange them into the truth. "Nic?"

His eyes returned to mine. "Yes, Andromeda?"

"Will you help me?"

16

"You want to go where?"

I slid into Stanyard's car and slammed the door. "Somewhere out of town. I need to connect to a cell tower that's nowhere near home—or base."

He hesitated, his hand on the gear shift. "Why?"

I buckled my seatbelt. "Just do it."

"Yeah no, I'm not playing that game." He took his hand off the wheel and leaned back in the seat. "If I'm going to drive you to the middle of nowhere, I need to know why."

I glared at him, but the frown on his face told me I'd have to try harder than that. I fingered the straps of my backpack. I hadn't planned on telling him what I was doing until it was over—mainly so that he didn't try to stop me.

"Come on, Phil, please," he said when the silence had grown long. "At least involve me if you're going to do something stupid."

Well, that's one way to put it.

I sighed. "Can I trust you?"

"Of course," he said, almost before I'd finished the question. "But do you?"

I stopped and looked at him. He let me search him, eyes wide and unbarred. When he spoke again, his voice was a gentle invitation. "Do you trust me?"

He held out his hand, and for the first time, I didn't see greasy alleys and flashing lights. I saw smoke and stained concrete, heard praying and chaotic singing. I saw the tears in his eyes and his fists beating the floor as he prayed, prayed for mercy. And through it all I saw his hand reaching out to me, begging me to share in an experience I didn't yet understand.

I won't go without you.

I looked back up into his face. "Yes, I do."

He smiled. "Okay." He put the car in gear and pulled away from the curb. "What are we doing?"

I unzipped my backpack and pulled out Carnegie's phone. "I need to make a call."

He slammed on the brakes, nearly sending me into the dash. I dropped the phone and braced myself. "Stanyard!"

"Sorry." He glanced in the review mirror to make sure no one was behind us on the street, then put the car back in park. "But if you're going to do what I think you are, I can't let you do that."

"I didn't ask." I fished the phone off the floor. "And it's my only hope."

He let out a long, rickety sigh. "Phil, those people want you dead."

"Yeah, and if I don't get that tube thawed, my dad will be. You said yourself we're running out of options." I shook the device at him.

He turned away from me and glared out the window, silent and stewing.

"If it will save him, I have to try. And I need you to drive me. I can't take the bus—Andromeda isn't supposed to be logging any activity away from home right now. And I know Jayde won't let me do it from base."

He still wouldn't look at me. I reached over and grabbed his knee. "Stanyard, please. I need your help."

He tensed, and so did I. He looked down at my hand, seemingly as shocked as I was that I'd put it there.

Slowly, he slid his hand under mine and entwined our fingers. I didn't pull away.

"All right," he said. He squeezed my hand, then let go to take the wheel. "But we need to make it quick. That's a registered device—they'll know as soon as you bring it online."

Nic had warned me about that, but it was a risk I was willing to take.

Stanyard copied my silence as he navigated rush hour traffic. It took over half an hour to reach a mall in the suburbs—somewhere far away from home, but busy enough that if they did trace the call, they'd have trouble figuring out who was responsible.

Stanyard parked on the edge of the lot. "Are you sure about this?"

For an answer, I turned Carnegie's phone on and handed it to him.

He didn't argue as he deftly navigated the settings with his thumbs. A few seconds later, he passed the device back to me. "It's online. Make it fast."

I opened Carnegie's texts and clicked on the most recent one.

YOU FOOL

Stanyard read over my shoulder and said nothing.

I took a deep breath, muttered a prayer, and dialed the number.

The line picked up after two rings.

"I thought you were dead."

Maybe it was because I'd had such a string of bad luck with men lately, but I was more than a little surprised to hear that it was a woman. She had a curt voice with perfect pronunciation, but there was a subtle Chinese clip to her words. The greeting was spoken with no affection at all, and while I knew she was talking about Carnegie, I realized the statement could equally apply to me.

I swallowed and forced my voice to be cold and confident—the same tone I used with Andes. "Funny, that's what I wanted you to think."

There was a sharp intake of breath and rustling. She'd lost the upper hand and with it her composure; her next words were harried and almost obscured by her natural Mandarin accent. "Who is this? How did you get this number?"

Stanyard gripped the gear shift, ready to move. I put my hand up and spoke calmly and clearly.

"This is Philadelphia Smyrna, and I believe I have something you want."

There was utter silence, and for a second I thought she'd hung up.

"Fascinating," she said finally. Her perfect English enunciation returned. "You really are a clever girl."

I winced. "So I've heard."

"Philadelphia." She rolled the name slowly, as if measuring how it fit me. She finished with a contemplative *hmm*, then continued. "To what do I owe the pleasure of this call?"

I put the phone on speaker. "I believe you're expecting a delivery."

"I was."

The past tense was definitive, as was the patient silence that followed.

I measured my words, making sure to repeat them exactly as Nic and I had rehearsed. "I apologize for the delay, but I'm hoping we can still make arrangements."

She barked a laugh so sharp it made me flinch. "Oh really?"

I swallowed. What if she called my bluff? I only had one shot at this. "Yes," I said, forcing myself to sound aloof and annoyed—like the way Nic used to talk to me. "That is, if you're still buying."

"Oh, I am." She composed herself. "I just didn't think you were selling."

"You and I both know he's as good as dead in there," I snapped. The words felt bitter on my tongue, and the pain was not an act.

Stanyard touched my knee. I reached down and grabbed his hand, gripping it like the railing of a capsizing boat.

She was silent for a beat. "I'm sorry," she said finally.

I tried to weigh how genuine the condolence was, then decided it didn't matter. "So, what's he worth to you?"

"What do you want?" The question was honest.

"Money," I replied without hesitation. I was very grateful Nic had helped me plan what to say; I would never have been able to come up with a believable answer around the swirling in my stomach. "Enough to get far away from you."

She laughed again, a sarcastic tinkle this time. "Charmed. But I'm sure we can come to an arrangement. Bring the tube and I'll bring the money and a plausible excuse for transferring it to you. Do you want to set the meeting place, or shall I?"

"I—I will," I stuttered, a little startled that she'd agreed so quickly. "I will text you the details from this line by 1400. We meet tonight, or not at all."

"I would expect nothing less."

Stanyard tapped the dashboard clock with his other hand. I nodded. "And there's one more thing."

"Of course there is."

Jesus, please let this work.

I took a deep breath and molded my words to be cold and slippery. "You'd better come prepared to unlock the tube."

There was a pause, which told me all I needed to know: She knew Carnegie had password-locked the tube, and she had the code.

"Why do you care?" Her tone shifted, and I could tell I was losing her. So I did exactly what Nic had told me to do—avoid the question.

"You want him or not?" I droned, as if the whole thing were beneath me. "Because if you're not paying, there are plenty of other people who are. So unless you want me to sell Red Rain to the highest bidder, you'll unlock the tube while I'm watching."

"Philadelphia," she murmured, voice slick with admiration. "How mercenary of you."

"It's been a long week," I muttered. "Do we have a deal?"

"We certainly do. I will await your text." I heard the smile in her voice as she added, "I look forward to meeting you."

"The pleasure is all mine," I said, and hung up.

*

"You did what?"

I'm not sure who was more upset: Ephesus or Jayde. We'd gathered everyone, including Tower, Lev, and Mrs. Nolan, in the command center to tell them the plan, and now the entire room was staring at me in mortified silence. It took only seconds for both Ephesus and Jayde to go from shocked to irate, although each for completely different reasons.

"I can't believe you brought that phone online!" Jayde snapped, every muscle in his neck pinched.

"And you let her do it!" Ephesus reeled on Stanyard, flapping his sling like a disgruntled bird. "Why didn't you call me?"

Stanyard shrugged, and only I could see the smile in the corner of his lips.

I didn't have time for their theatrics; the woman was expecting meeting details in three hours. "You got a better idea?" I demanded, knowing full well that they didn't. "She has the code—this will work."

Jayde growled and gripped his hair in a way that looked painful. "We don't even know who this woman is! She could be the commander in chief of the United, and you want to meet her for coffee."

He wasn't entirely wrong, and given the fact that the lady was distinctly Asian, the chances of her being a top United official were high. But it didn't matter.

I had to save my dad.

"What if they capture you? They could torture you for information," Tower grunted in a way that suggested he had experience in such matters.

"He's right, we can't risk it," Jayde agreed. "There's no way they'll let you out of that room alive."

"Then I'll go alone," I snapped, and meant every word. "If they catch me, the worst that could happen is they read my prints and realize I'm going by Andromeda. They won't be able to trace me to the base—that's the whole reason I've stayed offline."

"They'll know about Nic and the Vons, though," Mrs. Nolan whispered.

I turned to her. "I know. I already talked to Nic. It's a risk I—we—are willing to take."

"Nic, if this doesn't work, and they—"

"At least I'll see them coming."

"Phil, please," Ephesus begged, pulling on every string of sibling affection he could find. "I can't let you do this."

"And yet you'd do the same thing if you thought it could save Dad." I grabbed his good hand and looked up into the chocolatey eyes I had trusted for so long. "If you help me, we can pull this off. I get to pick the meeting place. You can stake it out—surround the whole place with snipers if that makes you feel better." I directed the last sentence at Jayde.

He folded his arms across his chest and didn't relent.

Lev leaned close to his ear. "She's too valuable," he hissed, as if I weren't there.

"I'm not asking permission," I declared, loud enough for everyone to hear. I let go of Ephesus's hand and drew myself up. I spun a slow circle, trading glances with everyone in the room. Two days ago, these people were willing to let me lead a rebellion. Couldn't they help me save one man's life?

"I'm going. We're going to set up a heist to get the code from this woman and save my father, and we're doing it tonight." I turned to look at Jayde again. "So unless you're prepared to lock 'Blue Fire' in a cell, I suggest you help me."

"I am," he said without hesitation, making me regret my choice of words. He unfolded his arms. "But I heard it didn't go well for the last two men who tried it."

Stanyard nearly choked on a laugh as he tried to stifle it.

Jayde made all his displeasure known in one slow, grumbling breath. "Well? What's your plan?"

Ephesus grabbed my shoulder. "You aren't really thinking of dragging Dad in there, are you?"

"No..." I said, my brain returning to all the problems I needed to solve. "But Nic had a suggestion about that."

Ephesus saw the look on my face and paled. "Oh no..."

Jayde arched an eyebrow.

I faced him. "How many bodies do you have in the morgue?"

He cast one final glance around at his troop. Tower nodded.

"Just the one," Jayde said, turning back to me. "But you're welcome to him."

18

Apparently nothing good happens in abandoned parking garages.

It was the second time in so many days that I'd been in one—and not the same one, which made me wonder how many there were in this city. But I could see why Jayde had chosen it as the meeting place: The split levels made it possible for his men to watch just out of sight, rifles ready. Several more crouched behind the concrete pillars on the other side of the room.

I stood alone in the middle of the floor, leaning against one of Jayde's SUVs. The boys had folded the seats down to make room for the coffin-sized glass tube. It lay there, crusted with frost, screen flashing an angry red as it counted down.

Our decoy was convincing. We'd bought—thanks to a connection of Andes's—an identical model. Stanyard and Ephesus had altered the control panel and rigged it with what was essentially a fancy credit card skimmer. When the woman typed the code on the screen, it would send the password to Stanyard's computer so he could input it on the real tube. If all went well, Dad's tube would be unlocked before the woman even realized she'd been scammed.

Of course, it would all be over if she looked too closely at the body in the ice. I hadn't watched while the boys dressed and froze Carnegie. I'd found an empty room to pray in and asked God to forgive me for desecrating the dead to save the living.

"We're live. Blue Fire, are you receiving?" Stanyard radioed in my ear.

The unwanted nickname was somehow even more vile coming from his lips; he had never called me anything but Phil, except in front of the Vons. But we were communicating over wireless, which could be intercepted, so Jayde had insisted on using callsigns.

I felt the microscopic transmitter with my finger. It fit neatly in my ear, almost invisible to passersby. "I hear you, Augustine."

"Remember, get the code and get out. The money is optional," Ephesus chimed in. He'd agreed, at the collective behest of Jayde and me, to stay behind and help monitor things from the command room. He'd volunteered to—more like insisted on—going in my place, but I wouldn't let him. This woman was expecting to meet me, and I wasn't about to scare her off by sending someone else.

"T-minus two minutes," Jayde said. I knew he was posed just out of sight on the level above me, the one who would be the first to shoot if this woman pulled anything.

"Car approaching," radioed an officer I didn't recognize. "Expensive, foreign make—guessing that's our target."

I turned and gave myself one last check in the car's side mirror. This woman knew me as Philadelphia, and I'd tried my best to bring that girl back. I wore a skirt I'd raided from Cea's closet and a drab military jacket one of Jayde's officers had loaned me. I'd removed my contacts and piercings and washed the makeup off my face. There hadn't been time to do anything with my hair, so I'd pinned it up under a scarf and hoped the woman wouldn't ask questions.

I looked like a prisoner of war more than anything else, but in a way, that's what Philadelphia had been.

Not anymore.

"Yup, I think that's her," the officer continued. "Chinese, early forties, and everything she's wearing costs at least ten grand."

"She parked a block away and is walking in," another confirmed. "She's alone. Definitely not dressed for combat."

Someone grunted, crackling the line. "She's either stupid or desperate."

"If we're lucky, she'll be both," Jayde said. "Let her in."

I closed my eyes and prayed. Stanyard did the same under his breath.

"She's coming up the elevator." Jayde's sigh clogged the line. "It's all on you, Blue Fire."

I opened my eyes and turned to face the elevator.

Holy Spirit, pave the way.

The light above the elevator flashed green, and the doors opened.

She looked exactly like I imagined she would. She was old enough to be my mother, not that you could tell with how flawless her skin was. She was about my height, with features that were somehow both sharp and curved at the same time. She had confident black eyeliner and bloodred lips, and her crisp white-on-black skirt set looked like it cost more than a small car. Her long, dark hair was done up in a sophisticated updo and fastened with pearls.

She stood in the doorway just long enough to take me in, then walked towards me, stiletto heels clipping on the concrete.

"You came," I said, not sure how else to initiate the conversation.

"Of course." She stopped in front of me and smiled. "Asia," she volunteered, and offered her hand.

I eyed it, then extended my scrutiny to her distinctly Chinese features.

She winked. "It's not my real name, but it was easier for the boys in Washington to remember."

I gingerly accepted the handshake. "Philadelphia."

She *tsked*. "I like Andromeda much better. It suits you."

I froze, my hand glued to hers with sweat. Someone on the radio cursed.

She mercifully released her grip. "Thames is—was—an old friend of mine. There's no reason to be afraid."

I took a slow step back. "Forgive me if I have trouble believing that."

"I understand. I know this whole ordeal has been very traumatic for you. You must believe me when I say it was never supposed to be this way." She gave me a slow once-over, expression thoughtful. "But I think you know that."

"That's what they tell me," I muttered, and waited.

Her eyes came to land on my scarf. "Can I see? What you did with your hair."

"Phil, don't—" Stanyard warned in my ear.

I reached up and undid the scarf. I pulled out the pin keeping the twist in place, and my ashy blonde locks tumbled to my shoulders.

Asia stretched a pale hand towards me. I didn't move. She used her impractically-long manicured fingernails to detangle my sweaty kinks.

"Hmm," she murmured. "Needs some toner, but I like it. It's a good color for you." She stepped back until there was a socially acceptable distance between us. "If you need a good hairdresser, I have one in Beacon Hill I can recommend."

"I'll keep that in mind," I said. I weighed her tone and tried to decide where she fit on the spectrum of my enemies.

"Don't let her stall," Jayde hissed on the line.

"Right," I acknowledged them both. "Shall we?" I stepped back and gestured at the car.

"Yes, of course." She opened her pocketbook and pulled out a phone. "I have the money ready to send. I've categorized it as an appearance fee—so if anyone asks, you spoke at a conference for entrepreneurial young women for me. Something about overcoming the challenges of being recently assimilated to start your own business."

"How charming."

She shrugged. "It's my favorite way to launder money. Shall I send it?" She showed me the screen.

"First, code." I opened the passenger door so she could easily access the keypad.

Her eyes glinted as she smirked. "As you wish."

She stepped up to the car and keyed in a code. The access panel flashed up a loading screen—a feature installed by Ephesus to give us a delay.

Jayde had a backup plan if the woman gave us a bogus code. But I didn't like how his plan ended.

I gripped the car door, praying fiercely.

Oh God, please save my dad.

I listened for confirmation from Stanyard, but the silence on the line was deafening. He should have tried the code by now. Was something wrong? What if the wireless malfunctioned and he hadn't gotten the password?

"Did it work?"

I started and looked up at Asia.

She smiled. "Did it work? Because if not, there's one other number I can try."

The blood was pounding so loudly in my ears that I barely heard Stanyard's shout of victory.

"We're in!"

Asia laughed. "Don't look so surprised, honey. I know this is a setup. I know you have friends listening."

The line erupted in barked orders. Ephesus started yelling at me to get out of there.

I pulled the transmitter out of my ear and held it up for Asia to see.

She winked. "I knew that if I allowed you to pick the meeting place, you'd come with backup. You can assure your friends I'm unarmed. I have no intention of hurting you."

I believed her, but that opened up more questions than it answered. "Then why did you agree to come?"

She spread her hands. "I wanted to meet you. And besides, you needed the code, didn't you?" She rapped the tube with her knuckles. "This is a rather impressive decoy, though. I do hope you don't have a real body in there."

"It's Carnegie," I answered. "He's yours if you want him."

In my peripheral, I saw one of Jayde's men slide around a pillar and aim his gun at Asia. I put up a hand to stop him.

Asia rolled her eyes and didn't bother to turn around. "Yet another mess of his I have to clean up. Did the code work?"

"Yes," I said. "And thank you."

The soldier lowered his gun.

"Of course," Asia crooned. "You know, you could have saved yourself all these theatrics if you'd just asked me for the code. I would have given it to you."

"Really?" It was a challenge.

"Absolutely. I never wanted to freeze your father. I never needed him in the first place. Red Rain was Carnegie's obsession." She picked a stray hair off her tailored suitcoat. "Melting cities with acid rain? Too messy for my tastes. And I can't *stand* unnecessary messes."

"But Carnegie was going to sell him to you," I argued, remembering the texts.

She shrugged. "Sometimes we compromise for our allies."

Carnegie had said the same thing to me—and I abruptly realized I had no idea where their tangled alliance of deception began and ended.

I knew Jayde must be screaming at me on the radio, but this might be my only chance to get answers. "If you're so benevolent, why not just give me the code over the phone? Do you know how much time we've wasted setting this up? I could have had my dad thawed by now."

She was unashamed. "Would you have agreed to meet me otherwise?"

"No," I admitted.

"That's all I wanted, Andromeda—a chance to see you face to face. I knew as soon as you got the code, you'd disappear back to Mars, and we'd never speak again. So when you called, I knew it was my only chance to meet you and give you this."

She reached back into her pocketbook and withdrew a jewelry box. "Happy birthday, a few weeks early."

She held it out. I didn't take it. "Birthday?"

"Did you know Andromeda's birthday is July 25th? That also happens to be the date of some big, boring state dinner we're all obliged to attend. Thames was going to bring you along. We all joked it was your coming out party."

I imagined a ballroom filled with flowing dresses and immaculate suits— and Thames flaunting me like a trophy as he introduced me to all the officials who wanted my people dead.

I shivered. "Who's 'we'?"

She ignored the question. She opened the jewelry box and admired the contents. "I'll admit, I'm disappointed you won't be making it. I was looking forward to inducting you into high society. Cynthia—Mrs. Nolan and I had arranged a day out on the town dress-shopping, the spa, everything."

She snapped the box shut and looked back up at me. "It's not too late, you know. You can still come with me. There's a mansion in Back Bay with your name on it."

The thought that I might have inherited more than money from the Nolans never occurred to me—but it all seemed irrelevant. "Last I checked, the United had several warrants out for my arrest," I reminded her.

She laughed. "I am the United. You let me deal with the boys in Beijing."

"Thames seemed pretty afraid of the boys in Beijing," I commented, memories of his anguished cries and the fatal gunshot echoing in my ears.

"Thames was a coward, I'm sorry to say," Asia declared with anything but remorse. "But you're not, are you?"

I frowned at her.

"You're not a coward, Andromeda. If you were, you wouldn't be here. You'd still be on Mars."

I should still be on Mars.

She reached out and pinched the sleeve of my army jacket with her fingers. Her face contorted in a grimace. "You don't belong here, Andromeda. You're not one of them."

"Them?"

You want to do this? You have to learn to be like us.

She gestured at the floor above us where Jayde and his men were hiding. "All this scheming and fighting and scrabbling in the dark like rats. You're not a terrorist."

But I don't want to do this. I'm not like you.

"Thames said I was."

She spread her hands. "All part of the PR. The media lies about everything, and your life story is no exception. But I know the real you, Andromeda."

"Do you?" I wasn't even sure I knew myself, not anymore.

"You're a Nolan." She laughed, as if it were that simple. "You're one of us now. You don't belong down here, on the street. You belong with us, in Washington, in Beijing."

Beijing was the last place I belonged.

Asia held out her hand. "Come with me, Andromeda."

Come with me.

I slid back. "Maybe you're right. Maybe I'm not one of them. But I'm definitely not one of you."

I expected her to be offended by the slight, but I was disappointed. She just smiled, coyly, as if that was the answer she had been hoping for. "As you wish. At least take this." She held the box out again. "Please, I picked it out for you."

When I hesitated, she chuckled. "It won't explode or anything. That would be an unnecessary mess."

I slowly took the box and opened it.

A single strand of pearls lay on a bed of blue velvet. Underneath the necklace was tucked a linen calling card embossed with silver gilding.

"If you ever need anything in the future, please, call me directly. You're a friend of the family now, which means my line is always open to you."

I fingered the necklace and didn't answer.

She pulled her phone out and tapped a button. "I sent the money—to help with revival costs."

I stared, unsure whether to thank her or run for my life.

"I really am sorry about what happened. When he gets through therapy, I would appreciate a call letting me know that he survived."

"Sure," I said, even though I had no intention of doing any such thing. I closed the box.

"Well, my driver is waiting. Thank you for meeting me. It was a pleasure." She turned and walked towards the elevator.

"Goodbye," I declared, not with any affection—desperately hoping that the words would be the end of our relationship.

"Goodbye, Andromeda." She stepped into the elevator and called her floor. "Oh, will you tell Cynthia that I miss our coffee dates?" She pressed the button to hold the door. "Tell her I can make this all go away. I can have her file cleared. All she has to do is call me."

She didn't wait for me to acknowledge that. She stepped back and allowed the doors to close. "Until we meet again, Andromeda."

She winked as the doors sealed shut.

19

When we got back to base, I was crushed to find that Dad was still very much frozen.

"It's going to take time," Mrs. Nolan said. She'd transformed back into a nurse, scrubs and all, and was sanitizing a new machine with gloved hands. "We have to bring him to temperature slowly, and then he has to be placed in stasis while we work on him."

She knocked on the machine with her knuckles. It looked like a giant incubator. The side was crusted with control panels and buttons, and an octopus of wires and tubes dangled from it.

"This machine will essentially do the living for him while we replace his damaged organs. Once we're sure he's viable and everything is functioning independently, then, *and only then*, will we be able to bring his brain online and work on bringing him to consciousness."

I walked over to Dad's tube and peered through the ice. Dad's face was still frozen in agony, but for the first time, the sight didn't fill me with horror. For the first time in days, there was hope—hope my father would be coming back.

I put my palm on the glass. "I'm sorry, Dad," I whispered one last time. "But it's going to be okay."

Mrs. Nolan stripped her gloves. "It's going to take at least seventy-two hours to bring him back to temperature. And most of that time will just be spent monitoring the machine while it does the work." She gestured at the control panel, which glowed yellow and displayed a chaotic readout.

I spun around. "Will you stay with him?"

She tipped her head to the side and waited.

"Someone has to supervise all the technicians and make sure everything's getting taken care of. I can't be here all the time, and you know more about this than me." I looked into her eyes. "He needs a doctor."

She smiled. "I'd be honored."

"Thank you," I said, and returned the gesture.

She went back to prepping the machine. I watched her in silence for a minute. "There is something I need to tell you."

She acknowledged me with a busied *hmm* as she grabbed a cloth and wiped the outside of the glass.

"Asia wanted me to pass along a message."

I saw her hand tighten around the rag, but she did not look up. "And what did she say?"

"That she misses your coffee dates." I pondered the next words before spitting them out. "And that she can make this all go away, if you just call her."

"I'll keep that in mind," she said in a tone as walled as a prison. "Anything else?"

I rolled Asia's invitation around in my mind, debating how much I wanted to share. "I guess my birthday is July 25th."

"It is. That was my mother's birthday."

"And apparently there's a state dinner that was supposed to be my coming out party."

Mrs. Nolan gave up any pretense of working as she stared at her reflection in the glass. "We talked about it."

"She says I don't belong here," I continued. I had to know how much of Asia's story was the truth—and how much Mrs. Nolan agreed with her. "She says I belong with them, in Washington. That I'm one of you now."

Mrs. Nolan finally turned and looked back at me. Her face was straight, devoid of any criticism or longing. "You were supposed to be."

She didn't offer anything more, perhaps because there was nothing else to say.

I stayed with Dad all night and into the morning. I'd called the Vons and told them I was sleeping over at a friend's house, and then called again several more times throughout the evening in an attempt to reinforce that fact. There was no telling whether or not they'd remember, but it would have been too late to take me home by the time we got back from meeting Asia.

So I stayed by my dad's side through the next day, praying and watching as Mrs. Nolan and Ephesus monitored the machine's progress. Mrs. Nolan claimed the procedure was going well, but I couldn't see any change yet. Some of the frost on the glass had turned into condensation, but inside the cryoprotectant still looked as solid as ever.

Ephesus convinced me to go home for the night. After all, the sleepover excuse probably wouldn't work a second time.

I went to find Stanyard. I'd seen him a few hours ago, but he'd wandered off, saying he had programming to do. Something about disguising the power drain from the defrost procedure. I searched the base from top to bottom and even asked several strangers where he was, but no one had seen him or Tower.

Someone finally directed me to Jayde.

"I sent them on an errand," he said without any more explanation. "I can take you home."

I inwardly grimaced and hoped the gesture didn't make it onto my face. "I'll wait."

Jayde shrugged and glanced at his watch. "Suit yourself, but you'll be at least an hour late getting home."

I weighed my choices: I could be stuck in a car with Jayde, or I could spend my entire evening putting the Vons back together.

I chose the former.

Lev came with us. We took Jayde's giant black SUV, and I begrudgingly accepted shotgun when Lev offered it to me. Mercifully, neither man was feeling conversational, so I spent the ride looking out the window and trying to pray.

It was going to be a long month—or more—while we revived Dad. Nic said we should leave as soon as Dad was viable, but there was no telling how long it would take just to get him breathing on his own. Should I have his prints altered while he was in surgery? What if he needed memory care like the Vons had? I wasn't ready to admit that my father might lose his mind, but it was a possibility I had to consider. Was there someone on Mars that could do neurotherapy if we went home?

I was jostled out of my thoughts when Jayde slammed on the brakes to avoid someone merging lanes. "Sorry," he offered.

I looked around and abruptly realized that we'd been driving for longer than usual—and we were nowhere I recognized. I sat up. "Where are we?"

"There's something you need to see," Jayde said, and my blood ran cold.

Jesus, help.

I grabbed the door handle. "Stop the car."

Without taking his eyes off the road, he reached down and punched a button on the dash, locking all the doors.

I yanked on the handle anyway. "I'm getting out."

"No, you're not," he said, still refusing to look at me.

"You can't do this!" I shrieked, the panic warping my voice.

"No one's going to hurt you," Lev said from the backseat. "Relax."

The coarseness of his Russian accent had the opposite effect on my nerves. "Then tell me where we're going."

"My house," he replied.

"Your what?"

His ashen blue eyes searched me. "Just wait and see."

That was the exact opposite of what I intended to do. "No—no. I'm not going. Either you pull over and let me out now, or I'll—"

Or you'll what? You don't even have a phone! Jesus Jesus Jesus...

"Don't be stupid," Lev said, as if reading my thoughts. He reached up and pushed on a panel in the roof of the vehicle. It dropped down to reveal two assault rifles. The weapons were practically bigger than he was. Lev tossed one on the seat and slung the other over his shoulder.

I didn't know if he meant that as a threat or not, but I certainly took it as one.

I turned back around and scanned the road, searching for a landmark. Nothing looked familiar. Then Jayde turned a corner, and a quaint clock tower appeared. I'd seen the iconic image in many a stock photo and knew exactly where we were: Brookline.

Thankfully the suburb was only fifteen minutes from Allston. If I could get away from Jayde, I could easily call for help or catch a bus ride back to the Vons.

I watched the street, making note of all the open businesses where I could seek refuge. Coolidge Corner was busy enough—it was a tourist trap, after all—but the further we drove down the road, the thinner the crowds became, and the dirtier the buildings. Coolidge had been propped up with a constant flow of government funding, but the surrounding district had been left to die. The buildings grew rapidly more dilapidated until they were abandoned entirely.

We finally reached a dead end; the road was blocked off by a gate emblazoned with the United seal and a stiff warning against trespassing.

"We're here." Jayde parked the car and reached back to accept the rifle Lev handed to him. My hopes of making a break for it evaporated.

Jayde finally turned and met eyes with me. "Make this easy and I'll get you home in time."

I swallowed and got out of the car.

Ahead, the whole block was cordoned off with electrified chainlink. It probably wouldn't have stopped a determined vandal—and, judging by a few gaps in the fence, it hadn't—but it certainly looked official. It definitely wasn't the kind of place Andromeda should be seen.

"I don't think we—I—should be here," I stammered.

"I've got clearance," Jayde said, but that fact did nothing to ease my anxiety. He walked up to the gate and pressed his thumb against the keypad. It chirped, and the whole fence crackled as the electricity turned off. He shoved the gate open. "Let's go."

Once more the will to refuse flashed through me, but Lev walked up behind me, his hand on the strap of his gun.

Oh God, protect me, I muttered as I followed Jayde through the gate.

The street beyond was eerily dark, even though the sun hadn't set. It took me a minute to realize why: The electricity to the block had been cut off. Silent traffic lights hung like blind eyes from sagging wires, and the streetlamps had grown cold. No light shone from any of the storefronts, making the buildings look like soulless skeletons.

The whole block had the vibrancy of a morgue, and it smelled like one, too. Trash decayed in the streets, greasy water stood stagnant on the road, and the air hung stiff and silent. There were no birds, no dogs, not even a rat. The only movement was the dying sunlight glinting off the broken glass that salted the pavement.

Jayde stopped in the middle of the road. "This is Brookline," he announced, even though I was well aware. "It's the biggest Jewish community in Boston. Or at least it used to be."

Suddenly the abandoned buildings and stale air made sense. Like Christianity, it was illegal to be Jewish, whether by creed or by blood. And Jews, based on the few I'd met, were generally not willing to deny either.

Jayde continued walking, the glass crunching under his boots like dried bones. I reluctantly followed, leaving as much of a gap between us as Lev would allow.

"This is what happens when the United razes a whole neighborhood," Jayde narrated, gesturing at the empty buildings. "Nobody noticed when the first wave of unassimilated disappeared—take a few here, take a few there, and the world moves on. Someone else steps in to fill the gap they left at work or school, and you never even know they're gone."

I knew that was true. That's what happened to us.

Jayde stopped in the intersection and faced west, his eyes on something unseen around the corner. "That didn't work with the Jews. There were too many of them, too close together. And when you rip a whole neighborhood up by the roots, sometimes there's no one to fill the void."

I stared into the window of the shop next to me, my face reflecting off the dark glass. "How long has this place been abandoned?"

"Seven years," Lev answered, voice husky. I turned to him and was startled to find that his eyes were wet.

"They took everybody." He shrugged his gun from his shoulders. "They blocked off the street and banged down every door. No one escaped. It was cruelly… efficient."

"In and out in an hour," Jayde muttered.

Lev brushed past me. He abandoned his gun on a rusty park bench and disappeared around the corner. Jayde watched him, his face stretched in an expression I had never seen him wear before: Regret.

I stayed where I was, glancing between Jayde and the gun. "What happened to them? Did they take them to a containment camp?"

"No," Jayde snapped. The answer was quick—angry.

I looked up. He flicked his hand at me.

I shook my head. "No."

"Yes," he said, and gestured again. "You need to see this."

I backed up.

He shifted his gun. "You're not leaving until you do."

I took one step forward, then another.

"Not everyone is as lucky as you, Phil. Not everyone gets put up in an apartment paid for by the government."

"It was a prison," I reminded him.

He glanced at me. "These people never made it to prison." He pointed straight ahead.

Inertia carried me forward as the blood pounded in my ears, drowning out all other sound. I rounded the corner and saw that Jayde was right.

These people never made it to a containment camp.

The world spun around me and flashed white and black. I stood completely still, my heart frozen and the prayers dried on my tongue.

Oh Lord, have mercy.

Jayde came and stood beside me. "This is where I met him." He gestured at Lev, who knelt at the edge, motionless.

"Is he...?"

Jayde nodded.

My heart broke free and rammed itself against my ribs. "Then his family..."

Jayde nodded again. I pinched my eyes shut and waited for the roar of grief to subside. Lev would have been only seven, maybe eight.

My eyes flew open as my mind reached the horrible conclusion. "But if you were there..."

Jayde bravely met my eyes. "Someone had to pull the trigger."

I slapped my hand over my mouth.

"It was my first big assignment. I thought we were going in to do another relocation, but not that day. I didn't realize what was happening until they gave the order to open fire." He fingered the strap of his rifle. "That's when I realized I'd joined the wrong side of the war."

I tried to decide whether that confession should inspire fear or admiration—maybe neither.

"But Lev..." I ventured.

"He was supposed to die, too. But I missed."

I didn't ask whether the misfire had been accidental or planned. I knew it didn't matter.

"I came back for him later." Jayde looked back up at Lev, and I saw a roulette of emotions in his eyes: guilt, grief, responsibility, love.

All the emotions I didn't know he was capable of.

Jayde let out his breath. "Brookline won't be the last. Things are changing. The government is tired of paying for the room and board of a bunch of noncompliants. There's talk of relocation, of condensing the camps—or worse."

I didn't have to ask what "or worse" meant.

Assimilated or removed.

"If we're going to stop them, we have to do it now. We have to act while people are paying attention—while they're angry. Your videos made them angry. They will shoot if we give them a target. But if we wait—if we let this die—then people will forget about us, about you, about the camps, about the unassimilated. They'll forget, and then the United can do whatever they want. No one will even know we're gone."

He turned to me, and I knew what he was going to say before the words left his mouth.

"We need you, Blue Fire."

"Jayde, I..." I tried to shift through the emotions that washed over me, but all I was left with was a muddy mess. "You know why I can't. Andromeda can't go on air."

"No," he agreed, and the admission silenced the argument I had ready to follow. "But Philadelphia can."

"I don't... I don't understand."

"I don't need Andromeda—I need Philadelphia. You don't have to disguise yourself to go on air. You can just be you."

I instinctively reached up and fingered my blonde braid. *Just be me?* But I was Andromeda—wasn't I? Did Philadelphia even exist anymore?

"But my prints..." I shook my head. It didn't matter how much makeup I had or didn't have; I couldn't put my family at risk like that. "If I get caught, and they find out about my file, it will implicate Nic and the Vons. I can't do that to them—to Nic."

I braced myself for the angry arguments, but they never came. Instead, he studied me, eyes roaming up and down as if I were a code to be cracked.

"There was a time when Nic was willing to fight for freedom," he said finally. "He was willing to risk a world war just to save a few."

He wasn't wrong, and that made me furious. "Yes, but he's different now," I snapped.

Jayde arched one eyebrow. "Is he?"

"Yes!"

"How?"

I scrambled to put the feeling—the feeling I wasn't sure I even understood—into words.

Jayde beat me to it. "It's because he cares about you."

The revelation wasn't a surprise to me, but it still flooded me with emotion to hear it spelled out from a stranger's lips.

The door's still open.

"That's why he was willing to help you find your father, even though he knew it was a death sentence. If not for you, then for him. He knew what was going to happen."

Look, I'm aware Andromeda has put herself—and, quite frankly, the rest of us—in a dangerous position. But that was her choice.

"He's not stupid, Phil. He knew what could happen. You said yourself yesterday—it was a risk he was willing to take."

He was right, and with each word, I felt like he was chipping away the ground I stood on. Nic did care, and he knew the risks—that's why he hadn't wanted me to go in the first place. That's why he told me to keep my head down.

That's why he wanted me to come back to Mars.

I think you know what I would do.

"Do you care about Nic, Phil?"

"Of course," I said, even though I knew I was walking down a path I'd regret.

"Would you risk your life to save him?"

Pretty sure I've already done that a couple of times. I frowned at Jayde and didn't gratify him with a response.

He didn't wait for one. "Then why won't you sacrifice for your friends in the camps?"

All my excuses evaporated as I skipped my next breath.

"They're still your friends, aren't they? Cami, Aid…"

Their faces flashed before my eyes as the near-forgotten names echoed in my ears.

"What about Stanyard's parents? Don't you think he wants to see them again?"

I wasn't so sure about that, but I knew Stanyard's family was worth fighting for—just as mine was worth fighting for, broken and shattered though it was.

"I don't know how long they have. I don't know how long we have before the camps end up like this." Jayde gestured at the shell of a neighborhood around us. "If the United has its way, soon all the unassimilated will be like Lev's family."

I looked to where the teen knelt on the concrete, weeping over the graves of his people.

Would my people be next?

"You can save them, Phil." Jayde drew my attention back to him. "You can fix this. Blue Fire can."

I can fix this.

I looked into his eyes. He dropped his defenses and spread his hands, the vulnerability rushing back into his face. "Please. Help me."

I didn't answer him. I didn't know what the correct answer was, not anymore.

What do I do, God?

"What... what are you asking me to do?" I whispered.

Something close to a smile stretched his lips. "The same thing you've been doing. I need you to get on there and tell people it's time to fight back. Turn over tables of chemicals, light a weapons factory on fire, get on social media and tell the world the truth—whatever they need to do."

He was right—I'd done all of those things. And I'd do them all again if it meant saving one family, one life.

"But how is that supposed to end the concentration camps?" I asked, desperately hoping there wasn't a catch.

He was grinning now. "If we all stand up together, they can't make us all sit down."

He traced in the air like he was drawing on a map. "Operation Blue Fire isn't an assault; it's a demonstration. If we can rally people across the country to all stand up and break something on the same day, they won't be able to catch us all. You can crush scattered resistance, explain away a lone factory fire with clever media coverage. But you can't silence us all. Not if we speak together. If we knock the legs out, the table will collapse."

His plan made sense—terrifying, exhilarating sense.

We can do this.

"I'm not asking you to lead a war, Phil." He silenced my unspoken fear. "I don't need another soldier. I just need you. I need you to get on there and remind them there's something worth fighting for."

What's worth fighting for? I thought I knew the answer to that question. God was worth fighting for. My family was worth fighting for. Innocent lives were worth fighting for.

Was Operation Blue Fire worth fighting for?

You never should have quit.

"Or." Jayde shouldered his gun, letting the word linger. "You can go back to Mars and live your life as Andromeda Nolan. That's what you want, isn't it?"

There was accusation in his eyes and his tone, and I didn't know how to answer him.

Is that what I really want?

He started walking away. "You can do it. I won't stop you. Take your money and your fancy file and run. Let Earth figure out its own problems."

He stopped at the corner. I turned to watch him.

"Maybe Asia was right," he said without looking back. "Maybe you are one of them."

He continued towards the car. I stared after him, my thoughts and prayers clashing like waves in a hurricane.

You don't belong here, Andromeda.

"For such a time as this."

I started. Lev appeared beside me, his elbow almost brushing mine. His eyes were dry and his face had been rearranged into the stoic expression I was used to from him.

"What?" I asked.

He didn't repeat himself. He just pressed something into my palm.

It was a star of David pin, its silver crusted with dirt and ash.

I looked up into his face. He saluted.

I stared into his white-washed eyes for a long moment. Then I closed my fist around the pin.

20

"Captain on the bridge."

Everyone in the command center shifted to welcome me. I forced myself to return the salutes with nods, even though I felt frail and drab next to all of them. They were all so practiced and precise, with their pressed uniforms and shiny guns. I looked out of place in jeans and Stanyard's hoodie, the most non-descript outfit I could find, my hair pinned up under a scarf. I'd removed my piercings and my contacts. I didn't even have any makeup on.

I stumbled as my feet questioned my decision. *Can I really do this?*

Jayde steadied me. "Relax. Just be yourself."

I nodded, a frantic motion that looked more like a seizure, and followed him across the room.

Tower and Ephesus were there, adjusting the settings on the camera. It was nothing like the setup Thames had rigged. On Mars, I had a whole soundproofed studio to myself. Here, they'd wired a camera directly into the command module. I would be in the center of the action, the entire database at my fingertips, just like the other officers.

Because, in a way, I was one.

Ephesus came to stand beside me. He gripped my elbow and bent over until his lips nearly brushed my ear. "Is this what you want?"

It didn't matter what I wanted anymore. I knew that now.

"It's what Dad should have done," I said, glancing at Tower.

He nodded.

"Then I'm with you." Ephesus squeezed my arm and went to stand on the other side of the terminal.

Jayde dropped a pair of earbuds into my hand. "You'll need these."

I put them in, and the noise of the room faded away, replaced by an unfamiliar voice doing a sound check. But I could still hear Jayde when he spoke, his voice dampened but sharp.

"Are you ready?" It was a question, an invitation—my last chance to walk away.

My answer felt disembodied, echoing back to me through the earbuds, but even I could hear the confidence in my voice. "I'm ready."

He guided me over to the terminal and centered me in front of the camera. The playback flickered on, and my face appeared on the curved monitor. The lighting was dank and gloomy, which was just as well. You couldn't tell what color my hair was, let alone where I was streaming from.

Jayde's voice came through the earbuds. "All systems go?"

"All systems go, lieutenant."

Lev joined the conversation. "Just press the button when you're ready, Blue Fire."

I looked up to see him staring at me from across the terminal. He mouthed the words *thank you.*

I swallowed, suddenly too nervous to acknowledge him.

Someone brushed my hand—Stanyard. He stood in the shadows, just out of sight of the camera. He didn't say anything. He just reached his hand below the control panel and wove his fingers with mine.

I searched his face for an answer, permission, admiration, anything. But there was none. His face was blank, eyes calm and steady. He wouldn't tell me what to do.

Because this was my choice.

I looked down at the terminal. The *start stream* button glowed red and inviting.

The line went silent as everyone waited.

I closed my eyes and counted down, just like Thames used to do.

Holy Spirit, teach me what to say.

I gripped Stanyard's hand and pressed the button. There was a subtle beep, and the timer started ticking up.

I looked into the camera. My face on the screen was pale and haunting, cast into sharp relief by the uneven lighting. But my eyes glistened deep and clear as I opened my mouth and spoke with a confidence that was not my own.

"This is Blue Fire. If you're hearing this, I need your help."

FIRST LIGHT

RED RAIN #5.5

JUNE 2076
PRESENT DAY

1

It was the fourth time she'd died this week.

She'd died every night since Sunday. Only Wednesday night had spared her, but that was due to my self-imposed insomnia and not any luck on her part.

Now it was Thursday night—or, more accurately, the inhumanely early hours of Friday morning—and I knew as soon my head hit the pillow that she would not live to see daylight.

There was no variety to the murders, which irked me. In another life, my subconscious had been more creative in inflicting punishment, but apparently I was losing my touch.

Every night was the same. It started with the smell—the burning stench of rusted metal that seared my nostrils. Then there was the clanging of decapitated machines, the wailing of unhelpful sirens, and the swaying of the broken platform as it bucked beneath my feet.

And then, before I could even orient myself and regain control of my muscles, she fell.

Sometimes she screamed. Sometimes she was silent. Sometimes, when I was feeling particularly self-loathing, she called my name. But each time, she hung eerily mid-air, her descent slowing until I fooled myself into thinking I could reach her in time.

But I never did. Every time the world restarted, and every time she dropped like a rock. And in this reality, there was nothing to break her fall.

Tonight, I didn't even try to save her. I walked to the edge of the platform and gripped the railing, ignoring the burn of Red Rain on my fingers. I watched her fall, her dark hair rippling in slow-motion like she was floating in a river, and willed her to die. I wished she would hit the ground so I could wake up.

And then, suddenly, I did.

I shattered into reality. A shrill ring pierced my ears; I glanced at the tablet on my bedside table and realized someone was calling me. Normally I would have cursed the intrusion, but this time, it could not have been more opportune. I took a deep breath, relishing the darkness of the room, and toyed with the idea of being grateful.

Then I noticed the caller ID and remembered I had absolutely nothing to be thankful for.

I sat up and grabbed the device. She'd only called me once since she left. And while there had been a very valid reason for that call, she *should* have been calling me every day. I was the only responsible adult in her life, despite what her father might say, and she needed me.

But she was too stubborn to ask for help, and I was too stubborn to point that out, so we'd barely talked since she left. Which meant, if she was motivated enough to call me, it could only be bad news.

My nightmares weren't over. They were about to become reality.

I rubbed my temples even as I accepted the call. I didn't have the emotional energy for any of the pedestrian chatter she might use to try and frame her confession, so as soon as the line picked up, I declared:

"Who died?"

My prophetic accuracy stunned her long enough for me to flip on a light and stumble over to the coffee maker I had on my dresser for just such emergencies.

"Uh... what?" she finally managed.

I sighed and tossed the tablet on the dresser. One of these days she would realize that I knew a lot more than she gave me credit for, but today was not that day. "It's the middle of the night over here." I walked her through it as I fumbled with the safety seal on a coffee pod. "So either you forgot to look up interplanetary time zones, or someone's dead."

She was silent, and I had my answer. It would be nice to be wrong once in a while.

"Well," she hesitated, as she always did when she was guilty, "no one's dead yet..."

Oh, how my sanity swings on that operative word. I jammed the pod in the machine and punched the button. If only the relative force would make the relief brew faster.

"...that's why I need your help."

My inner tirade derailed as her words flooded me with an emotion that was entirely inappropriate for the situation.

By way of invitation, I softened my tone. "What happened?"

She didn't take me up on my offer. She went silent again.

Before I could repeat myself using more affirmative language, another voice inserted themselves into the conversation. "I can explain if you want."

"Who's that?" I snapped. My muscles immediately went on the defensive, although I think it had more to do with the fact that the voice was distinctly young and male than with the fact that I couldn't place him.

"Stanyard," she answered, and then rudely made me figure it out for myself.

Memories of the dark-haired bundle of angsty hormones came into focus, and I became even more confused. "The kid?" I coughed. She could do so much better.

"Wow, specific," he muttered.

I was more than happy to remind him of his claim to fame. "The one who abandoned you in an alley—"

"Yes, yes," she cut me off in a fluster, which confirmed my suspicions. "Ephesus is here too."

Logically, I knew that her brother being with her was an improvement of her situation, if only a marginal one. But the fact that they'd miraculously reunited overnight—when a mere twelve hours ago she'd had no idea where he was—told me that she had not been laying low like she promised.

Suddenly, there were a lot of words I wanted to say. But I opted not to waste my breath on them and instead just swore.

Ephesus returned the sentiment from somewhere in the background.

I abandoned my coffee and strode back to the desk. "Well, this ought to be an excellent bedtime story." I flicked my monitor on and pulled up a note file. "Start from the beginning, Andromeda."

She hesitated again. I contemplated threatening her with her real name but decided I'd better not forfeit my ace so early in the conversation. Instead, I settled on, "And if you were thinking of holding anything back, let me remind you that this app encrypts calls."

She mumbled her defeat. "You said it wasn't bulletproof…"

"It's a risk I'm willing to take," I announced, and hoped she would appreciate the sacrifice. "Start talking."

She finally obeyed me, and that was where the warm fuzzy feeling ended.

Her story was a nightmare, worse than any I'd been concocting lately. She'd blown her cover; her dad had been cryogenically frozen; and my former assistant had nearly murdered her. It was a trainwreck of one ghastly mistake after another, and unfortunately for all involved, she could not be blamed for all of it.

I was used to a baseline of idiocy from her. I knew how to do damage control on her stupidity. But I hadn't planned on being slapped in the face with my own.

"Carnegie must have picked him up outside of Andes's," she confessed, and waited for me to put the nail in the coffin.

I did so without thinking. "Oh, I'm quite sure that's exactly what happened," I snapped. I hadn't intended to vocalize my frustration, but it was preferrable to the physical demonstration I was considering.

As usual, she pitifully assumed all anger in the room was directed at her. "I know, I'm sorry, I should have—"

There were a million ways to autofill that sentence, and I regrettably chose the least helpful option. "You should have waited to contact Andes until you had your father with you, like I *told* you to!"

Would that have averted disaster? If anything, Carnegie might have just gotten two birds with one stone, and I would have handed them to him. I was the one who referred Philadelphia to Andes. If I'd remembered my manners, I would have sent her with gift wrap and a bow.

She continued to blunder through her tale, but I mentally minimized the window and devoted my processing power to berating myself. Of course Carnegie knew about Andes. He had been there the last time I had contracted Andes's services, hovering at my elbow like the wraith that he was. I hadn't thought a thing of it because he had been my assistant, a fixture of the room more than a human being.

I got up to retrieve my coffee, not that I expected it to do any good. It would take something much stronger than caffeine to dull my mood at this point. As usual, my dreams had been prophetic in more ways than one. I was too late to prevent her from crashing.

And, yet again, it was my fault that she fell.

I returned to the desk only to realize that she'd finished her story and was waiting for a response. The window to apologize had passed five minutes ago, so I decided not to make it awkward and continued with damage control. I plied her for the morbid details about her father and helped her plan her next move. I plastered on some sarcasm in an attempt to make my advice easier to swallow, but slapping lipstick on a pig would have been a more profitable endeavor. Neither of us was in any way comforted by my emotional disinterest. I was grateful when she gave me an out to end the call.

I shoved my chair back, grabbed my now-cold coffee, and strode from the room. It was well past midnight, and the base was in power-saving mode. Keypads and fluorescents that were normally blinding had gone dark, and the lonely Martian sky above the glass dome lent little light. Only the low security lamps near the floor traced out the borders of the hallway.

I could have used my security clearance to override the lights, but I didn't need to. Unlike Phil, I could get to Wing 74 without a map.

The base grew increasingly quieter, the hum of generators and monitors fading like the breath leaving a dying man, as I neared the abandoned wing. I stepped over a roll of insulation and gingerly picked my way through the maze of construction paraphernalia. I would have preferred to demolish the entire wing rather than remodel, and it probably would have been the cheaper solution. But there was one room that I had been unable to condemn for eight years, and I was under no delusion that I'd find the courage to do so now.

I tapped the keypad to wake it up and swiped my hand over it. It was one of the few areas on base that only I could get into; even Phil didn't have access to this room yet. I stepped in, let the doors shut behind me, and waited for the silence to return.

There were no security lights or windows in this room, making it as dark as a grave—which in a way, it was. I let the utter blackness envelope me, appreciating the cold air caused by the cavernous space. Even my heavy breathing echoed oddly around the near-empty dome.

I waited until the familiarity of the space calmed my nerves, then let my mind replay the conversation with Phil. After a few more sips of coffee, my engineer's brain kicked in. I sketched out the conundrum before us, as if writing an equation on a mental whiteboard, and started searching for solutions.

But there were none; I knew that. I could solve some of her immediate concerns, of course, but like Hilbert's problems, the most critical ones had no solutions.

I leaned against the wall and closed my eyes. My nightmares seemed like a mercy now; at least my subconscious had the decency to put her out of her misery quickly.

Reality was not so kind. Her father was dead. If not literally, then effectively. But it would take her weeks, possibly months of scraping at the barrel of hope to figure that out.

And I of all people knew what a hell that was.

2054
TWELVE YEARS OLD

2

"You made this?"

It was a rhetorical question—Dad's favorite literary device—so I answered it with an eyeroll. "No, I dragged you across town to look at some other kid's project."

As usual, he ignored my wittiness. Mom always appreciated my jokes more.

We were at the observatory, where a conference room had been converted into a science fair. The room was crammed to the overflowing with homemade machines and displays, of which mine was the grand prize winner.

I watched as Dad continued to circle my device. I could tell his stone-gray eyes had switched from surprise to scrutiny. I knew he was breaking my machine down in his mind, reducing it to a mental schematic and list of parts. He folded his arms behind his back and frowned, pondering—judging.

I tested the ice. "Besides, none of the other kids are smart enough to pull this off."

It was a factual statement, but I could tell by the glare he shot in my direction that I was about to get it. "Nic, we talked about this. We should always be..."

"I know, I know." I sighed in defeat. "We should always be kind to people."

Even if they're stupid, Mom would have added.

In their defense, only two of my classmates were classifiably stupid, although over half of them were trailing behind the grade average, judging by how difficult it was for them to grasp basic algebra. But none of them were even remotely capable of building what I had created.

At first glance, it looked like a regular glass terrarium, except for the bulky environmental controls on the side. A patch of alfalfa sprouted under a grow light, irrigated by a slow drip of water. It all looked boring and ordinary—until you realized that the plant was thriving in red Martian dirt.

Getting the alfalfa to grow in the alien soil wasn't the impressive part; it had taken Sardis, my project partner, only a weekend to come up with a fertilizer blend that would feed the plant for six months with one capsule. What got us a blue ribbon was my wickedly efficient greenhouse dome and irrigation system. If my calculations were correct—and they always were—my greenhouse would require only sunlight and a conservative amount of water to grow a field of food. And for Mars, which lacked in both sunlight and water, that was a scientific breakthrough.

My dad of all people would know this. But if he was impressed, he wasn't letting it on. He tapped the glass. "Where did you get these supplies?"

"Mr. Garner donated most of the parts," I explained, referring to the owner of the nearest hardware store.

Dad's eyebrows jumped off his forehead. "He *donated* all this? How'd you convince him to do that? The parts for that temperature regulator are worth at least a couple hundred."

"I explained to him that this was an important contribution to the advancement of space colonization." I pointed at the gaudy *Garner's Gears* bumper sticker that was plastered on the base of my machine. It detracted from the beauty of my device, but it was a worthy sacrifice for free parts. "And I reminded him that some very important scientists—such as yourself—would be looking at the projects."

Dad knotted his eyebrows together, like he always did when I suggested something he deemed outlandish.

I cleared my throat. "I also mowed his lawn for a month."

Dad's face erupted in a smile like a forgotten volcano. "Now *that's* ingenuity, son. See, that's what happens when you're nice to people and show them what you can do for *them*, not the other way around. Why can't you treat your classmates that way?"

I shrugged. "None of them had sheet copper."

Dad laughed. He turned back to my machine and ran a hand over the fluffy blonde mustache that stuck to his lip like a dandelion. "It's very impressive," he said finally. "I'm proud of you, son."

I grinned. "Just wait 'til it goes to nationals. I heard Dr. Chen is flying in from Beijing to judge. Maybe you'll get to meet him…"

I trailed off when I realized he was rubbing his neck the way he did when he was uncomfortable. "About that…" He sighed, and my dreams shattered. "I'm not going to make it to your competition next month."

"But why?" I exclaimed, and wondered if it was worth the energy to be mad. It was the third event he'd missed this semester.

"I have to go back to Mars," he said.

I indulged in a frustrated growl, although it was only to make him feel bad. It certainly didn't make me feel any better. "You said you weren't leaving until summer!"

He shook his head. "The schedule changed."

"So tell them no." That's what I would have done.

His head continued to shake, as if he were stuck in a perpetual motion machine. "It's not like that. I don't have a choice this time."

"Why?" I said again, and it wasn't an accusation. My father was in charge of the project; nobody could tell him what to do. There wouldn't even *be* humans on Mars without him.

"There's new laws I have to obey. It's…" Dad struggled for a moment, then gave up. "It's complicated. You'll understand when you're older."

"That's what you said about metaphysics, and I understand those just fine," I snapped.

He squinted one eye at me. "You are my son, aren't you?"

I shrugged. "That's what Mom says."

He laughed. "Then I suppose I have no one to blame but myself." He turned to study the experiment next to mine, giving himself a moment to collect his thoughts. "You know that file they ask you to sign every day at school?"

How could I forget? Every afternoon they pulled us "unassimilated" out of study hall and tried to convince us that our lives would be better if we bowed to the dumb government. Their propaganda was so terrible that it failed to be funny, and it was a waste of perfectly good research time. If it took me an extra semester to complete my first associates, it would be their fault.

"Well, the United recently passed a law that says people who haven't signed the file—like me—don't get to decide when and where they work," my dad continued. "The government has to approve all my job assignments. I can't even resign without their permission."

I snorted. That sounded like more pointless paperwork, which was exactly what our government loved. "Well, luckily for them, you don't want to quit your job."

"You're right, I don't." My dad reached down to finger the blue-tipped carnations my classmate had dyed for her copy-paste experiment. "But it does mean that if they tell me to go to Mars, I have to go."

I studied the wilting flowers. I was great at math, but this wasn't adding up. "Why can't you tell them no? You tell the government off all the time. That's why we won't sign the file."

He nodded slowly, calibrating. "Yes, I could refuse—but then I might end up in jail."

"Wouldn't be the first time."

He glanced back at me. "You want me to spend a week in jail just so I can attend your science fair?"

I glared at the floor. *Here we go with the rhetorical questions again.* Of course I didn't want my father to spend more time in solitary. But it would be nice to know that I was more important to him than some stupid government regulation.

He put his hands on my shoulders. I stiffened and refused to look up.

"Nic," he said, trying to patch the bridge, "I know you're upset. I am too. And there's a time—a lot of times—for telling the government no. But I'm not doing this project just because the government told me to. It's important to me too."

I felt the anger leave my body and tried to will it back. I knew how much my dad enjoyed his work; he often said he loved Mars more than Earth.

"And I knew that if I had a conversation with my very intelligent, very grown-up son about what was happening, he would understand why I had to leave early."

I groaned and looked at the ceiling. Why were adults always trying to use my intelligence against me? "You can't flatter your way out of this, Dad."

I heard the smile creep back into his voice. "You're a kind, caring young man, Nic."

"Not listening."

"And you have a brilliant mind."

"If I pretend to be stupid, will I get less homework?"

He brushed my chin, and I had to look him in the eye. "And as long as you don't let your brilliance outrun your kindness, you're going to go places and do great things—much more than I've ever done."

My sarcastic comeback stopped in my throat. My dad had reached the summit of human achievement. He'd appeared before officials in Washington and Beijing, and he'd built colonies on the moon and Mars. He was everything I wanted to be when I grew up.

Did he really believe I could do *more* than that?

I realized I was grinning and quickly shook my head to wipe the smile off my face, lest he think he won. I shrugged out of his grasp and stepped back. "Okay, does that mean I get to go to Mars with you?"

"Oh no, we are not playing that game." He crossed his arms, but the sparkle still danced in his eyes. "You know the rules. No interplanetary travel until you're thirteen."

I mimicked his stance. "Why? Does the United have a law about that too?"

"No, but your mother does."

I moaned. If there was one force more formidable than the United government, it was my mother's will.

Dad abandoned any pretense of looking stern. "Want to see where I'm going?"

I pinched the bridge of my nose. "Dad, I'm too old for that."

I remembered the first time Dad had left for a long-term assignment on Mars. I'd only been four or five and didn't have a good grasp of object permanence, so I'd been inconsolable. To prevent a catastrophic breakdown, Dad had set up the family telescope in the backyard and taught me how to find Mars so I would always know where he was.

Dad chuckled. "No, I mean, do you want to see the base I'm going to? I can show you live footage."

My curiosity got the better of me. "They've got a livecam set up?"

He waved his hand and started walking. "Even better."

I followed him out to the lobby of the observatory. It was close to closing time—the observatory always closed early on Mondays—and only a few visitors lingered around the gift shop. We walked past the children's planetarium and the queue for the viewing room to a door marked "Faculty Only." Dad pressed his thumb on the keypad, and it let him in with a chirp.

I tried to suppress my excitement. This was where the real science happened.

We took the elevator to the top floor, then walked all the way to the back of the building, where the hall was blocked off with construction tape. Dad ducked underneath it, and I followed.

"The dome's not quite finished yet, but she works." Dad shoved open the door at the end of the hall and ushered me inside.

I darted in and stopped—the room beyond was pitch black. Dad let the door drift shut behind us, plunging us into utter darkness. I held completely still while he fiddled with a keypad near the door.

Suddenly, a deep vibrating echoed from the walls. I braced myself, feet apart, as a deafening grind filled the room. A crack appeared in the ceiling, growing wider and wider as the panels in the dome parted. Moonlight flooded the room, revealing a brand-new telescope.

She was massive—standing almost two stories tall, even at an angle—and absolutely *gorgeous*. Her secondary mirror was at least fifteen feet wide, its honeycomb panels glinting in the muted light. An elegant lattice of titanium suspended her primary mirror high in the air like a diamond ring. The whole apparatus was cradled in a massive robotic base, making it look like a small spaceship.

Dad put his arm around my shoulder, and we stood there in silence for several minutes, admiring.

"Who funded this?" I managed when I finally found my breath.

"I did."

I gaped at him and tried to wrap my mind around how cool my dad was.

He winked. "They're going to put my name above the door, so you can tell your friends your name is on an observatory."

He strode over to the control panel and tapped the touchpad. An array of monitors brightened at his touch, and a gigantic flatscreen flickered to life above his head. "She's state of the art. Completely computer-guided, with the best atmosphere-filtering capabilities for the size. And just wait until you see how clean her image is."

"Wow," I whispered, and hoped my appreciation could be translated from that syllable.

Dad started typing rapidly. "She's not fully calibrated yet, but I know where to find Mars."

He paused, finger poised over the screen. He glanced back at me. "You want to try steering her?"

I darted to his side. "Show me."

He walked me through the basics of her controls. She was a smart machine, and within five minutes I had her where I wanted her. I savored the feeling of power beneath my fingertips as I slowly traced my hand across the touchpad. The robotics whirred in response to my command, adjusting the angle until it was just right. Dad flipped a switch, and the view appeared on the flatscreen.

There was Mars, displayed on a screen that was nearly as tall as I was, in startlingly high definition. The image was so crisp that it almost seemed three-dimensional.

Dad handed me another touchpad. I tapped and dragged the image, and to my surprise, the view zoomed in even closer. Each crater and gorge showed in sharp relief as I navigated across the planet's surface like a rover.

"This is where I'll be." Dad leaned over my shoulder to tap the screen. The image focused on the Elysium Planitia. He zoomed in further, and a small black speck appeared in the valley.

"Is that... the base?" I whispered.

He nodded.

I was about to mouth my admiration—then grunted when I realized I'd fallen for his tricks again. Despite my best efforts, it did make me feel better to know exactly where my dad was going to be.

"You sure I can't come with you?" I whined.

"Next year, I promise." He slid his arm around my shoulder again. "Who knows? Keep building greenhouses like that, and they might just give you your own base. Then I'll move in with you."

"I doubt it," I muttered, and smiled.

2058
SIXTEEN YEARS OLD

3

"This is so cool!"

"Thanks," I said, and tried to sound genuine. I personally didn't think the data was all that interesting, but Wesley, who was two grades and several dozen IQ points behind me, was too naïve to realize he was looking at a failed experiment.

He pressed his face and hands against the side of the testing chamber, leaving a sweaty smear on the glass. Inside was a model car he had contributed to the cause of science—or, I should say, what was *left* of his model car. I'd poured a vial of acid on it, and it had dissolved the plastic casing almost instantly.

The problem was that the innards of the car were made of a different kind of plastic which wasn't reactive to the compound I had made. The miniature frame and engine sat there like a skeleton, taunting me with my inadequacies. I was trying to come up with a compound that would melt both types of plastic, but after murdering half a dozen of Wesley's cars, I was no closer to the solution.

At this rate, I was going to have to do extra chores to buy him a new set.

I turned back to the whiteboard and studied my equation. I had a theory as to what chemical I could use to perfect my compound, but Dad had refused to loan me any.

"If your equation works..." he'd said.

"When," I'd corrected, and he hadn't argued.

"That compound would be far too dangerous to have in this lab."

I'd tried to convince him that I knew how to properly handle caustic chemicals; I'd experimented with far worse in the lab at the community college back on Earth. But Dad wouldn't budge. And since we were on his Martian science station, he controlled the code to the restricted substance cabinet.

And I hadn't yet figured out how to hack that.

Surely there was another chemical I could use to the same effect. I tugged on my lip and grimaced when the scratch of stubble reminded me of another of my failed experiments.

Wesley wandered over to my workstation and admired the colorful chaos of vials and flasks. "Wanna do something else?"

"No," I grunted as I set the testing chamber to neutralize the contents, "but a mental break is, unfortunately, my best option."

He rolled his eyes. "Does the great Dr. Von Nieuwenhuyse need a nap?"

"Don't call me that." I hated when people called me by my full last name; my brain got bored and moved on to another task before they finished all the syllables. That, and it made me sound old like my dad.

"Whatever, Dr. Nic," he muttered, and I accepted the compromise. "Let's play video games."

I grimaced. I'd watched Wesley play a few times and had nearly gotten a migraine from the flashing colors and stupid storyline. "I think I'd rather do my homework."

"Haha," he droned.

I glanced back at him as I started capping my open flasks. "That wasn't sarcastic."

He flushed red. "If you don't want to play with me, just say so."

"Okay." I picked up a vial and checked the label before putting it back in the holder. "I don't want to play video games with you."

"But why not?" His voice changed to a whiny wail that grated on my ears like scraping metal. "We did what you wanted to do."

"You volunteered," I reminded him.

"Yeah, because we're friends."

I hesitated.

"Look," he said, mercifully at an appropriate decibel, "I let you use my cars for your experiment. The least you could do is let me blow you up in battle once or twice."

I glanced at the testing chamber. He had a point—and playing video games for an hour was a small price to pay for the promise of his free labor tomorrow.

"Fine," I said, hoping the monument of my sacrifice was being properly conveyed. "But I need to put these chemicals away first."

I grabbed the vial holder, and he followed me back to the supply closet. The supply closet was adjacent to the server room that processed the trillions of bytes of data collected from all the station's labs. Even the readouts from my mini demolition derby had been recorded and packaged to be sent back to the sponsors on Earth. The hum of fans and overworked motherboards filled the cramped space.

I opened a chemical cabinet and started carefully filing my vials back onto the appropriate shelves. Wesley, who was more interested in computers than science, amused himself by studying the flashing lights on the wall of servers across the room.

I was halfway done when he rudely interrupted my concentration. "Hey, what's this drive for?"

"How would I know?" I said without looking back. Computers were not my favorite thing; I involved them as little as possible in my scientific process.

"It's not connected to the mainframe."

"What?" I turned around and saw the module he was pointing at: the one on the floor in the far corner, almost hidden underneath the massive steel rack that supported the other servers.

I swallowed as I abruptly remembered that I *did* know what that server was for.

And Dad had told me to protect the contents at all costs.

I tried to play dumb. "It's not? How can you tell?"

He knelt on the floor and gestured at the wires that must have meant something to him. "It's transmitting, but it's not connected to the database. It's running off another connection."

There was a very good reason for that—so that the government couldn't trace the data, like it could with all the other information that fed through the mainframe and bounced off a United satellite.

"Maybe they've got some super-secret research going on!" He grinned over his shoulder at me.

I struggled to return the gesture. "Maybe. It's probably just something dumb like environmental controls."

"Nah, even those they monitor from Earth. Maybe I can hook it to my computer and rip the contents." He grabbed the box and dragged it towards him. The cords on the back stretched and threatened to pop—and I panicked.

"Don't!"

He stopped and looked back at me. "So you *do* know what's on here."

I froze.

"It's your dad, isn't it? He's got something going on."

Yes, and he's going to kill me when he finds out we're having this conversation.

"What is it? Secret research? Illegal experiments?"

Oh, it's illegal all right.

When he saw that I wasn't budging—let alone breathing—Wesley changed his approach. He stood up and turned to face me. "C'mon, Nic, tell me." The whine returned. "I thought we were friends. You can trust me."

"Can I?" I snapped.

"Yes! I promise I won't get you in trouble. Besides, who am I going to tell? You're the only other kid here."

I rolled the vial I had in my hand between my fingers and hesitated. He had a point, and if I alienated him by refusing to share, I'd be back to wandering the halls of the station alone while my dad was at work. Wesley wasn't brilliant, but he was always willing to hang out with me.

"C'mon, Nic," Wesley repeated. "Friends always share secrets. Don't you want to be friends?"

I searched his face. He spread his arms wide and waited.

Dad will never know the difference.

I took a deep breath and let it out in a huff. "Fine. But if my dad finds out I told you—we're both dead."

He zipped his lips and winked.

I glanced out the door to make sure the lab beyond was empty before I turned back to him and declared, "It's Bibles."

He blinked, a reaction that was wholly disproportionate to the revelation I had just shared with him. "Bibles? You mean like, Christian Bibles?"

I nodded.

He took a half step back and eyed me. "So does that mean *you're* Christian? Dude, what?"

I pulled a face. *That's what surprises you about this conversation? Not the part where I said my dad was transmitting illegal media?* "Yeah? Why do you think my dad makes me get up early on Sunday?"

He snorted. "So you, like, believe a dead guy is going to get you into paradise when you die, right?"

I groaned and glanced at the ceiling. If I had known it would lead to this moronic conversation, I wouldn't have shared my secret with him. "The whole point is that He's *not* dead, but I wouldn't expect you to appreciate that nuance."

He guffawed—doubled over and *howled* like that was the funniest thing he'd heard all week. "Dude! Are you for real right now?"

My face and neck started to burn.

He struggled to swallow another laugh. "I can't believe the great Dr. Von Nieuwenhuyse is into that kind of stuff."

I clenched my fist around the vial. "There's a world of evidence proving—"

"There's a 'world of evidence' proving you're wrong." He mimicked my tone, flicking quotes in the air, then dropped his hands and snorted. "Bro, I thought you liked science and stuff. I thought you were *smart.*"

Rage flashed through me, and I answered the call. "Smarter than you," I hissed, and punched him.

He stumbled back, more from surprise than from the force of my blow. "Hey!"

"Take it back!" I shouted. I ran at him, slamming all my weight into him with my shoulder.

He tripped on the slick metal flooring and fell backwards. His skull cracked on the ground, and he cursed with words he shouldn't have known.

I leered over him. "Take it back!"

He wiped blood off his chin and struggled to rise. "Make me."

"Gladly." I kicked him to make him stay down.

He moaned, and the look in his eyes shifted. "Dude, I—"

"Take. It. Back." I raised my fist to punch him again—then remembered I had a vial of chemicals in my other hand. A vial of very caustic chemicals.

I held it up to the light.

He was smart enough to see what was coming. He tried to back away, but I had him against the wall. "Nic, I'm sorry, I—"

"Are you?" I challenged. I tipped the vial and watched the reddish liquid slide against the tube. "Tell that to Jesus."

I yanked the cap off—just as a shout echoed from the hall.

"Nic, stop!"

I turned to see my dad barreling through the doorway. "What are you doing?"

"He's going to kill me!" Wesley squeaked, hands over his face.

"I'm not going to kill you," I snarled. "And he insulted me—and God."

Dad slowly reached out and closed his hand around my wrist. "Wesley, go to your quarters."

Wesley scrambled up. "But he—"

"I said go to your quarters," my father repeated in a way that left no room for argument. "I will talk to your father later."

Wesley growled and stormed to the door. He paused and cast one final jab at me. "You're going to regret this."

I opened my mouth, but my dad was faster. "Wesley. Now."

Wesley huffed and ran off.

"Did you hear what he said? You have to stop him!" I exclaimed.

Dad did not seem concerned by Wesley's threat. He gingerly slid the vial from my fingers and screwed the cap on. Then he twisted the tube to read the chemical contents. His eyes went wide.

"It wouldn't have killed him," I said quickly.

"No, but he might have gone blind." Dad turned and put the flask back in the cabinet, then shut the doors and keyed a code into the lock pad. My heart sank to my stomach.

When Dad turned back to me, the adrenaline had left his face, leaving his expression etched with worry. "Nic, what were you thinking?"

"He called me an idiot!" I exclaimed, all the heat of the argument rushing back to me.

"That's it?"

"No, I mean…" I struggled to hold onto my rage, but something about my dad's presence sapped it out of me. "We were talking about religion, and he said I was stupid for believing in a dead guy."

Dad's eyes searched me. "Why were you talking about religion?"

"He found out about the Bibles," I blurted, and then too late realized what I'd done.

To my surprise, Dad's face remained calm. "He 'found' out?"

"Yeah, he asked why the server wasn't connected to the mainframe, and…"

I trailed off. Dad arched one eyebrow.

I looked at the floor. "I told him."

Dad sighed, and I could hear the fear in his breath. But it was gone as quickly as it came, and when he spoke again his voice was soft, gentle—disappointed. "I'll deal with that later. But, Nic, that wasn't worth blinding him for. He could have been very seriously injured, and then what?"

And then he would have never laughed at me again.

I didn't say the words aloud, but I didn't need to. My dad pulled them out of thin air as he studied me. "Nic, I know you care passionately about God's name—and your own. But violence is not the answer."

I sighed. I knew he was right—and that didn't solve any of my problems. "What was I supposed to do? Let him laugh at me?"

Dad shrugged. "That's what Jesus did."

I avoided his stare.

He reached out and touched my shoulder. "I know it hurts when people make fun of who you are. I deal with it every single day at work. But Jesus could let people laugh because He knew who He was; He didn't need their approval. Did you need Wesley's approval?"

When I didn't answer right away, he pinched my shoulder. "No," I begrudgingly admitted. *Some respect would have been nice, though.*

Dad kneaded my shoulder. "You're a brave kid, Nic, and passionate. I'm proud of you for not being ashamed of your faith, but throwing acid in people's faces won't win them over. You're not protecting God when you do that—you're only protecting yourself."

I sagged under his strong grip. "I'm sorry, Dad."

"Don't apologize to me. You need to apologize to Wesley."

I cringed. "But I—"

Turns out fate had a much crueler punishment planned for me, because at that moment someone screamed my dad's name. "Von!"

We both turned to see Dr. Crusher storming towards us across the lab. I panicked. Dr. Crusher was another scientist who wanted Dad's job but was too stupid to qualify.

He also happened to be Wesley's dad.

He stopped in the doorway. "What's the meaning of this, Von?"

My dad pushed me behind him. "I was just coming to find you. I've had a talk with Nic about his actions—"

"Not that." Dr. Crusher flicked his hand, like me almost burning his son's face off was a minor offense. "I meant about the Bibles."

My dad stiffened. I grabbed his arm as a frantic prayer left my consciousness.

Oh God, help.

Wesley peeked out from around his dad's lab coat, and I felt my rage returning.

Dr. Crusher savored the moment of power. "Transmitting from Mars, Von? That's a serious offense."

"What do you want, Jack?" my dad challenged, tone even.

Dr. Crusher laughed. "I'll get whatever I want after I turn you in." He gestured, and two more scientists materialized from the shadows in the lab.

Anger and fear battled for control of my nerves, and fear was winning. *Please don't do this, God! I'm sorry!*

"Paul," Dr. Crusher said with a grin, "it's my great pleasure to inform you that you're under arrest."

*

That night was the first time I ever had a nightmare.

It wasn't that I'd never had scary dreams before. Most of my dreams would terrify mere mortals. Even my mom, the only person I shared my dreams with, was disturbed by a lot of them.

My dreams never scared me, no matter how dark and devasting they were, because I only ever dreamed about what could be. My dreams weren't reality; they were *possibilities*. Some, arguably, were probabilities, the most likely solution to the math problem that was life. But no matter how realistic they were, there was no reason to be afraid of my dreams, because they could all be prevented.

Not anymore.

Suddenly, I was dreaming about things that were. That night, it was about my dad, locked in a dark cell somewhere while the government sentenced him to years upon years in prison. It was augmented, of course—there were monsters and fire and blood in places they shouldn't have been—but it was still reality.

And that's when I knew my gift had become a curse. I was dreaming of futures I couldn't change, stories I couldn't rewrite. These were dreams I couldn't control.

The next morning, they transported Dad to the nearest settlement for further questioning. There was some debate about what to do with me. Jails and foster homes were both in short supply on Mars, so after much-heated argument, it was decided that I would stay on the station under the watchful eye of another scientist until we could be deported to Earth.

My supervisor made me do school the next day like nothing had happened. It would be another week before the next transit flight, and in the meantime, the government had an education obligation to fulfill. So I was escorted to the conference room and made to sit through another series of pedantic video lectures. I turned in zeros on all my coursework that day.

Let them flunk me. I knew they wouldn't have the courage.

They refused to let me call my dad after school, so I ended up back in the lab. My access should have been revoked after the fight yesterday, but Dr. Crusher was so caught up in seizing my dad's throne that he'd forgotten to report it. So, I let myself back into the lab and resumed my acid experiments, hoping everyone on base would be smart enough to leave me alone.

I thought the challenge of actual science would distract me, but it didn't. Instead, I ended up standing at the table, holding the vial that had almost been my murder weapon in my hand, and wondering if this was all my fault.

It was my fault Dr. Crusher knew about the Bibles. I trusted Wesley, let him in on the one secret that could kill us all, and for what? A chance at a friendship that would expire as soon as our mission ended?

You're a fool.

I clenched the vial in my hand, tightly, viciously. The fragile glass shuddered in my grip, and I relished the feeling of danger. Anything was better than the rage of guilt.

And then I heard a crack, and I stopped.

My father's words whispered back to me. *You're only protecting yourself.*

I opened my hand and rubbed the hairline fracture I'd created in the glass. Maybe—maybe Dad was right. Maybe I should have been nicer to Wesley. If I hadn't threatened him, maybe he wouldn't have told his father about the Bibles. Maybe, if I had let the insult slide like my dad told me to, this never would have happened.

Or maybe... I thought as I weighed the vial in my hand, *I didn't go far enough.*

I whipped around to face the whiteboard. My unfinished equation stared back at me like a film on pause. I began running the numbers, forging the compound in my mind and imagining how the acid would burn and scar.

If only I'd had a jar of it when Dr. Crusher threatened us.

I swiped my sleeve across the board to erase the broken half of the equation and grabbed a fresh marker. My nightmare was about to get a new ending.

2062
TWENTY YEARS OLD

4

I hated parties.

As a general rule, they involved too many people and too little productivity. State dinners were even worse, as the majority of the attendees had no business being there. The dregs of society tended to wash up at government events, floating in on the sponsorship of privileged friends. They would cling like mollusks to affluent attendees, muddying the waters for those of us who had actual work to accomplish.

That's the only reason I came to this particular government function. I had been presented with an award and was a keynote speaker, but the only thing I wanted to walk away with was more sponsors for my experiments.

On account of said award, I could have had anyone in the room I wanted, but most of them were not worth my time. Because of the sensitive nature of my work, I needed a very specific kind of patron.

Those in the upper echelons of society weren't worth the risk; they had everything to lose and nothing to gain. Those in the lower ranks didn't have the resources I needed. But the aspiring politicians in the middle—those were my primary targets. They had enough money to be useful to me, and they had everything to gain. An underappreciated director with a shot at a higher seat was willing to bend the rules if it meant winning valuable allies. If I found one who was disgruntled enough, they might even be willing to help me break the system entirely.

I spent the evening filtering the crowd, searching for the up-and-coming. I would introduce myself, allow them to flatter themselves a bit, and then sow a seed of hope—the mere suggestion that I could be useful to them. Then I would walk away, leaving them to simmer in their imagination for a while. By the time I returned, they were ready to sign.

It was a delicate process that involved balancing a dozen active leads simultaneously. I couldn't afford to get distracted—which was why I was extremely annoyed when the daughter of Chairman Mong approached me.

Anyone else would have been beside themselves. As third in line to the General Secretary, Chairman Mong had earned the privilege of not talking to people. Instead, he spied out his prey from across the room and sent one of his lesser councilmen to make the arrangements.

His daughter, a chairwoman of some standing in her own right, also had the honor of being his carrier pigeon. She spent the evening watching his face for subtle nods and gestures. I knew this because she and I had inadvertently exchanged several glances.

As she strode towards me, her clicking stilettos heralding her approach, I realized that those glances may have been intentional on her part.

I decided to cut her off at the pass in hopes of keeping the intrusion brief. I met her halfway across the ballroom and offered my hand. "Madame Mong, I'm Dr. Nic."

She clasped my hand with a fearless grip. "Shi Min Tai," she offered.

I blinked. She'd skipped at least three phases of formal introduction and jumped straight to given names.

Well, that escalated quickly.

"Charmed," I said, and lightly pumped her hand. "Which do you prefer?"

"Excuse me?"

"If we are going on a first name basis, three given names seems excessive. Which do you prefer?"

She grinned, showing perfect teeth. "The boys in Washington call me Asia." She withdrew her hand from mine, slowly, her fingers brushing my palm. "But I prefer Min."

I hesitated, fully aware of the risks associated with that invitation.

She waited patiently.

I accepted the offer. "Pleasure to meet you, Min." In exchange, I offered her one of my rare smiles—the most valuable currency I had on me at the moment.

She seemed pleased with the sacrifice. "Congratulations on the award. From what I've heard, you deserve it."

"You seem to think so."

My prophetic insight stumped her, as it did with everyone. She arched one thin, penciled eyebrow. "I'm sorry?"

"Forgive me for noticing, but your father didn't send you over here."

She instinctively glanced back at him. Chairman Mong hadn't paid me any mind all evening, for which I was grateful. I was not interested in bargaining with him; he was one of the people I hoped would suffer when I succeeded.

No, Min had sought me out of her own volition—a fact I found extremely suspicious.

When she turned back to me, her dark eyes glinted like stars swallowed by a black hole. "You're a smart man, Nic."

"I wouldn't be worth your time if I wasn't." I shifted and glanced around the room. Several jealous—and prying—eyes were angled in our direction, no doubt wondering what wizardry I had pulled to secure Min's attention. Whatever she wanted, she'd better make it fast.

I turned back to her and spread my hands. "What can I do for you, Min?"

She devoured my subservience with a ravenous grin. "I want to sponsor your project."

"I'd be honored," I said, even though I wasn't. I did not like people who volunteered their money without first listening to my speech. That meant they had something to gain—something I hadn't sold them. "May I ask what interests you about my work?"

She opened her diamond-encrusted clutch and rifled through the contents. "The science speaks for itself, doesn't it?"

Of course it did—but not to people like Min. My project was, by design, deceptively mundane. I had developed a unique blend of plastic that was resistant to almost every acidic compound on the spectrum. The result had significant implications for the medical and industrial fields, but that was hardly the kind of advancement that concerned people of Min's status.

She withdrew a lipstick from her purse. "I think the science has other… uses, don't you?"

It did. That was the whole reason I developed it—because I ultimately intended to store something other than cleaning products in the canisters.

And that was exactly why I had to be very careful about who got involved.

I pretended to straighten my bowtie. "Is the Chairman interested in other applications?"

"Hardly." With a deft hand, she swiped a fresh layer of bloodred paint on her lips. "But I might be."

"'Might'?" I fought the urge to laugh. "As much as I love a good experiment, that is not a probability I want to test."

She clicked her lipstick case shut. "Not a man to take a risk, are we, Dr. Nic?"

The insult tickled my rage, and I realized I'd lost the upper hand in the conversation a long time ago. "I am quite comfortable taking risks," I snapped. "But only necessary ones."

"As am I. I hate an unnecessary mess." She dropped the lipstick in her purse and looked up at me. "But I can assure you this is a well-calculated risk."

Clearly, she was now trying to sell me on the deal, so I deferred the stage to her. "What are your terms?"

"I have some personal projects you may be able to help me with in the future." She looked up and met my eyes. "But in the meantime, I've looked at your portfolio. I know people who can fund everything on your list. I would be happy to introduce you."

I filtered her words through my mental translation program, trying to decode any pauses or inflections that might tell me what she was up to. If I said yes, I'd be dancing with the devil; her father could ruin me with a finger snap.

But if she meant what she said, I could have everything I wanted—and a clear shot at her father when I was ready to take it.

I held out my hand. "I expect my project to cost a great deal of money."

She took it with a smile. "Leave it to me."

*

"I'm so glad you made it!"

I turned to see Min floating towards me across the ballroom. I accepted the hand she extended and dipped my head. "I wouldn't miss it."

I didn't tell her that I'd almost thrown the invitation away. In this digital age, messages that came in paper envelopes were rarely good news, especially when they were emblazoned with the United seal. I usually ignored paper mail as long as possible, then threw it away if I didn't like the contents. After all, the United postal service was so unreliable—it was easy for mail to get lost.

But as I'd gone to toss the envelope in the trash, I'd flipped it over and noticed her handwritten note on the back:

HOPE TO SEE YOU THERE –MIN

I'd given her the benefit of the doubt and opened the envelope, revealing an invitation to the annual United state dinner in Beijing, the most prestigious event of the year. I'd stood there, gaping at the gilded linen card, vacillating between exhilaration and abject horror.

I was exhilarated because this was my chance to become one of them—to win over some prestigious sponsors and secure my own lab so I could practice my seditious science in peace. I was horrified because Min clearly thought this was a date.

It had been a few months since we'd met, and she'd been feeding me a steady stream of middling sponsors. It was enough to keep me invested in our relationship, but not enough to make me want to commit and reveal the full details of my project.

She seemed content with the balance of power. She contacted me constantly, but she never asked about the science. She didn't demand to see reports or inquire about progress. I don't think she cared what I did with the money at all. Instead, she wanted to talk about me. She plied me mercilessly with questions about myself, my family, my interests—knowing full well that I was in no position to turn her down.

She was teasing me, but to what end, I hadn't yet figured out.

I considered refusing the invitation, but I wasn't about to sacrifice my one chance at fame and fortune. So I rallied my courage, bought a nicer bowtie, and dressed the part.

Min had also dressed for the occasion. She wore a fitted dress that flowed off her frame like water, the ruffled hem barely grazing the ground. It was black and woven with the tiniest crystals, making it look like she was clothed in starlight. Her straight black hair was pinned up with diamonds and her neck was chained in pearls.

And her lips were, as always, the color of murder.

She basked in my scrutiny. "How do I look?" she taunted, running a pale hand through her dark mane.

She was stunning, although I daren't tell her that in polite company. I stared at her, suddenly unable to find words around the buzz in my head. Every compliment I could find seemed inadequate, and I realized, far too late to back out, that she wanted more than science out of our relationship.

Her appearance sent a clear message, and unfortunately, I could read.

She spared me the misery of coming up with a gentlemanly reply. "You look handsome," she praised.

"I was just wondering if I was underdressed." I tugged on my bowtie.

She pretended to ponder that. "You could lose the mustache."

"What?" I reflectively touched it with both hands. "You don't like it, do you?"

She winked. Before I could object further, she passed a glass into my hand and gestured at me to follow her. "Come on, there's someone I'd like you to meet."

So meet and greet we did. Min led me through the crowd and introduced me to her prime contacts, forging connections like a spider weaves a web. I let her exchange the pleasantries, and then I took over, selling my captive audience with a vision of influence and prestige.

Min posed at my elbow all night. She stood far enough away to be professional, but close enough to be an accessory in my entourage. The effect was magnetic: Like a light of wealth and power, she drew the moths to me, and I caught them. By the time the evening was winding to a close, I had signed four contracts and obtained phone numbers that could lead to a dozen more.

I was more than satisfied with the night's work, but Min was still on the hunt. "I saved the best for last," she whispered as she touched my elbow and steered me towards one final victim. It was an older Asian man who I was sure I'd seen on the news at some point.

"Councilor Wu," Min called, and I abruptly remembered where I'd seen his face. Wu was the state councilor over the North American region; he was the liaison between the entire Eastern Seaboard and the United leadership in Beijing. If I wanted my experiments shielded from government scrutiny, this was the man to talk to.

He turned to Min with a smile, face lost in welcoming wrinkles. "Miss Mong! Who have you brought me?"

He knows what's up. I bowed for respect, then offered my hand. "Dr. Nic, and it's my pleasure, sir."

He returned both gestures. "I am sure the pleasure will be all mine by the time we're done. Forgive me for asking, but I'm not familiar with your work. Is Nic your given or surname?"

I swallowed a groan. "Given, sir. My surname is not worth the breath it takes to say."

Most people accepted the joke with a chuckle and moved on. He, however, paused expectantly.

Min unwittingly cursed me by offering, "It's Von Nieuwenhuyse."

His face scrunched again, but this time, the creases were not endearing. "As in the famous Dr. Paul Von Nieuwenhuyse?"

"I like to think I'm the famous doctor now." I forced a laugh. I hated winning sponsorships based on my father's merit. Those people always ended up disappointed, because I was not my father.

The councilor, apparently, had already decided to be disappointed in me. He tipped his head and regarded me with the most vilest of expressions: pity. "It's a shame."

"Excuse me?" I snapped, even though I knew exactly what he was talking about.

"The court case. It's a shame he wouldn't accept the settlement—Mars will feel his loss."

"What's a shame is how your government is treating him," I hissed, too quickly to process that I had used real words.

Min sucked in her breath, a sharp sound through clenched teeth. The councilor was merely amused. "I take it you don't agree with their decision."

I answered that with a huff. I thought it was an inane decision. In response to my father's repeated religious infractions, they'd voted to ground him; he was no longer allowed to travel off-planet. It was a suicidal ruling on the United's part. They were denying themselves of their best colonization scientist; they'd be lucky if the whole mission didn't fail without him.

But even worse was watching my father's soul suffocate when he received the sentence. He would never get to see his precious Mars again.

At least he wouldn't until I completed my experiments.

Min seemed to recognize her error in introducing me and struggled to compensate. She laid one hand on each of our arms, as if she could forge a bridge with her presence. "Yes, it's a shame, but Nic doesn't share his father's beliefs."

I glared at her. *Have you even met me, woman?*

"Excellent," Wu slithered. "Because I can only trust my projects to men of science."

I turned back to him. "Meaning?"

He gestured vaguely, as if my religious identity was a crumb he could sweep off the table. "Well, someone who holds so fiercely to ancient mythology can't be a follower of the scientific process, now can they?"

I thought you were smart.

He watched me, eyebrow arched, waiting. It was a challenge, a test. And this was a test I was happy to fail.

I drew back and opened my mouth, but Min pinched my elbow. I started and glanced back at her. She leaned closer, her sculpted fingernails digging into my arm.

Subtly, very subtly, she shook her head.

I weighed my options. I could tell Councilor Wu what I really thought— that he was an idiot—and have the momentary satisfaction of proving that I would not be bullied.

Or I could let the offense slide and get everything I wanted. If my mission succeeded, no Christian, including my father, would ever have to suffer the United's intolerance again.

I popped my jaw and rearranged my face into my coldest smile. "Of course not, sir. Of course not."

2066
TWENTY-FOUR YEARS OLD

5

I was so close.

I told myself that every morning, even if it wasn't true. I had to set the tone; I had to walk into work believing with every fiber of my being that today was the day. That's what my sponsors needed to see—their generosity was mathematically correlated to my level of optimism.

But some days, I needed to hear it as much as they did. I wasn't a fan of talking to myself—it took twice as long to finish a thought that way—but I indulged in it while I ruefully shaved my face each morning. I told myself I was a genius, and charismatic, and courageous. I convinced myself that I would win more sponsors, complete the project, and save the world.

At least one of those statements was hyperbole, but if I hadn't slathered myself with flattery each morning, I would have given up years ago.

It wasn't that I didn't believe in the science. The science was brilliant. What I wasn't convinced of was my own ability.

The premise was simple enough: Develop an acid that could dissolve metal, plastic, glass, and concrete alike. With such a weapon, I could melt prime military and government targets off the map. It was the kind of weapon you only needed to use once, maybe twice, and I liked that level of efficiency.

The question, of course, was *how* to weaponize it. Bomb dispersal would be dramatic for a demonstration but too localized to win a war. Using a tanker truck and firehose was the cheap but childish option.

My favorite theory was crop dusting. Disperse the liquid weapon from the air and let it rain down fire and brimstone. I'd sadistically named it Red Rain to capture the spirit.

There were some complications with that plan; if released too high, the weapon would simply evaporate. But those were problems that could be solved; dispensing the weapon was merely a matter of physics. It was the base formula that was eluding me.

It was the same problem that had frustrated me while trying to mutilate Wesley's cars all those years ago. Metal, plastic, glass, and concrete all had unique properties, which meant they were reactive to unique acidic compounds. Add in the fact that there were different *types* of metal and plastic, and I had given myself the improbable assignment of creating a compound that reacted to all of them.

Or at least most of them. I would have loved to be able to dissolve an entire city in one swipe, mainly so that I could relieve Earth of the burden of Washington and Beijing. But I would settle for crippling infrastructure. As long as there was nowhere to run and nowhere to hide, my weapon would suffice.

Unfortunately, even after years of research, I was no closer to finding a compound with the right balance. I'd discovered at least half a dozen new acidic compounds with glorious applications for the medical and industrial fields. I'd secured numerous research grants and won almost as many useless awards. But none of those formulas had any value to me. I didn't care about anything unless it would help me break the United.

Min was patient. I'd progressively revealed more and more of my research to her. She still didn't have full access to my files, but she knew enough that, if she was at least half as smart as she appeared, she could infer what was going on.

She hadn't objected. She occasionally asked for a progress report, but I think she did it more to humor me than anything else. As long as we went on our weekly dinner date every Tuesday, she was content.

I was less so. I wasn't afraid of failure; being in the experimental sciences demanded that one make friends with failure. But there was an invisible line that separated the hypothetical from the fantastical, and I was worried that I had begun to cross it.

I was neck—or, rather, arm—deep in another failed test when the secretary paged me to let me know I had a visitor. With the help of Councilor Wu, I'd been given my own lab, an entire wing at a secluded research facility. It came with state-of-the-art equipment, endless materials, and complete privacy. Absolutely nothing in the lab connected to the internet without my permission, meaning my research was shielded from government scrutiny.

But the best perk was the lady at the front desk. She afforded me the luxury of turning away visitors, a service for which I paid her in smiles and coffee delivery.

"Dr. Nic," her voice crackled sweetly over the intercom. "There's someone here to see you."

"Not today, Athena," I answered as I struggled to yank my hands out of the Teflon gloves that allowed me to manipulate the testing chamber.

Normally she obeyed me the first time, but today she was feeling impertinent. "It's your father."

I groaned. Normally I let my father up without question, but that would not be wise today. I knew what he wanted to talk about, and it was too soon. He needed at least three more days to cool off.

"Today's a bad day," I answered.

There was a painful pause. "He agrees, sir. He says it's a very sorry day indeed."

I yanked my goggles off and threw them on the table. "Send him up."

I quickly flicked off the computer monitor, tucked the most telling papers under a folder, and pulled the projector screen over the whiteboard. My dad didn't know what I was working on, and today was definitely not the day to have that conversation.

The automatic door whooshed open. He stood there, arms crossed, feet apart, nostrils flared—and said absolutely nothing.

"If you don't step inside, that door is going to close again," I informed him.

He did so. His graying hair was unwashed and his mustache was running rampant across his upper lip. In the harsh light of the lab, the dark circles under his eyes made it look like he'd been punched in the face. He probably hadn't slept since he'd gotten the news.

When he still refused to initiate the conversation, I decided to be the better man. "I would give you an explanation of why I did it, but I don't think you're in a frame of mind to hear it yet."

"I don't need an explanation," he snapped. "I know exactly what you did and why you did it. You think I can't take care of my own daughter."

"Who is my sister," I reminded him, "if the structure of our family tree was in question."

"Well, you seem to have forgotten that I am also your father. Nic, what's gotten into you? Do you know how upset your mother is?"

"Yes, I know, she's tried to call me ten times." I didn't add how much it had killed me to ignore each of her calls. But I knew my mother, and I knew that we spoke the same language. When we're upset, we lose our filters, and we burn bridges like matchsticks. I didn't want my relationship with my mother to be tainted by all the things she—we—would say in the heat of the moment, so I'd silenced her calls.

"Then you must understand what this is doing to her. What were you thinking, calling CPS?"

"I was thinking about Cea," I returned. "Which is what you should have done."

If my father had been more like me, I would have expected a violent reaction to that statement. Instead, he struggled to properly express his frustration and ended up flinging his arms around like a strangled turkey. "You really think I don't care about my own children? Who do you take me for?"

I leaned my knuckles on the workstation. "Do you want an honest answer to that?"

He hesitated, then folded his arms across his chest. "Yes. I do."

I took a deep breath and ordered my words—like I would when I was trying to convince a sponsor that this was for his own good. "I think you're a brilliant man and an amazing father. But you're picking fights with hornets—fights you can't win—and you're putting Cea in danger."

My words gave him pause, but not long enough of one. "Nic, all we did was go to church—like you used to do."

I ignored the cheap shot. "That, and you tried to transmit illegal media from work even though the conditions of your parole clearly state the consequences for such an act."

Any camaraderie I had generated by complimenting his parenting skills washed away. "They're called Bibles," he corrected. "And since when have I been concerned with the consequences? Since when have *you* been concerned with the consequences?"

In his defense, he had a point. I didn't care about consequences, but I did care about winning. And when you're playing the long game, sometimes you have to lose some battles to win the war.

As soon as Red Rain was complete, I would kick the hornet's nest. But until then, I would avoid aggravating the hive. My father, on the other hand, seemed determined to get stung.

I didn't expect him to agree with my philosophy, but he still deserved an honest response. "In case you didn't read the court order, those 'consequences' involved a federal raid of your home, your access to public accommodations being restricted, and a sleepover at the prison—your third in so many months, I might add."

"I'll move into the prison before I let them take the Bible *or* my daughter from me," he snarled.

I rolled my eyes, and apparently that was going a step too far. He burned as red as Mars as he took a dramatic step towards me. "Nic Joseph Von Nie—"

"I'm listening," I cut him off.

"No, you're not, and that's the problem." Abruptly, he seemed to reach the astute conclusion that I wasn't going to grovel before his anger. He sighed, and his whole body sagged, as if rage was the only thing holding his muscles taut. "Nic, please. You need to talk to them. Recant your statement. Don't take Cea away."

"She's not being 'taken away,' Dad." I tried to soften my tone, vainly hoping that would invite him to see reality. "She's just at boarding school. She's literally twenty-two minutes and fifteen seconds from home. You can visit her."

"Yes, on Wednesdays and Saturdays," he snapped with absolutely no gratitude at all, "like she's in prison."

"It's better than her *actually* being in prison." I grunted and rearranged the vials in the holder on the table in front of me. I probably shouldn't handle caustic chemicals right now, but if I didn't busy my hands, they'd find something far more unhelpful to do.

My dad didn't respond, maybe, for once, because he agreed with me.

"Dad, I know you think I'm on their side, but I promise I'm just doing it to protect Cea." I tapped the glass containers and tried to steady my thoughts. "Every time you go to jail, she spends the night in some state house for girls, and one day, they're not going to let her come home. I don't want to see her end up with strangers—or in prison with you."

My dad was still silent, so I chanced a glance up at him.

I regretted my decision when I saw his eyes were blurred with tears. "So you sent her to an indoctrination camp full of people who hate her religion? Nic, have you even been there?"

"Yes, I toured the place before I recommended it." Despite the mediocre curriculum, it was better than prison.

He shook his head, but the motion was wobbly, imbalanced. "Nic, you don't understand. Please, don't do this to her—let alone your mother. I can't lose my daughter. Not after I've already lost my son."

I rubbed my temples. "You haven't 'lost' me, Dad. I'm literally home for dinner twice a week."

He tipped his head back, his gaze long and deep, like I was a chemical equation to be solved. "Haven't I?"

I looked away. "It's not forever." I spoke of Cea, but the statement applied to both of us.

"So when?" my father challenged. He finally came around the table to stand beside me. "When are my children coming home? What are you waiting for?"

I'm waiting until I'm powerful enough to keep the monster from assimilating us back in.

"What are you working on, Nic?"

His tone shifted, downwards, and I knew I had to end the conversation quickly. "I told you, Dad. I have a research grant from the medical board—"

"Nic, I'm not stupid, and neither are you. I know you're not just creating solvents for the hospital. You're planning something."

"I'm always planning something," I deadpanned. "Now I need to get back to work." I grabbed his elbow and herded him towards the door. He allowed me to steer him around the table—and then his eyes fell on the testing chamber, where a warped puddle of plastic represented my latest roadblock.

He studied it, his eyes blinking like a cursor tracking across a monitor. And then, like clouds blowing across the moon, sadness cloaked his expression.

He'd seen this all before.

I tugged on his arm. "Let's go, Dad."

He looked up at me. "You're creating a weapon, aren't you?"

"Dad, I told you, I have a grant—"

"Don't lie to me!" he shouted. His voice nearly cracked from the sheer weight of the pain it carried. He twisted his arm from my grasp and whipped around to face the whiteboard. Before I could stop him, he yanked on the cord and rolled the projector screen up with a snap, revealing the formula for Red Rain.

The equation wasn't complete, but someone with his intelligence could easily decode what I was attempting. He read the sequence once, twice, three times, his face twisting in recognition.

"Son," he breathed, the word choking at the top of his throat. "What have you done?"

"I haven't *done* anything yet. The formula's incomplete."

He shook his head. "Not for long," he said, his grief muddying the compliment that was so strongly implied.

I took a long, even breath, forcing my nerves back under my control. "Dad, this is none of your business. Please leave."

"None of my business?" Horror washed his aging face white. "Son, do you understand what this weapon would do?"

"Why do you think I'm creating it?" I hissed.

"Are you trying to start another world war? Because that's what this does." He flung both hands at the whiteboard, as if I wasn't fully aware of what I was creating.

"I'm not trying to start a war, I'm trying to win one."

"By burning people to death with acid?"

A lifetime of doubt, distrust, and utter disappointment was crammed into those ten syllables. I could have argued with him; I had a whole thirty-page report proving that the collateral damage would be minimal if we bombed a few key targets. I had no intention of committing genocide.

But explaining that to my father would have been a waste of breath.

"Son, you have to stop this." It wasn't a suggestion. "Delete the data. Now."

I folded my arms. "I've made up my mind, Dad. People are counting on me."

"Nic, no, please. You don't understand. I can't let you do this." He had the audacity to reach out and grab my shoulder.

I shrugged him off. "I'm not asking you to be a part of it."

"Son, listen to me!" His voice broke and bent, as if modulating the pitch could shatter the glass between us. "This isn't you. I know it isn't. I know you're a kind, caring—"

"Stop," I said, more to myself than to him. I took a generous step back from him and closed my eyes, searching for my center that had been mercilessly kicked to a dusty corner of my mind. I waited until my emotions had settled before speaking again. "We don't have to do this."

He searched me. "I do."

"No, you don't. Dad, I'm an adult. We don't have to agree. You don't have to understand me." I spoke the words with false conviction.

The anger evaporated from his face, leaving a watery grief that made me feel like I was already dead and buried. "You're right, son. I don't have to agree with you. But I do have to protect you—even from yourself."

I turned back to the whiteboard. "Just walk away, Dad."

He did. After a moment's hesitation, he turned and walked out the door without another word.

Two days later, the police showed up at the door. They cuffed me and forced me to watch as they razed the lab and destroyed my research. Papers shredded, hard drives bashed in, all my chemical compounds poured down the drain. Eight years of work, erased in twenty minutes.

They claimed they had been tipped off by an anonymous source. But I knew who had sent them.

6

Min came to visit me in jail three days later.

I heard her heels clacking on the concrete and knew it was her long before she rounded the corner. "Nic, baby, are you okay?" she cried.

I was too surprised to answer her at first. I hadn't expected to see her or any of my sponsors ever again.

She grasped the bars of my cell and pressed her face against them, looking even more pathetic than I felt. "Are you all right? Are you hurt?"

I stood and walked over. "I'm fine. It's a county jail, not a torture bay."

Her coy smile returned, bringing the glint back into her eyes. She flicked her sharp fingers at the guard who stood behind her. "What are you waiting for? Open it up. We're going to be late, and this man needs to shave."

The guard obeyed, swiping a keycard on the door of my cell, but he didn't look pleased about the whole ordeal.

I took the implied invitation and cautiously stepped out into the hall. "Late for what? And what's going on?"

She laughed and threw her arms around me. "You're being released, you silly goose. And did you forget it's Tuesday?"

I struggled to process three stimuli at once: I was being released, she was hugging me, and I had, in fact, forgotten that it was Tuesday.

At least one of those things was completely unacceptable.

I gingerly disentangled myself from her arms. "It might be the dank prison air impairing my brain function, but I don't understand."

"What's there to understand?" She winked. "I'm a Mong."

The guard grunted something foul.

Min graciously ignored him and started waltzing down the hall, gesturing at me to follow. "Come on, my driver's waiting. You only have an hour to get cleaned up. Do you still have the reservations?"

I hurried to catch up. "Unless the government called the restaurant to tell them I was indisposed, I would assume we're still on for 6 o'clock."

"Excellent," she chirped, punctuating with a finger wave over her shoulder. "Because I have a surprise for you."

*

"What about Mars?"

It was several hours later, and we were closing our evening with coffee and a shared dessert. In the interest of time, Min's driver had forgone my house and taken me to hers, where a butler magically produced a clean outfit in my size. Within thirty minutes I had washed the stench of incarceration from my person, and we made it to the restaurant just in time.

Min had deferred my multitude of attempts to thank her for the bailout. "It really is no trouble," she crooned, and I believed her.

She'd filled the evening with her usual routine of pleasantries and social interrogations. I was dying—and somewhat terrified—to ask her what my "surprise" was, but I knew she would not allow the dinner experience to be rushed.

Finally, she drew her tablet from her oversized designer purse and laid it on the table between us. On the screen was displayed the blueprint for a research base.

"It's yours," she declared.

I looked up at her. "You're going to have to forgive me for my relative unintelligence tonight, but I really don't follow."

She grinned. "You need to continue the project." It wasn't a request. "And you need a private place to do so."

I agreed with both of those statements. "And it's on Mars?" I wasn't sure what I found more shocking: the fact that she'd casually acquired a base on Mars in less than 72 hours, or the fact that I might get to govern it.

She shrugged. "It seemed more… secure."

I picked up the tablet and studied the schematic. "It will pose some environmental challenges for testing…"

"I would offer you a blank check, except nobody uses checks anymore." She folded her arms on the table, smirked, and waited for me to catch up.

I bought myself time by zooming in on the schematic. I couldn't argue with anything she was saying, but I was still missing one crucial piece: why she cared.

Anyone else would have ditched me at the first sign of trouble. That's what Dad's sponsors had done to him, time and again. Even I had lost a few by saying too much too soon and in the wrong company.

I realized Min had the resources to make everything go away, but it was still *work*. It took effort to pay off judges, wipe court records, and distract the media. Covering my arrest was a mess, and I knew how Min felt about those.

I looked up and searched the galaxies lost in her eyes. "And what do you get out of it? Because if I go to Mars, we'll have to reduce our dates to once every six months—and I heard the restaurants on Mars are not that great."

"They're not," she agreed. "But it's not forever, is it?"

That was the exact same thing I had said to my dad, and in that moment, I realized that Min knew exactly what was going on.

She knew I was trying to set the world on fire, and she was eager to watch it burn.

I took a slow sip of my drink. "I take it you don't have a great relationship with your father." As a top United official, he'd be one of the first to fall if I succeeded.

She stroked the stem of her glass with her fingernail. "He was never home. So..." She tipped her head to the side, her flat-ironed hair falling across her soft cheekbones. "What do you say, Dr. Nic?"

I arched an eyebrow and gave her one of the smiles she so desperately coveted. "I don't suppose I have a choice, do I?"

She laughed. "No, you don't."

✳

It was Base #9.

Well, Base #9.6.11 was the technical title, based on the entirely arbitrary coordinates system the early colonizers had conjured up. Dad claimed the system was idiotic, and I was inclined to agree, if only because Region #1 was not correlated to a static reference point like a pole or the equator. It was merely the crater where the first manned mission had landed. In any case, #9 was currently the only base in the region, so the extra numbers were superfluous.

It was a fairly old base by Martian standards, old enough that it was feasible my dad had helped lay the foundation. I couldn't decide how that fact made me feel, so I made the conscious decision not to devote any more processing power to it.

What *did* bother me was the design. The base sprawled across the valley like a toddler had spilled a bucket of blocks. Dozens of research domes were connected to a central wing by long hallways that snaked through the dirt like worms. Some wings fed into other wings, and some hallways ended in nothing at all. It was deplorably inefficient and a grotesque waste of space.

But at least there was room to grow. There was nothing but red wilderness for miles, and the nearest settlement was almost three hours away. That's just where I liked my neighbors: in a different time zone.

It was past nightfall by the time I arrived, but they'd left the lights on for me. The exterior beacons were all lit, and the docking bay doors were open to receive me. As soon as the gate sealed shut and the atmosphere was restored, the door to the lobby opened.

A wrinkled waif of a man stood there. He was of average height and build, but he was so pale, with his white lab coat and even whiter hair, that he probably would have reflected light like the moon. It looked like God had gotten careless and bleached the entire man in the washer.

"Dr. Von Nieuwenhuyse, I presume?" he said by way of greeting, and offered his hand.

I dropped my suitcase on the ground to accept the gesture and was pleased to find that he had a strong grip, which was impressive since I could feel every bone in his hand. "Just Dr. Nic," I corrected. "Or Nic if time is of the essence."

"Isn't it always?" He let go of my hand to gesture at himself. "Carnegie." He didn't add any qualifiers, which was just as well; Carnegie was already such an ostentatious name that I couldn't imagine adding any more syllables to it.

"What's your function here?" I asked as I bent to grab my suitcase off the floor.

He beat me to it, employing a frightening amount of agility. "Governor's assistant," he announced.

I hesitated, my hand posed awkwardly midair. "Then I suppose you're out of a job."

"Not unless you've brought your own people." He glanced behind me, as if verifying that I had, in fact, not brought his replacement.

I studied him. An assistant was something I desperately needed—but only if I could trust him to be more loyal to me than to the United.

He seemed to deduce the source of my hesitation. "Besides, Miss Mong said I had to play nice, or she'll remind the officials of my past, ah… indiscretions."

That was what I needed to hear. "All right then, your interview starts now. Walk and talk. I want the tour."

"As you wish." He turned, my suitcase in hand, and started walking down the main hall.

I regretted my request for a tour about five minutes in. If the outside of the base looked chaotic, the inside was even more so. The central hallway and Wings 1-12 were sensible enough, probably because they were original. After that, the layout devolved into utter nonsense. It was clear that previous governors had tacked on new wings whenever a project demanded it. The result was that rooms serving similar functions—like greenhouses—were spread out all across the base, and the numbering system was so arbitrary that they might as well have not labeled any of the doors.

As a prime example, about twenty minutes into the tour, we found ourselves in Wing 74, even though the previous hallway had contained doors labeled in the 30s.

To add insult to injury, Wing 74 wasn't even finished. I don't think it had ever been used at all. Wires and insulation sagged from the exposed ceiling, and Carnegie had to drag most of the doors open by hand.

"You're paying to oxygenate rooms that no one is using—it's a massive waste of resources." I dragged my finger across a ledge and came up with a wad of dust.

Carnegie shrugged as he opened the door at the end of the hall. "It's not my money."

I stepped through the doorway after him. "What was this room even supposed to be?" It was a stunning but useless design. The room was massive and round with a domed ceiling that arched three stories overhead. Just keeping the cavernous space at a minimal 60 degrees was probably costing the base thousands a month.

Carnegie furrowed his brow. "I'm actually not sure. Theater, perhaps?"

"Who has time for that?" I said, twisting around. But even as my eyes toured the room, a new idea started forming.

"Certainly not you." Carnegie rested his hands in the pockets of his lab coat. "What do you think, doctor? Do you find the amenities sufficient?"

"If I don't, then I'll just build something new, like everyone else has apparently done."

He acknowledged that with a chuckle. "Shall we begin at 0900 tomorrow?"

"Better make it 1000—it'll take me an hour just to walk to the lab." I stopped in the middle of the room and looked up at the ceiling—remembering, suddenly, a building on Earth with a room of this size.

A warm, soggy feeling tried to worm its way into my stomach, although whether it was hope or longing or something equally detestable, I couldn't tell. I usually didn't have time for either of those emotions, but maybe now was the time to indulge.

I finally had everything I needed. I had unlimited funds and a powerful benefactor willing to ignore laws to get me what I needed. I was completely cut off from United control; even if they did try to bust me, it would take them a week just to fly up here, and I'd see them coming from miles away. I even had a willing assistant so I wouldn't have to waste time on paltry tasks like paperwork and emails.

I could do this. I could still finish Red Rain.

I turned back to Carnegie. "We meet in the morning for a preliminary briefing. And in the meantime, I have something I want you to research. I think I have an idea for this room."

2067
TWENTY-FIVE YEARS OLD

7

"You can't do this to me!"

That was incorrect. I was her legal guardian now, and she was still a minor, which meant I could, in fact, tell her what to do.

She knew that, of course, which was why she was resorting to hysterics. Her frazzled curls stood on end as she stomped about my office, waving her arms. She was like a little frilled lizard—doing everything she could to make herself appear bigger and more threatening.

"You can't kidnap me like this!"

I rolled my eyes, hoping that was a gesture her teenage brain could translate. "You're not a prisoner, Cea. You can go anywhere on base, and you have unrestricted internet access. You can even go off-base if you want—as long as I know where you are at all times."

Even I realized how that sounded, although regrettably, I didn't recognize it until after the words had left my mouth.

She growled like a disgruntled kitten. "You're not the boss of me! I can't believe you. You tricked me!"

That was the first accurate thing she'd said all night. I had pulled what could arguably be called a "bait and switch." I'd invited my sister to visit me at the base on Mars for the summer, and she'd excitedly accepted. It was only after she'd been here a week that I told her the truth: I had been granted full custody of her, and she wasn't going home.

Lesser men might have called me a coward, and the insult wouldn't have been inaccurate. But I knew my sister, and I knew that if I told her in advance, she never would have gotten on the transit. Not to speak of the stunts our parents might have pulled to try and keep her on Earth. No, I knew that if we'd had this conversation in advance, the police would have gotten involved, and she'd be even more shaken than she already was.

I'd gladly accept the title of coward if it meant my sister had been spared some misery.

She seemed to finally recognize that I wasn't threatened by her dramatic hand gestures, so she crossed her arms. "You can't do this to me," she said again, as if I'd find the repetition intimidating. "You're not my dad."

I gagged on the thought. "Heaven forbid," I muttered, even though that was the most ironic expression I could have chosen. "I'm not trying to parent you, Cea. I'm not about to impose an 11 pm bedtime or tell you that you can't date. All I'm trying to do is keep you alive and out of jail."

She huffed. "I don't need your help with that."

No, but our parents do, I thought, and wisely didn't say.

She resumed her war dance, strutting back and forth across the rug. "I can't believe the government just handed me over!"

It was my turn to huff. That was the most believable part of this Shakespearean tragedy, and her naivety was a little concerning. The government had been *delighted* to give me custody of my sister, so much so that they'd pushed the paperwork through in a month—an Olympic record for them. After all, I was an assimilated citizen, a prestigious governor in good standing with the officials. My parents were none of those things. They were religious noncompliants who had been in jail three times in the past two months.

That's what pushed me over the edge. I'd been contemplating requesting custody of Cea for years but had lacked the means. Now I owned a base, which gave me a stable source of income and Cea a steady place to live. I'd applied to become a foster guardian with the United, secretly hoping I would never have to use the privilege.

And then Sardis called to let me know my parents had been put in jail again. This wasn't particularly concerning in its own right, and I almost hung up on him—he had called during an important meeting, after all. But then he started describing the prison, and I knew the tides had changed.

I'd grilled him for details and quickly figured out that the place they had been sent wasn't a typical jail. No, this was something new, something that hadn't made it to the media yet. The United was getting creative with solving their unassimilated problem, and it was only a matter of time before Cea ended up behind bars with them. I immediately filed for custody and invited Cea to take a leave from boarding school and come visit me.

My parents' incarceration didn't last long. Dad pulled his usual stunts and blew the place up (somewhat literally, I was told), generating a wave of nasty media attention. To save face, the government sent them home with the usual slap on the wrist of fines and felonies. Thankfully, by the time they had been released, Cea was already on the transit to Mars.

Everyone was none the wiser until today. An officer had served the papers to my parents this morning, and I had undertaken the harrowing task of informing Cea of her new situation.

It had gone about as well as I expected.

"I'm not staying. You can't make me," she challenged, punctuating with another stomp.

"In case you've forgotten, you're only fourteen," I returned. "So as much as I'd rather find more productive things to do with my time, if I have to make you, I will."

She blistered bright red. "You're lying."

I breathed a private sigh of relief. As much as I didn't enjoy having my integrity questioned by a teenager, I knew I was about to win the argument. Cea always resorted to crucifying my character when she ran out of other options.

I reached back and grabbed my mug off the desk. "Would you like to see the court order?"

She hissed like a pot about to boil over. "Dad won't stand for this. He'll come and get me."

"I'm well aware," I grunted, taking a rallying drag of coffee, "which is why I took out a restraining order on him."

She washed white and froze, all the resistance evaporating from her body.

I stared into the mug, measuring my words. "Neither he nor Mom are supposed to contact you for six months, until they—all of you—calm down."

"How—how could you?" she whispered, the accusation rasping against her throat. "How could you do that to them? They're our *parents!*"

As if the process had given me any joy. Nothing about this abysmal situation gave me any pleasure, despite what my dad might say. But I knew the nuance of my motivations would be lost on Cea, so I didn't offer them up to be scrutinized. "I did what had to be done. You live here now, and that's final."

"No, I don't. I'm going home." She meant it as a threat, but her tears warped her voice, turning the exclamation into a pitiful cry for help.

I turned away so she couldn't see the emotion that tainted my face. "You can't. If you try to board a transit, they'll pick you up and send you right back here."

An ugly sob ripped out of her.

I pinched my eyes shut. "This is your home now, Cea," I said, forcing each syllable to be even. "The sooner you get used to it, the sooner you'll feel better."

She was unnervingly silent. I made the mistake of looking back at her.

Her swollen eyes glowed with blood and water as she glared at me. "I hate you," she hissed.

"I know," I said, my tone not belying the pain in my chest. "It was a sacrifice I was willing to make."

She shattered. She slapped her hands over her face as fresh sobs poured out of her. I could only watch her retreating form as she turned and ran out of the room.

8

I knew it was a mistake to visit my parents.

It had been about three months since I'd taken custody of Cea, and at Min's behest, I had taken a last-minute flight to Earth to attend a symposium on Martian climate change or some equally pointless topic. I should have refused; leaving Cea alone on base while she was still sulking was an unwarranted risk. Carnegie was many things, but he was not a babysitter.

But for reasons I was unwilling to admit, Min often inspired me to act against my better judgment. To her credit, I'd secured three new commissions for the base out of the event, but I knew the invitation had been a farce to get me to come visit. I'd taken the hint and booked a late dinner for tonight. What was terrifying was how much I was looking forward to it.

I had a few idle hours before I needed to pick her up, which unfortunately meant I had the perfect opportunity to visit my parents. I'd spent the entire morning trying to come up with an excuse to avoid them but couldn't find one that would withstand the test of my advanced logic. So after wasting many choice swear words on the hotel bathroom mirror, I found myself driving to Alliston.

It wasn't that I didn't want to see them. This fact seemed too nuanced for them to appreciate, but I always wanted to *see* my parents. What I didn't want to do was talk.

But I knew that, no matter what the restraining order said, there would be words. As I approached the house, I told myself that it would be better for them to crucify me than Cea. Perhaps, if I let them vent now, the next time they had a visitation with Cea they could focus on dispensing the loving attention she so desperately craved.

In some bizarre act of defiance, their porch light was on. I decided to be gracious and ring the bell instead of letting myself in the back with my key. Technically, there was nothing in the court order about me, but I was no fool. I wasn't about to walk into a den of bears robbed of their cub without knocking first.

Mom answered before the dorky electronic ring had finished playing. She opened the interior door but made no move to touch the storm door and invite me in. She stood there, staring at me from the other side of the glass, for a solid ten seconds.

I let her.

"He's here," she announced finally.

"Coming," my dad called from somewhere in the house.

"Was there traffic?" Mom asked.

I frowned. "What?"

"Took you long enough to get here," she stated blandly. "Your symposium has been over for two hours. Was there traffic?"

I allowed some emotion to make it onto my face. "You knew I was coming?"

Her nose twitched. "You're not the only one who knows how to hack into a personnel file."

I acknowledged that with a nod, even as I wondered how long she had been watching me.

Dad appeared, shrugging on a jacket. "All right, let's go. You, car." He pointed at me.

"Excuse me?"

He gave Mom a quick peck and then joined me on the porch. "Car. Let's go. We'll be late."

"Late for what?" I demanded, even though that was the least of my concerns. Visiting my parents in a house with multiple exits was one thing. Being confined in a car was an entirely different matter.

He was already walking to the detached garage. "You know they close early on Mondays. Come on, we only have an hour."

If I had thought hard enough, I probably could have remembered what closed early on Mondays, but that information was a waste of processing power when I had no intention of going. I glanced back at Mom.

Her arms had returned to their default position—tightly crossed on her chest. "You owe him this much."

I grunted and followed Dad to the car.

I had hoped mutual distrust would keep my father from attempting conversation, but I was wrong. He kept asking questions—the same ones he asked me every time he called.

How's work?

What's the latest project?

How's Sardis? He found a wife yet?

What about the base? How is it holding up? Have you upgraded the air purifier yet?

I answered the first few interrogations with clipped responses, because I falsely assumed he didn't care. After about five minutes of being brushed off, however, he slammed on the brakes at a yellow light and turned to glare at me.

"Was the restraining order against me or you?"

"What?"

"Unless I misread the paper, there was nothing in the court order that prevented us from talking about work." He turned back to the road. "So you're under no legal obligation to be rude about it."

I relaxed back in the seat. "My apologies, I thought you didn't care."

He huffed. "It's my base. I built it. Of course I care."

His words prodded the question that I was still, after all this time, too afraid to ask.

Then why don't you care about what happens to me or Cea?

He was right about one thing, though—I was under no legal or moral obligation to be rude, so I gave him what he wanted. We talked amicably about work, about all the new research projects and scientific improvements that were going on at the base, as we drove to the outskirts of the city.

When I saw the bronzed dome peaking the horizon, I abruptly remembered what closed early on Mondays.

The observatory.

"Why are we here?" I asked as we parked. They'd taken away his designated spot to save face, but they conveniently hadn't reassigned it to anyone else, so he parked in it anyway.

He didn't look back at me as we entered the building. "It seemed like a better place to talk."

"Not if you want privacy," I muttered, glancing around at the scattered visitors in the lobby.

He shrugged. "You always seemed more comfortable here than at home."

He walked up to the faculty door and pressed his thumb to the keypad. The screen squawked in warning and flashed red.

I cringed. The clerk in the ticket booth started out of her stupor and glared up at us. She looked prepared to mouth off—and then she recognized who it was.

She got out of her chair and glanced around the lobby. Satisfied that the few remaining visitors had better things to do than pay attention to us, she pressed a button to unlock the door and waved us through. Dad winked at her as he opened the door.

I followed him up to the observation dome on the top floor. Again, a half-hearted attempt had been made to strip the building of his legacy. The metal letters above the door now just read OBSERVATORY, but you could still see the ghost of his name in the faded paint.

We stepped in, and Dad toggled the controls to open the dome. I took a visual diagnostic of the room and noticed that the technology had been upgraded since I was here last. The telescope had been augmented with several new robotic instruments, and the control panel was twice as wide. I wondered who had been pouring money into the place; Dad had been fined out of most of his.

He walked over to the control panel and flicked the monitors on. "Show me the base."

"You haven't seen it?" I had a hard time believing my dad hadn't looked the base up before now. I'd been governor for over a year, and it wasn't like he didn't know where it was. It was one of his models, after all.

"I want to see how big it's gotten." He stood back to give me room at the controls.

I did not take the bait. "If you want to see the new additions, there's livecams on the promotional website that are much better."

He frowned at me. "You know, you'd save yourself a lot of energy if you didn't insist on being such a jerk all the time."

"It's how I stay fit." I sighed and rubbed my forehead. "What's this really about, Dad? I know you didn't drag me out here just to stargaze."

"Maybe I did." He keyed coordinates into the screen. The whole room vibrated as the telescope began roaming automatically, searching the skies for an unseen target. "Not everything I do is rocket science. Maybe I'm just an old man wanting to look up at the stars with his son one last time."

I didn't want to believe that. I would have rather dealt with rocket science.

The telescope stopped. The viewscreen flickered on, and a crystal-clear image of Mars filled the life-size monitor. Dad tipped his head back and studied it.

"Maybe... maybe I just want to know where my children are."

The silence returned, hot and heavy.

I walked over to the control panel. I stretched my fingers over the keyboard, then stopped.

I unplugged the handheld touchpad from the panel and passed it to my dad. "You drive. I'll show you."

His face stretched in a small smile as he took the device from me.

I gave Dad directions as he navigated the telescope across the surface of the planet. Thankfully it was the right time of day, and the base, which sat just north of the equator, was in full view. Whoever had invested in the telescope had not wasted their money; the image was stunning, and we could zoom in so close that you could almost see the spider legs of the base stretching out into the valley.

"Do you like living there?" Dad asked after we'd appreciated the view in silence for a minute.

My personal preferences had not been a factor in choosing the base, but I daren't tell him the real reason I was up there. I shrugged. "Better than Earth."

"That's setting the bar real low, isn't it?" He chuckled, but the sound died before it was finished. "And what about Cea? Does she like it?"

I stiffened. "I don't think she's decided yet."

Dad's lips twitched. "If she's anything like you, she'll take to it like a fish to water."

Cea wasn't anything like me, but I was inclined to agree. She would learn to appreciate life on base, once she realized I was giving her privacy from the government's merciless scrutiny.

If only my dad could recognize what I was doing for my family.

I decided to rip the bandage off. "Are you mad I took custody of Cea?"

He shook his head. "They were going to take her anyway."

"What?" I exclaimed. I wasn't surprised that the government had been planning to put Cea in the system; what shocked me was that Dad seemed so resigned to it.

He nodded, his eyes wandering across the dome. "It was only a matter of time. I think the only reason they hadn't done it yet was they knew I'd raise a storm in the media, and they needed a good story to cover it."

I knew that was the truth. That's why I'd gotten a restraining order—to try and save my family a little dignity.

"No, what bothers me is that I don't think she's any safer with you than she is with them."

I jerked my head up to find his eyes boring into mine, cold and unforgiving.

"I'm sorry?" I spat. I didn't usually waste energy on being offended, but now seemed like an excellent occasion. "You'd rather she be in the hands of a psychotic government than with her own *brother*?"

He folded his arms across his chest. "I wish you would have left her in that boarding school."

"Oh, you mean 'indoctrination camp full of people who hate her religion'?" I threw his own words back at him.

He was prepared for the volley. "Last I checked, so do you."

I pinched the bridge of my nose. "I don't know what that word means to you, but I don't 'hate' your religion."

"It used to be your religion, too."

In his defense, I walked right into that one, but I was prepared to walk right back out. I put my hands up. "I'm not having this conversation with you."

"Then don't."

I arched an eyebrow. He shrugged. "You can leave. No one's making you stand here and talk to your old man. You're the one that came to visit me."

"A gesture that was apparently wasted." I glanced at the door and contemplated taking his suggestion.

"Then why'd you come?"

I turned around. He spread his hands. "Why'd you come? You know my opinions haven't changed."

"I'm well aware," I admitted. "But if you're going to insist on preaching this sermon, I'd rather you do it to me than Cea."

"If you think a restraining order is going to stop me from parenting my own child, then those PhDs are wasted on you. I will never stop trying to train my daughter." He sighed, and some of the sting left his voice. "Just like I'll never give up on my son."

Against all better judgment, I looked up and met his eyes.

"I know what you're doing, Nic," he said, voice glimmering with sadness. "I know what you're building on that base."

"Dad," I hissed, and hoped the room wasn't recorded.

He spread his hands. "Don't worry, you won't get any trouble from me. I learned my lesson—I know I can't stop you. I just wonder if there's room for me and your mother up there."

A shot of hope stabbed me, and I foolishly grabbed it. Was my dad asking to come to Mars? "All you have to do is say the word, Dad, and I can have you on the next transit. I know the people."

He shook his head. "That's not what I meant. I meant, is there room for me in your perfectly balanced ideology?"

"I don't know what you think my 'ideology' is…" I swallowed the sarcasm and braced myself, fully aware of the risk I was taking with my next words. "But there's always room for you in my life."

He smiled, and for one final moment, the world was right on its axis.

"I love you too, son." He blinked and failed to stop the tears from forming. "But you know that's not true."

The tectonic plates shifted, and I felt the magma of rejection seeping in. "So I'm a liar now?"

He didn't deny it. "Let's say I come with you. Am I allowed to disagree with how you run things?"

"I feel obliged to tell you that this is a completely ineffective use of the rhetorical question," I snapped, "but yes. I'm not afraid of your opinions."

As soon as the words left my mouth, I realized with a pinch in my chest how untrue they were—although not for the reasons he would have assumed.

"Neither is the government." He shrugged. "I can have an opinion. I just can't act on it."

"I'm pleased to inform you that there will be plenty of room in my... on my base for people to experiment with whatever they wish. Which you would know if you'd listen to me."

My statement must not have been as accusing as it sounded in my head, because he didn't flinch. "Perhaps, until it interferes with one of your experiments. What happens if I don't like what you're doing? What if I try to stop it? What are you going to do—lock me in my room?"

I groaned. "I'm thinking about it."

He shook his head. "No, Nic, you and I both know that there's only room in your universe for people who agree with you. As soon as someone threatens your power, you won't hesitate to toss them aside to protect yourself. Then you'll be no better than the United is—willing to kill anything or anyone who threatens your control."

I should have been angry. Anger would have been the safer way to end this conversation. But instead, I was a fool and chose grief.

"Is that what you think of me?" I whispered, my voice barely loud enough to breach the chasm between us. "I'm not a killer."

He didn't even hesitate. "You will be if you complete your experiment."

That wasn't true. I had dozens of reports, statistics, and simulations demonstrating how my weapon would save lives. I could prove it mathematically—and morally.

But I didn't try. I didn't want to. I just closed my eyes and tried to rearrange my reality around the fact that formed the black hole at the center of my universe: My dad would never understand.

"Nic—son." His voice shifted through a roulette of emotions as if he were trying to find the tone that would save our relationship. "You're a kind, caring young man."

"You don't really believe that," I muttered, and tried to make myself believe it. If only I could bend time and space and convince twelve-year-old me that his father didn't mean what he said. That all those words spoken over him were lies, and he would never measure up.

Maybe then I wouldn't have wasted so many years trying.

"And you're brilliant. You're gifted, Nic—and I don't mean with a science degree. I know you can see things, comprehend a reality others can't. I've known since you were born that you were destined to change the world. That's how you got this far—you wouldn't be doing what you're doing if you didn't think the world could be saved."

In a cruel irony, that was the most validating thing my father had ever said to me.

Then why won't you help me save it?

"But we both know how this ends." His voice hardened like a door slamming shut in my face. "This doesn't end with freedom. This ends with war, bloodshed, and more tyranny. This won't change the world, Nic. The world will end up right back where it started. The only difference is who's on top: You."

And wouldn't I be better than them? I didn't ask the question out loud. I knew what his answer would be.

"But you can do so much more, Nic. None of this is an accident. Your giftings, the base, even the friends you're making in Beijing—it's all for such a time as this."

I finally opened my eyes and looked at him. "What do you mean?"

"You're being put in place to change the world." He cast his hand around the dome, scooping the stars up in his fingers. "But you can't do it without Him."

"Him who?"

The only clarification he offered was a sly smile. "I know He talks to you."

A rap on the door spared me the misery of acknowledging that. "Doctor?" The door creaked, and the ticket clerk peeked her head in. "We're closing soon."

"Yes, of course, thank you." My dad acknowledged her with a benevolent nod. "We'll be right down."

She shut the door and retreated. My dad turned back to the monitor and tapped a key. The viewscreen flickered off, and the telescope hummed as it settled back into its neutral position.

If only the rest of the world would put itself back where it belonged.

Dad zipped his jacket up and walked towards the door. "When can I call Cea?"

I swiveled to face him. "What? That's it?"

"Is what it? And I asked you a question."

"In June," I obliged, "and I mean—that's it? That's all you have to say?"

He glanced back at me. "Do *you* have something you want to say?"

I hesitated.

His lips twitched. "You know you can talk to your old man any time, right?" He turned and swiped his finger across the panel by the door. The dome groaned and began to shut. "Any time you want to talk, feel free to call. I'm happy to help any time—but I can't help you if you don't talk to me."

He opened the door to the hall and paused. He didn't look back, but I could hear the smile in his voice as he added, "And neither can He."

Then he walked out into the hall, leaving me alone in the loud silence.

9

"Who are you thinking about?"

I came back down to Earth with an unpleasant start and looked across the table. Min smiled at me, her face flickering in the light of the candle that tried to lend some romance to our private booth. "Who are you thinking about?" she repeated. "Because it isn't me."

"I'm sorry," I said, but didn't deny it. There was rarely any benefit in lying to Min, which was one of the reasons I liked her.

She propped her chin on her slender hand and studied me. "So? Who's the lucky girl?"

I snorted. "My dad."

Her eyes narrowed, and for a brief moment, it was as if the candle between us had gone out. "You went to see him?" Her voice held all the accusation and doubt I had been simmering in for the last hour.

"Against my better judgment," I admitted.

"What did he say?"

That I'm the next Hitler and I need to talk to Jesus more, I thought but wisely didn't say.

Enough of the truth must have made it onto my face, because she frowned. "He tried to convince you to abandon the project again, didn't he?"

I nodded, even though I was beginning to realize that was only half of it.

"And?" she prodded.

I forced my vision to focus on her again. "And what?"

"This is the part where you say 'But it didn't work, and I'm even more convinced why this project must be completed, and you have nothing to worry about, Shi Min Tai.'" She paused to refill her lungs. "Or something to that effect, but with fewer syllables."

"Good, because that's more words than I have ever used in a single sentence." I snorted, hoping we could laugh the conversation off—but she wasn't convinced.

"*Do* I have anything to worry about?"

"No," I said, but I failed to put a pause before the word.

Her whole face tightened. "Nic, please. You're scaring me."

I almost laughed. *You think you're scared? I'm abjectly terrified.* "It's fine—we just argued about Cea, that's all."

She shook her head, her dark hair dancing dangerously close to the open flame. "No, there's something more, I can tell."

I couldn't have this conversation—not with her, not here. I straightened, putting more distance between us so I could regain control of the table. "Min, I promise everything is fine. He just got on my nerves. Tell me about your work. How is—"

"No, you're going to talk to me." She grabbed my arm and tried to pull me back in, emotionally and physically. "If this is going to work between us, you need to involve me."

If what is going to work? I thought but daren't ask.

Her long fingernails kneaded my elbow. "Please, Nic. You can trust me."

I wanted to deny it. Life was so uncomplicated when you didn't trust anyone.

But I knew she was right. This woman knew things that could get me executed at the snap of a finger, and yet here we were, having dinner at the finest restaurant in Charlestown. Even if I could trust no one else on this horrid planet, I could trust her.

"I suppose you did bail me out of jail," I said, and made a payment towards my debt by offering her a genuine smile.

She accepted the sacrifice with a twinkle in her eye. "Best hundred grand I ever spent. Now tell me. What's wrong?"

I closed my eyes and tried to pull usable words out of the whirlwind. "What if… what if he's right?"

"About the project?"

"No, about me." As soon as the words left my lips, the dust began to settle.

"What about you?" Min's words were slow, stretched taut with the anxiety I was trying so hard to ignore.

I pushed her voice out of my head, for a brief minute pretending she wasn't there. I opened my eyes and stared at the candle flame, focusing on the flickering light until a vision took shape.

This is not who I am.

"Nic…?"

I turned to her. "Min, don't take this the wrong way…"

Her eyes flashed wide.

"But I don't want to be your dad."

Relief rushed back into her expression, returning the color to her cheeks. "Of course not. That's the whole reason I like you—you're not like him."

I shook my head. "No, I mean, I don't want to *be* him. I don't want his job."

"I don't follow."

I tapped my finger on my unused salad fork, rallying the courage to say the seditious words. "I don't want to be the next dictator."

She didn't respond for a long moment. When she finally spoke, her voice was painted to be reassuring, soothing. "You won't be. You could never be like him."

"I will be if I do this," I whispered, and in that moment, everything my father had ever said to me came true.

"But, Nic, you have to. There's no other way—"

"No, I don't. Min, don't you see?" I grabbed both of her hands, as if by touching her palms I could drag her into the reality that was just beyond this one. "If we do this, we start the cycle all over again. There will be another world war."

She didn't pull away, but her hands were limp in mine. "Yes, and we'll win. Someone has to be in charge, Nic. Why not us?"

Why not us? That was still the question I couldn't answer—maybe because it wasn't the one that needed to be asked.

"We can't let them win," she continued. "Think of what they've done to your parents—and it's only going to get worse. We can't let them get away with that. That's not what you're suggesting, is it?"

I shook my head. *You can't reduce this to a rhetorical question.* "No, of course not."

She wove her fingers with mine, but the gesture was slow, tentative. "Then what are you suggesting?"

The question posed there like a cliff. I knew full well that if I answered her truthfully, I would walk right off the edge—and be trusting our relationship to break my fall.

I took a deep breath and cast a thought at the one other person I knew was listening.

You'd better be right about this.

I looked into her eyes. "I think there's a better way. I think we should abandon Red Rain."

Rejection flickered across her eyes, and I died. I felt her fingers slip from mine, saw her body pull away, and felt myself falling, falling...

And then she was back, her hands tightening around mine and pulling me down to solid ground like an anchor on a ship. There was still fear in her eyes, but her voice was calm as she whispered, "I don't know what that better way is, but—I'm with you."

Air rushed back into my lungs so fast I almost choked. "Min, I—"

She put her finger to my lips. "I want you to think about it. I want you to go home, take a break. Don't touch the lab for a week. This is not the kind of decision you want to make on high... emotion."

She glanced at my empty glass, and I acknowledged the truth of that with a grunt. She was right—I was working under more than one influence tonight. But I knew the difference between the voices in my head.

"Sleep on it, then we'll talk. And if that's still what you want to do..." She pinched her eyes shut, all the doubt drawing deep lines in her face. "Then I'll support you."

"Min." I tapped her chin, forcing her to open her eyes and share in the smile I wore. "Thank you."

She cupped her hand over mine, pressing my fingers to her face. "Nic, I..." Her voice hitched on some uncomforted fear. "I need you. I can't do this without you."

"You won't have to." As the words slipped past my lips, I realized what I was saying, promising.

Her eyes searched me, the hope flickering in and out of her expression. I saw her anxiety start to crack and realized I had the power to make it all go away.

I slid my hand behind her neck, pulled her in, and kissed her.

She hesitated, her lips not moving, as if she were savoring my initiative. Then melted and kissed me back.

I gently pulled away to whisper in her ear. "I brought you something."

I let go of her to reach into the pocket of my jacket that hung on the back of my chair. My fingers closed around the object, and I hesitated.

I'd never given Min a gift before. And this was the kind of gift there was no going back from.

"You did?" she exclaimed, and the surprise in her voice was all the motivation I needed.

I pulled a jewelry box out of my pocket and turned to lay it in her hands.

She gasped, and for a second, she seemed too terrified to open it. Then she gingerly lifted the lid.

It was a single strand of pearls nestled on a bed of blue velvet.

I searched her face, but she didn't react. She stared at the gift, her face stoic.

I felt hope slip away like sand between my fingers. "Do you not like it?"

"No, no, it's beautiful." She gingerly fingered the necklace. "I just... I was hoping it was a ring."

She looked up at me and grinned, and all the sunshine came back into the room—even as tentative excitement pricked my heart.

Is that what I want?

I reached forward and slid my hand under hers. I rubbed her ring finger, imagining—wondering.

I looked back up into her eyes and smiled. "Maybe next time."

10

The call came two weeks later.

I was in the middle of dazzling a potential sponsor—the kind who would fund the base for a year if I flattered him enough—when Carnegie tapped on my elbow and held out a tablet.

I apologized to my guest and stepped away into the corner. "This better be important," I hissed, even though that was a rhetorical statement my dad would have been proud of. Carnegie only interrupted me when it was important.

"It's the government."

"I said important."

"It's about your parents."

"Maybe I better add a qualifier. This better be important *and* urgent." News about my parents, while important to me, was rarely urgent. Dad getting arrested for the second time this month didn't need my immediate attention.

Carnegie just stood there, unblinking. "It is."

I sighed to make my displeasure known, even though he was an unworthy subject, and snatched the device from him. "Stall my guests. Our paychecks are riding on this meeting."

"They always are," he said, and floated up to the table to take my place.

I hurried out of the meeting room and ducked into my office. I looked at the caller ID on the tablet, and sure enough, it was my absolute favorite people in the world: the United, Reassimilation Services Division.

I unmuted the call. "Third time's the charm."

"Excuse me?" a painfully young voice responded. "Is this Doctor—"

"Nic? Yes. And I say third time's the charm because I'm assuming you're calling me to tell me that you tried the containment camp stunt again. I hope for your sakes that it works this time."

There was a beat while the poor soul recalibrated to my sense of humor. "What containment camps, sir?"

It was said with such guileless professionalism. *This kid deserves a raise.* "Sorry, I meant 'behavioral training facility.' I forgot to turn on my bureaucratic filter." I walked over and flipped on the coffee maker. If I was going to have to deal with the government, I needed a fresh pot.

"I'm not sure what you're referring to, sir." The kid cleared his throat in a vain attempt to regain control of the conversation. "I called to tell you that you're needed back on Earth."

In his defense, that was a new one. "Why?"

"We believe they will be much more responsive to treatment if administered by a trusted face—"

"Whoa," I cut him off. "Hang on."

"What?"

I ignored him, yanked the cup off the coffee maker, and took a swig, ignoring the dribble on the tray as the machine continued to dispense. I set the cup back on the machine and cleared my throat. "I'm going to need you to try again. I don't know what that stupid script they gave you says, but I'm pretty sure you're not supposed to lead with that."

"Actually, sir, that's exactly what it says…"

"Then rewrite it. What do you mean, 'treatment'? What sort of moronic pseudoscience are you trying on my poor folks now?"

He went silent, and my blood ran cold.

Once again, my careless words had been prophetic. And once again, I would have given anything to be proven wrong.

The kid still hadn't found his courage, so I decided to help him out. I sat down at the desk and opened a note file. "Start from the beginning."

He did. My parents had been put on trial again—the usual song and dance—and this time, the judge had risked recommission to issue a severe sentence: neurosurgery.

It was an unpopular corrective device, even for dealing with thorns in the flesh like my dad. It wasn't that it didn't work; if the intent was to force patients to forget about their religion, national identity, and other pesky idiosyncrasies that prevented assimilation, then the treatment had a perfect success rate.

The problem was that patients often also died. And while the United was not against executing people, there were far cheaper ways to do it. Even the government wasn't *that* grossly inefficient.

By some miracle, both of my parents had survived. But the more the kid described their condition, the more I realized their survival may not have been a mercy.

The kid claimed they had forgotten everything they knew, including the majority of their life and social skills. He described their condition as that of a two-year-old.

"The doctors believe that, with consistent therapy, they will be able to—"

"Show me," I demanded.

"What?"

I gripped the desk with both hands, forcing myself to say the words I knew would end in disaster. "I want to see them."

"Now?"

"No, I have an opening next Tuesday. Of course now!" My voice rose to a shout, my whole body lurching with the effort. The desk rocked.

"I—I suppose I can patch you into the hospital."

"Please do."

It took him a good ten minutes—during which I asked to see his manager twice—but he managed to call the facility and get their doctor on the line. The doctor tried to give me the same spiel, just embellished with more technical terms, but I didn't give him the grace. After I issued several veiled and unveiled threats, he finally enabled a video call and let me see my father.

Dad looked fine, which was the most disturbing thing about the whole ordeal. There was no scarring, no bandage, no stitches; neurosurgery was a completely nano-driven procedure. He was alert and seemed to be in perfect health.

But he looked so confused.

"What's that?" he asked, voice several pitches too high. He pointed at the tablet some nurse was shakily holding up to his face.

I turned on my camera. "Paul."

His head jerked around, as if he couldn't figure out where the sound was coming from. "Who's Paul?"

"That's you, remember?" the nurse offered oh-so-sweetly.

But he didn't. He clearly didn't.

I don't know why I said it. I knew what was going to happen, the disappointment I was inviting on myself. But I had to do it. I had to try one last time.

"Dad," I said, and I repeated the word until his eyes focused on me. I leaned towards the camera, as if that could span the millions of miles between us. "Dad, it's me."

His response was immediate. "Who are you?"

I ended the video.

The underpaid clerk was still waiting on the other line. "I know this is a lot to take in, sir."

Can't even bend your bureaucracy to apologize, can you? I sank back in the chair, letting my muscles melt like plastic dissolved by acid.

"But you're needed back on Earth immediately."

"Why?" *I'm never going back. You can keep your stupid planet.*

"You need to assist with administrating the therapy. They will need round-the-clock observation, and we believe their chances of success increase with…"

I laughed, the sound as painful as broken glass. "Absolutely not. I'm current on my taxes."

"Sir?"

"Government healthcare includes end-of-life care, does it not?"

"Y-yes, for fully assimilated citizens—"

The truth sank into me like a knife. "Which they are now."

He couldn't deny it. "The government wants—"

"The government got what it wanted. Now it can clean up the mess." I didn't give him a chance to counter that, if he was even intelligent enough to do so. "I want daily reports on their progress and access to their full medical files."

"Sir, I'm not authorized to—"

"You're not? No worries, I know someone who is. Surname is Mong."

I would never have bothered Min with something as paltry as this, but I knew I wouldn't have to. The clerk's stuttering reached a new pitch. "Mong? Of-of course, sir, I'll set that up right away."

I hung up without thanking him.

I shoved my chair back and stormed over to the coffee maker. I grabbed my mug, stopped, and stared.

The dark liquid rippled as my hand shook. My whole body—my arms, my legs, my mind, my universe—was shaking. And there was no gravitational pull that could put my world back in orbit.

All this—the base, Red Rain, the coup—was to protect my family. It was to save my parents, save Cea, save me, save everyone who looked and thought and talked differently. We were going to crumble the United so that we would never have to suffer their injustices again.

But I was too late. Red Rain was a failure.

I was a failure.

I screamed. The primal yell rasped against my throat and agitated the darkness that descended on my mind like a dust storm. I turned and hurled my mug into the wall, relishing the chaos as the ceramic shattered and the coffee splattered.

Something shoved its way up my throat. I fought it, tried to swallow it like unwelcome bile, but it flared into an urge I could not deny. What point was there in resisting? There was no point in fighting. Not anymore.

So I surrendered, collapsed against the wall, and wept.

*

The nightmares returned immediately.

Of course, I only slept a combined four hours over the next three days. It took twenty-four hours of vicious phone calls and blackmailing before I was finally granted full access to my parents' medical files. I spent the next forty-eight scouring the data, trying to figure out who had done this.

The court case had been completely classified. Even my black-market connections couldn't hack in. I could find absolutely no explanation as to who had charged my parents or even what they had been charged with. I scoured my parents' personnel files trying to figure out what they had done to anger the law, but they had been unusually compliant over the last several months. I could not find any reason why even the pedantic United would justify the procedure.

Why them? And why now? They'd done nothing—nothing out of the ordinary—and Dad was still on their payroll. He'd had enough of his rights stripped away over the years that he was little better than an indentured servant, but he was still their best scientist. From his government-monitored lab in Boston, he was doing more to advance the colonies on Mars than all the students at Stanford combined.

Or at least he had been, before they'd used a nanobot to rewrite his brain circuitry.

I turned to their medical files next. I researched the neurologist, the surgeon, the director of the hospital—even their anesthesiologist. I couldn't find anything suspicious in their records, no prejudice or bias or history of malpractice. None of them were even running for office. They had absolutely nothing to gain from the procedure. As near as the record showed, they had simply been hired to do a job.

And then, finally, I found who had hired them.

Deep within the recesses of Dad's medical history, I found a digital signature. Neurosurgery was a highly restricted procedure, and it required multiple layers of government approval. Most of the permission slips had been classified, but there are always redundancies with computer records. And in this case, they'd forgotten that the lab also had a copy of the release for the special anesthesia.

I decrypted the file, and a government ID popped up on the screen:

MONG SHI MIN TAI

I panicked, my heart and brain flying into survival mode like I was being held at gunpoint. Everything in me willed the universe to conjure up another explanation, some logic that would reconcile this information with the truth I needed.

I grabbed my phone. Min and I had spoken little over the past few days. Correction: *I* had spoken little. I'd told her the news, inciting a barrage of texts and calls from her that I did not return. She had expressed her sympathy repeatedly and offered her assistance—financial and physical.

I scrolled to the bottom of our message history, to the text she had sent a mere hour ago:

THIS IS WHY WE NEED RED RAIN

Suddenly, everything made sense.

The world flashed black and white, and in that split moment of pure rage, I considered calling her. But to what end? So she could snivel and beg and try to convince me that this was all for my own good? I didn't have time for that. So I blocked her on every platform and device and hoped she would take the hint.

She didn't.

Three weeks later, she showed up at the base. I was in the lab, buried in a pointless experiment designed to distract my mind from bigger problems, when Carnegie interrupted me.

"I have a docking request, sir, but I have no arrivals on the agenda."

I held two vials up to the light. I poured one into the other, not because I needed the compound, but because I had to see the color change, the molecules move, the liquid slide against the glass—anything to fill the void that had become my subconscious. "Who is it?"

"That's just it—the vehicle registration is classified."

I slammed the empty vial down on the table, shattering it.

"Doctor?"

I brushed the glass shards into a pile. "The only people allowed to classify information is the government, Carnegie. Tell her to leave."

He was being unusually slow. "Her?"

I didn't elaborate. "The docking request has been denied."

After a flicker of hesitation, Carnegie lifted the tablet he carried and keyed my command onto the screen. I crossed my arms and waited.

As I suspected, she didn't take no for an answer. Carnegie turned the tablet to face me. "They're requesting to speak to you."

"Regrettably for them, I'm booked solid."

"They're sending over ID... It's Min." The tablet chirped. "Correction, she's *ordering* you to speak to her."

I cackled. "She of all people should know I'm terrible at following orders."

Carnegie's eyes flickered. He probably would have gone pale had there been any shades between him and copy paper. Unlike me, Carnegie still had a healthy fear of Min's influence. "Do I need to remind you that she can have you defunded in about five minutes?"

"It would probably take her closer to ten with the signal delay, but no, you don't. I just don't care."

Carnegie frowned. "Well, I do." He punched the button to enable audio and held the tablet out to me.

I grunted a choice word. "You're fired," I snarled, and snatched the tablet from him.

"Nic," Min's voice crackled over the speaker.

I leaned against the table and waited.

"Nic," she repeated. "Nic? Talk to me. Please."

Carnegie arched an eyebrow. I picked at my teeth.

Min huffed, her breath rippling the line. "Nic Joseph Von Nieuwen—"

I grimaced. "If you're wondering how long I can sit here and let you babble into an empty line, the answer is *all* day. I'll even clear my afternoon."

"Nic." She breathed again, a relieved sound this time. "Please, let's talk about this. I can explain."

"Babe," I said with enough sucrose to rot a tooth. "You don't have to explain anything."

Her desperation must have made her deaf, because she fell for it. "I don't?"

"No, of course not." I let my benevolence hang for a moment before dropping the knife. "I know exactly what you did and why you did it."

"But I—"

"They were unnecessary, weren't they?" My pain leeched into my voice, making it sharp like vinegar and salt. "My parents were an unnecessary mess that you just *had* to clean up."

She hesitated a beat too long. "Nic, I'm sorry, I—"

"No need to apologize. I'm the one who fell for it—for you." I picked up a vial and tossed it in my palm. "It's a shame, really. If I hadn't hacked into the medical records… it might have worked."

I thought of the necklace and the kiss and the candlelit dates and realized just how true that was.

"Nic, please," she begged, and the impending tears were genuine. "I need you."

I laughed—long, cold, and hard. "Don't lie to me."

"But I'm not—"

"You don't *need* me. You have a copy of the research. Find another scientist."

Carnegie shifted.

Min had the manners to process that before replying. "You're right," she said, and took a deep breath. "I don't need you."

I pressed the vial to my lips, closed my eyes, and waited.

"But I want you."

I opened my eyes and stood up. "Regrettably, *Asia...*" I let the name close the lid on the coffin, "...I don't want you."

I ended the call.

I held the tablet out to Carnegie. It took an inordinate amount of time for him to gather his wits and take it. "Is your will drawn up, doctor?"

"What?" I barked, suddenly feeling very tired.

He swiped on the screen. "Because I think you just signed your own death warrant."

I spat another laugh. "One can only hope." If Asia wanted to put me out of my misery, let her. But I knew she wouldn't. Love was a cruel master, and in this case, it would work in my favor.

The tablet screeched. "She's still requesting to dock."

I sighed and turned back to my workstation. "Carnegie, what *do* I pay you for? Take care of it."

He hesitated, craggily finger posed over the screen. I saw the cowardly fear dance in his eyes and wondered if he was about to defect—and then, suddenly, his emotion evaporated. "Of course, sir." He spun and strode from the room.

I waited until the door had slid shut behind him before sagging against the table. In some sick way, it wasn't Asia's deception that bothered me. I had done the same to other people in the process of securing sponsorships. That was how the game was played—I went into these relationships expecting to use and be used.

I did not go into them expecting to fall in love.

I couldn't decide whether to vomit or flip the table. Since grief was a highly unpleasant emotion to process, I chose the latter.

I roared and swiped my arm across the table, scattering the instruments. A welcome symphony of destruction erupted as metal clattered and glass shattered. Spilled chemicals bled together, adding an accompaniment of fizzles and steam.

I watched as the contents of two overturned flasks pooled on the table. A stream of yellow hastened to marry a puddle of orange, and when they kissed, they turned to blood. The newly forged acid trickled over the side of the table, where it instantly scarred the linoleum.

I watched the caustic chemical eat away at the floor and, for the first time since my visit to Earth, regretted stopping the Red Rain project. It would be nice to watch the world burn.

The door hissed open. "I've taken care of—doctor!"

Carnegie grabbed a spill kit off the wall and darted over, but I put up my hand. "Wait."

"Sir?"

I watched as the stream dried to a trickle. *What if…*

I strode to the other side of the room, where a whiteboard was shoved in the corner. I dragged it out and spun it around.

My incomplete formula for Red Rain was still written on the surface in mismatched colors, right where I'd abandoned it a month ago. I traced the imperfect chemical equation with my eyes, compounding, simulating—imagining.

"It's too subtle," I thought aloud.

"Sir?"

"Red Rain. It's too subtle. Too localized. It's limited to how far and fast a plane can spread it—and they could always shoot the plane down. It would never win in a large-scale attack."

"Are you planning a large-scale attack?"

I didn't answer. I grabbed a marker and tossed the cap on the floor. Then I started scribbling on the whiteboard. "But what if it really is raining?"

Carnegie came to stand by my elbow. "Explain."

"It's all in the name—Red Rain. We make it an environmental weapon." I had no idea what the chemical compound would look like yet, so I tried to emphasize with pictures and a diagram. "I don't know how we'll distribute it—gas, probably—but what if we could contaminate the air? What if we could release this compound into the environment, and as soon as it started raining, it would turn into acid?"

"Sir," Carnegie said again, this time with admiration.

"You could decimate an entire city—country—and no one would be able to stop it." I threw the marker on the tray and paused, for one final moment appreciating what I was saying. "We could win any war."

Carnegie folded his arms, his winkled hands disappearing in the folds of his lab coat. "May I ask, doctor… is there a war you'd like to win?"

I knew what he was asking, challenging.

We both know how this ends.

I dragged my finger across the whiteboard, smearing part of the equation. "My dad was right about one thing."

Carnegie frowned but waited.

I looked up at the ceiling, where a flicker of the Martian sky shone through the windows. "I am no better than they are."

JUNE 2076
PRESENT DAY

11

I waited until the memories had run their course and slunk back into the recesses of my mind. As soon as the relative silence returned, I reached up and stroked my fingers across the keypad next to the door.

The room shuddered and moaned as the ceiling began to part. The panels folded in on themselves, revealing a seamless dome of glass. Mars' dim moons lent barely any light, but it was just enough for me to make out the shape of the telescope in the middle of the room.

She stood idle, her frame covered in dust and her mirrors still wrapped in protective film. I had almost finished building her when I got the news about my parents' neurosurgery. Out of defiance and hope, I completed the project. It took two years—two years of watching my parents go through humiliating therapy—before I acknowledged that it was a wasted effort.

The telescope had never seen first light. And she never would.

*

The invitation was late this year.

It usually came in March, several months in advance of the event, as was proper with a formal invitation. This year, the envelope didn't arrive until the middle of July—much too late for me to reasonably plan a trip to Earth, not that I had any intention of attending.

Had she forgotten? Had I finally been released from the prison of her memory? I squinted at the ornate United postmark. She had only mailed the invite two weeks ago and expedited it by private transit.

Overcompensating, as always.

I opened my lower desk drawer and prepared to add the envelope to my collection. For eight years she had been inviting me, and for eight years she had written the same message on the back of the envelope. For eight years I had allowed silence to be my RSVP.

And yet, for some reason—perhaps the same one that prevented me from demolishing the observatory I had built for Dad—I couldn't bring myself to throw the invitations away. So they sat, unopened, in chronological order, at the back of the drawer.

I flipped the envelope over and bent to file it—and froze.

She'd written a different note this year. She'd used a new color of ink and made the cursive letters larger and curlier so that I would be sure to notice. How kind of her—it would have been a shame if I had missed the carefully-articulated threat.

YOU REALLY MUST COME. AFTER ALL, IT'S ANDROMEDA'S BIRTHDAY –MIN

OPERATION

THUNDERBIRD

RED RAIN #6

JULY 2076

1

Punching my boyfriend in the face was not my idea of a fun date.

"Pull back, regroup, try again," my uncle Tower called from outside the ring.

We both obeyed. I slid a few feet back from Stanyard, my bare feet dragging on the padded canvas floor. We were in the gym on the lower level of the base, where we'd been spending most of our afternoons for the past several weeks. Every day we came down here to train, and every day I ended up on the ground, gasping for breath.

Today, clearly, would be no exception. Even though we were several floors beneath the ground, the cold air did nothing to stop me from sweating profusely.

"You good?" Stanyard asked, pushing his tousled dark hair off his forehead. We'd been going for half an hour already, but he barely looked winded. Probably because I hadn't given him much of a fight.

"Yeah," I lied, and wiped the sides of my face with both hands. I'm sure I looked anything but cute with my tangled blonde hair and smudged eyeliner. Why I'd bothered to put on makeup this morning was beyond me, but something about knowing Stanyard would be picking me up made me want to break out the blush and bronzer.

The frown returned to his dark eyes, but he didn't argue. "Ready?"

I nodded, not trusting my voice.

"On the count of three." Tower leaned both hands on the rope railing. "And let's try to act like you mean it this time."

My heart returned to its second home in my throat. *Please don't.*

"One... two... three."

Stanyard lunged forward and grabbed my wrist. I struggled to remember the motions even as his touch ignited a flurry in my stomach. I should have been feeling fear, adrenaline, the fight to survive. None of those could have been further from my mind.

It's not real, I coached myself as I yanked my arm back, using his momentum to pull him forward. I hit his chin with the palm of my hand—harder than I intended. I heard his teeth click and winced.

No one's getting hurt. I forced myself to grab his shoulder and shove him down. *This is just practice.* I pretended to kick him, knocking his chest with my knee. He grunted. *And he's not your boyfriend.*

But even as I pushed off him and darted away, I realized I didn't believe any of those statements.

"Good one," Stanyard coughed. He straightened and turned to face me.

I scanned his face, searching for bruises. "You okay?"

He wiped his chin on the back of his hand, his grin returning. "Never better."

Tower was not impressed. "You need to be faster, Philadelphia. Again."

Stanyard nodded at me, and we repeated the motions with what *I* thought was an increase in efficiency. I looked to my uncle for approval.

He shook his head. "Again."

I was really starting to hate that word.

Tower paced around the ring as Stanyard and I continued our morbid dance. "This isn't for show. A real attacker isn't going to be sluggish."

A real attacker also wouldn't be staring at me with a secret half-smile, one eyebrow raised in a gesture only I could interpret. I glared at Stanyard as I clipped him in the chin, wishing I could wipe the feelings right off his face and off my heart.

Tower had similar thoughts. "Stanyard, stop flirting. Pretend like you actually intend to hurt her."

The light went out of Stanyard's eyes, and I swallowed.

"And you," Tower pointed a scarred finger at me, "I want you to forget his face. Pretend it's not him. Pretend it's someone who actually hurt you—you have plenty of options."

He wasn't wrong, but no matter how hard I tried to conjure Carnegie, or Ambrose, or Thames, I couldn't superimpose a nightmare over Stanyard's face. I couldn't erase the kind words, the gifts, the *prayers* he had showered on me for the past month. I couldn't imagine him as an enemy, not anymore.

He grasped my wrist and yanked me forward, but instead of reacting, I just froze, all my complicated emotions icing over. I stumbled and crashed into him. He dropped my hand and caught me—like he always did.

He chuckled and set me on my feet. "Easy there."

Tower sighed and rubbed his temples, clearly wondering how his illustrious military career had brought him to this point.

"Sorry," I mumbled to literally no one, quickly stepping back. "I just wasn't paying attention."

"And now you're dead."

I stifled a groan as Jayde walked into the room. He was the commander of the base, and he was the one person I didn't want to watch me train. Probably because he was the one making me do it.

He grasped the railing and swung his muscular body into the ring. "If that happens on the street, you're done."

I rubbed my sore arm. "I'm trying."

He wasn't appeased by the sacrifice. "That's not good enough. You should be better than this by now."

His words stung like a slap across the face—because he was right. I should be better than this by now.

"Lay off her," Stanyard grunted.

"Why should I? No one else will." Jayde's combat boots sunk into the padding as he strode towards me, and I registered what was happening—a second too late. He grabbed my hair and yanked my head back.

I yelled as my mind blacked out in panic. *What do I do, what do I do?* I should know what to do; we'd rehearsed this. I struggled to recall the right move, but all I could see were flashing colors. I scrabbled at his arm, my sweaty fingers slipping off his thick wrist.

Jayde let me struggle. "Ambrose didn't lay off her. Carnegie didn't lay off her."

Stanyard shouted an objection, but Jayde blocked him with his arm. "Nic didn't lay off her."

Rage replaced the fear in my lungs. "Don't talk about Nic like that!"

Jayde's fingernails dug into my scalp as he gave me one last yank and let me go. I slipped on the floor and fell. The impact shuddered through my joints and threatened to knock tears loose.

Stanyard dropped down next to me. "Phil."

"Don't help her," Jayde snapped. "She gets up on her own, or not at all."

"Don't be a jerk," Tower called, but less kindly.

Jayde folded his arms over his chest. "If she wants to lead us, she has to train like us. My men won't follow a 'Blue Fire' who can't pick herself up." He spat my callsign like a threat, and I took it as one. He leered over me. "Get up."

Stanyard touched my arm, but I shrugged him off. I was weak, but I was not a failure. Even if I could do nothing else, I could always get up again. I'd proven that to Ambrose, Carnegie, even Nic. I would prove it to Jayde, even if it broke every bone in my body.

I am Blue Fire.

I planted both palms on the mat. With a breath and a prayer, I pushed myself up and turned to face Jayde. I slid one foot back, put both fists up, and stared him down. "Again."

He grunted, approval flashing across his green eyes. "All right then, show me what you've learned. Try to punch me." He copied my stance and crossed his arms defensively in front of his face.

I quelled a spasm of anxiety. *I can do this.* At least punching Jayde required less imagination.

Stanyard gave us a wide berth. I swung my right fist at Jayde, and he ducked. I followed with my left first and then my right again. He continued to roll, motion effortless.

"Focus," Tower coached from somewhere behind me.

I lunged, overcompensating. Jayde easily sidestepped, and I stumbled forward, nearly ending up on my face.

Jayde pulled back and waited for me to gather my wits. "Operation Blue Fire launches in three months," he said, not sounding the least bit winded. "These people are going to expect a warrior, not a victim."

I am not a victim. We squared up again, and I threw another punch, more purposeful this time. I had been a victim before, but never again. I chose this. No one was forcing me to be Blue Fire. I chose to join the rebellion because I believed it could be done. Because it was the right thing to do.

"We're asking them to risk their lives to stand up to the government." Jayde raised his arm and clipped my next strike out of the air. "They're going to expect you to do the same."

I swung again, not caring that I hit his arm—at least I was hitting something. I had already risked my life several times to resist the United, and this wouldn't be my last. Only this time, my rebellion would look a little different. This time, I wouldn't be blowing up a lab or destroying a weapons factory. I wouldn't be recording a video in an empty room, begging someone, anyone, to help. I wouldn't be fighting alone.

No, this time, I would be leading an army.

"We only get one shot at this. We have one chance to pull the trigger, and if we don't move the needle, the United will finish us off." Jayde deflected my next shot, then lowered his arm to give me another chance.

I took the window of opportunity, pausing to measure my movements. I focused on pivoting my foot and putting my hip into it, just like Tower had taught me. Jayde was right—we wouldn't get another chance. There were no do-overs with Operation Blue Fire. On the chosen day, I would go on air and tell everyone it was time to fight. At my signal, citizens across the globe—anyone who followed the thunderbird symbol—would stand up and say no. They would burn factories, go on strike from their government jobs, destroy paperwork—whatever it took to show the United that we would not conform anymore. The unassimilated were going to resist, and we were going to do it together.

There was no going back from that. Either Operation Blue Fire would succeed, and the government would lose its grip on society. Or it would fail, and we'd all be branded as criminals. Anyone who spoke out would be executed, and my people—Christians and other dissidents who refused to sign the file—would suffer in containment camps until the government decided to wipe us out.

Operation Blue Fire was a one-shot chance at freedom. And its success all came down to me.

I took a deep breath and focused all my muscles into coordinating the next punch. I missed, but not by much—my knuckles grazed his ear as he dodged.

He cracked his neck and straightened. "Better, but too slow. Stop reacting. You have to lead. Everyone's looking at you."

His words made my stomach clench with anxiety, and my next swing missed by a large margin. He snorted derisively.

Stanyard shifted in my peripheral. "C'mon, Phil." His tone suggested that if I didn't land a punch, he would.

I took a deep breath and closed my eyes. Everyone *was* looking at me whether I liked it or not. I hadn't wanted to be famous, and certainly not for insurrection. I hadn't intended to start a war when I blew up the factory on Rott. All I wanted to do was keep Red Rain, the apocalyptic chemical weapon my father had created, out of the hands of the government.

I'd done that, but now my story was convincing other people to join the fight. Jayde and his allies had blasted my videos all over the internet and made me the face of a rebellion. I was Blue Fire, the thunderbird. I was the one they were listening to. I was the one they trusted.

And now it was my job to lead Operation Blue Fire.

There were days I still doubted. Every time I went live, I stared at the angry red recording light and wondered if someone, anyone, would be better than me. Someone with more experience. Someone with more strength. Someone who hadn't stumbled into this by accident and almost killed her father in the process.

But mistake or not, I was here. I had been chosen—God had chosen me. Only He could have strung all the tragic pieces of my life together and turned them into something worth fighting for. Now it was up to me to finish the job.

I opened my eyes and focused on Jayde's face, tracing an invisible line through the air to his chin. I ground the balls of my feet into the padded floor, tracing the flow of power up my spine and into my arm. Shoving all other thoughts out of my head, I swung my fist with a lifetime of righteous indignation—and landed.

My knuckles cracked into his chin, and I gasped in surprise. The shock rippled up my arm with a burst of elation. *You can do this. You can be one of them.*

Stanyard made a noise of admiration, and I savored it a beat too long. Jayde popped his jaw and swung his foot, knocking my legs out from under me. I collapsed on the ground with a grunt.

"Seriously, dude?" Tower griped. "She got you fair and square."

"Yes, she did," Jayde consented. "And she'll do it again. Get up." He nudged my foot with his boot.

I groaned and struggled to obey. Fatigue seized my joints, reminding me that I'd been training for an hour already. I braced myself against the rope railing. "I need a minute."

I'll never know if Jayde would have relented, because a slamming door and pounding footsteps answered for him. I turned to see my older brother Ephesus jogging towards us.

I smiled at him, feeling a rush of involuntary comfort. His arm cast and nose splint were gone, and his dark brown hair was growing back in. He looked like my brother again, and the sight of him reminded me that there were a few things that hadn't changed over the past few months.

Unlike me. I could never go back to the long-haired, brown-eyed girl he used to know. Some people still called me Philadelphia Smyrna when they thought the government wasn't listening, but to everyone else, I was Andromeda Nolan. Even to my family.

He stopped and tried to return my smile, but I could tell the gesture was harried, nervous. "It's time."

My happiness faded when I remembered why I'd agreed to train this afternoon. Why I was in the basement punching things—so I could forget what was going on upstairs.

Ephesus gulped a breath. "We need you." The statement was directed at me, but he cast a glance at our uncle. "They're ready to bring Dad online."

2

"Online" was an accurate term, seeing as my dad was more machine than man.

He lay entombed in an incubator, looking like Snow White in her glass coffin. His newly regenerated skin was almost as pale as hers, and there were patches and wires connected to almost every square inch of his body. A tangle of tubes snaked from the incubator and tethered him to the half a dozen machines that were keeping him alive. Everything whirred and beeped and gave conflicting readouts, making the whole room twitch and vibrate like an old man having a seizure.

It was only a slight improvement over the block of solid cryoprotectant he had been encased in a few weeks before.

Today, a new monitor had been added to the chaos. It sat on a stand at eye-level, with a curved screen over four feet wide. On its display trilled an endless scroll of green code.

Andes, the Scotsman I'd hired to oversee my dad's revival, stood in front of it, his thick fingers flying over the screen with a surprising amount of dexterity. "You got me wired in yet, lad? I'm still not seeing any input."

There was a thud and an exclamation muttered in Russian from behind Dad's machine. Another grunt, and then Lev appeared, a wad of wires in his hands. "Try that."

The code on the display flickered and rebooted. Andes clapped his hands together, his tattooed arms bulging. "We're in!"

Lev navigated his lanky body around the tangle of machines. He stopped next to me and saluted, as he did every time we met.

I managed a smile for him. Lev, like me, had lost everything for refusing to assimilate. Only, unlike me, there was no hope that Lev's family could be revived. The United had been less patient with the Jews.

Lev returned the smile and saw himself out, nodding at Tower as he passed. My uncle took up station at the door, guarding the room in watchful silence, like he always did.

Ephesus brushed past me and joined Andes at the monitor. "Are we ready, Cynthia?"

His question was directed at Mrs. Nolan. She stood on the other side of Dad's machine, fiddling with an IV dispenser. "Give me a minute to stabilize his blood pressure."

The sight of the clear liquid flowing down the tube and into Dad's chest made me shudder. "Is he okay?" I asked, too loudly.

She glanced up at me. "He's fine. He's just recovering from the lung transplant, that's all."

I nodded and swallowed, trying to push the fear and guilt back down into my stomach. Mrs. Nolan's tone was guarded, but I knew she wasn't lying to me. We'd moved past that stage, although I don't think either of us knew how to classify our relationship anymore. To the government, she was my adoptive mother. And although she would never be a parent to me, seeing how she had put her nursing skills to use caring for my dad had proven that she at least wasn't an enemy.

"He's done remarkably well for how much freezing damage he suffered." She turned back to the incubator and navigated controls with swift hands. "His body accepted all the transplants and seems to be assimilating them well. The question is if his brain can support them." She looked up at Ephesus.

"That's what we're going to find out. Ready?" He deferred to Andes.

"I don't think I'm the one you should be asking." Andes glanced back, and the burden shifted, as always, to me.

I walked over to Dad's machine. Laying my hand on the glass, I closed my eyes and prayed. My pleas for mercy and healing battered against an impossible wall of *what-ifs*, but I shoved through them all to reach the only One who could save my dad.

Please, God, let him still be in there.

I looked up and nodded at Andes.

He reciprocated the nod and swiped a hand across the monitor. "Right now we've got an implant suppressing his brain function so that the machines can do the living for him. I'm going to release the hold on each organ one at a time so we can make sure he remembers how to breathe."

Ephesus picked up a tablet and keyed instructions onto the screen. "I'm monitoring the electrical readouts."

"And I'm watching his bios," Mrs. Nolan said, squaring herself in front of Dad's incubator.

"One heart, coming online." Andes tapped the screen, and a flicker of electricity arced from the pads on Dad's chest. He convulsed, his legs and arms smacking into the glass.

I tried to scream and gagged on the sound.

"It's okay, it's okay." Mrs. Nolan stuck her gloved hands into the machine and gently laid him back down. "It was involuntary."

I scanned Andes's monitor, as if I had any idea what I was looking at. He navigated menus, his fingers barely lifting from the screen. "I need more power. I'm getting a reading, but it's too weak."

"Coming now." Ephesus typed on the tablet, and another flash of electricity danced across Dad's body. This time, he only twitched slightly, and a new readout blinked to life on Andes's screen. A thin line danced across the corner.

At first, it barely flickered. But then, slowly, it gained strength, the line tracing sharp mountain peaks across the screen. After a few erratic flutters, it settled into a rhythm.

Dad's heart was beating.

Andes cheered and clapped Ephesus on the back. My brother braced himself against the monitor, mouthing prayers of thanks.

Mrs. Nolan donned a wireless stethoscope and laid the receiver on Dad's chest. She listened for several seconds, her eyes on her watch. Then she popped the earpiece out and handed it to me.

I cupped it to my ear with both hands. Dad's heartbeat thrummed, loud and steady.

Warm tears slid down my face. *Thank you, Jesus.*

Tower echoed the sentiment in Latin.

Mrs. Nolan ran several more tests, then Andes took Dad's heart offline again, letting the machine take over so they could focus on another part of his body. The process went on for two hours. There were some scares—his oxygen level wasn't high enough, and his blood pressure was all over the map—but Mrs. Nolan said all those problems were fixable. My dad was going to live.

I repeated those words under my breath until I almost believed them.

While the others worked, I sat in a chair next to Dad's machine and prayed. Stanyard ran in and out, fetching whatever Mrs. Nolan or Ephesus requested.

"Do you need anything?" he asked me when Andes paused the process so everyone could take a break.

"No," I said, not stopping to consider the question.

"Wrong answer," he grunted, and pressed a water bottle into my hands. I stared at the clear plastic for a minute before turning to look up at him.

He smiled.

"All right, time for the big test." Andes strode back into the room, adjusting his ponytail.

I grabbed Stanyard's hand. "Stay. Please."

His fingers held mine, his grip strong and steady. "Always."

Ephesus returned to his post next to Andes. "How are we doing this?"

Andes's fingers resumed their one-man waltz across the screen. "A friend of mine designed a synaptic program that will rapid-fire neural stimuli directly into the cerebral cortex. The computer will read and analyze the electrical responses and give us a good idea of how well he remembers common objects and basic language skills. Should take about ten minutes."

Ten minutes. Ten minutes to have the answer I'd spent weeks praying for. Ten minutes to determine whether my dad was truly alive or dead.

I watched as Mrs. Nolan reached into the machine and gingerly lifted Dad's head. She carefully straightened the wires protruding from the base of his neck.

Andes grunted in satisfaction. "Here we go." Then, without waiting for permission, he launched the program.

The motherboard kicked into high gear, its circuits laboring so loudly I could hear it over the other machines. Code flew across the screen at a pace too fast to humanly read.

The results started tallying in the corner of the monitor. At first, there was a series of comforting green checkboxes. One after another, my father's brain passed the tests.

Ephesus smiled. I leaned forward, my grip crushing Stanyard's hand, as I felt the praises rise on my tongue.

And then there was a red *X.*

And another.

And another.

The monitor made no sound, but my mind supplied the screech of denial I had tried so hard to forget.

Access denied.

The X's continued to pile up until they drowned out the green checkboxes. I closed my eyes, unwilling to stare at the sea of red.

Abruptly, the machine silenced, bringing an unwelcome stillness back into the room. Andes sighed.

"What's the damage?" Ephesus said, voice dampened to keep the emotion out of it.

"He's got some basic object recognition." If Andes was trying to be optimistic, his tone was having the opposite effect. "I'd say we're looking at about a first-grade language level."

Tower made the sign of the cross.

Oh God, my spirit cried, but the only sound my lips made was a moan. Thirty years of experience and two PhDs, gone in a moment. All of my father's expert intelligence wiped from his mind like a whiteboard being erased.

I pulled my hand from Stanyard's to hide my face. He found my shoulder instead.

Ephesus muttered a prayer. "What about his memory?"

"That's the next test."

I dared to look up and saw Andes pull a flash drive from his pocket. "Now we'll run a program of stimuli curated from his life specifically. Memories are stored in a different part of the brain—it's possible for him to lose language skills while still retaining memories."

I straightened. "How common is that?"

"It's not." He glanced back at me with a glare not intended to be cruel. "I warned you, lass."

I sank back in the chair.

Andes plugged the drive into the machine and loaded the program. "Ready?" he asked. Mercifully, the question was directed at Ephesus; I wouldn't have had the courage to answer.

Ephesus sighed and tapped the screen.

The computer whirred. Immediately, red X's appeared in the corner of the screen.

I wanted to look away. I *needed* to look away. But I couldn't. As the marks continued to pile up, the screen filling with blood, I couldn't turn my head. It was as if cold, invisible hands were gripping my face, forcing me to keep my eyes open as my worst nightmare became reality.

As if thriving off our misery, the program took an eternity to run. No one moved as the computer continued to sign off on Dad's death warrant. And then, finally, it stopped.

Not a single green checkmark was found. My father didn't remember anything. Not even me.

Ephesus stood there, his arms gripping his chest as tears ran silently down his face. I couldn't find the strength to cry. I couldn't find the strength to do anything. I didn't move, or breathe, or speak, or pray. Stanyard's fingers dug into my shoulder, but I barely felt them. Tower stared straight ahead, his glazed eyes drained of any emotion.

"I'm sorry, lass," Andes whispered, his voice suffocated by the heaviness in the room.

I stood up, my limbs feeling like they were treading water. I leaned over the incubator and stared at Dad, the reflection of my face on the glass hovering like a ghost over his sleeping features. I studied the nose and cheekbones that so matched my own and tried to accept the truth I'd spent the last month denying.

My dad was never coming back.

3

"I'm sorry it's late."

I glanced at the dashboard clock in Stanyard's car. It was 5:17. According to the Vons, my host family, that was *catastrophically* late when I was supposed to be home at five. I was somewhat surprised Mrs. Von wasn't pacing the sidewalk, seething.

"It's not your fault," I told Stanyard.

It really wasn't; I'd been trapped in the world's worst family meeting all afternoon. There had been no time to waste on grief. As soon as Ephesus recovered and stuffed his feelings back down where they came from, we immediately started planning what to do with Dad. Mrs. Nolan wanted to run more tests before we woke him up; Andes wanted to order a brain implant that might help supplement Dad's vocabulary. On top of that, Dad would need physical therapy, more cosmetic surgery, and round-the-clock supervision until he adjusted. There were therapists to contact, bills to pay, living arrangements to settle—all the planning and logistics for a reality I didn't even want to live in.

Andes had made a valiant attempt to console me. "His memories may still be in there, lass. He just can't access them because the neural pathways are damaged."

"Can they be repaired?" I looked up at him, trying to decide why he was telling me this.

His eyes wandered, which told me all I needed to know. "They've experimented with it. It hasn't been successful, but... maybe one day."

One day. I didn't dare attach any hope to that statement.

By the time Andes left, it was too late to get me home on time. I didn't care. I had bigger problems than keeping Mrs. Von's universe in balance.

"Do you want me to come in with you?" Stanyard asked.

"No," I sighed. That wasn't exactly the truth, but it wasn't a lie either.

He didn't object. "Call me if you need anything."

"I will," I said, and looked into his eyes so he would know I was being sincere.

I let myself in the back door with my key. No sooner had I shed my shoes than an imposing voice scolded me from behind.

"You're grounded."

I sighed. I'd been praying that the Vons would have a bad memory day and not notice I was gone, but no such luck. I looked up to see Mrs. Von glaring at me, her feet apart so she could fill as much of the hallway as possible.

I put my hands up in surrender. "I'm sorry, I—"

She didn't even give me a chance. "Where have you been? You're," she glanced at her watch, "twenty-one minutes late. You have some explaining to do, young lady."

I had absolutely no intention of explaining the real reason I was late, but I was too tired to come up with a believable excuse. I just stared at her, struggling not to cry. *I can't do this tonight.*

She stopped when she saw my face. "Andromeda? What's wrong?"

What's wrong? I just found out my dad is going to end up exactly like you.

Roseanne and Paul Von Nieuwenhuyse had also lost their minds, although they were the victims of a botched neurosurgery, a failed government attempt to beat the noncompliance out of them. It had taken years of therapy before they were able to take care of themselves again. Despite all their progress, their memories still had the stability of a house of cards, and even the slightest deviation from the pattern—like me being five minutes late—broke them. The only reason Mrs. Von even remembered my name was because I had been home at precisely five o'clock every evening for the past month to repeat it to her. Even now, she looked at me with eyes that were permanently veiled with a shroud of confusion, like she was second-guessing everything she thought she knew about me.

Suddenly, I understood why it was so easy for their daughter Cea to just walk away and pretend they didn't exist.

I'd given Cea a hard time for it once, swore up and down that I'd never give up on my family. But now that my own father had been stripped of his identity, reduced to a shell of a man with no ability to care for himself, I understood why it was so tempting to claim he was dead.

Because, in a way, he was.

"Andromeda?" Mrs. Von tried again. "What happened?"

"I just... got some bad news about a friend who's in the hospital, that's all," I managed. But even as the words "that's all" left my lips, I realized that *wasn't* all, and a fresh sob ripped out of me. I hid my face in my hands.

"Oh, sweetheart. I'm so sorry." Mrs. Von stepped towards me and put her arms out, then hesitated. She awkwardly patted my shoulders, like she forgot how hugs worked. "Here, come sit down."

She steered me into the kitchen and pointed me towards a barstool. I sat down and put my chin on my arms while she made a fresh pot of coffee. It seemed like an odd time of day for coffee, but I wasn't complaining. I gripped the mug and savored the heat, hoping some of the warmth would seep from my fingertips into my soul.

"Do you want any creamer?" she asked.

"No," I said, indulging in a small chuckle. "This is perfect."

She studied me. "Do you want to take your dinner in your room tonight?"

I looked up at her. "I'd really appreciate that." As much as I loved Mr. Von, I didn't have the strength to watch sterilized sitcoms with him tonight.

Her lips stretched in a sympathetic smile. "Have you told your dad about your friend? Wait." She hesitated, but before I could correct her, she barreled on. "You don't have parents, do you? But you have someone. You told me. He's…" Her face pinched as she struggled to fire neurons that weren't there.

I helped her out. "Nic. My guardian." *Your son,* I thought but didn't add.

"Yes, him." She smiled, but I could tell by the tone of her voice that she was just taking my word for it. "Have you talked to him about what's going on?"

"No," I groaned. "But I should."

I'd have to tell him. I hadn't called him yesterday, and he never let me go more than forty-eight hours without video chatting him. With a pang of guilt, I realized that I'd been trying to space out our calls more than usual over the past week. It wasn't that I didn't want to talk to him; it was just that our conversations had gotten painfully repetitive. I knew exactly what he would say every time, and some days, I just wasn't in the mood to hear it.

But he needed to know what was happening with Dad. And, in a cruel irony, he was the one person who would most understand what I was going through.

Mrs. Von nodded encouragingly. "Go on then. Oh—you have mail."

"What?" My exclamation was too loud for the room, but the situation warranted it. There was no reason I should be getting mail. First of all, paper correspondence had gone out of fashion almost fifty years ago. But more importantly, there were only a few people who knew my address, and the majority of them lived on Mars.

She slid an envelope across the counter towards me. I picked it up and almost dropped it in horror when my fingers brushed the embossed United seal. Mail from the government was the worst kind of correspondence.

It was addressed to *Ms. Andromeda Nolan*, and the return label was for one of the capitol buildings in Beijing. I swallowed a flash of panic as I flipped the envelope over.

Someone had hand-written a note on the back in calligraphic cursive.

YOU'RE STILL INVITED –ASIA

I shuddered. Asia, as she called herself, was someone with money and political influence, and that was all I knew about her. My old enemy Carnegie had been planning to sell my father—and the formula for Red Rain—to her, but she claimed she didn't need it anymore. Said it was an "unnecessary mess."

I didn't fully believe that story, but so far, she'd held true to her word. She'd gladly given me the password to unlock Dad's cryogenics tube so we could thaw him, and she'd even paid for part of the procedure. More importantly, even though she knew exactly who I was and could have me executed at any moment, she'd been nothing but respectful. She never called, never invaded my privacy, and never showed up unannounced.

And yet, she wouldn't *leave.* She texted every few days, asking how Dad was progressing. Twice she sent more money, even though I didn't need it. She even had her lawyer deliver the paperwork for some trust funds and stocks she discovered were in Andromeda's name.

She was, by all accounts, acting like my friend, and that was the last thing a United official from Beijing should be.

I gingerly sliced the seal on the envelope with my finger and pulled out a card. It was a beautiful piece of heavyweight linen, embossed with gold and inked in red. I scanned the elegant typeface:

HIS EXCELLENCE GENERAL SECRETARY MONG
REQUESTS THE HONOR OF YOUR PRESENCE
AT THE 43RD ANNUAL STATE DINNER
JULY 25TH, 2076
SUMMER PALACE, BEIJING

I ran my finger over the letters. Apparently, Asia still wanted me to come to my birthday party.

July 25th was my birthday—or, more accurately, it was Andromeda's birthday. When we met, Asia had said the state dinner was supposed to be my coming out party, my debut into high society. That was back when Mrs. Nolan and her husband Thames were planning on taking me home and making me one of them.

According to Asia, that's still where I belonged.

I shoved the invitation back in the envelope and slid it into the little black backpack that I always carried with me. "It's an invite for a sorority at school," I said in response to Mrs. Von's quizzical stare.

"Must be a fancy one if they're willing to waste paper," she remarked, and she had no idea how right she was.

I accepted the plate of food she handed to me and stood up. Thanking her, I trudged up the stairs to Cea's old bedroom. I threw my backpack on the bed and set the plate on the nightstand, then took my tablet off the charger.

As always, the screen brightened to a flurry of notifications. I wasn't allowed to have my tablet on base. It was registered to Andromeda Nolan, and even though Jayde cloaked the internet traffic, we couldn't risk having Andromeda check in anywhere near the base.

I'd gotten surprisingly used to not having a device on me all day, but Nic was less accepting. Even though he was fully aware I wouldn't be home until evening, he sent me salty texts throughout the day. In part to remind me that he disapproved of my off-the-grid lifestyle, and in part, I suspected, to make sure he was the first person I talked to when I came online.

I sat down on the bed and opened our encrypted messaging app.

YOU ONLINE?

I watched his avatar flicker green.

AM NOW

I braced myself and started a video call.

He appeared, sitting at the desk in his office. The pale Martian sky shone out the window behind him. He had one leg crossed over the other and a coffee cup in his hand, his smart blond mustache posed perfectly on the rim. He looked like the mad scientist from a bad movie, with his starched lab coat and gelled hair, and I half-expected him to start the conversation with *"I've been expecting your call."*

With a twinge in my heart, I realized our relationship would be a whole lot less complicated if he'd stayed a villain.

The stereotyped image shattered when he frowned and lowered his mug. "What happened?"

I tried to smile but failed to land the delivery. "Is it that obvious?"

"Judging by the state of your makeup, you've been crying."

I pressed a finger to my cheek and came away with a smear of mascara and eyeliner. I rubbed it and avoided looking at the camera. "We brought Dad online today."

I heard a clink and roll as he set his mug on the desk and dragged his chair closer to the monitor. "And?"

"And this is the part where you say you understand exactly how I feel." I sniffed, but the sound snagged on my throat. I tipped my head back and stared at the ceiling, hoping gravity would keep the tears in.

He was silent. I didn't explain anymore. I didn't need to.

"I'm sorry, Philadelphia," he said finally.

I knew his use of my real name was code for all the emotions for which there were no words. I accepted the offer of sympathy with a nod.

"What's the damages?" He clacked on his keyboard.

Propping the tablet on a pillow, I grabbed the plate off the nightstand and poked the mound of casserole with my finger, trying to rally the courage to eat it. "Andes thinks he has about first-grade level language skills and object recognition."

"And his memory?"

Nic may as well have put a period on the end of that sentence for all the inflection he used. He knew the answer.

I gave up and set the plate back down. "He's gone."

Nic stopped typing, and the silence brought a fresh wave of helplessness crashing down on me. This was a problem even Nic couldn't solve.

I pulled my knees to my chin, as if that could keep my reality from shattering. "Andes thinks his memories could still be in there," I offered for no reason at all.

"That's what I'm worried about."

"What?" I looked back down at the tablet.

He rubbed his goatee, parsing his words. "Remember how I said Carnegie only needed your father's brain?"

"Yeah?" I said slowly, and by the time I'd finished the word, the horrid memories came rushing back.

All he needed was the formula for Red Rain—which is in your father's memory banks somewhere...

Nic nodded. "If any of your father's memories are intact, it means Red Rain is in there, too. Just because he can't access them doesn't mean a synaptic device couldn't read them."

Any old synaptic device could read them. Your father wouldn't have to be "viable" for that to work.

I sank back against the headboard, the weight of failure squeezing the breath from my lungs. I'd sacrificed the last six months of my life trying to keep Red Rain out of the hands of the government. That was the whole reason my dad even got frozen; I'd nearly killed him trying to destroy the weapon.

Now, Red Rain was the only thing my father was good for.

"He's essentially a walking flash drive," Nic admitted. "And unfortunately, he's an even greater liability because he doesn't know who he is. If someone wearing scrubs told him he needed to submit to a brain scan, he'd probably comply."

I didn't argue. There was nothing to argue with.

"You need to come home."

The statement pierced through the haze in my mind. "Huh?"

"You need to come back to Mars."

I heard the shift in his voice, the compassion freezing over, and knew where the conversation was going. I picked the tablet up. "Nic, I can't."

"First of all, that's a grammatically incorrect use of that word. You certainly *can*; you've just chosen not to. Second of all, I don't think you have a choice anymore." He folded his arms across his chest and continued lecturing before I could get a word in edgewise. "Your father needs therapy, and lots of it. He needs to be in a secure, controlled environment. And controlled environments are one thing I specialize in."

"He could stay—" I squeaked.

"Where? On base? Surrounded by unfamiliar faces, dangerous machinery, and a questionable amount of weapons? Yes, I'm sure there's nothing that could trigger him there."

I bit my lip.

"And he absolutely can't stay at my parents," Nic continued, checking off an invisible list in the air with his fingers. "The last thing you need is *three* brainwashed adults in one house."

I sighed, purposefully loud enough for him to hear. He was right, as always. Dad needed to be in a safe environment while he recovered, and Nic's science station was the safest place I knew. My dad should be on Mars.

But that didn't mean I should be.

Nic gave me two beats to comply. "Are you booking transit tickets? Because I don't see your hands moving."

"Nic, I can't..." I grunted and tried again. "I *won't* leave. Not yet. The operation launches in three months..."

Nic swore and lurched out of his chair, leaving it to spin listlessly in frame. "How many times are we going to have this conversation?"

I felt the heat rising behind my ears. "I don't know—until you realize this is serious."

He stopped with his back to the camera. "I know *you* think this is serious, and that's what concerns me."

I opened my mouth to object, but the air died on my tongue. I knew it would be pointless, just like it had been pointless the last dozen times I'd tried to explain. No matter what I told him, no matter how hard I tried to convince him that Operation Blue Fire was necessary, he didn't care.

He didn't think I could lead the rebellion. And worse, he didn't think I should.

I looked away from the camera. This—this was why I had been avoiding our calls. "I don't want to have this conversation tonight."

"Good," he chirped without turning around, "because there's nothing to discuss. You're coming home, Andromeda."

I pinched my eyes shut. "Nic, please, not right now—"

"No," he snapped, a metric ton of anger crammed into the word. He whipped back around to face me. "I'm done. I feel like I've been very patient…"

That's not exactly how I'd describe you.

"…and let you play out your fantasy for the past month, but it's over." He gripped the back of his desk chair until his knuckles went white. "You are not a hero, Andromeda."

His words struck like a whip across my back. "I'm not—I'm not trying to be," I squeaked. *Is that what you think of me?*

"Oh really?" he sneered, tone like vinegar on a wound. "Then why are you still there? Why did you even go back to Earth?"

Please stop, I wanted to beg, but couldn't. I knew the answer. I knew my sins, but he listed them anyway.

"You went back because you thought you could fix everything. You thought you could save your dad. And look what happened."

Tears shot to my eyes. I dropped the tablet on the bed and wrapped my arms around my chest.

He was right. This was all my fault.

"They don't need you, Andromeda. They can do this without you." He made a herculean effort to soften his voice, but it just made him sound fake. "Your focus needs to be on your family right now."

I closed my eyes. *Please, just stop talking. You've made your point.*

He let out his breath. "You'll buy transit tickets tonight. I want to see the receipts."

I slapped my palms down on the blanket. "What, you don't trust me anymore?"

He showed no mercy. "The appropriate response was 'yessir.'"

I flinched. "Yessir," I whispered, and then ended the call before he could see me cry.

4

"Captain on the bridge."

The command room on the top floor of the base was full when I arrived the next morning. Everyone who needed to know—Ephesus, Tower, Jayde, Lev, Mrs. Nolan—was there, along with a plethora of soldiers. I rubbed my arm nervously as they all saluted. At least I wouldn't have to repeat myself.

"We're ready for you to stream," Jayde said, walking around to the other side of the glittering control module that dominated the center of the room. "I want you to talk about—"

"No," I said, and flinched when he jerked back. I swallowed and forced the rest out before I could stop myself. "I'm not streaming today. There's been a change of plans."

"What?" he barked.

Ephesus walked over, his brow furrowed in concern. "What's wrong, Phil?"

I took a deep breath and looked up at him. "We're going back to Mars."

There were gasps and muttered exclamations—some foul—from around the room. Tower shifted but said nothing. Jayde wasted no time in losing his temper. "You can't leave! We launch in three months, and I—"

"We can still do this!" I shouted to match his volume, mostly to convince myself. "I can record videos from Mars."

Even Nic had said as much. He'd texted me a few hours after we'd hung up, as if it had finally dawned on him that he was being a heartless jerk.

IF YOU REALLY FEEL THE NEED TO DO THIS, YOU CAN STREAM VIDEOS FROM HERE. THE STUDIO IS STILL SET UP

He was right, but it was too late for damage control. I didn't reply to the message.

The bickering continued around the room. "Why are you leaving?" my uncle asked. His tone was flat, as was the expression on his face.

"Dad needs a stable environment while he goes through therapy," I explained, reciting exactly what Nic had said, "and Mars is the safest place for him."

Ephesus slid his arm protectively over my shoulder. I searched his face for approval; he looked relieved, if anything. "She's right. Dad can't stay here, and we need to be there for him while he gets treatment. Phil can record videos remotely." He scanned the room, as if daring anyone to argue with his judgment as big brother. "After all, she started on Mars—she can finish there. No one will know the difference."

"We'll know," Lev whispered from where he stood in the shadows. He squinted and blinked, as if he couldn't decide whether to be angry or betrayed. I turned away, unable to look him in the eye.

"I'm trying to win a war here." Jayde slapped his hand on the control panel, eliciting a screech from the computer. "I can't have my revolutionary leader *on another planet.*"

"Then get a new leader," Stanyard spat.

Jayde ignored him, his fierce eyes still on me. "And why do you have to go? Your father doesn't need you anymore."

Ephesus stiffened. I was too heartbroken to object.

"As the only one in this room with any medical knowledge, I strongly disagree," Mrs. Nolan spoke for the first time. She crossed her arms and glared at Jayde. "She's been through enough. Let her go home and take care of her family."

"And what about the rest of us, huh?" Jayde threw his arms out and turned around, including the entire room in his statement. "What about the rest of us who suffer every day because the United decided we're not part of the system? What about all those people who agreed to join the operation? Are you going to hide out on Mars while the rest of us risk our lives?"

He swiveled back to face me. I returned his stare, unable to answer him. That was exactly what I'd be doing.

He snorted. He reached back and punched a button on the dashboard, and the playback from the camera appeared on the giant monitor that hung from the ceiling. There I was, larger than life, the circles under my eyes forming dark shadows in the dank lighting of the command room. The "go live" button flickered in the corner of the screen.

Jayde held his finger over the key. "You want to tell your followers that? You want to tell everyone that Blue Fire is abandoning them?"

Tower grabbed his wrist. "Don't be stupid. Let's think this through."

Jayde pulled his hand back. "Oh, I think she's thought about it plenty. She's already made up her mind, can't you tell?"

The room was silent. Ephesus squeezed my shoulder.

Jayde spat in my direction. "You're a coward."

"Shut up!" Stanyard yelled, and hit him in the back of the head.

Jayde barely flinched. He just reached up and ruffled his hair back into place.

Stanyard muttered something else under his breath, then walked over and touched my shoulder. "Let's go, Phil."

"Don't listen to him," Ephesus agreed, taking my other arm and following us.

I allowed them to lead me from the room, my eyes on the floor. I couldn't tell them that I thought Jayde was right.

*

"You're sure you'll be okay while I'm gone?"

"It's only for a week," I reminded him, and tried to keep the fatigue out of my voice. Ephesus hadn't had many opportunities to play the protective older brother over the past few years, and he was trying to make up for lost time with this conversation.

We were standing on the sidewalk outside the transit hub having a repeat of the same argument we'd had on the ride over, and the night before, and the day before that. Per Nic's advice, we'd booked separate transit flights in case one of us aroused suspicion. So far, Ephesus hadn't had any trouble buying a ticket or registering a new phone under his temporary file, but all of us were wanted for crimes worthy of death. We couldn't be too careful.

Mrs. Nolan wanted to keep Dad under for a little while longer, and then he would need at least a couple days of physical therapy before he would be well enough to fly. He and I would be leaving in about a week.

Nic was none too happy about the delay, but he couldn't argue with doctor's orders.

Ephesus scrunched his nose, like the whole situation smelled foul. "I don't like leaving before you."

He'd made that abundantly clear, but he'd forgotten that I was just as stubborn as he was. "I'm not leaving Dad."

"And why do you get to pick? I'm eight years older than you!" He flapped his hands, as if the wild motion could make me change my mind.

I crossed my arms. "Because I'm paying."

Stanyard, who waited a comfortable distance away next to his car, snickered.

Ephesus blanched. "You've been spending too much time with Nic."

I rolled my eyes. *You have no idea.*

Ephesus finally acquiesced with a grunt. "I'll be offline until I land. So if anything happens, call Nic."

"Of course," I fudged. Nic was the last person I wanted to call. I didn't plan to talk to him until I got back to Mars, and maybe not even then.

Ephesus looked over my head and pointed at Stanyard. "I'm trusting you."

Stanyard saluted.

I pushed Ephesus's arm down. "Tell Cea I said hi."

He grinned. "Oh, I will." The sparkle returned to his eyes, suggesting he would also tell her a lot more. I copied his smile. There were a few good things about moving back to Mars.

Ephesus wrapped me in a hug. "Stay safe, stick with Stanyard, and I'll see you soon."

"Yes, yes, and yes." I savored his hug for a moment more, then pushed him away. "Now go. You'll miss your flight."

He grabbed his suitcase off the sidewalk and waved at Stanyard, then turned and jogged towards the revolving doors. I waited until he had blended with the crowd and disappeared out of sight before I turned back to Stanyard.

He opened the passenger door for me. "Want to go back to base?"

"No," I admitted as I slid in. Base was the last place I wanted to be right now. I didn't want to see Jayde or record another video where I lied through my teeth about how we were all in this together. "But Jayde is expecting me."

Stanyard shut the door and got behind the wheel. After glancing to make sure there was no one waiting behind us, he leaned over and touched my knee. "If it helps, I think you're making the right decision."

"Thanks," I said, even though I meant the exact opposite. Three of the people I trusted most in the world thought going back to Mars was the right thing to do.

Then why did it feel so wrong?

Stanyard said nothing more and took his hand away to start the car. A few raindrops plunked off the hood as we pulled away from the awning and merged into traffic. I leaned my arm on the door and watched out the window as the rain increased to a downpour. The city blurred into an abstract painting as the lights reflected off the puddles on the sidewalk. I closed my eyes and let the pounding on the roof lull me into prayer.

What do you want me to do, God?

Nic wanted me to go back to Mars—that was my answer, right? After all, according to him, I never should have left. But the more I tried to accept that logic, the more I felt haunted by the fear that I was throwing something precious away.

I replayed the last six months in my mind, tripping over all the coincidence and happenstance that could only be called a miracle. Red Rain, Carnegie, the Nolans, Dad, the truth about my mother's death. All the horrible and tragic things that had somehow collided into this, into me becoming Blue Fire. God had taken my father's failure and turned it into a revolution—that had to be God, right?

I reached into my backpack and pulled out the star of David pin Lev had given me. I twisted it in my fingers, rubbing the tarnished metal, and remembered his words.

For such a time as this.

I jerked out of my stupor when we drove into a tunnel, cutting off the sound of rain. I looked up and watched the yellow fluorescents whip past.

And then, suddenly, there was a flash of blue paint on the concrete wall.

I twisted around and caught a glimpse just before the graffiti passed out of sight around the corner.

It was a thunderbird.

The image was unmistakable: The crude form of a hawk-like bird, its wings spread wide in defiance. In its claws was clutched a jagged bolt of lightning.

Stanyard craned his neck to look in the rearview mirror. "I'm surprised they haven't painted over that yet. Must be fresh."

I didn't respond. I closed my fist around the pin.

It was still pouring when we got back to base. I checked on Dad, then reluctantly went up to the command room. It was mercifully empty except for a couple of nameless guards.

I went to the control module in the center of the room and pulled up the streaming app. But instead of launching a video, I navigated to the search bar and typed in my name.

The government worked tirelessly to block any content featuring my name or callsign, but automatic filters weren't perfect and the internet was creative. It wasn't hard to find a repost of my latest stream that had escaped the censors.

The views were over five million, and that was just on this one repost. I scrolled through the lengthy comments section. Some people mocked me, but most were supportive. There was a user who claimed to be thirteen who said I was an inspiration. There was another teen who claimed he and his friends were going to walk out of class on operation day. Several users were throwing coded messages back and forth, coordinating a demonstration of some sort.

There were comments in Hebrew, Arabic, Mandarin. And all of them were punctuated with emojis of lightning bolts and fire.

"They trust you."

I jumped and turned. Jayde stood in the shadows behind me, his face faintly lit by the blue glow from the monitors.

I looked back at the screen. "I know."

"I trust you."

I glanced up as he came to stand beside me. "Really?" I'd never gotten that impression from Jayde. He appreciated my ability to rally the crowds, but we weren't friends. We didn't need to be.

He nodded. "I'm sorry I yelled at you the other day. I know that if you say you'll record videos from Mars, you will."

"I promise," I assured him.

"But," he said, and I flinched. There was always a "but" with Jayde.

He sighed and randomly flicked a slider on the soundboard. "I know you can do so much more than record videos."

I frowned. "Like what?"

He opened his mouth to respond, but we were interrupted by one of the guards. "Sir," he said, stepping between us, "I'm sorry, but there's someone at reception asking to see Blue Fire."

I straightened. "Me?"

Jayde's hand instinctively touched his holster. "Who is it?"

The guard hesitated, then handed a tablet to Jayde.

He took one look at the screen and swore. "What is she doing here?"

"She?" I repeated.

He didn't answer. He shoved the tablet back at the guard and took off at a jog. I raced to keep up.

We took the elevator to the first floor. The base operated out of the shell of a defunct business, and as far as the public knew, this office building was still staffed with a bunch of white-collar salesmen and accountants. To keep up that façade, reception had been converted into an elaborate security checkpoint. From the outside, it looked benign enough, with the potted plants and bored secretary, while armed guards watched everything from behind one-way mirrors.

A girl about my age was leaning over the counter, arguing with the receptionist, but I couldn't see her face from beneath her dripping hood. Jayde shoved past the guard at the door and burst into the lobby without ceremony.

"What are you doing here?" he demanded.

I came out behind him. The girl straightened. "I didn't come to see you," she spat at Jayde.

I choked on my next breath when I recognized her voice. *It can't be.*

I walked around the counter. The girl turned towards me and flicked her hood back, revealing her face.

Mira.

5

After three beats of awkward staring, I realized Jayde was asking the right questions.

"What are you doing here?" I exclaimed, and hoped she would give me a long, detailed answer to that question. Last I'd heard, Mira Dass had run away from home, abandoning her brother and dropping off the grid. Stanyard hadn't seen any activity on her file in months, and he'd been watching it religiously.

She didn't take the hint. "I'm here to see you."

And not your own brother? I thought, swallowing rage. Stanyard had been heartbroken when Mira left. He'd spent weeks trying to find her, and he still blamed himself for her loss. He wouldn't admit that in so many words, but I could see it in his eyes, the way he avoided saying her name.

The revelation that she'd been alive and well this whole time was filling me with the unladylike urge to hit her. I chose to use my words instead.

"I'm flattered," I snapped, "but there's several problems with that statement, first and foremost being that my name is not Stanyard."

She leaned back against the counter and arched an eyebrow. "You've changed."

"So have you." I studied her and tried to decide if that was a good thing. She'd chopped her hair; half of it was shaved, and the other half fell across her face in a sharp pixie cut. It was dyed an unnatural shade of black with a pink stripe. She had a stud in her nose and at least five in her ears, and a giant dragon tattoo covered the right side of her body. It looked like the animal was swallowing her arm and sinking its teeth into her neck.

And as she stared at me, I could see that there was nothing behind her eyes. Not even anger.

"What happened, Mira?" I whispered.

"Nothing." She shrugged. "I got out of camp and found a new life—just like you."

"But…" I retraced everything Stanyard had told me, trying to find out where things had gone wrong. "Stanyard said you ran off and married a soldier…"

The words died on my tongue. I stared at her dragon tattoo, then looked up at Jayde.

The Green Dragon.

"You guys are *married?*" I screeched.

Jayde snorted.

"We were going to be," Mira snapped, fixing Jayde with a glare that could boil water. She rubbed her bare ring finger in a gesture that was not lost on anyone in the room.

I grimaced. "And why didn't you tell Stanyard? You knew he was looking for her!" I directed the accusation at Jayde, even though I wasn't sure who to blame more.

Jayde shrugged callously. "She wasn't even talking to *me* then—we'd already broken up."

I turned my frown on Mira.

She avoided my eyes. "I didn't want him to know—and I still don't." She stood up and pushed herself away from the counter. "I'm not staying."

"And neither am I. I'm going to go find him." I spun for the door, trying to decide whether to cry or be sick.

"No, Phil, wait!" She lunged forward and caught my arm. "Please, just listen. It's important."

I tried to wrench my arm from her grasp and realized with a flash of shame that I couldn't. *This is why you need to train more.* I settled for glaring at her. "What's important is telling Stanyard the truth."

She met my eyes. "It's about our old camp."

I stopped.

She mercifully let go of me to reach inside her jacket. "The district office just issued an emergency order to have the entire camp relocated—tomorrow. Everyone's getting shipped out in the morning."

Jayde's cold warning flashed through my mind.

Things are changing. The government is tired of paying for the room and board of a bunch of noncompliants. There's talk of relocation, of condensing the camps—or worse.

"To where?" Jayde grunted the question I was afraid to ask.

Mira pulled a scuffed flash drive out of her pocket and twisted it in her fingers. "China."

I muttered in tongues, too horrified to speak in English. No one else said anything. We all knew a flight to China, the center of the United government, was a one-way trip.

And Stanyard and Mira's parents still lived in that camp.

"I'm not exactly sure where in China they're taking them, but it's definitely a labor camp." She held the flash drive out to Jayde. "I have a copy of the order and several text messages verifying the pickup time."

Jayde opened his mouth, but Mira put up both hands to stop him. "Don't ask me where I got them, because it was *extremely* illegal. But I can promise you, my source knows what they're talking about." She stuffed her hands in her pockets and flicked her eyes around the room, as if she were afraid her informant was going to leap out from behind a potted plant.

"But why?" I cried. "I mean, why now? And why our camp? There's less than a hundred people in there."

She turned to me, her face tightened in a glare. "Because of you."

I took a step back.

"You might not know this," she continued, the concession spoken without any mercy, "but they've been rounding up everyone who ever knew you and interrogating them."

I gripped the edge of the reception desk. "What for?"

"Why do you think?" she sighed, as if my ignorance was exhausting. "To try and figure out where you are—and if that doesn't work, find out what makes you tick."

The room toppled, and a wave of anguish tried to force my stomach up my throat. I bent over the desk, searching for my balance, but I couldn't find it. The United was interrogating—torturing—people because of me. This was my fault.

Nic was right. I wasn't a hero.

"They had Dad and Mom in yesterday." Mira's words were slow and purposeful, driving the guilt in like a nail. "Kept them in that room for twelve hours straight."

"I'm—I'm sorry," I gasped, more to God than to her.

She shrugged. "I got off easy. I left before you did, so they correctly assumed I didn't know anything."

Jayde stepped forward, shattering the tension between us. "Why didn't you tell me sooner?" he asked Mira. His face was softened in an expression that made me believe they had in fact had a relationship once. "I probably could have gotten in on the session with your parents. I was able to bail Aid out of his."

Mira didn't have an answer to that, but I had several follow-up questions. "Wait." I stood up, my gravity recentering as a weight dropped to my stomach. "You knew? You knew they were interrogating people?"

He blinked, unashamed. "What would you have done if I told you? Stopped recording? Canceled the operation?"

I snapped my mouth shut with a click. *I definitely wouldn't have let them keep torturing my friends.*

"Exactly." He folded his arms. "These things happen in war, and I couldn't have you distracted—"

"No," I snapped. When he looked like he was about to mouth off again, I repeated myself. "No. Not in my war. We're going to save them."

He frowned, but Mira beat him to words. "What?"

"We're going to break them out," I said, and only after the statement left my mouth did I realize what I was proposing. I forged ahead before I could attach any emotions or fear to my thoughts. "We can't let them get shipped off to China. We have to intercept them. How are they transporting them? How many guards?"

The questions were directed at Mira, and it took her several breaths before she complied. "It's not terrible—a couple of prison vans, maybe a dozen guards."

"We can handle that," I declared, and turned to Jayde for confirmation. "Remember when you broke me out of Thames's headquarters? You redirected the van."

He shook his head, but it was a rapid, recalibrating shake, not a doubtful one. "It's too late to forge orders—this has clearly already gone through the chain of command. We're better off breaking them out tonight, before they load them up."

"Okay then," I replied, and that was that.

Jayde arched an eyebrow. "So?"

I threw my arms out. "So what? Let's go." If I put any more logical thought into this, I might reconsider, and we didn't have time for that.

"Are those your orders, Blue Fire?" he returned with a bow of his head.

I sighed and realized it was on me to pull the trigger. This was my choice. This was my fight.

"Yes," I repeated, straightening and planting my feet apart. "We're breaking them out tonight. That's an order."

His face split in a grin. "Yessir."

6

"I'm not going with you."

"Yes, you are," I argued, and yelped when I stabbed myself in the eye with my mascara. If I thought dressing up as Philadelphia would mean less makeup, I was wrong.

After I had debriefed the other commanders on the plan, I'd gone home for dinner so I wouldn't upset the Vons' routine. The last thing I needed was the police out looking for me because Mrs. Von lost her marbles. So I'd eaten dinner like a normal person, packed a bag with a change of clothes and makeup, and told them I was going to sleep over at a friend's house. Mira even picked me up and corroborated my story.

Now she and I were locked in a bathroom on base, where we'd spent the last hour and a half putting Philadelphia back together. I'd sprayed my hair with temporary brown dye and pinned it up under a scarf so you couldn't tell how long it was. I'd plastered over the piercings in my ears and concealed the scratches and bruises I'd earned while training. In their place, I'd given myself a new identity marker: a fake thunderbird tattoo, drawn on the upper part of my arm with a fine-tipped pen.

"No, I'm going home." Mira twirled my powder brush in her fingers, her eyes avoiding mine in the mirror. "You don't need my help."

"No, but your parents do." I tossed my mascara in my bag and turned to face her. "Mira, please. What's wrong?"

"Nothing," she said for at least the sixth time that evening.

"Stanyard would beg to differ," I muttered.

After no small amount of badgering from both Jayde and me, Mira had agreed to come up to the command deck and tell us what she knew about the relocation order. Stanyard burst into the room moments later. He did exactly what I expected him to do: scream Mira's name at the top of his lungs and grab her in a hug.

She did the exact opposite of what I expected her to do. She didn't even hug him back. She just gave him a weird pat on the shoulder and then pushed him away, cutting off any more inquisition with a cold, "It's fine, I'm safe."

I almost regretted forcing the reunion when I saw the soul shatter behind Stanyard's eyes. He'd always suspected that Mira didn't want to see him again, but I think, up until that moment, he'd held onto a sliver of hope, the private belief that there was some other explanation. That there was something, anything, outside of her control keeping her away.

In the cold silence of the command room, as she turned her back on him and faced the monitor, we all realized the truth. Mira had stayed away because she wanted to.

"I just don't want to talk to him right now." She flicked the brush bristles.

"Then talk to me." I opened my arms and softened my voice. "You always used to be able to talk to me."

I'm not sure why I thought that would work. All she did was glance at me out of the corner of her eye and snort. "I'm just... not ready."

"Ready for what? To be a family again?" I scoffed, and too late realized how harsh that sounded.

She tipped her head back, her cropped hair sliding across her ear. "We were never a family."

Grief crusted with rage rolled through me. "That's a lie, and you know it. I know your father wasn't the greatest..."

"You have *no* idea," she hissed.

I ignored the comment. "...but one thing I know: Stanyard always cared about you. Everything he did was for you."

She looked down at the floor, and I thought I'd found the crack in her armor. "That's why you left camp, isn't it? You're the one that wanted to go."

She straightened and pushed herself off the counter. "Yes, I was. And do you want to know why?"

My conscience writhed. I could tell by the tone of her voice that I'd ruined the conversation, but she didn't wait for an answer. "I left because I was tired of dealing with stupid, self-righteous people like my dad. Like you."

I sucked in my breath.

She glared back at me. "You always thought you could fix everyone, didn't you?" she taunted, voice dripping with syrup. "Thought that if you played the peacemaker, were just so sweet and kind and forgiving to everyone, that you could make it all better. Well, you can't." Her tone hardened. "You can't fix the government, you can't fix Stanyard, and you can't fix me. So stop trying. I *don't* want your help."

Jayde knocked on the door and asked if we were ready, but I couldn't answer him. I couldn't move. All I could hear were Nic's words echoing in my head, around and around and around.

You are not a hero, Andromeda.

"We'll be right out," Mira called. She grabbed a pair of gloves and pulled them on, hiding the dragon tail that was drawn on her wrist. "I'm going to help you, because despite what you might think, I don't want my parents to die. But after that, I'm leaving. And if you have any decency, you'll let me walk away."

I did just that. She threw the door open and walked into the hall, and I just stood there, staring at the door until long after it had shut.

The team met us in the parking garage. Stanyard stared at his sister, gaping like a fish as he tried and failed several times to say something.

I gave him a less-than-subtle shake of my head. He finally shut his mouth and clenched his jaw.

"Put these in." Jayde dropped a pair of earbuds into my hand, then walked around the circle and distributed pairs to the other soldiers. "I want codenames only. Except for Ms. Smyrna over here, the government doesn't know our real names, and I'd like to keep it that way."

"Uh, what if we don't remember our code names?" a familiar voice chirped.

"Do we get to pick new ones? Say yes! I wanna pick a new name!" his partner screeched at a volume much too loud for the acoustics of the parking garage.

"John? Dowe?" I scanned the lot and spotted them a few cars away, dangling out the back of a suspicious white van. It looked like the kind of vehicle you'd commit a crime in, and for better or for worse, John and Dowe definitely looked like the strangers my parents warned me about. They were old enough to be grandparents, and they looked so creepily identical that I often wondered if they were the result of a failed cloning experiment.

The one who was probably John put his hand up. "No, no, I want to be Dowe this time. Except I'm going to spell it D-o-e and really throw people off."

"Basic," the real Dowe muttered. At least, process of elimination would suggest that he was the real Dowe. "You're going to make a terrible me."

"Your fault for being such a poor role model."

Jayde pinched the bridge of his nose. "Who invited these two?"

"I did." Tower stepped up, his jacket slung over his shoulder. "They volunteered. And besides, we needed the van."

"Does it even drive?" Stanyard questioned. He pointed to the massive patches of rust that were eating away at the bottom of the vehicle, like the van had been gnawed on by a shark.

"Oh, don't worry about that." John flapped his hand. "It was stuck in the ocean for six months."

"I don't think—" Jayde started to object.

"They're coming," I declared. John and Dowe were arguably insane, and I definitely wouldn't trust them with a loaded gun, but they were excellent at staging breakouts and distractions. And that's exactly what we needed.

"Fine, but you're riding with me," Jayde snapped, and I didn't argue.

"Your loss," John muttered. "This will definitely be the fun-vee."

Jayde clapped his hands, the sharp sound summoning all the attention in the room, and raised his voice. "All right people, listen up. This should be a very simple extraction. We've got about seventy individuals, most of whom are adults and should get with the program pretty quick once they realize what's going on."

He turned and gestured at the row of mismatched vans and SUVs filling the lot. "We're going to divide and conquer. Each vehicle is going to take ten refugees. Drivers, as soon as you're full, head out. Don't wait. You're all going in different directions and taking them to different drop-off points. If we arouse suspicion, I want the other teams to bail. I'm not losing the whole batch because one of us gets pulled over for a random traffic stop."

That's not going to happen, I prayed. *We're all going to make it.*

"Our latest intel suggests that this place is low security." Tower walked into the middle of the circle, keying on a tablet. He set it on the floor, and it projected a map on the ceiling of the parking garage where everyone could see it. I stared at the network of narrow roads and tiny homes and fought down a sickening sense of familiarity.

"Our biggest concerns are the watchtower and the fact that the only entrance is the front gate." Tower pointed to the north edge of the map. "However, that information was collected before Phil made herself famous. We know for a fact the United has been questioning her neighbors; they could have also upped security in case she came home."

I felt the shift in the room, the change in gravity as everyone looked at me. I glanced down and rubbed my arm, trying to hide the goosebumps.

"So be prepared for surprises," Lev grunted from beside me.

Jayde nodded. "Right. Now I've got a friend at the electric company who can cut the power for us—but there's two problems with that. One, we can only leave it off for about twenty minutes. Any longer and the government is likely to dispatch police as backup in case someone tries something. Two, when the power goes out at the camp, the backup generator will kick in and autolock the gate."

A murmur rippled around the group. I wrapped my arms around my chest and prayed harder.

"The plan is to use those twenty minutes of darkness to scale the wall and get everyone ready to move." Jayde circled the projection, tracing the perimeter with his finger. "Tower's team is going to break into the watchtower and take out the guards while the rest of us herd the evacuees towards the front gate. When the power comes online, Tower will use his knowledge of the system to radio an okay so the government doesn't send reinforcements. Then we'll open the gate and load everyone out."

"But the security cameras will be online," Stanyard objected.

"I'll be the only one watching," Tower assured him, "but corporate will review the footage after they realize what happened. So hoods up, heads down, and absolutely no electronics."

Jayde held up his phone for emphasis. "This is a blackout operation. No devices except our radios. I don't want anyone leaving a mark."

"Except me." I stepped forward, welcoming the shift in attention this time. I shrugged off my jacket, stripping down to a black tank top and revealing my hand-drawn tattoo. "I want them to know I was there."

Someone gasped. Stanyard gripped my elbow. "But Phil—"

I turned to him. "I know they're doing this because of me. The interrogations, the relocation—it's all to get back at me."

His kind eyes searched me. "It's not your fault."

"Maybe not." I shifted my gaze to Mira. "But I'm going to show them that it won't work."

She arched an eyebrow.

Stanyard turned pleading eyes to Tower, as if expecting him to stop me. But my uncle just folded his arms across his chest and smiled.

"All right, let's move out!" Jayde shouted.

"Anyone else want to ride in the fun-vee?" John hollered. "We have snacks!"

"They might be stale, though…"

"It's fruit leather. It was made for the apocalypse."

Jayde approached me, snapping the clip into a small pistol. "Here, you need this." He grabbed my wrist and forced the gun into my hand before I could refuse.

I held it away from my body, resisting the urge to drop it. "Jayde, you know I can't shoot."

"You can, you just won't," he barked, and sounded an awful lot like Nic.

He wasn't wrong, though. I did know *how* to shoot. Jayde had been making me practice in the range almost daily, and muscle memory was starting to override my hesitancy. I'd learned to handle the recoil, and my aim wasn't terrible.

But no amount of practice could silence the horror that screamed through my system every time the weapon fired. Each time the explosion pierced the protective headphones, all I could think about was Thames, and Carnegie, and Ambrose—all the people who had threatened me with guns or died by them.

I couldn't be like them. I couldn't kill.

"Don't worry, I'll shoot first." Stanyard checked his own pistol, then stuffed it in the pocket of his jeans. I could see he was carrying one in each pocket, and he probably had another in his coat. "I'll be right beside you the whole time."

"And I've got your back." Lev appeared at my other arm, adjusting the strap of his rifle.

I offered him a grateful smile. Checking to make sure the safety was on, I slid the gun in my pocket and tried to ignore the weight against my thigh.

Closing my eyes, I took a deep breath, and another, filling my lungs until the air drove the anxiety away. *You can do this.* Jayde was right; it was a simple extraction. And even if it wasn't, it was the right thing to do.

I'd blown up a lab to save my family. Now it was time to save Stanyard's.

7

I never thought I'd make it home.

I sat in the backseat of Jayde's SUV, buckled safely between Stanyard and Lev, as we raced through the suburbs of Boston. At first, the sleeping neighborhoods were cold, unfamiliar, the generic houses blending into a domestic blur. But then we turned a corner, and I recognized that park, that convenience store, that apartment with the faded *Now Leasing* sign that hadn't been changed in years. I began to anticipate the turns, brace myself for the bumps in the road, as if my whole body were slipping into a trance. I probably could have driven us the rest of the way as muscle memory took me down a path I had traveled so many times before.

And I hated it.

The familiarity wasn't comforting; it was suffocating. My body didn't just remember the directions—it also remembered the fear, the pain, the abuse. Every block we passed, it felt like the air was getting thinner and the car was getting narrower, as if we were already behind the containment camp walls. I felt like I was slipping, falling—shackling myself with chains I had tried so hard to forget.

I can't go back.

I reached out and grasped Stanyard's hand, desperate to keep my head above water. He weakly squeezed my fingers, his palm clammy. I glanced at him and realized he had gone pale. Sweat trickled down the side of his face as he stared out the window, his whole body rigid.

"You okay?" I asked, even though I knew the answer. This used to be Stanyard's home, too.

"Yeah," he said, but he sounded like he couldn't catch his breath. "Just… trying to figure out what to say to my dad."

My heart broke as the pain of that day came rushing back: the day Stanyard and Mira left camp. I remembered the sickening horror as we all stood in the parking lot at school while they informed us that they'd packed their bags and left without saying goodbye. I remembered wanting to scream and call after them but not being able to find the words. I remembered feeling like I was sinking into the concrete as I watched Stanyard walk away, turning his back on his family, God, and me.

But Stanyard had changed. The Stanyard I knew came back. He'd come back to me, and he'd come back to God in powerful ways even I didn't understand. Surely, he could come back to his dad.

I wove our fingers together, anchoring my hold on his hand. "Just tell him what you told me," I said, remembering how he'd knelt on the lab floor and given me the chance to forgive or reject him.

He shook his head. "It's not the same. It was… easier with you."

"Why?" I demanded. If anything, I would have thought it would be easier to apologize to his dad. All he had to do was tell his dad that he was sorry he'd left home, and Mr. Dass would forgive him, I was sure. Me, I'd been a traumatized mess and had *hit* Stanyard when he'd tried to apologize.

Stanyard couldn't quantify his feelings. "It's… it's different with you," he mumbled, and I caught the inflection behind his voice.

I gripped his hand and felt my own pulse thrumming against my palm. "Why?" I asked again. When he avoided my eyes, I repeated myself, louder. "Why am I different, Stanyard?"

I knew the answer. But I had to hear it from him. I had to know I wasn't imagining things, reading nuance that wasn't there.

He finally looked at me, face scrunched in annoyance as if he knew exactly what I was doing. "Because I like you, Phil."

I sucked in my breath as those five words displaced a lifetime of rejection. My head spun as a thousand prayers and timid daydreams collided. There was so much I wanted to say, and suddenly I couldn't find the words for any of it.

Jayde glanced at us in the rearview mirror and arched an eyebrow.

Stanyard noticed and ended the moment. He pulled his hand from my grasp and turned back to face the window. "Besides, it's different with Dad because… well, he's kind of the reason I left. And I don't think he's figured that out yet."

I remembered Mira's bitter accusation and wondered, for the first time, if Mr. Dass had expressed his anger with more than just words.

Jayde braked at a red light. "We're almost there. Hoods up."

He yanked a ski mask over his head, not that he needed any help looking intimidating. Lev snapped on a pair of night vision goggles and tied a handkerchief over his nose. Stanyard pulled the hood of his jacket up.

I couldn't see his face anymore, so I reached out with my words. "Well, if you can't forgive him, at least forgive yourself."

Jayde hovered at the intersection even after the light turned green. "Ten seconds."

Stanyard turned back to me. "For what?"

"For leaving."

At that moment, the power went out, plunging the entire block into darkness.

"It's go time," Jayde hissed, and slammed on the gas.

I braced myself against the passenger seat as we whipped around the corner, headlights off. The SUV's proximity sensor screamed in agony as Jayde barely avoided the shadowy forms of parked cars.

I felt my anxiety building like heat in an oven. I focused on taking deep breaths through my nose, forcing a prayer out with each exhale.

Holy Spirit, pave the way. The guards will be distracted and easy to take out. Everyone will be calm and cooperative. And the police will not investigate.

Jayde slowed the vehicle to a crawl. We cleared the last building, and there it was: Street 17 Containment Camp.

I craned my neck to look out the windshield. It seemed smaller than I remembered, the concrete wall somehow less imposing. The silhouette of the guard tower stood illuminated against the moon, the one-way mirrored windows reflecting the pale light like dead eyes. The panel next to the gate glowed yellow as it flashed a warning about low power.

Jayde rolled down the window and listened. The only sound was the hum of our engine and a dog barking several streets over. There were no alarms going off, no distant police sirens.

I unbuckled my seatbelt. *Thank you, Jesus.*

The other vehicles in our caravan converged from the side streets, taking up station on each corner of the building. Jayde parked next to John and Dowe's white van on the south side of the complex. Stanyard helped me out of the car.

John tipped his head back and admired the wall. "So this is your place, eh, Phil?"

"No wonder she never invited us over for dinner," Dowe muttered.

Jayde cupped his hand over his ear. "Tower, are you in?"

"Climbing the stairs now," Tower responded over the radio, sounding like he was running. "Guard at the front door neutralized."

"Be careful," a voice I didn't recognize chimed in. "There's only one other guard up here, which could mean there's one in the streets doing rounds."

"Copy," Jayde said, and nodded at me. "Stay close."

With the help of another guard, Lev dragged an apparatus from the car and dropped it near the wall. "Clear!" the other guard hissed, and cranked the lever. With a snap, a grappling hook shot from the machine and flew over the wall, dragging a ladder behind it. It dropped with a dull *thunk* on the other side of the wall.

Lev tested the hold, then scrambled up the ladder with enviable agility. I watched it buck and twist under his weight and tried not to be sick.

He crouched on the top of the wall and scanned the streets below, his goggles autofocusing in the dim light. Then he waved his arm at us.

Jayde gestured to me. "After you, captain."

I swallowed. Stanyard touched my shoulder. "I'll be right behind you."

I nodded rapidly to anchor my courage and gripped the ladder before I could reconsider. I climbed as fast as I could, thinking only about grabbing each rung in order, ignoring the burn of the swaying rope on my palms.

Lev grabbed my hand and helped me onto the top of the wall. I knelt there, catching my breath, and for the briefest moment took in the view. There was my old neighborhood, an austere network of tiny concrete boxes laid out in strict rows. It looked like a graveyard without the lights on, each house representing the headstone of the family who lived inside. Had I really called this place home for nearly six years?

Lev gripped my arm as I lowered my foot onto the ladder on the other side. Thankfully climbing down was a lot easier than climbing up.

I dropped into the alley behind the first row of homes and heard Stanyard scrambling down behind me. Jayde's voice came over the radio. "We've got ten minutes, people! Get your assigned rows to the gate. Blue Fire, I want you in the middle of the road where people can see you."

"Copy," I hissed. After glancing to make sure the alley was empty, I slipped in the gap between two houses and darted for the main road.

I stepped out onto the sidewalk—and someone grabbed me from behind. I choked on a scream as a gloved closed over my mouth.

"They told me you'd come back," a gravelly voice grunted in my ear. I recognized him as Lieutenant Clint, my old warden.

Someone shrieked a warning on the radio. I fought against him as adrenaline pounded in my ears. He gripped me to him, his arms like a viper. "About time you came home, isn't it, Miss—"

The threat ended in a groan. His grip loosened, and I jerked away. I whipped around and watched him drop to the ground with a thud, unconscious.

Stanyard stood behind him, the hilt of his gun raised. "I told you I'd shoot first. You okay?"

I nodded, fighting a wave of embarrassment. *You walked right into that one. Get it together! They're counting on you!*

Stanyard stripped the lieutenant of his weapons. He tossed one to Lev and one to Jayde, who came out of the alley behind us. Jayde cocked the rifle appreciatively, then jerked his head. "Watts and John Dowe, you take this row. Augustine and Blue Fire, follow me."

He took off at a run, and Stanyard and I followed. We came around the corner to the next street, where Mira and several other guards were already banging down doors. There was commotion and crying and hushed yells of surprise as familiar faces began to pour into the street. Half-awake people stumbled onto the sidewalk, struggling with jackets and sobbing children.

Someone shrieked my name. "Philli!"

I turned to see my old friend Cami barreling towards me. She collided into me and nearly knocked us both to the ground. "You came back!"

I gripped her as she sobbed into my shoulder. "It's okay, you're going to be okay."

A ripple passed across the crowd. "Phil?" "Is that Smyrna's kid?" "It's Blue Fire!"

I looked up. The commotion on the street stilled as everyone turned to me.

Jayde touched my back. "Let them see you."

I disentangled myself from Cami and stepped out into the street. "Yes, it's me. You're not safe here anymore—but we're going to get you out. These soldiers are my friends." I nodded at Jayde. "Follow them and you'll be safe."

There was silence, and for a second, I thought they weren't going to obey me. Then Cami's brother Aid shoved his way through the crowd and came to stand beside me. "You came back for us," he said, his voice husky but bold.

I looked up into his face. "Of course I did. I couldn't leave you."

He smiled and held out a hand—then changed his mind and pulled me into a hug. I accepted it and felt the weight of responsibility crash into my shoulders. *I can't leave these people.*

Jayde clapped his hands. "You heard her! Move out!"

The noise on the street resumed, this time with purpose. I pushed Aid away. "Head towards the front gate. I'll meet you when you get there—I promise."

He nodded and grabbed Cami's hand.

I turned to Stanyard. He stood on the sidewalk, feet apart, staring straight ahead.

I followed his gaze. Several doors down, Mr. Dass stood on his top step, scanning the crowd in confusion.

I touched Stanyard's shoulder. "He needs you."

Stanyard sucked in more air than his lungs could hold and nodded. He turned to Mira, who stood a few feet away, watching us.

He held out his hand.

She stared at it for what felt like a cursed eternity. I held my breath and willed her to take it. *God, please, restore.*

Mira finally reached out and accepted the offer, grabbing his fingers loosely. Stanyard led the way and pulled her through the crowd towards their old house.

Mr. Dass spotted them. I couldn't see his expression in the dark, but I could read his body language—the jerk of surprise, the stiffened back, his hands gripping the railing.

Stanyard and Mira stopped on the sidewalk. If words were exchanged, I didn't hear them. I whispered in tongues under my breath.

The tension shattered as Mr. Dass shouted for his wife. I watched with grateful tears as Stanyard finally got the reunion he deserved: His father diving off the porch and crushing him in a hug. Even Mira accepted her father's embrace as he used both arms to gather his children to him.

I turned away—and came face to face with my old door.

There it was, House 79, right across the street from the Dasses'. All the curtains were drawn, and weeds stubbornly grew in the cracks on the sidewalk.

Jayde appeared beside me. He pressed a flashlight into my hand. "You've got two minutes before the lights come on. Hurry."

I nodded and ran up the steps.

The door wasn't locked. It creaked as I stepped inside. The musty air rushed up to greet me, stale but familiar. I flicked the flashlight on and panned it over the entryway tile—the same floor my mother died on.

I swallowed the thought and hurried into the living room. I scanned the flashlight over the furniture, searching for any belongings I could easily take with me. I knew there was nothing upstairs; Thames had sent all my personal effects to Mars. But surely there was something...

There. My flashlight landed on the digital picture frame hanging on the wall. Propping the flashlight on the coffee table, I ran over and grabbed the frame off the wall. It was wireless, so as soon as I touched it, the screen brightened to life, revealing my favorite picture of Daddy and me.

I gripped the frame. The picture had been taken before we moved into camp, and Daddy's eyes were still full of life and purpose. He was staring down at me as I wrapped my arms around his waist, my face scrunched in laughter and my long hair flowing in the wind. He smiled at me with all the love of a father—affection I'd never get again.

I hugged the frame to my chest, choking on waves of emotion. I didn't know whether to be sad or bitter or just plain angry—mad at everything that had been taken from me. My mom was gone. My dad was gone. I—Philadelphia—was gone. We could end the United and liberate the world, but the Smyrnas were never coming back.

Mira was right. I couldn't fix everything.

I knew what I needed to do. Turning around, I faced the living room—the worn couch where my family had shared so many tears and stolen moments of joy—and spoke into the darkness.

"Goodbye, Mama. I love you."

I sniffed and swallowed.

"Goodbye, Daddy. I'll miss you."

I choked on a sob. I stared at the ceiling and forced the last words out.

"I hope I make you proud."

Suddenly, the lights came on.

Tower's voice crackled over the radio. "Gate's open! Load out!"

Shouts echoed on the street. Wiping my eyes, I ran out the front door and left House 79 behind for good.

I stepped onto the porch to find the street nearly empty. Stanyard stood at the end of the block, flagging the last people around the corner. Jayde waited for me at the bottom of the steps.

"Smile for the camera." He gestured behind me.

I turned and saw the security camera on the light pole, its lens flickering as it rebooted.

"Want to leave a calling card?" John came around the corner of the house, shaking a can of spray paint in each hand.

"You brought spray paint?" Jayde exclaimed.

"We always come prepared to vandalize," Dowe returned.

John rattled the cans. "Pink or blue?" he asked me.

I grinned. "Blue," I said, and caught it as he tossed it at me.

I caught it and handed him the picture frame. Taking a step back, I studied my old house. Then I aimed the can and drew a jagged bolt of lightning across the front door.

"Blue Fire was here," I declared, then turned and stared straight into the camera, making sure the tattoo on my shoulder was visible.

Jayde nodded in approval. "All right, let's move out!" He jogged towards Stanyard, calling final instructions at his men.

I dropped the paint can and followed John and Dowe back to the wall. Orders ricocheted on the radio as each vehicle pulled out, carrying its precious cargo. *Oh Jesus—protect them!* I prayed.

"Race you!" John shouted at his partner, and they darted ahead of me.

A few yards behind them, I came around the corner to the last street—just in time to see Lieutenant Clint get up.

He moaned and rolled over. He pushed himself against a light pole and reached for his guns, cursing when he found them gone. He pulled out his radio and pressed the button.

"Stop!" I yelled, darting towards him.

He jerked his head around. I whipped the gun from my pocket. "Put it down!"

He let go of the button.

I stopped a few yards away and aimed the gun at his face. Muscle memory kicked in as I planted my feet apart, my hands steady even though I thought my heart was going to break a rib. "Put it down, or I shoot," I ordered.

He snorted. "Will you?"

I hesitated, my grip slacking.

"Blue Fire!" Jayde shouted from behind me.

Clint shook his head. "You won't. I know you, Philadelphia."

"Do you?" I hissed, taking another step forward.

He didn't flinch. "Your finger's not even on the trigger."

"Just shoot him!" Jayde called, still too far away to help me.

My eyes shifted from Clint's face to his uniform, with the shiny badge that represented the government that had tortured me for so long. I remembered the threats at gunpoint, the propagandizing at school, all the shouts and abuse as they told me over and over that I was worthless, broken, and unwanted.

My finger slid to the trigger, and I saw the light behind Clint's eyes change.

"Phil!" Stanyard shouted from somewhere in my peripheral.

I became aware of the weight of the gun in my hand as clarity rushed into my mind. Clint deserved to die—but without his radio, he was harmless. We'd be long gone before he could make it to the guard tower to call for help.

I adjusted my grip. "I'm not going to ask you again. Put. It. Down."

After a flicker of hesitation, he threw the radio on the pavement. It skidded towards me.

I kept the gun aimed. "Phone."

He grunted and fished it out of his pocket, tossing it at me.

I waited until it had spun to a stop on the pavement. Then I drew my foot back and stomped on both devices, crushing them.

I lowered the gun. "When you get back to headquarters, tell them Blue Fire sent you."

He didn't say anything. He just stared at me, eyes narrowed.

I turned and ran.

8

I didn't take a full breath until we were back at base.

As soon as I climbed into the SUV and slammed the door shut, the reality of what we'd just done collapsed on me—along with the reality of what I'd almost done. Stanyard rode with his family, so I was alone in the SUV with Lev and Jayde. Jayde barked directions into the radio as he raced through the alleys, but I didn't hear a word anyone was saying. I stared at the gun in my hands and felt the cold touch of the lethal metal on my fingertips.

You almost shot him in the face!

"Hey, you don't need that anymore," Lev muttered, followed by some words in Russian. He gingerly slid the weapon from my grasp and set the safety.

I stared down at my hands, so pale and shaky and streaked with substances I dare not identify, and wondered if they still belonged to me.

Lev pushed his goggles back and pulled the handkerchief off his nose. "You good, boss?"

"I almost... I almost killed him," I whispered, afraid the words would kill me too as I spoke them.

"What?"

"I almost killed him. I almost killed him!" I shouted, as if the volume could force me to accept this new reality that I'd created.

"You should have," Jayde grunted, his eyes finding mine in the rearview mirror.

"But you didn't." The inflection in Lev's voice was somewhere between a statement and a question, his brow furrowed as he studied me.

Most of the vans dispersed across the city, taking the refugees to different drop-off points to avoid suspicion, but the Dasses and Cami and Aid's family were coming to base at my request. Tower had personally agreed to transport the Dasses, and Cami and Aid's family rode with John and Dowe.

As soon as we all arrived back at base, Cami barreled into me, gushing all over again. Her parents hugged me and then plied me with all the well-meaning adult questions I didn't have the energy to answer truthfully: *"Where have you been? What's going on? Where's your father?"*

I looked for Stanyard, but he was busy getting his family settled. So I let them have their privacy and took Cami and Aid up with me to the command floor, where we waited for the other teams to check in. We stood around the module with Jayde, Lev, and Tower, watching the screen. A map of the city with all the drop-off points was displayed on the monitor, while a police scanner tracked the ongoing state of emergency.

It didn't take long for our jailbreak to reach headquarters and send the government into high alert. Within an hour they had the highways closed down, traffic scanners set up at a dozen major intersections, and police out on every corner looking for suspicious vehicles.

The silence on the radio was cruel. I pinched my eyes shut and repeated my prophetic prayers over and over.

They're all going to make it. No one will get pulled over. Everyone will be safe—

And then, suddenly, the first team checked in.

Air rushed back into the room as the soldiers murmured gratefully. I opened my eyes and watched the dot on the map representing the first team turn green. *Thank you, Jesus.*

One by one, the other captains called in, until every last team was accounted for. I stared at the map, now splattered with green dots, and blinked away tears.

They all made it. We did it. We won.

Jayde stepped forward and offered me his hand. "Congratulations, Blue Fire. Mission accomplished."

The room erupted in applause. Cami squealed and hugged me. Lev laughed, his face crinkled in the largest smile I'd ever seen him wear.

I felt hands slide over my shoulders. I looked up into my uncle's face, his smile hidden under the shadow of his shaggy hair. "Now *that's* how you lead a revolution."

I scanned the room and watched as the soldiers exchanged hugs and high fives and tears. Someone started a military chant, and the whole room joined in, pumping their fists in time. I listened to the war cry reverberate through my bones and finally admitted the truth.

This is where you belong.

*

Stanyard met me in the cafeteria when I stumbled down for breakfast the next morning.

"There you are," he said, turning and gesturing to the open bench beside him.

I wanted to say the same thing; I hadn't seen him or Mira since we got back to base last night. I joined him at the table, setting my backpack down on the floor, and accepted the mug of black coffee he had ready for me. I smiled at the rippling brown liquid. "Were you waiting for me?"

"Always," he said, and grinned. "How are you feeling?"

I arched my back. "Sore," I admitted. The stiffness hadn't hit me until this morning, when the adrenaline finally dried up.

He hesitated, then gently reached over and rubbed my back. When I didn't shy away, he pressed harder, grinding his knuckles in between my shoulder blades. I laid my forehead on my arms and flopped out on the table with a relieved sigh. I let him work, wondering, not for the first time, when he'd become so kind—or if he'd always been this nice, and I just never noticed.

I stiffened and sat up when I remembered what else had transpired yesterday. "But what about you? How did it…?"

"Ask me when I've had more sleep." He snorted and lowered his hand. "I don't think any of us slept more than a couple hours. It's a lot for Mom and Dad to take in."

Of course it was, but that wasn't what I was asking. "Did you and your dad have time to talk?"

He nodded, staring at the stain in the bottom of his empty mug.

I laid my hand on his knee. "And?"

His shoulders heaved as he took a deep breath. "I apologized. And… so did he."

I gripped his leg, my heart bursting with praise.

He looked up and stared at the wall, brow furrowed as if he was still trying to comprehend his new reality. "Now we have to figure out how to live with each other again."

I smiled in spite of myself. "And what about Mira?" I dared to ask.

He tapped the handle of his coffee mug. "She needs more time."

And Jesus, I thought but didn't add.

"You were right about one thing, though."

I looked up at him. "Yeah?"

He turned to meet my eyes. "I have to forgive myself first."

I studied the creases around the corners of his mouth and wondered if he hadn't quite accomplished that yet. "I forgive you," I reminded him. "And… I'm proud of you."

He started slightly, for a brief moment pulling back. Then he leaned towards me. "Thank you," he whispered, his eyes flickering with an expression I understood but dare not put words to.

I stared at him, wanting for all the world to say *yes* to the unspoken question between us. Before I could second guess what I was doing, I slid down the bench and laid my head on his shoulder.

He relaxed into me, slowly, as if he were afraid he'd displace me. His hand found mine beneath the table.

I closed my eyes and had just found my peace when Stanyard's phone buzzed.

He stiffened but made no move to pick it up. It pulsed three more times, vibrating irritatingly against the metal table.

I groaned and lifted my head. "If that's Jayde..." *I'll fire him.*

Stanyard sighed and grabbed the device, flipping it over to read the screen. His brow scrunched. "It's Nic."

I sat up straight. "What?"

He flipped through the notifications. "He's mad you didn't check in last night."

I hadn't even looked at my tablet last night when I'd stopped in at the Vons'—I'd had more important things to do. "And he's texting *you* about that?"

Stanyard shrugged. "He's also asking if you saw the news."

"I try not to. Why?" But as soon as I said it, I knew what had happened.

I hadn't told Nic what we were doing last night. There hadn't been time, and this was definitely a situation where it would be better to ask for forgiveness than permission—or, better yet, not tell him at all. But apparently the media had done my job for me.

The phone buzzed again. "He's asking me to call him."

"Don't," I said emphatically, standing up and grabbing my backpack.

"Or, never mind, I guess he's calling me." The phone trilled, and Stanyard answered it before I could stop him. "Hello?"

"Where is she?" Nic demanded, voice rigid with anger.

My palms started to sweat as my fight-or-flight response kicked in, but I willed it back. This didn't involve him, and I wasn't going to let him bully me this time. I did what was right.

Stanyard held the phone away from his ear and looked up at me. "She's right here."

"Of course she is." Nic sighed, and I pictured him aggressively rubbing a hand across his mustache. "I hope you're leaving room for Jesus."

Stanyard flushed red. "Huh?"

"Never mind. Put her on."

Stanyard offered the phone to me. I didn't take it.

"Philadelphia," Nic barked, "don't be a coward."

I snatched the device and walked a few feet away. "Don't be a jerk."

"I'll think about it. Who signed the parental waiver?"

"What?" I sighed, and hoped he wouldn't keep beating around the bush. I knew he was upset, but it would be a lot easier to deal with if he'd just be honest with me.

"Your tattoo. Who signed the parental waiver? Because I sure didn't."

"It's temporary," I admitted. Why was I humoring him? It really wasn't any of his business.

"That's a relief, because it's ugly."

My face burned as his words stung a part of my soul I didn't realize he had access to. *It's not ugly... I'm not ugly, am I?* I glanced down at what was left of the drawing on my shoulder.

Stanyard stood up and waited by the table, watching me.

"Anyway," Nic continued, his voice a starched façade of calm, "are you aware, Miss Smyrna, of how insufferably moronic you've been the last twenty-four hours, or do I need to explain it to you?"

My hand tightened around the phone. If he wanted to take cheap shots, two could play that game. "Why don't you explain it to me, Dr. Von Nieuwenhuyse? Enlighten me with your three PhDs."

I knew he hated his full name, and I could tell by the shift in his tone that I'd hurt him where he hurt me. "Watch your attitude, young lady."

"I learned from the best," I hissed.

He couldn't deny it, so he ignored it. "All right then, I hope you're taking notes, because there will be a quiz in the morning. First of all, thanks to your little outing last night, your name and image are now plastered all over the news—again."

That was, of course, the idea, but I daren't tell him that. "They already knew my name."

"Yes, well, now they have live footage proving you're in town, and they have visual descriptions of several of your 'friends.' What in the world were you thinking?"

The anger in his voice cracked, making room for genuine fear. I heard the desperation in his words and remembered why we were having this conversation. Nic was a jerk, yes, but he really did care about me.

"Nic." I took several breaths to regulate the tone of my voice. "That was my camp. Those were my old neighbors."

"'Old' should be the operative word there."

"No, Nic, listen." I tried to cram a brick in the door while it was open. "They were going to deport them."

He was silent.

I looked to Stanyard for support as I continued. "We intercepted orders from the regional office. They were all going to be deported to a labor camp in China in the morning. They… weren't coming back."

"I know." Nic sighed, but I couldn't tell if the gesture was a concession or not.

I swallowed and tried to force my heart out through my words, desperate for him to see my side. "They did it because of me, Nic. I just found out that they've been interrogating everyone I knew, trying to get to me."

"And that's exactly why you should have left it alone."

"What?"

His voice hardened again, each syllable thick with disappointment. "They baited you, Phil, and you played right into their hand. You should have walked away."

I'm not sure which upset me more: his disapproval or the horror of what he was suggesting. "You think I should have let them get deported?"

"It's what I would have done," he stated with absolutely no remorse at all, and in that moment, I remembered why he had once been the villain.

"Nic!" I cried. "They would have been *killed!*"

"It would have been their own fault," he stated.

Stanyard stiffened. Nic blathered on with no regard for the grave he was digging for himself. "Last I checked, the jewelry counter at the store has more security than those containment camps. If they wanted to break out, they would have done so before now."

I didn't want to think about the fact that, had it not been for Nic and the Red Rain fiasco, *I* would still be in that camp.

"You should have left it alone, Phil," Nic repeated, his voice grave. "These people that you're playing with—the officials in Beijing—they're out of your league. Trust me, I know. You need to walk away while you still can."

No. I was tired of turning a blind eye while the government destroyed people's lives. The whole reason the world was in this mess was because people had walked away, content to hibernate in their cocoon of security while freedom fell. That's what Nic had done. He'd built his castle on Mars and never looked back.

I wouldn't make the same mistake.

"I'm sorry I'm not more like you," I spat, withdrawing the affection from my voice.

"Well, let me know how that works out for you," his tone tightened in kind, "because you just made things so much worse."

My anger evaporated as my heart dropped to my stomach. I shared a panicked glance with Stanyard. "What do you mean?"

"Oh, you haven't heard? Maybe you should go turn on the TV, 'Blue Fire,'" he threatened. "You may have won a battle last night, but you're about to lose a war."

I hung up on him and started running.

9

We raced up to the command floor, paging Jayde as we went. A few bored guards were lounging around the controls when we arrived. Mira leaned against the dashboard, chatting with one of them.

She straightened when we entered. "What's wrong with you?" She gave me a once-over, her eyes distinctly avoiding Stanyard's.

I brushed past her. "Turn on the news."

"Why?"

One of the guards obeyed me without question, his fingers flying across a control pad. I saw the screen in front of him light up, the image dancing across the reflection on his glasses. He uttered something that could have been taken as either a prayer or an oath.

I gripped the dashboard. "Put it on the screen."

The door whooshed open and Jayde walked in just as the monitor above our heads flickered on, displaying the morning newscast. Clips of security footage from last night's raid played in the background, superimposed with the panicked words *Breaking News*. I watched as an eerily high-definition, black-and-white version of myself spraypainted a lightning bolt on the door of my old home.

Then I looked down at the ticker. I watched the words roll past, spelling out the doomed headline:

BEIJING OFFICIALS VOTE TO RESTRUCTURE ASSIMILATION ASSISTANCE PROGRAM

Stanyard muttered in tongues. I couldn't find anything to say as I listened to a plastic anchorwoman read off her tablet.

"Officials say the instigator behind last night's violent demonstration is Philadelphia Smyrna, a runaway from a Boston remedial home."

"'Remedial home'? How charming," Stanyard muttered.

To reinforce the veneer of benevolence, they popped up a quaint picture of me coloring with chalk on the sidewalk at camp. It was a grainy photo, clearly ripped from a security camera and zoomed in to crop out the watchtower and concrete fence in the background.

I remembered that day; it was not long after we'd been taken into camp, and I was only eleven or twelve. Dad had smuggled some sidewalk chalk home from work, and I'd amused myself for a week, drawing castles and unicorns to transport myself somewhere else.

I'd shared my treasure with Mira. I looked up at her where she stood across the room and wondered if she remembered, but if she did, it wasn't a pleasant memory. She was frowning at the screen, her arms crossed.

The anchorwoman continued narrating.

"Smyrna went missing shortly after being removed from a high school special ed program. People close to the suspect claim she was a well-adjusted girl before being forced to graduate early, leading many to blame the school system."

They cut to a clip of my homeroom teacher. *"She was an excellent student,"* he crooned, which was the exact opposite of what he'd always told me. *"Eager to learn, very responsive to redirection. She was really trying, but the system was designed for her to fail."*

"That's because I wanted to fail," I snorted, but the laugh stopped in my throat, like it was food I couldn't swallow. This wasn't funny—it was terrifying.

"Psychological experts say Smyrna's actions display classic signs of conduct disorder and borderline personality disorder. And there's mounting scientific evidence that both of these disorders can be caused by conditions in the remedial homes."

The screen flashed to carefully curated clips from my streams—the ones that looked shaky, amateur, and childish. The ones that made me look like a scared teenager with a laptop.

"This young woman should have been diagnosed years ago," some random guy with a bunch of letters after his name droned. *"It's been clinically proven that these 'homes' are actually preventing kids from rejoining society."*

So this was how they were going to cover their mess: By making me sound sick and diseased, like a lab rat. But in some disgusting way, they were right. The camps did turn me into the monster they thought I was. I did what I did because of the camps—because I didn't want anyone else to suffer like I did.

Suddenly, Asia appeared on the screen.

She stood behind a podium emblazoned with the United seal, cameras flashing in the background. *"This 'rebellion' is clearly a troubled young woman's cry for help. Children like her need our aid, not our punishment..."*

"That's her!" I lurched back and pointed. "That's Asia, the woman who gave me the code."

A murmur rippled around the room. Jayde stepped up beside me and swore. "Then you're in big trouble."

I looked at him. "What?"

He pointed to the corner where Asia's real name was displayed:

MONG SHI MIN TAI, COUNCILOR

The commotion in the room escalated. My mind struggled to peg the familiar surname, and when it finally did, my heart stopped.

Oh God, no.

I yanked my backpack off my shoulders and struggled with the zipper. I grabbed the invitation and ripped it out of the envelope, holding the cursed calligraphy up to the light.

HIS EXCELLENCE GENERAL SECRETARY MONG

The room faded as I remembered everything they'd taught us in school. Asia was the daughter of the General Secretary, the highest-ranking official in the United government.

And she knew exactly who I was, dual identities and all.

Jayde grabbed his radio and yelled for Tower, then started shouting orders to his men. I turned my focus back to Asia, squinting at the video and trying to read the motivation behind her expression. What was she doing? My rebellion threatened her government, her position in society. She should have been the first one to turn me in, but she hadn't. What did she want?

I tuned into her words as the video kept rolling.

"We are failing our children. None of this would have happened if the state had placed Philadelphia in a loving home instead of locking her behind bars. And now we have officials calling for her execution? Please, I'm begging my friends in Washington: Let this poor child come home."

She looked up and smiled benevolently at the camera, as if she knew I was watching. I took an instinctive step back. She wanted me to come home. She still wanted me to become Andromeda, to accept a life of affluence and live like one of them, and she would move heaven, earth, and hell until that was the only choice I had.

But why? Why was I so important to her? For that matter, why had I been so important to Thames? He had picked me out long before my dad had created Red Rain. I'd been a pawn in the end, but that's not how it had started. He had chosen me. Why?

Stanyard touched my elbow, his eyes narrowed, searching for answers to the same questions. I gripped his hand as the anchorwoman appeared on the screen again.

"These developments have experts all across the globe calling for reform of the reassimilation program. In an emergency session early this morning, Beijing officials voted almost unanimously to close the North American branch of the program and relocate detainees to compounds in China."

The room devolved into a hurricane of curses and shouts of rage. Stanyard turned away from me and rammed his fist into the nearest desk. Lev muttered in Russian. Even Jayde went silent, his face pale and pinched as he gripped the dashboard.

Mira moved beside me. "Look what you've done," she hissed.

I slapped my hands over my ears as Nic's accusations came ricocheting back.

You may have won a battle last night, but you're about to lose a war.

I could barely hear the recording as another United official came on the screen and praised the decision.

"This debacle clearly demonstrates the inefficiencies of the North American system. It is critical that these people are transferred to a stable environment before more lives are lost. We can assure you that the detainees will receive the finest medical care and psychological screening..."

The roar from the soldiers drowned him out. The room was spinning, spinning as I dropped the invitation and staggered for any handhold, finding only the dashboard. I braced myself against the controls and fought alternating waves of nausea, tears, and guilt.

You should have stayed on Mars, sweetheart.

No. I slammed my palm down on the control panel, freezing the stream. This can't be how it ends. I'd come too far, survived too many miracles, for this to all be a mistake. I wasn't going to give up, not this time.

God had brought me to this point, and I wasn't going back to Mars until I found out why.

"No," I said again, this time aloud. I whipped around and repeated myself, strong enough to be heard. "No."

The commotion stilled as everyone shifted to look at me. I accepted the responsibility and straightened. "We can't let this happen—*I* can't let this happen."

I am Blue Fire.

"And what are you going to do about it?" Mira threw up her hands. "Liberate the camps one by one and hide people in the basement? You can't fix this, Phil. The only reason this is happening is because *you* felt the need to show off."

"Mira," Stanyard hissed, an unfamiliar anger rising in his eyes.

"No, no," I muttered, mostly to myself, giving my mind time to catch up. She was right, of course—we couldn't save all those people, not like that. But there had to be something else I could do. We'd managed to rally an army just with one video; surely that wasn't for nothing.

I took a step back, as if the motion could help me see in another dimension, and my foot slipped on the invitation. I stared at the gilded lettering peeking out from beneath my scuffed shoe and remembered the handwritten note on the back of the envelope.

YOU'RE STILL INVITED –ASIA

I bent and picked up the card, and suddenly, I understood why God had chosen me.

I looked up at the group. "Let me talk to her."

"Who?" Stanyard demanded, instantly suspicious.

"Asia—Councilor Mong. She loves me. She's been trying to be friends since we met—and she can fix this. Maybe if I talk to her, or go to the party, she will—"

"What party?" Jayde interrupted.

I shoved the invitation at him. I paced a tight circle around the middle of the floor, trying to anchor my thoughts. I had no idea what I would say or how I would approach her, but I knew this was what I was supposed to do. *This* was why—this was why Thames had taken an interest in me. This was why Asia had befriended me. This was why I was a Nolan.

I realized the room had gone silent. I looked up at Jayde. He was frowning at the invitation, eyes dark and cold.

"Everyone out," he ordered. "I need to talk to Blue Fire."

10

After a flicker of hesitation, the soldiers obeyed him, filing out of the room.

Lev and Stanyard held back. Lev cast a questioning glare up at Jayde and rattled off something in Russian that apparently Jayde understood.

Jayde shook his head. "I said everyone."

Lev turned and hurried out. Stanyard frowned, planted his feet apart, and didn't move.

Jayde tensed, but Mira intercepted. She grabbed her brother's shoulder and steered him towards the door. With a final glance back at me, Stanyard relented.

Jayde waited until the door had shut behind them. Then he walked over to the dashboard and pressed down on a key. "Blackout," he declared into the empty room.

With a dying whir of electricity, all the computers in the room shut off. The dashboard grew cold as the buttons stopped flickering, and the monitor went black, plunging the room into near darkness. The only light left in the room came from the blinking sensors on the wall of servers.

I groped for a handhold. "Jayde…"

I heard his boots clumping on the floor, and then a lone desk lamp flickered on. He stood there, his back to me, holding the invitation under the yellow light.

"Why didn't you tell me about this sooner?"

It was none of your business would have been the correct answer, but I was quickly realizing that, as Blue Fire, everything that happened to me was someone else's business.

"I didn't think it was important," I settled for, and up until moments ago, it hadn't been.

"Phil…" He turned and shook the paper at me. "Do you understand what this is an invitation for?"

"Yeah, some state dinner." Asia had specifically called it a "boring" state dinner.

"Not just any state dinner. *The* state dinner. This is the most prestigious government event of the year. Don't you remember seeing it on the news?"

I thought we'd established today that I didn't watch the news, but even if I had, a state dinner wasn't something I would have paid attention to. Watching rich people crossbreed at parties was the exact opposite of entertaining.

"Only the most elite get invited. That's how they decide who's in and who's out for the next round of government commissions." Jayde paced, his face passing in and out of shadow. "Everyone who attends gets to meet the General Secretary, and it's all televised on live TV."

And I'm one of those elite. I tried and failed to grasp the complexity of that revelation.

"If I had realized that's what this woman was inviting you to when you met..." Jayde stood still and blinked, recalibrating his reality around a dimension of *what-ifs*. He shook his head and turned towards me. "Phil, if you go, you'll get to meet the General face-to-face."

That sounded like a reason why I should *not* go. The General Secretary was the last person I wanted to get a close look at me. Asia may know who I was, but logical deduction assumed her father did not. If he did, I wouldn't still be breathing.

Jayde studied me, watching to see if I was tracking the implications. When I didn't produce the desired reaction, he gestured behind me. "Sit down."

I glanced at the nearby desk chair. "Why?" I demanded, and tried to figure out why that command was vaguely threatening.

"Please," was all he said.

I refused.

He inhaled through his nose and pinched his eyes shut. "This is going to be very difficult for you to hear, but I need you to listen carefully." He opened his eyes. "I know how we can win this war."

"How?" I said, knowing full well that I didn't want the answer.

He spoke slowly, each word metered like the steady bang of a drum. "You need to accept the invitation," he held it out, "meet the General, and kill him."

"What?" I breathed. I'd heard him the first time. I just didn't want to accept it.

He repeated himself even more slowly. "You will go to the party, meet the General, and assassinate him."

No, I started to say, but the word died as soon as I formed it. *I can't.*

"You can," he countered my thoughts. "It's just like Asia said—you're a Nolan. You're one of them. And if your family is as famous as she makes them sound, the General will definitely want to meet you and shake your hand."

"But Thames—" Mr. Nolan had fallen out of grace with the United, and he'd decided he'd rather die than deal with the consequences. And his crimes were petty compared to mine. Surely his sins had tainted the family name.

"Asia can take care of that," Jayde declared without even the slightest hesitation. "She already has. Do you think you would have gotten this invitation if they suspected Andromeda?"

I remembered how Asia had so sweetly offered to clear Mrs. Nolan's file and realized he was right. If the Nolans were being penalized for their involvement in Red Rain, I would have heard about it by now. Asia had made the whole thing go away.

Perhaps, I recognized for the first time, because she had been in charge all along.

"You can do this," Jayde repeated, sealing the verdict while there was nowhere for me to run. "You can get close enough to him. Andromeda can."

He was right. Andromeda could do this.

But that didn't mean Philadelphia would.

"I won't," I said, and wished my voice had come out stronger, more convicted.

"You have to."

He stepped forward. I stumbled back, tripping over my backpack and spilling the contents on the floor. I heard a makeup tube roll away, thudding softly into a cabinet across the room.

He stopped on the edge of the light from the desk lamp. "This is how we end this, Phil. This is how we end the United."

"But Operation Blue Fire..." *That* was the plan. To revolt, to stand up together, to raise our voice and tell the government that we would not surrender. No one had to die for that plan to work. No one had to kill.

Jayde shook his head. "Operation Blue Fire will break the system, but it won't end it. No matter how many citizens join us, the United will still control the government. They're going to have their strongholds, and we'll have to fight them tooth and nail for control. It will be all-out war, Phil. Do you know what war means?"

Bloodshed. Death. Destruction.

I knew that. I knew the operation could lead to war; I'd known that this whole time. I hoped—and prayed—that things would go another way, that there would be enough resistance and the system would collapse on itself without the need for outright war. But war was always a possibility, and it was a sacrifice we were willing to make.

Was it possible that I could prevent war entirely?

"If you take out the General, it will throw the government into chaos." Jayde gestured in the air like he was drawing a battle plan on a map. "They'll be scrambling to replace him—and that's when we strike. That's when we launch Operation Blue Fire."

I wanted to refute him. I wanted to reject his plan and point out the flaws in his logic—but there were none.

"If we strike while they're weak, we can destroy the whole system. We can remove the government and build a new one."

Jayde's voice reached a fever pitch, but in my head, he sounded distant and small. There were dozens of questions I should be asking: *How are we going to get rid of the rest of the officials? Who will replace them? What kind of government will we build?* But I couldn't process any of that. All those hypothetical realities slipped through my fingers like sand as I choked on the bitter truth that underpinned them all.

You have to kill a man.

"You're the only one who can do it, Phil. No one else can get close enough. They won't let me anywhere near him—they don't know me. But they know you."

I finally took Jayde's advice and collapsed in the chair behind me. I heard rather than felt my breathing turn fast and shallow, became aware of the thrumming of my pulse as I gripped the arms of the chair. "I—I can't," I cried, but the word came out as a gasp, like I was drowning and couldn't keep my head above water.

"Yes, you can. I'll help you. We'll figure out a way to make it quick and bloodless. You won't be able to come at him with a traditional weapon—you're not going to have to stab him to death or anything."

Was that supposed to make it any better? "No, I can't!" I forced the words out with resolve, even though I was losing feeling in my hands and face.

"Phil—"

"I won't!"

The declaration echoed between us, drawing a line I wouldn't cross. Jayde stopped and waited until the silence returned. "Why not?" he asked finally, the question unnervingly calm.

"Because it's wrong," I answered reflexively. *Thou shalt not kill.*

"How is it any different than what you're already doing?"

I'm not murdering anyone.

He scoffed, crossing his arms over his bulky chest. "You signed up for this, Phil. When you agreed to be Blue Fire, you agreed to lead a revolution. You may not be on the front lines, but it's still war. If you don't pull the trigger, someone else will."

"So let them!" I screeched. *Anyone but me.*

"But if you do it, you can save so many lives," he pleaded, his voice softening again. "You can end this war before it starts."

I looked away. Every nerve in my body was screaming in refusal, but I couldn't find the words. Everything I could think to say felt weak, inadequate. Cowardly.

Jayde resorted to begging. "Phil, please. You have to be the one. I can't—" He stepped towards me, and his boot crunched on something. He bent to pick it up, rolling it over in his fingers. I couldn't see what it was in the shadows.

When he spoke again, his voice was soft, a cool whisper. "What if this is the reason you're here?"

I looked up at him and waited.

"You said yourself—Asia loves you. The Nolans chose you. Why?"

I wish I knew.

Jayde walked over and dropped down on one knee in front of me. "You're one of them now—but you're also Philadelphia. You're Blue Fire. You're the only one with a foot in both worlds."

He took my hand and gently spread my fingers. He pressed something cold and metallic into my palm.

I could tell what it was by the shape: the star of David pin Lev had given me. I stared at it as it glinted faintly in the darkness.

For such a time as this.

Jayde closed my fingers around the pin and gripped my fist. "This is why you're here, Phil. No one else can do this but you. Will you help me? Will you help me save the world?"

*

I closed the door to Cea's bedroom and sagged against it, relieved to finally be alone. Mr. Von had exacted vengeance on me for skipping out on dinner the last two nights and bullied me into watching six episodes of his current show. My mind was numb, and I was exhausted from the fake laughter—both the TV's and my own. It was nearly eleven o'clock before he finally let me escape.

I could only hope it wasn't too late to make a call.

I walked over to the nightstand and picked up the jewelry box Asia had given me. I opened the blue velvet case and fingered the single strand of pearls. Asia had claimed it was an "early birthday gift," and at the time, the gesture had seemed strange, unwelcome. Now, I was grateful for the gift. In one week, I would have an occasion to wear pearls.

Underneath the necklace was tucked Asia's calling card. I slid it out and ran my thumb over the gilded embossing. She'd said I could call anytime I needed anything. I was about to find out if she was telling the truth.

Sinking down on the edge of the bed, I took my tablet off the charger. There were several unread messages from both Nic and Stanyard, but I cleared the notifications and ignored them. If I didn't do this now, I'd lose my nerve.

I brought up the call screen and dialed Asia's number. She picked up after one ring.

"Andromeda!" she crooned into the phone, sounding wide awake. Her controlled Mandarin accent made her voice warm but spicy, like ginger. "It's so good to hear from you."

"Hi," I managed, but the word stuck in my throat.

Am I really doing this?

She latched onto my fear like a wolf. "What's wrong? Are you in danger? Do you need anything?"

I took three deep breaths through my nose and remembered what Jayde had said. *"Act frightened, like you've seen the light,"* he'd coached. *"If she asks, tell her you heard the news and realized you made a mistake. She won't question your change of heart—after all, that's what she wants."*

I swallowed and didn't try to suppress the stutter in my voice. "I—there's something I need to ask you."

"Yes?" she said, the question eager, too eager.

I pinched my eyes shut and squeezed out one last desperate prayer.

This is why you're here.

I opened my eyes and looked down at the screen. "Is it too late to RSVP to my birthday party?"

11

"This is going to hurt a lot."

"I know," I said, and hoped the pain medication Jayde had given me was working.

It was the next morning, and we were in the lab above Andes's shop. For the second time in so many months, I found myself strapped into the laser-guided surgery machine used to alter fingerprints.

Only this time, I wouldn't be changing my identity. This time, Andes would be weaving a network of wires and circuitry beneath the skin of my right hand, building a computer in my palm.

Andes snapped a magnifier over his right eye and blinked until it autofocused. Then he used tweezers to pick up a filament of wire, no thicker than a hair's breadth, and feed it into the machine.

"Brace yourself, lass," he warned, and lowered the needle into my thumb.

I shuddered. Whatever substance Jayde had given me was taking the edge off, but it didn't dull the horrifying feeling of the cold wire sliding into my skin. It was like a parasite, infesting me and turning me into a bomb.

That's what I was now: a walking weapon.

Jayde laid his warm hand on my shoulder, grounding me. "You're doing the right thing."

I nodded, not trusting my voice. He was right—he had to be. This is why I had been given all this privilege. This is why Thames had chosen me. This is why I was Andromeda Nolan.

I repeated that to myself over and over as Andes labored. It took an agonizing two hours, during which I cried out in pain more than once, before he was finally ready to install the motherboard.

Andes picked up the microscopic battery and held it close to the magnifier, his brow creased like a ravine. "What do you need this much power for, lass?"

I swallowed. I couldn't answer him truthfully.

I need that much power to kill.

The hardware was fairly simple. The computer would be programmed to deliver an electromagnetic pulse that would stop the heart and send the victim into cardiac arrest. Quick, bloodless, and irreversible.

All it needed was a microchip programmed to react to the General Secretary's DNA.

Andes arranged the battery on a sterile tray along with the other components of the motherboard. "I think you're missing some programming," he said. He directed the implied question at Jayde.

"It will be installed later," was all Jayde said, voice even.

Andes shifted his gaze back to me. He squinted, his right eye unnaturally large and bulbous behind the lens of the magnifier.

Please don't ask questions, I silently begged. Operation Thunderbird was a blackout mission. I couldn't even tell Stanyard.

Andes didn't ask for details, perhaps because he knew they wouldn't change anything. "Is this what you want, lass?"

I almost laughed. Maybe I should have; maybe the sound would have relieved some of the pain in my heart. No, this wasn't what I wanted. The last thing I wanted to do was kill.

But it was necessary.

I took a deep breath. "Do it."

Jayde squeezed my shoulder.

An eternity later, Andes finally released me from the machine. I stumbled out of the chair. My entire body was numb. My head pulsed with the reality of what I'd just done, what I'd just become. I rubbed my palm, trying to feel the wires and convince myself that this was real, but it was like my fingers weren't even there.

"How much?" Jayde grunted.

Andes put his hands up. "On the house. Consider it my investment in the new world."

I offered him a dizzy smile.

He stood up and grasped my shoulder, steadying me. "*Thig ar latha*, Thunderbird."

I used his brawny arm to pull myself upright. "There is one thing you can do for me."

He arched an eyebrow.

I rolled my sleeve up, baring my right shoulder. "I need a tattoo."

*

"I swear that hurt worse than the implant."

Jayde chuckled as he put the SUV in park. "You're the one who wanted it."

"Well, it's definitely my last." I gingerly rubbed the bandage that covered my new ink. For such a small design, it had taken almost thirty minutes of repetitive stabbing to create. I had been in complete agony the entire time; the pain medication had worn off, apparently. How people like Andes could willingly cover themselves in tattoos was beyond me.

"Hey." Jayde shut off the engine and swiveled to face me. "Thank you."

I tried not to look surprised, but my eyebrows had a mind of their own. "That's a new one coming from you."

He snorted. "I know. I don't say it often enough. But I couldn't do this without you."

"Do you really mean that?" I blurted with more transparency than I'd intended. Jayde was always telling me I was irreplaceable, but was it true? Nic thought the rebellion didn't need me. Even Stanyard thought I should just go home.

Jayde nodded. "I always have. I've always believed in you."

I eyed him, not sure I trusted this mushy and emotional version of Jayde.

"What?" he returned with an expression that was cross between amused and annoyed. "Do you think I would have tracked you across the entire Boston metropolitan area if you could be replaced?"

I rolled my eyes. "Way to kill the moment."

"Sorry." He laughed. "But think about it. If anyone else could have done it, don't you think I would have tried that before now? But I knew you were the one. That's why I put all my money on you."

I glanced at him out of the corner of my eye. "Was it a good investment?"

He leaned back in his seat and studied me. "You really don't see it, do you? You really don't understand what you've done."

I felt heat rising in my palms and up the back of my neck, but it wasn't a scary feeling.

"Phil, we've been trying for *years* to build what you've created in a matter of months. Ever since your dad…" He hesitated, chewing on his anger until he'd reduced it to a piece we could both swallow. "Ever since the original Operation Blue Fire failed, we've been trying to rally the people, but they've been too scared, too divided, too… distracted."

I thought back to all the years I'd spent willingly languishing in prison and realized he was right.

He drummed his finger on the steering wheel. "You're the first person I've met who wasn't scared."

"But that's not true. I am scared," I admitted, mostly to myself. *I'm terrified.*

His vivid green eyes found mine again. "Maybe. But you never let it stop you."

I stared down at my palm, still flushed and tender from the procedure. All my life I'd been afraid of something or someone, and I was still afraid now. I was afraid of the government, I was afraid of Asia, I was afraid of what would happen if someone found out what we were doing.

And, in a cold cruelty, I was afraid of what would happen if I succeeded.

I'd always been afraid, but somewhere in the halls of Wing 74, I'd found my courage. When I flipped over that table of chemicals, I'd made the decision that fear wouldn't make my choices for me. I could fight through the fear because I knew I was doing the right thing.

And because I knew Who was with me.

Jayde opened the car door. "There will always be something to be afraid of. There will always be someone bigger and scarier telling you what to do. The question is if you're going to obey."

He got out and slammed the door. I hesitated with my fingers clenched around the handle.

We must obey God rather than man.

I swallowed a prayer and opened the door.

"Where in the world have you been?"

I looked up to see Stanyard planted in the parking lot. His cheeks were flushed and his hair was disheveled, a sure sign he'd spent the morning pacing.

I cringed with embarrassment. I hadn't told Stanyard what we were doing; I'd hardly talked to him at all in the past twenty-four hours. Jayde and I had been behind closed doors all yesterday afternoon, working out the mission details and making calls. He'd taken me home, and then, to add insult to injury, he'd picked me up this morning and taken me straight to Andes's.

I'd responded to Stanyard's texts briefly last night to let him know I was okay, but almost everything I told him was a lie. I couldn't tell him what I was really doing, so all I could do was make up platitudes that sounded fake and disinterested. I'd muted the app and turned my tablet off before he could come online and try to call me.

I hated lying to him. I would almost rather not talk to him at all.

Unfortunately, it was a lot harder to avoid him in person.

"What were you doing this morning?" he repeated when I didn't answer his interrogation fast enough. "You didn't even respond to my texts."

I heard the hurt seeping through the anger in his voice and looked away. "I had an appointment."

"For what?" He paused and answered his own question. "You got a *tattoo?*"

He sounded absolutely horrified. No, worse than that—he sounded *ashamed.* He sounded just like Nic.

I slid my hand over my bandage.

"Dude, back off." Jayde stepped forward, shielding me. "It's none of your business."

Stanyard took that as an invitation to rear himself to his full height. "Yes, it is."

Jayde simply eyed him over the edge of his nose like he was a bug to be squashed. "How so?"

"She's my friend," Stanyard returned. The statement was incredulous, but the look he cast me was anything but.

Don't you still trust me?

I do, I wanted to answer him. *But I can't. Not with this.*

Jayde spared me the misery of another lie. "Yeah, well everyone in this building is her friend, so lay off it," he grunted. "This doesn't concern you. C'mon, Phil."

He started across the parking lot, and I ran to keep up with his long strides. I threw a glance over my shoulder and prepared to mouth an *I'm sorry* at Stanyard.

I changed my mind when I saw the anger burning on his face.

Jayde led us into the building and straight to the elevator. "What are we doing?" I asked as the doors closed.

"You have training to do."

All the camaraderie he'd generated with his motivational speech evaporated. I groaned. "I just spent four hours getting stabbed by needles, and now you want me to train?"

He didn't even gratify that with a response. We descended to the basement and walked to a room I knew all too well: the gun range.

My hands cramped at the very sight of the room. "Jayde, what's the point? I'm not going to need a gun at the party." I probably wouldn't have a gun on me the entire trip; I'm sure Asia's security was better than that.

"This isn't about your aim." He walked up to the control panel and pressed his thumb to the keypad. With a beep, all the dangling targets retracted back into the wall.

He swiped his fingers on the screen, and suddenly, the entire room went dark. With a crackle of electricity, a gridwork of purple laser light lit up, turning the room into a giant piece of graph paper. Jayde keyed in more commands, and the light began to congregate in the middle of the room, focusing until it formed the rough shape of a human. The figure was expressionless, like a mannequin.

"Here, put this on." Jayde held out a visor. It was thick and shiny but surprisingly light. I gingerly slid it over my eyes and turned to face the gun range. I couldn't see the laser light anymore. Instead, I could see a man.

He was stiff and robotic, his eyes refusing to blink, but he looked uncomfortably real. His skin was tan and marked with believable scratches and bruises. His clothes were soft, fabric rippling as he breathed in and out.

And his eyes. They were blue. Such a bright, bright blue.

"Earplugs," Jayde said from somewhere on my left. I turned, and he appeared in the viewscreen, his whole body highlighted in an angry red.

I lurched back. "Why are you red?" I took the earbuds he handed to me and popped them in.

His voice came through the plugs slightly warped. "Because you don't want to shoot me." He grabbed my wrist and forced a gun into my palm.

The balance of the room swung upside down as I realized what he was proposing. I looked back at the eerie hologram in the middle of the range. "Jayde, I—"

He didn't patronize me this time. "You have to. Phil, I'm not going to sugarcoat it. You're going to Beijing, and you're going to kill a man. And we both know what happened the last time you needed to kill someone."

Images of Lieutenant Clint lying on the concrete flashed through my mind. "But he didn't have to die."

"Debatable," Jayde muttered, "but this time, there's no other option. Either you kill the General, or everyone in the camps dies. Those are your choices— and you cannot afford to hesitate."

The electric gun vibrated in my palm, warm and ready.

Jayde grabbed my shoulders and steered me around so I was standing square in a booth. "We'll start slow and easy with a non-moving target."

How is that any easier? If anything, it made it worse. The holographic man was just standing there, taking it. Unarmed. Innocent.

Jayde stepped back. "Shoot him."

Instinctively, I put my body in position, sliding one foot back and steadying the gun with both hands. But I did not put my finger on the trigger.

"Shoot him," Jayde repeated, less kindly.

I slid my finger over the trigger and willed myself to pull it, but I couldn't. *It's just a hologram!* I derided myself. *Just do it and get it over with!*

"Phil," Jayde threatened, all of the patience leaving his voice.

I tried, I really tried to pull the trigger, but the world was frozen. I couldn't breathe. I couldn't feel my heartbeat. My fingers were cramped and stiff, like rigor mortis had set in early. All I could hear over and over was the scream of my soul, the last sliver of my identity begging for its life.

I am not a killer I am not a killer I am not a killer!

Jayde sighed loud enough for me to hear him through the earbuds. There was a beep, and suddenly, the hologram came to life. The man lurched into motion, face contorting in rage. A knife spawned in his hand. Without even a flicker of hesitation, he roared and charged at me.

I screamed and fired.

The shot shattered the air like thunder. The electric bullet arced forward and hit the man square in the chest. The hologram shattered into a million pieces, scattering on the floor like spilled rice.

I braced myself against the booth wall as the adrenaline collapsed like a demolished building. The hologram faded, but the image was burned in my memory. I played it over and over—the crack of the bullet, the gasp of the breath leaving his lungs, the roll of his eyes as his mind went dark.

You killed him.

"Good." Jayde's voice echoed from far away, bobbing in on the waves of nausea that coursed through my system. "Restart program."

The hologram regenerated in the middle of the room, a different man this time. This one was bigger, angrier. I swallowed. "How many times do I..."

"Until I'm confident you can pull the trigger."

The image flickered, and my digital assailant roused himself, wicked glare focusing on me. He shifted, then reached into his jacket and withdrew a gun.

I shot first.

"Better," Jayde grunted. "Again."

I stared at the pixels as they melted into a pool of blood on the floor. Jayde's words echoed in my head like a fading gunshot.

Until I'm confident you can pull the trigger. Until I'm confident you can kill.

12

"Again" turned into three days of solid training.

Jayde kept me in the range most of the rest of the day. We broke only to meet with Tower and a few other officers to debrief them on the operation as the morbid details came together.

Jayde would be going with me to Beijing. He had worked for Thames, which meant he technically worked for me. It was very easy to draw up a contract and claim he was my bodyguard. Even Asia fell for the ruse; when I told her Jayde would be flying with me, she didn't even bat an eyelash.

Meanwhile, Blue Fire went into hibernation. I recorded a short video claiming my position had been compromised and I needed to lay low for a few weeks. Jayde crafted my script carefully. It was worded so that Asia would believe I was stepping down; if I gave her any reason to suspect I had ulterior motives for coming to Beijing, it would all be over.

She texted me a mere thirty minutes after the video went up to say she was proud of me for making such a brave decision.

Privately, I also hoped Nic would see the video. Maybe if he thought I was taking his advice and retiring, he'd leave me alone and not ask questions.

So far, it was working. He texted once to make sure I still had the reservations for my transit flight to Mars. When I showed him the confirmation receipt, he went mercifully silent.

My followers were less accepting of my retirement. The comments on the video descended into a hailstorm of panic, fear, and accusations. Some people claimed they would quit if I wasn't involved. Jayde and his team worked tirelessly to try and convince people that Operation Blue Fire was still on, but the damage had been done.

The people would understand as soon as they saw the footage of me assassinating the General Secretary.

Tower took me home that night. He, as usual, did not have much to say. But he did tell me that he was proud of me.

I asked him if he thought Dad would be proud too. He didn't have an answer for that.

The next day was more of the same, only this time, the training was worse. Every time I shot a hologram, Jayde would load another one, not even pausing to let me process the virtual life I'd just taken. I killed again, and again, and again, but it was never enough for Jayde.

As the day wore on, I could have sworn that the projections began to look familiar. At first, I thought I was hallucinating it, my exhaustion projecting ghosts that weren't there. But, one by one, I started to recognize the digital faces.

At first, it was just people I'd heard of on the news. United officials, councilmen, military generals. But slowly the likenesses grew closer to home. The district governor, the chief of the Boston police, the principal of my old school.

Lieutenant Clint.

I failed that one. Jayde tried a dozen simulations with a dozen scenarios, and each time I hesitated a beat too long. No matter how cruel and threatening and dangerous the computer made Clint appear, all I could see was the fear in his eyes as he gave up the radio to save his life.

I begged Jayde to change the program. He refused. Again and again the computer threw the hologram of Clint at me, and again and again I spared his life at the expense of my own. No matter how much Jayde coached me, no matter how bitterly he cussed me out, I couldn't do it.

Tower finally rescued me when he came to say it was time to go home.

I passed out as soon as dinner was over, but I regretted sleeping when my dreams became a repeat of the simulation. All night long, I saw Clint lying on the sidewalk. This time, he was injured, bloody, and helpless. He groveled on the concrete and begged me to spare his life.

But in this dream, I didn't. In this dream, when Jayde told me to fire, I did.

In a cruel irony, I overslept. Mrs. Von finally came and roused me, saying I had company. I stumbled down to the kitchen to find Stanyard sitting at the counter. He'd clearly been there awhile; his plate was licked clean, and he was on his second cup of coffee.

He shoved his stool back as soon as I entered. "Phil—Andi, are you okay?"

"I'm fine," I croaked, even though everything about my appearance sent the opposite message.

He wasn't blind. "No, you're not." He strode over and opened his arms like he was about to hug me. My heart lurched at the same time my body recoiled. I wanted to collapse in his arms and sob, but I knew that was the last thing I should be doing. I couldn't tell him what was wrong. I couldn't tell him what I was training for. He couldn't know about any of this. As far as he was concerned, everything was fine.

And I knew that if he touched me, I wouldn't be able to lie to him again.

I stepped back and put my hand up. "I just couldn't sleep. I'm… sore from all the training. Please don't touch me."

He obeyed.

No sooner had I stepped foot on base than Jayde summoned me back to the range. "Jayde, please," I begged. "I can't do this today." Everything still hurt, and I had a blinding headache. Never mind the fact that I felt like I could have a mental breakdown at any moment.

"You're not leaving this room until you pass this test," he announced without even looking at me, and I knew he meant it.

I heard the door creak and turned to see Stanyard slip in. *No, anyone but him. I can't let him see this. I can't let him see me kill.*

Jayde put the visor and earbuds in my hands. "Again."

"But…" I hesitated, my eyes still on Stanyard.

"The sooner you do this, the sooner you can leave. Again." He thrust the gun at me.

I shoved the earbuds in and grabbed the weapon with a growl. Snapping the visor on, I whipped around to face the range. "Make it quick."

Stanyard's voice echoed hesitantly through the earbuds. "Phil…"

"Shut up," Jayde snapped at him. He punched the control panel, and the simulation flickered to life. There was Clint, in fatigues and carrying a rifle that was practically bigger than I was.

My anger wavered.

"Ready, set… shoot!" Jayde barked.

The simulation lurched to life. Clint charged at me, and I felt my muscles seizing up, the fear clenching my nerves.

I closed my eyes to block out the image and fired. *It's not real. It's not real!*

The program shrieked as the hologram died. I turned away, unwilling to look at the digital remains, and pushed the visor up on my forehead. "There. You happy?" I spat at Jayde.

He shook his head. "This time, eyes open."

I moaned and turned around, suddenly aware that my headache was worse. It was thicker, heavier, the weight shifting to one side of my head as if my whole body were out of balance. I braced myself against the booth wall.

"Again," Jayde shouted, and Clint reappeared. This time, all he had was a knife.

I pried my eyes open, willing myself not to blink, as I mechanically raised the gun and fired. The hologram disintegrated, and I winced. Was it just me, or were the colors getting brighter? I blinked, but ghosts of Clint's face still danced across my vision. Was the visor malfunctioning?

"Again."

The room went dark, and for a minute, I could see no one. Then I heard scuffling, and I looked down.

Clint lay on the ground a few yards away, moaning.

Oh God, no.

"Shoot him," Jayde commanded from somewhere behind me.

I can't.

"He's not innocent, Phil," Jayde coached, as if he could read my thoughts. "He's part of the system. He's the problem."

I took a step forward. Clint jerked around, his wild eyes searching mine. His hand cradled some unseen injury as he panted for breath.

"But he's injured," I argued, this time aloud. "He can't hurt me."

He never hurt me. Clint had been the warden, yes, but he had been reasonable. He'd never been cruel. He'd never touched me, never threatened me, never demanded more than what was expected of him. He'd never been a threat to me.

"Doesn't matter," Jayde spat. "Even if he's just pushing paperwork, he's helping the enemy."

I took another step forward, then another, feeling the floor of the range slope upwards beneath my feet.

"The government and anyone who helps them is the enemy, Phil." Jayde's voice came through loud and clear, louder than the throbbing in my ears. "If you don't stop them, they'll kill everyone you love. Do you want to be responsible for that?"

I flinched, the accusations of a thousand failures washing over me. No, I didn't want to be responsible for the loss of any more life. I couldn't. I had to save them.

I stopped only a few inches away from Clint. I put my foot back and lifted the weapon.

"Remember who the enemy is, Phil."

I am Blue Fire.

"Kill him."

And this is my war.

I fired.

The hologram shattered with a scream—a scream that kept echoing and echoing. My ears started ringing as the sound continued to ricochet, as if the explosion from the gun never stopped. My headache throbbed, and random colors flashed across the room. Was the hologram glitching? Where was Jayde? What was happening?

I took a step back, but the floor wasn't there. My mind pitched like a ship rolled by a wave as I fell.

"Phil!" Stanyard screeched, and caught me as the world went black.

13

"I'm not going to ask what you were doing. I'm just going to tell you that you were doing it wrong."

I'd only blacked out for a second. I came to as Stanyard was carrying me to the elevator. I heard Jayde in the background, radioing for Mrs. Nolan. I tried to tell Stanyard that I could stand on my own, but he ignored me. He didn't even look me in the eye. I just felt his arms tighten around me as the elevator rushed upwards.

I almost had my bearings back by the time we arrived in the lab, but Mrs. Nolan promptly stabbed me with a needle, and I lost them again. Everything suddenly became warm and fuzzy and *oh so calm*. I didn't resist as Stanyard laid me in a chair and Mrs. Nolan threaded an IV into my arm. I just sat there, completely unaware of the passage of time, watching the fluid *drip, drip, drip* down the tube.

I might have slept. I wasn't sure. It was the middle of the afternoon by the time I finally got a grip on my surroundings. I sat up and stretched, slowly, finally regaining control of my muscles.

I looked around the room. Stanyard was gone. Mrs. Nolan stood over Dad's incubator, typing notes into a tablet. She heard me moving and started lecturing without even looking up.

"If you're going to traumatize yourself, at least try to stay hydrated."

"Sorry," I mumbled.

"You're fine," she answered my unspoken question. She set her tablet down and came over to remove the IV. "But you need to rest. And yes, I already told Jayde."

I held still while she pulled the needle from my arm, then stood up and tested my balance. Mercifully, the world stayed upright.

Mrs. Nolan walked back to Dad's machine. "When are you leaving for Beijing?"

I froze. "How did you—"

"Jayde told me." She adjusted a dial on the control pad. "Asked me if I would go with you."

A shot of hope ramrodded my heart. "Will you?"

She shook her head and picked up the tablet. "You don't need me."

"Yes, I do," I insisted. "You've been there. You know these people. You know how to dress, how to act…"

She snorted. "Don't worry, Asia will tell you everything you need to know. I'm sure she has it all planned out already."

"But…" I struggled to quantify why her disinterest was so disappointing. "I thought this is what you wanted."

"It was," she admitted, too quickly. "But you're not going to Beijing because you want to be a Nolan, are you?" She glanced back at me then, one eyebrow raised in accusation.

I swallowed. "How much did Jayde tell you?"

"Not much." She resumed typing notes into the tablet with one hand. "But I know you better than you think. And I know this is not what you want."

Which part? I almost blurted, but caught myself.

"I just hope you realize what you're throwing away."

I stiffened. "What?"

She kept her back to me, swiping aimlessly on the tablet. "We gave you a gift. Andromeda was a gift, and she's irreplaceable."

The clump of anxiety found its way to my throat again when I realized she was right. As soon as I shook the General's hand, Andromeda's spotless reputation would be ruined. I'd no longer be able to hide behind my clean file, my money, and my privilege.

"It's your choice what to do with her," Mrs. Nolan continued, the permission in her voice a blank check. "It always was. Just know that once Andromeda is dead, even Asia won't be able to bring her back to life."

It was true. By midnight Saturday, Andromeda would be dead—just like Philadelphia was. Would Philadelphia get to come back to life from the ashes? Or would I just be Blue Fire?

Did it matter? Did it matter who I was if I could save my friends, my family? Wasn't that why I had been given these identities—so I could make a difference?

"Do you want me to keep him under until you get back?"

I started as Mrs. Nolan's words splashed me in the face with a consequence I hadn't even considered. *My father.* We were supposed to be waking my father up tomorrow. And I wouldn't be here for him; I'd already be on the flight to China.

I walked over and stared down at my father's sleeping face. He was beginning to look more like a living person; his skin had developed some color, and he was regaining weight. He was almost completely weaned off life support, and only a few wires were still connected to his wrist and his head. His chest rose and fell gently as he breathed on his own, the inside of the oxygen mask fogging with each exhale.

"Can you do that?" I asked, looking across the machine at Mrs. Nolan.

She shrugged. "He's been under this long. Another week won't hurt him."

I almost said yes. I wanted to be selfish, to keep my father under until I was ready to deal with the tragedy of his new existence on my own terms. But that wasn't fair to him. My dad deserved a chance at life, whatever that life might look like.

I slipped my hand into the incubator and grasped Dad's limp fingers. "No. Do what you need to do. I trust you," I declared, and I meant it.

Tower took me home shortly after, where I discovered that coming home early was just as traumatic for the Vons as getting home late. Fortunately, Mr. Von was easily appeased when I agreed to watch TV with him for the rest of the day. After all, I was under doctor's orders to do nothing, and watching mindless sitcoms was the most effective way to keep my complicated thoughts offline.

We'd finished dinner and started on a new show when I became aware of an incessant ringing. It was faint and distant, and I thought it was coming from the TV at first. But when it wouldn't stop—and neither Mr. nor Mrs. Von made any move to answer it—I got up.

I excused myself and walked out into the hall. I could hear it more clearly now; it was coming from upstairs, from Cea's bedroom.

And that's when I recognized the ringtone. It was my tablet.

I charged up the stairs and threw the bedroom door open. My tablet almost vibrated off the nightstand as it rang again and again. It rang out as soon as I picked up the device. The home screen was cluttered with notifications for ten missed calls.

Before I could unlock it and read the caller ID, the device rang again.

Nic.

I almost didn't answer. I didn't want to talk to him, but worry outweighed my reserve. Nic never called me. Told me to call him, yes. Called other people and demanded to know where I was, also yes. But he'd never once initiated a call with me, and if he'd called ten times in a row, it must be bad news.

What if something's wrong with Ephesus's transit? That was the worst but most plausible explanation I could think of. I offered up a quick prayer and answered the call. "What's wrong?"

"Why don't you tell me?"

His voice came through before the video did, but I didn't need a camera to tell me what expression he was wearing. He was angry. Very, very angry.

"N-nothing's wrong," I stuttered. "You're the one that called me."

"And why do you think that is?" His video connected, bringing me face to face with his fury. He was using a handheld device, and he leered creepily close to the camera, his head filling the entire screen.

I held my tablet away from me, as if that could restore my personal space. "I-I don't know!" I yelled, and my confusion was genuine. As far as he knew, there was nothing wrong. Unless…

He confirmed my worst fears when he spat, "You're not planning on coming back to Mars, are you?"

I was too stunned to answer, and that was all the confirmation he needed. His face contorted with rage—and then, suddenly, he relaxed. He blinked, as if he'd just woken up out of a dead sleep and was adjusting to reality.

When he finally spoke, his voice was calm, a statement. "You lied to me."

"I didn't lie," I snapped, faster than I could recognize that I'd just done it again.

"No, I suppose not," he grunted, the sarcasm returning like a layer of smoke. "You just conveniently changed your mind after booking the transit tickets."

Unironically, he wasn't wrong. But that was because so much had changed—so much he didn't know about. "Nic, they're closing the camps. They're going to deport everyone to—"

"I have eyes. I saw the news. What I want to know is what you're planning on doing about it, and why it involves you shooting men in the face until you pass out."

My retort died on my tongue. "How did you—"

"Stanyard told me."

I sank down on the bed as this information altered the playing field.

Nic did the same, sitting in a chair and holding the camera a safe distance away from his face. "Phil," he sighed, the concern overriding the bitterness in his voice. "What's going on?"

I wished he would stay angry. It was so much easier to refuse him when he was angry.

"I—I can't tell you," I managed, and braced myself.

He worked his jaw in silence for a minute before replying. "What's scary is that I actually believe that."

I stared down at the screen.

He shifted so he was square in the frame. "Are you being threatened?"

I shook my head rapidly. "No, no—it's just classified."

"Always is. Are you in danger?"

Not immediately. I shook my head again. "I'm fine. I just overdid it today, I promise."

"Okay, then you can tell me what's going on."

It was not a suggestion. "But, Nic, I—"

"Phil," he interrupted, but not unkindly, "whatever it is, I promise I can protect you. And I promise that no one will know we had this conversation. You can talk to me."

I grasped at the only other excuse I could think of. "I don't want to put you in danger—"

"Hasn't stopped you yet."

It was spoken dryly, but that was all it took to release the dam of memories.

Look, I'm aware Andromeda has put herself—and, quite frankly, the rest of us—in a dangerous position. But that was her choice.

"Phil," Nic said, speaking in time with the images flashing through my mind.

It's a risk I'm willing to take. Start talking.

"Talk to me."

The door's still open.

"I can't help you if you don't tell me what's going on."

I dragged my knuckles across my face, pushing the emotion back in. "I'm going to China."

If that revelation surprised him, he covered it well. "When?"

"Tomorrow."

"Why?"

I closed my eyes and tried to find the same conviction I'd had yesterday. "I was invited to the state dinner—"

He swore.

There was a beat, and then he did it again. And again. He threw his device down and stormed out of frame, repeating the same swear word over and over.

"Nic—"

"Why are you going?" he snapped from off-camera.

I couldn't decipher his tone of voice, and that made me panic. "I—I'm going to meet the General Secretary," I stammered.

Silence.

"And I'm going to shake his hand."

Still more silence.

"And I... I'm going to kill him."

The confession sucked the breath from my lungs in a gasp. Jayde had talked about it, we'd been planning it, and I'd been training for it. But I'd never actually said it, admitted it.

I am going to kill the General Secretary.

"You're lying," Nic declared, voice cool.

"What? No! That's the truth, Nic, I swear." I shook the tablet, as if that could force him back into frame. I expected him to be upset; I didn't expect him to not believe me at all.

He answered the summons, reappearing and picking up his device. "Then you're lying about being threatened. Who's in charge? Is it that carrot-topped military brat?"

"Jayde? Yes—I mean, no, I mean, I'm doing this willingly. We're in this together."

"Then you're both idiots." He delivered the insult effortlessly, like a backhanded slap. "You can't kill. Who do you think you are, Phil?"

I am Blue Fire. "Yes, I can, and I will."

His entire face puckered as he snorted. "Really? What are you going to do? Throw the Bible at him?"

I'm about to throw the Bible at you. "Of course not. I'm going to shake his hand."

Nic contorted his eyebrows and looked downright amused, like I'd just said I was going to sprinkle pixie dust on the General and turn him into a frog.

I glared at him. "You don't believe me, do you?"

"Oh, I believe you," he chirped. "I'm just waiting for you to realize how *incredibly* stupid and childish you're being right now. What did I tell you about being a hero?"

I stiffened. "There's a computer embedded in my palm. It's programmed to his DNA. As soon as I shake his hand, he'll have a heart attack." I thrust my hand at the camera. "Call Andes if you don't believe me. He installed it."

He blinked at the screen, nursing the silence for a long moment. "You're serious."

"I have been this entire time."

He sighed, a long, grating sound that caused the connection to crackle. "You're coming home."

Not this again. "No, I'm not. Are you even listening to me?"

"Regrettably, I am, and I'm done bargaining with you." His fingers swiped across the screen as he toggled menus in the background. "Pack your bags. I'm calling the police. They'll put you on the next transit."

My nerves tensed, but I held my ground. "I'm not going."

"Tell that to CPS."

I volleyed the threat right back at him. "They can take it up with Jayde."

He stopped, wisely deduced that physical threats wouldn't work, and resumed the verbal abuse. "You're a fool."

My cheeks burned as his words fed the monster of shame that lurked just below my heart. But I steeled my nerves and pushed past the feeling. I would not let him bully me, not this time. "No, I'm not."

"You're right, my bad. You're a hypocrite, which is even worse."

My self-control shattered beneath the accusation. I'd been called a lot of things by a lot of people, but hypocrite was never one of them. "Excuse me?"

"I mean, if I knew you wanted to play dirty, we could have saved ourselves a lot of trouble and just finished Red Rain."

It was spoken frivolously, heartlessly—and with so much hate.

Every nerve in my spine bristled with the implication. "This isn't like that! I'm not like you."

"A shame, really. At least my plan for WWIV had *style*."

Did he honestly think that was what I was trying to do? Did he honestly think I intended to slaughter *millions* of people just to get my way? "I'm not trying to start a war—I'm trying to end one."

He squinted one eye shut. "By murdering the highest government official on live TV at a party surrounded by his most loyal followers? That's not how politics *or* parties work."

"No, don't you see?" I begged, even though it was clear to both of us that he didn't. "I can get close to him. I can do this cleanly. This is why I'm a Nolan. This is why I'm here. God chose me!"

He laughed, the abrupt sound causing his video to glitch. "God didn't 'choose' you for anything, Phil. You're delusional."

"And you're a coward."

The accusation left my mouth before I had time to filter it. It hung there, echoing in the sudden silence between us.

That was when I finally admitted how true those words were—and how long I had wanted to say them.

"You have no idea what it's like to be unassimilated," I continued, my feelings slowly forming a usable shape out of the darkness. "You have no idea what it's like to live in a camp and be told you're worthless because of your faith. You've always had privilege, and money, and your college degrees. All you've ever wanted was to cut yourself off from the world and live in your own little kingdom, safe and protected from everyone's problems."

He didn't deny it. He just stared at the screen, his face stoic, unyielding.

"Well, I'm sorry, but my world doesn't work like that. For the first time in my life, I have power, and I'm going to do something with it. I'm not going to run back to Mars and hide while the world burns. I'm not like you."

As I spoke, I began to see the chasm between us for what it really was.

He saw it too. "Is that what you think of me?" It was a statement, not a question.

It was too late to lie, so I told him the truth. "I think you only care about yourself. That's why you created Red Rain. You don't care about Earth or the unassimilated. You don't care about freedom. You don't care about Ephesus, or Cea, or my dad. You don't care about me."

And you never did.

He finally moved, shifting and sitting up straight. His voice was calm and cold, the same tone he'd used when we first met on Mars.

"I'm disappointed in you, Philadelphia."

Then his screen flickered and went blank.

Did he hang up on me? I tapped his avatar and got a horrendous screech in reply. An error message popped up, and I stared at the contents in disbelief.

He'd blocked me.

14

"Resume program."

The gun range was mercifully empty when I arrived on base the next day. I'd called and asked Tower to pick me up in the morning, because he was the only one I could trust not to ask questions. Stanyard was nowhere to be found when we entered the lobby, and neither was Jayde. He'd texted to say he was making the final preparations to install the microchip in my palm—the piece of programming that would turn the computer in my hand from an inert web of wires into a targeted weapon.

I would be meeting him in the lab in an hour. After that, we would go by the Vons to pick up my tablet and luggage and say goodbye, not that I expected them to remember I was leaving. Then we would meet Asia at the airport, and I'd be on my way to Beijing.

That meant I had an hour to kill. And kill was exactly what I wanted to do.

The visor and gun were abandoned on the floor in the middle of the range, right where I'd dropped them yesterday. The simulation was still loaded on the control panel. Donning a pair of earbuds, I retrieved the gun and visor and centered myself in a booth.

"Random opponent."

The laser light congregated in the middle of the room. Snapping the visor on, I saw that the computer had generated some nameless military officer. *Perfect.*

"Begin," I announced to the empty room, sliding my foot back and putting the gun in position.

The hologram roused himself. I waited until he had taken two steps and then shot him where he stood.

"Again."

The computer continued to spawn random assailants. Most of them were faceless, but a few I recognized. It didn't matter. I took them all down, most of them before they even had time to draw their weapon.

I let the next one get closer. He charged at me with a knife, mouth open in a primal scream. He was a mere two feet from me—so close that I could see the glitching in his soulless eyes—before I dropped him.

I watched his pixels disintegrate and sighed. This was too easy.

"Increase difficulty level by twenty-five percent."

The computer rose to the challenge. It began to spawn enemies from different corners of the room; one even sprung out from the booth next to me. Some of them hit the ground running; many of them had their weapons already drawn. I missed several of them, but it didn't matter. Anything for a challenge. Anything to feel something.

"See, Nic?" I hissed as I hit another square in the chest. I watched his digital remains spill at my feet. "I can do this."

The next opponent generated in the corner next to the booths. I lunged out from around the metal divider and shot him—but not before he got a shot in at me. The digital bullet arced past my shoulder, barely missing me, and slammed into the wall with a shower of sparks.

I stared at the pixels as they faded away, relishing the adrenaline that pounded in my chest. Beneath the panic of near-death, I felt a new sensation, one I'd never felt before. Victory. Power. Pride.

I am one of them.

Jayde had been right about me all along. This was where I belonged. I didn't belong in a camp. I didn't belong on Mars. And I definitely didn't belong in Washington or Beijing with the elites. This—this is who I was.

"No, it's not."

I whipped around. The voice came from the next opponent: Lieutenant Clint.

He strolled towards me from the far side of the room. He was unarmed, but I shot him anyway.

He respawned in the opposite corner. "You won't shoot me."

I proved him wrong. He immediately reappeared.

"Random opponent!" I yelled at the computer, but nothing happened. *What is wrong with this thing?*

Clint continued to approach slowly, as if he'd cleared his afternoon and had nowhere better to be. "I know you, Philadelphia."

"You don't know me!" I shouted, but my voice came back warbly and distant through the earplugs. He couldn't hear me—nobody could hear me.

I shot him again, and he respawned mid-laugh. "Look at you. This is pathetic."

He stopped in the middle of the floor and waited until I took him out for the fourth time. He reappeared in exactly the same spot, his head wagging in a derisive gesture I knew all too well. "Isn't it about time you came home?"

"I am home!" I screeched, and fired.

His hologram didn't even disintegrate this time. He just stared at the hole I'd made in his virtual chest and snorted. The image flickered, and he regenerated, good as new. "You're not a hero, Andromeda."

I killed him almost before he got the words out. "Yes, I am!"

The image blinked and respawned, so I shot him again.

"You can't control me!"

And again.

"You don't get to decide who I am!"

And again. The explosions echoed around the room, layering one on top of the other in a broken symphony. The hologram pulsed as it respawned over and over.

I strode up to him. He didn't move, just sneered down his nose at me as if I were no more annoying than a stray cat.

I shoved the gun under his chin, savoring the rush of power as the hologram glitched and struggled to recalibrate.

I stood on my toes until my eyes were mere inches from his. "And I don't need you."

"Phil!"

I whipped around. The computer had spawned a second opponent, and he was running right at me, his entire frame glowing red.

I took aim.

"Wait! Don't shoot!" He skidded to a stop.

"I will!" I threatened. "Don't come any closer!"

He raised his hands in surrender. "Phil, it's me!"

The familiar voice cut through my subconscious, and that's when I remembered that holograms weren't red. Red meant it was a real person.

I yanked the visor off. *Stanyard.*

He stood a few yards away, panting, his eyes wild with fear as he looked between me and the gun.

The weapon clattered to the floor.

He lowered his hands. "What are you doing?"

I spun around, but Clint was gone. In fact, the whole program was off, the range dark. Dozens of scorch marks peppered the walls and floor where I had shot at a hundred imaginary opponents.

I buckled and landed on my knees, hard.

Stanyard kicked the gun a safe distance away and dropped down beside me. "Phil, you're sweating. What's wrong?"

I swiped a hand across my forehead and stared at the perspiration glistening on my fingertips—the fingertips that had almost pulled the trigger on my best friend.

"I almost killed you," I whispered.

He said nothing.

"I almost killed you!" I repeated, louder. I looked up at him and begged him to corroborate the story. I had no idea what was real anymore.

"Yes," he said, very slowly. "You did."

I wanted to apologize, but the words clogged in my throat. *What have you become?*

"Phil…" Stanyard grabbed my hand, and his touch ignited a dozen emotions I wasn't prepared to feel—didn't *deserve* to feel. Stanyard deserved better. He deserved someone who didn't scream at him, hit him, try to kill him. He deserved someone who didn't lie to him.

My dad had lied to my mom. He'd lied and failed to involve her in his revolution, and that's why she died. And now I was doing the exact same thing to the friend who had tried so many times to save me.

I tried to yank my arm from his grasp and stand up. "I need to go."

"No, Phil, please!" He tightened his grip and pulled me back down to the ground. "Don't do this to me. Don't shut me out."

"But I—"

"I can't lose you again."

I stopped and stared at him as memories of his panicked text messages came rushing back.

I THOUGHT I LOST YOU

He took a breath and shifted, sitting cross-legged next to me. "Do you know what the worst moment of my life was?"

"When you left camp?"

He snorted. "No."

"When you… left me in the alley?" That wasn't necessarily the worst moment of my life either, but it was definitely on the list.

He shook his head. "No. It was when you blocked me, after you asked me to check if the road was clear."

I remembered. I hadn't known it was Stanyard then; I'd known him only by his online alias, Aurelius, and I thought it was Jayde talking. I was being chased by cops and had asked him to radio and see if the intersection was clear. The underground had used the opportunity to catch up to me.

That's when I realized I'd been lied to and cut Aurelius off.

"As soon as you hung up on me, I realized something bad was about to happen—and it would be my fault because I was too afraid to tell you the truth.

If I had just told you who I was and apologized in the first place, none of that—Carnegie, your dad getting frozen—would have ever happened."

I searched his face and tried to imagine that alternate universe. I didn't blame him at all—I'd made a lot of mistakes and brought most of my misery on myself—but he wasn't wrong. If I had known it was him, things would have gone very differently.

Stanyard cradled my hand in both of his, rubbing my knuckles with his thumbs. "I made the same mistake with Mira. She started changing, going down a path I knew was wrong, and I didn't say anything. I stayed quiet and played the supportive older brother because I didn't want her to shut me out."

I thought of Mira's dramatic change in appearance and suddenly realized why Stanyard had been so upset about my tattoo. It wasn't about the ink; it was because he'd seen this all before and knew how it ended.

He stared at my shoulder. "Can I see?"

I loosened my hand from his and rolled my sleeve up, revealing the emblem permanently etched on my upper arm: a thunderbird.

I tried to read his reaction, but there was no emotion on his face. "Do you like it?" I ventured.

His eyes returned to mine. "Do you want the truth?"

"Yes," I said, even though my heart said no.

"I'm not a big fan of tattoos," he admitted, "but what concerns me is what it means."

I jumped to the inevitable conclusion. "You don't think I should do this."

"Phil, I don't even know what 'this' is anymore. I..." He took a deep breath, closed his eyes, and tried again. "Look, after what happened with your dad, I promised myself—and God—that if I was ever worried about one of my friends again, I'd say something. I would tell them the truth, no matter how it made me feel. No matter if they rejected me."

Heat flashed across my cheeks.

He opened his eyes and bravely met my stare. "I'm going to tell you how I feel. And when I'm done, if you want to tell me it's none of my business, then okay. But please, just hear me out."

I nodded.

He found my hands again. "I'm worried about you. I know you and Jayde are planning something, and the fact that it involves you training to kill concerns me. You've been withdrawn and anxious, and you're avoiding everyone. That's why I called Nic."

I winced and looked down at my lap. Stanyard was right; I'd been pushing away everyone who was trying to help me. Especially Nic.

Stanyard squeezed my hands. "Did you talk to him?"

I nodded, and the motion shook loose the grief I'd been avoiding since last night. I'd ruined my friendship with Nic, and now I couldn't even get ahold of him to apologize if I wanted to.

A few tears fell and splattered on Stanyard's hand.

He pulled me closer, and I let him. I laid my head on his shoulder and tried to find the words, the emotions, the prayers I needed to express what I had to say.

He wrapped his arms around me and spoke gently in my ear. "Can you tell me?"

Underneath the chaos in my soul, I felt the tiniest whisper of the Holy Spirit. *You can talk to him.*

"I'll—I'll try," I said, and obeyed. In between sobs and bursts of silence as I tried to come to grips with what had happened, I told Stanyard everything. About Operation Thunderbird, about the implant in my palm, about my argument with Nic.

I broke down crying then. Stanyard just held me, praying in tongues under his breath, and waited until my tears had dried.

He set me upright and brushed my tangled hair out of my face. "What do you think you should do?"

I stalled my answer by rubbing my eyes with my palms. "I... I don't know."

"Why not? What's holding you back?" he said in a way that suggested he'd already come up with his own answer.

I wished it was that easy for me. "I just... I just don't see how this *can't* be God. Me being Blue Fire..." I traced my hands in the air like I was connecting strings on a corkboard. "Too much has happened for this to *not* be God. This can't be a mistake. I can't be making this up."

"I agree," he said with conviction.

A small bit of reassurance found its way into my heart, so I pressed on. "And this party... I mean, it's on my *birthday*. How is that an accident?"

"It's not."

"So why..." I looked up at the scorch-marked ceiling and tried to order my thoughts like a deck of cards. "So why am I here, if not for this? I didn't choose this. Thames chose *me*, and Asia has gone out of her way to make me a Nolan. God clearly gave me this identity for a reason. If not this, then why?"

"I don't know," Stanyard admitted. He tapped his finger on the concrete, giving us both a minute to think. "But you've never stopped to find out."

I frowned at him.

He shrugged and spread his hands. "I think you're right. I think God made you a Nolan for a reason. But I think you've spent the last two months running from Andromeda instead of asking why she exists."

He was right again. I'd only adopted the identity to survive. Up until a few days ago, I'd never intended to be a Nolan in anything more than name. I never saw Thames as anything more than an enemy, and Mrs. Nolan was only an unfortunate ally. I'd never once asked God why all this had happened to me.

"Did you ask Him about the mission, Phil?"

I blinked and focused on Stanyard's face.

"Did you ask Him if He wants you to kill the General?"

I didn't say anything. The burn on my cheeks was answer enough. I hadn't prayed about this—I hadn't prayed about this at all. I'd just assumed, because there had been so much happenstance and coincidence and miracle involved in getting me there, that it must be God. I hadn't actually asked Him what He wanted me to do.

Because, I realized just then, I'd been afraid of the answer.

"What do you think He'll say?" Stanyard prodded.

I closed my eyes and turned my thoughts inward. The answer was instantaneous, like it had been hovering in my peripheral the whole time. I just had to turn and look.

I opened my eyes. "I need to talk to Jayde."

Stanyard scrambled up and offered his hand. "Do you want me to come with you?"

I let him help me to my feet. "No, this is something I have to do."

His phone buzzed. He pulled it out of his pocket and glanced at the screen. "Looks like I have to go back to work anyway. Come find me afterwards?" He followed me to the door.

"Of course. And hey." I turned and touched his elbow. I waited until he met my eyes, then forced as much overdue gratitude into my words as I could. "Thank you."

His face warmed in a smile that sparkled deep behind his eyes. "I'd do anything for you."

He would, and he had.

"If it means anything..." He gently grasped my shoulders. "I think you're making the right decision."

"That means everything," I said, and it was the truth.

"Killing... that's not you." His thumb pinched my shoulder where my tattoo was. "You don't kill people, Phil. You save them. You give them second chances when they don't deserve them—like me."

My heart flinched. "Of course you deserved a second chance. Everyone does."

He chuckled. "And there she is. *That's* the Philadelphia I know."

I sucked in my breath. Stanyard rarely used my full name, but I liked the way he said it: slow and sweet, like he had all the time in the world for me.

"That—that compassion, that innocence—is why I believe in you. That's why I came back for you. That's why I…"

He hesitated, and I felt the tension stretch out between us—all the unspoken gestures and emotions strung together in a line, a line that had turned us from strangers into something else.

"Why, Stanyard?" I demanded. "Why what?"

His hand brushed the hair off my neck and then stayed there. He met my eyes and declared without a flicker of doubt, "That's why I love you."

I expected my world to bottom out, but it didn't. Instead, I felt like the earth came together under my feet, like I had something to stand on, rely on. Someone who would support me no matter what, someone whose arms would catch me if I fell. Someone who loved me for who I was. Not for what I could do. Not for any of the titles I wore. But for me.

I wanted to tell him all of that, but words seemed cheap. So I kissed him instead.

He reciprocated—gently, sweetly, one hand cradling the back of my head. The kiss was short—too short—but he held me for a moment longer, letting our silence put a period on the promise we'd just exchanged.

When he finally pulled away, he was grinning. "I'll take that as a yes."

"Yes," I laughed, "I love you too."

15

The flutter in my stomach lasted to the elevator, and that's where the giddy feeling ended.

I braced myself against the wall as I ascended alone, forcing my breaths to be slow and steady. My heart continued to pulse, this time for an entirely different reason. I knew how this conversation would go, and it would not be pleasant.

Holy Spirit, I need you now.

Jayde was waiting for me in a lab on the tenth floor. He stood behind a worktable with a young man I didn't recognize. They were both bent over a laptop that looked advanced enough to be sentient. Scattered on the table was a morbid array of implements and wires.

In the center of it all was the kill chip.

It was microscopic; it would have fit on the eraser of a pencil. It was plugged into a docking port and shielded by a glass case. The port's flashing lights illuminated the miniature circuitry as it sat there, taunting me with the morbid reality of what I'd almost done, what I'd almost become.

The men stopped their conversation as soon as I entered. Jayde didn't greet me, but the other man offered me a cavernous smile. "Blue Fire!"

I deferred with a nod.

He slammed the laptop shut and unplugged it from the docking port. "You're good to go, man."

Jayde clasped his arm in a brawny handshake. "Send the bill."

"You know it." The man came around the table and gripped my hand in both of his. "It's an honor to finally meet you. Data."

I remembered hearing the callsign on the radio back when I was trying to make contact with my father. "Charmed," I responded.

"Good luck," he said, and pumped my hand one more time. Then he threw a salute at Jayde and let himself out.

Jayde was fiddling with a device and didn't look up at me. "Shut the door."

I obeyed, leaning against it and taking a long breath through my nose.

Jayde arched an eyebrow. "Everything good?"

I pushed away from the door. "Yes," I said, because in a way, it was. I walked over to the table. "Jayde, we need to talk."

"Do we?" He flicked the device on. It was shaped like a gun, but I could see the tip held a laser-guided needle, not unlike the machine Andes used to alter fingerprints.

I swallowed when I realized what it was. That was the device that would implant the kill chip in my palm.

I forced the words out, drawing on the reservoir of courage the conversation with Stanyard had given me. "Yes. Jayde, I... I'm not going to do it. I'm not going to kill the General."

He slammed his hand down on the metal table with a violent smack.

I flinched but pressed on. "I'm not going to Beijing. This isn't right—this is not how we win this war."

Shadows hid his expression as he bent over the table, but I could see the tension rippling up his muscular arms. "And what," he hissed, each word like the stab of a knife, "do you suggest as an alternative?"

"I don't know," I admitted, and hated how pathetic that sounded.

"Because the only other option I see is war." He straightened, finally bringing his blackened eyes to meet mine. "Is that what you want? Would you like me to send a hundred thousand men to storm Beijing and die trying to get to the General?"

"No, but there has to be another way—"

"There is no other way!" He roared and paced in a tight circle. "Phil, there is no other way to end the United. They're too big, too powerful, and control too many resources. Either we take them down from the top, or they wipe us out. Those are the only choices."

There was always another choice. I'd proven that time and again—with Thames, with Carnegie, with Nic. There was always a third option if you were brave enough to take it. "Jayde, just listen. I—"

"No, you listen!" He whipped back around to face me. "I am sick and tired of dealing with your self-righteous idealism. The world is not a fairytale. This is life and death, and either we fight back, or they kill us all. I thought you of all people would understand that."

"Of course I understand! How do you think I got here? The only reason you even know I exist is because I wouldn't lie down and take it."

He couldn't argue with that, and his hesitation gave me enough time to get a word in edgewise. "Jayde, I'm not saying we shouldn't fight back. I'm asking you to reconsider how—"

"No, *this* is how," he cut me off, louder than before. His words escalated as he pounded the table with his fist. "We have to break the system. We have to hit them where they're weak and take out their power structure so they can't retaliate. We have to kill—"

"Maybe you're right!" I shouted.

He silenced, although whether because of my volume or my consent, I'll never know.

I took a deep breath. It did nothing to smooth my words as they tumbled over each other. "Maybe we do need war. Maybe we do need to kill the General. Maybe—maybe we should have used Red Rain. Maybe Nic was right. Maybe Thames was right."

Jayde cocked his head. "You don't believe that."

"No," I said, and with that one word, my conviction fell into place. "But I don't have to decide what's right for the world. I just have to do what's right for me."

"This isn't about you, Phil," he snapped, patience taut and fragile.

"When it's between me and God, it is." I straightened and found, for the first time in weeks, that feeling of courage beneath my feet. "I don't have the answers, and I don't need them. I don't need to decide what's right for everyone else. But I have to do what's right for *me*, what God told *me* to do. Me. Not you. Not Nic. Not even Dad."

I looked down at my right hand, pinching the motherboard beneath my skin. Jayde, Nic, Ephesus, Thames, Carnegie, even Dad—they had all made different choices, and if they were standing in my place right now, they'd probably make a different choice than I was. But I wasn't responsible for their choices. I was only responsible for mine.

I didn't know what was going to happen, but I knew one thing: God did not tell me to kill the General Secretary. This was not why I was a Nolan. This was not my time.

I looked back up at Jayde, parsing the words slowly and clearly to make sure I was understood. "I am not going to Beijing. I will be your Blue Fire. I will stay on Earth and lead this revolution. But I will not kill the General Secretary."

I braced myself for the rage, the arguments, but they never came. He just stared at me, his whole body rigid, his eyes flickering with emotions I dared not decode.

Then he shifted and pulled his phone from his pocket. He dialed and held the device out, the call on speaker for both of us to hear.

It rang once, twice, and then a distinct Russian voice picked up. "Yes, boss?"

Lev.

"Where's Stanyard?" Jayde asked, the question smooth, his eyes locked with mine.

All the air in my lungs went to my throat.

"He's here with me," Lev answered with a trace of boredom. "We're installing the new server, just like you asked."

My reality began to crack, the room shattering around the edges, as the truth caught up with me. Jayde had planned this, he'd planned it all along. He knew I might refuse and had prepared insurance.

"Do you have your gun on you?" Jayde said into the phone.

"Don't—" I started, but he put a finger to his lips.

Oh God, oh God, help.

"Always," Lev grunted. "Why?"

"If I give the signal, take Stanyard out."

Jayde spoke the command with no mercy, no fear, no regret. He arched an eyebrow and angled the phone towards me, daring me to make a sound and pull the trigger.

I said nothing.

There was rustling on the line. "Sir?" Lev repeated, and for a flicker of a moment, I could hear the scared youth in his voice. I briefly dared to hope that his innocence might be my saving grace. After all, he had been the victim of so much cruelty; surely, he wouldn't want to be the cause of more.

Jayde had no doubts. "If I give the signal, kill him," he repeated.

There was a beat, two. "Yes, boss," Lev answered finally, his voice cold again.

Jayde ended the call.

I stumbled back and gripped an exam table with both hands, digging the sharp metal edge into my fingers. "You're a monster," I hissed, but the shot felt weak, like an arrow falling short.

He shrugged and picked up the implant device. "Shall we?"

I didn't move. I stood there, frozen, scraping my mind for any excuse, any argument, any threat I could wedge into his hardened soul.

"But what about Mira?" I gasped. "You wouldn't do that to her."

He laughed, the sound hard and dry. "It was her idea."

My vision flashed red, then black.

"She won't miss him. But you will." Jayde tipped his head back and studied me. He didn't smile, but his words stretched, thin and sinister. "Don't think I haven't noticed. I've got security cameras in the range. I saw that kiss."

I tasted bile and slapped my hand over my mouth. I should have known he'd be watching, should have known he'd see what was going on between Stanyard and me. I should have been more careful.

"It's basic math, Phil." He turned to the table and scanned the contents, his fingertips grazing the array of lethal instruments. "I can sacrifice one life to save millions."

"Please," I whispered, throwing my last plea at his feet. I wanted to scream *You can't, you wouldn't,* but I knew they were lies. He could, and he would.

He selected tweezers. With a slow hand, he lifted the glass cover and removed the chip from the dock. He held it up to the harsh fluorescents like a sacrifice. "I thought you of all people would understand that equation."

I did. This was exactly why my dad had created Red Rain, why he'd bargained with the devil and given the government the keys to the apocalypse: because they'd threatened to kill me.

"My life isn't worth millions of others."

"It is to me."

A sob pushed past the blockage in my throat. I'd tried so hard for so long to undo the damage my dad had done. I'd sacrificed everything to avoid being like him, and only now did I finally understand how he felt.

And in that moment, I knew that I would be no better.

"The choice is yours." Jayde slid the chip in the chamber of the implant device and clicked it shut. "You can help me end the United, or you can die on your self-righteous hill and take Stanyard with you."

He turned to face me and held out his hand, the device throbbing and buzzing. "But I have a war to win, so I'll ask you one last time: Are you with me, Blue Fire?"

16

"You're going to love Beijing."

The inside of Asia's private jet was the most luxurious thing I'd ever seen. The interior design had been perfectly sculpted to match the plane's curves; the paneling seemed to flow off the walls, as if the whole room were in motion. The cabin was decorated in shades of white and cool gray, contrasted against real mahogany tables. Everything was rimmed with soft fluorescent lights, making it look more futuristic than the actual space stations I'd been on.

Unfortunately for me, the plane was little more than an opulent prison.

Asia sashayed up to my seat, her stiletto heels sinking into the plush carpet. "Your family has a summer home that's the envy of the neighborhood. Wait until you see the pool—do you like to swim?"

I couldn't remember the last time I'd had access to a pool, much less the desire to jump in one. "I didn't pack my swimsuit," I deferred.

Truth was, I hadn't packed *anything*. As soon as Jayde had finished implanting the device in my palm, he'd taken me down a back elevator and forced me into his car, where we'd driven straight to the transit hub. I hadn't even been allowed to say goodbye.

Asia flicked her fingers, as if the thought were no more inconvenient than a fly. "Just buy a new one."

I snorted when I realized she was right; I could afford to buy a whole wardrobe. I'd even picked up a few essentials at the transit hub, just so it wouldn't look suspicious that I was boarding without a suitcase.

If Asia noticed my light packing, she hadn't commented on it. If anything, she took it as an invitation. "I'll take you shopping tomorrow. We won't have as much time as I'd hoped, since we also have to cram in all your appointments, but we'll make it work."

She pushed her sleeve up and regarded her watch, as if that could conjure more minutes from thin air. "As soon as we land, you've got an appointment for a facial and waxing. I want you looking at least halfway decent for tomorrow's dinner—I've invited some old friends and you need to make a good impression. But we should be able to hit a couple of boutiques afterwards. We need to at least get your dress so your stylist has time to fit it."

"Sounds great," I managed with a smile that I'm sure looked as painful as it felt. The nonstop schedule sounded like torture, made worse by such sinister words as "waxing."

She was too engrossed in her digital calendar to notice. She used two pointed fingers to key commands into her watch's screen. "I'm going to see if I can move your nail appointment to Friday. Maybe I can have the jeweler pick out some pieces and deliver them instead of taking you to the gallery. That might help..."

She evidently didn't expect me to contribute to the next seventy-two hours of my life, because she bustled off without waiting for a response. I let out my breath and sank back in my seat. I had no idea being Cinderella was so exhausting.

Maybe it wouldn't be so bad if I actually *wanted* to go to the ball.

"Try to look more excited."

I started and looked up to see Jayde leering over me. He'd cleaned up well; he'd traded his fatigues for a pressed and tasseled dress uniform. With his black hat and white gloves, he looked like a proper military escort, which as far as Asia knew, that's what he was.

He bent towards me, one hand folded behind his back and the other extended. It was a polite, fluid motion—and oh so threatening. "You need to act more excited, like you can't wait to buy a new dress." His hot breath brushed my ear as he spoke in a harsh whisper. "She's going to suspect something."

I tried to squirm away from him, but there was nowhere to go; my shoulder was pressed against the window. There was already a long list of rules I had to obey if I wanted Stanyard to live: *Don't damage the implant. Don't tell anyone what you're doing. Don't mention Blue Fire.* Did I have to add "enjoy playing dress-up" to the list? "Sorry, it's hard to be excited about shoes when I'm being held at gunpoint."

He stiffened, and I knew I'd gone too far. He glanced around the cabin, but Asia had disappeared into her private room.

"Then fake it, princess," he slithered. His hand brushed aside the hem of his jacket, revealing his phone clipped to his belt. "Or I'll have to make a call."

I pinched my eyes shut and turned to the window. "Okay, okay, I will. Just please, leave me alone."

He straightened slowly, letting the threat linger, then withdrew to the other side of the cabin.

I grabbed my phone and tried to look busy—not that there was anything on it. Jayde had given me a new device so Andromeda could check in online, but he'd blocked most apps and given himself remote access. There was no way for me to call for help on this phone.

Not that there was anyone to call. Stanyard was halfway around the world being held hostage by Lev. Ephesus was on a transit to Mars, completely cut off from communication. And Nic wouldn't help me even if I could get ahold of him.

As usual, he'd been right about me. He'd been right about everything.

I'm disappointed in you, Philadelphia.

I turned the phone off and suffocated the feelings. If Jayde caught me crying, it would all be over.

I picked up my backpack—the one personal belonging I'd been able to bring—and rifled through it. I'd been allowed to keep the paper Bible Stanyard had given me—a bitter mercy. All the precious artifact did was remind me of the friend I was putting in danger and the God who had stopped talking to me.

I'd been praying fiercely all day in every spiritual and earthly language I knew. I prayed that the implant machine would malfunction, or someone would catch us in the elevator, or even that a stranger at the transit hub would recognize me and stop us. I begged God to send someone, anyone to save me.

But no one came, and the kill chip was now embedded in my palm, the scar hidden by a layer of regenerated skin. And throughout the whole process, the Holy Spirit had remained silent. I didn't get a rush of courage or any brilliant ideas; I asked for wisdom and heard nothing.

I was alone.

I shoved the Bible aside and reached to the bottom of the bag. Cold metal brushed my fingers, and I pulled the object out: the star of David pin.

I twisted it in my hand, feeling a rush of miserable anger. I thought Lev and I had a camaraderie, an understanding forged by mutual grief. We both knew what it was like to lose our families and our freedom for our faith, but apparently, he wasn't afraid to shed more blood for the cause.

"Are you all right?"

I looked up to see Asia standing next to me. I took stock of my face and realized I hadn't been doing a very good job of keeping my emotions masked. I glanced around the cabin, but thankfully Jayde wasn't in sight.

I plastered on a smile. "Just thinking about my dad." I dropped the pin in my backpack, zipped it up, and kicked it under the seat.

"I understand." Asia slid into the seat across from me and set two drinks on the table. Hers was bubbly and fancy—mine was plain black coffee.

I took it skeptically. "How did you know how I liked it?"

She winked. "You seemed like the type."

I accepted the peace offering and slipped it slowly, grateful to have something to do with my mouth other than fake a smile.

"How is your father doing?" Asia asked after I'd had a few minutes to rally my courage in my coffee.

"He's still in therapy," I said, careful to keep it vague. "But he's progressing well."

"Did you talk to him before you left?"

I didn't talk to anyone before I left. "We haven't woken him up yet," I said, swirling my mug. "Mrs. Nolan says he needs more time."

At least that was one thing I didn't have to worry about. Mrs. Nolan would take care of my dad, especially once she realized I was gone. She shouldn't let anyone touch him.

"And his memory?"

I looked up at Asia, debating how much to share. It was really none of her business, but then again, maybe it would be better if she knew Red Rain was dead. "It's gone," I whispered.

She pursed her lips. "I'm sorry," she said, voice thick with disappointment. "I can recommend some neurotherapists."

I'm sure you can. I shrugged and returned to my coffee.

She tapped her glass with her manicured fingernail. "Maybe when he's well you can both move to Beijing. We'd love to have you."

"I'm sure he'd like that," I lied, and tried not to laugh. I wouldn't be welcome in Beijing after this trip. After this mission was complete, Andromeda would be dead, just like Philadelphia was.

No, after this trip, there would be only one place I'd be welcome. Jayde claimed I could go free, but it was a technicality. We both knew there would be only one identity I could wear after I killed the General Secretary.

I am Blue Fire.

17

If Asia's itinerary sounded aggressive on paper, it was even more exhausting in practice.

Her driver met us on the runway when we landed the next day. He helped me into the car, sparing me the misery of holding Jayde's hand, and then whisked us across the city. As he navigated traffic with wizard-like efficiency, I stole my first look at China through the tinted windows. The traditional colors of gold on red blurred with the silvery-blue of glass and steel. Towering apartments pierced the clouds, while historic archways and shrines watched with shuttered eyes. Everything was splashed with neon and emblazoned with the United seal—reminding us, always, who was in control.

We soon reached downtown, where I was escorted to an exclusive spa on the top floor of a high-rise. Jayde, thankfully, was forced to wait in the lobby, but I got no reprieve as a trio of technicians set about sculpting me into a porcelain doll. Asia gave them a laundry list of specifications, like I was a sewing pattern to be stitched together. No one asked my opinion.

What was most infuriating was how little effect the procedure seemed to have. Despite all the poking and plucking and stripping and *pain* of the humiliating four-hour appointment, I came out looking exactly as I had gone in. I stared in the mirror and tried to figure out what was different, except for the fact that my eyebrows were a little thinner.

At least Asia seemed satisfied. While I was on the table, she'd taken it upon herself to pick out my dinner outfit: a ruffled blouse and pleated ocher skirt, paired with a lavender blazer that I'm sure was the height of fashion somewhere. I felt like a quaint schoolgirl, especially next to her with her deadly heels and immaculate white suit.

She hustled me across town to an opulent restaurant, where she introduced me to a dozen people as affluent and terrifying as she. There was a mix of native elites and imported American and European politicians, all of which had names and titles I'd never remember. But they all had one thing in common: They were dripping with praises about how *thrilled* they were to meet me. They slathered me with condolences over Thames's death and gushed about how lucky I was to have been plucked from the trenches, each of them offering to introduce me to this or that activity or take me on this or that outing.

I forced a pretty smile, repeating platitudes about how honored I was to be here. But inwardly, each benevolent smile and patronizing pat on the arm had me recoiling in disgust. This was why I'd never wanted to become a Nolan, why I never wanted to go with Asia: I didn't want to be a trophy.

At least no one expected a trophy to do anything but smile and nod. The rules of etiquette were simple, as Asia had reminded me repeatedly on the ride over:

Speak only when spoken to.

And if someone does not offer you their hand, bow.

Almost everyone that night offered me their hand. I accepted each unspoken invitation of friendship, struggling not to think about the bomb in my palm. I reminded myself over and over that it would only trigger for the intended target, but that didn't stop my hand from sweating or my fingers from shaking. Thankfully, everyone thought my nervousness was charming, and the meal passed without incident. Even Jayde gave my performance a pass.

By the time we'd finished dessert, I was dead on my feet. But Asia would not be deterred from her schedule, and she dragged me to a boutique where each price tag had more zeros than I could count. I'm not sure why I needed to be there, because unsurprisingly, Asia had already conjured a precise picture of the dress I should wear to the gala. All I did was sit on the velvet ottoman, sipping metallic sparkling water and trying to avoid my reflection in the octagonal mirrors that turned the fitting room into a horror funhouse.

After a dozen styles were brought and refused, Asia finally allowed me to try one on. The clerks helped me slip into the sheath of black velvet, then put me on a stool so they could fiddle with the hemline. I finally looked my reflection in the eye and tried to decide if I liked who I saw.

To her credit, Asia had picked out an understated, if not demure, gown. It was modeled after a qipao, with a starched collar, three-quarter sleeves, and a flared skirt with a slit to the knee. The black velvet was embedded with tiny crystals, making it look like the dress had been dipped in starlight. It was pretty, to be sure, but it looked like something Asia would wear.

I suppose that was her intent.

It was long past dark by the time we made the trek back to the Nolan estate. The city glowed in technicolor, but I was too exhausted to appreciate it. I could only hope Asia had reached the end of her itinerary, and I could put a closed door between me and Jayde.

I jerked out of my stupor when the car rocked to a stop in front of the most magnificent house I had ever seen. In fact, calling it a house seemed like an insult: It looked like a tiny palace. It was modeled after a traditional villa, with a two-story ring of rooms framing a private courtyard. The walls were made of stone so pale it appeared to glow in the moonlight, and the black-tiled roof was sloped and capped with statues of dragons. Giant iron phoenixes stood guard on either side of the front door, their flared wings sweeping up to the sky.

"Gorgeous, isn't it? Some of the masonry is original." Asia brushed past where I stood gawking on the sidewalk and led the way through the gate.

I followed her gingerly, almost afraid to put my feet on the sparkling tile walkway. "I get to stay here?"

"Stay here?" Asia cackled. She stopped on the top step and looked back at me. "Darling, you *own* this house."

I gaped at her.

She gestured at the keypad next to the door. "Try it."

I slowly climbed the steps, casting a nervous glance up at the massive phoenixes. They glared down at me with carved eyes as I passed under their wings, and I briefly wondered if they were about to come alive and devour me for being an imposter.

I cautiously approached the door and pressed my thumb to the keypad. It chirped and flashed green.

Asia echoed the sentiment as she pushed the door open. "Welcome home, Andromeda."

I stepped into the entryway and was taken aback by the sudden shift in aesthetic. Where the exterior of the home was traditional, the interior was egregiously Western. It was minimalistic to a fault, with glaring white space and blank walls. Everything was white and black and clean and sharp, with square corners and harsh edges. The only warmth in the entire space was the massive fireplace that formed the wall straight ahead, its silent flame flickering a gas-fed blue.

"Nolan Xiaojie." A posh voice and soft footsteps greeted me. I looked up to see a butler approach. He matched the aesthetic of the house perfectly, with his crisp white-and-black uniform and plastered hair. He stopped in front of me and bowed. "Peng Bai, houseman."

"Pleased to meet you," I said, and hoped that was somewhere on the scale of polite behavior.

He smiled. "It is my pleasure to make sure your estate runs smoothly. Please, if you require anything, simply say the word and I will be happy to assist."

"Thank you," I managed, and was surprised when my voice shook. Did this all really belong to me? Money was one thing, but *servants*? Is this who I was now? I fiddled with the hem of my jacket, suddenly feeling very small in my childish pleated skirt.

Thankfully, Asia had no trouble assuming command. "Peng, will you see to it that Andromeda's baggage is taken up? And show the lieutenant to the servants' quarters."

I glanced back to where Jayde waited in the doorway. He stepped forward. "I would prefer to stay close to Miss—"

"I said," Asia sneered without even looking back, "will you show the lieutenant to the *servants'* quarters?"

Jayde flushed almost as red as his hair. He stiffened and looked prepared to mouth off—then changed his mind. He gave a curt half-bow. "Goodnight, Miss Nolan." Then he shot me a glare that only I could interpret and followed Peng out of the room.

"I could have him hanged if you'd like."

I started and looked at Asia. "What?"

She tapped her lip with a pointed fingernail. "He's such a drag. I'm this close to having him arrested just to watch him squirm."

I wasn't sure how to respond to that.

She laughed disarmingly. "It was a joke, darling. But do let me know if he's bothering you. Remember, there's nothing money and a well-placed phone call can't fix."

I frowned. She certainly didn't sound like she was joking—and part of me wished she wasn't.

She didn't give me time to contemplate the implications. "Well, don't just stand there—come see your room." She clipped towards the stairs, her heels popping sharply on the tile floor, and I hastened to follow.

She led me up the spiral staircase and down the hall to a double door that was nearly as big as the front entrance. She grabbed both handles and threw them wide open, revealing a bedroom set in the stars.

A mural of screens paneled one wall, displaying a softly moving image of a purple-blue nebula. In the middle of the room sat a massive four-poster bed piled high with blankets and pillows in varying shades of plum and navy. A fur rug softened the gray wood floor, and the furniture was a mix of mahogany and stained birch. Above it all hung a net of fairy lights that was strung from the ceiling like a constellation.

It certainly looked like a room belonging to someone named Andromeda.

"I hope you don't mind, I had it decorated," Asia said from behind me. "I thought you might find it more inviting."

"Yes," I said, and meant it. I took a slow step into the room, my shoes sinking into the plush carpet.

"One of the staff will come get you when it's time for breakfast. Be ready to leave by 8 A.M.—we've got a full day of appointments, and you need to meet with your stylist."

The thought of another day of beauty appointments filled me with dread, but I forced a nod.

"Call me if you need anything—I'm only minutes away." Asia grabbed the handles and started to close the door, then stopped. "It's good to have you home. You deserve this."

Do I? I scanned the room and tried to understand what I had done to earn this. The only reason my name was on the deed was because Thames had chosen me—and I still didn't fully understand why.

Asia didn't expect an answer. She gave me one more smile—softer, kinder this time. "Goodnight, Andromeda," she said, and closed the door.

I waited until her footsteps had faded before venturing further into the room. It was huge; the entire first floor of our old home in the containment camp would have fit inside. To the right, a mirrored hallway led to a gigantic closet and in-suite bathroom. Straight ahead, solid glass doors opened to a private balcony that overlooked the courtyard.

I stepped out into the warm night air and looked around the yard—*my* yard. More balconies lined the upper floor of the square pavilion, although all the other bedrooms were dark, curtains drawn. Below, iron statues and exotic plants decorated the stone patio that surrounded an Olympic-sized pool. The immaculate water reflected the starless night sky, the moon balanced perfectly on the still surface.

Gripping the railing, I stared at the glassy water and wished, for the very first time, that I could live here forever. I didn't even know how to comprehend such wealth. It was one thing to have enough money to buy what I needed—*this* was luxury I couldn't have dreamed up had I tried.

Of course, it would all vanish Saturday night when I shook the General's hand and ruined Andromeda's reputation.

Unless...

I told Asia what was going on.

I sank down on the ground and leaned my head against the railing, using the cool stone to center my swirling thoughts. Asia had teasingly said she could take care of Jayde, and I believed her. She practically owned the government and had unlimited resources; with one phone call she could put Jayde away *and* get Stanyard to safety. No one had to die.

But I would have to tell her that I'd been planning to kill her father.

How would she react? A normal person would have me arrested, but Asia had proven herself to be anything but normal. She knew all my identities and had every reason to order my execution, but she hadn't for her own mysterious reasons. She'd made it clear that she was prepared to ignore the crimes of Blue Fire and Philadelphia Smyrna if I would only agree to be Andromeda Nolan.

No, based on her behavior tonight, I had every reason to believe that if I told Asia what was going on, she would make it all go away.

I traced the ornate pattern on the railing with my finger. All I had to do was say the word, and she'd remove Jayde. She'd have my record expunged and overturn the warrants for my father's arrest; he wouldn't even need a new file. She would get Stanyard, Tower, and Mrs. Nolan to safety. Then we could all move to Beijing. We could live behind this iron gate, watched over by carved dragons, and forget the containment camps, forget the rebellion.

And I would become Andromeda Nolan forever.

I rubbed my palm, feeling the chip flex beneath the surface. Maybe Asia was right. Maybe I was one of them.

18

It turned out Peng wasn't the only servant at my command. I was woken by a maid barely older than myself who asked if I wanted help getting ready. Thankfully, she took no for an answer.

I almost regretted sending her away when I stumbled into the closet and discovered that it was crammed full of clothes, all of which were miraculously my size. Why Asia thought I needed to go shopping was beyond me; someone had clearly gone to a lot of trouble to build a wardrobe for me. I didn't dare ask whether that person was Asia or Thames.

I rifled through the hangers until I found something that looked like it cost less than a thousand dollars. I didn't waste too much time on my appearance and threw on a minimal amount of makeup. There was no point when Asia was going to have it all redone anyway.

I went downstairs and wandered around until I found the right kitchen (there were three), where a chef had gone overboard preparing breakfast. He was French and seemed over the moon to have someone to cook for. He served me an elegantly layered bowl that was probably the most nutritious thing I'd eaten all year.

I dared to ask about Jayde and was more than a little gratified to hear he'd been served with the rest of the staff.

Asia kept her word and pulled up promptly at eight. She whisked me away to another two-hour torture session, followed by a nail appointment where it took a suspiciously long time just to give me plain white French tips. By then it was supposedly lunch time, even though I was still full from breakfast, followed by coffee, which I was more amicable towards.

At long last, it was finally time to go see my fabled stylist. The driver pulled up to a classy all-glass building in an artsy part of town. The massive front windows revealed a gaudy array of dresses, all edgy styles clearly designed to provoke. The neon sign was written in Mandarin characters, and the doorbell trilled zither music as we entered.

The lobby was empty. The place had the aura of a spa, with an abundance of potted plants and a waterfall concealing the entire back wall. I scanned the empty salon chairs while Asia rang the bell impatiently.

There was a muffled shout from somewhere in the back. Footsteps approached, followed immediately by a screeched, "What in the *world* did you do to your hair?"

I turned around to find Narissa glaring at me.

I blinked to recalibrate my reality, then realized that I shouldn't be surprised. After all, Narissa had known Thames; he'd hired her to be my stylist back when we were on Mars. She'd since changed her hairstyle to a daring asymmetrical pixie cut, but otherwise, she looked exactly like she had when I'd met her. Her simple black outfit and sharp winged eyeliner gave her a fierce elegance as she scrutinized me with palpable distaste.

"Hello again," I offered.

She didn't return the greeting. "Some nerve you have coming in here with *that* haircut," she hissed. "I tried to get you to cut your hair, but *no!* And now look at you. What even is this?" She strode up to me and grabbed chunks of my hair with both hands, holding them out from my head.

"It was necessary," I confessed.

"It was necessary when I wanted to do it!" She growled like a cat.

"Can you fix it?" Asia asked.

"Fix it? No, the only way to fix this crime against humanity would be to shave it all off and start over."

I swallowed.

"But..." Narissa sighed and dropped my hair. "If I add some toner and lowlights, I can make her presentable."

I spread my hands. "That's why I hired the best."

Narissa finally shifted her gaze from my hair to my eyes and smiled.

"This will also need to be fitted." Asia laid a dress bag on the counter. "And her makeup will need to be—"

Narissa cut her off with a flick of her hand. "Trust me, I know all about making this one look like something she's not. I'll handle it."

Asia seemed a bit miffed to have been interrupted, but she deferred with a nod. "We'll be back to pick you up for dinner, Andromeda." Another tinkle of zither music escorted her out the door as she left.

"Andromeda, huh?" Narissa picked at her lip. "So you did decide to take the old man's name."

I looked back up at her. "Didn't really have a choice."

Something close to a smile pinched her face. "At least tell me you've been conditioning."

I shrugged sheepishly.

She rolled her eyes and grabbed the dress bag off the counter. "Well, we've got work to do. This way."

She walked to the back of the store. I followed her around the waterfall to a hidden elevator, where we descended two floors below.

The doors slid open to reveal an underground studio lit as bright as daylight. Seamless screens wrapped the entire room; the image slowly shifted between different patterns and textures, all in shades of crimson. The floor was cluttered with a drafting board, cutting table, and half a dozen headless mannequins. But the crown jewel was a gigantic dress fabricator.

It was almost as tall as I was, and it had more wires and flashing displays than Dad's cryogenics tube. In the central chamber, multiple robotic arms flashed in and out, stabbing needles and weaving threads. I walked up and watched in fascination as the bodice of a dress began to form on the table. The robotic fingers wove each line of thread, conforming the bust to some invisible pattern, almost as if the dress were being conjured out of thin air.

I breathed a sound of admiration. "Can it sew anything?"

"As long as I can dream up the pattern. It takes my sketches and turns them into a 3D model that I can tweak, then it fabricates the garment from scratch." Narissa held up a tablet with a half-finished sketch on the screen. She tossed it aside and laid the dress bag out on the cutting table. "Now, what did you bring me?"

There was the sound of a zipper opening, and Narissa retched.

I glanced back. "Asia picked it out."

"I can see that." Narissa pinched a chunk of the sparkly fabric between two fingertips, as if she were afraid it was going to bite her. "No, no—you're not wearing this."

Then she scooped it up, bag and all, and tossed it on a pile of forgotten fabric.

"But—"

"First of all, that'll make you look like you're forty-five. Second of all..." She turned back to me and hesitated, the light shifting behind her eyes. "It doesn't really scream... revolution, does it?"

I stiffened.

She shrugged. "I know what's going on. I was there when it started."

I looked into her eyes and waited.

She took a deep, rallying breath. "You're not here just to attend a party, are you?"

I took a step back. "I can't—"

"No, no." She put her hands up. "Don't tell me. I don't want to know. I just need to know how high to make the slit. Are you going to be running?"

I never should have stopped running. "No," I admitted. That was what made the whole plan so sinister: All I would be doing was shaking someone's hand.

"Good, that gives me options. Up." She gestured at a stool that stood against the back wall.

I kicked off my shoes and obeyed, stepping on the stool and standing up straight. Narissa took one slow lap around me, eyes scanning up and down while she muttered to herself.

After she'd been computing in silence for a long moment, I ventured, "Why are you helping—"

"I said I don't want to know," she snapped. She straightened and glanced around the room. "This color is all wrong though. I need... blue."

At her command, the screens on the wall shifted to display a gradient of royal blue textures. Narissa shook her head. "Too bright. Try... periwinkle."

The screens flickered again. "Nope, too purple. Maybe... slate."

The image changed one more time. This time, a roulette of storm clouds, deep water, and quartz painted the whole room a muted gray blue.

"Much better." Narissa took a step back and eyed me from a distance. "You're about a twenty-seven and a quarter inch waist, right?"

I flushed self-consciously. "How did you..."

She glanced around the room, as if verifying that we were alone. Then she reached up and popped her contacts out. Blinking, she looked back up at me, revealing two eyes that weren't human at all.

Two robotic orbs sat where her eyes should have been. They looked like miniature computers suspended in glass marbles. The artificial lenses focused on me while the microscopic motherboards flickered with an unintelligible readout.

"You're... blind?" I finally managed.

She nodded. "With special glasses, I could see a little, but not enough to do what I really wanted." She reached out and fingered the fabric that was draped over the chair next to her. "My parents tried every surgery they could afford, but it wasn't enough to get me into design school. Every time I tried to apply for a grant or enter my dresses in a competition, they denied me."

Her artificial gaze shifted back to me. "The United doesn't like imperfect people any more than it likes religious brats."

I knew that was true.

She looked down, rolling her contacts around in her fingers. "Then, one day, I hear about this new program. The government was giving away implants—*free*—to anyone who needed them. I could have brand-new augmented eyesight, completely paid for by the United."

She laughed suddenly, the sound shattered and cruel. "Unfortunately, I failed to read the terms and conditions."

I connected the dots. "Can they…"

She tipped her head back and slid her contacts in, blinking and rolling her eyes until they adjusted. "The government can hear everything I hear and see everything I see. That's why I say… I really *don't* want to know."

I instinctively grabbed my upper arm, where my thunderbird tattoo was hidden under my shirt and a bandage.

"Don't worry," she assured, "I doubt anyone's listening. I haven't caused trouble in a long time. But if I were to say the wrong thing—say, the callsign of a certain revolutionary figure—it might trip the algorithm."

I nodded rapidly, feeling all the dread and fear slip to my stomach.

"It has its perks, though," Narissa said, her cheerfulness salted with pain. "I can take measurements, send sketches to my machine, even ask the computer to match your foundation shade. And it's not like it pops up in the corner of my vision like a stupid visor—I just *know*."

A little sense of wonder found its way into my consciousness. "I assume it wasn't hard to get into design school."

"Top of my class. And—I didn't have to sign the file."

"What?"

She picked up a tablet and started sketching. "They don't do files here— that's an American thing. You people like choice, so they let you pick what kind of government control you want."

I'd never thought of it that way, but I realized, with a sickening weight in my chest, that she was right. You could choose to assimilate and obey the rules of the system, or you could live in a containment camp under complete surveillance. Either way the government was in control. Either way the United won.

And apparently, we could accept that as long as we got to sign off on it.

"Here, we prefer more fashionable solutions. There's thirty million people in this province alone—we don't have time to be checking people's paperwork. No, we let the computer do the heavy lifting." She tapped the side of her head with her stylus. "I don't need a piece of paper to tell me where I can and cannot go when the algorithm will let the boss know if I get out of line."

I rubbed my arm. "Can they… shut it down remotely?"

"Probably," she muttered in a tone that suggested she'd spent years convincing herself not to think about it.

I started to pray for her, then realized I had no idea what to even ask for. The only thing worse than a prison was one you carried around with you.

She set the tablet down and grabbed a remnant of chiffon. "Everyone gets to pick their chains, Andromeda." She started circling me again, bunching the fabric in different ways to see how it hung on my frame. "Be careful which ones you choose."

I held my arms out and let her work as I chewed on her words. All my life, I'd chosen to be unassimilated—to live at the bottom of society so I could salvage some semblance of autonomy. But if I stayed in Beijing, I'd be trading all of that for another containment camp. This one had a chef and a butler and a pool, but it was a containment camp nonetheless. The Nolan estate was a prison—it would only protect me so long as I played the role of Andromeda. If I failed to follow the rules, if I failed to be the perfect daughter Asia wanted me to be, the system would kick me out.

Narissa was right—Andromeda was just another set of chains. Was she the chains I wanted?

19

"Open your eyes."

I hesitated, almost afraid of what I would see. It was Saturday afternoon, and I'd spent the entire day in a chair at Narissa's salon. She salvaged my hair, adding toner and lowlights to bring some warmth back into the bleached locks. She fixed my hack job by meticulously scissoring in layers, then twisted my hair up and clipped on an extension to give me an elegant curled updo. Then she spent an hour painting on my face, each stroke of contour and eyeliner done with precision.

At long last, she had me stand on a stool and told me to close my eyes while she helped me into the dress. I felt the rustle of cool silk slide over my arms and suddenly felt exposed and unprotected. I was walking into the most dangerous party of my life, intent on starting a war, and I was wearing heels and had bare shoulders.

"You can look now."

I swallowed, opened my eyes, and stared at the woman in the mirror.

The dress was a barely-there pale blue that seemed to shift in and out of gray, like the underside of a cloud. The boned bodice was understated, with ruched cap sleeves that just grazed my shoulders. But where the bodice was reserved, the skirt was captivating. Layers of sheer chiffon flowed off the waist. Hidden on the second and third layers was a bold network of silver embroidery. The lines were jagged and random, making it look like the skirt was made from shattered glass. When I moved, the metallic thread flashed in and out of the light, like lightning flickering behind the clouds.

I was a thunderbird.

I looked down at Narissa. "But why…"

She finished adjusting the hem and straightened. "I figured if you were going to make a scene tonight… you needed to dress the part."

She offered her hand and helped me down from the stool. I squeezed her fingers, a wave of guilt crashing into my mind. "But what about you? If they find out who made this dress…"

"Oh, they'll know." She reached up and adjusted my sleeve. Only a thin layer of fabric covered my tattoo today, because soon there would be no reason to hide it. If I went through with this, one fatal handshake would turn me into a war hero. On live TV, I would initiate the revolution—and become Blue Fire forever. And I'm sure the government would not be thrilled with the designer who had turned me into the thunderbird.

"But I can't… I won't be able to protect you," I managed. *They'll kill you,* was the truth I was too afraid to say.

Her cold hands grazed my skin as she clipped the strand of pearls Asia had given me around my neck. She stepped back and met my eyes in the mirror, hers blinking and unafraid. "Do what you came to do."

Jayde was waiting on the bench outside the salon in full regalia. He stood up when I exited, his eyes taking in my dress as the embroidery crackled in the sunlight. I could tell the meaning of the design was not lost on him when he grinned.

He bowed and offered his hand. I took it and allowed him to assist me into the car, but only because the driver was watching.

Asia had said she would meet us at the party, so she sent a pearl white stretch limo to chauffeur us around—an excess, as usual. Despite the fact that the car could have seated twenty, Jayde sat uncomfortably close to me on the padded leather bench. He asked the driver to turn up the music, then leaned and whispered in my ear.

"The party will be spread out all across the compound. There will be food in the Hall of Dispelling Clouds by the docks, and the General Secretary will be taking visitors in the Tower of Incense, which is in the middle of the complex. Everyone who's invited to the party gets a chance to meet the General, but you have to wait to be called. When it's your turn, if Asia has done her job, he'll want to shake your hand."

I instinctively rubbed my palm.

Jayde grabbed my wrist to stop me. "You can do this. I know you don't see yourself as a leader, but I still believe in you."

"It's too late for camaraderie." I yanked my hand from his grasp.

"Then just follow my lead." He adjusted his white gloves. "As soon as the deed is done, there will be chaos. I've got several friends at the party; one of them is going to grab you and take you to safety. Stick to the plan and you'll make it out alive."

I nodded and scooted away from him down the bench. It wasn't me I was worried about. Jayde had made it abundantly clear that Lev would be watching the party on TV. If I did not shake the General's hand, Stanyard would die.

One way or another, I was going to murder someone tonight. The question was who.

The sun was just beginning to set when we joined the long line of cars entering the outer grounds of the Summer Palace. All the VIPs, of which I apparently was one, were being escorted over the Bridge of Seventeen Arches and ferried across the lake so they could get a full view of the palace. The vast complex was lit with hundreds of lanterns, making it look like the hills were blanketed in fireflies. The descending sun turned the lake to blood as we docked and were escorted through the arch into the first courtyard.

The stone pavilion was crammed with affluence. A mix of Western ball gowns and Eastern qipaos mingled with suits and ties. Live musicians played traditional instruments while the guests kept time with their laughter. Lanterns drifted from every tree branch, and fires burned in ornate kilns. The kilns were filled with incense to keep the bugs at bay, blanketing the entire courtyard in perfume.

And everywhere there were cameras and press, capturing the entire party on film.

The Hall of Dispelling Clouds was straight ahead. The brilliant red-and-gold structure was decorated with ornate carvings and luscious calligraphy. Light poured out of the geometric windows, and the smell of decadent food floated from the open doors.

Jayde hooked his arm with mine and guided me towards the steps. "Do you want something to eat?"

"No" would have been the truthful answer; I was sure that if I tried to cram food into my clenched stomach, I would vomit. But I would rather hold chopsticks than Jayde's hand, so I nodded and followed him into the hall.

Inside, a table as nearly as long as the building was burdened with delicacies. I allowed Jayde to play the gentleman and serve me. I accepted the small plate he handed to me and tried to rally the courage to eat it.

Thankfully, I was spared the misery when someone called my name. "Andromeda!"

I looked up to see a couple approach. "I'm so glad you made it! It's great to see you again," the man said. He was American—Southern, specifically—and I loosely recognized him as someone who had been at dinner the first night.

I gratefully handed my plate back to Jayde so I could offer the man a bow.

"Oh please, none of that. You're a friend of the family." He grasped both of my hands in his and pumped them warmly. "I was telling Ivy all about you— wasn't I, honey?"

"Yes, he was! I'm so thrilled to meet you." The lustrous woman at his side let go of his arm to reach for me. I offered her a handshake, but she forwent that and came in for a hug and a kiss on the cheek instead. I was too stunned to refuse or reciprocate the gesture.

Vaguely, I registered the flash of a camera in the background as some insolent press member captured this momentous moment in time.

The woman held me at arm's length and admired me. "And look at this dress! Aren't you stunning? Thames undersold how beautiful you are."

Thames thought I was pretty? I tried to grasp the thought and gave up.

"Come on, you simply must meet the Yangs." The woman grabbed my hand and dragged me across the room, where the whole process of gushing handshakes and hugs was repeated, punctuated by the ever-present flicker of cameras. This went on for the next hour until I could have sworn I'd met everyone in the complex and had my picture taken a hundred times.

Everyone, it seemed, had heard about me from someone. Many of them were friends of Asia, but several said they'd heard about me from Thames. Apparently, Mr. and Mrs. Nolan had been talking about me since I'd moved to camp; some of these people claimed they'd been waiting to meet me for years.

I told them I was flattered, and my surprise was genuine. There was nothing special about me, or at least there hadn't been when Thames had met me. What had he seen in me?

Too bad I would never get to ask.

Unfortunately, tonight my fame would be a curse. If everyone else at the party had heard of me, surely the General Secretary had as well. And that was not good news.

My worst fears were confirmed when a smartly dressed guard interrupted us. "Beg pardon, Miss Nolan, but General Secretary Mong would see you."

20

The noise of the party died away as my vision flashed black.

Oh God, help.

Jayde hooked his arm through my elbow before I could even think about resisting. The guard led us out of the hall and across the courtyard to the winding stone steps that led up to the Tower of Incense. It was an agonizingly long climb that only gave me more time to panic. Each step reminded me that it was too late to turn back, and each step brought me closer to my death.

No matter what I chose, part of me would not leave that building. Either Andromeda would die, or Blue Fire would.

Finally, we reached the top. The three-story tower loomed over the pavilion, its octagonal eaves strung with lanterns and banners bearing the United seal. The most privileged of the guests decorated the patio, and every three steps was another guard, several of which exchanged subtle nods with Jayde. All eyes were on me as I was escorted up the stairs and into the building.

The tower had once been a temple, but the religious artifacts had long since been stripped away and the first floor repaneled into a throne room of sorts. Guests and guards milled around the perimeter and supplied the ambiance while butlers ferried drinks. In the center of it all, General Secretary Mong stood on a raised platform, receiving guests in a line.

He was not a large man, which was somehow all the more threatening. His hair was feathered with a proud gray, and his face was folded in a practiced smile. The way he carried himself reminded me of Thames: Everything about his movements was calm, if not understated, and yet he projected a power that formed the center of gravity in the room.

He was flanked by several guards, all of whom were bejeweled with military medals, and his top staff. Asia stood a few feet away to his left. She spotted me as we entered. I saw her eyes scan my dress, face contorted in confusion. But then her expression lit up and she grinned, broad and catlike.

Jayde tugged on my arm. I followed his gaze to the side of the room, where a cluster of press people manned a camera. I heard the reporter quietly narrating each introduction, inflating the egos of each guest as they passed in front of the General.

"Everyone is watching," Jayde whispered, as if I needed to be told. "As soon as you shake his hand, the war for freedom starts."

Yes, I'll start a war—but will it bring freedom?

As if sensing my hesitation, Jayde laid his hand over mine. "You can do this." I looked into his eyes and saw that they were wide, genuine. "I believe in you, Blue Fire."

He did—he really did. I could tell by his excited, hopeful expression. He truly believed this was the right thing to do.

But did I?

God—Jesus—what do I do? I mentally cried, fighting to get the prayer out through the whirlwind of doubts and fears.

The silence in my soul was deafening.

The line shifted forward. I looked ahead and watched as the General received the next guest. A guard introduced the woman at the head of the line, and then the General judged her. I saw the General weigh the lady's life in the scales with a single glance. Then, after a moment's hesitation, he offered her his hand. She accepted it with gushing praises. A couple of pleasantries were exchanged, and then the woman was shuffled away to make room for the next guest, who was not so lucky. The foreign diplomat behind her received only a nod in greeting. He bowed shakily and scuttled away.

And then, as if time had skipped forward, it was my turn.

I reflexively lifted the hem of my skirt as Jayde helped me onto the platform. He let go of my arm and melted into the crowd, leaving me alone with the General and my screaming thoughts.

Asia winked at me in silent welcome and beckoned me forward. My ears rang as I approached the General. The click of my heels on the wooden floor sounded like gunfire—could everyone else hear them?

Vaguely, I registered that someone was introducing me. "Nolan Xiaojie."

I froze.

The General glanced at me. He spared me only a breath—the briefest pause in his sentence—before turning back to the man at his side and continuing his conversation.

Hope fluttered through me. I meant nothing to him. Maybe—maybe he didn't want to shake my hand. This could all be avoided if he didn't offer me his hand. *Thank you, Jesus—*

Suddenly, Asia touched her father's arm and leaned towards his ear. "This is the girl I told you about. This is Thames's daughter."

The conversation stopped, and so did my heart.

The General turned back to me and gave me a second look. His eyes lit up. "Ahh! So this is Andromeda."

The attention of everyone in the room shifted to me. I heard whispers in the background and saw the camera lens focus and knew the entire world was watching.

The General smiled. "It's an honor to finally meet you."

And then he offered his hand.

At that moment, the God who had been quiet for so long rushed in my ear. *For such a time as this.*

I stared at the General's hand as mine instinctively slid forward.

And then I grabbed my skirt and bowed.

"The honor is all mine," I said, and was surprised when my voice came out clear and strong.

Yes, God had made me Andromeda Nolan for a reason. But this was not it.

Someone gasped. I looked up and realized it was Asia. She'd gone as pale as her Chinese complexion would allow. And then, suddenly, the color came rushing back into her expression as she glared at me, her eyes filled with disgust. Several people around us muttered in surprise.

I swallowed. Had I violated some unspoken rule of etiquette? Was I about to be executed for refusing the General's handshake? I hadn't planned on making it out of this party alive, but being beheaded for social ineptitude hadn't been on the list of options.

The General, however, seemed unoffended. He laughed, his grin cracking the sides of his face, as he slid his hand to its neutral position behind his back. "Such a polite young woman. Thames taught you well."

I donned my prettiest smile as I straightened. "He always wanted the best for me."

It was my turn to look surprised. Where had that come from? The words were graceful, elegant—and they weren't even a lie.

"That he did. I want you to know that I am deeply sorry for your family's loss." The General dipped his head in condolence. "How are you handling it?"

Did he want an honest answer to that question? The look in his eyes said yes, but I couldn't imagine why he cared. I glanced at the people standing nearby, searching for a social clue, but everyone just seemed surprised that the General and I were even having a conversation. Even Asia couldn't seem to recalibrate as she glanced back and forth between her father and me, her brow knotted.

After taking a breath to check my tone of voice, I gave him a modified story. "It's been difficult these past few days, sir, seeing the house, the wardrobe, the staff—everything he meant for me to have."

His smile returned, gentler this time. "It's your first time in Beijing, isn't it?" When I nodded, he winked. "Feeling a bit overwhelmed by it all?"

A beautiful laugh bubbled out of my throat before I could stop it. "In the best way possible, sir."

He echoed the sound. "I can only imagine. Have you thought about moving back here? We'd love to have you and your mother nearby."

His tone of voice suggested that he genuinely meant that, so I gave him the answer he wanted to hear. "After seeing the pool in the backyard, I don't think I have a choice."

That time, even some of his advisors laughed. He smiled benevolently at them, as if soaking up their mirth, before turning back to me. "I know what you mean. I've been there several times."

"We—I—would love to have you visit again. It would be my deepest honor to serve you."

The collective breath left the crowd again. Asia looked mortified, if not a little impressed. I resisted the urge to clutch my throat as I tried to figure out where the audacious words had come from.

Did I just invite the General over for dinner?

I couldn't even remember thinking the words; they just rolled off my lips as fluidly as a prayer.

And that's when I recognized that it wasn't me speaking.

Do not worry about what to say or how to say it. At that time you will be given what to say.

The smile remained on the General's face—poised and powerful—as he weighed me with his gaze. After a moment, he bent forward in a bow. "I would be delighted to receive your invitation."

And he just accepted?

I picked up my skirt and dipped as low as I could. "Thank you for honoring my family in this way."

A murmur erupted from the bystanders, and I caught several envious glances being shot in my direction. I twisted my skirt in my fingers as a new feeling of power rippled down my nerves.

I am Andromeda Nolan. And this is how I will fight my war.

The General started to say something else, but one of his advisors leaned over and whispered in his ear. He rolled his eyes. "It's always something. My apologies, Andromeda, but I must step away. Once you've chosen a date, forward the details to my daughter—she knows my calendar." He gestured at Asia, who recovered from her shock long enough to nod politely.

I bowed one more time for good measure. "Thank you for speaking with me, your excellence."

I turned to see Jayde standing at the edge of the platform, holding out his hand. His expression was unreadable.

Panic immediately displaced the feeling of victory in my head as I mechanically offered him my arm and let him help me off the platform. *Oh Jesus, protect me now.*

"The pleasure was all mine. I hope to see you again very soon," the General said as he allowed his advisors to herd him away. "Oh, and Andromeda..."

Jayde froze, his fingers pinching my arm. I glanced back.

A strange light glinted behind the General's eyes. "Next time I offer you my hand... don't refuse it."

I swallowed. "Of course, sir."

He disappeared into the crowd as the motion of the party resumed. Asia gave me one last stare as she hustled after her father.

Jayde pushed me towards the side of the room. His entire body was taut as he struggled to conceal his anger. "I hope you enjoyed your little *chat* with the General," he hissed in my ear, and then spat something very foul.

The adrenaline returned, bringing a wave of fear crashing down. I saw the hate burning in Jayde's eyes and knew I had only moments before my world ended. What would happen to Stanyard? My dad? What about the rebellion? What about—

And then I remembered Narissa's confident indifference in the face of death, and I finally understood.

I sucked in a breath and centered myself around the truth that my dad had failed to find: It was God's job to protect my family. It was my job to do what was right.

I found my courage and my voice. "Jayde, listen. You don't—"

"Shut up," he hissed, and pulled me towards the stairwell. One of his associates was there waiting. With a glance around at the crowd, he swiped his thumb on the panel and let us in.

The door slammed behind us, plunging us into the near darkness of the unused stairwell. I tripped on my skirt twice as Jayde hauled me up the stairs. "Jayde, stop!"

"You don't get to call the shots anymore." With a final yank, he pushed me through the door at the top of the stairs. I stumbled out into the warm night air and realized we were on the third floor.

Jayde slammed the door and advanced towards me. "You had one job."

I glanced around, but there was nowhere to go on the narrow balcony. This floor wasn't open to the public, so there was no one in sight. I could hear the laughter of people in the courtyard far below.

"Go ahead, scream," Jayde threatened, his words slurred with rage.

I swallowed and contemplated doing just that.

"They'll never make it in time." He reached into the folds of his uniform and pulled out a knife, flicking it open. I slid back and rammed into the railing. Against my better judgment, I turned and looked down.

It was a three-story drop to the stone courtyard below.

I gripped the railing as my courage buckled. It wouldn't be the first time I'd fallen from a great height. But this time, there would be nothing to break my fall.

"Jayde," I panted, trying and failing to find the peace I'd had moments before. "Please."

He shook his head. "Do you have any idea how much damage you've done? You missed the signal. You failed! And because of you, Operation Thunderbird never happened. It's going to take me years to build back what we had!"

He lurched forward and slammed into my shoulder. A scream died in my throat as I almost flipped backward over the railing, but he grabbed my arm and held me down. I hyperventilated as the world spun.

His hand closed around my throat, cutting off my airflow. His breath burned hot on my ear as he growled, "I do hope the people love a martyr, because that's what you're about to be."

He pressed the blade of his knife to my chin, and I closed my eyes. *Jesus, save me.*

"Well, that's just rude."

Jayde jerked back. My world stopped and restarted as I recognized the voice.

"Nic!"

He came around the corner of the balcony, clearly dressed for the occasion. He wore a white suit jacket paired with black pants and a smart bowtie, and a single red rose was clipped to his lapel.

"Sorry to intrude on your emasculated display of power." He regarded Jayde as if he were the worm inside of an apple. "But I believe she promised me the next set."

Jayde contorted his face. "Q? What are you—"

Nic put his finger up. "First of all, that's Dr. Von Nieuwenhuyse to you. Second of all, last I checked, I have a piece of paper stating that the woman you're about to throw off a balcony is my daughter, so frankly the rest is none of your business."

The statement was delivered with his usual dose of salt and disinterest, but his words sent relief and forgiveness rushing through me.

Nic came back for me.

Jayde recovered from the shock. "How charming," he grunted. He lifted the knife. "But don't come any closer."

"And now I'm bored." Nic whipped an electric pistol from his pocket and flipped it on in one smooth motion. "I'll make the math easy for you. Let her go, and I won't shoot to kill."

Jayde didn't even blink. "Is that how you want to do it? Two can play that game."

He reached up and grabbed my styled curls, yanking my head back in a motion that was all too familiar.

But this time, I remembered.

I reached up and grasped his hand with both of mine. Hours of practice kicked in as I ducked and turned, wrenching his arm. He yelled as his wrist twisted. I broke free and ran to Nic.

He pushed me behind him, and suddenly, I knew I was safe.

Jayde gaped at me as horror washed over his expression. Then his eyes shifted to the gun, and for the first time since I'd met him, he looked afraid.

Nic clucked his tongue. "Did I say I wouldn't shoot to kill? Because I'm strongly reconsidering that position. It's something about your face."

Jayde clenched his fists and tried to regain control by raising his voice. "I have people! They're waiting for me downstairs."

"So? There's another stairwell," Nic chirped, and fired.

Bright blue electricity arced from the gun to Jayde's chest. He gasped as all the life was sucked from his lungs. He jerked once, then stumbled forward and collapsed without a sound.

I slapped a hand over my mouth. "Is he…"

Nic looked down at the settings on the gun. "Ah, what a shame, I had it on stun. He'll thank me in an hour." He powered off the weapon and concealed it in his jacket. "Let's go."

I gathered my skirt and followed him around the building to the other stairwell. My brain caught up with my new reality, and I realized we had only minutes before Jayde's people figured out something was wrong. "Nic," I panted as we pounded down the stairs, "wait. There's something you should know—"

"I'm sure there's a lot of things. Act natural." Nic paused at the bottom of the stairs and reset his hair.

I shook my skirt out and shoved my hairpin back in. "No, listen, Stanyard—"

"Already taken care of." Nic scooped my arm in his, opened the door, and dragged me outside. The stairwell opened to the back of the porch that wrapped the tower, mercifully away from any prying camera lenses. We waited until a servant passed by with a tray of food and then followed in his wake as we walked around the building, down the steps, and merged into the crowd in the courtyard. The rhythm of the party continued undisturbed—but I knew that wouldn't last long.

I gripped Nic's arm and hoped the gesture looked elegant and not panicked. "But how—"

"I had Ephesus make the calls—everyone's fine. I sent Pizza Boy to stay with my parents. This way." Nic steered me towards the stairs that led back down the hill.

The fear that had been driving me for days evaporated, leaving me breathless. Stanyard was safe—and had been all this time. God had protected him.

Through Nic.

And Ephesus. I tried to imagine Nic and my brother working in harmony and couldn't decide which was more impressive: The fact that they'd cooperated towards a common goal, or the fact that the common goal was my safety.

Of course, the real miracle was how Nic even knew what was going on. "But how did you know he was in trouble?"

He gave an eyeroll so passionate that every muscle in his face moved. "You're not complicated, Andi. I knew that if what's-his-face back there had convinced you to go through with this against your will, then he was holding someone at gunpoint. Process of elimination suggested it was Pizza Boy."

"He's got a name," I reminded him.

"Everyone does."

I dropped the argument and struggled to keep up as he descended the stairs a little faster than was proper. The math still wasn't adding up. "How did you know I was going against my will?" I remembered our final conversation and winced. Last Nic knew, this was what I wanted.

And last I knew, he was prepared to abandon me to the consequences of my decision.

He didn't answer me until we reached the bottom of the stairs. "Mom called."

"What?"

He stopped under a tree and waited for a cluster of giggling couples to pass us. The aroma of food still soaked the air as the crowd continued to wine and dine, completely oblivious to the crisis that had just been averted.

"When you didn't show for dinner, she went up to your room and found your tablet," Nic explained. "She appropriately freaked out and called your emergency contact—me."

I felt as if I were floating as Nic guided me across the courtyard towards the docks. I could see it now—Mrs. Von's religious adherence to her schedule, the contact settings on my tablet—all the dominoes that had been put in place to save me. God *had* answered my prayer for salvation—the moment I'd asked.

And He'd sent Nic of all people.

Nic paused under the last archway and checked to make sure we were not being followed, but no one questioned our premature exit from the party. We hurried to the docks and boarded a waiting ferry. Mercifully, there were no other passengers, so we had the boat to ourselves except for the servants, who gave us a respectful berth. Nic lowered me into a seat by the stern and then sat down a comfortable distance away.

I stared at him, reliving our last conversation. I pictured his face twisted in rage, the curses flying off his lips. I remembered the hateful accusations I'd thrown at him as I tore our relationship down with my words. And I heard the hideous screech of my tablet as he blocked me and put a *"the end"* on our friendship.

I'm disappointed in you, Philadelphia.

I waited until we were almost across the lake before voicing my thoughts. "You came."

He was watching the approaching shore and didn't even turn to look at me. "Why wouldn't I come?"

"Because I..." I choked on the words, not sure which I was more afraid of: my mistakes or my feelings.

Nic had no qualms against either. "Oh, you mean because you betrayed me?"

I twisted my hands in my lap. "That's not exactly what I'd call it—"

"You betrayed me," he continued matter-of-factly. He leaned back against the railing and checked my sins off like a grocery list. "You betrayed my trust, you betrayed our friendship, you betrayed everything we ever stood for. You let me down."

There it was—the crushing rejection that took my world out from under me. The boat rocked to a stop, and he got up and started walking without even a glance at me. I hurried after him, fighting my skirts and the impending need to cry. He strode down the path to the bridge, oblivious to both.

"Nic, stop!" I gasped.

He halted, back to me.

I caught up to him and spilled my heart before he could interrupt. "If that's how you feel, then why are you helping me?"

He looked up at the night sky. "Why?"

I braced myself as the tears I'd been swallowing all evening splashed across my vision.

He finally turned and, for the first time that night, met my eyes. "Do you think I care for you so little that betraying me would make a difference?"

"I mean… yeah?" I admitted, and blushed. That is exactly what I thought.

And I'd never been more grateful to be proven wrong.

He blinked. "Sometimes I wonder. Come on, let's go." He started across the bridge.

"No, Nic, wait."

He glanced back and arched an eyebrow.

I took a deep breath as my universe rediscovered its center of gravity. "Thank you."

"You're welc—"

He gagged on the word when I hugged him.

He let me savor it for three seconds—just long enough for it to be awkward—before he shoved me away. "You're welcome," he repeated, "but don't *ever* hug me again."

I wasn't sure whether to laugh or cry, so I did both.

He rolled his eyes again. "Let's get out of here. I need a coffee."

"I'll buy," I teased, and followed him onto the bridge.

"Leaving so soon?"

Nic froze, every muscle in his body rigid.

I whipped around. Asia emerged from the trees on the shore and came to stand on the end of the bridge behind us. She posed under the light of the lamppost, hand on her hip like a femme fatale in a frame.

Nic refused to turn around. "You know I hate parties."

His tone was cold, easy, familiar, and I suddenly realized that I should be very afraid. "You two… know each other?"

"More than I'd like," Nic hissed.

"And not as much I'd hoped," Asia cackled at the same time. She strolled towards us with the ease of a cat who'd cornered its prey. "But we can make up for lost time. Won't you two join me? They're just about to serve dessert." She gestured across the lake at the party.

"Regrettably, Andromeda is an extremely busy woman, so we'll have to catch up later." Nic grabbed my hand and started to pull me across the bridge.

"Nic, don't be so cruel. I've waited *eight years* for you to accept my invitation—the least you could do is spare fifteen minutes." Asia flicked her fingers, and armed guards emerged from the trees behind her. Several more materialized at the far end of the bridge, cutting us off from both sides. There was nowhere to go but into the water.

I gripped Nic's hand as my throat closed in fear. *Oh God, no.*

Asia flashed a perfect smile. "Dr. Von Nieuwenhuyse, you're under arrest."

LAODICEA

RED RAIN #6.5

JULY 2076

1: EPHESUS

"Nic needs to see you."

I groaned and dropped my luggage in the lobby of the research base. Those were my five least favorite words to hear. They usually meant I was about to get threatened, or ordered to do something illegal, or—when Nic was feeling particularly spicy—kidnapped and declared dead.

Of course, I knew we'd moved past the stage of wanting to kill each other. Nic's time in prison had shown him that there were bigger fish in the pond, and his narcissism had become much more manageable as of late. In fact, based on what he had done for my sister, I even dared to hope he had turned over a new leaf.

But he still wasn't my favorite person in the world, and he definitely wasn't the person I had flown all the way to Mars to see.

I grabbed both of Cea's hands in mine. "He wants to see me? Well, he'll have to wait, because the person *I* want to see is *you*."

Maybe it didn't come out as romantic as it sounded in my head, but the effect was lost on her. She immediately pulled one of her hands back to tuck her golden curls behind her ear. "Oh no, he doesn't *want* to see you," she clarified. "But he *needs* to see you."

I knew what that meant: Nic needed my help, but he was too proud to ask. No doubt he had done something arrogant and self-centered, and I needed to clean it up before he got us all killed. It wouldn't be the first time, but it could wait while I kissed my girlfriend, whom I hadn't seen in two months.

"I'll take care of it. But how are you? I missed you." I rubbed her palm and drank in the sight of her—her agile frame, her sharp nose, her heart-shaped face that seemed to have a permanent flush to it, like she was always burning with passion beneath the surface. I had missed that face while we had been on the run, and now, seeing her right in front of me, I realized I needed to do whatever it took to keep from losing her again.

Unfortunately, if Cea was having any feelings, she wasn't showing it. She wasn't even looking at me; her eyes wandered down the hall of the base as she turned to lead the way. "I'm fine," she intoned. "We need to go. It's important. Your—"

"It's always important with Nic," I interrupted, trying to reclaim the moment. "He'll live for another five minutes. It's you I care about. I was so worried—"

"Ephesus," she yanked on my arm to cut me off, "it's about Phil."

I froze. I'd left Philadelphia—my sister—behind on Earth to care for our father, who had just been brought back from the dead after being cryogenically frozen. Both of them were wanted by the law, and the only things keeping Phil from being executed for starting a revolution were a haircut and a new set of fingerprints. Leaving her behind wasn't my favorite arrangement, especially since Dad was in no position to protect her, but I hadn't been given much say in the matter.

Just like I hadn't been given much say in the last two years of my life.

Phil was supposed to be hiding out while Dad finished therapy, and then they would be getting on the next flight to Mars. Any news about her could not be good news.

I tensed—then closed my eyes, took a deep breath, and prayed to the count of ten. As much as I wanted it to be, my sister's safety was not in my hands. I wouldn't be able to fix anything by flying into a panic.

I opened my eyes and squeezed Cea's fingers. "I'll handle it. Whatever it is, we can take care of it. God's brought her—and us—this far. He won't abandon her now."

My confidence brought her peace, like it always did. She managed a smile, and I tried to capitalize on the opportunity and pull her close.

She jerked back. "Ephesus, please, not right now. Can't we do this later?"

I kept my hand around her wrist, briefly contemplating making her stay. It was always "later" with her.

I saw the anxiety on her face and thought better of it. "Okay," I relented, letting go of her hand, "as long as you promise you'll meet me for dinner. I have something to give you."

She looked up and met my eyes.

I struggled not to get lost in the freckles that smattered her face like stars in a galaxy. "I brought you a *very special* present from Earth."

My inflection did the trick. Her cloud-gray eyes sparkled with curiosity, and she squinted like she suspected I was up to no good. I winked. She had no idea.

"Deal," she agreed, and leaned forward to give me a peck on the cheek.

I caught a whiff of her perfume—just enough to make me want more. I reached for her, but she saw it coming and sidestepped. "Later," she snapped.

I knew better than to argue with that tone of voice. I grumbled my defeat, grabbed my suitcase, and strode down the hall towards Nic's office.

It was early morning on Mars, and the base was still waking up. The distant sun had just peaked the red-dirt bluffs and was casting soft light through the glass dome of the central wing. I slowed my pace as the familiar sights and sounds set in—the clap of my shoes on the metal floor, the quiet whir of gravity augmenters, the slightly stale taste of the oxygenated air. I wanted to love it; I felt the same excitement and trepidation I'd experienced when I'd arrived on base for the first time, the glorious anticipation that I was about to be part of something amazing. But I also felt fear and loneliness—the helplessness I'd suffered through while I was trapped in Wing 74, never knowing if I'd make it home alive.

I suffocated the feelings, intending to detangle them later. I opened the gate to Wing 2 and navigated to Nic's office.

I heard him cussing and ranting through the walls while I was still three doors down. I winced. Nic avoided talking to himself—and others—as much as possible. Cea was right; something was very wrong.

Holy Spirit, give me strength. I braced myself and pressed the doorbell.

He took a breath between expletives to bark, "Go away."

"It's Ephesus," I said, knowing he'd never get around to asking. "Cea said you needed to see me."

His sharp laugh made the speaker crackle. "I never *want* to see you, Ephesus."

"I wasn't asking," I returned, and waved my hand over the sensor on the door panel. By sheer providence, he'd forgotten to lock it, and the door whooshed open.

He whipped around to face me from where he stood by the desk. "Get out."

I stepped in. "You look terrible."

He did. He'd clearly slept in his clothes, if he'd slept at all, and his hair was a crunchy mess of day-old styling gel. His mustache hadn't been trimmed in a day or two and was slowly creeping down the sides of his face, threatening to merge with his scraggly goatee.

A quick glance around the room showed that his office had fared no better. It wasn't unusual for Nic to live in a little bit of chaos, but this was disturbing. There was trash scattered on the floor, and every flat surface had at least one plate of abandoned food on it. It looked like he'd ordered a dozen dishes and refused them all. Dried coffee stains streaked his desktop, and something was splattered on the far wall. There was a dent in the plaster and a pile of broken ceramic on the floor—like he'd thrown a mug of coffee into the wall in a rage.

I kicked a piece of dirty laundry out of my way and approached him. "What's going on? What's wrong with Phil?"

"You want a list?" He tipped his head to the side and squinted at me with bloodshot eyes, like he was debating whether to kick me out of his office. He decided I wasn't worth it and instead took a swig from the mug he had in his hands.

I grabbed the trash can and started dumping dried food into it. "Is she safe?"

He scoffed. "I'm done trying to keep that stupid girl safe."

That wasn't what I had asked, so I narrowed the question. "Where is she?"

"How would I know?" He took another gulp.

I dropped the trash can. "What do you mean, you don't know? You're supposed to be keeping an eye on her!"

He shrugged. "Haven't talked to her."

"How have you not talked to her? She talks to you more than anyone."

It was only after the words left my mouth that I realized how much bitterness and rejection was attached to them.

He was too absorbed in himself to notice. "I *can't* talk to her," he enunciated like he was breaking down a chemistry equation for me, "because I blocked her."

I struggled to stay in control as adrenaline flooded my system. "You *blocked* her?"

He had absolutely no appreciation for how depraved that confession was. "She wasn't listening to me anyway."

I grabbed his tablet off the desk. Phil's messaging profile was still on the screen, her avatar grayed out. I skimmed the chat history and saw that they'd had a call the day before—a call that had, apparently, ended abruptly.

I threw the tablet down. "Nic, what were you thinking?"

He flicked his fingers like he was seasoning a filet. "I don't have to put up with her disrespect."

I pinched my nose and gave myself three beats to channel the Holy Spirit before replying. "First of all, you sound like a teenage girl. Second of all, yes, you do. You're the adult in this relationship."

He paused and reconsidered whatever insult he had been about to fire. "At least someone recognizes that." With a grunt, he tipped his mug back and chugged the contents.

I snatched the cup from his hands. A splash of clear liquid sloshed in the bottom. I sniffed it and grimaced; it definitely *wasn't* water.

Nic was unashamed. "If you want to ask for a raise, now would be a great time."

I walked over to the bathroom and rinsed out the mug in the sink. "Well, I was going to ask you if I could marry your sister."

"What?" he shouted over the running water.

"Never mind." I turned the faucet off and came back out into the office. "Sit down."

He surprisingly obeyed, flopping dramatically in his desk chair.

I set the mug on the coffee maker on the bookcase—one of three brewers Nic had in his office. "I'm going to need you to explain this to me nice and slow. What happened?"

He gestured sloppily with his hands. "Oh, Phil's just got it in her head that she's the hero of the universe, and she's going to China to assassinate the General Secretary."

There were way too many stimuli in that sentence to process in one breath. "I'm sorry, what?"

Unfortunately, Nic decided to elaborate on the least important part of that revelation. "Yeah, I guess they rigged up some sort of kill switch in her palm—"

"I don't care," I cut him off. "She's going to *China*?"

"I know, right?" he crowed. He looked delighted that we finally agreed on something, like this was a breakthrough in our friendship. "She got invited to the state gala, because apparently 'Andromeda' is a celebrity now, and so Jayde's decided that this is their opportunity to save the world. So they're going to have her assassinate the General, which is an absolutely *ludicrous* plan if you ask me, because—"

I put my hand up. "Just stop." I punched the button on the coffee maker and took a deep breath. *Jesus, please help me.*

I looked back up at Nic. "We're going to start from the beginning."

It took an hour and three cups of coffee—two for him and one for me—before I had what I thought was the full story. Apparently, in the four days I had been offline while on the transit from Earth, my sister had gone rogue. With the help of our friends in the underground, she'd broken into our old containment camp and freed our neighbors. The government had retaliated by ordering the relocation of all the unassimilated to Chinese prisons, and Jayde, Phil's military contact, had decided to escalate the conflict by attempting to assassinate the General Secretary, the leader of the United.

And he was using my little sister to do it.

I agreed with Nic: It was a ludicrous plan. Phil was in grave danger, and I knew that killing the General would not bring the change Jayde thought it would. There would be chaos, yes, but chaos was just an excuse for lesser men to seize power. Philadelphia was going to start a war, and we'd all be lucky if a greater evil didn't take the General's place.

I was furious, but I didn't blame my sister. She was seventeen, for crying out loud. If anything, I blamed myself. I never should have let her start recording propaganda for the underground. Our dad never should have created the weapon that started this whole conflict in the first place.

And Nic never should have let her go back to Earth.

I sighed and gathered my courage. "Nic, do you have any idea what you've done?"

He glowered. At least he had started to dry up and was processing sentences like an adult. "Enlighten me."

I got up to refill our mugs. "First, you let her go back to Earth *by herself* to look for our father…"

"Oh, we're blaming me now? Love that."

I ignored him. "And then, instead of explaining to her why she shouldn't go to China, you alienate her by calling her an idiot."

"It wasn't a lie…" he said, but more quietly this time.

I walked back to the desk and slammed the mug down in front of him. "And then, to top it all off, you block your *seventeen-year-old dependent* on all your accounts, stranding her on a hostile planet with no way to get ahold of you."

That finally got through to him. He stared at the liquid sloshing around in his cup for a long moment before he replied. "Thank you for summing that up," he mumbled.

I sat back down across from him. "So, what are you going to do about it?"

He grunted and grabbed his coffee. "Not my problem anymore. I don't care."

That was a lie, and if we were going to save Phil, I needed him to see that. "Could've fooled me."

He contorted his face. "Excuse me?"

I shrugged and swirled my mug to disperse the creamer. "Could've fooled me. If you didn't care, you wouldn't be shut up in your office trying to drink your way out of feelings."

He flushed and looked down at himself, noticing, perhaps for the first time, what a state he was in.

"Hate to break it to you, Dr. Nic, but it sounds like you care an awful lot—which, granted, is *really* unusual for you." I slathered the accusation on thick. "Since when did you start caring about other people?"

"I don't," he said haltingly, as if trying to convince himself that it was still true.

"So why'd you agree to be her legal guardian? Why put yourself at risk like that?" It didn't make any sense to me either. This couldn't be the same conniving mad scientist who had locked me in a basement for two years just to protect his secret project.

"Because…" Nic squinted at the steam rising from his mug. "She cares. She cares about everyone. Which means someone has to care about her."

He looked back up at me, and in that moment, I was convinced the mad scientist was gone.

Or at least he was on his way out the door, even if he was getting dragged kicking and screaming by Nic's better self.

"Okay then." I set my mug aside. "Fix it."

He frowned at me.

I shoved the tablet across the desk towards him. "You're the one who blocked her. Fix it."

He stared at the device, his eyes flickering as he recalibrated his life choices.

And then he made the right decision.

He picked up the tablet—and at that exact moment, it rang.

I did an abysmal job of stifling a laugh as he yelped and nearly dropped the device and his coffee. He regained his grip, looked at the screen, and swore.

"What?" I asked.

He swore again, but it wasn't a curse of anger. It was an oath of disbelief as he stared at the screen. The device continued to trill.

"Who is it?" I repeated.

He looked up at me, probably unintentionally. "My mom."

I opened my mouth, then realized I had no idea where to go with that. Nic's parents hadn't called him in almost a decade—if only because they didn't remember him, thanks to a botched government neurosurgery.

Nic accepted the call. "Hello?"

A female voice came through the line. "Hello? Is this Doctor…" There was a pause, and then she enunciated the name slowly, as if she were reading it off a piece of paper. "Nic Von Nieuwenhuyse?"

Nic gasped like the woman had just asked him to marry her. "Yes, it's me," he exclaimed with way too much emotion.

"Yes, hi," Mrs. Von continued. "Sorry to bother you, but—"

"You're not bothering me at all," he interrupted. He sniffled.

"Are you crying?" I scolded.

"Shut up," he hissed. He turned away and swiped his face on the sleeve of his dirty lab coat. He must be *really* drunk.

"Glad to know I'm not being an inconvenience," Mrs. Von deadpanned. "Anyway, I'm calling because you're listed as Andromeda Nolan's emergency contact."

The joy evaporated from the room. Nic straightened, sobriety instantly returning to his eyes. "What happened?"

"That's just it, I don't know." Mrs. Von's voice faltered, as if she was struggling to hold on to reality. "She didn't make it home for dinner, and when I went up to check her room, her tablet was still here."

Nic threw a questioning glare at me, but I shrugged. That didn't sound catastrophic. Phil always left her registered electronics at the Vons' so she could keep her legal identity—Andromeda Nolan—clean. She was probably just late getting home.

"It's been two hours, and now I have no way of getting ahold of her. Does she have another device that you're aware of?"

Nic spun his chair back around and started typing on his computer. A couple of clicks, a concentrated frown, and then he angled the monitor so I could see.

He'd pulled up Andromeda's file. The most recent entries indicated that she had, in fact, registered a new cellphone under her account—just earlier today in Earth-time. There were a couple of shopping transactions, and then she'd boarded a nonstop flight to Beijing.

My heart plunged from my throat to my stomach. *We're too late. Oh God, help.*

"Let me see if I can reach her," Nic said into the line, voice intentionally calm. "If I can, I'll have her call you."

Mrs. Von took the bait of his false confidence. "Thank you," she said, relieved. "And if I hear from her first, I'll update you."

"I'd appreciate that. And hey, Mom?"

I winced. *Now's not the time, man...*

"What did you just call me?" she barked.

He ignored the question and leaned towards the screen. "Thank you for calling and letting me know."

She accepted the offer of his sincerity. "Of course," she agreed, and hung up.

He took a deep breath. I gave him a minute. I knew what it was like to lose a parent—literally and figuratively.

He blinked away the feelings and turned back to his desktop. "Something's wrong."

"We're too late," I admitted, fighting to keep the hopelessness out of my voice. "She's already on her way to China."

He shook his head. "No, something's not right. There's no reason she wouldn't have taken her tablet with her—after all, Andromeda is the one that's going to the party."

He had a point, and the realization replaced the dread in my stomach with something far more sinister.

He swiped his fingers on the tablet and attempted to call her new number. The line clicked, and a computerized voice said, *"The number you have dialed could not be reached. Please try again."*

"You try," Nic demanded.

I pulled my phone out of my pocket and dialed the number on her file. I was also greeted with the same message.

"She has no reason to block me," I said, stating what we both already knew. "You, I'd understand. But me?"

He grunted his acknowledgment. He yanked his desk drawer open and rooted around until he found an outdated smart phone. Wiping off the screen with his sleeve, he powered it on and tried to call her one more time. No luck.

I connected the ominous dots. "I don't think that number is set to receive inbound calls at all. It's a dummy device."

He glared at his desktop, scrolling aggressively with his mouse. "These purchases—they were all made at stores at the transit hub. That's where she got the phone, too."

He looked back up at me. We both ruminated in horrified silence for a minute before I finally had the courage to declare, "She didn't go willingly."

He rolled his eyes. "Better late than never, sis."

"Excuse me?" I yelped.

He shoved the chair back and strode across the room to the closet. "I mean, she's clearly had a come to Jesus moment and realized this is a terrible idea—better late than never."

I stood up to follow. "Now is not the time for your nihilistic sarcasm, Nic. She's going to get herself killed."

"She's certainly trying." He grabbed a duffle out of the closet and started taking a lap around the room, shoveling electronics and personal effects into the bag. "She probably told Carrot-Top she wouldn't do it, and he pulled a gun on her."

I knew he meant Jayde, and he was most assuredly right. My sister was a compassionate person who was more in tune with God's heart than she realized. She would have known, deep down, that killing the General wasn't His plan for her. She had clearly figured that out—a second too late.

And now we were a second too late to save her.

Nic stopped, his hand on the knob of a cabinet drawer, his eyes on the floor. "What?" I prodded.

"I just came to the uncomfortable realization that—if she had this change of heart this morning—it means she *was* listening to me."

I folded my arms. "Of course. If I were a teenage girl, and the man I looked up to told me he was 'disappointed in me,' I would definitely have a come to Jesus moment."

His whole face simmered in guilt, and I let him. He deserved it.

He yanked the drawer open and grabbed an electric pistol. "Well, let's see if I can't get there before she pulls the trigger."

I caught up. The transit I had just gotten off of would be returning to Earth in a few hours. If we hurried, we could make it. I grabbed my suitcase from where I'd abandoned it by the door. "I'm still packed. Let's go."

"No, I need you to stay here."

Absolutely not. I'm not sitting by the sidelines this time. "She's my sister!" I argued.

"No one's debating that." He stepped into the bathroom and grimaced at his disheveled reflection in the mirror. "But you'll just get in my way."

"Didn't realize I was such a nuisance to you," I snapped.

"Really? Because I feel like I've been pretty clear about that fact over the years." He tried to comb a hand through his crusty hair and only made it worse. He gave up and walked over to me. "Ephesus, put your ego aside and think logically about this. You're riding on a temp file—if you try to walk into Beijing, they're going to flag it and arrest you."

He was right, which left me with no ground to stand on.

"Besides, I have an invitation to the party." He rooted through the stack of papers on his desk and pulled out a gilded envelope.

I sighed my defeat as a coldly familiar emotion seeped into my soul.

You're useless. Again.

I threw my suitcase back on the floor with more force than was necessary. "Surely there's something I can do."

"Of course," he said, and it wasn't patronizing. "Call the transit station and tell them I'm coming. Then call Stanyard."

"What can he do?" Stanyard was a childhood friend of the family and one of Phil's contacts in the underground. He was supposed to be keeping an eye on her while she was earthside, but if she'd already gotten on a plane to Beijing, he wouldn't be of much help.

"I have a hunch." Nic tossed his soiled lab coat on the floor and fetched a clean one from the closet. "I don't know how well you know your sister..."

"Better than you," I snapped, even though I wasn't sure it was true.

He let me have it. "...But if she's doing this against her will, then Carrot-Top probably has a hostage. Seeing as your dad is basically dead—no offense—Pizza Boy is the next logical option."

I had to admit that was another astute observation. Stanyard himself had confessed to me that he would love to be something more than friends if Phil would ever give him the chance.

At least *he* had the grace to talk to me before he talked to Nic.

"Call Stanyard, call my parents back, and see if you can't get ahold of Mrs. Nolan. If she went with Phil to Beijing, that might help us." Nic zipped up his duffle and slung it over his shoulder. "I'll call you when I land."

So that was it—I'd make three five-minute phone calls, and then I'd go back to being an NPC, stranded over a hundred million miles away while someone else saved my sister and the world.

I collapsed against the wall. *God, where did I go wrong?*

Nic brushed past me on his way out the door, then hesitated. "There is one other thing you can do for me."

2: CEA

Ephesus was late for dinner.

He called before 6:30 to let me know he was running late because he was "finishing up something for Nic." I got us a table and waited in the cafeteria, milking an appetizer longer than was proper. Now it was nearly seven, and I hadn't heard a word from him.

I wasn't offended so much as I was surprised. He concealed it well with his gentle attitude, but I knew Ephesus was a very exacting person. When something was important to him, it was done with precision. He had never once been late for a date before—which meant something was wrong.

I pulled out my phone and called him back.

"Hey baby," he answered in a tired tone that said he'd given up on salvaging our evening.

"Where are you?" I asked, trying not to sound worried. "There's only so long I can eat these chips and dip by myself before it looks suspicious."

He sacrificed a chuckle. "Well, if you can believe it, I'm actually in the kitchen. Er, dry good storage room, to be specific."

What's he doing back there? "I'm on my way." Abandoning my sad guacamole, I used my security clearance to let myself into the kitchen. I walked past the row of industrial ovens, still hot from feeding the base's residents, and opened the door to the warehouse where all the food was kept.

Food storage took up a sizeable portion of the base. Even though we grew most of our own food—Mr. Sardis saw to that—we were still prepared for the worst. If all our greenhouses failed, we still had enough canned and freeze-dried food to feed everyone on base for two years.

I wandered up and down several rows of dried goods before I found Ephesus. He was up on a ladder, cramming cans of beans onto an overflowing shelf. He balanced three commercial-sized cans in his arms as he struggled to read the dates on the labels. An open shipping crate took up the middle of the floor.

I stopped beneath the ladder and looked up. "What are you doing?"

He gave me a weary smile. "Finishing Nic's chores."

"What?"

He gestured at a tablet that lay on the edge of the crate. "He asked me to finish his to-do list since he had to run to catch his flight."

I picked up the tablet. A lengthy task list was displayed on the screen, everything from performing a safety check on the environmental controls to putting away the most recent shipment of food. No wonder Ephesus was late; I wasn't sure even Nic himself could have gotten this all done in one day.

I scrolled through the list of green checkboxes Ephesus had dutifully logged. "You know this means he trusts you, right?"

Ephesus grunted his disagreement as he shoved a stack of cans to the back of the shelf.

"No, seriously. This base is his pride and joy, and if you mess up something like the environmental controls, you'll kill us all." I waved the tablet at him. "He trusts you."

Ephesus paused and considered the compliment. "Well, then I owe him an apology when he gets back," he admitted. "I didn't realize he did all this himself."

"Normally he has people to do most of this, but since Carnegie…" I shrugged. We'd been running on a skeleton crew since the fallout with Thames. "You want some help?"

"That'd be amazing," he sighed. "These dates are all messed up. Some of the stuff they just sent us is older than the cans we already have—I wonder if this crate sat in the warehouse for a while before they sent it."

"Probably. Did you detox the shipment before you started putting it away?" I tapped the screen, noticing that was one of the few items not checked off.

"Yeah, I checked it, it's clear. Some of the dry goods weren't packed well—I found several bags with tears in them. I wrote up a list; hopefully he can get credit for them." He jumped off the ladder with a grunt.

I set the tablet down and walked over to him. "I see that—you're all flour-y." I brushed off his shirt and released a cloud of white dust.

He caught my hands in his, like he always did when he was about to make a confession. "I'm sorry about tonight, baby."

"Don't be." I pecked him on the cheek. "This is important."

"You're important," he returned, his voice thick with disappointment.

I chewed my lip. Our date *was* important to him, and I hated to see him so sad. He looked exhausted. No doubt he had run himself ragged trying to get everything done in time, and now he was wallowing in his failure. He'd probably been beating himself up for the last hour.

I couldn't let the night end like this.

I reached up to straighten his collar. "Hey, why don't you let me finish putting this crate away while you get our table ready?"

His face instantly brightened, the life returning to his intense brown eyes. "Would you?"

I winked. "Maybe I just want my 'very special' present."

He wrapped me in a tight hug, smacked me on the lips, and then set me back down. "I'll make it worth your while."

I brushed off the smear of flour he'd left on my blouse. "You'd better," I teased as I bent over the crate and pulled out more cans.

He grabbed his tablet and abandoned jacket. He started to run for the door—then stopped, his oxfords squeaking on the tile. "Hey," he said, turning around.

I stopped and looked up at him.

He smiled. It wasn't the closed-lip smile he usually gave others just to be polite. This was a broad, vulnerable gesture, the kind he gave when he wanted you to know he was being sincere. His eyes glimmered like he'd opened the doors to his soul just for me.

"Thanks for helping me," he said.

He walked away. I stared after him, remembering the first time he had said those words to me.

TWO YEARS AGO

"I think I'm lost."

I stopped and turned around. A scientist stood in the middle of the hall, looking lost indeed. His brow was furrowed, and he clutched a tablet and lab paraphernalia to his chest like he was a high schooler late for first period. I didn't recognize him, but that wasn't surprising. There were always so many scientists coming and going for Nic's experiments that it was usually a waste of time to get to know them.

"Probably," I admitted. "Where are you trying to go?"

He glanced at his watch. "Lab 8A.5."

"Yup, you're lost. Wing 8 is clear on the other side of the base."

He sighed dramatically. "Late on the first day. I'm fired."

I chuckled. "Come on, I'll show you. We can take a shortcut across Wing 5." I gestured with my arm and started walking.

He hustled to catch up. "How *do* you find your way around here?"

"You'll get used to it," I said, which was really the only explanation I could give. "Give it time. You'll figure out your own landmarks."

He snorted. "Probably faster if I just code my own GPS system."

I took another look at him. He was about my age, with fluffy brown hair that stuck up a little in the front. He wasn't smiling, but his expression was relaxed and approachable. He seemed like the kind of guy who would help you find the cereal aisle in the supermarket.

"First day, huh?" I prodded. "When did you land?"

"This morning—er, yesterday. My brain hasn't adjusted to the time zone yet."

I laughed as I led us through the gate to Wing 5. "First time on Mars, I take it."

"Yeah," he replied, and I heard in his voice the awe and wonder that all first-time colonists had. I wished Mars still excited me like that. But I'd been living here for over five years, and now it was just another house to me. Only difference was you couldn't walk into the backyard without putting on a spacesuit.

"I'm Ephesus, by the way." He juggled the gadgetry in his arms to offer me a handshake.

I accepted it. "Cea."

"Oh, so you're Nic's sister."

I flinched. I was always "Nic's sister" to people. It was inevitable, since my brother owned this base, but I hated being an accessory to his entourage. It would be nice to have a function on this planet other than "dependent." But I wasn't a scientist, and there wasn't anything left for me on Earth, so my options were limited.

"My one claim to fame," I said dismissively. "You got any family up here?"

He shook his head. "My father and sister are back on Earth," he mumbled. The clip in his tone made me wonder if his family relationships were just as complicated as mine, so I let it drop.

"This way," I said, and waved us into a storage room.

Ephesus hesitated in the doorway. "What are we doing in here? Besides getting murdered."

I laughed, the sound echoing eerily off the metal walls. I didn't blame him; it was a creepy room. It was outdated and unused—most of the lights didn't work, and the air was stuffy. But it had one benefit: There were two entrances, and the second door led straight to Wing 8.

I ran ahead and opened the opposite door. "Ta da."

He followed and stepped blinking into the bright lights of the hallway. "Snazzy."

"Go through Door A," I pointed, "and Lab 8A.5 will be like the third door on the right."

"Got it. And hey." He turned to face me. "Thank you for helping me."

I looked up at him, and he smiled for the first time. It was a warm, broad gesture that instantly transformed his whole face.

I found myself returning the sentiment. "Of course."

He shifted the gear in his arms. "Would you like to have dinner with me?"

It was said with such unequivocal confidence that it startled me. "You... what?"

"Would you like to eat dinner with me?" he repeated, unfazed. "I think I get off at six o'clock."

I struggled to process what he was asking me, and he mistook my silence. "If you don't, that's okay. But I'd like to get to know you better."

"No, I mean sure, I just..." I finally got a handle on my feelings. "I'm just surprised you asked, is all."

The smile was toying at the corners of his lips again. "Why? You're a girl my age who's been kind and friendly. I just got dumped on a foreign planet and have no friends. Seems like a logical order of events to me."

"Well, when you put it that way," I deadpanned.

He shrugged. "The world is already so complicated... I'd rather not complicate this if I can avoid it." He gestured between us.

I tipped my head to the side and studied him. He waited patiently, eyes open and honest.

He was right; my world *was* complicated, especially once you threw my brother's various illegal projects into the mix. It would be nice to enjoy a simple pleasure for once, and dinner with a cute guy was definitely on the list of acceptable options.

"Six-thirty?" I offered.

He grinned. "Six-thirty it is."

*

It was almost nine o'clock by the time I'd finished putting the food away, gotten cleaned up, and found my way back to the mess hall. But that suited me just fine, because the place was deserted. Ephesus and I had the whole room to ourselves.

He'd taken advantage of that fact. He'd shoved other tables out of the way and dragged a loveseat from the lounge in front of the bay windows. On the coffee table was spread our dinner, illuminated by a trio of flickering tea lights in glass jars.

"Where'd you find candles?" In a base pumped full of artificial oxygen, candles were an Earth luxury we were not allowed to have.

"They're from the lab," he admitted. "And don't tell Nic."

"I have no intention to. And did you cook this yourself?" I walked over to the coffee table and inhaled the oregano-spiced scent of our dinner. It was a fancy pasta dish, perfectly portioned for two and topped with a sprig of fresh parsley that was no doubt clipped from Mr. Sardis's personal garden.

"Best I could whip up on short notice." He tugged on his tie. He'd ditched his lab coat in favor of a suit jacket. I could tell he had borrowed it from someone—the sleeves didn't quite fit—but he looked incredibly handsome, nonetheless.

I reached up and helped him fix his tie. "You did all this in less than two hours? Now I feel underdressed." All I had done was thrown on a cute top, heels, and some red lipstick.

He wrapped his arms around my waist. "You look beautiful. Now, about that kiss you were going to give me earlier..."

He didn't wait for permission, not that he needed it. He put one hand behind my neck and drew me in for a kiss that made up for the two months we had been apart.

I felt my heart fluttering against my ribs. I'd been avoiding the feeling—suffocating it, denying it—for months. There had just been too much going on, too many dangers to fight, too many unknowns. But here, now, in the abandoned mess hall, stationed on Mars millions of miles away from the people who hated us—love felt, perhaps for the first time, safe.

I was sad when he finally pulled away. He took my hand and led me to a seat on the couch, his devious grin returning. "Now, if you will allow me the honor of serving you..."

And serve me he did. He guided me through a delightful dinner and even more delightful conversation. He knew just what questions to ask and what topics to avoid to keep me laughing and focused on the present. I spent the evening drunk in his kindness and wit—just like I had on our first date, when I'd agreed to meet him in the cafeteria for dinner.

Our candles had almost burned out by the time we were finished with dessert. For the first time that night, Ephesus had gone silent as he stared out the window at the pitch-black landscape.

I poked him in the knee. "I thought you said you had a 'very special' present for me."

He instantly returned to this reality. "Oh, I do, but first..." He twisted to face me and grasped both of my hands. "You have to listen to a very sappy speech."

I laughed, mostly because Ephesus was never sappy. "Um, okay."

He cleared his throat, and his voice changed pitch, like he had been memorizing the words for weeks. "Laodicea, I missed you. I know I said it earlier, but I'll say it again: *I missed you.* It wasn't just that I was worried about you. It's like something was wrong with my life and I couldn't fix it. I don't know how else to explain it except to say that I felt incomplete without you."

"You're right, that *was* sappy." I gigged; he was so sincere about it, with his wide chocolaty eyes. "But, thank you. I missed you too."

He kissed my hand, and I noticed he wasn't smiling. "Can I be honest with you?"

I swallowed a sudden wave of nervousness. "Well, I hope you're not being anything else."

He massaged my fingers. "I've felt that way since Wing 74."

I tensed as the unwanted memories of locked doors, strained conversations, and unspoken goodbyes came washing back. "Ephesus, I don't want to talk about—"

He shushed me. "Just listen, please. I'm trying to tell you that I've loved you for a very long time. I've had two years to think about it, and no matter what happens, I keep coming back to you—to us."

Us. How I wanted to believe in that word, to embrace it and let it define my future. Little did Ephesus know that I kept coming back to "us," too. No matter what happened, my thoughts and dreams orbited around him. I was in love with him, and I'd given up lying to myself about that six months ago.

But how could there be an us when the world was on fire?

I tried to slip my hand from his grasp. "Ephesus, please. I don't—"

"No." He gripped my hands, pulling me towards him. "I promised when we met that I wouldn't complicate our relationship. This is me telling you how I feel and uncomplicating things: I love you, and I don't want to lose you again."

He slid off the couch to the floor, and suddenly, I knew what my "present" was.

Oh no.

Getting down on one knee, he reached into the pocket of his suit jacket and pulled out a small velvet box I'd seen before.

Not now.

Before I could find my breath to object, he opened the box and held it up. His eyes finding mine, he asked with all the innocence in the world:

"Laodicea, will you marry me?"

I stared at him, at the tiny diamond glinting on the red velvet, and panicked as that unsafe feeling crept back in.

"Ephesus, I..."

Before I could answer him, the power went out.

3: EPHESUS

This wasn't what I had in mind for a "candlelight dinner."

Just as Cea was about to give me her answer, the lights flickered. They hesitated, as if gasping for breath, and then they went out, plunging the room into unnatural darkness.

Cea squeaked. I shushed her, listening hard. I strained into the sudden silence and caught the faint whir of the gravity augmenters, the grind of the furnaces circulating air.

I let out my breath in relief. "The environmental controls are still online. It's probably just a blown circuit in the lights. Nothing to worry about."

"We should go see what's going on," she said, sounding extremely worried. She started to rise.

"No, Cea, wait—look." I pointed out the window. As my eyes adjusted, I saw that the dark Martian night was actually alive with light. The landscape of stars, unfiltered by the thin atmosphere, exploded in the sky like a shower of sparks. Phobos, one of Mars' lumpy little moons, cast a pale glow over the desolate wilderness, revealing the outlines of the rugged plateaus. The whole scene was unmarred, a masterpiece of uncharted space.

"It's beautiful," I murmured. It was the perfect backdrop for an engagement; I couldn't have planned it better myself.

Nice one, Jesus.

I turned to Cea, but she wasn't looking at me or out the window. She'd pulled out her phone and was typing rapidly. The glare of the backlit screen disrupted the ambiance and threw her features into harsh relief. "Looks like the nonessential power to this entire wing is out."

I sighed. If it was nonessential, then it could wait ten minutes. We wouldn't get another moment like this. Why couldn't she see what I saw—the beauty that was right in front of her?

TWO YEARS AGO

"Wanna see something cool?"

"Always," Cea said, slamming her laptop shut. I'd found her in a lounge near the dorms, sipping a soda and scrolling mindlessly on her device. No one else was around—the perfect opportunity to do something slightly against the rules.

I gestured for her to follow. "This way—but you have to promise not to tell Nic."

"Oh, I'm *in*." She grinned, tossed her device aside, and stood up.

I led her out of the lounge. We crossed the central hallway, cut through Wing 3, and then started down a long, dimly lit corridor that wrapped around the exterior of the base.

"Where are we going?" she asked, suspicion edging her voice.

"Wing 11."

She halted in the middle of the hall. "But that wing's been decommissioned for years."

"Exactly." I grinned and kept walking.

She didn't follow. "What could possibly be back there?"

"You'll see. Come on!"

"Is it safe?" she called, her voice getting farther away as she refused to move.

I turned around to face her and walked backwards. "I promise—but you'll need one of these."

She finally started moving towards me—slowly. I stopped in front of the gate for Wing 11. Each door in the base was equipped with a storage compartment for emergency supplies. I yanked on the bright yellow handle and pried the access panel off, pulling out two oxygen masks.

I tossed one at her. "The seals in the hallway are leaking, so the air's a bit thin."

She barely caught the mask, holding it away from her like it was a venomous snake. "Ephesus, I—"

"Once you get in the room, it's fine." I strapped my mask on. "I promise it's worth it."

She was not convinced. "Look, I don't—"

"Cea." I raised my voice to be heard through the plastic mouthpiece. I touched her arm. "Do you trust me?"

She stared at me, eyes flickering as she ran the numbers like a computer. Then she gingerly slid her mask on.

I grabbed her hand. "Follow me."

I pressed my thumb to the keypad; the lock was old and had been easy to pick. The doors slid open slowly, their hydraulics lacking grease. The hall beyond was cold and abandoned, lit only by the slit of daylight that filtered through the grimy windows. We navigated around abandoned equipment and fallen ceiling tiles as I led her to the door at the far end of the hall.

I paused in front of the door. "Close your eyes."

She glared at me, then obeyed. Her rapid breaths fogged the inside of her mask.

I opened the door and took both of her hands, guiding her into the room. "Keep coming, almost there... Here." I stopped her in the middle of the room. I tossed my mask aside, then reached up and gently removed hers. "Okay, you can look now."

She opened her eyes—and gasped.

The place was a jungle. It was a greenhouse, one of the original ones from when the base was first built. It had been decommissioned years ago in favor of newer models, but evidently a few seedlings had been left behind. Those plants had multiplied, turning the place into an enchanted forest. Tangled foliage spilled over the edge of the raised beds and pooled on the floor, and fuzzy moss concealed the rusting metal walls. Flowering vines snaked up the beams that supported the honeycomb glass ceiling, making the room dance with speckled shadows.

"How..." Cea spun in a slow circle, her curls bouncing on her shoulders. "I thought they cut the power to this room."

"Me too, but they wired it wrong. This room is on the same circuit as Wing 12, so the sprinklers are still running. It 'rains' in here twice a week." I inhaled deeply. The air was rich with the smell of wet dirt and living things. If you closed your eyes, it almost smelled like Earth.

I watched her bask in the sight, appreciating how lovely she looked with her head tipped back, her eyes wide, her face flushed in awe. "Do you like it?" I prodded.

"It's amazing. You should show Sardis," she murmured, running her fingers through a trailing vine.

I chuckled. She was right; the base's horticulturist would be in heaven amongst all these wild plants. But he could wait.

"I will," I promised. "But I wanted to share it with you first."

She glanced back at me. She frowned, but her stare wasn't suspicious—it was questioning. Hopeful.

I reached out and gently took her hand. "I'm enjoying this."

"Me too," she said, looking up at the dome again. "It's beautiful."

"No, I mean I'm enjoying *this*." I tugged on her hand. "Us."

Her eyes returned to mine. We stared at each other, souls open, wading into deep waters as we both tested what it would feel like to orbit our lives around that word. *Us.*

Slowly, she threaded her fingers with mine. "I am too."

*

I yanked my eyes away from the starry sky. I had let too many perfect moments pass us by—too many opportunities to start forever. I wouldn't make the same mistake again.

I pinched her knee. "Cea. Please. I need an answer."

"Ephesus," she groaned in a tone as cold as a slamming door, "not now. We need to go check the generator."

She brushed my hand away and stood up. I knelt there, staring at the jewelry box in my palm, struggling not to drown as rejection sucked the oxygen out of the room.

I was no fool; I knew what her gestures meant. I had the answer I'd spent two years waiting for.

She was going to say no. Again.

4: CEA

I can't marry you.

I ran for the door, leaving Ephesus kneeling on the floor. I didn't look back at him. I knew what I would see—the frown on his face, the pain in his eyes, the tightness of his muscles as he gripped the couch to keep from losing himself in a storm of rejection. We'd been through this whole song and dance before. There had been nowhere to run then, nothing to do but awkwardly bid each other goodnight as he blinked away the tears he thought I couldn't see.

How I wanted to say yes. I wanted nothing more than to accept his proposal and let him sweep me away into happily ever after. But that future didn't exist, not yet. Not when his name was on the government's most wanted list, and his sister was starting a war, and Nic was running to Beijing, the most hostile city on Earth, to try to prevent it all.

Why couldn't Ephesus see that? Why couldn't he understand that this was not the right time? I loved him; surely he knew that. But we couldn't do this. Not here, not now.

The control panel for the cafeteria doors was out, screen an eerie black. I pried open the emergency panel and yanked on the manual release lever. I let out my breath in thanks when it worked; the doors ground open, hydraulics hissing.

The comforting glow of artificial light shone down the hall. I ran back to Wing 1 and was relieved to find that the power in the rest of the base seemed to be operating normally. Everything was running at full capacity, the buzz of fluorescents and grind of distant generators omnipresent in the hallway.

"Looks like just Wing 7 is out," I declared, knowing without looking that Ephesus wasn't far behind me. "Let's go check the control room."

I led the way, jogging to stay three paces ahead of him—just far enough to prevent polite conversation. I heard his feet pounding behind me, but he wisely said nothing.

I scanned the passing labs and hallways as we ran, but the rest of the base seemed undisturbed. The few people who were still on shift were going about their business as if nothing had happened, making me hope it was just a localized glitch.

Sydney was on staff in the control room when we arrived. Sydney was the kind of person who volunteered for the graveyard shift because he would rather stare at a monitor than talk to people, or so he claimed. He'd been here for five years, ever since he was an intern in college, and in that time I'd never heard him have a full conversation with anybody.

He frowned at us as we entered, like we were disturbing his private sanctum. "If this is about the power outage in Wing 7, I'm already on it."

Ephesus walked up to the desk and took charge. "Yes, it is—we were in the room when the power went out."

"Oh." Sydney pushed one side of his headphones off his ear. "You guys good?" he asked in a tone that suggested he didn't really care one way or another.

"It was just the lights," I answered dismissively. "What happened?"

"Well, according to the diagnostic I just ran, the power supply is fine." He angled the monitor to face us, revealing a program that proved he had, in fact, been doing actual work. "There's power going to that wing. So whatever the problem is, it's localized."

"Thank God," Ephesus murmured. "So is it a fuse, or…?"

"Probably a relay module," Sydney droned. "Those wear out sometimes. I'll fix it."

Ephesus nodded. "Let's go see."

Sydney frowned. "I said *I'll* fix it," he repeated with absolutely no tact.

Ephesus drew himself to his full height—all five feet, eight inches—and folded his arms. "Dr. Nic left me in charge of the base," he said, which wasn't quite true, but I appreciated the authority. "So forgive me if I want to make sure that this is just a simple relay failure."

Sydney eyed him, then relented with a dramatic sigh. He made a scene of removing his headphones and getting out of the chair. He noisily rooted around in a supply cabinet, leaving us standing there for longer than was probably necessary.

He finally emerged with a tool hit and a headlamp. "After you."

Ephesus led the way back to Wing 7. Sydney pulled a tablet out of his bag and brought up a live feed of the base's power grid. "Looks like the problem is here." He pointed to the screen, where the network of green lines ended in an abrupt red *X.*

We came around the corner and entered the hallway that connected the food storage rooms to the kitchen and cafeteria. The entire hall was dark; even the security lights in the baseboards were out. Sydney flicked on his headlamp, which cast a circle of white light in front of him.

We followed him about ten paces down the hall, staying close so that we didn't trip in the dark. Sydney knelt on the floor and rooted around in his bag for a drill. "Relay box should be right here."

With a few whirs of his power tool, he removed the screws and set the panel aside. He scanned the crevice with his lamp, grumbling to himself. Then, without any explanation of what he was doing, he stuck his head into the hole in the wall, taking most of the light with him.

Ephesus and I stood in the uncomfortable silence while we watched Sydney grunt and dig around in the wall for a minute. Then Ephesus moved beside me. He stepped close to me, his shoulders brushing mine in the shadow.

I tensed. *Not now.*

He felt around with his hand until he found mine. "I'll wait," he said, quietly enough that Sydney couldn't hear. "But I need an answer. I have to hear it from you."

I closed my eyes. "How long can you wait?"

His response was instant. "As long as it takes."

TWO YEARS AGO

"Drop what you're doing."

Ephesus obeyed me, quite literally. The test tube he was holding almost ended up on the floor as he whipped around. "Cea! What are you doing here?"

"Kidnapping you," I announced. "I've got a surprise for you."

He arched his eyebrows suspiciously, and rightfully so—it was quite the role reversal for us. He was usually the one planning surprises, showing up at lunch with cookies he'd baked, giving me gifts when I least expected it. But Nic had been working him around the clock for the last several weeks, designing something for his precious Wing 74. I hadn't seen Ephesus in days, so I decided to take the initiative.

"Sounds amazing, but I'm not supposed to go on break until—well, ever," Ephesus grumbled, even though he was already putting caps on the open tubes.

"I may or may not have bribed Sydney into helping me fudge the time logs…" I flipped my hair in triumph. "Just don't tell Nic."

He laughed. "You're amazing."

"I know." I shoved a small cooler into his vacated hands. "Follow me, and hurry!"

I took off running, and he matched my pace. I led us around the back way, taking side halls and ducking through storage rooms to avoid Nic. We were both out of breath by the time we reached our destination.

I stopped in the middle of an abandoned hallway. After glancing around to make sure we were alone, I knelt and pried a panel off the wall, revealing a service ladder. I ducked into the hole, grabbed the rungs, and started climbing. "This way!" I shouted back at Ephesus.

"Well, this is a tight squeeze," he muttered, his voice bouncing off the cramped metal enclosure. He balanced the cooler on one arm and followed me as we climbed the ladder up the inside of the wall.

I crested the top and waited for him to catch up. He reached the top rung and stopped, slack-jawed. "Wow."

"Isn't it great?" I crooned. We were in Wing 1, where the ceiling was made of a glass dome. In the crevice between the exterior and interior walls was a service walkway that stretched the entire length of the hall. It formed the perfect hiding place and offered an unobstructed view of the countryside.

Ephesus climbed up beside me. "Do you come here often?" he asked, pointing at the pile of stolen blankets I'd used to decorate the space.

"It used to be my favorite place to get away from Nic when I was younger." I handed him a pillow to sit on. "I figured if he never found me here, he won't find you while you're playing hooky."

"What was that like—growing up with Nic?" Ephesus fluffed the pillow and settled in.

I shrugged. "I didn't really 'grow up' with him. He was away at college by the time I could talk, and I didn't move to Mars with him until I was a teenager."

There was a lot more to the story than that—including how my brother had essentially kidnapped me and taken out a restraining order against our parents—but I didn't want to talk about it. I didn't want to talk about the fact that my brother, as tactless as he was, had been right. He'd saved my life by bringing me to Mars, and now I had to wonder if he was right about other things—including the sinister experiments he was doing in Wing 74.

Ephesus didn't push it. He opened the cooler and started pulling out the plastic containers I'd meticulously packed. "Did you make all this?"

"No," I snorted. "Mrs. Sardis helped me. You don't want to taste my cooking."

"I'd be willing to take the risk." He looked up at me with a sly smile, his eyes glittering with an unspoken invitation.

My heart slipped out of rhythm as I realized what he was suggesting. I fantasized about what it would be like to keep a house and cook for my family—my husband. What would it be like to come home to someone, someone other than Nic?

Ephesus seemed to be imagining the same future. "Can I… tell you a secret?"

"Yes," I whispered, my mind auto-filling a dozen things I hoped he would say.

He set the salad aside to take my hand. "You make me think about staying on Mars."

I translated the implications. "You don't want to be here?"

He started to shake his head, then hesitated. "Well, I always wanted to come to Mars—who doesn't? But I don't want to be *here*. Not with Nic. Not like this."

"Same." I gave a bitter chuckle. Any base would probably be preferable to one owned by my brother, if it weren't for one inconvenient detail: Both Ephesus and I practiced a religion that was illegal. On any other base, we'd be criminals. At least Nic, for all his faults, was patronizingly indifferent about religion.

And if he had his way, one day religion wouldn't be illegal at all.

"But where else could we go?" I asked, putting words to the hopeless question I'd failed to answer for the past six years.

"I don't know. But I just… I miss my family," he admitted with a pure simplicity. He looked into my eyes, and for a moment, I saw the heartbreak he tried so hard to conceal. "They're stuck on Earth in that camp, and I can't even call them because Ambrose is such a stickler. Mom's gone, and Dad's at work all the time, and my sister is literally growing up in a prison all by herself. She's barely fourteen."

That's how old I had been when Nic had taken custody of me, and I remembered how many lonely days I'd spent wandering the cold halls, feeling trapped and forgotten.

"When I first got here, all I wanted was to go home to Earth. But when I'm with you…" Ephesus scrunched his nose, as if he realized how sappy his words were. He hesitated, then decided to take the plunge. "You make this home, Cea."

I gripped his hand involuntarily, wanting for all the world to take him up on his offer. I wanted to open the door to my heart and invite him in, invite him to remake our lives around each other.

Except, if he was going to move in, there was one thing he should know.

I slid closer to him, leaning my head on his shoulder. "Can I tell you a secret too?"

He relaxed into me, stroking my fingers with his. "Please."

I took a deep breath and then offered him my greatest gift: "My name isn't really Cea."

"Oh?" he said in a tone that suggested he'd been wondering.

"Yeah. It's short for Laodicea." I looked up at him and waited for his reaction.

He smiled, slow and wide, as he put the pieces together. "I like it."

"You do?" I returned, more incredulously than necessary. Most people tripped around my real name like the elephant in the room, privately wondering what had possessed my parents to curse me like that.

"You don't?" he returned almost as quickly.

"Oh no, I *love* being named after the 'lukewarm church.' It made picking a childhood nickname real easy," I snarked, remembering the schoolyard taunts. Thankfully, religion had fallen so far out of fashion by the time I was in school that most of my classmates were none the wiser—but there was always that one know-it-all who looked it up on the internet.

Ephesus shrugged. "God only disciplines those He loves," he quoted loosely.

I flushed as my entire childhood refocused. I had never considered it like that—that some of the seemingly cold, heartless things that had happened to me might have been mercy.

Do you love me? I whispered into the air.

Only after the thought formed did I realize I was waiting for an answer from more than one person.

Ephesus stared down at our joined hands. "Mine's not much better. I was told to 'return to my first love' or I'm going to be cast out of my place. Real cheery."

The sarcasm in his voice was as dry as a cracker, and I couldn't help but giggle. "I don't think you have anything to worry about. You're the most faithful man I know. You're so calm, so consistent. It's like... the law doesn't even bother you. You're the only Christian I know who isn't ashamed to let everyone know he's unassimilated."

As I laid each word out in the open, I realized I was building a case against my own half-heartedness—and building a case for why I was falling hard and fast for Ephesus Smyrna. I would never find another man like him.

Ephesus pondered the compliment. "What's there to hide?" he wondered aloud, even though, in a world where being a Christian could get you locked in a camp, there was plenty to hide. "I know who I am. And so do you."

I pulled back from him in surprise. I didn't know who I was—because there had been no reason for me to show up. I was who my brother needed me to be, and until something changed in the world, that was the role I would play. I was Cea, Nic's little sister. Nothing more.

Ephesus was not convinced. "Think about it—you can't be 'lukewarm' without first being hot or cold. The Laodicean church fell from something, and so did the Ephesians."

What did I fall from? I wondered but dare not ask. I knew I'd get an answer I didn't like.

Ephesus twisted around to face me and took both of my hands in his. "We're not that different, you and I. We both know what we should be—we just have to have the courage to obey."

It was easy for him to say. He woke up with courage. He was living out his identity every day, resisting the system, challenging Nic, asking questions that no one else dared ask. I didn't have that courage. I knew what the world was like, let alone my brother.

Ephesus let go of one hand to reach up and brush my curls off my shoulder. "I've seen the real you. I know you have a passion for justice and a desire to defend the innocent. That's who *God* made you to be. That's who you are. You don't have to be the person your brother made you to be, Laodicea."

I gasped. I'm not sure which startled me more—the content of his sentence, or how warm and intimate my full name sounded rolling off his tongue.

Suddenly, I wanted to be that person. I wanted to do everything I could to hold on to that feeling, to become the person Ephesus thought I was. Bold. Fearless. Holy.

But was that person even real? I didn't know what life lived outside of my brother's shadow would look like. Who would I even be if I wasn't afraid of him?

I combined the swirling questions into one hesitant, "I don't… know if I can."

Ephesus cradled the back of my neck with his hand. His eyes locked with mine, expression deep and unafraid. "I'll help you."

Yes, my spirit answered, and I kissed him.

I saw it coming—the flicker on his face as he leaned forward—and I took it. I let him pull me to himself, and I initiated, lifting my lips to meet his. The gesture was gentle, unhurried, like he would have held me for a thousand years until time stopped. I'm not sure how long we sat there before he finally let me go.

"Well," I said as we shifted apart and struggled to pick up the conversation. "Now you *really* can't tell Nic."

"Oh, I'm going to tell him," Ephesus declared. "When I'm ready to ask you to marry me."

It was stated so forthrightly, without even a hint of sarcasm, that I had no idea how to react except to blush.

He winked. "What? I told you I wouldn't complicate things. I'm going to marry you, Laodicea. I just wasn't planning on it being *today*, so I haven't bought a ring yet."

The comforting sarcasm returned to his voice. I laughed and snuggled back up next to him. "I'll wait."

*

"Well, good news and bad news," Sydney grunted from inside the wall.

I quickly shook off Ephesus's hand and stepped away. "Good news?" I asked, desperate for some.

"I was right, it's the relay module. The power connection is fine," Sydney explained, voice muffled by insulation.

"And bad news?" Ephesus prompted. He mercifully put some space between us.

For an answer, Sydney sighed and sat back on his haunches. He turned to us and held up a wire into the light of his headlamp.

The end had been cut.

5: EPHESUS

"Who would do this?"

The ruined power module sat on the desk, mocking me with my failure. Nothing like this had ever happened while Nic was governor. He'd managed to kidnap a dozen people and keep an entire wing full of secrets under lock and key for nearly a decade, and he never had any incidents until Philadelphia turned him in. I'd been unofficially in charge for less than twenty-four hours, and already someone had sabotaged the station.

My secret dream of owning my own base on Mars faded back into the recesses of my mind. If Nic had trusted me before, he wouldn't after he heard about this.

"It had to be intentional. Right?" Cea said too loudly, her volume begging for another explanation. She fidgeted in the chair across from me. "There's no way three wires just 'wore out' at the same time."

I agreed with her. It definitely couldn't be chalked up to faulty wiring. Someone had done this intentionally, and what's worse, it looked like we were dealing with an amateur. Sydney had removed the damaged module from the wall and discovered three separate wires had been cut, like the perpetrator had tried several before they found the one they wanted. The cuts were gnarly, the ends of the wires split and frayed, as if the villain had used scissors too dull for the job.

At this point, we were lucky they hadn't cut something critical.

But who would want to sabotage the base? I twisted a damaged wire in my fingers, echoing Cea's question. No new colonists had moved onto the station since the fallout with Thames, and all his accomplices had long since fled and dropped off the grid. Everyone left had lived on base for at least a year, which could only mean one thing.

They'd just been waiting for an opportunity.

I turned to face the computer. "Who has access to that hallway?" I asked aloud, even as I ran a search for that information.

Cea frowned in concentration. "The kitchen and food storage are on a security level five—so, basically everyone but visitors."

That didn't limit the playing field, and the security cameras were no help either. That had been my first thought—to look at the cameras and catch the perpetrator in the act. But the access panel for the power relay was tucked around a corner, conveniently out of sight of the cameras. It was a busy hallway, and it connected to the kitchen, the food storage rooms, and three other wings. Dozens of people had walked down that hallway last night, and as soon as the lights went out, there were ample ways for the vandal to escape unseen. It would be nearly impossible to pinpoint any suspects, and even if we could prove that someone had gone down that hallway, it would all be conjecture.

I grunted my frustration and raked my hands through my hair. A saboteur was roaming the base, and I had nothing to go on. I'd spent most of the night and all of today scouring the activity logs, looking for anything out of the ordinary, but even the base's AI hadn't flagged any suspicious behavior. At this point, my best mathematical probability was to wait for the perpetrator to strike again and correlate the similarities.

I didn't like that solution.

Cea took a breath, long and tentative. "What are we going to do?"

I closed my eyes and prayed for wisdom. We—I—had to do something. Cea needed me; the base needed me. Nic was gone, and it was up to me to keep this place running until he got back. I finally had the opportunity to be an active player in the game, and I wasn't going to sit around waiting for my opponent to make the first move.

I sat up and resumed typing. "I'm increasing the sensitivity on the algorithm—if there's even the tiniest blip in the power, I want to know about it."

Cea nodded, but she didn't look at all comforted.

I rapidly swiped through menus as I narrated my actions. "And I'm raising the security clearance on all the critical infrastructure—the kitchen, the greenhouses, the generator—to level two. I want all common doors locked at all times. No one goes anywhere without leaving a DNA log."

"Good idea," Cea echoed, her tone shifting. She sat up straighter and looked impressed.

I tried not to let it go to my head. "Sydney and I are going to conduct safety checks on all the major systems. If this vandal has tampered with anything important, we'll find it." I stood up and grabbed a tablet from the desk.

Cea jumped up to follow. "I'll help."

I grinned.

Just then, the computer screeched at me. I glanced back at the monitor and saw that my modified algorithm was doing its job—it had already kicked out an error.

"What's wrong?" Cea asked, squinting at the screen.

"The computer found an anomaly." I bent over the keyboard and pulled up the report. "The power is flickering in and out in a handful of rooms. It could just be a loose connection…"

"Or our vandal could be in the act," Cea voiced my suspicions. "Let's go."

I pulled up the location of the outage on the map—and for a brief moment, I lost my courage.

Of course it would be there.

My trepidation must have made it onto my face, because Cea stepped closer to me. "Ephesus? What is it? Where's it coming from?"

I sighed. "Wing 74."

TWO YEARS AGO

"What are you doing?"

I reacted, closing the program and slamming my laptop shut in a motion that was anything but casual. I whipped around—and realized who it was.

"Cea." I let out my breath and tried to put the brakes on my heart rate. *If it had been anybody else…*

She stood behind me in the darkened hall, her frame silhouetted by the dim security lighting. "What are you doing?" she repeated.

"Nothing," I fudged, even though it was an obvious lie. It was 2 in the morning, and I was kneeling in the back hallway of Wing 74 with my laptop wired into the security panel for a door. I was obviously doing something.

But for the first time since I'd met her, I wasn't going to tell Cea the truth. I didn't want her involved in case I failed. Nic would kill me—for real this time— if he found out what I was doing, and I wanted Cea to have culpable deniability. He'd already threatened to revoke her access to Wing 74 after he caught her visiting me; I hated to think what he'd do if he found out she'd helped me escape.

Unfortunately for me, Cea wasn't gullible. I couldn't see her expression in the shadows, but I could hear the suspicion in her voice. "Were you trying to—"

"There's been power failures in this hallway," I cut her off. I spoke loudly for the benefit of any cameras that might be within range. "The lights keep flickering on and off. I couldn't sleep so... I decided to try my hand at it." I enunciated the words slowly, prompting her to take the bait.

She didn't. The doubt in her voice cracked, replaced by genuine fear. "Ephesus, no, please. Don't do this."

What else am I supposed to do? I was locked in a secret lab with an unhinged mad scientist who was determined to destroy Earth with a chemical superweapon. I'd finally found out what Nic was building on Mars—and why he needed me—and I wanted nothing to do with it. But Nic wouldn't take no for an answer. He'd kidnapped me, locked me in Wing 74, and given me a choice: I could help him build his superweapon and start a war against the United, or I could eat a bullet.

I didn't like either of those options. Meanwhile, my family thought I was dead because Nic had quite dramatically staged my death to cover his tracks.

So of course I was trying to escape. Currently, my best plan was attempting to hot wire the locks on the doors. It hadn't worked yet, but I'd at least managed to hack into the program that controlled them. I'd been copying the database to a laptop when Cea found me.

I took a deep breath and started unplugging my cables from the wall. "This doesn't involve you, Cea," I said, even though that was another lie. Nic was her brother; she was more involved than she wanted to admit. "Just walk away."

"No, Ephesus, please, listen to me. If Nic finds out..." She glanced behind her, as if making sure her brother hadn't materialized out of the shadows.

She didn't have to finish the sentence; I was aware of the risks. "I know, and I don't care."

"But I do."

I stopped and looked up at her.

She knelt beside me. "Ephesus, if they find out what you're doing, they *will* kill you. Carnegie thinks Nic should have killed you three weeks ago. If you try something, I'm not going to be able to convince him—"

"What do you mean?" I turned around to face her, then rephrased the question. "What did you do?"

She gnawed on her lip, as if realizing she'd gone too far. She weighed her choices and mercifully decided to let me in on her secret. "I talked Nic out of killing you."

I sat in silence as I struggled to reboot my universe around that revelation.

She fidgeted with her curls, her eyes still hidden in the darkness. "After you tried to alert the authorities, Carnegie wanted to kill you. They were going to do it, but I happened to hear them shouting in the hall and... I convinced Nic to forge the paperwork instead."

The fact that Cea had begged for my life—and Nic, the soulless scientist, had allowed it—shed new light on both characters. But even more disconcerting was the realization that my girlfriend, the one person I loved on this planet, had been involved in faking my death and lying to my family.

I struggled to find a center of gravity to fix my emotions on, then realized there was only one solution. If Cea and I were going to survive this, I had to do what I'd always promised I'd do: Uncomplicate things.

Jesus, help me.

I scooped both her hands in mine. "Thank you for saving me."

She just nodded, her gaze on the floor.

I pulled her closer. "But we both know that what Nic's doing isn't right."

She still didn't respond, and I felt her body tense—making me wonder if, in fact, she *didn't* know that.

"Cea." I tugged on her hand. "This is wrong. Red Rain is wrong. Tell me you agree."

"I..." she croaked, barely managing to get the first word out. "I don't... I don't know anymore."

I weighed my tone of voice. "You think it was right for him to kidnap me and lie to my family?"

"No," she snipped immediately, giving me some hope.

I rubbed her fingers. "Then you must know that the rest of this is wrong. Bombing Earth—that's not the solution."

"But what else can we do?" she cried, still refusing to concede.

I could think of several alternatives, but that was irrelevant. She knew better. She could have stopped her brother a dozen times before now, and she hadn't, even though she clearly hated what he was doing. Why? I chewed the silence, shifting through her words and trying to decode the fear, the lie that was driving her to do something I knew she didn't want to do.

The Holy Spirit breathed in my ear. I repeated His words slowly, salting them with all the affection I had stored up in my heart for this woman. I knew that if she could just see what I—what we—saw in her, she would know what to do. We could fix this. Together.

"This isn't justice, Cea," I began. "What Nic's doing—it won't save people. It will kill them. It won't bring freedom, and it won't create tolerance for people like us. If Nic succeeds, the world will be worse off than it started—and we'll have helped him get there."

She didn't argue, her fingers limp in mine.

I leaned forward, allowing the hope to build in my voice. "There is another way. We don't have to do this. *You* don't have to do this."

I cupped her chin and forced her to look at me. She stared back, her eyes a swirling galaxy of confusion.

"Laodicea." I parsed the name out, pulling her identity from the darkness. "This is not you."

She looked at me, hoping, believing.

And then she closed her eyes.

"Ephesus," she sighed. Her tone walled up even as tears threatened to seep through the cracks. "You don't understand."

But I did understand; she had no idea how well I understood what she was going through. "But I do—"

"No." She slapped a period on my arguments. "You don't understand what you're up against. You don't know what Nic's like. I do—I've lived with him for six years."

And that's exactly why you are the way you are.

I struggled with how to tell her that—how to make her see that her brother was controlling her. But she didn't give me a chance to find the words. "This isn't a joke to him. He's spent years building this project, and he's not going to let you ruin it."

As she talked, her words gained speed and venom. For a terrifyingly eerie moment, she sounded exactly like Nic.

She barreled on. "He's got weapons, and he will use them. He will kill you to protect his project, and I can't... I can't lose you!"

Her anger crumbled like a house of cards. All the fear and pain came pouring out as she collapsed in my arms, sobbing. "I can't lose you!" she screamed, her voice jagged like broken glass. "You're the only good thing in my life, and if Nic kills you, it will be my fault, and I can't, I can't..."

I pulled her into my lap and held her tightly, wishing I could suffocate the sound of her tears. Each shattered cry scraped at my soul and exposed the only emotion that could keep me in this place.

"What... what do you want me to do?" I whispered in her ear.

"Please don't fight him," she cried, gasping out each word in between sobs. "Please, just give it time. We'll... we'll figure something out. Maybe... maybe it won't work. Maybe the project will fail. He has to let you go sometime. He promised you could come back when he's ready."

Nic had told me as much. In a bitter irony, I knew he would keep that promise.

Cea sucked in air and struggled to control her sobs. "Please, Ephesus. I can't lose you. Not like this. Promise me you won't push him."

I stared over her head at the long shadows in Wing 74—the prison I would be calling home if I agreed.

She wasn't comforted by my silence. She grabbed my shirt like I was the only thing keeping her head above water. "Please, Ephesus. Do it for me."

Those four words slammed into my conscience like nails on a coffin. "Okay," I said, even as nauseating anguish swelled up my throat. "I'll do it for you."

She relaxed, her dead weight sagging in my arms. "Thank you," she whispered, and fought down another sniff.

I pulled her to me, rocking us both as I waited for the world to settle around the terrifying promise I'd just made. "I'll wait," I repeated. "I'll wait for you."

*

It all came rushing back. The screech of locked doors, the guilt-induced nightmares, the cold loneliness as I waited for a girl who never came back—it all washed over me like a flood. I felt like I was treading through chest-deep water as we drew closer to Wing 74, my breaths becoming fast and shallow.

Cea must have noticed, because she did something she hadn't done in years. She slid up next to me and took my hand. The warmth of her fingers brought life back into my nerves, and I immediately remembered why I'd sacrificed it all.

"We're here," she announced unnecessarily. I knew exactly where we were. It looked so different, so benign from the outside. The entryway was plain and undecorated; you would never imagine that anything important had happened behind the door.

Cea mercifully took the initiative and opened the gate. We stepped inside, her leading the way, and I was shocked to find that I didn't recognize the wing at all.

My sister had off-handedly mentioned that Nic had been remodeling Wing 74, but she'd undersold his enthusiasm. In a mere month, he'd managed to strip the wing down to its shell. The wall ahead of us had been knocked in, revealing the skeleton of what used to be a lab. Insulation sagged from the ceiling, and we had to pick our way around stacks of paneling and over slippery paint tarps. I scanned the hallways, made foreign by the rapid construction, and tried to decide if the unfamiliarity made me feel better or worse.

I pried my hand from Cea's to open my tablet. "The power fluctuations are coming from Rooms 12 through 14. I think those used to be storage rooms."

"Used to" was definitely the operative word. Room 12 was the first one we came to. I opened the door, revealing a mess that rivaled the clutter in Nic's closet. All the old storage containers had been pushed against the wall and half-heartedly covered with tarps. The center of the ceiling was ripped open, exposing the heating duct. The handiwork was inglorious at best. Ceiling tiles had been haphazardly shoved aside, and insulation and loose wires dangled from the hole, like the roof had thrown up its guts.

"Well, this won't pass inspection," I muttered. I attempted to turn the lights on to no avail. The electricity sputtered, the displaced fluorescents crackling sinisterly, before the room went dark again. "I'm guessing the power is just fluctuating because of the shoddy electrical job."

Cea shifted by my side. "Do you smell something?"

I paused and took a stock of all five senses. There were a lot of foreign odors competing for dominance—paint thinner, sawdust, the manufactured smell of new plastic. "Not really."

She took a few steps down the hall, nose twitching. "I think it's coming from Room 13."

I followed her to the door across the hall. I thought I caught a faint whiff of something, but I couldn't place the smell. I looked at my tablet and flipped through the notifications. The sensors for Room 13 were all over the map, including an elevated temperature reading that had triggered just a moment ago.

I frowned at the screen. The sensors must not be properly installed; if the computer was to be believed, the temperature in the room was over a thousand degrees. *There's no way...*

I reached out and brushed the closed door with my fingers, then yelped as the hot metal seared my hand. I jerked back. Too late I registered what was happening. The heat, the distinct smell seeping under the door...

"Cea, don't—"

She didn't hear me. She swiped her hand over the panel, opening the door and releasing a billow of smoke into the hall.

The room was on fire.

6: CEA

I stumbled back, hacking. I could barely process what I was seeing through the stinging smoke: The room was engulfed in flames. The exposed insulation and loose building materials created the perfect catalyst as the fire licked around the metal room, searching for an escape. Sparks leapt through the open door and caught on a roll of carpet that was sitting in the hallway.

Ephesus yanked his shirt over his nose and darted forward, trying to stamp the carpet out with his shoe. "Close the door!" he yelled, voice muffled. "We have to keep it from spreading!"

I copied him, pulling my shirt over my nose. I ducked and tried to find the door panel through the burning haze. Smoke was billowing out of the room and flooding the ceiling, spreading down the hall towards the nearest smoke detector.

And then I abruptly remembered what would happen when the fire alarm went off.

"Leave it!" I screeched, grabbing Ephesus's sleeve and dragging him back. "We need to get out of here!"

He followed me as I started running down the hall. "But the fire—"

"If the alarm goes off, it will lock the whole wing down!"

The emergency system on a space station was merciless. Fire spread rapidly in the artificially oxygenated air, and a breech in the hull could depressurize the entire building. In the event of an emergency, the computer would lock the entire wing down, deactivate the air circulation, and cut the power to save the rest of the building.

Tough luck if you were stuck on the wrong side of the door.

I ran for Gate A, praying Ephesus would keep up. We had only seconds. If we could just make it to the door—

Too late.

The fire alarm went off. The sirens wailed, colliding with the adrenaline ringing in my ears. The hall plunged into darkness as the power died, and then the battery-operated emergency lights kicked in. I stumbled forward and reached the gate just in time to hear the hydraulics groan as the airlock dropped in place.

Oh God, no.

Ephesus crashed into me. "Pull the emergency release!"

"There is no emergency release!" I screamed. Wing 74 was a prison; it didn't have the safety features of the rest of the base. If you were stuck inside, you were expected to go down with the ship.

"I am *not* dying here!" Ephesus roared. "There has to be another way out."

There wasn't. Gate A was the only way out of the wing; that was the whole point. "There isn't—"

He didn't let me finish. He grasped me by the shoulders and shook me. "There has to be a way! Think!"

I wasn't sure if he was yelling at me or himself, but I didn't have an answer for him. "I don't know! You're the one who lived here! I can't—"

"Laodicea." The sudden calm of his voice was completely dissonant from the chaos around us. He tipped me back and stared into my eyes, enunciating each word clearly. "Think. We can do this, but I need you to work with me. What about the manual extinguishers? Where's the CO2?"

"It's too late—" I started, then hacked. The fire was spreading rapidly down the hall; smoke was already clogging the entryway. There was no way Ephesus and I could put the blaze out by ourselves. There probably wasn't enough portable CO2 in the hallway to suffocate the flames—

Suffocate.

An idea spawned. Ephesus and I couldn't put the fire out by hand. But if we could vent the wing, the thin Martian atmosphere would do it for us.

I shoved Ephesus out of the way and ran across the hall. The remains of Labs 1 and 2 were there. All the delicate machinery had been removed, but the supply shelves were still in the corner. The racks were loaded with a sparkling rainbow of jarred chemicals.

I grabbed the edge of the shelf and pulled, trying to drag it away from the wall. "Help me!"

"Why?" Ephesus exclaimed, even as he grabbed the other side of the rack.

"I'm taking a page from your sister's book!"

I didn't wait to see if he understood my meaning. With an adrenaline-powered heave, I managed to drag the rack an inch away from the wall. A bottle rocked off the shelf and shattered on the ground.

Ephesus pushed me aside. Bracing his foot on the wall, he shoved all his weight into the rack and knocked it over. The metal shelf landed with a terrific crash and the shattering of a hundred bottles. I couldn't hear the hissing and cracking over the sirens, but I could see the steam and bubbles as the chemicals began to mix.

"Get away from there!" Ephesus hauled me back, coughing. The lab was filling with smoke. I glanced behind us and saw that we had only minutes before the flames reached the spill.

"We have to get as far away from here as possible!" I shouted.

He didn't need to be told. He grabbed my arm and ran, dragging me down the hall in the opposite direction of the fire. We raced into the depths of Wing 74, closing each door behind us. I counted down in my head.

Ten... nine... eight...

"Here!" I pointed to a food storage locker. Its thick, insulated walls were our best bet. I pried the emergency panel off the nearest door and grabbed the oxygen masks, throwing one at Ephesus. He caught it and held the door to the locker open for me. We darted inside, and the heavy door slammed shut just in time.

An explosion rocked the wing, muffled through the thick steel. I dropped to the floor and covered my head. Ephesus threw himself over me and shielded me with his chest. Another explosion shattered the atmosphere.

I pinched my eyes shut and prayed.

There was another explosion, and another. The room shuddered, and a forgotten can fell off the shelf and dented the floor. I heard Ephesus muttering in togues, his panicked breaths brushing my ear.

Jesus, save us!

And then, suddenly, there was silence.

Ephesus waited one minute, two, and then he sat up. I straightened and looked around. The walls of our bunker had held. The hall outside was quiet except for the distant wail of sirens.

"You're insane," Ephesus muttered. Then he laughed, the sound a pitiful attempt to relieve the tension.

I joined him. "It worked for your sister. Do you think that explosion was big enough to puncture the hull?"

"We'll be lucky if it didn't take the whole ceiling off." He pulled his tablet out of his lab coat pocket and flipped through the apps. "Most of the wing is still online, so that's a good sign. The temperature and pressure are dropping rapidly."

I let out my breath. It worked. *Thank you, Jesus.* "How long do you think the oxygen will last in here?" I rapped the textured metal floor with my knuckles.

"Long enough for them to find us. I'm calling them now."

I waited while Ephesus called Mr. Sardis and walked him through the situation. Sydney ran a systems check and confirmed that we'd punctured the hull in the lab, depressurizing the wing and putting out the fire. Thankfully the damage was minor enough that a rescue crew could get in. We'd have to wait while they put out the last of the fire, patched the breech, and repressurized the wing. But our portable oxygen would hold until then.

I put my mask on. "Do you think the vandal started the fire intentionally, or were they just stupid and cut a live wire?"

Ephesus adjusted the strap on his mask. "I don't know, but hopefully the door logs will tell us something." He paused and regarded me.

"What?" I prodded.

Even the mask couldn't conceal the smile on his face. "I was right."

I frowned. "About what?"

He winked. "You did have the answers."

NINE MONTHS AGO

This is a mistake.

I tried to talk myself out of it as I ran to Wing 74. I shouldn't involve him; it would only make things worse. It would be better for all three of them to live in blissful ignorance until I could figure out what Nic was up to. This was going to end in disaster or heartbreak or both, and I should stay out of it.

But no matter how much I lectured myself, no matter how many warnings went off in my head, I knew I wouldn't sleep if I didn't tell Ephesus. I'd kept a lot of secrets from him these past two years, but this would not be one of them. He deserved to know.

I stopped in the hall and looked at my phone. Nic was outside doing his monthly check of the perimeter security system. That meant I had an hour tops to get in, get out, and edit the logs before he noticed.

There was no rule preventing me from going to Wing 74. I still had access to all the common doors. But I knew that if Nic found out I'd gone back there today, after all that had happened, he'd suspect something.

After all, I hadn't visited Wing 74 in almost six months.

I braced myself for the torrent of emotions and memories and unlocked the door.

Ephesus was in Lab 1, where he usually worked. The door to the hall was open, and he was bent over the desk with his nose to the screen. He didn't hear me approach over his noisy clacking on the keyboard. I stopped a safe distance away and broke the bubble.

"Ephesus."

He froze, his hands limp on the keys. He hesitated with his back to me, almost as if he were afraid to turn around. He was probably worried I'd vanish as soon as I appeared.

"Cea," he breathed. There was affection and disbelief and elation all muddled in his tone, and it made me sick. Abruptly, he came to life, shoving his keyboard and coffee and the entire desk away from him as he jumped up and ran for me. He opened his arms.

I saw what was coming and sidestepped. "There's something you need to know."

He stopped, hovering on the edge of acceptable distance. "What's wrong?"

There would be no easy way to tell him this, so I took a page from his book and just came out with it. "Your father and sister are here."

He tried and failed to assimilate that information. "What?"

For an answer, I pulled up a video on my phone and handed the device to him. It was security footage from earlier today showing Philadelphia accidentally breaking into Wing 74.

"All these halls!" her recording muttered nervously to herself.

Ephesus held the device close to his face. He replayed the video once, twice. Then, slowly, as if he were afraid the image would shatter like a hologram, he laid his hand on the screen, tracing his sister's silhouette.

I saw the longing stained with anguish flash across his eyes and almost regretted telling him. His family was so close—and it would do him no good.

He blinked, shoving the emotion back where it came from. "What in the world are they doing here?" he asked. He sounded just as incredulous as I had when I'd found out.

"Your dad got called up here for that new project they're doing in Wing 38—the one with all the big government funding."

Ephesus folded his brow and handed my phone back to me. "Does Nic know we're related?"

"He has to. He has access to all the paperwork." That was the only logical conclusion, but I hadn't yet found the courage to confront Nic about it.

"Seems like an unnecessary risk when I'm supposed to be 'dead,'" Ephesus muttered. For a brief moment, his analytical brain overrode his emotions as he ran the numbers. "It doesn't make any sense for him. Why would he do that?"

He looked at me for a better explanation, but I had none. I agreed—it didn't make sense. Ephesus may be stuck behind a locked door, but there was still evidence of his existence, quirks in the system that couldn't be explained away. Even Philadelphia had picked up on that, and she'd barely been here twenty-four hours. It seemed like an incredible risk to bring Ephesus's family here if Nic wanted him to remain dead.

Unless, of course, my brother didn't expect to be keeping secrets much longer.

I shuddered and shoved the implications out of my mind. "I think he wasn't planning on you finding out," I said dismissively.

Ephesus paused and reconsidered the situation. "Thank you for telling me."

I just nodded, suddenly afraid to speak. The silence returned, bringing with it all the questions and accusations and pain and longing that formed the chasm between us.

Ephesus, as always, had no fear of breaching the gap. "I missed you," he said gently. There was no criticism in his voice, but my conscience more than made up for it. It had been months since I'd seen him, and our last meeting was only a passing glance, a hurried *hello* from across the hall as I fled in the other direction. It had been even longer since we'd had a private conversation.

He stepped closer. "Where have you been?"

I flinched. "I went back to Earth for a visit," I said reflexively, even though that only accounted for three weeks of my absence. The real reason was that I couldn't bear to see him.

It had been fine at first. Awkward, yes, but we'd made do, sneaking visits late at night, sharing packed lunches in the lab when Nic was away. The pain had been raw; I could tell Ephesus was stressed. The knowledge that I could unlock the door tormented him almost as much as it tormented me. He'd asked once or twice if I could help him get a message through to his family, but I knew Carnegie would find out when he reviewed the logs. I'd begged him to stop asking. He'd obeyed.

After that, he'd plastered on a veneer of compliance. I knew he was doing it for my benefit—the smiles, the quiet tones of voice, the way he forced himself to walk slowly down the hall like he had nowhere to be. He was faking it for me.

And then, one day, he wasn't.

I saw the change, slow and gradual. He reached an unspoken impasse with my brother; Ephesus agreed to work on a different project, and Nic agreed not to kill him. After that, Ephesus began to settle into the rhythm of the lab. His calm was no longer an act, his patience no longer thin. His sarcasm came back, and even though he didn't smile very often, he seemed at peace.

And I hated it.

He'd become just like everyone else on base. He'd accepted that this was a war he couldn't win, and he stopped bucking the system. He gave my brother a wide berth and minded his own business. He compromised, just like everyone else who had been bullied by my brother.

Just like me.

That wasn't the Ephesus I knew. That wasn't the Ephesus I'd fallen in love with. The Ephesus I loved fought the system, held his ground, asked the questions no one else was asking.

But that Ephesus was gone. He was gone because I'd asked him to leave.

If Ephesus noticed the change in himself, he wasn't letting it stop him from pursuing me. "Would you like to have dinner with me?"

I winced, remembering the first time he'd asked me that—and wondered, suddenly, if I could have saved him a world of pain if I'd turned him down. "I can't. Nic will be getting in soon."

He didn't push it. "When are you coming back?"

I wasn't sure whether he meant the question figuratively or literally, but I didn't want to have this conversation. Not now. "I need to go," I repeated, turning way.

"What are you going to tell Phil?" he called after me.

I froze. I had no idea. I had no idea where I was going to go from here. I'd opened a door I knew I shouldn't have, and now I couldn't shut it. "I don't know," I said honestly and a little bitterly.

"She's going to ask questions," he warned.

"She already has," I snapped, glancing back at him, "and I don't have the answers for her."

He frowned at me, but it wasn't an accusatory frown. It was a thoughtful, pensive frown, like he was studying me and parsing his words. "You've always had the answers, Cea."

No, I don't. There are no answers.

He mistook my silence as an opportunity. He reached out and grabbed my hands, just like he always did when he was about to open his soul to me. "You don't have to do this. You don't have to go along with this. This isn't you."

I yanked my hands from his grasp. That—that was the other reason I had been avoiding our meetings. I didn't want to hear what he had to say.

"I have to go. Nic will be back any minute." I turned and walked away before he could question that excuse.

"Laodicea," he called when I reached the door.

I hesitated, my hand hovering over the panel.

He took a breath—that same sigh that always prefaced his confessions. "I'm still waiting for you."

I opened the door and ran.

He wisely didn't follow. I darted into the hall and ran through Gate A, then Gate 73, then Gate 34—racing to get as far away from him as possible. I stumbled through the hallways, taking back routes and looping over my tracks as if I were trying to lose a ghost.

But you can't outrun feelings. If anything, the pounding of my heart and my shortness of breath made it worse. With every step, the emotions beat into my chest like hailstones. My guilt and regret hurled accusations and shame at me like I was being stoned alive. I hid my face and crashed through the halls until I finally collapsed out of exhaustion.

I slumped on the floor in an abandoned corner. The world continued to spin as my guilt solidified into words.

You don't deserve him.

I didn't, I truly didn't. I was a terrible person. I'd helped forge his death, and I'd been an accomplice in my brother's crimes. For two years I had turned a blind eye as Nic had abused Ephesus and forced him to build a world-ending armory. I'd watched my boyfriend suffer for two years, and I'd said nothing—when all the while I'd had the power to unlock the door.

On top of all that, I'd let my guilt come between us, and I hadn't even visited him. I'd walked away to spare myself and left him in Wing 74, alone, hanging on promises I'd never fulfilled.

And yet, he was still waiting. Waiting for me.

Why? I'd secretly believed—hoped, even—that Ephesus had moved on. This would be so much easier if he would just give up on me, on *us*. But he hadn't. I'd seen it just now in his eyes, in the brush of his hand. His galaxy still revolved around a future with us together.

And I couldn't tell him that mine did too.

I leaned my head against the cold metal wall and struggled to breathe. There was no "us," and there never would be as long as Nic was in charge. Until Red Rain was complete, Ephesus would have to stay locked in the basement with all of Nic's other secrets. And how long would that be? Nic had been working on Red Rain for over a decade, and he was no closer to finishing. It could be years before the project was complete or he gave up and moved on.

And what if he *did* complete the project? What if he succeeded in defeating the United and liberating Mars? Did I really think there was a future for Ephesus and me in the ashes of Nic's cruel empire?

This is not justice, Cea.

I pinched my eyes shut. Ephesus was right; what Nic was doing was wrong. I'd known that, I'd known that all along. I just didn't want to admit it, because if I agreed, if I drew that line in the sand, I would be accepting the responsibility—the responsibility to change things.

You've always had the answers.

I stared down at my hands, the palms that contained the DNA that could unlock the door. I could change things. Ephesus's family was right here, and I had the power to fix it. I finally had the chance to make up for two years of silence.

Was it worth the risk? Was it worth it for family? For justice?

Was it worth it for him?

I drew a deep breath and sat up. I couldn't get Ephesus out of Wing 74, not right now. Nic would know immediately that he was gone, and he would probably kill the entire family. There was no way I could get Ephesus out safely, not while Nic and Carnegie were on base.

But I could get Philadelphia in.

*

Within two hours the rescue crew had restored the atmosphere, and Ephesus and I gratefully emerged from Wing 74. We submitted ourselves to an obligatory health check by the base's medic, and then Ephesus took charge in a way that would have made Nic proud.

He immediately tasked a crew with fireproofing Wing 74, fixing wiring and removing building materials to prevent another blaze. Meanwhile, he ran a full diagnostic of the base, checking every system and access port to make sure nothing else had been tampered with. He stopped all projects and drafted every inhabitant on base to help, and they all responded willingly. He was probably too busy to notice, but I could tell that the other residents appreciated his confidence and respected his authority, just like I always had.

I barely saw him the rest of the day, or the next. I made myself useful and helped with the cleanup of Wing 74. It gave me plenty of time to think about Ephesus's words and everything that had happened in the last two years. It also gave me plenty of time to pray.

It was early Saturday morning when Ephesus finally called me into his office. I preemptively brought him a coffee and sandwich, rightly deducing that he hadn't had much time to eat in the last thirty-six hours.

He was bent over his computer monitor when I entered. He hadn't shaved and his hair was an adorably disheveled mess, but his eyes were clear, making me hope that he'd at least slept a little.

"Hey baby," he called when the door opened. "I've been reviewing the logs, and I think—"

He stopped when I plunked the plate and coffee mug down in front of him. He looked up at me, and his tense expression melted into a smile. "I could just marry you."

"I'm thinking about it," I said, and too late realized I'd attached a lot of emotion to the statement. The truth was that I *had* been thinking about it since the fire, but now was not the time to start that conversation. I sat on the edge of his desk and pointed at the monitor. "You were saying?"

535

He scarfed a bite of sandwich and spoke around it. "I've reviewed all the door logs and security footage from Wing 74."

"And?"

He swallowed a mouthful of coffee and shook his head. "Absolutely nothing. There was a construction crew in there the day before, but they weren't working anywhere near those rooms. I can't find any evidence that anyone broke into the wing after-hours. The digital logs are pristine—there's absolutely no evidence of tampering."

I chewed my lip. Ephesus was an expert coder; if someone had left a digital trail, he would have found it. "So it was an accident?"

"It's possible."

I caught his inflection. "But you don't think so."

He leaned back in the chair and raked his hands through his hair, making it stick up even worse. "I just don't understand why *now*. There were plenty of fire hazards in that wing, but it's been that way for weeks. The power fluctuations we saw—those just started two days ago. If it wasn't someone tampering with the system, then what changed?"

I drummed my fingers on the desk—and then remembered we weren't in this alone. I closed my eyes and asked God to give Ephesus wisdom.

Ephesus took the opportunity to finish his meal. I let him eat in silence for a minute before asking, "Have there been any other anomalies in the system?"

He chugged the last of his coffee. "None that I've found—"

As if mocking us, the computer screeched.

"Shouldn't have said anything," Ephesus muttered. He sighed and opened the program—then squinted at the screen.

"Another power fluctuation?" I guessed.

"No," he said, voice clouded with confusion. "It's a motion alert."

I straightened. "From where?"

He frowned up at me. "Nic's office."

TWO MONTHS AGO

"Why not?"

It was asked with such simplicity and innocence—and for once, I wished Ephesus wouldn't be so honest.

He knelt on the kitchen floor of my apartment in the containment camp, a ring box in his outstretched hand. He'd gotten down on one knee and asked a four-word question that had ended my world and brought our relationship to a crashing halt.

We'd been doing fine for the last six months. After Philadelphia had turned Red Rain over to the government, they'd sent Nic to jail and evicted me from the base. Left with no functional family and no job, I'd sulked around Boston for a few days, avoiding the Holy Spirit like the plague.

He finally got through to me when Ephesus managed to sneak a text message past the censors:

WOULD YOU LIKE TO HAVE DINNER WITH ME?

I took the hint and accepted.

I turned myself in at camp and had great fun telling the clerk at the assimilation office that I was a Christian and proud of it. They'd never had anyone recant their file before, so it took them an entire workday to figure out how to handle the paperwork. They finally gave up and called Ambrose to come take me to camp.

Ephesus met me on the other side of the gate with open arms.

We then spent the rest of winter catching up on what we should have been doing for the past two years: dating. We cooked together, watched movies I smuggled into camp, and stayed up talking into the wee hours of the morning. We got to know each other and fell in love all over again. Ephesus took it slow, as if we'd just met for the first time, and I loved it.

And then, just when I thought I knew myself again, he popped the question.

I refused him immediately, so fast that it sounded like I was offended by the question. I wasn't, and he wasn't offended by my refusal—but I almost wished he would be. It would be so much easier to escape the conversation if he was upset, or guarded, or accusatory. Instead, he did what he always did and asked a simple, uncomplicated question that stripped away all the pretensions I wanted to hide behind.

"Why not?"

He knelt there, ring box still open, and waited. When I didn't answer, he verbally backed me into the corner. "Remember when you showed me your hiding place in Wing 1?"

I swallowed. Of course I remembered.

He took my silence as consent. "You were prepared to marry me then."

"That was before Wing 74," I snapped.

He shrugged. "What changed?"

Everything.

"You made mistakes and so did I," he said without accusation, "but that's behind us now. Red Rain is over, and we can both make our own choices. So, what changed between us?"

His deep, chocolate-colored eyes searched me. His gaze was so fierce and yet so kind, and I knew that if he stared at me much longer, he would pry the layers off my heart and expose the truth. I looked away, but there was nowhere to hide in the cramped kitchen.

He closed the ring box and slid it in his pocket, then laid his hand on my knee. "If something has changed... if there's something I said or did that changed your mind, and you don't want to be with me, tell me. I won't be upset at you, I promise. If I can fix it, I will. But if not, I'll walk away."

I clenched the edge of the chair with both hands. I knew he was telling the truth. If I told him to leave, he would.

"But you have to tell me what it is," he prodded, again putting all the responsibility in my lap. "Because nothing's changed for me. I still love you, Laodicea."

I love you too, I thought but didn't say. I did love him; I'd loved him for years. Nothing had changed on my end. But this wasn't about how much I loved him. Why couldn't he see that?

He was still on the floor, waiting for an answer, and I knew he wouldn't leave until I gave him one. "I'm just... not ready."

That was a cop-out, and I knew he wouldn't accept it. "What needs to change for you to feel ready? Is it something I can fix?"

I didn't know the answer to that. It wasn't a feeling I could quantify; I didn't have a list of boxes that needed to be checked before I would feel ready to get married. I just *knew* I wasn't ready. But I couldn't explain why, and I knew *he* knew I couldn't explain why, and that made me furious.

"I'm just not. First of all, we live in a prison, and second of all, I have no idea what's going on with Nic. No one will tell me what prison they put him in, and the records are all wrong. Something's going on, and until I figure out what, I... I just can't think about getting married."

At least that was a halfway truthful answer, and to my surprise, he didn't argue with it. "I agree. I think the government is hiding something about Wing 74, and I want to find out what."

Finally, we'd reached a truce. I took a deep breath, but before I could finish the inhale, he continued. "But I want to find out together."

I froze, the air caught in my throat.

"I know the world is a mess," he continued. He gently pried my hands from the chair and wove our fingers together. "We're criminals, our religion is illegal, and we live in a containment camp. There's a hundred things wrong with our lives right now, and most of them I can't fix. But if I'm going to live in a world on fire, I want to do it with you."

Squeezing my palms, he found my eyes again. I was too terrified to look away.

"The world is complicated, Laodicea, and I can't promise that will ever change. But I can promise you one thing."

I heard the shift in his tone and knew exactly what he was going to say.

"I can promise you that I will never complicate our relationship. So this is how I feel: I want to spend the rest of my life with you, and I don't want to wait for the world to catch up before I say yes to us."

I knew that was the truth, and as usual, there was no way to argue with his honesty. But no matter how hard I tried to see the world the way he saw it, I couldn't push past the choking feeling that saying "yes" was a big mistake. That getting married would open the door to more heartbreak in a world I couldn't control.

It wasn't safe.

I knew Ephesus would demand a verbal answer, so I struggled to put the thought into words. "I know that's how you feel…"

His face pinched, and I closed my eyes. "But that's not how I feel. I just can't think about marriage when there are so many unknowns. I'm just *not ready.*"

He took a breath like he was going to argue, so I spoke faster. "I know you want a better answer, but I don't have one. I'm just not ready, and that's all I can tell you."

He was silent. I kept my eyes shut, waiting.

Slowly, like a ship drifting out to sea, he pulled his hands from mine.

I felt him stand up. "Can I ask you again in the future?"

I hesitated, knowing it was fully within my power to shut and lock the door forever. But that's not what I wanted either. "Yes, you can."

"Thank you," he whispered, and I heard the choke in his voice. I dared to look up at him and saw the glisten in his eyes before he quickly turned to go.

He let himself out. I got up and followed, stopping in the doorway to the kitchen.

He opened the front door and paused on the top step with his back to me. He glanced over his shoulder, gaze barely catching mine. "I'll be waiting," he said, voice suddenly strong again.

Then he shut the door and left.

7: EPHESUS

"Are you sure?" Cea questioned, even though she was already on her feet.

I opened the notification on the computer. "I'm sure. He locked it and set the alarm when he left—and now I've got a motion alert. Someone is definitely moving in there." Nic's office was the most secure place on Mars; he had more alarms and motion sensors in that room than all of Wing 74 put together.

"How'd they break in?"

"That's just it—they didn't." I opened another app to verify my findings. "According to the system, the door's still locked. Is there another way in?"

She shook her head. "Not that I know of—and it's not like they can just break a window."

I nodded; the pressure in the room was normal, which meant they hadn't compromised the hull. But they'd gotten in somehow, and I wasn't going to let them get away.

I stood up. "Well, let's go ask them, shall we?"

Cea caught my sleeve. "But how are *we* going to get in? Nic's office is on a Level 1 security clearance. Even I can't open that door when it's locked."

I growled, as if the sound could shake loose a brilliant plan. I had no idea how we were going to override the security on Nic's door, but we needed to do it fast if we were going to catch the vandal in the act. If they found a way in, they had a way out, and we needed to catch them before they lit anything else on fire.

I brushed away the panicked thoughts to give the Holy Spirit room to talk. "The door locks... do you know where the reprogram disc is?"

She rolled her eyes, which told me all I needed to know. "His office, of course."

I grunted. Maybe I could hack into the system and add myself to the door. I knew my DNA was already on file in the database...

"That's it!" I shouted. "Nic's DNA. If I can get a copy of his DNA off the database, I can trick the door into thinking it's him." All the door scanners did was read the DNA off a person's hand and compare it to the database. If I had the code for Nic's DNA, I could wire myself into the system and bypass the scanner entirely.

I bent over the computer and started typing. "Any idea where on the database they store the DNA files?"

"Nowhere you're going to be able to access on any of your computers. Nic doesn't trust you *that* much."

I slapped my hand on the keyboard. *Of course not.*

Cea was silent for a beat. "But… he does trust Phil."

"What?" I looked back at her.

I could see the gears turning as she worked her jaw. "He gave her Level 2 security clearance. She can get into more places than I can."

That was an astounding revelation that I did not have the emotional energy to process, but I didn't see how it helped us. "She still can't unlock his office."

"No, but she can definitely get into some rooms where Nic has computers—and if the DNA glitch works both ways, you should be able to open those doors too. If we can get into a room with a computer that's got access to that database, we can download the file."

It was a solid theory. Back when I'd been trapped in Wing 74, a glitch in the system had allowed my sister to unlock doors set for me. That was how this whole mess had started. And if the Lord was on our side, that glitch might still work.

"But wait," I said, my engineer's brain catching up, "shouldn't you be able to unlock doors set for Nic? You're his sister."

She was shaking her head before I finished the sentence. "You and Phil must share a higher percentage of DNA than we do. If it worked for me, Nic would have discovered the glitch years ago."

"Fair enough." I glanced back at the monitor. There was still motion in Nic's office. We had a chance, but we had to hurry. "Any idea where we can find one of these computers?"

Cea was already jogging towards the door. "Follow me."

She was right: I was able to use my sister's security clearance to access a control room with a terminal that was connected to the restricted database. I easily found the code for Nic's DNA. In fact, it appeared at the top of the search results because it had been modified recently.

I sacrificed an extra sixty seconds to look at the log. Someone had opened and downloaded the code for Nic's DNA in the last week—and the IP address wasn't from this planet.

I pointed it out to Cea. "I think I know how our vandal has been getting around."

She squinted at the screen. Then, without a word, she strode over to the wall, opened a cabinet, and pulled out a pistol. She cocked it and turned to face me. "Let's go."

I couldn't help but laugh. "I just love you."

She rolled her eyes and waved me out the door, but I caught the smile in the corner of her lips.

We ran back to Nic's office. A quick check of the logs said our intruder was still in there. Thankfully, it took me only minutes to hot wire the door, even working quietly.

"Ready?" I whispered, finger above the key.

Cea took aim and nodded.

Jesus, we're gonna need You, I prayed, and ran the program.

The door whooshed open. Cea scanned the room with her pistol, then hesitated, her stance slacking. "There's no one in here."

I scrambled up and joined her in the doorway. She was right—the room looked exactly as Nic had left it three days ago, rotting food and all. He had kicked me out and not let me finish cleaning up, so the room reeked of overripe fruit and stale coffee.

I stepped over the trash on the floor and scanned the desk, but it didn't look like anything had been tampered with. Nic's tablet and stacks of papers were still there, and all the filing cabinets were locked.

Cea walked up beside me. "Could the sensors just be on the fritz?"

"I mean, I guess so." At this point, I didn't have any better explanations. Maybe there was no vandal. Maybe the fire in Wing 74 was a freak accident; maybe the power relay module was just poorly installed. Was I so paranoid about proving to Nic that I could manage a base that I'd imagined the whole thing?

I walked towards the corner of the room, where one of the motion sensors was mounted near the floor. The carpet was cluttered with trash and a plate of uneaten food. I bent down to pick up a discarded shirt—and that's when I saw it.

I froze. "Cea."

She spun around. "What?"

"Stay very still. And… put the gun down."

"Why?" she said, all her distrust coming out in one dragging syllable.

"Because I don't want you to shoot when you see what it is."

She hesitated. I watched out of my peripheral until I saw her set the safety and slide the weapon in her pocket.

I took a careful step towards the corner. My prey hesitated, obsessed with the food on the abandoned plate. I took another step, and it ran—but I was too quick. I lunged and trapped its tail under my shoe.

Cea squealed almost as loud as the vermin did. "A *mouse*?"

I knelt down and grabbed the little brown critter by the scruff of the neck. I flipped it over and pinned it in my hand so it couldn't bite me, then held it up for Cea to see.

She took a step back. "*That's* what caused all this mess?"

"Apparently," I grunted, not sure whether to laugh hysterically or murder the rodent in a rage. "It must have chewed on the power relay—that's why the wires were so frayed."

"And if it bit a live wire in Wing 74, it could have easily caused a spark that started the fire." Cea regarded the critter with something close to admiration.

That was the last thing I was feeling for the mouse. I held it up and watched it squirm. "But if this is our vandal, then who was messing with the code for Nic's DNA?"

"No idea, but we need to solve this problem before it becomes an infestation." Cea pointed at the rodent.

She was right. I glanced around the room and easily deduced what had attracted the vermin to Nic's office. "I bet you came in here because of all this food, didn't you? Nice of Nic to leave it out for you."

"What did I do?"

Cea screamed again, louder this time. I spun around and nearly fell over. Nic's face appeared on the computer monitor as the screen brightened to life.

I hastily cupped the mouse in my hands and prayed it wouldn't bite me.

"What are you two doing in my office?" Nic demanded, his voice obscured by the roar of the busy street behind him.

Cea gestured at the screen. "How are you…"

"Of course I can remotely video into my office. I can video in to half the base." There was a grunt as he ducked into a cab and slammed the door. He rattled off directions to the driver in Mandarin, then turned back to face the camera. "Care to tell me what's going on? I land and am immediately assaulted with an intruder warning for my office. There had better be a *delicious* explanation for this."

I shared a glance with Cea. She discreetly shook her head, eyes panicked.

I agreed with her. Now seemed like a terrible time to tell Nic that a mouse had nearly burned Wing 74 to the ground. Unfortunately, I didn't have any plausible alternative stories. "I, uh…"

"Wait." Nic's voice hardened in a way that would have put the fear of God in anyone. "Are you *proposing*?"

I glanced down at myself and realized how it must look: me on one knee, with my cupped hands held out to Cea.

Nic didn't give me a chance to deny it. "Am I seeing this right? Are you actually proposing to my sister *in my office*?"

"I... yes. Yes, I am," I declared before I could second-guess myself.

"What?" Cea screeched.

Well, no going back now. I straightened and looked into her eyes. "Laodicea, will you marry me?"

"Are you serious right now?" she squawked.

Nic spat something far more colorful.

"Of course I'm serious," I returned. "I was serious the last time I asked."

"You've already asked her?" Nic yelled.

I glanced at the screen. "Twice, actually."

He blinked as he ran the numbers. "Do you not know how to take a hint?"

I shrugged. "Nope."

Cea crossed her arms. "You really want to do this now?" she deadpanned.

"Yes, I want to do this now," I returned, letting some of the annoyance seep into my voice. "I'm tired of dancing around the question. You keep saying 'later' and then later never comes. I deserve an honest answer, Cea. After all we've been through, you owe me that much."

She jerked back, as startled as I was by my demands. Nic snorted. "Way to kill the romance, hero."

"Shut up," Cea snapped at him without looking back. "He's right. He's been nothing but good to me, and he deserves my honesty."

It was my turn to stare in surprise. That was the first time Cea had ever defended me in front of her brother—and that was all it took for me to find my courage.

Cea sighed and unfolded her arms. "Ephesus, you know I love you. I always have."

"News to me," Nic muttered, then wisely silenced when Cea glared at him.

Her eyes returned to mine. "I want to marry you. I do. But." She winced as if injured, and if I didn't have a scrabbling rodent in my hands, I would have dropped everything to wrap her in my arms. "I just don't see how you can think about a wedding with everything going on."

"Is now a good time to remind you why I'm on Earth?" Nic inserted. "Speaking of people lighting the world on fire, your sister is first in line."

"I'm aware. But you know what? There's nothing I can do about that." My fear of being a helpless bystander came knocking, but this time, I faced it bravely. "I can't do anything to save my sister, I can't do anything to save my dad, and I can't do anything to save the world. There's a ton of problems in my life right now that I can't fix."

Cea sensed my pain and mirrored it, her gray-blue eyes watering. "Oh, Ephesus," she whispered, those four syllables giving me all the encouragement I needed.

I smiled at her. "But there is one thing I can control: my relationship with you. I promised when we met that I wouldn't make it complicated."

"Ironic, because this situation is *extremely* complicated," Nic commented.

Neither of us acknowledged that. "You've kept that promise," Cea assured me.

"So let me make you a new one." I shifted and centered myself in front of her. "Laodicea, I know you're scared. I know the world is a mess and we have no idea what's going to happen tomorrow—or tonight, even. I wish I could promise that I could keep you safe, but I can't. I can't even promise that I can always protect you."

She nodded wordlessly, a tear escaping down her cheek.

"But I can promise that I'll always be there for you. I can promise that whatever comes, we'll face it together. I will stand by your side and fight with you. I will always support you, I will always love you, and I will always help you be the person God called you to be."

She laid her hand over mine. "You've done that."

"So let me keep doing it. Let's agree to do this together—right here, right now. Look, I know this is a *really* dumb time to propose..."

"I'll say," Nic grunted, and the squirming mouse in my hand agreed with him.

I tightened my grip and ignored them both. "But I don't want to wait until tomorrow. The first time I asked you to marry me, you said 'maybe later'—and you know what, 'later' almost never came. The very next day, Thames arrested you, and I thought I'd never see you again."

"I know," Cea whispered, and I wondered if she, too, had spent several sleepless nights agonizing over the what-ifs.

"I'm not going to let that happen again," I declared, raising my voice for her, for Nic, for myself. "I'm not going to miss another opportunity. So either agree or let me go, but this time, *please* give me an answer."

She didn't object. Even Nic went silent.

I took a deep breath, offered up a prayer, and then looked into her eyes. "Laodicea, will you marry me?"

She smiled even as the tears started running freely down her face. "Yes, I will."

I almost collapsed in relief. *Thank you, Jesus!*

She laughed and wrapped her arms around my neck. I used the cover to stuff the mouse in the pocket of my lab coat and pull out the ring box that I'd been carrying for the past three days.

Cea pulled away. I slid the ring on her finger while she used the other hand to vainly wipe her eyes. She looked stunning—with the diamond glittering on her finger, the smile blushing on her cheeks, and the beautiful tears sparkling in the corners of her eyes. I gripped her hand as the reality of what had just happened caught up with me and sent my pulse soaring. *She said yes she said yes she said yes...*

Nic shattered the moment. "Well, this week can't get any weirder." He flopped back in the seat of the cab and rubbed his face. "When's the date?" he groaned in defeat.

I stood up and looked at the monitor. "Does that mean you approve?"

The glare he shot me could have frozen water. "Let me assure you, *nothing* about this situation has my approval, brother-in-law." He wretched a little after he said it, and Cea giggled. "But, luckily for you, I'm a bit preoccupied right now keeping Andi alive. So at least tell me when I should clear my calendar so I don't double-book."

"How about now?" Cea suggested.

"What?" both Nic and I said together.

Her eyes sparkled with mischief. "We could get married right now. I mean, if you want to." She reached out and grasped both of my hands.

"I'm not opposed," I admitted, even as my brain struggled to process what she was suggesting. "I just have some questions."

"I have *so* many questions," Nic echoed.

Cea pulled me towards her. "Why not? There's nothing left to wait for."

I grinned.

She winked. "Nic, you can marry us because you're a governor, right?"

He pointed a finger at the screen. "Can and will are two very different things."

She didn't even look back at him. "He *will* marry us, because even though he's never actually said it, he loves me and wants me to be happy."

I gawked at her as a shiver of adrenaline passed up my spine. This new, fearless version of Cea was *terrifying*—and wildly attractive.

Nic broke off into mutters, sounding like a disgruntled chipmunk. "I mean, it's basically just a tax form. But you know how I feel about paperwork."

"I'll fill it out for you," I offered. "Then you just have to sign it."

He blinked. "You know me well, and I hate that."

I deferred to my bride. "Okay, so what do we do?" *Is this happening? Am I really getting married, right now?*

"I think you've already made a vow to me, so let me make one to you." Adjusting her grip on my hands, she sobered as she met my gaze and gave me what I always wanted: her heart.

"Ephesus, I promise to be faithful to you. I promise to put our relationship first and to always be open and honest with you about everything. I promise to support you in everything you choose to do. I choose you, and I will never, ever change my mind about that."

My heart swelled so hard that my head buzzed. I drew her to me, wrapping one arm around her waist and putting the other behind her head. "And I will never back down from my commitment to you, Laodicea."

She searched my face, her gorgeous eyes glimmering with the reality of the future we'd just created. "'Til death do us part."

"'Til death do us part," I echoed, then tipped her back and kissed her.

"You didn't even wait for me to say 'you may kiss the bride,'" Nic groused.

Cea wrapped her arms around my neck and returned the affection, but our passion was cut short when she pressed against my leg, crushing the mouse. The little varmint squealed and nipped me. I yelped and nearly dropped my bride on the floor. She stumbled back, laughing hysterically.

Thankfully, Nic didn't hear the mouse. "I can't believe I have to declare under penalty of perjury that I witnessed that debacle."

Cea composed herself. "We'll email the form to you tonight."

"No hurry, I still need to save your sister-in-law. I'll video chat you after I have her in tow so she can yell at you for leaving her out of your wedding. That'll be a riot."

I coughed and gave the situation the sobriety it deserved. "Thank you. For what you're doing for my sister."

He sighed. "You're making it really hard to stay mad at you."

"I love you, Nic," Cea said, and then ended the call to save him the misery of replying in kind.

We appreciated the silence for a moment. "So... *wife*," I said, sidling up to her and wrapping my arms around her from behind. "What would you like for your wedding night dinner?"

She stood on her toes to plant a kiss on my cheek. "Well, before we worry about cake, I think we should take care of our little friend." She pulled away and pointed at the squirming lump in my pocket.

I sighed and opened the flap to stare at the furry troublemaker. "I guess you were an okay best man."

The practicality returned to Cea's voice. "Where did it come from? We haven't had an infestation in years. Do you think it snuck in on your luggage?"

"I doubt it." I tried to think what else had arrived on base in the last few days, and it dawned on me. "Remember how I said there were a couple of torn bags in the food shipment?"

She slapped her hands over her mouth. "Oh no. I thought you said you detoxed it!"

My neck began to burn when I realized that we may have two very different definitions of what that word meant. "I mean, I checked it…"

"Ephesus!" she shrieked. "You can't just 'check' food shipments. There's a whole radiation detox process you have to go through just for this very reason!"

I spread my hands. "I didn't know…"

She tented her fingers and took a deep breath. "Hopefully it was just the one, and—"

"Ephesus? Cea? You in there?"

I turned towards the door as Mr. Sardis approached from the hall. He paused in the doorway and took in the situation. His face erupted in a grin. "Oh, you finally gave her a ring? It's about time."

"Tell me about it," I muttered. "What's going on?"

Mr. Sardis folded his arms across his chest. "Well, hate to break up the party, but I've got bad news."

I rubbed my temples. "I'll add it to the list. What is it?"

"I was checking the greenhouses like you asked, and I've got a whole bed of freshly planted seeds that's been ripped up. I think we've got some vermin on base, probably mice."

I swallowed. "You don't say…"

He nodded gravely. "Yeah, and judging by the amount of droppings I found along the wall, I'd say we're dealing with a large infestation. Probably got at least a couple dozen of them already."

My wife crossed her arms and arched her eyebrow at me.

I cleared my throat. "So, you know how I said, whatever comes, we'd face it together…?"

She couldn't keep the smile off her face as she shook her head. "You'd better be glad I love you."

I laughed. "Oh, I am."

TO BE CONTINUED…

WANT EXCLUSIVE BONUS SCENES?

Become a Patron and get access to **exclusive bonus scenes** for this series! This bonus content is not available anywhere else, and I post a new scene every month. Plus, you can get digital ARCs, signed paperbacks, collector's edition hardbacks, and merch, or read my WIP as I write it!

Become a Patron at:
patreon.com/rachelnewhouse

Or sign up for my newsletter and be the first to hear about new releases—plus get sneak peeks of upcoming books, cover art, and more!

Sign up at:
rachelnewhouse.com/subscribe

DID YOU LOVE THIS BOOK?

Please consider leaving a review on Amazon or Goodreads! It's one of the most important things you can do to support an indie author. Thank you!

HI FROM RACHEL

Rachel Newhouse is an author, wife, secretary, and Sunday school teacher from Kansas City, Missouri. Her obsessions are sci-fi, dystopian, and kid lit. When she's not writing, she's cooking Asian food, growing chilis that are too spicy to eat, and watching wildly age-inappropriate shows like *My Little Pony* and *Gravity Falls* with her husband, Joe. She also really likes glitter. You've been warned.

Connect with Rachel:
bio.site/rachelnewhouse